ASCENSION

ASCENSION

THE NECROMANCER'S KEY: BOOK FIVE

MITCHELL HOGAN

This book is a work of fiction. The characters, incidents and dialogues are products of the author's imagination and are not to be construed as real. Any resemblance to any persons, living or dead, events, or locales is entirely coincidental.

ASCENSION

Published by Mitchell Hogan

First Printing, 2023

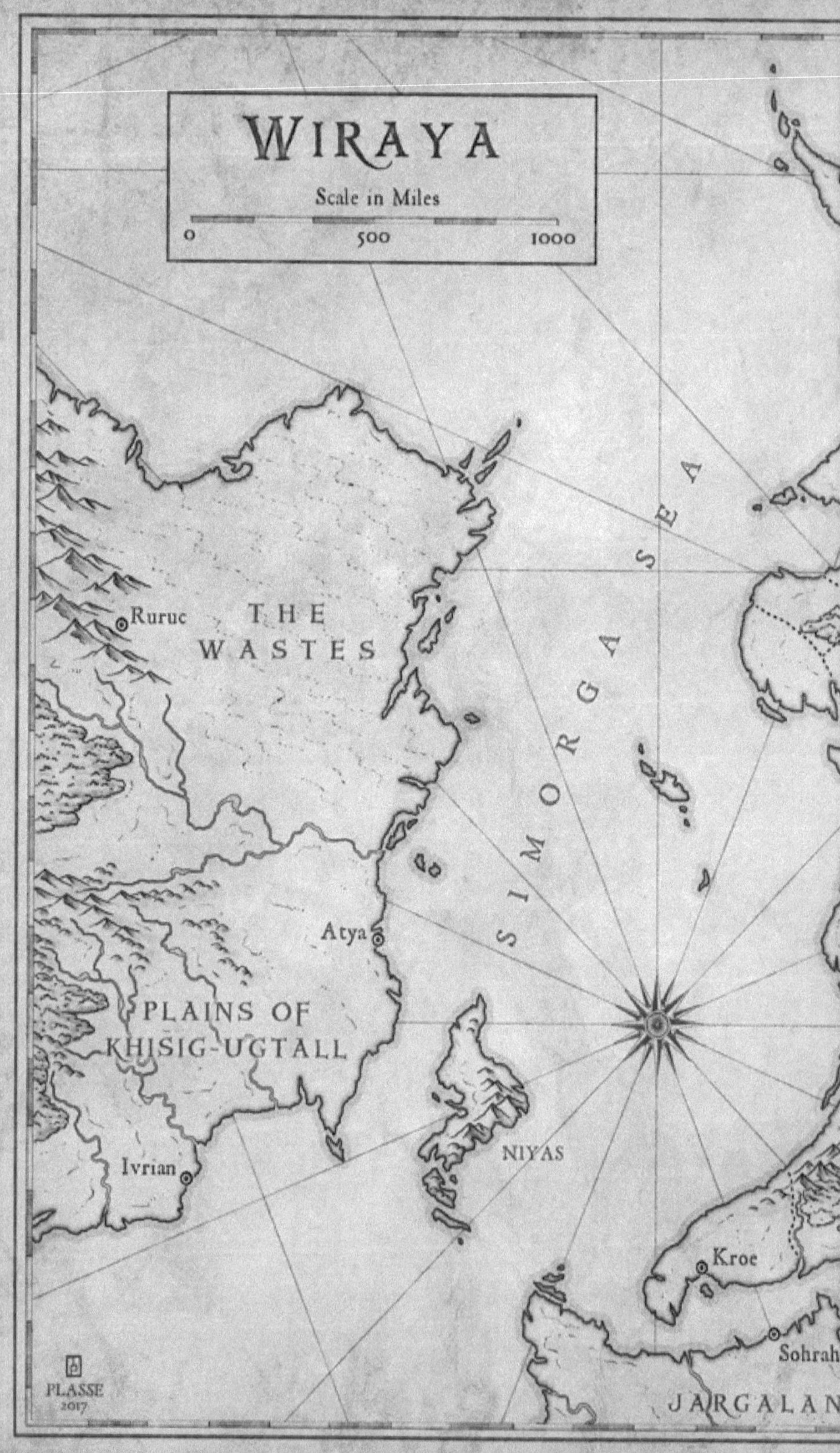

WIRAYA
Scale in Miles
0
500
1000
THE
WASTES
Ruruc
SIMORGA SEA
Atya
PLAINS OF
KHISIG-UGTALL
Ivrian
NIYAS
Kroe
Sohrah
JARGALAN
PLASSE
2017

YMALTIAN MOUNTAINS
OUSAND LAKES
Caronath
Crystal River
Nantin
TATES
OCEAN
TRACKLESS
Kyuth
KAILES
Sansor
Nagorn City
STARTS
OMBINE
Valborg
MOUNTAINS OF SOUTHERN EALYSIA
GREAT
Mazin
AK-SETTUR
SEA
OF
MINGOL
Manela
Gessa
JARGALAN MOUNTAINS

WHAT'S GONE BEFORE

NECROMANCY BEGAN ON THE island of Niyas, when the peoples of Wiraya were little more than savages roaming the wilderness. The dawn-and dusk-tides were already known, but Niyandrian sorcerers discovered the corrupted tidal forces absorbed into the earth. They grew obsessed with the earth-tide's promise of immortality and with the secrets of the dead.

When Queen Talia of Niyas sought to raise her people to eternal life, the powerful countries of the mainland conspired to put an end to her rule. Allied armies invaded Niyas. Battles were fought with steel and sorcery. Thousands died. Cities fell. And, at last, the mainland allies, led by the Order of Eternal Vigilance, prevailed. Queen Talia died when her capital, Naphor, fell, and Niyas was placed under mainland occupation.

But there were rumors of a child: the heir to Niyas, the daughter of Talia, the Necromancer Queen. In secret, a guardian was appointed to protect the heir.

BOOK ONE: INCURSION

Carred Selenas, Captain of the Last Cohort and Queen Talia's former lover, leads the resistance against the foreign invaders as they await the return of the Necromancer Queen and the reemergence of the Niyandrian people and culture. But it has been years since Talia died, and her people are losing heart. With one failure after another, Carred's resolve crumbles, but duty keeps her searching for the lost heir—the symbol all Niyandrians could rally behind and the key to Queen Talia's return from the dead.

Anskar DeVantte has been raised in the sacred disciplines of the Order of Eternal Vigilance, the military arm of the Church of Menselas, God of Five Aspects, his entire life. Born with the mark of sorcery and the ability to manipulate the dawn-tide, Anskar must endure the Order's brutal initiation trials if he is to become a consecrated knight. Against the Order's rules, he assists a Niyandrian postulant, Sareya, with the sword she is forging for the second trial, and they become lovers.

The blind sorcerer Luzius Landav arrives with his assistant, a dwarf woman named Malady. Landav brings the trainees crystal catalysts that will enable them to draw upon the dawn-tide for their protective sorceries. Landav senses Anskar also has a dusk-tide repository and, more disturbingly, can also store the dark-tide.

Using their catalysts, the trainee knights imbue the blades they forged during the trials with strengthening cants using the dawn-tide. Anskar names his sword *Amalantril* ("Moontouched") after Sareya's Niyandrian name.

Anskar, Orix, and Sareya are among the seven trainees to pass the trials and are raised to the interim rank of knight-liminal. The Seneschal, Vihtor Ulnar, declares he will take Anskar under his wing.

Anskar questions Vihtor about his past and his parents. The Seneschal is guarded and forbids him from asking again.

Landav and Malady implant the catalysts beneath the skin of the trainees. Anskar's body rejects the dark-threaded crystal, and he grows critically ill.

As Anskar recovers under the care of the priests of the Healer, a golden-eyed crow disturbs him in the middle of the night. Anskar enters a fugue-like state as he follows the crow through the wilderness to a Niyandrian ruin atop Hallow Hill. There, a wraithe—one of the ancient beings that haunt Wiraya—urges Anskar to enter the ruin, where he finds a statue of a woman carved from bone, upon her forearm a vambrace crafted from a peculiar silver alloy.

Carred Selenas receives word from her spies that one of the Order's newest knights, a woman named Sareya, could be the Niyandrian heir, and also that Hyle Pausus, the Grand Master of the Order of Eternal Vigilance, is on his way to Niyas from the mainland city of Sansor. She comes up with a plan to bloody the Order's nose and snatch Sareya away from them.

Carred and her rebels are attacked by Luzius Landav and Malady, and in the ensuing fight, Landav transports himself and Carred to a shadowy realm, where she meets a secret consortium who put pressure on Carred to disband her rebellion. She refuses and uses a ring Queen Talia gave her to break Landav's power and return to Wiraya. The rebels capture Landav, but Malady escapes. Carred cuts off the sorcerer's head.

Anskar approaches his namesake, the knight Eldrid DeVantte, to ask about his mother and father. Eldrid claims to know nothing except that he gave Anskar his surname at the request of Vihtor.

The trainees undertake their first mission, each mentored by a fully consecrated knight. To everyone's surprise, Vihtor announces he will join them. Ambushed by rebels, they lose almost half their number, including the trainee Petor.

As dusk approaches, they find a farm with a cottage to shelter in before dead-eyes attack in the night. Anskar hears a woman screaming inside the cottage. He and Vihtor investigate, only to find the cottage empty apart from the corpse of a woman recently killed.

After nightfall, dozens of sickly, spindly-limbed dead-eyes attack. Anskar uses dark-tide sorcery to hold up the ceiling, which bows under the weight of dead-eyes. Sareya uses dusk-tide sorcery to incinerate the rest of the dead-eyes with violet flames, and then, exhausted, she collapses.

Carred discovers that Niyandrians are being rounded up a few at a time and sold by the Order of Eternal Vigilance as slaves. After years of failures and self-doubt, she cannot stand by. She frees Niyandrian slaves from a warehouse and burns down the building.

Carred receives word that her rebels attacked a group of knights and their trainees from Branil's Burg, but were driven back by a young knight who bristled with sorcerous energy, aided by a young Niyandrian woman, Sareya. Carred speculates that, if Sareya is Queen Talia's daughter, the young knight may be the heir's guardian. Both must have been conditioned by the Order, unaware of who they really are.

After the knights' expedition returns to Branil's Burg with Petor's body, Anskar examines his vambrace using dark-tide power. He has a vision of a full suit of intricately forged plate armor and is inexplicably overcome with a burning need to possess the armor.

Luzius Landav's servant, Malady, turns up at the Burg, carrying Luzius's severed head in a sack. The decomposing head seems to speak to Anskar, who is horrified. Malady is revealed to be a demon, and tells the Grand Master that he was deceived by the new Niyandrian converts. Malady escapes, and, fearful of betrayal, Hyle Pausus orders the recently branded Niyandrians killed. Four of the Niyandrians, however, cannot be found.

The trainees are raised to the rank of knight-inferior. In another year, they will be expected to either take solemn vows or leave the Order and never return. To clear his head, Anskar rides from the Burg, intending to find some space. When he returns, he finds Naul's dead body, which speaks to him, telling him to help Sareya. Anskar finds Sareya bound and gagged, kneeling at the center of a circle formed from a golden chain. Within the circle stand four Niyandrians: the four escaped converts.

As Anskar fights two of the men, the dark-tide within him bursts its bindings. One Niyandrian's hand withers, and the second's face putrefies. The Niyandrian woman, a sorcerer, confronts Anskar, her dagger dazzling with silver fire. But she holds back and gasps with reverent awe: "*Melesh-Eloni!*"

Anskar escapes his kidnappers and causes the carriage to crash. The Niyandrian sorcerer begs Anskar to come with her, but knights of the Order arrive. Vihtor kills the sorcerer and is shocked to see that Anskar's eyes are now somehow cat's eyes, like those of a Niyandrian.

Back inside the Burg, Anskar is sure Vihtor knows more than he is revealing, but Hyle Pausus decides Anskar is a gifted knight-inferior and will take him to Sansor with his retinue. Vihtor doesn't voice an objection, and agrees that it could be dangerous for Anskar to remain in Niyas.

Anskar visits Sareya in the infirmary, where she tells him that *Melesh-Eloni* means "godling."

Anskar departs Branil's Burg by ship the next morning, consumed by questions that he feels he may never get answers to.

Carred and a small group of her followers watch the passage of the lone galleon as it heads out to sea.

One of the slaves Carred rescued, a young woman called Noni, is possessed by the spirit of Queen Talia and tells Carred that there is no daughter: the heir to Niyas is Talia's son, the knight-sorcerer Anskar DeVantte. Talia reveals that Carred is Anskar's guardian, and now is the time for her to step into that role.

Carred vows to bring Anskar back to Niyas so that the entire country will rally to her cause. Under Anskar's lead, the faithful will take back Niyas for Niyandrians. Queen Talia will return. And the dead will live forever.

BOOK TWO: CORRUPTION

Entrusted by Vihtor Ulnar to the protection of the knight Lanuc of Gessa, Anskar DeVantte sails on the *Exultant* across the waters of the Simorga Sea to Sansor. Anskar and Orix discover Niyandrian slaves chained in the bilge. The *Exultant* detours to the coastal city of Atya, where the Grand Master plans to sell the slaves.

That night, Orix is set upon and almost raped by one of the knights. Anskar uses dark-tide sorcery, which corrupts the knight's arm, and then Orix runs the man through with his sword. Instead of disciplining Anskar, the Grand Master tells Anskar that, if he plays his cards right, he should fit in well at the Mother House in Sansor.

Carred Selenas is visited by Queen Talia, who possesses Noni and speaks through her. Talia exhorts Carred, Anskar's guardian, to find him and keep him safe—Anskar is the key to returning Talia from the realm of the dead. She commands Carred to find the old Niyandrian sorcerer Maggow, and enlist the help of Malady the demon and the abyssal realms.

Maggow summons the demon Malady and binds her to his will. He also informs Carred that the *Exultant* is heading west, away from Sansor. Carred procures a ship and gives chase.

The *Exultant* arrives at Atya, where Anskar, Orix, and Lanuc go ashore for a few days to explore the city while the slaves are sold. They are approached by a woman named Blaice Rancey, who claims her business is ransacking ancient tombs and that she's an old friend of Lanuc's.

Blaice claims to have knowledge of a recently unearthed ancient ruin, and the Grand Master Hyle Pausus puts together an expedition to explore the ruin and claim its treasures for the Order. As they journey to the ruin, they are joined by Niklaus du Plessis, who claims to be the

Chosen Sword of the goddess Sylva Kalisia. Lanuc explains to Anskar that gifted knights and sorcerers, including Lanuc himself and now Anskar, are not only tolerated in secret but are called upon by the Grand Master to sacrifice their purity in the defense of the Order.

Blaice and Niklaus decipher the code that unlocks the entrance to the ruin and lead the group inside. They come to an inscribed brass circle set into the floor of a chamber—a portal. Anskar, at Hyle Pausus's urging, uses dark-tide sorcery to activate the portal, and the group are transferred to the fabled city of Yustanwyrd, buried underneath the ruins of the seven cities that succeeded it.

Carred crosses the Simorga Sea and lands near Atya, and then finds her way to a Traguh-raj tribe. The tribe's leader agrees to lead them to the unearthed ruin in pursuit of Anskar. Carred and her new companions capture Orix and Lanuc, who were left outside the ruin as guards.

Blaice leads Anskar and the rest of the group to a building atop a hill of granulated quartz, where they are attacked by eight statues holding black wavy blades. They resemble the ancient wraithe Anskar encountered atop Hallow Hill. There is also a massive reptile's head with jaws that open onto absolute blackness.

Anskar's vambrace grows warm and tugs him toward the lizard's maw with increasing urgency. Anskar passes between the statues, continues into the reptile's gaping mouth, and is pitched into the void.

Anskar finds himself confronted by a group of wraithes, who know that he is the child of the Necromancer Queen of Niyas. The ancient beings also reveal that Anskar's vambrace is a step on the path to godhood. They deny the existence of the portal stone Blaice and the Grand Master seek, and state that the members of the expedition have seen things they shouldn't have, before using sorcery to send him back to his companions.

Anskar rejoins his companions in a chamber littered with crystal boxes. From one container, Blaice and Niklaus remove a severed hand with an ebony ring.

Fearful of the wraithes' warning, the companions flee back to the entrance hall, only to find the eight statues are now living wraithes. In the ensuing fight several companions are killed, along with a wraithe. Hyle Pausus and Anskar are overwhelmed, but then Anskar's vambrace flares with brilliance, and he briefly finds himself in the realm of the dead. The shade of Queen Talia appears, with a golden-eyed crow perched on her shoulder. The Necromancer Queen says that the vambrace is not enough, and that there is much more to be done before Anskar comes for her. She sends him back to Wiraya.

Anskar, the Grand Master, Niklaus and Blaice flee, with the wraithes sending birds made of smoke to attack. Anskar's sword, *Amalantril*, is ineffective against the smoke birds, as are all their weapons. Only Niklaus's sword, which bears the image of his goddess, has any effect against the birds. Niklaus saves the Grand Master and tells him and Anskar to flee. As they do, Niklaus is smothered by hundreds of the birds and is lost.

Finally free of the disastrous ruin, Anskar, Blaice, Hyle and the rest of the survivors stumble back to their camp, only to find Orix and Lanuc tied with rope. Lanuc shouts at them to run, but before they can, Traguh-raj warriors cut off their escape. With them are Carred Selenas and the demon Malady.

To Anskar's dismay, Carred reveals to all that he is the son of Queen Talia. Anskar demands to know who his father is, but Carred is unable to answer.

Anskar is exhausted, his repositories depleted, and so is unable to muster a defense. When Carred agrees not to harm his companions, Anskar agrees to go with her. Carred takes Anskar back to Atya. When they near the wharves, Anskar draws on the dark-tide and shadow-steps away to where the *Exultant* is moored. As knights come to his aid, Malady pursues him through the shadows. The demon slaughters a few knights and is about to capture Anskar when the dawn-tide arrives. Anskar uses the dawn-tide power flooding his repository against Malady, and she flees. Carred, seemingly admitting defeat, departs on her own ship.

Safe aboard the *Exultant*, Anskar is heartened when Lanuc, Orix, Blaice, and the Grand Master return unharmed with the remaining knights. On the final night in Atya, Blaice seduces Anskar.

One night aboard ship while they're bound for Sansor, Queen Talia visits Anskar in his sleep and begins to teach him sorcery in a twilight dreamscape. The next day, Carred's ship attacks, and the knights and rebels fight with steel and sorcery. Amid the slaughter, and at the Grand Master's behest, Anskar uses dark-tide sorcery to turn the tide of the battle, killing the old Niyandrian sorcerer Maggow in the process. Unable to seize Anskar, Carred and Malady abduct Orix instead.

The *Exultant* finally arrives at Sansor, and Anskar and the knights find refuge at the Order's Mother House. Anskar makes the acquaintance of Gisela of Gessa, Lanuc's daughter, who is a priestess of the Five and a healer.

Carred is once again beaten down and depressed at another failure to secure Talia's heir. She briefly contemplates giving up, but instead goes against her better judgment and gives Malady a task: capture Anskar and the demon can go free.

Anskar wanders the Mother House and finds himself at a forge, where he meets Braga, a foul-mouthed blacksmith. He watches her working for a time, and despite her surliness, they strike up an unlikely friendship.

After Carred's failed attempt, Talia once again possesses Noni and speaks through her. Talia tells Carred to seek out the necromancer Tain and to use his knowledge to create a suit of Armor of Divinity as a fallback plan, in case Anskar fails to make his own.

The Grand Master Hyle Pausus summons Anskar and, in front of senior priests, urges Anskar to make peace with his burgeoning abilities and harness them for the good of the Order. Hyle Pausus sends Anskar for further training under the ancient Abbess at the Abbey of the Hooded One, in an attempt to cure him of his disillusionment with the Order of Eternal Vigilance.

Arriving at the Abbey, Anskar is given a cold welcome by the Abbess. He is confined to a cell and left to contemplate for long lengths of time, only broken by meals, prayer, and brief talks with the Abbess. Anskar's preconceptions about the Order and its morality are broken down little by little. The Abbess's talks are his only lifeline, and Anskar clings to them as if his sanity depends on it. They speak of demons and demon lore; Malady, Carred, and Niyas; Menselas; and balance, despair and death, as the Abbess challenges everything Anskar has grown to believe.

When the Abbess declares Anskar ready, he summons and binds the demon Malady to his will. Malady takes him briefly to the abyssal realms, then swiftly on to Carred before a winged demon can attack them. Malady reveals that knowing a demon's name grants a sorcerer power over that demon, and makes him a gift of the winged demon's name.

Anskar confronts Carred and Orix, who has been converted to the rebel's cause. Carred attempts to bring Anskar to her side, explaining the faults of the Order and the good Anskar could do if the Niyandrian people were liberated. Anskar rejects Carred, and Malady spirits him away, back to the abbey.

When they arrive, Malady tries to kill Anskar. Malady proves too powerful, until the Abbess arrives and slays her with sorcery. Afterwards, the Abbess, clothed in the illusion of Carred Selenas, forces Anskar to copulate with her, again and again, until he loses consciousness.

The next day, Anskar is summoned to see the Abbess, and still reeling and confused, he is taken to a vast chamber in which are gathered all of the priests and priestesses of the Hooded One. The Abbess reveals that she is a member of the Tainted Cabal, and that with Anskar joining their ranks, she believes they will be powerful enough to return the demon lord Nysrog to Wiraya.

Led by the Abbess, the congregation begins a ritual of summoning. Anskar is torn between extremes of savagery and terror. However, the demon lord Nysrog does not fully manifest and the summoning fails.

The Abbess is jubilant. She believes they only need to become a little stronger, and then, because of Anskar's abilities, Nysrog will once again walk upon the face of Wiraya.

Anskar comes to his senses and is horrified. He has to get away from the abbey before it is too late for him, and too late for the world. Swallowing his repugnance, he forces himself to go along with the Abbess and her deranged followers until an opportunity presents itself. As the Abbess and the priests begin an orgy, Queen Talia makes contact with Anskar, and he flees into the night.

Running for his life, Anskar is cornered by demons the Abbess has sent to capture or kill him. Unarmored and without a weapon, Anskar believes he is doomed, but Queen Talia shows him how to use the earth-tide, the power behind necromancy, to summon the dead spirit of a warrior and send it for help.

Anskar fends off one demon, using his vambrace to keep its fangs from his flesh. Help arrives in the form of Lanuc, Braga, and knights of the Order.

The Grand Master sends knights to the abbey, but they find the priests all dead, their veins turned black by some poison or sorcery. Of the Abbess there is no sign.

Once Anskar has recovered from his ordeals, he and the Grand Master walk the grounds outside the Mother House, discussing demons and the Tainted Cabal. The Grand Master's bodyguards are all slain by an assassin sent by the Abbess. The assassin incapacitates the Grand Master, and Anskar skewers the man with his sword *Amalantril*, only to find that there is no blood, and the assassin isn't slowed down by the wound.

Queen Talia tells Anskar to summon the dead using the earth-tide. Desperate, Anskar obeys and raises the Grand Master's dead guards. The assassin disposes of the animated corpses, but when Anskar scours him with dark-tide fire, the assassin is revealed as a demon.

Anskar recognizes it as the demon Malady pointed out to him in their brief sojourn in the abyssal realms. He halts the demon by uttering its name, then kills it.

The Grand Master declares that the Tainted Cabal have infiltrated the Order of Eternal Vigilance, and all must keep their eyes and ears open to detect the taint of corruption. Anskar is ordered to join Lanuc and a hundred knights on a mission to the Thousand Lakes kingdom, where they are to assist King Aelfyr, who is beset with problems from the Soreshi of the Ymaltian Mountains.

Breaking his promise to Talia, Anskar re-establishes the wards he had set against his mother, believing this new mission to be a manifestation of the mercy of Menselas and a way for him to atone for past sins and to give his life over to the providence of the Five. He feels free of Carred Selenas, free of the hold the Abbess had over him, and most of all he feels free of the specter of his mother.

BOOK THREE: SUBVERSION

Anskar DeVantte rides across Kaile, one knight among many among the Order's forces led by Lanuc of Gessa. Anskar vows never to use sorcery again, believing it is the source of all the ill luck that has befallen him and that it weakens his faith. Also afraid of his mother's influence, he blocks Queen Talia out.

As the forces journey toward the Kingdom of the Thousand Lakes to assist King Aelfyr, one of the Warrior's priests traveling with the knights takes an unhealthy interest in Anskar. Another priest of the Warrior, Josac, explains that the angry priest is Gann Harril, brother of Beof, whom Anskar severely injured during his trials and who had been sent away in disgrace. Anskar is warned that Gann wants revenge for what happened to his brother.

Carred Selenas continues her journey with the head of the necromancer Tain, along with Orix and Noni, in their search for the Armor of Divinity Tain claims to have created. Tain reveals that the helm that encases his head—all that remains of his Armor of Divinity—is the only thing keeping him alive.

Meanwhile, a woman driving a wagon approaches the Order's forces from behind: Braga the blacksmith, who tells Anskar she was urged to accompany the knights by a "ghost lady": Anskar's mother, Queen Talia.

The next day, Josac appears, bloodied and bruised. Gann, paranoid that Josac has sided with Anskar, attacks him with the Warrior's Fire, a divine ability gifted to priests by Menselas. Ashamed of his defeat, and telling Anskar he must fight Gann, Josac begins to teach Anskar how to use the Warrior's Fire. Anskar is hesitant, unable to embrace the Warrior's Fire until Josac demonstrates the power and beats him senseless.

Gisela of Gessa tends to Anskar's injuries and fully heals him. Although she is wary of what she has learned of Anskar from his confession, she agrees to attempt to teach him the way of vicarious suffering, a Healer's technique that involves taking the suffering of others upon oneself.

Anskar uses his newfound healing powers to take Josac's injuries upon himself, and the pain renders him unconscious. In the morning, Gisela relieves Anskar's pain by taking it upon herself, explaining that she has built a tolerance to suffering and will heal in a few hours. Having accepted at least this limited use of sorcery, Anskar embraces the dawn-tide as the sun rises.

When the Order's forces arrive at Kyuth, a coastal town in the north of

Kaile, they meet with Franklin Gore, mayor of Kyuth, and Brother Stevos, a priest of the Elder. Brother Stevos appears less devout than is usual for a priest, and is strangely accommodating to all of the other faiths, proclaiming it is no sin to worship with others for the sake of friendship.

Braga and Anskar strike up a friendship. When they are out one night, Anskar shows her his sorcerously imbued vambrace. Braga believes it is crafted of divine alloy, and that the only remaining knowledge regarding the metal is held in the scriptorium of King Aelfyr in the Thousand Lakes, and that the king's master blacksmith, Hrothyr, is the only person to have access.

That night, Gann makes his move and surprises Anskar with a vicious attack from behind. Fighting Gann off, Anskar taunts him in an attempt to enrage Gann beyond reason and give himself an edge. But immersed in the Warrior's Fire, Gann remains calm. After trading blows, Anskar desperately uses Menselas' gift of healing combined with the dawn-tide to snuff out the Warrior's Fire within Gann. The stolen fire is subsumed by Anskar, and he pounds Gann into a bloody mess. As Anskar lies insensate after the effects of the Warrior's Fire, Braga disposes of what's left of Gann along with Anskar's bloody clothes. When Anskar wakes, they agree not to admit to the killing. Anskar still feels a kernel of the Warrior's Fire within himself, now a part of him.

Lanuc tells Anskar and Gisela they must attend a ceremony worshiping the Lady Sylva Kalisia, at the behest of the mayor, Frankin Glore, and the priest of the Elder, Brother Stevos. Reluctantly, they agree, but as the ceremony progresses, both Anskar and Gisela feel more and more uneasy, believing that followers of Menselas should have nothing to do with heathen worship. Gisela eventually storms out, disgusted with her father's weakness. Anskar follows, telling Lanuc that he's already made too many compromises.

Carred's expedition arrives at an interconnected cairn of massive stones: the location of ancient suits of Armor of Divinity. Inside, they descend steps into a dark pit at Tain's urging. They investigate the tombs inside until they find a corpse clad in armor. But the armor is guarded by undead shades, a result of the necromancy used by Tain to murder the people who first helped him excavate the site. Taloc is killed by the shades, and Carred and the others only just escape. Tain urges them to continue to another location, where another suit of Armor of Divinity might be located.

Anskar and the force of Order knights continue their journey north. At Anskar's urging, Braga tries to remove the vambrace, but is unable to even scratch the metal with a hammer and chisel. They realize it will take great heat to work the metal, a heat that can be found in Hrothyr's forges in Wintotashum in the Kingdom of the Thousand Lakes.

Anskar tries to persuade Gisela to mend her relationship with her father, but Gisela is still angry with Lanuc for committing what she believes to be an abomination.

As soon as they arrive in the Kingdom of the Thousand Lakes, the knights are trailed by Soreshi scouts. The Soreshi grow bolder, and as the days pass, they no longer bother to hide their presence.

Meanwhile, the Tainted Cabalist Castellac furthers his plans among the Soreshi. For it is the Tainted Cabal who have deceived the Soreshi and caused them to attack the Kingdom of the Thousand Lakes. Castellac plans to break into the Scriptorium at the capital, Wintotashum, and steal the memory crystal of Morudjin, the priest of the Elder responsible for summoning the demon lord Nysrog into the world. The Cabal believes this will give them enough knowledge to return Nysrog to Wiraya.

The knights fight skirmishes with the Soreshi, who prove to be adept with sorcery. When the knights are almost overwhelmed, Anskar responds with potent cants of dawn- and dusk-tide. But the vitriolic gouts burn away all of his self-imposed bindings, and the dark-tide bursts forth, immolating the Soreshi around him. With dawn-, dusk-

, and dark-tide coursing through him, Anskar loses all restraint and revels in his power, ruthlessly slaughtering the Soreshi with sorcery.

The next day, the knights capture a Soreshi sorcerer named Zek, and Anskar stops them killing him out of revenge for the deaths the Soreshi caused. Over the next few days, Anskar and Zek talk about how sorcery works and how the tides interact. To the Soreshi, the dawn- and the dusk-tides are two ends of the same day. They have different applications, but neither is good or bad.

When the knights are attacked by mulag, supernatural creatures that travel with the mist, Zek saves Anskar by replenishing his dwindling dawn-tide repository, and the two become friends.

Arriving at Wintotashum, the Order knights are taken to greet King Aelfyr and a priest of Menselas named Brother Bonavir. King Aelfyr isn't impressed with the Order's small force of knights and makes his displeasure known. Aelfyr explains he plans to take the fight to the Soreshi, into the mountains.

King Aelfyr takes offense at Zek, a Soreshi, in their midst. He questions Zek, who reveals he believes an evil taint has corrupted many of the Soreshi. Aelfyr isn't convinced, but for the time being allows the Soreshi to remain with the knights.

Anskar and Zek talk more of sorcery, and Zek reveals that most Soreshi have braided their dusk- and dawn-tide repositories together seamlessly. As Anskar and Zek discuss religion and sorcery further, Anskar again becomes troubled with doubts about Menselas and the Order.

Queen Talia visits Braga and shows the blacksmith a full suit of armor, with Anskar wearing it. Braga believes Talia wants her to examine Anskar's vambrace and forge him a suit of armor using the same sorcerously imbued alloy. Brother Bonavir claims that Tain's notes are kept in the Scriptorium at Wintotashum.

Braga takes Anskar, Zek, and Bonavir to see Hrothyr, where they find out that Braga used to be married to him. Hrothyr admits he made the vambrace for Queen Talia, under duress. Hrothyr agrees to help them smelt the divine alloy required and to forge a full set of Divine Armor. Brother Bonavir says they will need the Ethereal Sorceress's aid in procuring the rare metals and minerals required, but her help will come at a price. Zek says he can steal the Necromancer Tain's notes from the Scriptorium using sorcery.

At another audience with King Aelfyr, Brother Bonavir talks up Anskar's sorcerous abilities, to Anskar's embarrassment. Aelfyr decides that Zek may be a spy and orders him imprisoned.

Anskar visits Zek in prison, and they further their friendship, discussing sorcery, Queen Talia, and the Armor of Divinity. Zek urges caution, as Anskar is in the dark regarding Talia's plans. Zek also teaches Anskar how to more effectively use the dusk-tide, and to crudely braid his dawn- and dusk-tide repositories. With Zek incarcerated, Anskar decides to break into the Scriptorium.

Queen Talia contacts Anskar, and he lowers his wards to speak with her. Talia approves of his plans and shows Anskar a way to break into the Scriptorium, using the same methods her spy Lengar previously used when he accessed Tain's notes for the knowledge that resulted in the creation of Anskar's vambrace. She also reveals that Lengar is still alive and might be of help.

But when Anskar breaks into Lengar's rooms, he finds the spy dead, killed by a man and a woman who are still there: Castellac and Haleki. The Tainted Cabal had come looking for a way to break into the Scriptorium in order to steal the memory crystal of Morudjin, the key to their summoning of Nysrog.

Castellac tries to persuade Anskar to join the Tainted Cabal, but Anskar refuses. At Talia's urging, Anskar uses the dark-tide to solidify shadow into lethal shards, and he shreds Haleki. Castellac shadow-steps away.

Able to break into the Scriptorium from Lengar's rooms, Anskar steals Tain's notebook. Brother Bonavir begins to copy the instructions for the creation of Armor of Divinity from the notebook. Next, they have to gather the rare ingredients.

Anskar visits Sheelahn the Ethereal Sorceress. She agrees to procure most of the ingredients required by Anskar except for the *nietan* horn, which Anskar must gather himself if he agrees to her contract: two unspecified services from Anskar sometime in the future. Reluctantly, Anskar agrees, and Sheelahn makes use of what she calls an *izindel* to transport Anskar to another of her depots close to where the *nietan* reside.

Carred and her group travel north to the Niyandrian coast at Tain's urging. The necromancer directs them to a shipwreck, where he claims a suit of Armor of Divinity is to be found. Carred has no idea how to retrieve the armor, until Queen Talia, through a possessed Noni, reinvigorates Carred's disused dawn-tide repository. Now able to use a cant to enable her to breathe underwater, Carred dives down to the shipwreck and takes the armor from an ancient skeleton.

Anskar steps out of Sheelahn's depot and finds himself somewhere under a blazing sun, with a dusty village nearby. A Traguh-raj woman arrives to greet him, Uraxa of the Agalot. Uraxa states that she is knowledgeable regarding the region and the *nietan*. They enter a crystal wasteland, all that remains of a once mighty city destroyed by sorcery in an ancient cataclysm. Uraxa takes Anskar to a crystal crevasse, wherein lies the *nietan*'s lair. After wandering through a warren of crystal passages, Anskar comes across a cavern with hundreds of smooth crystal eggs. The *nietan* appears, and Anskar is shocked that it looks like a small child with a crystal horn in the center of its forehead. In Anskar's mind, Talia urges him to kill the *nietan* and take the horn, but Anskar hesitates. He re-forms his wards and shuts his mother out of his mind.

The *nietan* transforms into a horned beast formed from compacted crystal. Rather than fight the creature, Anskar decides to leave it alive, and he retreats to safety. Believing he has failed, Anskar is relieved yet angry and disappointed that he will be unable to forge the Armor of Divinity.

Scurrying out of the lair, Anskar joins Uraxa. Holding her hand is the crystal child. The *nietan* offers its horn freely, and Anskar accepts. Translating for the *nietan*, Uraxa urges Anskar to cease following this path, and to remove the vambrace and cast it into the sea. Both Uraxa and the *nietan* weep tears for Anskar, for he is devoid of choice, swept along by his mother's plans.

Anskar returns to Wintotashum and the smithy, where Hrothyr says the rest of the ingredients needed for divine alloy have arrived by cart, courtesy of the Ethereal Sorceress. When Braga and Brother Bonavir arrive, Anskar implores them to remove the vambrace. Hrothyr attempts to, using pincers with tips made from divine alloy. Anskar's body convulses, and he passes out. When he wakes, the vambrace has been removed, and Gisela has been brought to heal him.

Anskar, Braga, and Brother Bonavir later discover that Hrothyr has been murdered. Hrothyr has a discolored forearm and they surmise he tried to put on the vambrace, which somehow killed him. They search for the vambrace, and when they find it, it leaps up and fastens itself to Anskar's arm. Bonavir reasons that only Anskar or Queen Talia can wear the vambrace, and anyone else who tries is rejected or killed. Using sorcery, Anskar returns Tain's notebook to the Scriptorium before anyone realizes it has gone missing.

Anskar joins the Order knights as they march against the Soreshi, reinforcing King Aelfyr's six hundred soldiers with their hundred. The Soreshi Zek accompanies them, although he is still guarded. On the way, they encounter many burned villages and corpses, along with signs of destructive dusk-tide sorcery, which Zek claims is considered an abomination by his people.

The King's forces take the fight to the Soreshi, and they attack an occupied town. The Soreshi sorcerers imbue their arrows with dusk-tide sorcery to penetrate the knights' arcane wards and their armor. As the Thousand Lakes soldiers hide behind a shield wall, Lanuc orders the knights to charge. Anskar unleashes the full potency of his braided repository, shielding the entire center of their line and allowing the knights to burst through the town's gates.

As the knights, Thousand Lakes soldiers, and Soreshi fight a bloody battle, Anskar comes face-to-face with a Soreshi sorcerer. Almost completely drained of the dawn-tide, Anskar attacks her with *Amalantril*. The woman blasts him off his feet, and the only thing that saves him is his ward sphere, which subsequently collapses under the strain. As the Soreshi sorcerer is about to finish Anskar off, he reaches for the dusk-tide, and his anger somehow also invokes the Warrior's Fire. He slaughters the Soreshi horde, blasting them into ash.

Anskar feels the tug of the dark-tide, and sees a man in black plate armor, who shadow-steps away. They now surmise the Tainted Cabal is behind the Soreshi insurgence.

The Armor of Divinity breastplate Carred retrieved from the shipwreck is damaged, but Tain uses the earth-tide to repair it, heating and shaping the metal. Tain uses Orix's essence to power his sorcery, as well as the iron and astrumium alloy in Orix's sword, destroying the blade. Orix almost dies in the process, and his face is warped, the features misplaced. Sick of Tain's deceptions and certain that he was deceiving her for his own ends, Carred yanks Tain's head from the Armor of Divinity helmet, and it crumbles into dust.

King Aelfyr and his forces celebrate the victory over the Soreshi with carousing and drunkenness. The Order knights and Anskar are subdued. In adherence to the strict ideals of the Order of Eternal Vigilance, they must remain sober and focused when on campaign.

Aelfyr has Zek locked in the town's dungeon as a precaution, and Anskar visits to keep him company and to continue learning all he can about the tides. Zek coaches Anskar on how to rebuild his crudely braided repositories to match his own: a latticework of gossamer strands of the dawn-tide interwoven in perfect balance with the dusk, each thrumming with a measured flow.

Later that night, Anskar joins Brother Bonavir and Braga at the town's smithy. Braga has been able to use the raw materials to forge three ingots of divine alloy. However, Braga says there's only enough *nietan* horn left for a few smaller pieces of armor. As they discuss the ingots and armor, the Tainted Cabalist Castellac appears. Castellac disintegrates Bonavir with sorcery. Anskar protects Braga with his arcane ward. Laughing, Castellac flees, but not before summoning a minor demon to attack Braga. Anskar's sorcery fizzles out, and in desperation he calls on Queen Talia for aid. But he is too late, and the demon grabs Braga and drags her into the shadows, where they disappear. Anskar snatches up the divine alloy ingots and pouch of powdered *nietan* horn, along with the copy of Tain's notes, and escapes the smithy.

With all of his confidants dead, Anskar confesses to Lanuc almost the entire story, and Lanuc informs King Aelfyr that the Tainted Cabalist Castellac was there and has killed Brother Bonavir and Braga. Learning from Anskar that Castellac wanted to break into the Scriptorium, King Aelfyr surmises he is after the memory crystal of Morudjin.

Queen Talia speaks to Anskar again, explaining that the vambrace was made for him alone and urging him to find another blacksmith to complete the Armor of Divinity. When Anskar balks, Talia says she can teach him how to raise Hrothyr from the dead to complete the work. Anskar is appalled, and he shuts her out again.

Angry and confused, Anskar seeks out Gisela in order to make his confession. She rejects him, and Anskar's anger grows. He is sick to death of being pulled between Menselas and his mother. He resolves to reject them both and pledge his allegiance to King Aelfyr in the morning.

Carred and the others arrive back at Naphor, the site of the old Niyandrian capital destroyed by Queen Talia. Orix despairs because of his disfigurement and has trouble eating and talking. Through her possession of Noni, Talia guides them to a ruined mansion and then explains that her ring, which Carred has carried with her all this time, is made from demonic void-steel. Talia says they need far more void-steel to complete the armor and that Carred must travel to the abyssal realms to procure more. Hidden in the vicinity of the ruined mansion is a portal chamber, and before Carred can object or agree, Talia sends her to the abyssal realm of Vulthanor to trade with the ruling lord.

Back in Wintotashum, King Aelfyr calls a full war council in order to drive the Soreshi out once and for all. Aelfyr reveals that the Tainted Cabal are behind the Soreshi and have insinuated themselves into the Ymaltian Mountains, taking over a long-abandoned Soreshi citadel. The previous night, the King reveals, the Scriptorium was entered and all the guards within slaughtered, mutilated, and defiled, and the memory crystal of Morudjin was taken.

Convinced that destroying the Tainted Cabal stronghold and retrieving the memory crystal is their only way of preventing a second demon war, King Aelfyr orders his army and the Order knights north to the Cabalist stronghold. Before they leave, they receive word that Gisela has been kidnapped by Castellac and will only be released if Anskar exchanges himself for her.

King Aelfyr forbids Anskar to go, but Anskar shadow-steps to escape the king's guards and breaks Zek out of prison to help him. They steal out of the city and ride in pursuit of Castellac's carriage.

Having been kept underground and unable to replenish his repositories, Zek partakes of the dusk-tide as night falls. To Anskar's astonishment, Zek's dawn-tide repository is also filled. Zek explains this is the benefit of a properly braided repository, and that the tides were never meant to be separated.

As Anskar and Zek approach the citadel gates, they are met by Castellac and a woman Anskar had hoped never to see again: the Abbess of the Abbey of the Hooded One, along with her son, Uspeth. Having no further need of Castellac, who is disfigured and broken from an attempt to summon a higher-order demon, the Abbess uses dark-tide to dissolve Castellac into a dark stain.

Anskar demands that they release Gisela now that he's here to give himself up. The Cabalists release Gisela, but she has been tormented and abused and driven insane. Gisela manages to mount a horse and ride to freedom with Zek.

Anskar is led deep into the citadel until they reach a summoning chamber with scores of dark-robed Cabalists painting symbols and polishing broad strips of brass riveted to the floor within a circle of quartz. The Abbess gives Anskar the memory crystal of Morudjin, and Anskar's mind is transported into Morudjin's memory of his disastrous summoning of Nysrog. When he returns, the Abbess and Uspeth are relieved Anskar's mind hasn't been damaged, and exultant with the knowledge he brings: that Morudjin's mistake was to try to coerce the demon lord with the dark-tide, which shattered Nysrog's mind into fragments.

Anskar refuses to participate further, so the Abbess uses sorcery to compel him. Anskar calls on his mother for aid, and Queen Talia answers with curses, saying that this is what they wanted all along: for Anskar to call on Talia's spirit in order to control her. After a sorcerous battle of resolve, the Abbess and Uspeth bind Talia to their will. Talia explains that they must use the earth-tide in order to complete their summoning of Nysrog.

Led by the Abbess and Uspeth, the Cabalists begin to summon the demon lord. As Nysrog begins to form, the Abbess forces Anskar to add his power to the summoning, and then commands Talia to use the earth-tide to reshape the demon lord. Nysrog's form begins to solidify, and the Cabalists rejoice, believing they are successful. But Talia has deceived them and was never bound to obey their will. The summoning deteriorates, and Nysrog's flesh slops in steaming puddles to the floor as he decomposes before their very eyes.

The Abbess is livid and tries to kill Anskar, but Nysrog recovers and destroys all of the Cabalists, then snatches up the Abbess in a clawed hand. Uspeth flees, shadow-stepping to safety, as Nysrog returns to the abyssal realms, taking the dying Abbess with him.

Anskar, exhausted from his use of the dark-tide, allows Talia to take the life force of the dead Cabalists and feed it to him. Anskar wonders how far he has fallen that he is willing to take for himself the very substance of these dying souls.

Anskar shadow-steps out of the citadel but is pursued by surviving Cabalist sorcerers and Soreshi. Under a terrible sorcerous assault, Anskar cedes control to Talia once more, and she uses earth-tide necromancy to summon a legion of skeletons from an old battle fought close by. Spent of all his sorcerous power and utterly exhausted, Anskar is carried by skeletons to safety while many more fight and delay the Cabalists and Soreshi.

But Uspeth has not fled, and finds Anskar in his exhausted state. Uspeth attacks Anskar, who unconsciously slings earth-tide power at him and uses the tide to create an arcane ward. Zek appears, having waited for Anskar once Gisela was safe. Anskar and Zek fight against Uspeth, the Cabalists, and Soreshi, holding them at bay with Anskar's earth-tide sorcery and Zek's braided repositories. But Zek is run through with Uspeth's sword and slain.

Anskar uses the dark-tide, but Uspeth's mastery is greater and the attack fails. In desperation, Anskar reaches for the earth-tide again. Uspeth has no counter, and the earth-tide corrupts his flesh, withering his limbs and rotting his body into a pool of pus.

But Anskar is sorely injured, and when Gisela attempts to heal him, she cannot. After being defiled by the Cabalists, she has lost Menselas' gift of healing. King Aelfyr arrives to mop up the remaining Cabalist and Soreshi forces.

King Aelfyr's army and the Order knights return to Wintotashum in triumph, the Soreshi insurgence quashed and the Tainted Cabal routed.

Anskar consoles Gisela, who believes her god has forsaken her.

Sareya, his ex-lover, arrives at Wintotashum. The Seneschal Vihtor Ulnar is dying, having been struck by a poisoned arrow. Vihtor has sent Sareya to bring Anskar back to Niyas before he dies.

BOOK FOUR: CONVERSION

C Vihtor Ulnar, Anskar's father and the Seneschal of Branil's Burg, is dying, struck by a cursed arrow. Anskar travels to the port city of Dorinah in Niyas via the Ethereal Sorceress' teleportation device, the *izindel*, in order to see his father before he dies. Vihtor implores Anskar to remember his training in the Order and the holiness of the god Menselas, and to not get involved with Carred Selenas and her plans to return the Necromancer Queen to life. As Anskar begins to disclose his plans, Vihtor dies from his unnatural wound.

Some days later, Sareya arrives for the funeral rites, along with General Monash, the new Seneschal, and Governor Niyas. Anskar tells Monash he will never use sorcery again, and plans to have his catalyst surgically removed. Monash urges him to reconsider, as the Order has need of his powers. She tells Anskar that Archduke Peleus, the father of Colvin, the knight who attempted to defile Orix and who was subsequently killed, has taken out a blood feud against him and Orix.

As Anskar processes the death of a father he believes did nothing except lie to him, part of him longs for his mother, Queen Talia, but another part hopes that she is gone forever. Determined to restore his purity as a Knight of the Order of Eternal Vigilance, Anskar scours the slums of the City of Dorinah until he finds an old Niyandrian sorcerer who agrees to remove his catalyst.

During the procedure, Anskar passes out from the pain and the trauma of severing his connection to his catalyst. Sareya finds him dumped in a canal, having tracked Anskar by his use of the dark-tide. Anskar's repositories are now a flaccid ruin, and he is unable to perform sorcery. But the removal of his catalyst was like the destruction of a dam, and the inheritance he had received—his earth-tide and dark-tide powers—surge with renewed vigor, as if finally unconstrained.

Back in Branil's Burgh, Seneschal Monash tells Anskar that he is to take a ship to Sansor, where the Grand Master of the Order, Hyle Pausus, will deal with him.

Meanwhile, Carred Selenas arrives in the abyssal realms on her quest for void-steel. Finding herself amidst an unending sea of massive standing stones, Carred wanders until she almost passes out from dehydration. On the verge of death, she is captured by a demon with alabaster skin and sapphire eyes, but she escapes his clutches by flinging powdered star-metal into his face. She flees, and after more excruciating wandering in the parched wastes, finds a stream to drink from.

Only partially recovered, Carred encounters another demon, who binds her with sticky threads. Believing she is doomed, she is startled when a woman rescues her. The woman claims to be able to take her to the Demon Lord Domatai, ruler of the realm.

One night before Anskar leaves for Sansor, the shade of his mother Queen Talia returns to speak with him. She admits she had hidden his dark-tide from him as a child, and the removal of his catalyst has awoken his latent power. When she begins to revile Anskar's father Vihtor, he flies into a rage and screams at her to leave. Believing him to be possessed, the Order perform an exorcism to cleanse his spirit of any taint, and Queen Talia's presence disappears.

Believing that Seneschal Monash and Grand Master Hyle Pausus represent the greatest threats to his newfound freedom, Anskar persuades his old friend Blosius, who is about to be expelled from the Order, to join him in fleeing the citadel. They travel to a depot of Sheelahn the Ethereal Sorceress, and she proposes a bargain: she will employ Blosius as a functionary, but refuses to transport Anskar anywhere. Out of options and on impulse, Anskar decides to go looking for Carred Selenas. After asking around the Niyandrian Quarter of Dorinah for Carred, Anskar is struck from behind and rendered unconscious.

He awakens in a hidden wilderness camp, a prisoner of the Niyandrian rebels, and is interrogated by Vilintia Yoenth, their leader in Carred's absence. Orix is among the rebels, and for the first time, Anskar sees the aberration the necromancer Tain has made of the Traguh-Raj lad's face. Noni is also there, fiercely protective of Orix, her mind warped from Talia's possession.

A Niyandrian necromancer named Eadgith explains to Anskar that Noni may be able to fix Orix's face, but not without her help. Anskar admits to Eadgith that it was probably a mistake to have removed his catalyst and lost access to the dawn- and dusk-tides. She agrees to do her best to help him control the earth-tide. With the help of her vile potions and rough teachings, Anskar begins to wrest control of the earth-tide *and* the dark-tide. Orix and Anskar settle their differences, and Orix reveals that Carred took a portal to the abyssal realms in search of void-steel, the missing ingredient to finish crafting the Armor of Divinity she'd recovered with the help of the necromancer Tain.

Anskar spends time with the rebels, especially Eadgith, Orix, and Noni. Eadgith is a font of information, and he slowly comes to understand Niyandrians and their ways. Under Eadgith's tutelage, his necromantic abilities develop at a startling pace.

In the abyssal realms, the woman leads Carred to two of her companions. All three are demons who are going to kill and eat her. Carred struggles in vain against a glamor they cast on her. Other demons, wearing armor of shadow, kill the three and take her to Lord Domatai.

Carred finds herself imprisoned by the demons in a dismal cell, but is soon visited by Domatai, Queen Talia's father. The Demon Lord explains that he killed and ate Talia's mother after she gave birth, and he strikes a bargain with Carred to trade star-metal for void-steel.

Under Eadgith's guidance, and with some insights from Noni, Anskar realizes the earth-tide is also a shaping tide, and that the basis of necromancy was re-ordering and re-forming rather than decay. Using this knowledge, he experiments with Noni's help, but further stokes Orix's hatred when she is caught kissing him.

Among the Niyandrian rebels, Anskar learns more of their ways and their history. Coming to understand them, he is more at ease, especially with Vilintia. At a feast to remember the fall of Naphor, the old Niyandrian capital, the dark-tide rises within Anskar, and he is overcome with a silent rage—an anger at Talia, the Order, Vihtor, and most of all himself. He is brought back to earth by Vilintia. With both of them drunk from the feast, they console each other and spend the night together.

In the morning they learn that Orix and Noni have left the encampment, and Anskar believes it's his fault. Searching the wilderness for them, Anskar is surprised to find a carriage sent by Sheelahn the Ethereal Sorceress, and a masked functionary he believes is Blosius. The functionary has been sent to take Anskar to Sheelahn's depot, because his debt is due.

With Sheelahn is Blaice Rancey, the tattooed and pierced treasure hunter Anskar had first met in Atya. The Ethereal Sorceress tells Anskar he is to join Blaice on an expedition to the abyssal realms to obtain star-metal. Their only way to return would be via a sorcerous miniature depot Sheelahn hands to Anskar.

Sheelahn transports Anskar and Blaice to one of the abyssal realms, and for hours they travel under a hot sun. Seemingly familiar with the demon realms, Blaice leads them to a large settlement. But before they can reach their destination—the city of Artuum-Nak'Urdim—they are set upon, and they fight their way through a mob of minor demons, only to come face to face with their master, a major demon. In the ensuing fight, Blaice flings star-metal at the demon, severely weakening it, before Anskar kills it. Without knowing what he's doing, Anskar presses a cut on his arm against the severed neck of the demon and subsumes its essence. The demon's life-force grants Anskar a measure of power, and he finds his dark-tide abilities strengthened. But Anskar hasn't just taken essence, he has absorbed memories as well. The demon's essence—its very being—is locked within a hard shell inside his mind.

Sneaking into the settlement in search of food, Anskar and Blaice try to blend in, pretending they're demons who have shape-shifted into human form. Following the star-metal indicator Sheelahn gave Blaice, the pair move closer to their goal, traveling along canals and through sewers and seldom-used tunnels. But just as they reach their goal, they are subdued and find themselves trapped in separate cells. Before long, Anskar is brought before seven demons who will decide his fate. They perceive he has the essence of another demon inside him, and torturing him for further information, they realize he is the son of Queen Talia. Deciding to take Anskar's power and essence as their own, the demons begin to tear down Anskar's defenses, until they are stopped by another powerful force—the Demon Lord Domatai—who is surprised to find that he has a grandson: Anskar. Domatai guides Anskar in controlling his dark-tide powers, shows him how to generate wings made of shadow, and tells him about other shadow abilities. Domatai reveals that he wants to use Anskar to summon Talia back to the realm of the living, which he can only do by using Anskar's blood link to her.

Anskar questions Domatai's motives, which stirs the demon lord to anger. Domatai uses dark-tide power to force Anskar to summon his mother back from the dead. As Talia's spectral form appears, the demon lord attempts to subsume her essence, but Talia evades his clutches and slips through the void to Niyas, following a link to Carred's lover, Marith. Marith, herself an accomplished sorcerer, captures the weakened spirit of Talia in a bottle.

Domatai incapacitates Anskar and begins to drain his blood in order to transfuse it into himself, in the hope of gaining immunity to starmetal. But the demon lord's plan fails as, according to Domatai, Anskar bears "the taint of Menselas." Domatai is furious, but tells Anskar he may still be of use, as a pet trained like a dog to serve him. He also reveals that he is a member of the Consortium, a shadowy council of powerful figures and organizations dedicated to enriching themselves on the spoils of Wiraya.

Domatai leads Anskar to where he has Blaice imprisoned, and Anskar despairs at her state—filthy and dehydrated, hung up by her ankles among animals awaiting slaughter. As despair creeps into Anskar, Domatai reveals Carred is also a prisoner. The demon lord asks Anskar to choose which one of the two women will be eaten.

Overcome with rage at Anskar's passive state, Carred lashes out, punching and kicking him. The violence and beating shakes Anskar from his daze, and in an instant he and Carred are on the offensive. Anskar manages to snatch the demon lord's sword and wound him, while Carred takes on lesser demons. With Domatai wounded, the pair flee, leaving Blaice to her fate. Carred and Anskar head to the chamber where Anskar's belongings are, intending to use Sheelahn's miniature depot to return to Wiraya.

With a horde of angry demons about to descend upon them, Anskar activates the miniature depot, and they find themselves back in one of Sheelahn's depots. But the Ethereal Sorceress and the depot come under sorcerous attack, and Sheelahn is grievously wounded. She urges them to escape via her teleportation device, the *izindel*. Carred makes sure to take some void-steel ingots, though she's still uncertain about telling Anskar that void-steel is an essential ingredient in the Armor of Divinity: without it, he'll end up just like the necromancer Tain.

They find the *izindel* chamber overrun with Knights of the Order, led by Sareya. Anskar is angry, and protests about what the Order has done, attacking the depot and killing the Ethereal Sorceress. But Sareya is unrepentant, and Anskar attacks her with sorcery. The fight is short-lived, and neither gains the upper hand. Sareya reveals that she has been hired by Archduke Peleus to capture Anskar and Orix.

With a surge of dark-tide, Anskar forms shadow-wings, scoops Carred into his arms, and escapes the depot, flying out into the city of Dorinah.

At Queen Talia's urging, Marith heads to Dorinah, where she says she can sense Anskar. She releases Talia from the bottle she's imprisoned in, and Talia lends her power to Marith. They assault the city gates, intending to rescue Anskar.

Weak from blood loss and his recent ordeal, Anskar cannot maintain his shadow wings. Sareya tracks them by getting inside Anskar's mind with sorcery. Anskar tries in vain to banish her with the dark-tide. In desperation he reaches for the corrupt earth-tide— necromancy—and drives Sareya from his head. The exertion is too much, and he collapses, leaving Carred the only one standing against Sareya, Seneschal Monash, and at least fifty knights.

Believing the situation hopeless, Carred is determined to go out fighting. But Anskar is not finished yet, and reaching for reserves of power and grit he never knew he possessed, he throws himself deeper into the corruption of the earth-tide.

Sareya attacks with sorcery, but Anskar's earth-tide shield repels all her efforts. And then Queen Talia, via Marith, blows the gates of Dorinah apart, and the Niyandrian rebels invade the city.

In the chaos of the ensuing battle, Anskar's powers tear apart dozens of knights, and he absorbs their life essence to further fuel his earth-tide sorcery.

Meanwhile, the rebel Niyandrians and Order knights do battle, with heavy losses on both sides. And Noni, having come with the rebels, finds Orix and sacrifices her own life to fix his deformed face.

Anskar chases down Sareya and bests her with sorcery, but his powers continue to build within him until he all but loses control. Before he destroys the fleeing Order knights and unleashes a cataclysm on Wiraya, the likes of which has not been seen in centuries, Carred brings him back to his senses.

Victorious, the rebels celebrate the defeat of the knights and the retaking of Dorinah, the old Niyandrian capital. Having witnessed Anskar's dark powers, they acclaim him the true *Melesh-Eloni*.

And all the assembled Niyandrians kneel to him.

And Now the Conclusion...

ONE

THE CHURCH OF THE FIVE was burning. Flames razed the timber frame, erupting from the steeple in a roaring blaze. Black smoke plumed into the sky, wafting towards the battlements of Branil's Burg, both a warning and a goad to the knights cowering inside the citadel.

Anskar stood as close to the conflagration as he dared, heat prickling his face as he watched the building being consumed from the inside out. Acrid fumes irritated his nostrils, making his head swim and filling his mouth with the taste of soot. Pews crumbled into charcoal, and tapestries went up in whorls of brown and green smoke. Behind the altar, the five-headed statue of Menselas smoldered within a corona of fire.

He should have been appalled. He had seen the church under construction that first time he'd left the Burg with Vihtor, one of many built in the wake of the mainland conquest; yet all he felt was a hatred so cold it simmered inside and froze his heart. He had been duped his whole life. The powers from overseas—those who had raised him— were oppressors. The mainland rulers were the empire builders, not

Queen Talia. Wealth, not Menselas, was their god. That much had been made abundantly clear when Sareya and the knights under her control had come for him, doing the bidding of Archduke Peleus. The Knights of the Order of Eternal Vigilance acting as paid thugs, if not assassins! Hypocrites, the lot of them. The Order was a sham; the Church of Menselas a five-faced lie. His mother had been right all along. Pity was, she wasn't here to see it.

In the street behind him, Niyandrian rebels cheered as they hacked apart the bodies of Order knights and hurled limbs and heads at the walls of the citadel. Anskar's jaw clenched, his veins throbbing with a savagery to match that of the rebels. He was one of them now. Niyandrian barbarism was in his blood. And yet… He closed his eyes, inhaling deeply of the air aswirl with ashes. The effect was like plunging a white-hot blade into a slack tub. Thoughts, images, desires, and regrets hissed and steamed through his mind as his hands repeatedly clenched and unclenched.

He glanced over his shoulder at Carred Selenas, shuddering as her lover, Marith, consoled her. But consoled her for what? They had won, hadn't they? For once the rebels had won. And it was no secret why. Anskar's sorcery had been too much for the knights—too much even for Sareya. He couldn't quite suppress a swell of pride at that. When they had been trainee knights together—when they had been lovers—she had always been one step ahead of him in sorcery. Maybe Carred's problem was that the victory was his, not hers. All she had achieved over the years was a litany of failures. And yet… it didn't feel like victory to Anskar. The guilt clumped in his guts made it feel more like a betrayal. These knights had once been the only family he'd ever known. His eyes stung with unshed tears, and he took a deep breath.

Marith glanced at him, giving the impression she somehow knew his thoughts. Anskar returned his gaze to the blazing church. There had been a smug look on Marith's face, and he didn't think it was gloating that she had Carred and he did not.

What was going on? Why was Marith even here? Some niggling feeling tugged at him, urging him to look back, but he fought against it. He had already sensed it during the fight against the Order of Eternal Vigilance, before the hundreds of rebels who stormed into Dorinah had sent the knights scurrying behind their walls. Marith was wearing a satchel over one shoulder, and there was something within that called to him. Something familiar.

He saw Orix emerge from one of the buildings the rebels had commandeered. At the close of battle, the Traguh-raj lad had carried Noni inside, the young Niyandrian woman dead and disfigured—as disfigured as Orix's face, the eyes where the mouth should be, the whole thing a jumbled mess. An effect of the earth-tide, apparently, one he had not previously heard of. His mother had only shown him the earth-tide's power over the dead, and then only as much as she'd thought he needed to know, the minimum to keep him alive in a crisis.

Orix glared across the street, his eyes seeming to say, *You could have saved Noni if you had wanted to. You could have raised her to new life, and you didn't. Why, Anskar? Are we no longer friends?*

Were we ever? Anskar wondered as he turned away.

A gust of smoke stung his eyes and caused him to step back, coughing. He looked up at the citadel, but still no knights manned the parapet. It was as if they didn't care about the desecration of the church. As if they didn't really believe in Menselas. They had, after all, converted the chapel of the Hooded One into a vault for mainland wealth. You didn't do that if you really believed in a fair and just god.

"Come fight me!" Anskar yelled, and hundreds of Niyandrian voices jeered at the empty battlements.

How could they call themselves knights when all they did was hide behind the walls of their stolen fortress? It had been Niyandrians who had built those walls, all that now stood between the Burg's garrison and death.

"Niyas has risen!" Anskar cried, and the army roared. They understood him, even though he had spoken in Nan-Rhouric. No doubt they had been forced to learn the tongue, else be excluded from the broader society foisted upon them by the mainlanders. He repeated himself in Niyandrian, and this time the roar was even louder.

Carred's rebels had come, right at the moment he needed them most. It was a sign. *Of course it was,* a sarcastic inner voice said, and he silenced it with a whiplash of thought. He was done with indecision, and he no longer believed in coincidences. This was the time.

"I'm right here!" he yelled, voice hoarse from the smoke and the ash. "Come out and fight me!"

No reply.

Nothing but the spit and crackle of flames, the crash of falling timber sending up showers of sparking motes, and the taunts of the rebel army. Anskar was tempted to unleash them, his red-skinned dogs of war. But were they his to command? Carred had bent her knee to him, so surely they would do whatever he asked—even leap into the roaring flames, if he so desired it. Probably they thought he could bring them back to life afterwards; make them live forever. Belief, he realized, was such a strong goad. A single blast of sorcery and he'd have them through the gates. Nobody should think he couldn't do it. He was the son of the Necromancer Queen. Just look at what *she* had done to Naphor!

Power boiled in his blood, and he spoke a cant. Emerald light suffused his skin.

"Anskar, no!" Carred cried.

She had been at Naphor, where she'd seen the devastation wrought by Queen Talia's last act of defiance.

"Do you want to win this war, Carred?" he said softly, sorcery carrying his voice above the storm wind of his power. "How about victory for a change?"

Shards of green light burst from his hands, weaving together in a chaotic sphere above his head. The heart of the sphere pulsed in time with Anskar's breaths, and the emerald light grew dense and heavy as it swelled with force.

"You'll kill us in the blast!" Carred yelled. "And you'll die too, just like your mother."

"Until we rise again," Anskar said. "We are Niyandrians. Death cannot hold us."

Anskar's feet rose from the ground. He opened his arms and arched his back, pouring tidal essence into the agitated sphere, laughing as it throbbed and strained.

"Marith!" Carred screamed.

At once, the sphere fizzled out, and his surging power drained from him.

Anskar's boots struck the ground with a thud, pain jolting through his kneecaps from the impact.

"What have you…?" he croaked, no breath left in his lungs for rage. His lips, when he licked them, tasted of tar.

Violet light radiated from Marith's satchel, already starting to recede. "No more Naphors," she said in a voice enhanced by sorcery—it sounded like two voices entwined, a harmony of betrayal.

And perhaps it was. *The love of my love,* Queen Talia had said when the demon lord Domatai—her father—had summoned her shade to the abyssal realms. When she'd tried to escape, Talia's instinct had been to flee to Carred, her lover in life, but Carred had been as trapped in the abyssal realms as she was. Not Marith, though. *The love of my love…*

"Marith's right, Anskar," Carred said. "A piece of Niyas died that day. We must not lose another."

Anskar was barely listening. His mind was awhirl with implications. If Talia had indeed flown to Marith, why hadn't she let him know? Was his mother angry with him for being instrumental in her summoning by Domatai? Or didn't she need him anymore? If her spirit had been ripped from the realm of the dead during the summoning, perhaps she no longer needed the Armor of Divinity; no longer needed him to wear it in order to bring her back. In some way he couldn't yet discern, she was right here, right now. The Queen had returned, and not at all in the manner he had expected.

"You started this, Carred," Anskar said. "Don't you ever see anything through? It's no wonder Niyas is losing the war."

"Niyas lost the war," Marith said. "Carred was there at the end, remember, when Naphor fell. But don't blame her for this." She glanced at Vilintia Yoenth, stiff and straight, knotted with ropey muscle—Anskar had seen for himself; felt the strength of her embrace. Vilintia's prematurely gray hair was speckled with blood, and her hands and forearms were smeared with it. "And don't even think of blaming Vilintia. The attack on Dorinah was my decision, and I stand by it."

Anskar's senses prickled at some response from within Marith's satchel. The dark-tide flowing in his veins seethed but could do nothing more. Marith's sorcery had rendered him impotent.

Vilintia was watching him, but she swallowed and looked away when he noticed. Perhaps she had read his mind. She disgusted him. How could he have lain with her? With any of them? The Abbess, for Menselas' sake! Blaice Rancey. Sareya. Though when he thought about Sareya, it was anger he felt, not disgust. Violence and lust. She had been paid to capture him, part of Archduke Peleus's blood feud. She had challenged him in the streets of Dorinah. Almost bested him. Some friend she had turned out to be! She was a traitor to her own people, fighting for the Order of Eternal Vigilance. She was supposed to be moontouched, a sorcerer of unusual power, chosen by the ancient gods of Niyas. Before Anskar had left for the mainland, Sareya had constantly complained about the Order—pointed out its oppression of her people, its excesses, its evils. She had painted her nails, for Menselas' sake, with the symbol of Black Wing, the spirit name of Queen Talia. Then, the moment Vihtor died, she had switched her allegiance to the new Seneschal—probably jumped into bed with her. Filthy, cheating, turncoat Niyandrian whore!

He became aware that Marith was waiting for his response, Carred at her elbow, a little lost child clinging to her mother. Carred frowned and shook her head. It was as if she said, *You've got it wrong. I'm torn. Between my hope for you, Anskar, and my disappointment; between loyalty to my queen and fear of her son.* Well, she was a fool, then. She had nothing to fear from him. He was only doing what she had wanted all along: assuming the role that had been destined for him, uniting the people and ending the tyranny of the mainland occupation.

Because that's what he needed to do: end it. A line had been crossed. There was no turning back now.

"We must attack," he said. "Take back the citadel for Niyas."

"Why bother?" Carred said. "If we maintain a siege, starvation will force them to surrender."

"I could have destroyed them," Anskar said, "if you hadn't interfered." He directed his ire at Marith. "Dorinah could have been ours, the first stage of our reconquest of Niyas. It's what they would do, were our positions reversed."

"And then what?" Carred said. "Destroy the next stronghold, and the next? And even if you could, what then? Reduce Niyas to rubble so you can be king of the ruins? Think, Anskar. You used to be better than this. Something happened to you in the abyssal realms. You changed."

"I awakened," he said. "This is who I am; who I've always been."

"No." Carred shook her head. "You're not right. You're out of balance. Prone to extremes."

"Now you sound like my old mentor, Brother Tion," Anskar said.

"Maybe he was right."

"And maybe you should put out the fire," Anskar said, gesturing at the church. "Because you're starting to sound like a lily-livered devotee of Menselas, not of the old gods of Niyas."

Carred drew in a sharp breath through gritted teeth, and Anskar noticed Marith squeeze her hand.

"Fine," he said. "Have it your way. I'll not destroy the Burg with sorcery. Happy now? We'll storm the walls instead. Marith and I can use sorcery just to breach the gates." He liked how Marith's attention sharpened when he included her in his plan. Some energy shifted within her—or was it within her satchel? All he had were his passive senses, no dark-tide tendrils with which to explore. Not without Marith's consent. Not unless she restored his power.

"There are too few of us for an all-out assault on the citadel," Carred said.

Hundreds of Niyandrians filled the street in front of the burning church. Anskar hadn't realized how quiet they had grown, listening to him and Marith and Carred. Did they still accept his leadership? Had their enthusiasm waned now that Marith's sorcery had held him back—at Carred's command—and revealed he was no godling? He quashed the thought that he could incinerate every last one of them, show them who was the rightful ruler of Niyas; because he wasn't sure that was true. Marith had snuffed out his power as if it were nothing. Not just Marith, though; he was certain of it. She was being aided.

"More Niyandrians are on the way," Marith said, eyes fixed on Anskar. "Word has been sent. The sleepers will come."

"Who sent the word?" Carred said, with a fierce look at Vilintia. "I gave no such command. What sleepers?"

"Peace, love," Marith said, still watching Anskar. "We have entered the end game. Anskar is right: we should storm the citadel. It is what Queen Talia wishes."

Anskar gave Marith a knowing look. Much better. Now perhaps they could get on with it. Without Marith's backing, Carred was nothing.

"You know all this how?" Carred asked. She snatched her hand away and confronted her lover. A ripple ran through the lines of rebels. Vilintia gripped the pommel of her sword, eyes flitting between Carred and Anskar.

"I was going to tell you… " Marith started.

Before she could finish, someone yelled and pointed up at the battlements.

There were figures there now, visible between the merlons, sunlight glinting from weapons and helms. Anskar strained to see, looking for Sareya among the defenders, but she wasn't there. Disappointing. Nor was Seneschal Monash. He spat into the flames. Coward. Some leader she'd turned out to be. Vihtor would have stood his ground. He would have rallied the knights to ride outside the keep and fight.

"What were you going to tell me?" Carred asked.

"Later," Marith said. "When we're alone."

"Just make sure you don't leave me out," Anskar said. "I want to know too. I am the *Melesh-Eloni*, after all."

Carred swallowed as she nodded. "No secrets," she said. "If you two are right, and this is the time, we need to act as one."

"If we are to act as one, we need trust," Anskar said. "Whatever you've done to block my powers, Marith, you need to stop it… for the sake of Niyas."

Marith glanced at Carred.

"Carred's right," Anskar said. "I'm not myself. I swear I'll follow her lead until I grow into my new powers. Until my mother's return." He paused to see if Marith would react. Her jaw might have tightened. "Or until I am crowned in her place."

"I agree," Carred said. "We can't do this if we are divided."

Marith closed her eyes, lips moving, either in a cant or in consultation.

Dark-tide essence fizzed through Anskar's veins, the tinder of its power crackling into a blaze that rivaled that which had consumed the church. The tidal force felt different somehow. Evolved. Or perhaps more primal. His back arched as heat shot up his spine. Marith took a step toward him, but he held up a hand.

"It's all right," he said. "I'm all right. It's just the shock of you unblocking the flow of my power." He quelled the tide rising within him and spread his palms. "See? Nothing to worry about."

It was an effort keeping a calm demeanor. Magma bathed his insides, scorching hot. Dark-tide swelled like a head of steam, threatening to burst free of his control. Instinctively he sent his senses plunging below ground till he found a connection with the earth-tide and let it bubble up through his boots. Its cold effluence flooded his veins, quelling the darkness and keeping it in check. The two tides swirled around each other in a dance of courtship that swiftly turned to rejection. Anskar gave an involuntary shudder. Eels writhed through his guts, but then they seemed to clump together and grow still.

He breathed deeply, his focus turned inwards as he drove his senses through his organs, his limbs, the marrow within his bones. The dark-tide had grown dormant, coaxed into sleep by the earth-tide. He had regained control—or at least the illusion of control. His knowledge of the dark and the earth was too scant for him to trust either tide, but for now they had both settled down, which was just as well. The last thing he needed was for Marith to negate his power again. Without it, he was nothing defenseless and scared.

When his focus turned outwards again, his eyes once more fell upon Marith's satchel. Coaxing a few strands of dark-tide back to life, he sent them questing into the satchel, but sorcery repelled them. It hadn't come from Marith: her repositories were perfectly still, and no essence shifted within them. And she only possessed the dusk- and the dawn. Yet it had been an effect of the dark-tide that had warded against him. And not just any old dark-tide; this he recognized, almost as if it were his own.

So, he was right. The Necromancer Queen had returned. But in what form? The one consoling thought: if she were here, then Queen Talia had permitted Marith to restore his power. Perhaps she still needed him after all. Maybe even loved him?

"Look!" Vilintia cried, pointing up at the battlements.

A knight was waving a white flag, at the same time gesturing to the west, where the barbican stood.

"They're coming out?" Carred asked.

Anskar was still staring up at the knight with the flag. He thought he knew the man.

"Vilintia, stay here," Carred said. "And keep half our force watching the side gate, just in case. The rest of you, with me."

Anskar flashed Carred a look. The knights had retreated to the Burg through the side gate. Did they now want to leave via the main road that led away from Dorinah?

"You think the white flag is a ruse?" Vilintia asked.

"If it is, they'll pay for it," Anskar replied.

"I'll come with you," Marith suggested. She almost sounded motherly.

"Of course." Anskar started down the street toward the edge of town, Niyandrian rebels falling into line behind.

It was a lone knight that emerged from the barbican gates. He was wearing poorly fitting armor and walked with a pronounced limp, a dog trailing behind.

Anskar bit down a rising tide of emotion. He would have recognized the man by the flicker of his malformed ward sphere alone.

"That's it?" Marith said. "The Seneschal is too busy? All we get to talk to is a lame old man with a shoddy ward sphere?"

Carred looked at her askance, as if she didn't quite approve. But before the tension between them could grow, she deflated it with a shrug. "Unless we're supposed to negotiate with the dog."

"Stay here," Anskar said. "Both of you stay."

Marith shrugged. "You know him?"

"I do. I know him."

Anskar met Larson halfway. "You think that ward will make any difference if my people fire on you?" he asked. The rebels who had followed him with Carred and Marith started to creep forward, but he stopped them with a glare.

"Probably not," Larson said, banishing the sphere with a wave of his hand.

Anskar couldn't meet the stablemaster's eyes, so he crouched down and petted Rosie instead. The ridgeback hound drew back, snarling, and Anskar snatched his hand away.

"It's me, girl," he said as he stood. The rejection smarted. "Have I changed so much?" he asked Larson.

"You tell me, son." The stablemaster jerked his head toward Carred and Marith, who had advanced a step to be at the head of the rebels. "Changed who you associate with, for one thing. And if what they're saying is true, you've changed inside, too."

"What are they saying? Who?"

"The knights who saw what you did in the street. Seneschal Monash. That girl you were so hung up on not so long ago. Sareya, wasn't it? Going places, that one is, and I don't just mean up the new Seneschal's ass."

"Sareya has power," Anskar said.

"She's not the only one."

Anskar puffed out his cheeks and looked over Larson's shoulder at the barbican. Through the partially open gate, he could see that the portcullis was only half-raised. Beyond, in the bailey, white-cloaked knights were gathered in ranks. He recognized several knights-liminal among them, who had been made up the same time as he. None of them would have expected active duty before taking solemn vows, but perhaps there had been no choice. A lot of knights had died in the streets of Dorinah. The garrison was getting thin.

"You told me you didn't know about my past," Anskar said, still not able to look at Larson.

"And I didn't. None of us did."

"Save Vihtor. Did you hear he was my father?"

"Vihtor?"

Anskar finally met Larson's eyes, gauging the stablemaster's reaction. "Monash didn't mention it?"

Larson shook his head. "I had no idea. I know I should have done. It makes an obvious sort of sense now. But why would he…? I mean, how?"

"Oh, so you've heard about my mother, then?"

"Talk of the Burg, son."

"And you're not scared."

"I know you, Anskar. I know what you're capable of… and what you're not."

"That was before you found out I was the Necromancer Queen's son. Before I found out."

"It changes nothing."

Anskar sighed. For some reason he felt like laughing. Not a good reason. Not a funny one. "Why did they send you?"

"No one else had the nerve."

"But you did."

"Like I said… "

"So what happens now?" Anskar asked. "What does Monash want?"

Larson took a step toward him, shortening Rosie's leash as she barked and growled. "To withdraw. She knows you've got us beat, Anskar. Let us go. There doesn't need to be more bloodshed. More killing."

"And what do you think will happen if you do that?" Marith said, striding toward him. "They'll set sail for the mainland and come back with more ships, more knights. There are powers at work who will not let our victory stand, Anskar. This is our land. Ours!"

He nodded slowly, knowing she spoke true. "Carred?"

"The mainland armies will come anyway," she said. "Word will carry from Branil's Burg to the other strongholds. They have ways and means—pigeons, for one thing. It's only a matter of time before the strongholds send to the mainland for help. I say let them go. A little mercy shown now might help us in the future."

"No!" Marith said. "I forbid it."

"*You* forbid it?" Anskar asked. He glanced at her satchel, and Marith didn't miss it.

Anskar let the silence simmer for a moment, then turned back to Larson.

"Tell Seneschal Monash this for me: Tell her to leave my isle, and to take everyone with her. Tell her to send messages to the strongholds: leave now, or be next."

Behind him, Marith let out a sigh, apparently appeased.

Anskar stuck his face in Larson's, as if the stablemaster were the new Seneschal and not just her mouthpiece. "When the mainland armies come, we will be prepared. I will be ready. She knows what I can do already, but how much more will I be capable of by the time an invasion force is raised? I'm still growing, Larson. Even I don't know how much is left to come."

Marith let out a low chuckle. Oh, she knew; Anskar was growing ever more sure of that. Queen Talia knew. But how strong would she let him grow? That was the question. This had always been about her return, not seeing him placed on the throne.

"There's only one galleon in the harbor," Larson said. "What if there's not enough room on board for everyone?"

"There are fishing boats," Anskar said. On clear days, he had sometimes watched them bringing in their catches from his bedroom window. "Just tell her to go. How isn't my concern."

Larson tried to mask his expression, but Anskar could tell he was disappointed. Not with the outcome of their meeting; that was as good as he could have hoped for. Disappointed with the lad who used to muck out the stables, take care of his old horse Hazel and Monty the donkey. As disappointed as Rosie was fearful of him now. Of what he'd become.

The stablemaster gave a stiff nod and turned away, his flimsy ward flickering back on around him, in case Anskar wasn't as totally in control as he would like to believe. In case someone among the rebels agreed with Marith's first take and saw blood as rightful vengeance and the first step to cleansing the isle of all the corruption that the mainlanders had done.

"Larson…" Anskar said, and the stablemaster stopped without looking round. "Thank you for everything. I'll not forget how you helped me growing up."

Larson reached down to stroke the crest of hair on Rosie's neck. "Nor will I, son. Nor will I."

As Anskar watched the stablemaster enter the barbican and the gates shut behind him, his hand drifted to the hilt of his sword. His fingers curled around the hilt, and he felt a sudden urge to draw the blade and thrust it through Marith's heart. She was standing beside him now, as if they were equals, as if she had a bond with him, over and above the one she had with Carred.

"Was that man a friend of yours?" she asked.

"Is," Anskar said. "He *is* my friend."

"Split loyalties?" Marith asked. "Is that how your mother would wish you to proceed?"

"Marith…" Carred said. She shook her head in warning, and Marith smiled an apology. "We should get back to Vilintia. Theltek only knows what will happen if these bloody sleepers start pouring into Dorinah, or if some of our own stragglers show up. It'll be all an idiot like Fult Wreave needs to assert his command, and I don't know about you two, but a return to the Ickthal Dynasty and their perversions is not the kind of Niyas I want to live in. Anskar?"

Was she asking his permission? With a nod, he granted it, ceded control back to her, at least for the time being.

You will have to deal with them, a thought said, each word in time with the vibrations coming through the hilt of his sword.

"Carred and Marith?" Anskar asked, aware of the bizarreness of speaking with *Amalantril,* yet at the same time feeling it was totally normal. His blood seethed, sending pulses through his fingertips. He felt certain there was no need for him to speak. The sword could feel his thoughts.

Marith and your mother, Amalantril replied. *You have already intuited this. You are nothing to the Necromancer Queen save the means of her return. But what need has she of you now? What need of the Armor of Divinity? She is here already. You know this, Anskar. You have felt her presence. Sooner or later, you are going to have to fight her.*

TWO

"MARITH, I HAVE TO KNOW," Carred said. "Does Talia speak with you?"

"Is this your definition of alone?" Marith said, indicating the thousands of newcomers massed in the square, filling every tributary street, and the thousands more still pouring through the city gates. "I said we'd speak when it was just the two of us."

Carred had given up greeting the new arrivals; she'd stopped listening to their boasts of what they had done, how they had overpowered Order patrols, driven mainlanders from their villages. She would have been more impressed if they had laid siege to strongholds; the fact that they hadn't told her the uprising wasn't quite as universal as she'd been led to believe. That made her cautious—even more than she usually was. What in Theltek's name was Marith keeping from her?

There were old seasoned warriors, many of whom had fought in the war, with youngsters among them, daughters and sons. She could feel the pressure of powerful, sorcerous wells, but the majority were ordinary Niyandrians: villagers, townsfolk, and farmers. Had they just abandoned their crops and their flocks, their shops and their livelihoods, at an anonymous word of command?

Frowning, she looked around for Fult Wreave and his supporters, but saw no sign of the Ickthal standard. Maybe the arrogant prick was running late, or he was too busy fomenting a rebellion of his own—against her. She hoped Wreave wouldn't come, then worried about what it would mean if he didn't. What if Wreave went over to the other side in return for concessions from the mainlanders that might elevate the Ickthal Dynasty to its former prestige? Would he do that? Was even Fult Wreave capable of such a betrayal? Of course he wasn't, Carred told herself. He might have been an idiot with a silver spoon shoved up his ass, but he was a Niyandrian idiot. Give it time. He would come.

But seeing the thousands pour into the city, one thing was undeniable: her rebellion had gone from the remnants of the Last Cohort to a leviathan that could soon get out of control.

"You think we'll have a chance to be alone—in this? You think I can wait that long? Tell me now, Marith. And don't deny what I know is true. There's something different about you. You've changed."

"No," Marith protested. "I haven't. I'm the same Marith." Her smile looked a mad one, not congruent with her eyes. "I still drink too much wine, and I still feel cold in bed at night."

Carred's heart skipped a beat. "One thing you never were was cold; you were permanently in heat. And let's not forget it was you who used to throw the covers off."

"Of course I was cold. Surely you remember?"

"That was Talia, Marith."

Their eyes locked, and Marith swallowed and then looked away. "You told me about Talia, but that doesn't mean I'm not the same. Lots of people feel the cold."

"True," Carred said. She became aware she was hugging her arms across her chest. "I… "

"Are you the cold one now, sweetie? Want me to—?"

"No." Carred turned her head aside. "What I want… I'm sorry, love, I don't know. I don't know what to do, or what's going on."

"You've just got back from the abyssal realms," Marith said. "It's no wonder you feel overwhelmed. Theltek knows I do too. It's all moved so quickly. You need time to recover, time to readjust, to think."

Maybe, Carred thought, but something definitely felt wrong. She couldn't even look Marith in the eye as she muttered, "You're right, love. I'm sorry. I've not felt myself since the portal ripped me apart and put me back together in the abyssal realms. And the return journey wasn't any easier."

"It's all right," Marith said, touching Carred's cheek with her fingertips. "I understand. You've been through a lot. Anyone can see that."

Of course they can, Carred thought wryly. *It's not you that's changed, it's me. I'm the crazy one. Are you sure you're not really a man, Marith? Not that a real man would have implied any such thing; certainly not a man like Kovin.* She almost smiled, then almost wept. *The memory of Kovin weakened her—his inability to wear masks around her; his unashamed simplicity; his honest, open lust.*

"Can you be here?" she asked, meeting Marith's gaze, willing her eyes to smile with her mouth. "Help Vilintia? The poor girl looks like she's drowning over there. She keeps looking at me for instruction, but it's not me these people have come to see."

"No, it's not," Marith said. "Your job is done, Carred, after so long. It's Anskar they've come to follow."

"You're sure about that?"

"Who else? They've come to see the *Melesh-Eloni,* to answer his call."

"Do they even know who he is?" Carred said. "Are these the Sleepers you spoke about? It wasn't you, Marith, was it? Tell me you didn't summon them."

"Why would they listen to me? I just… I hear things."

"From Queen Talia? Can you hear her now?"

"Later, Carred. What I have to say is for your ears only. Go. Do whatever you need to do. Think, rest, get some sleep."

"With all this going on?" Carred looked towards the tavern at the edge of the square. Vilintia had told her that was where Anskar had gone after speaking with the lame knight, Larson.

"Go speak with him, if you must," Marith said. "I'll be right here. I'll take care of everything." She waved at Vilintia, who extricated herself from a group of Niyandrian nobles and approached, relief etched into her face.

"Thanks," Carred said, then hurried off toward the tavern before Vilintia could corner her.

The Brief Repose seemed to Carred a name more fitting for an embalmer's than a tavern. Appropriately enough, the atmosphere inside felt like that of crypt as she let the door creak shut behind her, deadening the sounds from outside. The interior was no more than a gray room with empty tables, cold ashes in the hearth, and a stale beer smell in the air. A fat Niyandrian was wiping out glasses behind the bar, casting nervous glances at the one customer seated on a stool, head dipped, hands clasping an untouched mug of beer.

The touch of gossamer threads danced across her well, measuring her, knowing her.

"Carred," he said without looking round.

"Anskar, I…"

"I told Vilintia I wanted to be alone."

"Bet she loved that," Carred said, standing her ground by the door. "There's a bunch of disgruntled Niyandrians outside in the road, clutching empty mugs. What did you do to scare them off?"

He swiveled round to face her.

"Oh… " Carred said.

He had a crazed look about him, his eyes bloodshot, though that could have been from drinking. But it was more than that. He looked tormented. Lost. Somehow, that betokened danger.

"Well," she said, "I guess that explains what put the fear of the Corpse Maker in them. Theltek's asses, Anskar, you look terrible. And I thought it was just Marith I had to worry about."

"What's up with Marith?"

"Nothing I can't handle." A lie, but she wasn't ready to trust him—a man with glassy black eyes—with her suspicions.

He caught her frowning and turned back to his untouched drink.

"It's not the first time my eyes have changed," he said. "The last time, it was the dispelling of an illusion—that I was really a mainlander."

"And this is the same?" Carred asked. "There are layers to the illusion?"

She felt the urge to go to him, but something held her in place. It might have been fear; might have been Anskar's will.

"I don't know what's happening to me, Carred." He looked longingly into his beer, but still didn't take a sip.

"How long have you been here, Anskar… just sitting?"

"Too bloody long," the bartender said. "Costing me money, he is. Costing me customers."

"Watch your mouth," Carred said, anger breaking the spell that held her immobile. She strode toward the bar. "Do you even know who this is? You should be on your knees, you fat bastard, never mind daring to speak."

"Let him be," Anskar said. "He's the only one who's said anything… real… since we got back from the abyssal realms. Save maybe Larson."

"Real?" Carred said. "Enlighten me. What did you say to him?"

"Called him a maudlin, self-absorbed little prick," the bartender said.

"And you let him?"

Anskar's grip on his mug tightened, and he spilled beer. Nevertheless, he smiled. "He knows what I'm capable of," he said. "When I entered this place, the others fled at one look from me. The fact that he didn't… "

"Speak truth to power," the bartender said. "That's what my mother taught me."

"Maybe she didn't like you, then," Carred said. She was the expert in such things. Her mother had made no secret of what she thought of her daughter. "Speak truth to the wrong kind of power and you'll end up like the ashes in the hearth: cold and dead."

"You saying you want me to get the fire going again?"

"That's not what I… Yes, that would be nice. A fire to chase some of the chill away, don't you think, Anskar?"

"I'm not cold."

"Well, I am. Down to the bloody bone."

With a *tsk* and a sigh, the fat man came round the bar and set about rebuilding a fire in the hearth with a box of kindling and logs from a cast iron rack.

Carred leaned over the counter and grabbed herself a half-empty bottle of wine, pulling the cork with her teeth. The bartender glared at her over his shoulder, then shook his head and got back to laying the fire.

"So, where is Marith?" Anskar asked.

Carred took a long pull on the wine, then wiped her lips as she set the bottle down.

"Helping Vilintia with the new arrivals."

"Organizing them, you mean? Isn't that your job? Or aren't you the leader now?"

"Not around you, I'm not. But would you look at us! Anskar DeVantte, son of the Necromancer Queen, the *Melesh-Eloni*, the great hope of Niyas; and Carred Selenas, Captain of the Last Cohort, ringleader of the rebellion, sitting in a tavern together, while outside the monster rises."

"Monster?"

"You think it will be anything else?" Carred asked. "All these people swarming to our side. To do what? Take Branil's Burg? Lay waste to the isle, just so they can call it theirs again? In whose name? Did you order this, Anskar? I don't think so. And it definitely wasn't me."

"Marith?" Anskar asked. "What brought her here?"

"She knew I was in trouble, I suppose. Even when we were in the abyssal realms, she knew."

"She has that kind of power?"

"You tell me. She nullified your sorcery easily enough."

"That wasn't her," Anskar said. "At least, she wasn't acting alone."

Carred met his black eyes; felt herself sinking into their depths and looked away. "So, you felt it too." Then she whispered, "Talia."

"It's all right," Anskar said. "She can't hear you. Not here, not now."

She became aware of a heaviness in the atmosphere around them, a tightness in her scalp. "You're warding us?"

"With the dark-tide," Anskar said. "It's easy for me now. As easy as breathing."

"And that's a good thing?"

Anskar returned his gaze to his beer. This time, he took a drink. "Do you think…" His hands were trembling, and when he turned his head to face her once more, his dark eyes glistened with moisture. "Has Menselas cursed me?"

"No!" she said, as if the idea were absurd. But maybe it wasn't to him. "Of course he hasn't. This… What's happened to you, Anskar… It's not your fault."

"I know that. But it's what I am." He broke down then, and started to shudder. "I'm a demon, Carred."

"Half," Carred said. "No, quarter. That's not so bad."

"This isn't a joke!" Anskar said. "You saw what I almost did back there. I could have annihilated the entire city."

"Like mother, like son?" Carred said. "Only you're not like Talia, are you? She would have actually done it."

"But Naphor," Anskar said. "You were there. Did she have a choice?"

"We always have a… " Carred started, then stopped herself. Was she being unfair? "I don't know. Maybe not. We had already lost the war."

"So, if you were in my mother's place, you would have just surrendered?"

She'd thought about that a lot these past eighteen years. Would she have surrendered, given the hopelessness of their situation? Or would she have gone out in a blaze of glory, just to spite the invaders?

"Could you imagine Queen Talia a prisoner?" she asked. "Do you have any idea what they would have done to her, these mainlanders you used to think you were one of? Beaten her, tortured her, humiliated her before her people, and much, much worse. And I'm not just talking about the secular soldiers, either."

"I know," Anskar said. "I've seen what the Order of Eternal Vigilance is capable of. The spies you sent to the Burg disguised as builders, for example. I wish I could forget what was done to them."

Carred closed her eyes and pinched the bridge of her nose. "I was given sketchy details."

"Then let that be enough. You say there's a monster forming outside, but maybe it takes a monster to fight a monster. You think that's what I am?"

"You're no monster, Anskar."

"Are you sure?"

Carred's eyes fell upon the hilt of the sword hanging at his hip. It loomed suddenly in her vision and expanded to fill her mind. A wave of pure hatred slammed into her, and she fell back against the bar, gasping for breath.

"What is it?" Anskar asked, rising from his stool.

Carred's eyes lifted from the sword to his face. There was concern in his frown, but it wasn't reflected in his eyes. Nothing was. They seemed to swallow the light.

"I'm okay," Carred said, taking another swig of wine. "Just hungry, is all."

"I suppose you'll be wanting something to eat now," the bartender said, returning from the hearth, where fire spat and crackled in the grate.

"I'll pay," Carred said. "For both of us. For the drinks, too."

"You'd better, because I don't care who you think you are, the pair of you. No freeloaders in my tavern."

Anskar shook his head and chuckled. "I like him," he said as the man went out back to the kitchens. "In a funny sort of way, he reminds me of… Oh, you didn't know Braga, did you? She was a blacksmith. Plain speaking didn't do her justice. She was vile and bloody rude. But at least I knew where I stood with her."

"If you want me to insult you… " Carred said.

"Believe me, I don't. Not right now. I doubt I could handle it."

They drank in silence till the bartender slapped down a bowl in front of each of them.

"Eel stew. And before you go whining, no, it's not fresh, but you've only yourselves to blame for that. Whole city's shut down on account of the fighting and the influx of troublemakers."

"Think of them as loyalists," Carred said. "Niyandrians who've come to fight a war."

"Like we need another bloody war," the bartender said. "I still haven't gotten over the last one. I'll be in the kitchen if you need me. Washing up. 'Cause if I don't do it, no one else will. Bloody kitchen hands didn't show up for work today, and you know who we can thank for that?" He jabbed a finger at Anskar, then at Carred, before heading back through the door to the kitchen.

"He's not wrong about the stew," Carred said after her first mouthful. The meat was stringy and the taste bitter. She set her spoon down. "Still, it's cured my hunger. Yours too, by the looks of it."

Anskar hadn't so much as looked at his stew. Like a man who had reached a decision, he raised his beer mug and downed what was left in one. When he'd finished, he wiped his lips on his sleeve. "More!" he called.

"When I'm good and ready!" the bartender said, voice muffled by the door.

Anskar turned on his stool and stared at Carred for the longest time. Her skin crawled under the scrutiny of those dark eyes.

"How did you know Marith was under my mother's influence?"

"Because I know Marith, that's why; enough to know she's not herself."

"And, of course, you knew my mother… equally as well."

"You're not going to ever get over that, are you?" Carred asked.

"Did you?"

Carred drummed her fingers on the countertop. "It took a while."

"You loved my mother?"

"In a way."

"You mean, she didn't give you a choice."

Carred sighed and leaned back against the bar. Theltek's eyes, she was thirsty. "Where's that beer?" she yelled. "Make it two, if you can count that high."

"Hold your bloody horses," the bartender said, coming through the kitchen door. "Two now, is it?" he started to refill Anskar's mug from a tapped keg. "And you couldn't tell me that before?"

"I wasn't thirsty then."

"Typical. Next you'll be wanting me to drink it for you and take a piss for you after."

He slammed Anskar's beer down on the bar, then poured a fresh one for Carred.

"You take payment in queens?" Carred asked, fishing out some Niyandrian coppers.

"Queens! What good are queens nowadays? Real money's what we accept here. Mainland currency."

Carred slapped a mainland silver coin on the bar. "Not for much longer, the way things are going. Have you thought about that? Whose side are you on, little man?"

He gave her a sly look, then pocketed the coin. "The side that wins."

Anskar watched the bartender exit through the kitchen door, then said, "Domatai… "

"The demon lord is your grandfather. I got that. The father Talia never wanted to speak about. The demon she was always so terrified of."

"He made me summon her, Carred."

"He what?"

"I summoned my mother from the realm of the dead."

Carred sipped her beer. "You can do that?"

"I couldn't before. She was petrified. All she did was scream and spin about, looking for some means of escape. Why is she so afraid of her own father?"

"You're asking me?" Carred said. "If he's anything like mine, or worse still, my mother… "

"She screamed your name, Carred. I think she wanted to flee to you, but she couldn't."

"Because I was in the abyssal realm at the time?"

Anskar nodded. "Domatai's domain, yes. So she fled to the only other person she could think of. Someone she knew you trusted. Someone you knew inside and out."

"Marith," Carred whispered. "But Marith's moontouched. Not even Talia could get through her defenses if she didn't permit it."

"Maybe she didn't," Anskar said. "Marith's still herself, but Talia is influencing her, I can sense it. Something about that satchel she carries."

"Talia's in the satchel? I've seen stranger things—like the severed head of a necromancer still jabbering away inside his helm. Speaking of which, does that mean you no longer need the Armor of Divinity? After all we went through?"

"I don't know," Anskar said. "My mother has returned from the dead, but only in spirit. She lacks substance, lacks a body."

"Explain this to me," Carred said. "What would have happened if you'd worn the Armor of Divinity and fetched your mother from the realm of the dead? Were you supposed to bring her back with you— inside you? Is that how it works?"

"I don't know."

"Maybe she planned to take the armor from you… and leave you behind in her place."

She couldn't tell if the idea shocked him when he looked at her; his eyes conveyed no expression.

"You think she would be that callous?" Anskar asked.

"You tell me. She's your mother."

"Don't play around, Carred. A lot hinges on this. You knew her better than most."

"Yes, yes, I was her lover. That was a long time ago, Anskar. People change. I've changed."

"Ah, but do the dead change? Can they?"

"I suppose we're going to have to find that out."

"Will you serve her?" Anskar asked.

Carred raised her mug to her lips and left it there while she considered. "That depends. I'm your guardian, remember?"

"Because she made you so. But what if… "

"If you and Talia come into conflict? Which one will I serve? Well, assuming I don't just knock your heads together… "

A colossal roar came from outside.

"What in Theltek's name?" Carred said.

Anskar raised a hand for silence.

A second roar came, this one rolling into wave after wave of jeering and cheering, amid the clangor of steel; and then a booming detonation shook the tavern to its foundations. The bartender came stumbling out of the kitchen door, covering his ears. Echoes of destructive sorcery blasted through Carred's well. She met Anskar's empty gaze, and together they stood and rushed outside.

The disgruntled drinkers Anskar had scared from the tavern were staring off into the near distance, up at the walls of Branil's Burg, which were limned with emerald light. Cries sounded form the parapet, followed by a succession of cracks and the seething rush of masonry cascading toward the ground.

"Sweet Menselas!" Anskar swore, as an entire section of curtain wall came tumbling down amid plumes of dust and the scream of knights plummeting to the street below.

The devastation was greeted with deafening cheers, and then thousands of Niyandrians surged through the breach in the walls, sunlight glinting from swords, spears, and axes, coruscating streamers of sorcery streaking through the air.

"Marith… " Carred breathed. "Theltek, what has she done?"

THREE

SAREYA TRAILED HER HAND THROUGH the water, as if the icy cold could leech away the heat of her anger. Sent away with two rowers and a fishing boat, to get her out of the bay and onto one of the mainland galleons patrolling Niyandrian shores! Hardly a dignified escape from Branil's Burg.

And it wasn't even like she wanted to escape. Varensi—*Seneschal* Monash—had been too quick to capitulate. Worse, she'd not even had the courage to go out and negotiate the surrender face to face. She had sent the bloody stablemaster, for Kaythe Nurglich's sake! Larson, of all people, and his bloody dog. Sure, Larson had more of a relationship with Anskar than Monash did, but not more than Sareya. That would take some beating.

"I'll go," she had said.

"And do what?" Monash replied. "Overwhelm Anskar with your sorcery? I think you already tried that, and failed."

Bitch. Self-important, manipulative, using bitch.

"Failed? He surprised me with how much his powers have grown, that's all. I'll make adjustments. It won't happen a second time."

"No," Monash had said. "It won't."

Which is when she'd pulled rank and charged Sareya with a mission, if that was what you could call it. A craven bloody errand, more like. Take a report to Sansor, so the powers-that-be would descend upon Niyas in force. Why you would need a moontouched sorcerer and the new Seneschal's lover for that was beyond her. Any half-rate postulant could have gone in her place. She should have stayed behind to fight. But that was sort of the problem; the reason Varensi wanted her out of the way. The Seneschal had decided it was better to surrender than to go down fighting with honor. Not that Sareya was big on honor, but the Order of Eternal Vigilance was supposed to be. Menselas's five faces, she'd just started to change her tune about the Order—something Varensi had been instrumental in—but now… Now, she just felt betrayed.

Worse, she felt like a rat, the way she'd scurried through the tunnels beneath Branil's Burg—more evidence of the genius possessed by the Niyandrian architects who had designed the citadel in a bygone age.

She should have remained at Monash's side. The entire garrison should have suited up and ridden forth for one last glorious charge. Not that it would have necessarily been final, she kept telling herself. With her sorcery, unfettered from the Order's strictures, they could have won. *She* would have won.

Anskar's too strong, love, Varensi's last words to her repeated in her head. *You're right, he's grown; but grown into what? I'll not risk you, my scarlet beauty. No more arguments. Go now.*

A shared bed on the way back from Sansor, when Varensi had received the commission to take over Branil's Burg following Vihtor Ulnar's death; snatches of heat when no one was looking. That's all it was: a mutual itch that needed scratching, a primal desire as old as time. At least to Sareya, it was no more than that, no more than she had experienced with Niv Allund or any of the boy knights. With Tion, even. But Monash seemed to think it gave her rights over her, a power of command that exceeded her rank as governor of the isle. Sure, Sareya liked the prestige and the attention, but part of her was left feeling like the great majority of red-skinned Niyandrians under the heel of the Order's rule: a slave. Theltek's hundred pricks, had she been so stupid, so easily swayed by a show of fake interest, the prospect of respect, of a smidgen of power?

Out of all her lovers, only Anskar had been different, but it was a curse to admit it. A knotty clump of rage formed in Sareya's guts whenever she thought about how she had stolen his innocence.

It wasn't love, she told herself. *I was converting him, showing him who he truly was.*

Right! She could imagine Varensi saying the same about her—how she'd brought a heretic Niyandrian fully into the fold. The fact she'd broken rules to do it, given in to the sin of lust, didn't matter to Varensi's type. The ends justified the means. They always did.

For a while it was undeniable that Monash had been successful. Sareya stopped painting her nails with the soul name of Queen Talia, Niyas's last legitimate ruler. Anskar's mother! She'd shunned the company of the other Niyandrian trainees at the Burg, stopped invoking the names of Niyandrian gods. Until now. Kaythe Nurglich, the Corpse Maker! When had that name last passed Sareya's lips? Or that of Theltek of the Thousand Eyes?

She looked up at a break of the oars cutting through the water. The two Dorinian fishermen who'd been commandeered for the task—both dusky-skinned mainlanders—rested their oars in the tholes as the boat drifted toward a bank of fog so thick it seemed a wall of white.

"Why have we stopped?" Sareya asked.

"Listen," one of the men told her, cupping a hand to his ear.

Beneath the skirl of the wind, she could hear it now: the snap and flap of canvas, the creek of wooden yards flexing.

"Starboard," the other rower said, and they dipped the oars back into the water, altering course.

Sareya pulled her white cloak around her, wrapping herself in the authority it signified. Would the ship's captain permit her to board? Probably not, if she hadn't been carrying a letter from Seneschal Monash. There were more than a few consecrated Niyandrians in the local garrisons, but among the crews of the mainland patrol ships, dark skin, not red-tinged, was more often than not the norm.

As she peered into the thickening fog, a twinge pricked the base of her dusk-tide repository. Some instinct made her turn around and then scoot to the stern. High above the waterline, Branil's Burg loomed like a saw-toothed mountain, the quays of Dorinah's harbor sprawling away from the buttressed curtain walls. The bridges and towers and the scattered tenements of the city rolled away into the hazy distance. The citadel had been her home since childhood, when she'd been ripped from her family and raised to serve a foreign god.

As she let her eyes run along the Burg's parapets, her dusk-tide repository clenched like a held breath.

An emerald sunburst exploded in the sky above the citadel, followed by a colossal boom. The air crackled and fizzed. Waves surged outwards from the base of the Burg, shunting the boat forward. Sareya clutched the gunwale to stop herself falling overboard. The rowers glanced over their shoulders nervously, then redoubled their efforts, propelling them toward the fog.

The echoes of the boom reverberated around Sareya's skull, sending fluttering ripples through her repositories. The stench of burnt metal reached her nostrils on the wind. Screams sounded from the far side of the citadel. The crash and rumble of falling stone. Dust billowed into the air, shrouding the Burg's highest towers. And still people screamed, a spreading wave of despair. Then there were voices raised in jubilant triumph. Niyandrian voices, breaking out into the ancient paean of victory that had last been heard before Sareya was born, before the empire Queen Talia had been in process of building had started to collapse in on itself as the mainlanders curbed her power.

"Turn back!" she yelled at the rowers.

The two shared a look, but neither responded.

"We have to go back!" Sareya said, grabbing a rower by the shoulder.

"And do what?" he snarled. "Listen! That ain't the sound of a battle. That's the sound of a massacre."

"I order you… " Sareya started, then swallowed as the prow of a massive ship emerged from the mist, sails bellied by the wind, the five-pointed star of Menselas in red upon the pennant streaming from the main mast.

FOUR

ANSKAR BENT DOUBLE, COUGHING AND spitting out dust, as he and Carred climbed over the rubble of the curtain wall and entered the bailey. Smoke plumed from the charred grass, and a molten stench abraded his nostrils. Emerald motes danced around him—dust set alight by sorcery. It scorched as he breathed it in, prickled his face and the back of his hand when he covered his mouth and nose. Carred's red skin had paled to almost pink as she stared around in shock, her cat's eyes bloodshot and glistening. Anskar's own eyes streamed as he blinked sparking motes from them. Through a coruscant haze, he could see burnt bodies strewn across the bailey, dismembered by the blast.

"Do something," Carred sputtered. "I can't breathe."

She was the only one with him. The entire rebel force roared ahead of them, oblivious to the billowing emerald dust, driven on by rage and revenge, or, he suspected, sorcery.

With a surge of dark-tide, Anskar muttered a cant and blew the dust cloud away from them, then threw up a ward of glistening opacity around himself and Carred. He saw the walls of the keep beyond as if through twilight, but at least he could fill his lungs without burning them.

"We were right," he said. "This is way beyond what Marith's capable of."

"But how can you be sure?" Carred asked. "Marith's moontouched. She has exceptional control of the tides."

"The dawn and the dusk, maybe, but this is more than that."

There was powerful sorcery in the air, stronger than any he had felt before—save for perhaps when he had almost incinerated the Burg, before Carred had talked him down. He sensed it was dusk-tide mainly—the source of the devastation that had brought down the walls. But he also recognized the residue of the dark-tide, and his innards clenched in revulsion at the sewer-stench (was he the only one who could smell it?) of the corrupted earth's putrid flow.

As they followed the rebel horde through the shattered doors of the keep, there were butchered knights and servants everywhere. Most of the servants were Niyandrian, but that hadn't saved them.

"Who would do this?" Carred asked as she surveyed the bodies. "Marith would never... never... "

But she had. The skin of Anskar's face tautened with rage. His fist ached from clenching too tightly. It had been bad enough how the Niyandrian servants had been treated by the knights, but this... Butchered by their own kind. And for what? Because they had been forced to serve the enemy? Because they were too weak to refuse? He couldn't help himself: he looked for Jonita among the dead, the kitchen hand he had worked alongside as a child. If she was there, he didn't recognize her; but then didn't recognize any of the slaughtered, the butchery was so extreme. Menselas, some of them looked as though they had been half devoured by wild beasts.

Blood drenched the floors and spattered the walls and ceilings. The injured and dying moaned and cried out, but he forced himself to press on. He wasn't even sure they really were alive. It wouldn't be the first time he had heard the dead.

"Stop!" Carred commanded a cluster of rebels outside the Dodecagon, blades rising and falling as they cut down a group of postulants, all of whom wore no armor beneath their blood-drenched white cloaks. "I order you to stand down!"

The rebels turned on her, red skin a shade redder with the blood of their victims. At first, Anskar thought they were going to attack, but they simply approached the dark ward sphere that protected him and Carred, outstretched hands coming to within a hair's breadth of its glistening surface. Eyes at once frenzied and blank, they turned away and resumed their grisly business.

Beyond the rebels, through the wide-open doors of the Dodecagon, the broken bodies of knights lay slumped across the thrones that lined the walls.

"We have to find Marith," Carred said.

"Before it's too late?" came Anskar's acerbic reply. "It's already too late." Cold dread gripped him as the full implications of what was happening sunk in. Faces like ghosts rose to fill his mind. "Sweet Menselas… Larson!" He froze as he thought of all the people he stood to lose; people he had known all his life. "Sned," he muttered. "Vaila, Crosbyn… " Good people, all of them. "Sareya… " He'd come close to killing her during the battle outside in the streets of Dorinah. He'd wanted nothing more. But now…

The dark ward vanished. He lacked the focus to sustain it.

"Why…?" Carred asked, but Anskar was already running, sword in hand.

He beat back futility as if it were a spell of despair. He had to find Sareya, Larson, all the others.

He could hear Carred breathing hard behind him as they raced along corridors, up stairs and down, following the footprints in the blood, the screams of the dying, the bodies of the dead. There were slain rebels among them, an entire group pulverized against a wall by a ward sphere turned into a bludgeoning fist of force. He hoped it was Crosbyn or Vaila; hoped they were still alive and that he could stop this—stop Marith—before there was no one left.

The air grew hazy with heat as they drew nigh to the smithing hall, where the fighting was still fierce. The glow of the forges reflected orange from clashing blades, and the clangor of steel echoed from the stone walls.

Anskar and Carred approached the backs of a Niyandrian mob, who threw themselves against a wall of silver ward spheres. Dusk-tide streaked from outstretched hands, fizzing, igniting upon impact with the wards and erupting in prismatic bursts of fire. Several ward spheres buckled. Others flickered, close to failure. Anskar strained on tiptoe to see if he knew any knights still alive.

In a fury, Carred grabbed a Niyandrian woman from behind and spun her round. It was Vilintia, cat's eyes burning with madness. Carred let go and stepped back in shock. Vilintia's sword darted toward her throat, and in that instant, Anskar felt it… felt the corruption that infected her; *saw* the inky thread that penetrated her skull. Before he realized what he was doing, he flung out his senses in a wide net. They found blood and the bodies of the fallen. With a thought—less than a thought—he drew their ebbing essence into himself and bound it into an intention; an intention that grew solid, becoming a shard of razor-sharp bone that streaked towards Vilintia and severed the connection with her mind. Vilintia's sword clattered to the floor and she pitched to her knees. A compost stench rose in Anskar's nostrils, its rank odors effusing from his skin.

Carred stepped in and cracked Vilintia on the jaw with a left hook, spinning her to the ground.

"What in Theltek's fucking assholes are you doing?" she stormed.

The fighting continued unabated, sparks showering from the clash of blades, the zip and flash of sorcery. The Order knights backed up through the doors of the smithing hall, ward spheres sputtering. Before the Niyandrians surged in after them, taking them from view, Anskar glimpsed Crosbyn, his bald head and mustache speckled with blood; beside him stood Vaila, gaunt and open-mouthed as she struggled for breath. And he saw Seneschal Monash at the same time as she saw him, her one eye narrowed to a venomous slit. And he realized then: she hated him in that moment. She believed—they all did—that he had gone back on his word to Larson; that he had betrayed them.

"I thought we'd accepted their surrender," Vilintia told Carred in Niyandrian. More than it had ever done, it disquieted Anskar that he had learned the language from a ghost, and in so little time. The spirit of his mother. The language, the slaughter, the rebels, frenzied and possessed, the presence he had felt in Marith's satchel—right now, at this moment, he felt them rolled into one, a confluence of impressions, an illative sense that saw the true hand behind the slaughter. "But Marith said you countermanded the order. She told us to attack."

"Did she now?" Carred said. It looked like an executioner's sword she held. "Since when did I give her a position of command? Marith has no authority. What are you, Vilintia, a soldier or an idiot?"

"But—"

"You think because I sleep with someone, that qualifies them to give you orders?"

"Of course she doesn't," Anskar said. "If that were true, Orix would be a bloody dictator."

"Oh, for Theltek's sake, grow up!" Carred snapped.

Her words stung Anskar like a slap. But she was right: he was being an ass. Was he really so immature, so bitter because she'd rutted with Orix instead of him? Because he had only slept with an illusion worn by a brown-toothed crone?

"I wanted to wait for you to confirm," Vilintia sobbed, looking to Anskar as if he would back her up—as if what they'd done together at the rebel camp meant something. Realizing she would get no help from him, she turned back to Carred. "But then… but then… Oh, sweet Theltek, what have I done?"

"You did nothing," Anskar said, reaching down with his hand. Vilintia took it, tears tracking down her dust-grimed cheeks. "This was done to you." Before Carred could object, he locked eyes with her and said, "They're under the influence of mind-altering sorcery."

"Dark-tide? Marith told me she would never—"

"Not the dark," Anskar said.

With his help, Vilintia stood.

One by one, Anskar began to sever the tendrils of earth-tide infecting the rebels, and as he did, they flopped exhausted to the flagstone floor.

"Where's Marith?" Carred demanded, but Vilintia pushed her away, appalled.

"Stop what you're doing!" she yelled at Anskar. Then to Carred: "Tell him to stop!"

Noxious vapors rose from the flagstones, roiling through Anskar's insides. Cold sludge oozed in his veins. His heart thudded once, then grew deathly still. With growing efficiency, he severed connection after connection, but Vilintia had drawn his attention to what he'd been too wrapped up in his sorcery to notice: as the Niyandrians slumped to the floor, the knights took advantage, powering forward, sticking the prone rebels with their swords.

Instantly, the earth-tide slopped away from Anskar, through his boots back down to the vile pit it had come from.

"Seneschal, stop!" he cried at Monash. "You don't understand. Please, stop!"

"Oh, she understands right enough, boy," Crosbyn growled. "We all do."

The old sergeant flung out his ward sphere like a fist. Instinctively, Anskar's dark ward came up. Crosbyn's luminescent fist swelled in Anskar's vision and then hit the ward with concussive force. Anskar staggered under the impact, and his ears started to ring, but his ward sphere held. Crosbyn's knees buckled, and he stumbled.

Anskar stepped toward him. "This isn't what I want!"

Still the knights hacked into the prone rebels. He felt a surge from Vaila's repository, but Anskar was faster. Taking his cue from Crosbyn, he projected his ward outwards, not as a fist but as a billowing sheet of blackness that flew over the heads of the rebels and dropped like a curtain between them and the knights. Swords struck the dark-tide barrier, sending rills and ripples across its surface. Vaila's fist of force slammed into it, buckling the center then sputtering out.

Holding his shadow wall in place with a thought, Anskar pushed through the rebels as they regained their feet. There were only eight left. On the other side of his barrier, twice that number of knights were still alive, ghost-like through the wall's opacity. He pressed his face up close to the barrier, and then, with a deep breath, he walked straight through to the other side.

Monash came straight at him, sword arcing toward his face. Anskar's hand lashed out. He caught her wrist and squeezed. Spittle sprayed from the Seneschal's mouth as she cursed, straining to reach him with her blade. She was stronger than her willowy frame suggested, but her resistance quickly ebbed away. She'd fought too long already, and she knew her efforts were futile. The last spark of hope fled her one eye.

Anskar held on to her wrist, drilling his eyes into her pinched and hollow face. Her white leather eye-patch had come dislodged in the struggle, revealing the puckered scar and the empty socket beneath. Her gray hair, shorn close to the scalp, was spattered with Niyandrian blood. The ermine collar of her white cloak was showered with it, and the cloak itself was torn and ragged. She was lucky to be alive, Anskar surmised, judging by the dent in her steel breastplate.

"Let it go," he breathed. "This ends now."

She hesitated, then her sword arm went limp. Anskar released his grip, stepping back to survey the other knights. None of them had moved. No one had come to the Seneschal's aid. They were afraid, he realized. Afraid of him; of what he had become.

"This wasn't me," he said. When he elicited no reaction from Monash, he sought out Crosbyn, but the old knight was gray with exhaustion and barely keeping his feet.

"You half-blood bastard," Vaila snarled.

"Silence!" Monash said. She resituated her eye-patch. "If he wanted us dead, we would be."

Anskar glanced behind at his barrier. On the other side, he could make out the blurry form of Carred watching him. Vilintia and the other Niyandrians stood motionless, as if they no longer knew what to do.

"You lied, son," Crosbyn said. The old sergeant gave a hacking cough, and Vaila grabbed his elbow to support him. "You broke your word to Larson."

"No!" Anskar said. "I didn't. It wasn't me who ordered the attack. You have to believe me!"

Monash studied him, her good eye narrowed. Words were exchanged among the other knights.

"Whether we believe you or not," the Seneschal said, "Branil's Burg has fallen. Or are you going to order your new friends to just hand it back? If you're anything like your mother, maybe you'll bring our dead back to life. Because anything less than that, and I don't give a damn who started this massacre. You reneged on your vows to the Order. You betrayed everything your father stood for."

"I surrender," Anskar said, stooping to lay his sword on the flagstones.

"Anskar, no!" Carred cried, her voice muffled by the dark barrier.

"Just you?" Vaila said. "And your army?"

"Like I said—I didn't order them to attack. Someone else had control over them."

"Then what difference does it make if you surrender?" Monash said. "You think these Niyandrian scum will just let us go?"

"Course they won't," Vaila said. "Because they know what'll happen if we find our way back to the mainland."

"War," Monash said. "Are these savages ready for another war, Anskar? The last one didn't go so well for them. The next will be worse."

"Please," Anskar said, despising himself for the tears rolling down his cheeks. "Let me try to make this right."

"I don't think you can," Monash said. "A line has been crossed, so you might just as well kill us. I would, in your position."

"And you would be right to," a woman's voice said, as Anskar felt his connection with the dark-tide barrier break and the shadow curtain dispersed into the air.

"Marith… " Carred gasped from behind him.

Marith came from the far end of the corridor, trailed by dozens of rebels. Her red skin effused emerald light, and her hair writhed like serpents. The stench of forge-heated metal and rot accompanied her, causing Anskar to gag. More than one of the knights turned aside to retch. In one green-glowing hand, she held a leash of inky vapor that pulsed with a murky phosphorescence; the other end was wrapped around the neck of a squatting aberration, an old woman, hump-backed and twisted, knuckles trailing the ground. Her bloodless face, froggish and melted like wax, was so misshapen he almost didn't recognize her, and when he did, he wished he hadn't.

"Eadgith?"

The squatting horror gibbered, thick ropes of drool spilling from her lipless mouth. She tried to speak again, her bulbous eyes bloodshot and glistening with tears, but Marith yanked on the leash, causing Eadgith to choke. Sickly light pulsed along the leash, still glowing as it entered beneath the skin of Marith's hand and coursed through her veins. At the same time, Eadgith contorted and cried out. When she ceased, she looked thinner, diminished.

"Let her go," Anskar said.

"A bit late for that," Marith replied. "Eadgith's dead."

Anskar swallowed bile. The earth-tide swilled all around Marith and the moribund old woman, drawn through the soles of Marith's feet, but it was strongest elsewhere… it coalesced within the satchel she wore over her shoulder.

Dead?

Eadgith still crouched at Marith's side. Essence passed between them along the umbilicus that was the lead. But her eyes… he should have seen it earlier. Not just bulbous and veined with red: they were sightless, like a dead-eye's.

"You killed her?" Carred said. Her advance was checked by a sharp look from Marith.

The rebels behind Carred stood in hushed awe. Anskar couldn't tell if they were petrified or reverent. The Order knights watched with undisguised horror. Monash's single eye was on Anskar, as if she'd read the situation and decided he was all that stood between them and death.

"I chose Eadgith to serve," Marith said, "and still she serves. She will serve until she is flaccid, dried up, no more than an empty husk."

"Then what?" Carred asked. Her chin was trembling. "Who will be next?"

"You think it should be you, lover?" Marith said. She smirked as Carred took a step back. "Because it can't be Anskar—not my precious little *Melesh-Eloni*."

"You think I'd let you?" Anskar said.

"You think you could stop me?"

With the merest stroke of his will, shadow armor wreathed his flesh. A dark helm formed around his head. He risked a glance toward *Amalantril*, abandoned on the floor.

Marith smiled and the armor dissolved into the air. "Bad boy," she said. "So much still to learn. Such as your place!"

Marith flung out her hand and Anskar was punched off his feet. He flew back into the rebels, scattering them. Air exploded from his lungs as he slammed into the ground on his back.

"Marith!" Carred cried. "You have to stop."

Suddenly, Marith's face contorted with anguish. "Love, I can't!"

Carred screamed as she lunged in with her sword. Marith's hand came up, and Carred's legs gave way beneath her, as if the bones had been ripped out. She collapsed, her legs bent at unnatural angles. Shuddering as she whimpered in agony, Carred pushed herself up on one elbow, her free hand scrabbling about for her sword.

"Poor little Carred," Marith said, "left all alone in the woods. Naughty Mommy didn't want you. Naughty Daddy—all that drink. Slap!" She swiped the air. "Slap, slap, slap, thump, kick—and Theltek knows what else they did. You never did tell me. Did it hurt? Tell me, lover, did it hurt?"

"Marith, please… " Carred said, fingers curling around her sword then recoiling as if it were molten.

"Please what? Please stop? Why would I listen to you? What use are you now?"

"Marith, I love you."

"But I have another love. You have to move on."

"It's Talia," Anskar said, wincing at the throb in his skull when he lifted his head. "Queen Talia's controlling you, Marith. You have to fight her."

"Have to? What if I don't want to?"

"Marith, please!" Carred cried. She tried to stand, but her legs gave way and she slumped back down, screaming in pain.

"Sniveling girl!" And there was no disguising the voice now: icy and cruel. The voice of the Necromancer Queen, though it came from Marith's mouth. "You were only ever good for one thing."

"Then that's one more than you," Anskar snarled as he made it to his feet. The dark-tide surged within him, bursting from his pores in quills of fuligin. He took a step in the direction of his sword, but realized he didn't have time to reach it. The dark flooding his insides coalesced around his hand and extended into a blade woven from shadow. He'd taken barely one step toward Marith when the power left him. Like a ruptured wine skin, he seemed to deflate as the dark-tide dispersed into the air, cut off from its source.

Marith raised an eyebrow and smiled. Beside her, Eadgith bellied like a wind-filled sail and then collapsed in a pile of soot.

"It's really no use fighting me with sorcer—" Marith started, but she whirled round as Seneschal Monash charged and swept down her sword. The blade crashed into Marith's head… and shattered, pieces clanging to the stone floor.

"Silly old hag," Marith said as she advanced, and Monash backed away. "You shouldn't have done that."

One of the knights stepped in front of the Seneschal, thrusting with his sword. The blade pierced Marith's guts and exited her lower back. Without so much as wincing, Marith reached out and brushed his face with emerald-tinted fingers. Luminescent veins spread across the man's face, ran down his neck beneath his tunic, and then he slopped into a puddle of offal and pus. Marith pulled the sword from her guts amid a spurt of blood, and then flung the blade to the flagstones. Anskar expected viscera to spill from her wound, but instead the blood congealed in an instant and the skin knitted back together.

As Marith advanced another step toward Monash, Anskar gritted his teeth and plunged his senses through the floor, dredging up the effluence that pooled at the core of Wiraya—the earth-tide. He despised himself as putrescence gushed through him, spraying from his mouth and nose, slinging like spiderweb from his fingers. But where the necrotic essence touched, the dead began to stir—the bloodied corpses of Niyandrians and knights. Broken-limbed, wide-open wounds spilling viscera, white-cloaked mainlanders stood on creaking limbs, red-skinned Niyandrians gasping the air of new life as they rose to join them, all of them, every single one of them, obedient to Anskar's will. But Anskar was rotten inside and out, a lifeless husk putrefying in his own juices. At least, that was how he felt as he fought back his revulsion and sent the risen stumbling toward their prey.

Marith's eyes burned violet, and she actually looked surprised, perhaps even a little impressed. But then the knees of a Niyandrian corpse buckled and it collapsed. A white knight followed, bursting apart in a shower of blood as it hit the ground. One after another, the fledgling army of the dead fell down and stayed down.

Anskar swallowed as he looked Marith in the eye, petrified by the malice he saw in those violet depths.

"Don't look at me like that," Marith said. "I did nothing. This is down to your lack of experience. It's all very well picking up things from the sorcery I worked through you, but that's no path to true mastery."

"So, you really are my mother," Anskar said, unable to look away from her eyes.

"Of course," Marith said. "You suspected from the moment you saw me outside in the streets."

"Your satchel… " Anskar said, and Marith lay a protective hand over the bag. "How?"

"What's important," Marith said, stalking toward him, "is that you failed. Without me, you are nothing, *Melesh-Eloni*. For what is a godling compared with a god?"

"You're no goddess, Talia," Carred said.

"Really? Then how can I do this?"

Marith flung out a hand and Carred lifted into the air, clutching her throat, feet dangling a foot above the flagstones.

"Levitation," Carred gasped. "Doesn't… make you… a god."

"Then how about this?"

Whatever she'd been about to do, Anskar had seen enough. Guided by fear and intuition, he scoured his veins with his senses, scoured his organs and his marrow, till he found a pebble of darkness wedged deep at the base of his mind. In a timeless moment, he studied its woven structure, its impossible density. It was a plug, formed from the dark-tide and damming the flow of his power. With a surge of rage, he thrust his senses into it and the dam burst. Darkness spouted up from within him, welling at his core.

Marith's head snapped around. She caught him with her violet eyes. Anskar tried to lash out with a tentacle of the darkness, but the tide no longer obeyed him. It sluiced through his veins, seethed beneath his skin, rose to flood his mind. Marith grinned. She knew she had him. With a circling motion of her finger, she made him turn around to confront Monash and the last surviving knights in the smithing hall. Dark vapors effused from his outstretched hand, and the knights backed away toward the forges. Anskar shook as he fought against his own sorcery, trying to will it to abate. But Marith was stronger than he; his mother even stronger. He felt Queen Talia's malignant presence steering his dark-tide sorcery, using Marith as a puppet, albeit a puppet with her own enormous power.

"Anskar," Crosbyn said, as he put himself between Vaila and Monash and the cloud of noxious sorcery. "This isn't you, son. You're stronger than this."

"Is that what you think, old man?" Marith said. "He was born to be a pawn, a puppet, no more than that."

"Anskar!" And now it was Carred who appealed to him.

A second cloud of darkness formed from the fingertips of his other hand, curling through the air toward the Niyandrians. Sweat beaded on Anskar's forehead as he fought tooth and nail, stinging as it dripped into his eyes. Ice walked its way up his spine and rimed his mind, compacting his thoughts and his will, making them one with Talia's. And he knew then—knew he was doomed to watch old comrades die, new allies die, new friends die. *Menselas, no,* he prayed.

He could feel Queen Talia's presence now, seething within Marith's satchel. To his sorcerous sight, she was a pulsing glow seen through the leather. Not free, though—he perceived that much. Contained somehow, yet connected intimately to Marith.

The knights had backed away to the forges as far as they could go without being burned, the rebels retreating into the corridor outside the smithing hall. But not Carred. Still she dangled, feet above the ground, face purpling as she struggled to breathe. The black cloud should have touched her already; the other should have smothered the knights; but somehow, through his helplessness and failure, Anskar knew he was the only thing holding them back.

Marith flashed him a look of annoyance, and the darkness within tightened its hold. Anskar could feel his restraint ebbing. Menselas, it was like hanging by his fingertips from a precipice, though when he inevitably let go, he wouldn't be the one to die.

The grate of metal on stone drew his eye. Marith's too. *Amalantril* shifted on the flagstones.

"What is this?" Marith demanded. "What are you—?"

The sword skittered across the floor and leaped into Anskar's hand. In one fluid motion, he whirled and flowed toward Marith, and rammed the blade between her breasts. At first, Marith rolled her eyes, as if to say—*Really? Have you learned nothing?* But then *Amalantril* began to sing—a mournful note yet overlaid with hunger, with lust. The blade flickered between silver and black, and Anskar could feel an arterial pulse through the hilt as the sword… drank? Not blood, though. Something more fundamental to *being*. The sword sucked on her essence. Her soul.

Marith shrieked. Behind Anskar, Carred let out a wail of utter despair. It was enough to make Anskar rip the blade free. But even before Marith's wound healed over, he thrust with the sword at the bulge within her satchel.

This time it was Queen Talia's voice doing the screaming, and before the blade reached it mark, there was a thunderous discharge of energy, a molten stench, and Marith was gone.

Sparkling motes wafted to the floor where she had been.

Anskar stared at his sword. No streak or stain of Marith's blood tainted the blade. No more pulsing blackness. Just silver once more, inert. A dead blade.

"What did you do?" Carred asked, staring wide-eyed at the sword.

"I don't know."

Some quality of the forging process—the astrumium he had added to the blade? He sought out Seneschal Monash's good eye but found only shock and bewilderment there, no answers. It made no sense. If astrumium imbued weapons with this kind of power, he would have known. Every trainee knight who passed the trials would know.

Then what was it?

"Did you kill her?" Carred was insistent, her red face turning purple with anger. "Did you kill Marith?"

Anskar's fingers splayed, and he dropped *Amalantril* to the floor. It barely even clattered, and it never quite stopped moving—at least to his sorcerous sight.

"Good for him, if he did," Seneschal Monash said.

Carred whirled on her, but Vaila stepped between them.

"Good for him," Monash repeated, "but it changes nothing."

"I should have realized," Anskar said. He sought out Carred's eyes, but only saw accusation there, and despair. "The satchel… I should have acted sooner."

"Whatever you think you should have done," Monash said, "you didn't. You had no such trouble, though, doing what you should *not* have. You reneged on your vows, boy. You betrayed your own Order."

Vaila nodded sternly. Crosbyn glowered. Anskar had diminished himself in Crosbyn's eyes. He was no more than a demon; a malefactor to be resisted, beaten, slain.

But at least the heat had gone out of the rebels. They all looked bewildered, wiped out, ashamed. You'd have thought they were the losers, not the Order knights—who, though blood-spattered and exhausted, still held their heads high. Their arrogance astounded Anskar; made him want to thrash it from them. *Amalantril*, at his feet, turned in an agitated circle on the ground, as if sensing his rising anger and wanted to stoke it.

He placed a booted foot on the blade to still it. "You should leave," he told Monash, not quite able to meet her gaze now. If he did, he might throttle her.

"A line has been crossed, DeVantte," the Seneschal said.

"I said, leave!" Shadows effused from his pores, causing the knights to back away. "Now!"

Monash shrugged. "War is inevitable now, Anskar, whether Niyas is ready or not. You do understand this, don't you?"

"It's not what I want."

"No one ever does, when they realize they've awakened a sleeping monster. Don't think you'll survive what's coming." She let her eyes rove over the rebels, pausing on Vilintia, then Carred, and finally Anskar.

"I guess we just kill the bitch, then," Vilintia said, starting forward with her sword raised.

"No!" Carred said, snapping out an arm to hold her back. "No more acting without orders. *My* orders. Understood?"

Vilintia glanced at Anskar, then nodded.

"You too," she told Anskar.

"This wasn't my doing… "

"You too, or I turn around and leave. We all do."

"Better and better," Monash said. "An enemy divided is a peril halved. Now, perhaps one of you might be so kind as to tell us how we are to leave? Sareya must have rendezvoused with the only galleon within a day of Niyas. She'll be well on the way to Sansor by now."

"Sareya?" Anskar said. "You sent her to Sansor?"

"Someone had to get word to the mother house. I imagine Hyle Pausus will be most displeased with you—unless, of course, you're one of his special boys, in which case he might just give you a good spanking."

"Special?" Anskar turned to Carred for an explanation, and she rolled her eyes.

"There's fishing boats in the harbor," Crosbyn said. "We might make it across the Simorga in those… " He didn't sound confident.

"They're Niyandrian boats," Vilintia said. "They belong to us."

"Take them," Carred said. "And go, before I change my mind."

Monash gave a faint smile and saluted—four fingers and a thumb on her chest.

"And our dead?" Vaila said, glancing behind at the bodies strewing the floor of the smithing hall.

"We will bury them," Anskar said without raising his eyes.

Monash stepped in close. "You might want to consider a pyre. There's a lot of dead. You were here a long time. I daresay you know some of them. Maybe considered them friends once. Till we meet again."

Anskar stood with his head down while the knights filed out of the hall, Monash's parting words to him lingering after she had gone. One in particular: *friends.*

In a sudden panic, he rushed in among the white-cloaked dead, peering at faces, closing eyelids with his thumbs, and then with a wrench of his heart he found what he was looking for beneath one of the forges. Or rather, whom.

Anskar threw himself to his knees, sobbing as he cradled the battered head, its unruly hair slick with blood. It was then he saw the big forge-blackened hands, crimson with gore, vainly attempting to stem the flow of blood from a stomach wound—a wound about as mortal as they got.

"Assling," Sned said. The forge master stank of booze. "Missed the bastard that gutted me." He winced as he inclined his head toward the mallet on the floor. "It's the drink messing with my aim."

"You're going to be all right," Anskar said. "Help! Over here!" he called to Niyandrians. "We need a healer."

Carred turned her back on him, arms folded across her chest.

"Don't… " Sned said, hand on Anskar's, hot and slick with blood. "I ain't no surgeon, but I know I'm buggered. Why'd you do it, lad? Why'd you turn on us?"

"I didn't… The attack wasn't my… "

But Sned grew limp in his arms, no longer breathing.

FIVE

MARITH'S TEETH CRUNCHED TOGETHER AS she slammed into the ground, flat on her face. White exploded in her skull; before, there had been only blackness, featureless and void. With a jolt she became aware of the agony in her mouth—she must have bitten her tongue. Blood streamed from her nose; she wiped it with her sleeve, which is when she realized she had no sleeve. She was naked, her red skin beaded with sweat and smelling faintly of cooked meat. A high-pitched ringing pierced her eardrums. The buzz of a thousand insects filled her head, and she retched.

Theltek, what just happened? she wondered as she spat out bile, hands scratching for purchase on the hard, abrasive surface. Stone? She pushed her head away from the ground, blinking spots from her eyes until she could see. A paved road? It was dusted in places with golden-brown leaves. Trees leaned down either side, the road a scar that carved its way through dense woodland of russet and yellow—the leaves that had yet to fall. Beyond the shedding branches, the sun dipped toward the brow of a sloping hill. Rassik's Head! That meant she was midway between Brittling Down and her smallholding. But coming or going? She was buck naked, so perhaps she had been returning after a night out at the taverns? That didn't seem likely. It was way past morning, and in any case, she never drank that much in public, only in the privacy of her own home, where there was no one to take advantage—unless Carred was visiting. Admittedly, she had been drinking too much lately, to suppress the voices in her head—the voices of traders, movers and shakers, the financiers beneath the veneer of the mainland governments. She'd heard them refer to themselves as the Consortium.

But if it was drink that had led her here, why was there no taste of mistberry wine in her bile? And she felt… off… vile somehow, as if she'd bathed in something festering. But there wasn't any smell. And it still didn't explain why she wasn't wearing any clothes. Would she not have passed out fully dressed? She panicked that someone would see. The locals already viewed her as strange, the mad woman who lived all alone since her husband's passing. Even the people who worked for her whispered behind her back that she was a crazy witch. She had no evidence to support that, but she could tell. She was sensitive to such things—part of the joy of being moontouched.

Marith picked herself up, vainly attempting to cover herself with her hands as she scurried out of the sunlight and into the trees. The first thing she did when she was sure she was out of sight was to examine herself for bruises, cuts, and bites—any indication she had been assaulted. There was nothing save the hard-to-put-her-finger-on feeling that something wasn't right with her. She felt… dislocated. De-centered. Her mind, she realized, when she touched her fingertips to her temples…. Usually, she felt her consciousness, her sense of who she was, in between her ears somewhere, but now she seemed spread thin, like too little butter scraped over too much bread. No, that wasn't right: she was stretched out around an unrecognizable core, her awareness not located within her head but somehow everywhere at once, dispersed beneath her skin.

Then, like a lightning-struck tower, it hit her.

"Theltek," she breathed. She remembered. "Dorinah… Blood and fire! Branil's Burg. Carred. Oh, gods, Anskar… his sword." They had fought with sorcery. She had won. But then his sword… sentient somehow. Hungry. It had drunk her. She clapped a hand over her mouth to keep from crying out. It had sucked at her soul.

Something shifted within her, rattling the bones beneath the awareness of her skin. But it was deeper than her bones: a granite clumping, a pressure that squeezed her outwards. And it *knew* her. It could hear her thoughts.

[I underestimated the child of my womb.]

Marith's heart hammered within her ribcage. The voice seemed to come from beneath her, yet it was somehow within. Deep inside her organs, her marrow, in every drop of her blood.

The satchel with the glass bottle: it had gone, along with the clothes she had been wearing at Branil's Burg…

The solid core that had driven her out from herself shivered, and Marith's heart skipped to a frantic pitter-patter. She felt like nothing so much as a cloak worn by the cuckoo that had ousted her from her nest; or rather the entity, the presence that was…

"Queen Talia?"

[Don't sound so surprised. What else was I to do? This was all I could think of to get us out alive.]

"But how?" It shouldn't have been possible. Talia had tried to enter within her before.

[You still think your moontouched blood makes you too strong for me? Perhaps you are right, but during Anskar's attack, your defenses were down.]

"And so you took full advantage," Marith accused.

[Don't be obtuse. We both would have perished if I'd not acted when I

did. You felt the power of his sword. You knew what it was doing to you.]

"So, you nested yourself within me? No wonder I feel turned inside out. And you tapped into my innate sorcery to transport us here? I had no idea I was even capable of such a feat."

"Alone, you are not. Neither am I. But together… Just think, Marith, how much more we could do together."

Marith felt the urge to throw up. Her skin itched with revulsion. No longer burning, it was frigid now, cold as a corpse.

[Peace, Marith. Accept my presence within you. Succumb to the will of your queen.]

"Get out of me!" Marith growled through gritted teeth. "I want you out." She reached into her mind for her repositories, but they were oil to her sorcerous senses, still tangible but slippery and impossible to hold onto.

"I am within you, Marith. You cannot cast me out. That horse has bolted. You think I am incapable of learning? Of taking from you all that I need? Once I was inside, all that you possess became mine—your senses, your moontouched abilities, your thoughts, your memories. And I must say, you have some very exceptionally entertaining memories. Do you know, I think Carred favors you over me. I'm not sure if I should feel insulted or betrayed."

"Get out!" Marith screamed. "Get out!" She snatched a rock from the forest floor and dashed it against her temple—not enough to do any real damage, but enough to convey a threat. "I mean it."

[You think that would help? Go ahead. By all means, smash your brains out. Admittedly, your lively intelligence is a bonus, but all I need is the vessel of your body. I'm a necromancer, Marith. I animate dead things.]

Marith bashed the rock into her forehead. This time it hurt. White-hot motes sparked behind her eyes. Blood oozed down her brow and onto the bridge of her nose. She made ready for another strike, but her hand spasmed, and the rock went flying into the woods.

[It won't be forever, Marith. Not if you help me.]

Marith dropped to her knees, scrabbling about in the leaves for something else she might harm herself with.

[Desist, Marith. You do not need to do this.]

Marith was suddenly overcome with lethargy. She crawled to the base of a tree and slumped against the trunk, tears of frustration, tears of anger, tears of despair running down her cheeks.

[I only want what's best for you. What's best for Niyas.]

"And what about what I want?"

Marith scratched around in the roots of the tree, searching for another rock, a sharp length of wood, but her fingers froze, and both arms went numb.

[Serve me, and I will give you Carred.]

"Carred's not yours to give."

[Oh, you'd be surprised what is mine to give. Carred is a puppet. A plaything. A body I once used to keep myself warm at night.]

"And you wonder why she prefers me to you?"

[Cease your futile struggles, Marith. I will overlook your insolence if you put the fate of Niyas above your own petty desires. Serve me. Serve the new empire.]

"I thought that's what I was doing back at Dorinah—of my own free will. You didn't have to take advantage. I would have done as you wished. But not like this."

A shiver ran through her innards, the presence within shifting, seething, then settling down.

[Try to understand, Marith. If there had been another way, I would have taken it. When Anskar did what he did... with that infernal sword... I had to move fast. He would have taken your soul. He would have taken mine. It took all my power and yours to bring us here. There was not enough for your clothes, for the satchel, for the bottle that contained my spirit and kept me hidden from my father. Without the bottle, Marith,

I would have sooner or later been drawn back to the realm of the dead. Domatai would have found me there. He learned from Anskar when together they summoned me. Without the bottle, I need a body of flesh and blood in which to hide. It won't be forever, I promise you. Please, Marith, a little longer. I need you to help me.]

Marith put her head in her hands, felt the stickiness of the blood that oozed from her forehead. The wound stung, but that was a good thing—something she could latch onto.

"Help you how?"

[The Armor of Divinity. Carred found a suit. You must retrieve it, alter it, and then we will both be free.]

"Carred found the Armor of Divinity? I didn't know she was even looking… You made her find it for you?"

[I prompted her, it's true. For Niyas, Marith. Carred has always understood this. It is always about Niyas.]

For the good of the people, Marith thought bitterly. Of course it was. Nothing to do with the Necromancer Queen wanting to live forever, controlling everyone around her, everything. Nothing to do with Talia wanting to be a goddess.

"So," Marith said, "I help you find the armor—"

[You simply take me to it. I already know where it is. Just think, Marith: with the Armor of Divinity we will be unstoppable, and all Niyas will rally to the true ruler, not to Carred the failure nor Anskar the pretender. I have already issued a summons… to one most likely to sense an opportunity. After, more will come to our cause.]

"I thought you needed Anskar."

[Not anymore. Not now you have provided me with an anchor in the world. You have seen what he has become, Marith. What his sword almost did to you. This is not the Niyandrian way. This is his grandfather's demonic influence.]

Marith snorted. "What, so Anskar's a demon now?"

[He was always a demon, in part. The half I inherited, halved again.]

Ice sluiced through Marith's veins. Self-loathing? Queen Talia was revolted by her own demon descent?

[But the sword… this is worse. Demon lore above any I have known. It can only be occult knowledge, the preserve of a select few. Domatai, my accursed father… I have long suspected he is affiliated with the Order of the Black Sun.]

"And they're an Order of demon blacksmiths, I suppose, who specialize in soul-drinking swords?"

[Oh, the sword is more than that. It is an agent in its own right. As it supped on you, I felt the crawl of its sentience.]

Marith wiggled her fingers and felt the prickle of blood returning to the veins of both arms. Had Talia forgotten to control her, or was it a concession? She raised her hand and dabbed at her head wound. The blood was already clotting, no longer dripping down her nose. Was that thanks to Talia as well? Her cuts didn't normally heal so quickly.

"What I don't get," she said, "is what a sword would want with a soul."

[I suspect the sword is a conduit, passing the lifeforce on to its wielder. Anskar would have subsumed your soul, and probably not known about it.]

"But he would have felt different, yes?"

[Invigorated. Euphoric. Powerful beyond his dreams. And he would have felt hunger. The lust for more souls. The higher-order demons have no need for swords to do their absorbing for them. The theft of essence is innate to demonkind. Anskar is but a quarter demon.]

"So, he needed a helping hand?"

[You see what Domatai is doing to him? Why Anskar can no longer be accepted as the Melesh-Eloni, the key to my triumphal return? Domatai seeks to create an addiction within him, the drive toward becoming a demon lord like his grandfather.]

And now Anskar was the head of the rebel alliance, who had already struck a devastating blow against the Order of Eternal Vigilance—no small thanks to Marith, albeit not exactly by choice.

[As always,] Talia continued, her spirit voice tight with bitterness, *[Domatai seeks to thwart my plans. It was he, I suspect, who instigated the war that enslaved Niyas and consigned me to the realm of the dead. What kind of father could so despise his daughter?]*

"You obviously never spoke to Carred about her drunken sot of a father. Although he was nothing compared with her mother. But as for Anskar, Carred will see through him. She'll never permit a demon to take the throne of Niyas."

[Oh, Marith,] Talia sighed. *[Carred is not the woman you think she is. She swore an oath of service to me, yet now she has betrayed me and put all Niyas in peril. I will bring her back to you, I promise; but we must not be blind to the difficulties ahead. It is down to you and me now, Marith, to raise Niyas from the dead. Anskar was the key to my return, to the salvation of the Niyandrian race, but now… Now that mission falls to you.]*

Marith laughed with scorn. "Oh, please. I may be many things, but I'm no key. I'm nobody in the grand scheme of things, just a lonely widow who takes what little comfort she can from a love not quite requited. Theltek, do you think I don't care that Carred has lovers all over the isle? I told her I didn't, but I was lying. Of course I care. She is all I have, all that keeps me tethered to this miserable existence. Pathetic. Bloody pathetic is what I am. The only key I could ever be is the one that unlocks the drinks cabinet."

[You are moontouched, Marith. The gods do not lightly touch their chosen ones. You are favored. You are destined for this very moment.]

"Destined, my foot! Moontouched is just another word for lunatic. My mother always said I was an odd child."

[You deny you possess exceptional powers of sorcery?]

"Well, no, but… "

[Moontouched, Marith. And now you must be the new key.]

Marith clutched her shoulders. Theltek, she was cold. Violent shudders passed through her body, and her teeth began to chatter.

"So, I collect this armor for you, and then what?"

[Later. First, take yourself home. Wash, rest, find something to wear. We will confer once you have recovered.]

Thanks, Marith thought. *You're all heart.*

Laughter bubbled up from within her. It wasn't her own. *[I heard that,]* Queen Talia said. *[I hear all your thoughts.]*

"Well, hopefully you won't hear the voices too."

[I hear their echoes now, playing in your mind. The vile Consortium that squats at the heart of the mainland, forging and breaking alliances, shifting the balance of power. You hear the true enemy of Niyas, Marith, the forces that plotted the downfall of my empire, no doubt prompted by my father. You think this a coincidence? You hear because the gods wish you to hear.]

"Of course. I suppose I'm one of Theltek's thousand ears?"

[How do you know you are not? And if Theltek hears the machinations of the Consortium through you, does it not stand to reason that he expects you to act?]

"I thought you were the god controlling my every move."

[Niyas has many gods, some too ancient to be remembered. Some,] she added with a quaver in her spirit voice, *[who should be forgotten forever.]*

"And now we need another?"

[It is the way of things. The way it has always been. Sylva Kalisia was once a mere woman, Menselas a man—albeit a confused one. Even Theltek once walked Wiraya, with only two legs, two hands, two eyes.]

"Which is more than I have, now that you've taken control."

The temperature dropped as the sun sank toward the horizon. Marith hugged herself for warmth as she scrabbled through the woods. By road and on a horse, she'd have been home in next to no time, but sticking to the cover of the trees, scouring the fallen leaves for sleeping serpents and anything else that might bite her bare feet, it took more than an hour—closer to two—for her to reach the boundary of her land.

She crouched in the shadows beneath an oak tree, watching the flickering firelight in the window of the lodge that overlooked the main approach to the house. The shadows of the couple who acted as caretakers for the property passed back and forth—drying plates and cups, from what she could make out. The wait was interminable, but she didn't want to risk being seen. At last they settled down, and she made a last quick dash for home.

And, of course, the front door was locked! For bloody once. Normally she left it open, but since the assassins had come for Carred, she'd taken to locking it when she was away, and she had added an additional bolt for when she was asleep indoors at night. Each evening since the attack, she'd cast dusk-tide wards on both entrances and all the windows, but even so, you could never be too careful—not if the Order of Eternal Vigilance had been behind the assassination attempt, or worse, this mysterious conniving Consortium. It occurred to her that the Order might even be bound up with the Consortium, considering it was a secret group of the rich and the powerful, from what she could make out. It wouldn't have surprised her if the Church of Menselas was in it up to the neck, too, and Theltek only knew who else. Or perhaps he didn't. Maybe that's why he needed her to act as his ears and eavesdrop on the clandestine meetings. It would be nice to know. Why did gods have to be so cryptic all the time?

[*You think they would survive long if they weren't?*] Talia said. [*Obfuscation is the road to power for most of them.*]

"But not you."

[*Oh, I can obfuscate along with the best of them, but not with you. There are no secrets between us now, Marith.*]

"Then you won't mind telling me where I'm supposed to go to retrieve this suit of oh-so-precious armor."

[*Get the door open first. Bathe. Put some clothes on. Eat, drink. Then we can talk.*]

"I never knew you were so kind and considerate."

[*Marith... I am your queen, remember. Do not forget that.*]

As if I could. "Sorry," she quickly added to that errant thought. It was a bloody nuisance having someone entwined with your mind. A person should be able to keep secrets, to bitch and whine to themselves. She'd had a lifetime of practice, and old habits would be hard to break.

[*Then don't break them,*] Talia said. [*I already know your desires, your motives, and I fully understand your reticence. But I also know the limits of your power to resist, and of your will.*]

"You mean I'm weak and totally useless against you?" Marith said. "I think we both worked that out earlier. Now, if you don't mind, I've a door to open."

She reached into her dusk-tide repository, but it was as empty as her resolve.

"Theltek's hairy assholes!" she cursed, then sat down with her back to the door. "Now all I need is some bloody farmhand to come and collect their pay, and all the rumors will be confirmed: Mad Marith sits naked under the stars, gibbering to herself in the dark."

[*It's not yet dark, Marith. Not quite dusk.*]

An unnatural wind came skirling through the woods that enveloped her lands. A wind that came from the west.

"Oh! Of course," she said, then stood and opened her arms as the dusk-tide blasted through her, scouring her inside and out. Thrills of near ecstasy ripped through her nerves. Her back arched and she gasped. Lightning shot up her spine and she collapsed, shuddering, to her knees as the eldritch wind passed.

[*Better?*] Talia asked, the hint of a tinkling chuckle behind her inner voice.

"I should be able to manage that door now," Marith said as she stood. She was no longer cold; a pleasant warmth suffused her skin. She might have felt euphoric but for the presence within, which had ousted her from her own skull.

This time, the dusk-tide came eagerly from her repository, manifesting upon her fingertip as a lurid green spark. She touched her finger to the lock and discharged just the right amount of force. There was an emerald flash, the stink of burning metal, and then a click. Marith took hold of the door handle and let herself in.

The first thing she did was to run a bath from the rainwater tank and heat it using the dawn-tide. Then she poured herself a glass of mistberry wine—just a little, she reassured Queen Talia, enough to relax her, not to get drunk. She lay in the scented bath water, sipping and sighing. She closed her eyes and succeeded in forgetting about Talia for a moment, about Anskar and his sword. About Carred. She wallowed in the bliss of oblivion, but only because Talia permitted it. The realization snapped her eyes open.

[Relax, Marith,] Talia said. *[You are going to need all your strength.]*

Marith drained the contents of her glass and then laid her head back. She'd reach for the sponge in a minute and scrub her skin clean of the detritus from the forest. *In a minute,* she repeated. *Once I've had a good—*

She sat bolt upright, splashing water over the side of the tub. Voices filled her head—too many, speaking all at once. Snatches of conversations, phrases, single words, questions, retorts. She gripped the sides of the tub so hard her arms hurt. Little by little, she could discern individual voices, and the incessant babble separated out into disparate conversations, all happening at the same time.

A woman's voice came clear—something about her bid on a piece of land. A second woman cut her off, said her offer was better, that she would put the plot to more industrious use. A man's voice pointed out the land wasn't technically for sale. "Yet," someone else replied, and everyone laughed at that. "If you want my advice,"—a voice that reverberated like a clap of thunder directly overhead, as the other voices hushed, as if cowed—"I'd say you should speculate on Niyas."

[*That voice,*] Queen Talia said. [*The skull helm. The voice of my father, Domatai! Shut him out, Marith! If you can hear him...*]

"Don't worry," Marith said, climbing out of the tub and pinching the bridge of her nose, "they don't hear me. At least, I don't think so. How could they, above their own gods-awful noise?"

[*Sever the contact!*] Talia said. [*Now! You must!*]

"If you insist," Marith said, dripping water over the floor as she crossed the room to fetch her wine bottle. She didn't bother pouring another glass. Instead, she upended the bottle and downed it in one glugging pull. "Course, I might be unreachable for the next several hours."

Already her mind was cloudy. In a minute or two, she would be sound asleep.

"Funny," she muttered to herself, knowing Talia would hear.

[*What is funny?*]

"Your father Domatai is one of them—a member of the Consortium. Else why would he be there? No wonder their blasted alliance was so successful!"

[*How else would Niyas have fallen?*] Queen Talia said.

"But it'll be different next time, huh?"

[*Next time, I will have the Armor of Divinity. Next time, I will be a god!*]

"Ess," Marith said with a yawn as she entered her room and flopped on the bed. "You'll be a god-ess. But I still don't understand this fear of the demon lord Domatai. You're his daughter."

[*No, I am not. I refuse him. And that is something he can't abide. If he can't have me under his control, I am a pest to be exterminated, and all Niyas along with it. What demon lords cannot control or subsume, they destroy.*]

And that's all there is to it? A likely story!

[You question my word?]

"Actually," Marith said dreamily as she pressed her head into the pillow, "I was musing to myself, and you're a naughty queen for listening in."

[What I am,] Talia said, *[is impatient to leave. More so now I have heard Domatai speaking in your head. I must have the armor, before someone else finds it.]*

"Who's looking? Who even knows where it is? Save Carred, of course. And she probably told Anskar. Don't worry." Another yawn. "Just need forty winks. I'll be right as… "

She was suddenly drifting down an endless chasm, Talia's voice wafting around her like scented rose petals. How blissful. How utterly wonderful and soothing.

Her thoughts ceased being words; they were incandescent motes circling her, bees in search of nectar. They winked out one by one till the only sense left was sound. She heard a tinkling brook and drifted towards it; but when she got there and let its cool waters wash over her, the tinkling was replaced by an animal sound—some distant drakkon roaring, or perhaps just breathing. Or was it the sound of her own snoring?

SIX

SAREYA HAD ASSUMED SHE WOULD be welcomed aboard with at least some military honor, some degree of respect, given her rank and white cloak and the letter she carried. But instead she had been virtually ignored since the crew lowered a rope ladder for her. She had waved Monash's letter, told them it had urgent orders for the ship's captain, but was only met with shrugs and promises to let the captain know. By the time she had stood at the gunwale for an hour or more, she began to regret sending the two men who had rowed her out to sea back to Dorinah.

The crew ignored her for the most part, save one hunch-backed seaman who seemed to do nothing but roam the decks carrying a tray, handing out drinks to the sailors. He brought her one too, as if she weren't a stranger, as if her skin weren't red. Even gave a little bow of respect at the sight of her white Order cloak. Not that hers was the only one on display. The decks were full of Order knights, conversing in groups, lounging on the benches around the gunwale, playing dice with the crew. It was as if no one cared about what was happening ashore. Not that she expected them to head into port and take the fight to the rebels—far from it. A shipload of knights would make no difference at all. But they might at least bring her to the captain, insist that she be seen. Insist that they set sail at once for Sansor.

She waited another half hour, until the sun went down. Until the dusk-tide came skirling over the wavetops and slammed into her. And she let them see as she threw back her arms and shuddered while the tide ripped through her. That certainly grabbed their attention. All hands on deck watched her with frowns or wide eyes. Several of the knights touched four fingers and a thumb to their breasts—the sign of the Five's protection. She was one of them, couldn't they see that? Didn't they know who she was? But why would they? Monash had made a big deal out of her on the voyage to Dorinah; more so after their arrival at Branil's Burg. People she had trained with, or trained under, had seen she was someone now; but these knights, this crew, only saw what they wanted to see: a Niyandrian playing dress-up. Menselas, did they think she was a spy? Idiots.

Fired by the dusk-tide boiling within her repository, she strode for the cabin beneath the poop deck. A knight moved to stop her, but backed away when she turned a glare on him, a trickle of dusk-tide causing her eyes to flash like lightning. She let him know she could incinerate him without breaking sweat, and in response, he spoke a cant and his ward sphere sprang into existence around him. She gave a derisive laugh, and the silver sphere flickered and fizzled out.

And then she was at the door. She thumped it once with her fist and let herself in.

Smoke swirled about her, irritating her eyes and getting into her lungs; it was both pungent and sweet, an aromatic tobacco, and it came from the pipe hanging limply from the mouth of the fat man lounging in a comfy chair, booted feet crossed on the cabin's lone table. And fat wasn't doing him justice: he was truly obese, a quivering blob of a man whose several chins melted into his chest like wax. He wore a white jacket so huge Sareya could have camped in it and a white shirt with frills that disappeared beneath his chins. Amid the wine stains on his lapel, she spotted the five-pointed star of the Order embroidered in red. Atop the table, surrounding his bare feet, were empty wine bottles, an overflowing ashtray, and a battered fiddle with a horsehair bow.

It took a moment for his squinty eyes to register her, no doubt on account of whatever it was he was smoking—her best guess would be cravv, a narcotic.

The man took the pipe from his mouth and used it to gesture with. "What the bloody abyss do you think you're doing, barging in here like this, you bloody savage?"

"My name is Sareya—"

"I don't remember asking your name, girl. What makes you think I care what an animal calls itself? Now get out, before I have you slung over the side for the sharp-tooths."

"I have a message—"

"Did I grant you permission to speak? And even if I did, you will address me as sir, is that understood?"

"Sir, I—"

"Out, out, out with you!" He slid his feet from the tabletop, scattering the wine bottles and sending one to the floor, where it miraculously didn't shatter, and instead went rolling across the cabin till it hit the wall.

A knight appeared at Sareya's shoulder. "Everything all right, Captain?"

"No, it most definitely is not!"

Sareya shunted the knight away from her with a blast of dusk-tide. He flew back across the deck and landed flat on his back. Several ward spheres winked on as swords were drawn and knights came towards her, but she stepped fully inside the cabin and pulled the door closed, welding the catch shut with another measured burst of sorcery.

The fat man stood, tugging down his rumpled jacket and squaring his shoulders.

"Now, look here, you—"

"Disparage me again, you fat pig, and I'll liquefy your innards then feed them to you as soup."

He swallowed, one eyebrow arched, and then glanced at the door which was being hammered on by the knights outside. "You can do that?"

"Shall we find out?"

The Captain held up a hand to placate her, then shouted, "Enough of that, or you'll break my door!" When the clamor subsided, he took a swift puff on his pipe and set it down in the ashtray, where it sent up a wispy plume of smoke.

Sareya was starting to feel lightheaded. Stay in this atmosphere too long and she wouldn't know up from down, left from right; and if her past experience of cravv was anything to go by (Niv Allund had insisted she try it), she'd have nightmare visions of the Corpse Maker.

"I am a junior officer," she said.

"Pah," the Captain responded. "A likely bloody… " He trailed away when flames began to dance on the tips of Sareya's fingers.

"A junior officer from Branil's Burg," she continued. "Which, you may or may not have noticed, is under attack." Or was. As far as she knew, the fighting could all be over now. She should have been worried about Monash and the others, but infuriatingly, all she could think about was Anskar. What he was doing—whatever it was—touched a nerve in her. Anskar with the Niyandrian rebels. She had always taunted him about his blood, always displayed her painted nails and spoke of her proud Niyandrian heritage. So, why was it they seemed to have exchanged places? She should have been on the side of the rebels, and yet… And yet her old life was lost to her, swallowed up by the Order's training, the years of what she had always known was indoctrination.

"I wondered what all the clamor was," the Captain said.

"And you didn't bother to find out?"

He spread his pudgy hands. "Orders, my dear girl. You should understand."

"And your orders are?"

"Why, to patrol, of course. The *Callixonis* is an integral part of the naval blockade of Niyas, a check on the trade that goes in and out."

"In case the mainland nations miss out on their tariffs, is that what you mean?"

"Without tariffs, the standard of living we mainlanders enjoy would soon decline."

"By the looks of you, Captain, that might not be such a bad thing."

His jaw dropped, and his hands went to his belly as he breathed in.

"*Callixonis?*" Sareya said.

"Named for the Patriarch, Callixonis III, who paid for the ship to be built, Menselas bless his holy generosity. Now, I assume you escaped the Burg by the skin of your teeth. With permission, or are you a deserter?" A hard edge crept back into his voice.

"I was sent, against my will, with a message from Seneschal Monash."

"Oh."

Clearly he had heard of the name. Monash had quite the reputation in Sansor, and it wasn't for meekness.

Sareya brought the missive from her pouch and handed it to him.

The Captain took it and collapsed back into his chair. "It's Gulbert, by the way," he said absently as he proceeded to read Monash's letter. "Captain Ilaire Gulbert."

When Sareya didn't reply, he looked up. "You must forgive my earlier surliness, and any… injudicious comments I may have made. It has been a long stint at sea, and I do not do well with the constant bobbing of the ship."

"I can see how that might make you disparage my skin color," Sareya said. "Now read."

The Captain tsked and shook his head as he perused the letter. "No, it's no good. It can't be done. Leave my position? Who will relieve the *Callixonis*? Our replacement isn't due for another few weeks. I'm sorry, my dear, but we all have our orders, you and me both. You must find another passage to Sansor."

"Captain," Sareya said, "by order of Seneschal Monash, I am commandeering your ship."

"Now look here," the fat man said, starting out of his chair, then slumping back down at the look she shot him.

"Give the order, Captain, to raise anchor and turn this ship around. Or do I have to give an order of my own—to have you removed?"

"That would be mutiny," he said.

Sareya raised both eyebrows: *So?*

"Oh, very well, but I do so only under protest."

"Noted."

"And if there's a sudden rise in smuggling—"

"I'm sure you can make up the shortfall in tariffs if you cut back on the wine, the tobacco, and the food. Oh, and let's not forget the cravv—is it legal now for the navy?"

His jowls quivered as he blew out his cheeks. "Right, then, best open the door—I'm assuming you can?"

Sareya directed a thin stream of dusk-tide at the latch and burned a hole right through it. "You'll be able to find a locksmith in Sansor," she said as she held the door open for him, and grinned at the confused looks on the faces of the knights outside.

SEVEN

A CHILL WIND NIPPED AT Anskar's skin, blew hair in his face, stung his eyes and made them weep. He stood atop Branil's Burg's battlements, looking out across Dorinah to the bay, where he could still just about make out the specks of two dozen fishing boats riding the waves as they entered the Simorga Sea.

He had come alone to think, and to watch Monash and the Order knights leave. Their Niyandrian servants—those who had not been slaughtered during Marith's assault—remained behind.

He could feel the icy throb of the sword at his hip, even through the scabbard. *Amalantril* wasn't the weapon he had deliberated over for so long, then sweated to turn into a reality in the smithing hall. He almost choked as he recalled Sned's suggestion that he was overreaching himself, that the design of the sword was too complicated. But when Anskar had succeeded in crafting such a masterwork, Sned had been the first to congratulate him. The weapons master had been proud of him, in his uncouth, insulting way. And now he was dead.

Amalantril, though, felt far from dead. It was no inert sword forged from steel. It had a pulse—an almost tangible one. And he could feel its presence—its sentience—scratching at the back of his mind. Whether that was a good thing or bad, he had yet to find out. But one thing was undeniable: the sword hungered for souls. It wanted to feed them to him. He'd felt something similar before, in the Kingdom of the Thousand Lakes, when a black thrall had come over him and he had slaughtered Soreshi sorcerers. But feeding on souls! The idea revolted him. And yet, as far as he could tell, the change in *Amalantril* had nothing to do with his mother. Talia had been afraid of the sword. He had heard her scream.

Time seemed not to pass as he grew mired in ruminations, but when his awareness was drawn back outside his head by the blanketing twilight, he could no longer see the boats. The refugees from Branil's Burg would be cold enough as it was, but they would freeze to death if their fragile vessels capsized under the weight of overcrowding. He almost uttered a petition to Menselas on their behalf, then stopped himself. Did he really want them to make it to the mainland?

"Save them," he whispered to the Mother aspect of the Five. "Aid them," he petitioned the Healer. "But make us strong," he asked the Warrior. "So that, if the mainland armies come—when they come— we will be ready."

Anskar felt a sudden pang of loss for his catalyst. Another bad decision. He should never have had it removed. Under Zek's tutelage he had started to gain in proficiency. His dawn- and dusk-tide repositories had braided together—the way they were supposed to be—and then he had been an idiot and had the crystal cut from his chest. Ever since, there had been just the dark and the earth. The stuff of demons and the putrid ooze of corrupted dawn- and dusk-tide at the world's core that granted power over the dead.

As the last glimmer of sunlight dissolved into gray, and the red sun sank towards the horizon, he closed his eyes but felt... At first there was nothing, but then he heard the dusk-tide wind as if from afar, a steady susurration, not its usual skirling roar. No gusts blasted through him, but if he focused hard enough, there was a breeze, and it felt as if it entered through a crack in some indiscernible bubble that encompassed him to brush lightly over his skin.

He pressed his senses deeper, and started to perceive something he had not been aware of before, though he knew it had been part of him all along: there was indeed some kind of insubstantial bubble. Nevertheless, it felt like a hard shell all around him, invisible, but now that he was aware of it, most definitely tangible. Something he had heard somewhere before: the serpent within the egg, waiting to hatch—in the legend, behind enemy lines. And now the dusk-tide had found a crack.

He drilled his senses into that crack. Had he been the one to make it? How? He wrestled with it in his mind, and when that didn't work, he drove threads of dark-tide into the perceived gap, played it all out in his imagination, saw his hands on a crowbar of shadow, prying the fissure wide. Lightning shot up his spine. He cried out, clutching his head. It felt as though his skull shattered into a million fragments. But it was the egg that had shattered, not his mind. He dropped his hands to his sides, stood tall, and breathed in the frigid air atop the battlements. His veins began to fizz. Pores opened all over his skin—the widening of hungry mouths.

And then the dusk-tide slammed into him. He threw out his arms and arched his back. Eldritch forces blasted through him, scouring him inside and out. He moaned, gasped, silently screamed in rapture, then slumped to his knees, panting, aware of just how close he'd come to falling backwards over the parapet.

He was sweat-drenched yet euphoric. He wept with relief and gratitude. No catalyst, and yet the tide had come. The tide had come! Because of his Niyandrian blood? Niyandrians never used catalysts, yet they were accomplished natural sorcerers. What if he was too? What if his innate abilities had been stifled somehow, suppressed, crushed by exposure to the mainlanders and their sorcery-hating god? Or had Queen Talia done it to him, the same way she had hidden his dark-tide power until a time of her choosing? But this wasn't of her choosing. He had been the one to discern the egg, to crack it, to shatter it. He clutched that thought as if his life depended upon it. It wasn't much, but it was an act he could at last call his own. Talia might indeed have intended him to be the serpent that took down the Order and its mainland allies, but had she considered that the wyrm might turn and use its powers against her?

He felt different inside. His mind was afire, his skull bristling with force. His braided repository… it was bursting with essence, and not just the dusk-tide. It no longer seemed to differentiate between the dusk and the dawn. Zek had been right. The mainlanders were stunted in their sorcerous development, their repositories malformed. And when anyone who worshipped Menselas showed signs of aptitude, they were herded into the Order or into the Church, told their dusk-tide abilities were anathema to their god, and taught to screen them out in favor of the dawn. Then they made up for the atrophy of their innate abilities with a specially grown crystal catalyst to focus their arcane powers. And he'd believed the lies. Gone along with them. Until he'd met Zek, he'd known no better. But now… Now he *knew*.

He could feel the interplay of the dawn, the dusk, and the dark within him. On a sudden impulse, he rose to his feet and dredged up the effluence of the earth. Its cold seepage entered through his feet, but where it met the roiling tides within, they curled away from it. There was no unity of the four: it was three against one. But it felt like progress—though progress towards what? It also felt like another act of his own volition. That made two now, and he was keen for more, to snatch them greedily up, to be his own man. He'd been for so long the puppet of his mother's insidious schemes; so long under her spell, even when he didn't know it. And if not his mother, it had been the Order's tune he'd marched to. But he was no one's plaything anymore.

A voice reached him from below.

Orix?

He looked down to see the Traguh-raj lad waving, and felt a wave of sadness mixed with revulsion at his friend's malformed face, with his eyes, mouth, and nose jumbled across his face. There were Niyandrian warriors moving among the dead in the bailey; servants too, separating their own from the white-cloaked knights who had perished, some of them burned by Marith's sorcery, all of them bloody.

"Come down here!" Orix yelled in a voice thick with emotion. "There's something I want to show you."

Anskar's heart thudded, a death knell. Hadn't he suffered enough for one day?

Whispering a cant, he stepped from the parapet, Orix's cry in his ears echoing and far removed as he plummeted.

But then Anskar's fall slowed to a wafting descent, and he grinned. His hands when he brought them before his face were ghost-like and insubstantial. His arms, his legs the same; his skin sheathed with a flickering amalgam of all four tides, a mottling of light and dark.

But when his boots touched the ground of the bailey, it was with an impact that, while not slight, only jolted his knees. He should have broken bones.

"Sweet Menselas!" Orix said, running towards him. "I thought... I thought...."

"You thought what? That I'd had enough? That I wanted to end it all?" Anskar chuckled, but there was no humor in it, and Orix backed away when Anskar extended a hand intended to slap him on the back. "Well, maybe I have, and I do. We'll have to see. Now, what is it you want to show me?"

The shimmer of sorcery left his skin, but the dawn, the dusk, and the dark still embraced within him, the reunion of lovers following a prolonged separation. And the three that were one continued to spurn the earth-tide, which seemed to seethe with resentment.

It was hard to gauge Orix's expression, with his eyes where his mouth should have been, but his body was taut, his gesture awkward and stiff when he beckoned Anskar to follow him.

Head down—maybe it had to be, so he could see—Orix led Anskar across the bailey, past bodies left where they had fallen, past others dragged into neat lines for burial or burning. Anskar grimaced as he tried to shut out the voices of the whispering dead. There were so many, it was impossible to distinguish one word from another, and irrational as it felt, he couldn't help thinking they condemned him, that somehow this was all his fault.

Orix waited at the gateway to the stable yard, and Anskar's heart clenched. He hesitated, and almost turned back. He didn't need to be a prophet to know what was coming. His brief sense of agency was gone, dispelled like a beginner's sorcery, throttled by the reimposed hand of a higher fate. Need compelled him more surely than any coercive sorcery, more insistently than the crow that had led him to Hallow Hill so long ago. As Orix held the gate open for him, Anskar walked through, as somnambulant as the night he'd first left Branil's Burg.

There, face down on the grass, as if he'd been fleeing toward the stables, was Larson. Atop the stablemaster's prone body lay Rosie.

A lump formed in Anskar's throat as he approached. Pressure built behind his eyes, but a hope he knew was hopeless wouldn't yet let him cry. He dropped to his knees beside Larson, taking in the congealed blood that bloomed on his back, the slit at the center, right through his jerkin: a sword thrust from behind as he ran. Was there no honor among Niyandrians?

"It wasn't me!" he said as the tears began to fall. "I never gave the order to attack. I promise it wasn't me!"

His only answer was a muffled whine; it came not from Larson but from the dog sprawled atop him. Still alive? Rosie was still—!

As he felt her fur, she snapped at his hand, eyes rolled up in her head, teeth bared.

Anskar fell back on the grass, and Rosie leapt, snarling and snapping. He caught hold of her by the throat, and she yelped. With a shift of his hips, Anskar got back to his knees, holding the dog on her back beneath him, careful not to use too much weight. She growled, but her aggression soon ebbed. He felt her relax and released his grip, and Rosie just lay there, docile, all the rage gone from her eyes; they were soppy and brown once more, and she offered her belly. When he tickled it, the dog squirmed, but not happily like she used to. She was scared of him. She only lay there because he was stronger than her. But was she scared of his physical dominance or the changes within? Dogs were sensitive like that, Larson used to say; they could feel the movements of sorcery, and they could tell good sorcerers from bad.

"It's all right, puppy," he told her as he withdrew his hand. "I'm better now. Whatever you sensed outside the Burg, it's gone." *Blended with the other tides. I'm balanced,* he wanted to say. *Like Menselas, god of five aspects.* But he didn't know that. Didn't know what it meant that three of the tides were now intertwined and interacting inside him, the fourth sullen, rejected, a simmering rival.

Absently, he petted Rosie as his eyes returned to Larson's corpse. He didn't turn the face but left it buried in the grass so that he didn't have to see the dead eyes.

"I'm sorry, old friend," he whispered. "I'm so sorry."

This wasn't your doing, son, Larson said, his voice a feather's touch beneath Anskar's scalp. *I may have been many things in life, but stupid wasn't one of them.*

"Larson?" Was the dead man's spirit speaking to him, or was it just his imagination?

Make this right, Anskar. Not for me. For Niyas. For the mainland. For all of us. Make it right.

"I don't know how… "

Trust in yourself, son. When the whole world's lying to you, it's all you can do.

Anskar dropped his head to Larson's back—stiff and cold. He hugged the corpse, drenching it with his tears.

"I can't trust myself," he sniffed. "I don't even know who I am anymore. I never knew! It's you I trust. You and Sned and…" And who? Who else did he trust? Vihtor had kept him in the dark about who he was for most of his life. Carred? Certainly not his mother! Then who?

He felt a hand on his shoulder. He turned as Orix pulled him into an embrace, and he sobbed uncontrollably.

"We'll bury him," Orix said as he stroked Anskar's hair. "We'll bury all of them."

Anskar angled his head for one last look at the stablemaster's body. Rosie brushed herself against his leg, whining.

"Don't worry, old friend," Anskar said, wiping his nose with the back of his hand. "I'll take care of her for you."

"He's gone, Anskar," Orix said. "He can't hear you."

"He heard me," Anskar said. "Same as I heard him."

An uncomfortable silence followed, during which Anskar rested his head on Orix's shoulder.

"That bloody Marith did this," Orix said. "Not you. I saw, and by Menselas, she has to pay."

"You saw?"

"It was just the Niyandrians who ran off," Orix said, "like some crazy mob. I followed when it seemed to be over."

"You didn't feel the control? You weren't swept up in Marith's sorcery?"

Orix held Anskar out at arm's length. "I heard the commotion…

when I was with… ”

“Noni?”

Orix's face was an anguish of misplaced features, twitching and grimacing, as he tried to hold in whatever he felt. Now it was Anskar's turn to hold his friend, and Orix shuddered as he wept.

“She's gone, Anskar. Noni's gone. I love her. Don't ask me why, but by Menselas, I do.”

“I'm sorry,” Anskar said. “For everything.” He wiped tears from his friend's face, and recoiled. Beneath his touch, the skin sloughed and churned, and within himself, the tides rippled and went from a torpid ooze to a burning breeze to the feel of crisp air and cool water. Not just the three: the earth-tide gushed up through his feet of its own accord, and the other tides weaved around it.

Orix gasped, and Anskar backed away, blinking. But it wasn't tears blurring his vision that was the issue; it was Orix's face, distorting as it bubbled, blistered, and set.

And when it was over, when the boiling tides inside Anskar had settled back into their background flow, when it was once more three against one, Orix was staring at him wide-eyed—eyes where they were supposed to be, nose and mouth below.

Orix touched his own face with the tips of his fingers, tracing the contours of every feature.

“It's back to normal,” he breathed. “Anskar, I felt it. I felt you heal me.”

Anskar trembled. He was no healer! Gisela of Gessa had taught him what she could, but it wasn't enough. Not for this. “How? I have no idea… How did I…?”

“The earth-tide.”

He turned, startled. Carred Selenas stood behind him. He'd not heard her approach. She'd spoken in Nan-Rhouric—presumably because Orix was present.

“What do you know about the earth-tide?” Anskar asked. “Did my mother tell you anything?"

"Talia told me next to nothing—especially when it came to you."

"Tain," Orix said, then he spat on the ground, as if he wanted to prove he could spit properly now that his mouth was restored to its proper place.

Carred nodded. "The necromancer Tain used the earth-tide to distort Orix's face."

"Because it's for shaping matter and not just raising the dead!" Anskar said, recalling what Eadgith had told him, though still not understanding how it worked nor what the connection was between the sorcery of the dead and altering the form of things. But there was a connection, he was sure of it, one that nibbled away at the back of his mind; a connection that Orix already seemed to have made, though it was likely drawn from hope rather than deduction.

"You have the power," Orix said. "The power to bring Noni back." He turned to appeal to Carred. "He can bring her back."

Anskar just stared at him, the implications of what Orix had just said slow to form.

"Can you?" Carred asked.

"No!" he said, hands clutching his head.

"You can!" Orix said, moving toward him.

Carred placed herself between them. "Now, now. There's been enough fighting for one day."

"I'm not..." Orix protested as he took a backwards step. "I wasn't going to fight. I just... Please, Anskar, do this for me."

"You're presupposing that he could," Carred said. "And what if he can? What then? Should he raise everyone who's died? Even if it were possible, would it be the right thing to do?"

Orix ignored her. "Anskar..."

"I can't," Anskar said as he turned away, Rosie following at his heels.

"Won't, you mean!" Orix yelled after him. "You won't even try!"

EIGHT

ANSKAR STOOD WITH ROSIE IN the shadowed north court of the bailey, watching former comrades burn. The dog lay at his feet, her head on her paws, her brown eyes sad and forlorn.

His setting fire to the church of Menselas earlier felt like an ill omen now, as he cremated the Five's servants. The pyre for the dead knights roared into a violent conflagration, sending sparks streaking into the turbid air. Anskar followed the plumes of black smoke, watching as they were driven by the gusting wind out over Dorinah. The smoldering skeleton of the church he had earlier torched lay that way, and it struck him then as a premonition of the Niyas that was to come. Was it a liberated Niyas he was creating or a burning abyss? Had he made the right choices? Menselas, how could he tell?

The smell of burnt flesh drew his eyes back to the blaze. He felt a sudden longing for his fellow trainees—old antagonists, one-time friends. Memories of their faces, the way they moved, the things they said competed for place of honor in his mind. He was content to let them fight it out, distracted as he was by the plaintive chant of a myriad Niyandrian voices coming from the other side of the keep. The rebels had started their own pyre there and had gathered in full force to sing their fallen to the realm of the dead. He'd seen Orix go to stand with them. The Traguh-raj had decisively chosen his side. Anskar thought he had too, but it was difficult to let go of the people and the Order who had raised him. Without them, there seemed no frame to define his life. Without them, what would he be, where would he go? Without order in his life, what depths would he plummet to? He'd always known he would have to choose where he stood, but the choice had been made for him, which was another way of saying it was no choice at all. For all his recent experiences, his travels, his friendships, his battles, he was still subject to the random buffets of fate; or more likely, the carefully orchestrated machinations of Queen Talia. But had she gone too far and revealed her hand, the way she had hijacked Marith and started a war? Because the mainlanders would come in their thousands now, united in one cause. Could the same be said of Niyas? Marith's actions—Talia's—felt a betrayal too far, a knife in the back that had the potential to split the loyalties of the isle.

Rosie yipped, then let out a succession of half-formed barks. Anskar stooped to stroke her, then realized she had fallen asleep and was dreaming.

The wind turned, blowing smoke in his eyes. He swiped smoldering ash from his shirt and pants. He was too close to the blaze, but he couldn't take a step back. It would have felt a dereliction of duty, foolish as that sounded. He'd defied the Order of Eternal Vigilance, sided with the rebels against their oppressors, but he still felt a responsibility for the Order's dead, and the eyes of Menselas still scrutinized his every action and weighed it in the Five's divine balance.

The smoke brought stinging tears to his eyes. It seemed to him that the spirits of the dead knights were borne along with the smoke, and that the wind was some hitherto undisclosed tide of sorcery, or even the will of Menselas drawing them home into the carcass of the burned out church. But what would be their reward? An eternity in which to find their own inner harmony, and the deeper harmony of union with their god of five aspects?

The only real union these dead knights and their servants would achieve, he thought bitterly, was union with oblivion, the final revelation of a delusory belief.

But no, he couldn't accept that. Wouldn't. He had felt the presence of Menselas, a warmth within; fleeting, but nevertheless…

The memory of prayers answered dispersed like the smoke on the wind. It might have been true, and by all five aspects of Menselas he wanted it to be true. Sned and Larson were among the burning dead. There had to be somewhere for them to go other than some featureless void. There was, an errant thought reminded him: the realm of the dead. But that was no paradisal rest for the loyal servants of Menselas. He'd glimpsed what it was when his vambrace had activated: a gray limbo, a misty abode of twilight within which drifted the spirits of the unquiet dead. Compared with that, oblivion didn't seem so bad.

A wail startled him, and he looked round. No one was there. There came another, keening and drawn out, and his eyes returned to the pyre. Within the flames, char-blackened corpses melted and crumbled. A skull coated in steaming, gelatinous tar dropped lower in the flames as the bones beneath it collapsed. Its jaw hung slack, and its empty eye sockets stared at him.

Half-blood, it said in a voice like the wind, *you did this. This is your fault.*

Rosie snarled, then shook herself as she awakened and stood, ears pricked up, tail erect.

Traitor! said another voice out of the pyre. *The Five curse you!*

Die, half-blood! A woman's voice this time.

Die! came a chorus of the dead from within the conflagration, a chant in Anskar's mind that drowned out the song of the Niyandrians. *Die! Die! Die!* The flames flared in time with the chant, and now Anskar took a step back. Ashes spat towards him amid the sizzle and pop of flesh and fat. Fire whiplashed out of the blaze, and he stumbled back, pitching to his backside. He muttered prayers like an exorcism, but the flames roared even higher. He changed his prayer to one of contrition, begging the Five's forgiveness for the part he had played, for the failures, the betrayals. But every word he spoke to his god was met with ire and iridescence. Flames seared the sky. Black smoke roiled towards him, inexorable as death.

Back, a familiar voice said. *Back away. Leave the lad alone.*

Obediently, the smoke started to curl away from Anskar, drawn back to the pyre.

Rosie let out a pathetic whine and sat on her haunches, a deep frown etched into her blunt face as she watched Anskar, as if he knew what to do.

"Larson?" he asked, trembling with loss and hope.

Aye, son, it's me. You comfort that poor dog now, you hear? She feels I'm near, but she knows something's not right.

Anskar knelt to stroke Rosie behind the ear. She licked his face and whined, her tail curled around one of her hind legs.

Assling, another familiar voice said—Sned, the forge master. *You self-pitying little prick, this ain't your doing. The others are scared, they're angry, and it blinds them. But me and Larson know you, son, and we're on your side.*

Anskar drew some small comfort from the fact that Sned, even in death, still insulted him. It was a mark of affection. He almost wished the forge master's wooden mallet would come hurtling from the blaze and hit him on the head; it might scatter the warring serpents that had taken up residence in his skull.

You know who you are, son, Larson said.

"No," Anskar replied, and he was speaking to the pyre. "No, I don't."

Course you know, lad, Sned said. *You're an asshole. You've always been an asshole.*

"I thought it was 'assling'…"

Same difference, save maybe the size. Listen to Larson, assling. He's the one that talks sense. Me, I was always too drunk. But I know people, and I say you're all right.

No one worked harder than you at the stables, Larson said. *And no one took the rules of the Order more seriously. And them animals—Rosie here, Monty and Hazel—they love you, Anskar, and I always said animals are the best judge of character.*

"They're still here… Monty and Hazel?" Now he felt as though he'd betrayed the donkey and the horse as well. They had been his companions on those frosty early mornings, when everyone else was tucked up in bed. It had been just him and the animals greeting the rising sun, and no dawn tide to worry about back then.

They're still here, Larson said. *Still doing nothing but grazing and eating too much grain. Go see them, son. You can learn a lot from the beasts. Helps to keep things straight.*

Learn a lot from the forges, too, Sned put in. *You have a talent for metal work, assling. Don't let it go to waste.*

Anskar mouthed a "Thank you," even as he wondered what he would make. Another demon-possessed sword? The Armor of Divinity? Any comfort he might once have taken from the smithing hall had been destroyed by the blood pooling on the floor and the bodies of the people slaughtered there. The memory of Sned.

Look after Rosie for me, Larson said, his voice quieter now, farther away.

Little things, assling, Sned said, his words drifting away on the wind. *Little things is what's important.*

"Don't go," Anskar wanted to say, but doing so would have been an admission of his isolation, an admission of his fear. He racked his brains for something else to say, something that sounded less like pleading, less like a child frightened of the dark.

"Are you all right?" he asked. "Are you with Menselas?" *Are you both in the realm of the dead?*

Nothing.

No answer.

He felt the weight of a presence behind him and turned with the same terror he might have felt were it a wraithe or a dead-eye.

It was Carred.

"Sorry I startled you," she said.

Anskar turned his back on the pyre and went to her, the flicker of flames casting her crimson face in eerie animation. It could have been the face of a demon, if he'd not known demons better. It was hard to read her expression in the play of shadow and light. She might have been weeping.

"I thought you'd be at the other pyre," he said, coming to a stop mere inches from her, so close he could smell the wine on her breath.

"Couldn't stay. What happened here—it wasn't by my command. Wasn't what I would have chosen."

"Nor me," Anskar said.

Carred held out her trembling hand to him, and he took it.

NINE

ANSKAR RETURNED WITH ROSIE TO the Brief Repose and took a room on the third floor, where there was a better chance of being left alone. The proprietor welcomed him back with his earlier surliness, but it felt forced this time, and he ruined the mystique of anonymity by presenting his name: "Joal Pelzid at your service, *Melesh-Eloni.*" The formality made him seem less trustworthy somehow. Niyandrian rebels had apparently been gossiping during the wake for their dead. Anskar suspected the fat man had smelled prestige and coin now he fully understood whom he was dealing with. Pelzid couldn't hide the wrinkling of his nose at Anskar's dog, but with a change of character an actor would have been proud of, he fetched her a bowl of water and some kitchen scraps. With a guarantee that the new Niyandrian army would settle the bill, whatever Pelzid decided to charge in these trying times, Anskar left the dog in the proprietor's dubious care and then took a pitcher of beer and a mug to his room.

Carred had gone with Vilintia to organize the commandeering of buildings for the Niyandrian forces, nominating captains for each newly formed division. Already the Burg was being occupied, its walls manned. Anskar wanted no part of that. Yet it was the right thing to do—the only thing, considering the hornet's nest they had now poked. War was coming. It was unavoidable.

He sat for a while, drinking on the bed—the only furniture, and then only if the term were used in the loosest sense. At some point in the tavern's dingy past, an enterprising soul, likely Pelzid himself, had nailed half-rotted planks between two parallel fence posts. Of course, it could originally have been intended as a raft. The mattress was a straw-filled sackcloth alive with the black specks of fleas. For covers, there was a stinking sheepskin and a moth-eaten quilt, a patchwork of ravens, bats, and skulls—the sacramentals of the old gods of Niyas. The room stank of urine and damp. The ceiling was speckled with dark mold, and paint the color of ruptured bowels flaked from the walls.

The needle-sharp bites of fleas were an immediate irritation, the perpetrators gone before he could swat them or crush them between thumb and forefinger. Before he could worry about that, he had other needs to assuage, and within the space of a few short minutes he set the half-empty pitcher on the floorboards then sat cross-legged in the center of the bed, nestling the mug in his lap.

Power.

That was the word that consumed his impromptu meditation. How much did he have now, and was it truly his to command? What were his limitations? Orix assumed he had none; that he was only refusing to resuscitate Noni out of spite or some childish jealousy over Carred. Of equal interest, what were Marith's limitations as a moontouched Niyandrian? What were Queen Talia's? Clearly they both had them; neither had withstood the assault of his sword. But therein lay the rogue element in his deliberations: What role in all this did his strange sword *Amalantril* play?

He slapped at a bite on his neck, and then, almost absently, unleashed a steady flow of intermingled essence through his pores. His skin grew hot, and an uncomfortable heat radiated out across the mattress. In obedience to some buried instinct, the earth-tide rose through the floorboards, through the bed, and coiled about the swirling miasma within him. A rank odor reached his nostrils, and a cold and limpid mist effused from the mattress. He held the enchantment a little longer than he thought he needed to, then with a sigh let the earth-tide ebb away and the other three settle back within him.

Good, he thought as he picked a black speck from the mattress and flicked it to the floor amid the accumulated feculence of Menselas knew how many years. The fleas were dead.

So he had a degree of control, but what if the demands on his power were greater? Turn up the heat enough, and what could contain it? In the streets of Dorinah, when he had challenged the very walls of Branil's Burg, he had come close to finding out the answer—which he suspected was "Nothing."

But that still didn't mean he had enough power. In the fight with Marith-Talia, he'd been more-or-less impotent until his sword's intervention. Rely on that too much and he became the tool, not the other way around; and he'd played that part too long already. What he needed was knowledge, not just power raw and unadulterated. He needed to understand what he had, what he had been given. The return of the dusk and the dawn without need for a catalyst wasn't the issue; they felt like the reacquaintance of old friends. The dark had never left him, although its presence within his blood grew ever more overt and essential to who he really was—and he didn't know what that was yet, only that the veils that obscured the truth were getting as frayed as the patchwork quilt on his bed.

It was the earth-tide that most intrigued him, probably because it was the most recent manifestation of his powers, whether gifted or innate. It had been Queen Talia who had first worked the earth-tide through him outside the Tainted Cabal stronghold of Nax-ur-Vadim in the Ymaltian Mountains. Her mastery of the necromantic forces had seemed complete, unsurpassable, but he knew now that was because of his own inexperience. What if he held within him the potential to rival Queen Talia—not just in the use of the dark-tide but also the earth? One way or another, he was going to have to find out, because to his mind, war wasn't just coming from the mainland. At some point, he was going to have to face his mother again, and unless he was going to give her whatever she wanted—whatever she had birthed him for— there was going to be a different kind of war, a war of unearthly powers. As things stood, Marith definitely held the advantage with the dawn and the dusk, whereas Queen Talia was leaps and bounds ahead of him with the earth. In a dark-tide duel between him and his mother, Anskar felt he might hold his own; but things were never that simple.

Every winding path his thoughts went down led him back to the same conclusion: If he was to be anything other than a pawn, if he was going to survive, he had to learn, to practice, to improve.

And the guilt Orix had left him with was all the incentive he needed to begin.

He finished off the beer in his mug but retained his grip on the handle. For what he planned to attempt, he needed the touch of something solid, an anchor to pull him back to the world when the time was right, and a beer mug seemed just the thing. Not the vambrace. That would never do. When the wraithes of the lost city of Yustanwyrd had come for him and the Grand Master, the vambrace had transported him to the realm of the dead—not a place he wanted to visit again. Nevertheless, that brief translation to another realm had given him an idea.

And so he closed his eyes and plunged his senses downwards: through the bed, through the floor, the story beneath, down through the very ground itself. It was the route the earth-tide took when it came to him, and now he simply followed it in reverse. He sought answers there, at the source of the necrotic currents that gave power over life and death, though he had no idea what he would find. Almost at once he wondered if this was just his imagination, but as an overwhelming stench rose up to engulf him, he had to believe there was sorcery involved. He told himself Queen Talia had found a way to travel in spirit from the realm of the dead. Why should it be any different to travel from Wiraya to the underworld, where the tides of dawn, dusk, and dark seeped through layers of sediment to putrefy at the world's core, to make a fourth?

Suddenly the fumes no longer disturbed him. He *was* the fumes, roiling in a vertiginous descent, limbs a jumble of vapors that uncoiled as he reached the bottom and grew not quite solid. He'd expected to find himself in a subterranean sea, a mire of putrescence. He had imagined caverns of poisonous smoke, a brume of unbridled contagion. What he did not expect was shimmering walls of silver, a shiny pliant floor, a ceiling high above of burnished argent.

"Yustanwyrd…" he breathed with the voice of his spirit, a swirling susurration that seemed to come from everywhere and nowhere.

And there, apparently waiting for him, moonlit by the lost city's unseen light source, stood the wraithe he had first seen atop Hallow Hill. He was sure it was the same one, from the bedizened crossguard of the sword sheathed at its hip. He raised his arm, expecting to see the vambrace aglow with the lunar radiance of the chamber, but it was not there. He was naked, made of smoke, as ethereal as a ghost. The wraithe, on the other hand, looked entirely solid, down to the weight of its iron-banded boots.

"Your powers grow, young DeVantte," the wraithe said as it stomped towards him, the floor vibrating with each iron-clad impact.

Alarmed, Anskar turned to run, but run where? There were no doors, no arches, not even a window. It was a perfect cube that contained him. He shut his eyes, willing himself back to his room and his bed. A chill touch on his spectral shoulder caused him to open them with a start. The wraithe was gripping him with an iron gauntlet, as if he were solid.

"How can I be in Yustanwyrd?" Anskar asked, his voice howling like the wind. He waited for the echoing din to die down; considered whether he dare speak again; decided to await the wraithe's reply.

"You seek answers, do you not?" the wraithe said, no sign of motion beneath its cowl, just emptiness, utterly dark. "You seek power. It is ever the way with humans."

Warily, in case he caused a hurricane this time, Anskar whispered, "I seek only to understand the powers I already have."

"Of course," the wraithe said. "Power misunderstood is a hazard to our agenda. Power not understood is no power at all. But what you seek—knowledge and control of the dead—is under the dominion of one more ancient than I, more fundamental to the way things are."

"You're speaking in riddles," Anskar said, and now his voice was his own, without a hint of breeze. He felt heavier, more substantial. He shifted his weight from foot to foot, under the wraithe's inscrutable gaze.

"Riddles, like poems, like art in all its guises, are a veil that protects from the unmediated truth."

"Why would I want to be protected from the truth?" Anskar asked. Once he would have protested that Menselas was the truth, in the harmony of his five aspects. It troubled him he no longer thought that. Bereft of childhood beliefs, he was an enigma to himself, all potential with no guiding framework, thoroughly his own man—or more absolutely someone else's than he had ever been.

"Come," the wraithe said, turning away from him with a swish of its cloak. Its boots caused a fearsome clangor on the metal floor as it passed through an archway that had not been there before.

Anskar followed, his own footfalls shouting his weight. Part of him wanted to call out to the wraithe, to tell it he'd made a mistake coming here, that he wanted to go back to the world above. But truth was a lure he couldn't resist. He had to know, had to see for himself.

The gleam of the corridor, as silver as the room, hurt his eyes. He almost bumped into the wraithe as it stopped abruptly. The floor and walls just simply ran out, and there was nothing ahead save an impenetrable darkness. Anskar drew back, the confrontation with infinity hammering at his senses and making him reel. It was a blackness without end, an abyss that could never be filled.

When the wraithe stepped from the end of the corridor and plummeted through the dark, Anskar edged closer to the brink and risked a look down, only to see the wraithe's fall had slowed to a gentle drift. The reason he could see anything at all was because the wraithe had drawn its sword, and the gems on the crossguard shone like miniature suns. It wasn't the first unnatural descent Anskar had witnessed, nor the first he'd been called upon to undertake.

With a muttered curse as full of bile and spittle as a physical utterance, he stepped off the end of the corridor. For a second he plunged downward, then he too slowed into a timeless and carefree descent. He counted an entire minute, and still there was nothing but blackness all around him. A second minute, and he couldn't tell up from down, left from right. He began to panic that he had entered an eternal fall, then reached for the dark-tide, willing himself to sprout wings of shadow. Nothing. There was no power within him, no repositories, no blood, no bone. He was weightless once again, a phantom of mist, a thought, a dream.

Minute after minute he drifted down. Hour after hour. Time had no meaning here; there were no reference points by which to measure its passing. It could have been days, it could have been weeks or months, but at length he began to gain on the wraithe, and then the two of them stood side by side, and their descent stopped.

There was nothing solid beneath Anskar's feet. Below him, the infinite darkness continued. It spread away from him on every side. He felt its crushing presence pressing down from above, its light-eating walls closing in like unseen pincers, compressing him to a point. To keep from crying out in despair, he focused his attention on the scattered light coming from the wraithe's bejeweled sword hilt.

"Behold," the wraithe said.

Ahead, the darkness wavered, and Anskar stood, transfixed. By increments, the surrounding darkness advanced, the fist of utter nothingness relinquishing its grasp as the jewels on the wraithe's sword grew more radiant. The rippling dark took form now, chitinous and hard. The carapace of some monstrous insect swayed atop a coiled serpent's tail. Six spindly limbs projected from the body, rustling as they shivered. Lastly, the head came into view, bat-like but scaled, with the pronounced snout and vicious jaws of a wolf. A single bloodshot eye glared from the center of its forehead, excoriating with its intensity. The stench of rot rolled off the monster, everything vile and repugnant Anskar could think of.

He willed himself to back away, but he couldn't move. Tried to shut his eyes, but they were no longer under his control. Light retreated from his peripheral vision—the wraithe leaving him? He couldn't see. All he *could* see was the glistening horror before him, swaying like a charmed snake as it swelled in size till it towered above him—till it would have towered above the keep at Branil's Burg.

Not real, he told himself over and over, a mantra that, no matter how often he repeated it, banished nothing. *Menselas, what are you?* He wanted to scream—would have screamed, if he could have moved his lips. *I made a mistake,* he railed against the dark. *I shouldn't have come here. Please, send me back!*

"So," the monstrosity hissed, drool slopping from its jaws and dissolving into the fuliginous dark, "the Necromancer's Key seeks power for itself. For whyever else would you come to me?"

Tremors ran through Anskar's body. It felt as though his petrified flesh had cracked like an egg. Fissures of volition opened up within his mind. Fear sloughed away from him, and he found his voice.

"I came looking for knowledge, for control of the earth-tide, not… I did not seek you out. I don't even know who you are."

"Corpse Maker, the blood skins call me. Devourer of the Dead. Sower of Rot. The Putrescence."

"Kaythe Nurglich?" Anskar asked, the words the scantest of breaths leaving his lips. Sareya had long ago suggested Kaythe Nurglich as a name for his sword.

"So, you do know me after all. You seek control of the earth-tide, you say? I was spawned in its effluence. The earth-tide formed me. I am *it*."

"You are…" Anskar stammered. "You are a god."

"You bear the stink of Menselas," the monster said, its single eye flaring crimson. "Yet I know you from your blood: Queen Talia's get, the descendent of demons. You are at best confused, most likely a hypocrite; else why would you come in search of knowledge forbidden by your church?"

"To help my friend."

"Of course. Blame the friend. That way you can plead innocence before your five-faced god."

He's not my god, Anskar wanted to say, but some niggling voice within warned him not to; told him such a denial could lead nowhere good.

"He lost someone," Anskar said. "He thinks I have the means to bring her back from the dead."

"You do not," Kaythe Nurglich said. "But you could."

Anskar glanced around for the wraithe, as if that mysterious being might offer him advice. It was gone. Its absence felt like a betrayal, though why should he have expected anything less? A gloomy resignation fell over him.

"Do you know what your mother gave me in return for power over the earth-tide?" Kaythe Nurglich asked.

"Do I need to know?"

The wolf's jaws twisted into the semblance of a cruel smile. A twitching cloaca opened within the god's armor-like carapace. It contracted then dilated, and a knotted mass appeared at its mouth. Another contraction, and the knots untangled. Dozens of sinewy tendrils shivered from the sphincter, each tipped with a vicious barb of cartilage. They thrashed and writhed and weaved through the dark toward Anskar, venomous droplets of greenish fluid dripping from their tips.

"Accept the earth tide's fullness within you," the god said, "and your power will rival your mother's. Maybe even surpass it."

Anskar backed away. "Forgive me," he said. "I should not have come. I didn't know... I would never have asked..."

"If you had known what it is I demand in return?" Kaythe Nurglich's wolf jaws salivated. "A simple intermingling of essence, a blending of the tides. An infection, if you like, but one that empowers rather than enfeebles. And, you must understand, it would give me pleasure."

"I'm sorry," Anskar said. "I can't."

"I understand," the god said. It left its obscene tendrils swaying before Anskar a moment longer. Then, with a slurping sound, the vile worms retracted back inside the cloaca, and the cloaca itself disappeared beneath the carapace. "But you know where to find me when all looks hopeless."

"I don't understand," Anskar said. "What are you saying? That things will get worse? That I will have no choice but to come back?"

"There is always a choice," Kaythe Nurglich said as he retreated into the darkness. "Depending on how you define choice."

Anskar stood trembling, facing the oblivion from whence the god had materialized. A soft dweomer from his right made him turn.

There stood the wraithe, its gauntleted hand grasping the starlit hilt of its sword.

"I will walk you back."

"Walk?" Anskar said, lost in a daze of shock and revulsion and decisions he hoped never to have to make.

"A figure of speech."

The wraithe glided ahead of him through the featureless void, and Anskar raced to keep up, not daring to take his eyes from the sword's effulgence.

The wraithe turned and waited for him at the threshold to the silver chamber. Once Anskar was within, the wall closed up, sealing them in.

"Your mother and I had a pact," the wraithe said. "I fulfilled my part when I brought you her vambrace. She no longer desires what my kind desire. Her purposes are her own. But you, Anskar, possess all she once possessed… and perhaps more."

"If I accept Kaythe Nurglich's gift?"

"I would not," the wraithe said. "I regret that the leaders of my kind once did, an aeon ago, and that we are still enslaved by the needs the Corpse Maker engendered in us."

"You serve Kaythe Nurglich?"

"It is not easy to explain. Some would call us slaves, but we are not."

Anskar frowned as he paced the chamber, glad of its burnished floor as opposed to the disorienting dark. "I don't understand. How did you know I would travel in spirit to the world's core? Why meet me here? And why take me to that monster?"

"You assign to me knowledge beyond any I possess and choices not open to me. You ask if I serve, and I say it is not easy to explain. There are laws to these matters, laws as compelling as those that govern the stars, the moons, and the sun—yea, the four tides and one, even. You have the potential. Perhaps one day you will see further even than I. Perhaps you shall understand in whole what I comprehend only in part. I would help you."

"Help me? What would you want in return?"

"Nothing to compare with the depravities of Kaythe Nurglich. Perhaps I—we, for I acknowledge my brethren of Yustanwyrd in this matter—will send you teachers."

"What kind of teachers?"

"Those who would steep you gradually in the lore that you seek without the immersion Kaythe Nurglich would have granted. It is a point in your favor that you declined his offer."

"You brought me to him as a test?"

The wraithe sheathed its sword. "Again, it is complicated. A test, yes, but also a duty fulfilled. I am no longer bound to your mother, but older covenants still compel my acts and those of my kind. Let it be said: those who most desire power least deserve it."

"Your words… all these riddles… none of this helps me," Anskar said.

"This I acknowledge. Once I would not have wished it so."

"But not now?"

"Wishes are no longer accessible to me. They are but memories, ghosts as ethereal as you are to me now and as I would be to you in the world above. We are a passing race, young Anskar. Wiraya is all but done with us. But not so you. The tides will be one again, depending upon the path that you tread. I see unity. True balance, not the juggling of disparate forces that makes your Menselas such a difficult god to follow. Yes, I think I will indeed send you help."

"No pacts, though," Anskar said. Never again. He'd gotten in above his head with the Ethereal Sorceress. "I am my own man now."

"I understand. Consider it a gift; a tiny taste of what you are missing, what Kaythe Nurglich would have given you, complete, irresistible, but at a terrible cost."

"Why?" Anskar asked. "Why would you do this?" *What's the catch?*

"Because this particular choice is open to me."

The wraithe's gauntleted hand lashed out, an iron finger stabbing

Anskar between the eyes. Fire exploded in his skull, then images of bones and blood. The stench of effluence rose all around him—the same smell that had accompanied Kaythe Nurglich.

The bed creaked beneath Anskar as he came to in his tawdry little room. His hands shot straight to his eyes. Menselas, they hurt. Tears burned them like acid. He looked about for a mirror. Nothing in the room—no surprise there. But then an idea struck him, and he drew *Amalantril* from his scabbard. The sword shuddered as he gripped the hilt, seeming to purr with pleasure. He angled the blade so he could see his reflection, and maggots wriggled in his stomach in response. God of Five Aspects—the wraithe, unlike the Corpse Maker, hadn't even given him a choice. It had made an offer and acted upon it before he'd had time to respond.

His eyes!

Sweet Menselas, what was it with his eyes? First his Niyandrian kidnappers had altered, or revealed, his true eyes: cat's eyes, proof of the lineage he had tried so hard to deny.

And now this.

Menselas, what did it mean?

His eyes were wells of inky blackness that seemed to swallow the light, windows on a soul he was no longer sure he possessed.

But as he wrestled with the horror and the loss, he knew, as if a veil had been drawn back, exactly would he could do for Orix.

For Noni.

"No!" he cried, clutching his head and letting the sword clatter to the floor. "I'll not do it."

This reeked of manipulation, of playing upon his need to fix things with Orix. He wouldn't. Couldn't. Shouldn't. But Menselas, how could he not? Orix already thought he had the power to restore Noni, and now that he really did, could he in good faith withhold that power? *Yes,* a part of him said. The earth-tide was antithetical to the will of

Menselas. *So?* another thought said. The Grand Master had disabused him of the notion that Menselas never made exceptions as far as the forbidden tides were concerned. It all depended on who defined the god's will, on who was making the decisions.

His mind was an agony of recollections, of the things he had witnessed, the things he had done at the Abbey of the Hooded One. He heard again the persuasive arguments of the Abbess, a woman who could have convinced him that black was white, that two plus two equaled five, that she was Carred Selenas, panting and naked above him.

How could he trust himself to make the right choice?

How could he know anything at all?

He needed help. Advice he could trust. He wasn't even sure such a thing existed.

But if it did, he thought he knew where he might find it.

TEN

THE ROOMS CARRED TOOK AT Branil's Burg weren't exactly plush, but they were more than adequate. Embers still smoldered in the grate, and seasoned logs were stacked in the scuttle beside the hearth, enough to get a really good blaze going. But that would involve getting up from the dour but comfy couch.

She knocked back the rest of her mistberry wine with one swallow, poured herself another, then curled back up on the cushions, enjoying the heady feeling that washed over her. Vilintia had outdone herself in finding Carred's new quarters. There was an entire wine rack filled with bottles of mistberry. Sad that it reminded her of Marith, who was never short of a bottle; but at least she didn't have to share.

A woman had been the previous occupant, she decided. She'd found the bed perfectly made, not a crinkle in the satin sheets, and the pillowcases retained a lingering floral scent. It was why she had opted for the couch: messing up those pristine sheets would have made her feel she was in trouble with her mother, ludicrous as it sounded after all these years. And the scent: it reminded her of an ex-lover, though for the life of her she couldn't remember who.

An interesting woman, though, she thought as she studied for the hundredth time the artwork of perfectly proportioned ladies on every wall: dark-skinned San-Kharr beauties; crimson Niyandrians scarce out of girlhood; green-skinned and dark haired Ilapa; even a toned and muscular black-skinned Orgol posed against the backdrop of the Jargalan Desert; and strangest of all, but utterly delectable, a violet-skinned nymph with a pointy tipped tail. Her predecessor was clearly something of a connoisseur. If only Carred had met her. Then again, perhaps she already had. Rooms like these, so much larger than the others, better located—Vilintia had insisted on her taking them, and Carred had been too tired to argue—they were befitting a commander.

Oh, Theltek, she thought, suppressing the urge to vomit—although that could have been on account of too much wine. These were Seneschal Monash's rooms, the one-eyed harridan from the smithing hall.

That made her look afresh at the dainty little writing desk with the two inkwells in the corner, the loose pages of notes, and the book of poetry with pressed flowers between its leaves. Monash had looked hard as bone in a pinched-face sort of way, a little too manly for Carred's liking—not that she had anything against men. But the portraits and the poetry, the scent and the flowers… it all made for an enticingly complex impression. It just went to show, you should never judge a book by its cover.

She curled up on the couch and immediately became restless. Mistberry wine sometimes did that to her. In the past, Marith had been there to remedy the problem.

Marith…

Memories vied for her attention, and shutting her eyes only made the images that accompanied them more vivid. In her mind, she was mid-conversation with Kovin when she realized he was dead and she was here all alone. Theltek, poor Kovin. Her heart clenched in refusal of his absence. She could feel the heat of his body pressed against her. Absently, her hand glided over her shirt, tracing the contours of her breast. Kovin and his love of tits! Any tits, not just hers. She'd never had a problem with that. They were birds of a feather in that respect, seeking comfort, seeking a little joy, without all the complications others seemed to relish. If only her parents had been the same, rather than misers in love, jealously clinging to what they never had, too stubborn, too stupid, too bloody undesirable to see what a shambles their marriage was and move on. Mother used to say they stayed together for her sake. She really wished they hadn't made the sacrifice.

She stretched out her hand towards the wine rack, as if sorcery would bring another bottle to her, so she wouldn't have to stand and fetch it. Gods, why did she drink so much? She knew the answer, though she let it remain unformed. Too much had happened. There were too many responsibilities. Too many failures. Why did they have to be hers?

There was a knock on the door.

"I'm busy!" she called out. "Go away!" Chance would be a fine thing. It didn't matter what she tried to do, there were always demands. Probably bloody Vilintia again, wanting approval for the captains she had chosen.

"Carred?" came the voice from outside.

Anskar.

She sat up too quickly and her head swooned. She settled herself with a deep breath and then tried to stand, abandoned the attempt, and called, "Come in."

The door clicked open and Anskar slid through the gap, closing it behind him.

"What's wrong?" Carred asked. His head was down. His own reaction to the weight of responsibility, or something else? Shame, perhaps. Well, there was enough to go around.

He raised his eyes to hers, and she was appalled. They seemed set in deep cavities and had totally black, orbs of gleaming onyx.

"Sweet Theltek, Anskar, your eyes! What happened?"

His hand hovered above the pommel of his sword. Was he even conscious of the fact?

"The abyssal realms did something to me, Carred," he said. "Domatai, the Demon Lord, did something." She had the sense he was lying, withholding some less palatable truth.

"And it's just manifested now?"

He shrugged. He was a terrible liar, which to her mind was a good thing. At least she could read him, not like some she could mention. And now Fult Wreave sprang to mind—Fult Weasel, as she'd always thought of him. He'd not come in answer to Marith's call. Maybe that was a good thing, but she doubted it. It wasn't just Fult who hadn't come, it was the families loyal to the lingering remnants of the Ickthal Dynasty too, and so many more—good Niyandrians who must have lost faith in Carred's rebellion. Who could blame them?

"Carred?" Anskar asked, snapping her out of her head. "Are you all right?"

"Fine," she said. "I'm fine. Just caught up in my thoughts. You know how it is."

His black eyes took in the bottle on the side table—had she laid it down, or knocked it over?

"There's more in the rack," she said. "Join me in a glass?"

Anskar's cheek twitched as emotions warred across his face. Vaguely, he surveyed the room, nodded, then crossed to the writing desk and starting leafing through the book.

"You'll have to get it," Carred said, waving towards the wine rack. "Uncork it too. I've had a bit much."

"Maybe I'll decline, then," Anskar said. Something caught his attention in the book, and he lifted it closer to see.

"So you can still read, then?" Carred said. "With those eyes."

He didn't answer. He was starting to unnerve her. She'd seen Marith possessed by Talia. Who was to say something similar hadn't happened to him?

He held up the open book to her.

"I can't see from over here," Carred said.

He brought it to her, tossing it in her lap like a challenge, like a condemnation. On the flyleaf, an inscription in Nan-Rhouric: "For what you've shown me, for what we've done, for the confidence you've given me, the trust. Your dearest S."

"That's supposed to mean something to me?" Carred said.

"S is for Sareya, I'll bet," Anskar said.

"I wouldn't know."

Anskar turned away from her and did a circuit of the room. "These were Vihtor's chambers originally, then Monash's."

"I'd just worked that out," Carred said, smirking as she indicated the artwork that adorned the walls. Anskar didn't even smile.

"Why did you come here?" she asked, as she stood on wobbly legs. She found her balance on the way to the wine rack, selected a bottle, then wavered on her feet as she tried to locate the corkscrew.

"Here," Anskar said, finding it on the table beside the rack and passing it to her.

"I knew you were good for something," Carred said, and this time he did smile. One thing she'd never had trouble with was opening a bottle when drunk. When the cork popped, she grinned at Anskar, expecting a round of applause. He barely noticed.

"Everything all right?" Carred asked as she poured a glass and handed it to him. Seeing as she'd left hers by the couch she decided to drink from the bottle.

"Fine," Anskar said, sniffing the wine as if it might be poison. Either that or it was his first time drinking wine. "I'm fine. It's just... These rooms were Vihtor's. Monash changed them a good deal."

"And I will change them again. Sometime. Come, sit down."

She stumbled on the way to the couch but somehow managed to get there without spilling the bottle. Anskar waited till she sat with her feet up then perched on the end, as far from her as he could get.

"I don't bite," she said. Sometimes she did, though.

That brought a smile to his face, though it looked sinister, what with his eyes. He shifted closer, and she swung her feet down to sit beside him. He didn't pull away when she touched his face, then traced circles around the onyx orbs of his eyes. The surrounding skin felt hard and abrasive.

"Does it hurt?" she asked.

"At first it did, like acid burning my eyeballs. I feel nothing now. They're just numb."

"But you can see well enough?"

"I can see."

"Give me your hand," she said, setting the wine bottle on the table next to her empty glass. She snatched it and held it in both her own. "You're cold. Just like your mother. Bitterly cold."

Anskar shrugged, as if it were no concern of his.

"Do you feel cold?"

He ignored the question and instead gestured at the room. "Vihtor and I sat here after the trials, when he became my mentor."

"Before you knew he was your father?"

He nodded then looked her in the eye with his unsettling gaze, all darkness, no light, no one left inside.

"What are we going to do?" he asked.

"That's a bit forward," Carred said, glancing at the bedroom. He didn't laugh, so she manufactured her most serious look. On second thought, the sheets! "So, if not for my good looks and charm, why did you come here, Anskar?"

"Orix…"

"Mind your own business," she said, pulling her feet back up on the sofa and hugging her knees. "And don't tell me you've not made mistakes. Remember Blaice Rancey? Do I need to go on?"

"Not that," Anskar said. Embarrassment brought out a reddish hue to his otherwise dusky skin. It made him look more Niyandrian, more wholesome. If only the eyes would change back. "Orix thinks I can restore Noni to life."

"Can you?"

"I told him no, but now… Now, I think maybe I can."

There was more… something he wasn't telling her. He looked as though he were trying not to be sick.

"What is it, Anskar? What have you done?"

"Nothing. Yet."

Carred puffed out her cheeks and deflated them with a sigh. "If I'd known we were going to talk about such serious matters, I'd have made tea. Wine plays havoc with my brain and leads to bad decisions. Did I tell you about the time I ran out of money gambling in Ahz?"

"Ahz?" Anskar asked.

"I know, terrible name for a town, but quite appropriate, I thought. Anyhow, there was this man—well, he wasn't exactly a man. He had spines like a porcupine and… It doesn't matter. I'm sure you didn't come here to hear about my past mishaps. Noni… You want to know if you should raise Noni."

And of course, Carred was the expert on such matters. If only Marith were here. She'd have known what to do. But Marith was gone, perhaps for good this time. And even if she did come back, how could Carred ever look at her the same again?

"Well," she said, fumbling for the right thing to say. "Noni had a connection with your mother. Talia used to speak through her from the realm of the dead."

"So speaking to Marith's spirit could help?"

"Maybe. Probably not. I've never liked this kind of thing. To be honest, I've never been much good with sorcery. Stems from my upbringing, I'd say."

"But you're Niyandrian."

"Yes, and rejection of sorcery's my little rebellion. What else could I do to retain some semblance of control as a child and to piss off my parents? I've heard of kids who refuse to eat—the only power they think they have—but I like food too much. So, sorcery was my way of not being like them. Screw it, I said."

"And yet Marith's moontouched."

"Ah, but did the sly cow tell you she kept it a secret from me for years? By the time I found out, I was too far enmeshed." She winced as she remembered the night the assassins had come, and Marith had fought them off with wild sorcery and given her a chance to flee. It made her stomach clench, and she had to stifle tears.

Anskar noticed, though, and gripped her hand. "Did Marith ever use the earth-tide?"

Carred shook her head. "Nor the dark. She had standards, things she wouldn't do—more's the pity." She forced a grin, but her smile was lost on Anskar.

"So, you want my advice? I say don't risk it. Sure, it might be useful to have Noni back, to see if she could find out where Talia and Marith have gone, but necromancy's not like the dawn- or the dusk, Anskar, least not the way Marith used to speak about it. The dark-tide is for demons, but the earth… Even Eadgith never raised the dead with it, and I bet there was a good reason. Between you and me, I've never liked necromancers. Even less, having now met the infamous Tain."

"But you made an exception for my mother?"

"I was young. The more I think about it, the more I have to wonder if I was given a choice."

"It wasn't meant as a criticism," Anskar said.

"It certainly sounded like one."

He released her hand and stood. "Then I apologize. It's not easy… knowing what I now know."

"I can understand that." Carred reached for the bottle and refilled her glass. Anskar's remained untouched in his hand.

"Not drinking?" she asked.

With a nonchalant shrug, he upended the glass and downed the contents in one. His dark eyes closed momentarily, immediately softening his face. When he opened them again, he looked tormented.

"Mistberry not to your taste?"

"It's not that," he said. "The wine's good. Very sweet."

"Marith's favorite," Carred said, blithely taking another swig. "So, what do you plan to do as regards Noni?"

"I'm not sure yet." He moved back to the couch, put his glass on the table and took hers from her, halfway to her lips. "We both need level heads if we're to prepare."

"I'll prepare in the morning," Carred said, shoving his hand aside and reclaiming her glass. "And so should you. We've gone from one crisis to the next since the abyssal realms. Since before that. You could at least give me this night to unwind."

"You think war will come?" Anskar asked. He didn't sound committed to the question, as if there were more important things to say but he was uncertain how to arrive at them.

"You don't? We just drove the Order of Eternal Flatulence out of their principal stronghold on Niyas, so I'd say war is a good assumption." Not to mention the fact that Monash had promised as much, and from the little Carred had seen of her, the Seneschal didn't seem a woman given to making idle threats.

She sipped tentatively on her wine, watching Anskar over the rim of the glass. His jaw tightened with irritation, but he didn't raise an objection this time.

"So, what do we do?" he asked—a child seeking the advice of a parent.

Theltek, was that what she was to him? Was that how he viewed her—as some sort of surrogate Talia? The idea was insulting. Unconsciously, she ran a hand through her hair, then felt around her neck for creases. Suddenly, the way she'd been starting to feel, the inevitability of what she assumed was going to happen—because, in her case, it always did—no longer seemed so inevitable. Or desirable.

"My opinion, for what it's worth," she said, pausing dramatically for another sip of wine. "We press forward, or we die."

"It's that simple?" Anskar asked.

"What's simple about it? The mainlanders think it's already started, the culmination of years of rebellion. They think we're trying to take back Niyas. Whether we do or don't is beside the point. The mainlanders will come anyway. If we don't build on what we've done here, we won't be in a position to oppose them. That's when we die. Not necessarily in battle, going down in a blaze of glory, either. I've seen how these people operate, Anskar. It's not just the governors and kings we have to worry about, it's the whole shady bunch of bastards behind them."

"Who are?"

"They call themselves the Consortium." She thought back to when Luzius Landav had transported her to some other place, some liminal realm, where she had confronted the hooded collective. "I have to assume they're the money behind the mainland realms, the pullers of the strings. Probably nobles from Sansor. Fat merchants. I think I might have detected a robey type or two."

"Robey type?"

"You know," she said, draining her glass and pouring another, "a high up priest of the Church of Men's-arse. What do you call them?"

"Bishops?"

"Yes, them. Or maybe even higher. But what do I know? Save this: it won't be a simple matter of ships coming from overseas carrying an invasion force. Oh, it'll probably be that too, but not before the Consortium does its utmost to undermine our movement, persuade Niyandrians to come over to their side, and get us fighting among themselves."

"We're already doing that," Anskar said.

"So it's not just personal then?" Carred asked, not believing for one minute that it was. "Talia and Marith against me and you?"

"Did you ever think it was? My mother has been using me all along."

"Not just you, I suspect," Carred said. The admission turned the wine sour on her lips, but it didn't stop her taking another sip. "Do you know how long I've…? Of course you do. Since before you were born I've served your mother. Since the fall of Naphor, I've kept the hope of her return alive in my bumbling, delusional way. It's a wonder anyone has followed me for this long, what with all the mishaps, the defeats, the unfulfilled promises. I mean, would you?" Before he could answer that, realization struck her—not so much a lightning blast as a suffocating, sinking feeling. "Fult Wreave…" she muttered.

"Who?" Anskar must have sensed the change that had come over her. He perched on the edge of the couch. A few minutes earlier, she might have sidled closer, let him feel her warmth, but now she rested on her elbow and drew her feet up and away from him.

"A Niyandrian noble," she said, focused not on Anskar but staring blankly at the pictures on the wall opposite. Nothing arousing about them now; they were a blur as she tried to corral her wine-addled thoughts into some sort of sequence. "When Marith sent out the call to our rebel groups to descend upon Dorinah, he didn't come. Fult's an annoying little prick—and I don't mean that literally; I have no idea on that score and don't want to know—but he's descended from the Ickthal Dynasty, who ruled Niyas before your mother."

"And you think he plans to side with her?"

"It makes no sense," Carred said. "He hates Queen Talia and

everything she stood for. All Fult Wreave wants is for her to stay in the realm of the dead and for him to resurrect his ancestral claim on Niyas. Besides, how could he know that Talia's among us? Even you and I didn't know."

"Until Marith took it into her own hands to start a bloody war," Anskar said.

"It wasn't Marith," Carred said. "You know that."

"I take it this Fult Wreave commands warriors?"

"Just a few," Carred said. "Quite a few, actually. Hundreds. Maybe even thousands."

"And you say he didn't answer the call? Perhaps he didn't receive it."

"Let's hope so. But my gut tells me he did, and that he's hedging his bets. It wouldn't surprise me if that old snake is in negotiations with the Order and the mainland powers. Knowing how things work in the world, they've probably offered him the governorship of Niyas, if they don't want to install him as a puppet king."

"My mother would never permit that."

"As of yet, your mother lacks an army."

"Which is why we need to do something," Anskar said, searching out her eyes. His were slitted, intense.

"You're looking at me as if I hold all the answers," she said. "Listen, Anskar... *Melesh-Eloni*," she said, as if the name were a taunt. "I've done my part. You're supposed to lead from now on, aren't you?"

He swallowed and looked away. Stared too long at one of Monash's lewd pictures.

Carred's focus switched, as if it had a mind of its own. Heat flooded her belly. She started to reconsider.

"I don't think that would be wise," Anskar said. "You saw what I did back there; how I almost lost control. *Did* lose control, until you talked me down. I'm eighteen years old, Carred, barely out of boyhood. I can't make the kinds of decisions we face. What if I get it wrong? What if people die because of me?"

Carred set down her wine glass on the table—a statement that altered the atmosphere in the room. "You think I can make these decisions? You think I should be responsible for people dying? Because, let me tell you this, I already have the blood of way too many Niyandrians on my hands. Seventeen years' worth of blood. And for what? I still don't know what I'm doing, and it's very likely I've been played all along. So, yes, *Melesh-Eloni*, you're the one who needs to make the hard choices. And if you can't, then…" She'd not thought about what came next; she had no words with which to finish her sentence.

Anskar raised an eyebrow. *Yes?*

Carred sighed and pinched the bridge of her nose. "I told you to let me prepare in the morning. I can't deal with this right now. I've drunk too much mistberry wine."

"And I told you to stop," Anskar said.

"Which is a demonstration of your superior wisdom, and why you are the *Melesh-Eloni,* and I'm a drunken, needy, shriveled-up, good-for-nothing hag."

"Needy?" Anskar asked, and he looked genuinely concerned.

"So, you pass no comment about the other bits?"

"Well, you are undeniably drunk," he said with a shrug.

"Good for nothing? Shriveled up?"

"Your words, not mine."

"But are they true?"

She held his gaze now. Managed to fill her eyes with tears and cause her chin to quiver. He reached his hand toward her, then yanked it back.

"I have always thought…" he said, and she pushed herself upright and leaned toward him. He frowned, as if some hard memory had just scourged him. The reddish tinge to his cheeks turned a vivid crimson. "You are very beautiful."

"More wine?" Carred said, proffering the bottle.

Anskar didn't seem to notice. "If things are out of our control… If the mainlanders will respond to what we've done here with war… We should move on Naphor."

"That's a bold move, if ever I heard one."

"It's the only move," Anskar said. "We retake the old capital. After that, the people will come."

"Or they won't," Carred observed drily.

"All Niyas will rise once they see the *Melesh-Eloni* enthroned in Naphor."

Maybe. But would it be enough? Carred studied him for the longest while, let her sorcerous senses—which were as attuned as they had ever been, given their years of neglect—flitter around his repositories. She couldn't make sense of what she perceived—an amalgam of conflicting forces? An interwoven net? Then suddenly she was drowning in a mire of tar, her mind filled with images of rot, and she recoiled.

"You probably shouldn't have done that," Anskar said.

"I'll remember next time."

But she had seen and felt enough to know that, if there was any hope for Niyas in the event that the mainlanders came, it lay within Anskar himself. Even if the whole isle took up arms, how could they expect to stand against the might of Kaile, the City States, and all their mainland allies? How could even the best of Niyas's warrior-sorcerers compete with the discipline and the armor and the silver ward spheres of the Order of Eternal Vigilance? They had tried before, and they had lost. But Anskar: he was something different that had been introduced into the conflict. His was a new power—she'd seen just how devastating a power outside in the streets of Dorinah. But was it *his* power, or did it belong to another?

"I'll speak with Vilintia and the captains in the morning," she said. "We'll devise a strategy."

"And I'll send a missive to King Aelfyr of the Kingdom of the

Thousand Lakes," Anskar said. "I fought for him recently, and he may be inclined to aid us."

"I wouldn't hold your breath," Carred said. "If the mainlanders come against us and demand his aid, King Aelfyr will jump. They have all the money, after all. What could we offer him as an alternative?"

Anskar clenched his fist, but he knew she was right. For a young man, he'd seen enough of how the world worked. It was etched all over his face.

"Then what do you suggest?" Anskar said. "Go after Marith?"

"Do you know where she is?"

"Not yet, but I think I can find out."

Carred sucked in air through gritted teeth. "Noni again. Anskar, I have a bad feeling about this."

"So do I."

"We don't even know if Marith's alive," Carred said, although *she* knew. Surely she would feel something, some resonance in her repositories, some dread clenching of her gut, if Marith were to die.

"My mother possesses her," Anskar said. "One way or another, Marith's alive. I'd stake my life on it."

"Then we'll find her together," Carred said. "When we're ready."

Anskar's hand strayed to the hilt of his sword. "I'm ready."

"Not for that," Carred said, narrowing her eyes until he moved his hand away from the hilt. "You have to find another way. Promise me. Another way. Please. I want Marith to live."

Anskar nodded.

Carred let out a sigh and then swung her legs off the couch as she sat. She pressed her thigh against his as she reached for her wine. He didn't move away.

"So," Carred said as she took another sip, "what now?" She widened her eyes over the rim of the glass.

"I'm sorry," Anskar said, standing. "It's not you. It's me. Everything I touch…" Without completing the thought, he turned and left the room.

For a second after the door closed, Carred was the girl abandoned in the woods once more, afraid and alone.

Carelessly, she downed the rest of her wine, slumped back on the couch, and drew her legs up. After that, she didn't feel the least bit rejected. She knew all too well what her needs were: no different to the need for wine and sweet foods—anything to assuage the emptiness that had followed her through life; the hollow space within that made her nothing, made her prone to serve without thinking, to warm the Necromancer Queen's bed. Anything that made her feel real, feel needed, feel alive.

"Bloody hells," Carred muttered as her hand crept between her legs. "I need to stop drinking so much."

But there was to be no escape in pleasure. All she could think of was Marith with Talia inside her, growing like a cancer, *becoming* her. She forced back tears. She needed release, not more grief. But it wasn't happening. Curse Anskar for walking out on her like that. She needed a body—any body—just not her own.

With an angry growl, she stood and swiped her glass and the wine bottle off the table. The bottle bounced and rolled till it hit the wall, where the glass shattered. Good. She didn't need it anymore. Enough with addiction—of every kind. So what if she had a gaping hole inside her? She'd just have to stitch it up, same as her ragdoll Nally had been sewn together from old scraps of cloth.

And stuffed with straw.

ELEVEN

ANSKAR STORMED THROUGH THE BLOOD-STREAKED corridors of the citadel. His veins were on fire, his head a nest of insects that stung and poisoned his thoughts. His nostrils flared as he breathed in tainted air that carried the stink of death and sorcery. But none of those things bothered him. If anything, he drew strength from the sepulchral atmosphere inside Branil's Burg.

The meeting with Carred hadn't gone as planned. He'd come out as clueless as he'd gone in. But was that really the cause of his thundering mood? Outside in the bailey, he stopped, breaths ragged, and leaned against a wall. Of course it wasn't.

The venom in his mind dredged up the stench of rank mutton, the illusion of firm flesh pressed against his; of grinding and groaning, of kissing moist lips. Carred. The Abbess. Carred again, the two perpetually changing places. Since that day at the Abbey of the Hooded one, he'd been alternately inflamed and repulsed, his memories vacillating between unappeasable lust and gut-wrenching disgust.

Sweet Menselas, Carred had wanted him—practically begged him to take her, and he'd wanted to so much. But where his mind wished to go, his body wouldn't follow. It was as if that old crone the Abbess had cursed him deep within his flesh. Each time he'd started to respond to Carred's provocations, his skin tingled with revulsion.

As it should, an unbridled thought said. *She's too old for you. Too scarred. Too much of a failure.* By the Five, it sounded like his mother; only it couldn't be. Talia was gone from him. She had entered into Marith.

And still lust seethed within him, as puissant as a fifth sorcerous tide. It demanded satiety, and it didn't have to be Carred. *Never,* he told himself, as if he warded against possession.

He left the bailey by the east gate and roamed Dorinah in the muggy light from grimy alchemical globes suspended from iron posts. He was numb to the broken glass everywhere, glinting in the scant light. the kicked-in doors, and all the other hallmarks of looting. Rebels prowled the streets, taking whatever they wanted, be it food, drink, clothing, or women. Anskar's anger went up a notch as he passed sobbing victims in tattered clothes. Crowds of the dispossessed glared, as if he were personally responsible, all of them as red-skinned as the rebels, all Niyandrian.

Was this the new Niyas Carred had fought for all these years? The exchange of one oppression for another? At least the Order had ruled with law and justice, and treated the Niyandrians—in the main—with a degree of dignity. But this… This was chaos. It was the dog-eat-dog rule of the strong. Where were the commanders? Where was Vilintia? He knew where Carred was, and that did nothing to assuage his anger. She was lounging about, drunk, while her people committed atrocities against their own kind, against the people they were supposed to protect.

His fist grew lambent with emerald sorcery, drawing the eyes of rebel soldiers and citizens alike. Silence fell over the street. Dozens of Niyandrians watched as he dipped his head and hurried down the road, knowing if he hesitated, there would be carnage, and he wasn't ready for that. Yet. He could have stopped them. Should have. But he was consumed with an entirely different need. Not lust, either. The need for a friend.

He approached a couple of rebels sharing a bottle of alchemical brandy as they kicked through the refuse on the street, but they shrugged when he asked them where Orix was. "Never heard of him," one said. Anskar described him, and still they shrugged. Then they both paled when they saw his eyes and muttered apologies as they hurried away.

His eyes.

Black. Devoid of all light. Soulless.

The cost of the wraithe's gift to him? The price for raising Noni? Or the start of something else? A gift, the wraithe had said, not a pact. But one thing he had learned in his short life: there were no free gifts, least of all when it came to sorcerous power.

At once, he knew where Orix was. Another of the wraithe's gifts? There was no name of a place, no image, just an implacable drive to head in a certain direction. As he hurried along the streets, he became aware of motes of glimmering crimson that wafted like petals through the air: a trail he felt compelled to follow. He glanced at passersby, most of them drunk, most of them rebel warriors, but none of them seemed aware of the ghostly trail. It was his alone.

The sorcerous motes led him to a ramshackle townhouse. A middle-aged Niyandrian man sat in a rocking chair on the porch, smoking something pungent in a pipe. He muttered a curse around the stem of his pipe as Anskar came up the steps.

"I'm looking for a friend," Anskar said. He started to describe Orix, but the man glanced at him, saw his eyes, and stood, backing away.

"Inside," he said. "Just moved himself in. Darned well helped himself to our house, like they're doing all over the city."

"What do you mean?" Anskar asked.

"Warriors—you rebels. You're supposed to free Niyas, ain't you? Not steal people's homes and scare their families?"

"Has Orix harmed your family?"

The man thought about that then decided to tell the truth. "Not yet, he ain't. But what's he doing? Friend of yours, you say? What's he doing carting a dead body around with him? It ain't natural, I tell you."

"No," Anskar said as he opened the door and went inside. "It isn't."

He entered a long hallway with arched openings on either side and a steep flight of stairs leading to the next floor. The aroma of cooking came from the doorway at the far end, along with the clamor of someone working in the kitchen. Three children rushed through the left-hand arch as if they were expecting someone—their father presumably, who remained on the porch. They watched Anskar with a mixture of curiosity and wariness. The youngest of the children, a little girl of perhaps three or four, started to wail when she saw his eyes. A Niyandrian woman wearing an apron came out of the kitchen in response. There was fire in her repository and anger in her eyes, but she gave Anskar a wide berth as she went to her children and ushered them into the room beyond the arch. Finally, she faced Anskar, arms folded across her chest.

"What?" she said, as if she weren't as frightened as her children. As if he didn't have eyes as black as the void. Feelers of awareness probed at his mind then recoiled as if burned. The woman's face remained mask-like, but he knew she was appalled by what she had perceived.

"Forgive me for disturbing your home," Anskar said, dipping his eyes. "But I'm looking—"

"Upstairs," she said. "Taken over our bedroom." She shook her head and curled her fingers like horns. "He has a corpse with him."

"I know," Anskar said. "I'm sorry."

The husband chose that moment to come back inside, stinking of tobacco. When Anskar turned to acknowledge him, the man just stood there, deferring to his wife with his eyes.

"It isn't right," the woman said. "All across the street there's others like him, moving into people's houses. Even the Order knights never did that."

"I told him," the man said. "Happening all over the city, it is. Your kind," he told Anskar, "ain't helping. You're only making things worse."

They had no idea who he was. Save for his eyes, he was just a regular Niyandrian to them, albeit one with only a hint of crimson to his dusky skin, though if they looked down upon him for being a half-blood, they hid it well.

"I didn't want this," Anskar said lamely. When he glanced at the woman, he saw no understanding in her expression, only hardness. "I'll see what I can do," he said, as he headed up the stairs.

He passed two rebels on the landing, both passed out from drinking, bottles clutched in their hands.

The first room he entered smelled like a goat pen, and the floor was strewn with clothes, ornaments, even carved wooden toys. The three single cot beds were occupied by sleeping rebels. Anskar stood and studied them for the longest time, not quite sure if it was heat or cold that pulsed through his veins, fire or ice. He thought about the family downstairs, wondering where the children would sleep tonight, whether there was anything left to eat. One of the sleepers stirred—a fat Niyandrian man still wearing his armor, if you could call it that: rusty links of chain mail sewn onto a vest of animal hide. The man belched and rubbed his eyes, then noticed Anskar watching him and threw his legs out of bed. But then he saw Anskar's eyes and reconsidered whatever it was he'd been about to do.

"Wake your friends," Anskar said. Now it was definitely cold he felt, and he saw all three Niyandrians as pallid corpses riddled with worms. "Leave this house and don't come back."

The man nodded.

"The ones on the landing, too," Anskar said. "Everyone out."

With that, he turned on his heel and entered the room at the end of the corridor.

The first thing that struck him when he opened the door—he was too angry to knock—was the terrible smell. He was starting to think it was his destiny to be surrounded by the stench of a graveyard.

Orix sat bolt upright on the double bed, causing its iron frame to squeak. His face might have been restored, but it resembled nothing so much as a contorted death mask, frozen in its final torments. Only he wasn't the dead one. *She* lay beside him on the bed. Noni.

She'd not been dead long, but already she stank, as if her carcass were conforming itself to the malodorous presence of Kaythe Nurglich, the Corpse Maker. Is that where her soul was destined to go—into those nightmare depths, to be defiled by that monstrosity? Was she already there? Or was she a listless spirit drifting forever through the realm of the dead? Because even if it existed, there was no place for Niyandrians and practitioners of forbidden sorcery in the harmonious eternity of Menselas. He would do well to remember that.

"What do you think you're doing?" he said from the doorway. It was clearly the parents' room, their clothes hanging within an open closet, shoes strewn around the floor. Underneath the rot, there was a lingering floral scent, probably perfume, and there was a book and a half-empty wine bottle on one of the two nightstands.

"Get out," Orix said, lying back down, arm around the corpse. "Just leave."

"You leave," Anskar said. "You can't just walk into someone else's house and take over, Orix! There's a family downstairs. These are people—real people. You can't stay here."

"Noni feels safe here," Orix said as he stroked her hair.

Anskar strode across the room, grabbed Orix's arm and pulled it away from the body on the bed. "Noni's dead!"

Anger blazed in Orix's eyes. "Why are you here? Have you changed your mind?"

"Don't be absurd," Anskar said, matching his friend's ire. Nevertheless, his eyes strayed to Noni's corpse, and something fizzed in his brain. It felt as though oil were seeping beneath his scalp, and for a moment, dark specks blurred his vision and caused him to blink. He could do it, he realized, if he wanted to. He could bring Noni back from the realm of the dead.

Anskar shook his head and pinched the bridge of his nose.

"What?" Orix asked. He sounded eager now, hopeful, no longer driven by rage. He climbed out of bed.

"Keep away!" Anskar said with such vehemence that Orix flopped back onto the bed. "I need to… I need to think."

Could he refuse? If he knew how to bring Noni back, could he withhold her from her lover, his friend?

Of course you can refuse, the voice of reason told him, although it was frail, almost imperceptible amid the turmoil in his mind. *Don't do this. Menselas will curse you.*

Menselas! As if! What could that five-faced phony do against power like his? If anyone were a god…

"All I ask is that you try," Orix said in a tremulous voice. He might have been weeping.

Anskar glared at him. Sucked in air through clenched teeth. What did he have to lose—save his sanity, if that were still in his possession? Save his soul?

Images of writhing tendrils rose in his mind. A wolf's head. Shivering tendrils from a vile cloaca.

Consider it a gift, the wraithe had told him. *A tiny taste of what you are missing, what Kaythe Nurglich would have given you…*

He turned away, intending to leave. Behind him, Orix let out a groan of utter torment, and Anskar thumped the door jamb. He knew then he was trapped. He needed… he needed something from Orix. Something hard to define, something familiar. Something that wasn't to be found in Carred and her rebels, and definitely not in his mother.

He turned back and met Orix's pleading gaze. Friendship: it was all he had left that he could even begin to define. Everything else about him was new, unrecognizable.

"Get away from her," he said as he strode with resolve toward the bed.

Orix stood and stepped aside.

"Back," Anskar said. "Over by the door. I've never done this before, and I don't know what will happen."

But a part of him did. A part of him was certain.

With the confidence of someone who did this all the time, as if he were a necromancer who swam in such unwholesome waters, Anskar leaned over the bed and placed his hand over Noni's mouth and nose.

"What are you doing?" Orix cried, coming towards him.

"Back, I say," Anskar said. "It's not as if she can breathe, you dolt."

"Dolt?" Orix said, even while he obeyed and retreated to the doorway. "That doesn't even sound like you."

"Did I ask your opinion?" Anskar said. His voice sounded cold to his own ears. In his mind, Orix was an insect who could be crushed with but a thought.

He closed his eyes. Noni's face beneath his hand grew suddenly pliant, then limpid. There was a faint plopping sensation. It felt as though his fingers had ruptured her skin and were now submerged in viscous fluid. He wanted to look but feared what he might see. Feared it might be blood.

His arm started to stretch, unnaturally. His hand plunged deeper and deeper into the depths of Noni's face, down into a fathomless well, down through the cold and the wet. The stench of effluence filled his awareness. Diseased waters seeped through his pores, rising as bile within him.

For an instant, he was someplace else, wrapped in wriggling tentacles. Slavering jaws snapped at his face. He heard the bark of harsh laughter. The thud of his heart came from a long way off. Had he been duped by the wraithe and made a terrible mistake?

And then he was through, drifting in a gray limbo, surrounded by the ragged shades of the dead, who roiled around him, giving him a wide berth, as if they feared coming too near. One of them shivered with lunar light, and he sped toward it, a beast who knew his prey. With spectral hands he grabbed the ghost and ripped her from the realm of the dead. She screamed as he whiplashed back to his physical body and withdrew his hand from Noni's face.

"Did you…? Did you do it?" Orix asked, edging nearer. "Is she back?"

"I can't see," a thready voice said. It came from the corpse on the bed, but Noni's blue lips didn't part. "I can't move! Where am I?" she asked in a tone of mounting panic. "Orix!"

"Here, love," Orix said, shouldering Anskar aside and kneeling beside the bed. He took hold of a stiff and lifeless hand. "I'm right here."

"I thought you'd left me," she said, and still her lips didn't move.

"Bastard," Anskar muttered under his breath. "You conniving bastard."

The wraithe had given him a gift, all right. An incomplete gift—*a tiny taste.*

"What else am I supposed to do? What is it you want from me?" he shouted.

"Anskar?" Noni said. "Is that Anskar I can hear?"

"He brought you back, love," Orix said.

"Back?"

"Noni… You were dead. You died outside Branil's Burg, remember? You overreached yourself."

"Died?" She elicited a sound like a gasp, yet her mouth didn't open, and her chest didn't rise. "Overreached? I remember the earth-tide, a torrent within me. I had power, Orix, real power! But I died, you say?

Oh, no. He brought me back? Not like this! Please, not like this! Send me back to the realm of the dead!"

"Not like what?" Orix said, and now he was speaking to Anskar—an accusation.

"Her soul…" Anskar said, fully realizing what he had done, how the wraithe had short-changed him. "I brought her soul back from the realm of the dead, but I can't restore her body to life."

"Can't?" Orix said. "Can't!"

"I don't know how!"

"Then kill me, please," Noni said. "You can't leave me like this."

But how could he kill what was already dead?

"I'll find a way to fix this," Anskar said. But he had no idea where to start. Did the wraithe want him to return to Kaythe Nurglich, despite what it had said? Was its gift merely bait to get him hooked? He couldn't go back to that vile monster. Wouldn't. Not ever.

Noni began to whimper, then scream.

Downstairs, children started to cry.

"Let me return her shade to the realm of the dead," he told Orix. "When I know more, I can go back and retrieve her."

"She stays here," Orix said. "And that's final."

"No!" Noni wailed.

"It's better this way!" Orix snapped at her.

"Better for who?" Anskar said.

"Both of us."

Orix lay back down on the bed beside the corpse and held her close, pulling her face into his chest. Oddly, it muffled the screams, as if they really emanated from her lifeless mouth.

"If you truly loved her…" Anskar started, but Orix shot him such a glare that he looked away.

He headed toward the door, but stopped in his tracks when the corpse suddenly said, "I know where Queen Talia is."

"My mother? You still have a connection with her?"

"It never left me, even in the realm of the dead. Talia doesn't like to abandon options."

"Where is she?" Anskar asked, returning to the foot of the bed.

"Marith's farm, but not for much longer. She will return to her father's house," Noni said.

"She's going to the abyssal realms?"

"Her father's house near Naphor."

"Where? How do I find it?"

"Carred knows," the corpse said as she started to sob once more. "I feel entombed," she wailed. "Buried alive within my own body."

Orix cradled her head and looked at Anskar as if this were all his fault. "You have to do more."

"I will, I promise. But first we need to get you out of this house. Both of you."

"And go where?"

"I'll send rebels to help you move Noni. I thought maybe rooms in the Burg? Your old room, if you want?"

"Like when we were novices?" Orix said, something like hope in his voice. His face quickly dropped. He knew it was a false hope, that there was no going back.

Anskar recognized the feeling. He felt the same. He couldn't think about those innocent times without clenching up. He'd come too far.

He manufactured a smile that he doubted was in the least bit convincing. "Like when we were novices. I'll send help," he said as he turned away and headed through the doorway and down the stairs.

The Niyandrian mother was waiting downstairs, her arms around her three children. The youngest still had snot streaming from his nose, and his eyes were red from crying.

"I'm sorry," Anskar said, "for everything you've been through. I've told them all to leave. My friend and his... My friend will be leaving as soon as help arrives."

"To carry the body?" the woman said, with a wary glance at Anskar's eyes.

"I'll say it again," Anskar said. "I'm sorry. None of this should have happened. I'll see to it that no one else bothers you."

"Goodbye, Mister," the eldest boy said as Anskar headed for the door.

The mother shushed him, then glared as Anskar turned to respond. Accepting that no words of his would be welcome, he went outside and closed the door behind him.

The rebels Anskar had told to leave were making their sullen way across the road. It was dark, and they were probably fretting about where they would sleep. He really didn't care, so long as they didn't kick anyone's door down and commandeer their home. He paused for a moment to watch them go. He thought about saying something to the husband, once more seated on his rocking chair, smoking and drinking, but the man got there before him.

"Nobody asked us if we wanted to be liberated," he said, then punctuated his remark by spitting out a wad of phlegm.

"No," Anskar said, walking on past, down the steps and into the street. "No, they didn't."

TWELVE

 above Dorinah, enticing with their winks, hinting at others realms beyond this one. Indeed, to Anskar's weary mind, the stars could well have been pinprick openings onto the abode of the gods, if such a place existed.

He shrugged off the blithe blasphemies that flitted through his mind like the moths beneath the alchemical globes that lined the streets. The ideas he supposedly offended against seemed somehow beneath him, primitive, not serious gristle for him to wrestle with in his current state of growth. He was… He tried to think of some other way of putting it, but nothing else seemed to fit as well. He was contemptuous of the Five, of the knights, of the holy scriptures and the priests who had taught him growing up. He included Brother Tion in the mix, a weak man, possessed by his base instincts, little better than a low-order demon.

And he recalled, then, his sojourn in the abyssal realm of Vulthanor, the conversations he'd had with the demon lord Domatai—his grandfather. Domatai was no lust-enslaved beast. Far from it. The demon lord had been self-possessed to the point of serenity, and his intellect would have dwarfed even the most gifted priests of the Elder.

He wandered aimlessly, along street after street. A fog had rolled in from the Simorga Sea; it seemed like some eldritch drakkon's breath, the way it picked up the pearlescent glow of the alchemical globes. It swirled above the roads, moiling with the dark, keeping it at bay.

He stopped once or twice outside taverns still heaving with late night drinkers. Fights spilled over into the streets—more fallout from the rebel occupation. There was no one around to keep order, not now the knights had gone.

Ignoring the drunken brawlers outside a tavern called The Old Black Feather, Anskar went inside and shouldered his way to the bar. Smoke irritated his eyes and made him cough. Niyandrian rebels made up at least half of the drinkers, many of them getting friendly with the local prostitutes. The sight of the carousing and the drunkenness along with the sound of vainglorious voices boasting of the day's deeds caused his fists to clench at his sides. His skin itched amid all the filth, as if he'd entered a pen of goats, rutting, shitting, drinking their own piss. The image was like a blow between the eyes. He started out of his head, wondering what in Wiraya was happening to him.

"What are you having?" a woman said from behind the bar.

Before he could answer, she caught sight of his eyes and covered her mouth with a hand. Her reaction was contagious, and a corridor opened up around Anskar. The hubbub of voices, the clash and clang of mugs, stilled in an instant.

He turned slowly, taking in everyone in the tavern. No one could hold his gaze. He took their dipped eyes for obeisance, and he nodded to himself, satisfied that they knew his power. He was tempted to command them to prostrate themselves, certain they would obey. But then he felt suddenly awkward, a fish out of water. He didn't belong here. This place sullied him.

No one spoke as he made his way back to the door, but the moment the door shut behind him, he heard them start to speak once more, and that angered him, made him want to go back inside and cut their tongues out. It was only the shock of how different he felt, the strangeness of the thoughts in his head, the chill in his veins, that dragged him away. Was it what he'd done to Noni, or some effect of the wraithe's gift?

He lost all appetite for drinking, even more so for company. The cold seeping through his flesh and sluicing through his marrow demanded his full attention. It was a mild night, but he began to shiver as his thoughts turned to where he was going to sleep tonight. He dismissed with a scoff the idea of returning to Carred, at the same time knowing he would once have jumped at the chance. Nevertheless, he made his way back to Branil's Burg. He'd advised Orix to return to his own quarters. He should do the same.

The dead whispered as he entered the bailey through the east gate. He could still make out mounds of bodies piled up ready for burning, and their stench was thick in his nostrils, amid the residual smoke of the funeral pyres that had burned throughout the afternoon. With an effort of will, he shut out the groans and the moans, the ceaseless imprecations. He had no desire for the company of the living, let alone the dead.

The flap and flutter of wings startled him as a bird flew from the branches of a dogwood tree. His heart thudded, and he half-expected to see a golden-eyed crow, but as it flew through the ambit of Jagonath's crimson moonbeams, he saw that it was an owl, and he breathed a sigh of relief.

But why was he still scared of the crow? He'd crushed it underfoot. And besides, it had been a manifestation of his mother's shade, as far as he could tell. What had he to fear from her? He wrapped his fingers around the hilt of his sword. Nothing; not while he had *Amalantril.*

A gentle vibration passed through the hilt, traveling up his arm to his head. It reminded him of the purr of a cat. Something about that touch of the sword settled the turmoil that had been steadily growing within him, made him aloof from it. *It's just a change,* a thought reassured him. *You're growing, evolving, becoming who you truly are.*

The *Melesh-Eloni?*

The son of the Necromancer Queen?

More than that, his thoughts seemed to say. *The antithesis. What is it your mother most feared?*

"Anskar?" a woman said from the shadows beneath the keep.

"Vilintia?"

He eyed her coldly, dispassionately, as she came into the moonlight, wearing only a simple gray tunic and nothing on her feet.

"I couldn't sleep," she said when she saw him noticing. "So I thought I'd get in some training."

"With no boots on?"

"I only put on the tunic because there are people still awake. In Rynmuntithe Forest, I trained naked. It's better that way. More natural."

Anskar turned away, not wanting to give her any sort of response. Once had been enough for him, and the thought of replicating the experience made him sick to the stomach. Not because there was anything wrong with Vilintia—far from it. She might have been old enough to be his mother, but she took good care of herself; her hard body and chiseled lines were testament to that. And, he supposed, in a way that set her a rung above the level of the beasts. It showed she possessed discipline, that she strove to be more than she was.

"I was just heading inside to sleep," Anskar said.

He winced at the feel of her hand on his shoulder.

"Please don't. Not yet."

There was a quaver in her voice, and he turned, frowning. Her eyes glistened from recent tears.

"What is it?" he asked.

"Here," she said, leading him by the hand to one of the stone benches that adorned the cultivated gardens just outside the keep. He remembered walking here with Tion, but that felt a lifetime ago.

He sat beside her, impatient to leave, but for some reason he cared enough to stay awhile and listen.

"I…" she started, letting go of his hand and taking a deep breath.

For a moment, he thought she was going to bring up what had happened between them before, and he prepared himself to stand.

"I never thought I'd admit this," she said, "but I'm out of my depth."

Anskar relaxed. "You mean what happened with Marith? The sorcery?"

"With command. Carred left me in charge when she went off to wherever she went."

The abyssal realms. She'd gone looking for void-steel on behalf of his mother. He wondered how much Carred had shared of her mission, and decided it was better not to say anything.

"You seemed to manage," Anskar said. "Of all the people I can think of…"

"There's no one you'd sooner trust to be in charge?" She shook her head, then dabbed a tear from her eye. "That's what they all say. But do you want to know the truth? I'm afraid. Scared of screwing things up— and it wouldn't be the first time. Why do you think I train so hard?"

"To compensate?" And now he was interested, despite himself. "But you always seem so competent."

"I work at it. And I know I'm good at what I do. But that was when… before Marith turned up here and started a bloody war. Have you seen what our soldiers are doing in Dorinah?"

Anskar gritted his teeth as he nodded.

"I'm supposed to be able to control them, to stop such things from happening, but I don't know how."

"It's not your responsibility," he said. "It's Carred's."

"Really?" She turned into him now, so close her could feel the heat of her thigh pressed up against his. She felt so hot, like a furnace—no doubt because he was so cold. "I thought… I mean, you and Carred…"

"It was irresponsible of her to leave," he said. "More so for her to take this night off so she could get drunk in her rooms. If she's going to take over Vihtor's quarters, she could at least try to act like him. Even Monash did that." Now, there was a woman with a healthy degree of discipline. Though thinking of Monash led to thoughts of Sareya and the clot of shame that sat heavy in his guts.

"What is it?" Vilintia said, reaching out warily and stroking his hair. "What's the matter?"

Wasn't that just the question? He had no idea. Even as a novice, even when he'd believed all the nonsense about Menselas—before his experience at the Hooded One's Abbey had pulled the scales from his eyes—he'd not felt so repulsed by the idea of two bodies lying together as he did now.

"I'm just tired," he said. He tried to stand, but she gripped his arm.

"Anskar," she said, "during the fighting… What you did… what you…"

"Became? That's who I am, Vilintia. Whatever you think you saw, that's who I really am. I know that now."

She grew silent. He caught her looking up at the two moons, watching clouds scud across their faces.

"You're not afraid of me?" Anskar asked.

She gazed into his eyes. He could tell from the way she swallowed that she was disturbed by their inky blackness, but she tried not to show it.

"Should I be afraid?"

He manufactured a smile but failed to make it reassuring, judging by the way she broke off eye contact. Yes, she should be afraid. They all should. He was becoming more than they could ever dream of. More than even he could dream of. He knew he should have been troubled, concerned about why. He'd been changing since the abyssal realms—and so had his sword. But since the wraithe's gift, since he had brought Noni's shade back from the realm of the dead, the changes had taken on a different aspect. And what should have been most concerning of all was that he didn't care.

"You have nothing to fear from me, Vilintia." And why should she have? None of the Niyandrians had any reason to fear him, save those who refused to abide by his rules. Just what those rules were he hadn't decided yet, but he knew they didn't permit oppressing the citizens of Dorinah and taking over their houses.

A violent shudder ripped through Anskar.

"Are you all right?" Vilintia said.

"It's so cold out here. I really need to go to bed."

"You might be unwell," she said, touching her hand to his brow. "It's a warm night. Like I said, I would have trained..." She trailed off at the look he gave her. "You didn't use to be so serious," she said. "So... prudish. Back in Rynmuntithe, I thought..."

"We go forward," Anskar said, not even recognizing the aphorism as his own, "never back."

"You might," she said, "but I value my past."

"Because it made you who you are today? Because it made you underconfident and riddled with doubt?" He held up a hand. "Forgive me. I don't know what I'm saying. I think you're right: I'm not well." He hugged himself as he shivered.

"Come here," Vilintia said. She embraced him.

Her hand fell to his hip as she tried to squeeze even closer. He felt her breasts crush against his chest. Anskar started to pull away, but her lips suddenly covered his, and she kissed him urgently, her hand now on the back of his head, keeping him in place. He started to pull back, but her other hand was inside his pants now. His aloofness barked a silent protest, before he started to respond.

Next thing, he was kissing her back fiercely, tugging up her tunic.

"Someone might see," she said, batting his hands away. But then she stood, turned her back to him, and placed her hands on the wall of the keep. "Like this," she said.

Anskar released the tie of his pants and pressed up behind her. She gasped as he entered her and pushed back against him, panting, urging him on.

Cold clumped in his guts and swilled through his veins. He pulled out and lurched away from her, holding up his pants; then he doubled up and vomited, streams of stinking vileness that burned as it came up. Even in the moonlight, he could see it was no ordinary vomit: it was thick and glutinous, dark enough to be molasses. Or tar.

When he finished and turned back to her, Vilintia was watching him, a look of horror on her face.

"Don't come near me again," she said, then turned and hurried away inside the keep.

"You're the one that did it!" Anskar yelled after her. "I told you no! You sick, disgusting animal. No, I said!"

He fastened his pants, shuddering, grimacing at the thought of what they had done, fretting over why it should have affected him like this.

"What's happening to me?" he muttered. "Menselas, what is happening?"

As if Menselas would answer him! As if he could!

He felt an overwhelming need to bathe, to cleanse all trace of Vilintia's touch from him. Why did he feel so debased? All he wanted was to be left alone. Cleansed and left alone to wallow in the currents at war within him. He needed time, he tried to reassure himself. Time to get to know his evolving powers. Time to reassess who he was, what he could become.

And so he headed inside, once he was sure Vilintia was far enough ahead of him. And he followed the corridors back to his old room.

THIRTEEN

MARITH COULDN'T JUST HEAR THEIR voices, she could see them now: twelve figures, their faces obscured by some kind of masking sorcery, as if they feared being recognized. She took in several ermine-trimmed cloaks and the glitter of heavy chains of office. There were hooded robes, a white cassock among them; women in elegant gowns; a couple of tail-coated mainland banker types. The chamber they occupied was ill-defined and gloomy, and all the people were ghostly in appearance, though she sensed these were no shades of the dead. Patterns of motes sparkled in the air above where they sat around a vast circular table: wards against sorcerous intrusion, and likely the reason the assembled people appeared so insubstantial, their faces hazy patterns of shadow.

But why had the wards not kept her out? Because she wasn't here by sorcerous means—she wasn't attempting a scrying? Which was when Marith realized she was dreaming; or if not dreaming, in the throes of a divinely inspired vision. That almost made her laugh. The idea was absurd, and yet she couldn't quite shake off the feeling that it was real. So she wasn't just one of the thousand ears of Theltek now. She was also one of his eyes. To her mind, that made her the puppet of two masters, one without, the other—Talia—within.

"Fallen, you say?" one of the women said, her sumptuous gown revealing more cleavage than was decent, but with the woman's face obscured, Marith could find no place better to look. The cleavage was a not inconsiderable distraction, until one of the bankers spoke.

"Bran's… what did you call it?"

"Branil's Burg," a robed giant said, his voice resonant from within his hood, implying thunder. "You remember: the citadel of the Order of Eternal Vigilance on Niyas."

"On where?" someone asked—Marith didn't see who.

Madame Cleavage fanned her non-existent face with a long-nailed hand. "Never heard of it. Is it anywhere near the Pristart Combine?"

With measured patience, the robed giant said, "You recall, I assume, the war with the Necromancer Queen?"

"Totally before my time," the woman said. "Well, almost. I was still a child back then, and wars are such dreadfully tedious affairs for children. And they haven't gotten any more riveting as an adult, I can tell you."

"Perhaps not, but you won't deny, I assume, that there is nothing so profitable," a different banker said. "Our establishment did quite nicely off the back of that war. So much so, we were considering making Queen Talia of Niyas one of our patrons. Posthumously, of course."

"Our financial network was practically born from the carnage of Niyas," another banker said, "not to mention the arms transactions required to make certain our victory."

"But did any of you pay heed," the robed giant asked, "when I advised you to invest in Niyas not so long ago? The island is in a state of flux. Has been ever since the fall of its capital, Naphor. The Order of Eternal Vigilance has held a tentative grip on power, but there has been endless rebellion."

"Also good for business," the first banker said. "Which is why we have allowed it to run unchecked all these years."

"Just don't mention that at the Council of Bishops later this month," the man in the white cassock said.

Madame Cleavage let out a tinkling laugh. "As if any of us would attend!"

"You still haven't explained how you know about Branil's Burg nor why we should take your word for it," one of the ermine-trimmed noble types said. "For one thing, I've had no word of this alleged attack on the seat of the Order's power in Niyas, and I imagine no one else here has."

There were grunts of agreement, though the bankers didn't respond—perhaps they knew something the others didn't. Nor did Madame Cleavage respond.

"All I am willing to share," the robed giant said, "is that I know."

"Huh," the noble said. "And how do you know? I thought we agreed only to ever work in unison, whenever our actions have the potential to affect the balance of power in Wiraya."

"I fully agree," the giant said, "and have taken no unilateral action. I merely observe and intuit. You financiers might say I speculate. And I listen to the reports that so frequently come my way."

"You have spies in Niyas?" This from the man in the white cassock.

"I have ways and means. That is all you need to know."

They began to squabble, too many voices, too loud—about armor and weapons, a lucrative trade, it seemed. It came up that the Order of Eternal Vigilance's blacksmiths on Niyas were the major supplier of armaments to the mainland, which was no big surprise to Marith. But with Branil's Burg lost, who would now meet the demands of the mainland military, especially if there were another war? She heard mention of investment opportunities, of price gouging. One of the women spoke about her factory that could turn out arrow heads by the thousands, about her dozens of forges that could be kept fired day and night, and grindstones with teams of green-skinned Ilapan slaves (apparently the latest investment opportunity for the in-the-know speculator) to do the sharpening. Someone claimed they could supply arrow shafts, and there was talk of fletchers and of recruiting more apprentices from among the poor regions of the mainland—Nagorn City and its provinces was considered a good target region. A man mentioned the possibility of hiring archers from King Aelfyr of the Thousand Lakes, whose people trained with the long war bow from childhood and were the only people of the mainland with the entrained strength to pull the bow.

"So, we crush this uprising right away?" another noble type asked. "We mount a full invasion of Niyas, like before?"

That made Marith giggle—which didn't seem right. This was no laughing matter. After all, she had been the one to instigate the trouble at Dorinah, in a roundabout sort of way, and that made her feel six years old again and extremely naughty.

"Why show our hand at this juncture?" the giant said. "Let us see how things play out, and wait for the news to reach the ears of both our elected and our divinely appointed leaders."

There were sniggers at that.

"How much leeway do we give those buffoons?" a banker asked.

Suddenly the voices were muffled, and the figures seated around the table were gone.

Marith awakened in bed. Slivers of light came through the shutters. Theltek, it was day!

And still she could hear voices. Not in her head; they were coming from outside. Rather a lot of them, by the sounds of things.

She was naked from the night before, though not from doing anything that would have added to her burden of guilt, considering the unrumpled sheets she had fallen asleep on. Hadn't she taken a bath and been too tired to get dressed? She had only misty recollections of the night before. Misty, no doubt, on account of the kind of wine she had been drinking. When she sat up and swung her legs out of bed, her head started to throb.

A footfall came from the porch.

She froze, listening intently. Still people were talking. Someone turned the doorknob.

"Shit," she muttered, thinking about the assassins that had come for Carred.

She threw on her robe and was about to check the state of her dusktide repository when she was suddenly flung out of her skull, her awareness dispersing throughout her entire body.

Talia resumed center stage, and Marith was compelled to listen to her voice. And obey.

"I will handle this," the Queen said through Marith's lips, before propelling her forward, one stumbling step at a time, till the motions grew smooth and natural. "I had quite forgotten. The shade I sent to entice them with high-sounding promises must have led them here to me while you slept. It is of no matter. If anything, this works to our advantage."

Marith found herself walking into the living area and startling a man who had just entered through the front door. It was an unnerving experience, being aware of the movements of her body yet not having one jot of control over them. Even weirder to hear the words coming out of her mouth—and it was indeed her own voice, though she was not the one speaking. Nor could she have spoken if she had wanted to.

"Ah, Fult Wreave, the last heir to the Ickthal Dynasty," Talia said.

Carred had spoken about Fult Wreave on more than one occasion, usually when she was drunk. She had described him as a weasel, and she wasn't wrong in that assessment. It didn't say much for the Ickthals who had ruled Niyas until Queen Talia deposed them, if this was their heir apparent. Tall wasn't a word Marith would have used to describe Fult Wreave—he barely came up to her chin, and she was only of average height. He had a pronounced widow's peak, which seemed in the process of slipping right off the back of his head. Unkempt, curling eyebrows, and, by way of contrast, a neatly waxed mustache—had that ever been a fashion in Niyas? As far as she knew, it might have been an affectation in Sansor or one of the other leading mainland cities, but in a Niyandrian it was pretentious, bordering on treasonous, to her way of thinking. He wore a tarnished breastplate from a bygone era beneath a faded, moth-eaten red cloak. His black pants were tucked into knee-length riding boots with silver spurs—another mainland affectation. A long, slender sword hung from his belt in a fancy scabbard embossed with knotwork patterns of intertwining serpents.

"You got my message, then," Talia said in Marith's voice.

"I got something." Wreave's eyes were bloodshot, and he had the haggard look of a haunted man.

"Quite a fright, I imagine," Talia said. "But who better to awaken you to your destiny than the last great ruler of your dynasty, the shade of the last king of Niyas?"

"That was you?" Wreave said. "You sent a ghost—the ghost of a king!—as a messenger? You possess that kind of power?" He eyed her up and down, his gaze lingering a little too long for decency. Disgusting little man.

[I concur] Talia said in Marith's dislocated mind. *[Fult Wreave is a turd, but even turds have their uses.]*

Other than as compost, I shudder to think what, Marith replied.

Despite the inner dialogue, Talia coerced Marith's hips to sway seductively as she approached Wreave and put her hands on his shoulders. He swallowed, blinked, didn't seem to know what to do with his own hands as Talia-Marith whispered into his ear. "You want to restore your family fortunes?"

"Of course," he growled—not from anger, but from nearly ruptured self-control. His hands settled on her buttocks. Marith was in full accord as Talia reached back and grabbed his wrists, squeezing tight, far stronger than Marith had ever been. Wreave whimpered and bit his lip, drawing blood.

"You do not touch," Talia said. "Only I touch. You do not think, do not even speak without my leave."

Defiance sparked in his bloodshot eyes, so Talia squeezed harder, and Wreave dropped to his knees, wincing in pain.

"Would you like me to break them?" Talia asked.

"No! Please, stop!"

Talia released him, and Wreave let out an anguished sob as he checked both wrists. They bore the impress of Marith's fingers and angry red welts.

"Who are you?" Wreave asked.

"You mean you don't know?" Talia said. "I would have thought a disgruntled Ickthal like you would have kept tabs on all your rivals, real and perceived."

"The Selenas bitch used to hide out here," Wreave said. "I know that much. This is the Pelhur place."

"Good boy," Talia said. "Nothing escapes you, which is why you may yet become king. I am Marith Pelhur." Marith wasn't sure she liked where this was leading.

"And Carred Selenas knows you sent for me?" Wreave said. "We're not exactly on good terms."

"She does not. Carred and I have had, shall we say, something of a falling out."

Marith groaned internally—which was the only sort of groan she was capable of. *No,* she wanted to say. *No, we have not.* But in a way they had, thanks to what Talia had made her do back at Dorinah.

[Settle down, Marith,] Talia said. *[We almost have him. Don't worry about the things I say to win him over; they are only words.]*

But words like these had more the feel of invocations… or curses.

"Now," Talia said, Marith's lips now so close to Wreave's she could smell his mustache wax, "would you like permission to touch me?" She let her robe fall open. It made Marith want to suck in her stomach, and no doubt reading her thoughts, Talia did just that. "Would you like to cement our covenant, Fult Wreave, flesh to flesh?"

His eyebrows shot up, as if he couldn't believe what he was being offered.

Please, for Theltek's sake! Marith said. *If I had control of my guts, I'd be sick.*

Wreave reached inside her robe, but before he touched a breast, Talia unleashed a torrent of dusk-tide essence that lit up her skin. Wreave squealed as he flew across the room and slammed into the wall, convulsing and frothing at the mouth.

"Know your place, little man," Talia said. "To be a king, to be an emperor, is within your reach. It all depends on the choice you make today."

"What choice?" he asked miserably, teeth chattering, face twitching.

Something awakened within Marith: an aperture of darkness beneath her dawn- and dusk-tide repositories. There was no question in her mind as to what it was, but it was as off-limits to her as the repositories she had been born with. And then it burst its bounds, and its contents sluiced through her veins. The dark-tide. It was joined with some kind of effluence not quite physical that flowed up from the ground beneath the floorboards and through her feet, moiling about the dark-tide, both breaking around the defined bounds of her dawn- and dusk-tide repositories—islands within a churning sea of virulence.

"Prostrate yourself."

"I don't know what you—"

"On your face, weasel!"

Fult Wreave complied, trembling now from head to foot.

"Swear to obey me in all things," Talia said. "Not just with words. Swear from the very center of your wretched being."

"Please," he whined. "I can't. Not until I know who you really are."

"I have already told you: Marith Pelhur."

"No one has power like this!" Wreave said, and he actually sounded bitter about it.

"I am moontouched," Talia said, causing Marith's shoulders to shrug.

Wreave nodded uncertainly, at the same time frowning. He didn't quite believe her.

"Forgive my ignorance," he said, "and be patient with me, but you are more than moontouched. Are you…?" He licked his lips as he peered up from the floor. "Please don't punish me if I am being insolent, but are you a goddess?"

"Which goddess would you like me to be?" Talia asked. "No, let me guess: Sylva Kalisia? We all know how she torments her closest servants. Is that what you would like for me to do, little man: torment you? Tease you? Perhaps I will. And perhaps my teasing will lead to more, if you please me. If you consent to my dominion over you with your entire being. Do this, and you will take back Naphor, become a king, and perhaps I will show you how much more you can achieve. I may even permit you to ascend, to become divine. Even goddesses desire consorts."

Wreave reared up on his knees, a tormented man, warring with the budding seeds of covetousness. "You… you really think I could take Naphor? The Order's garrison there is too strong. I have only a few hundred warriors. The bulk of the rebels are at Dorinah, fighting for Carred Selenas."

"But not you," Talia said. "You ignored that particular summons of mine, but I do not count it against you."

"If I had known who you were... your power..." Wreave said, "I would have heeded your first summons. I thought you were—"

"Carred's woman?" Talia said.

I am! Marith protested.

[Hush, Marith. A little while longer and you will be free.]

"Well, yes," Wreave said. He looked her in the eye, seeking permission, then decided it was safe to stand. He tried to reclaim an iota of dignity by straightening his breastplate and squaring his shoulders, but he was fooling no one. Carred had been right: a weasel in every sense of the word.

"Why would I fight for that loser?" Wreave said. "I refuse to risk good warriors for her."

"Even if she once fought for me?" Talia said. "Even if I once trusted her above all others?"

"You? I thought you said... Oh." He swallowed thickly and backed away to the door. "You serve the Necromancer Queen?"

Talia chuckled. Marith had never heard herself sound so... chilling. "Are you so slow, Fult Wreave of the Ickthals? I *am* her. Be still!" she commanded, as he turned to flee.

Wreave froze in place, and Talia glided in between him and the open door. There were Niyandrians looking on from outside, dozens that Marith could see, though none of them approached, as if they sensed the power boiling inside her possessed body.

"You have nothing to fear, Fult Wreave," Talia said. "Your family were my rivals. They lost. I have no rivals now, save among the gods, and even they will not plague me much longer. Join with me and I will make you king of all Niyas. Let our once warring houses unite. If the people know you are my loyal servant, they will flock to you, and Naphor will fall. We will unite Niyas and drive the mainlanders from the isle. In time, we will take the fight to them. I will build for you an empire."

"You came back?" Wreave said. "Carred Selenas always said that you would, but I don't think even she believed it. How?"

"You really think you can understand the ways of the gods?" Talia said.

"So, you ascended? That must have been…" His eyes gleamed with excitement. "This is incredible! It can be done? The necromancer Tain was not lying?"

"Your questions are verging on impertinent," Talia said, and Wreave licked his lips, some of the color leaving his cheeks. "All I want from you is an answer. Do you want me to make you a king, an emperor? Are you willing to serve me?"

Does he have a choice? Marith wondered.

[In this, yes. In all other matters, no. The binding of people is not like the binding of demons, a simple matter of dominance, of force.]

You could have fooled me!

[You are not bound, Marith, merely ousted, and that only for a time.]

"I would like to serve you," Wreave said, "but how do I know I can trust you?"

"You need witnesses?" Talia said. "Then I will provide them."

A geyser of vileness spouted up through the floor, unseen but not intangible, and to Marith's dispersed senses it stank as it sloshed throughout her possessed body. Fult Wreave grew rigid with fear, eyes wide and unblinking, and then the air around him grew hazy. Figures formed from dust motes, coalescing into definition. First one, then two, three, four, five robed and crowned shades encircled him, ghosts of mist with sunken cheeks and pallid skin stretched thin over ancient skulls. Three were women, two men: the kings and queens who had ruled Niyas before Talia usurped the throne, the monarchs of the Ickthal Dynasty. A susurrus of whispers filled the room, building to the skirl and gust of an unnatural wind. Five near-skeletal hands with the consistency of smoke rose in unison, bony fingers pointing at Fult Wreave.

"Consent," they all said at the same time.

Wreave stumbled, as if his knees no longer had the strength or the stability to hold him up. He somehow managed to stay on his feet, trembling arms spread wide for balance, chin quivering, teeth audibly chattering.

"See?" Talia said through Marith's lips. "Your esteemed ancestors trust me. Is their witness sufficient?"

"This is necromancy," Wreave whispered, as if he feared louder utterances. "You have compelled them."

"It is true the last of the Ickthals and I crossed swords, in a sense, and that I ended the reign of King Yanos Duwint Ickthal sooner than he would have liked, but the realm of the dead is a great teacher of wisdom, and these your ancestors now accept that what I did was in the best interests of Niyas."

"You tried to create an empire," Wreave said. "You lost a devastating war and destroyed our people."

"And now I have returned," Talia said, steel in her voice, "and with you as the focal point for the reborn Niyas, I will make all things right. Now, Fult Wreave, will you submit to me? Will you serve?"

The five Ickthal ghosts closed in around him, a slowly tightening noose. "Consent," they said again.

"I..." Wreave said. He glanced over his shoulder, out through the open doorway at the warriors who had accompanied him to Marith's land. Many were on their knees, signing themselves with the many protective wards attributed to Theltek.

"Consent," the ghosts said, and this time they spoke gently, persuasively.

Talia walked through one of the incorporeal spirits to stand before Wreave. She ignored his pleading look, the stammered stream of babbled objections spilling from his lips, and instead unlaced his pants. She slid her hand—Marith's hand!—inside.

Wreave gasped and squeezed his eyes shut but made no attempt to pull away as Talia caressed him. He began to swell in Marith's hand, letting out little gasps and moans.

"Consent!" the royal shades repeated. "Consent!"

Marith's hand moved faster and faster, Wreave clenching every muscle in his body and groaning.

Please, Theltek, no! Marith thought. The first violation was bad enough—Talia invading her body— but this… She wanted to scream, wanted to stick her fingers in Wreave's eyes and gouge them out. Wanted to incinerate Talia's evil spirit and make sure it never came back.

[Oh, Marith, must you be so dramatic?] Talia said in her mind. *[I do this for Niyas. We do it.]*

"Consent!" the shades screamed at Wreave now, as his groans grew ever more urgent. "Consent!"

Talia withdrew her hand, and Wreave grew apoplectic. "Don't stop!" he pleaded. "Sweet Theltek, don't—"

"Consent!" the shades roared.

"All right, I consent!' Wreave said. "Now, please…"

He grabbed Marith's wrist and guided her hand back inside his pants.

Fire burst from her fingers, and he screamed. There followed the stench of burned flesh and a terrible wail as Wreave let his pants fall around his knees and stared in horror at his melted genitals. He shook and gasped, his face turning red, then purple. Mercifully, he fainted and collapsed in a heap.

"He'll be all right," Talia told the kneeling Niyandrians outside the door. The perverts had watched everything. Were they without shame? Was Talia?

[I never saw much point in it,] Talia said. *[The important thing is, we have him now, hooked like a fish.]*

With a wave of her hand, she dismissed the shades of the Ickthal dead.

Will he live? Marith asked.

[What do you take me for?] Talia said. *[Of course he will live. I have ensured that he does. Heirs, though, might prove a problem.]*

Dusk-tide sorcery surged within Marith's repository as Talia stooped and touched her hand to Fult Wreave's chest. Lightning arced between her fingers, and Wreave bucked. His eyes snapped open, and he sucked in air. Immediately jerked and then screamed, as he sat up and looked in horror at the melted ruin between his legs. Again a putrid swill rose up from the ground, discharging through Marith's fingers. Wreave sighed then whimpered as the livid flesh of his groin blackened as it cooled, until there was nothing there save shriveled, necrotic tissue.

"There," Talia said, as if she cared. "How does that feel? Better?"

"Numb," Wreave said, his voice raw from screaming. "But… how can I be your consort now?" he asked miserably.

"I have the power to shape flesh," Talia said. "When you succeed in restoring Niyas to Niyandrian rule, when you rule over the new empire, I will heal you, and you will know such pleasure!"

You can do that? Marith asked. It didn't seem likely.

[The earth-tide is principally about shaping and giving form to matter,] Talia said within her. *[It is a perversion of its power when we use it to raise and control the dead, an aberration introduced by a vile and loathsome god.]*

The Corpse Maker? Marith wondered.

A tremor passed through her body in reply.

"Promise me you will tell no one," Fult Wreave pleaded, glancing at the dead flesh of his manhood before pulling up his pants.

"You have my word," Talia said. "But until you have completed your tasks, you must pretend to lead. Give the impression of strength, of being the one in control, and I will not contradict you in public. Go now. Tell your followers you have spoken with a great prophet and that the shades of your dead ancestors confirm that soon you will be king. Send out word across Niyas, and bring those who would not follow

Carred Selenas to Rynmuntithe Forest, within half a day's march of Naphor. The ancient earthworks of our forebears… you know it?"

"The mount of barrows?" Wreave said. "I know the place."

Talia placed a hand on his shoulder. "Muster your forces. Await me there."

Wreave shuddered and then turned away, heading outside. His warriors rose from their knees as he moved among them, issuing orders.

With a chuckle, Talia closed the door.

Were those illusions? Marith asked. *Or really the ghosts of his ancestors?*

[Shades from the realm of the dead. So easy to control, as dimwitted in death as they were in life.]

So, what do we do now? Marith asked.

She could feel the skin of her face pull taut as Talia smiled. When she replied, the Queen spoke through Marith's lips, as if to emphasize the point that Marith could not. "So compliant, my dear Marith. Have I won you over?"

You might as well have done. It's not like I can resist.

"So you would resist if you could? A pity. I was starting to enjoy your company."

It's not easy for me, with you running my body. I've never exactly been the passive type.

Talia moved to the wine rack, selected a bottle, and studied the label. "It won't be for long, Marith. Once you retrieve the Armor of Divinity for me, I'll have all that I need to be fully manifest, and you will be restored."

It's that simple? As simple as the Queen telling Carred to wait for her return and then doing nothing for all those years?

"Of course it is that simple," Talia said. "But you are not convinced. Oh, Marith, you really must learn to trust me a little more. And yes, Carred did have to wait a long time, but there was a reason for that. My son had to grow into manhood."

For all the good it's done.

"Quite." Talia took up the corkscrew and opened the bottle. "Anskar had such potential, ruined since his little trip to the abyssal realms." The corkscrew slipped as she pressed it too hard into the cork, and it tore into the skin of her finger.

Ouch! Marith cried. *I felt that!*

Talia ignored her; more interested, it seemed, in the drop of blood slowly rolling down her finger.

"It has been a long time," she said, "since I last bled."

She tried again with the cork, and this time it came free with a plop. She selected a glass and filled it, and at least Marith got the benefit of tasting the mistberry wine as it went down.

Not my usual choice for breakfast, she said.

"These are exceptional times," Talia replied. "Enjoy the moment, for we do not have long."

Oh?

"One has been brought back from the realm of the dead." Talia wandered to a window and peered through the blinds at the greenery dappled with sunlight. Birds were chirping as if the world were at rights, as if it didn't share the petty concerns of people, of queens and gods. There was no sign now of Fult Wreave and his warriors save for the muddy gouges their horses had left in the grass. "One who knows things she should not."

You're not speaking about yourself?

"Her name is Noni. You would have seen her at Dorinah. Like a fast burning wick, she wielded power she was not prepared for; power she had no business using."

The girl who had wreaked such destruction during the battle in the streets. Yes, Marith had seen her fall, consumed by the power flowing through her. *What does she know that she should not?*

"Glimpses. Impressions of my intentions, my plans. We were once joined, as I am now joined with you."

You possessed her, you mean? A better term might have been "raped," spiritually.

"Guard your thoughts!" Talia said, almost spitting with anger.

Sorry. I forgot you could hear them, and they aren't always easy to control. Her thoughts were like wild horses, untamed. They were like fish scattering before a predator, or a myriad self-willed demons.

"Possession," Talia said, voice tight with control, "is a two-way street. True, I am the one in control, but the host is not without access to my mind."

I'll remember… Marith throttled the thought before she gave it full expression.

Talia shook her head, smiling. "I think we are coming to an understanding, you and I."

Noni was brought back, you say. Brought back by whom?

"I doubt it was some stray necromancer, one of those who loiter amid the ancient ruins, serving the gods of pre-history." A shudder again passed through Marith's body, a chill along her spine. Talia seemed to swallow old regrets.

You think it was Anskar?

"I have not unlocked such power within him. True, I have wielded necromancy through him, but not in such a way that he would possess it for himself."

Then how?

"How did he do it? How did he bring Noni back—if indeed he did? Poorly, I would have to say. Her return is in some way incomplete. She suffers beyond belief, a soul locked within the tomb of her own decomposing flesh. Anskar is a fool. There is but one he could have gained this knowledge from. I had sought to spare him the path he now walks. I made… mistakes when I was young, out of desperation. My father… He was not a good father, and though my power was great, it was never great enough to rival him, to ward him off."

What did you do?

"I sought help from the old ones... an old one, whose abode lies in the depths of Wiraya. It changed me. It changed Niyas. You will ask no more about it. I forbid it."

So, what does this Noni know? I assume she has told Anskar? Ah, I think I can guess: the location of the Armor of Divinity. Am I right?

"See how he works against me? How I underestimated the pervasive influence of the Order of Eternal Vigilance. Anskar was supposed to be the serpent's egg among them, waiting to hatch, waiting to foment true rebellion in the heart of the foe. And he was supposed to forge a suit of Armor of Divinity and use it to return me to life—not just this life, but divine life, for eternity."

You believe he has betrayed you?

"With his sword, he would have drunk my soul. And yours, Marith, let us not forget that. You are just as disposable to him. Enough talk now. We must hurry. You must again use the haste sorcery."

The one that almost killed me on the way to Dorinah?

"I will sustain you. And no, before you think it: I am sincere. You are not a mere horse to be ridden to exhaustion and then discarded in favor of a new and fresher mount."

Then why do I feel...? Sorry, Marith thought. *Errant thoughts...*

"Will no doubt be the death of you," Talia said as she clamped down on Marith's repositories and her mind, compelling her to commence the haste sorcery. "Probably quite soon."

FOURTEEN

BRANIL'S BURG HADN'T ALWAYS BEEN a stronghold of the Order of Eternal Vigilance. That much was clear as soon as Carred slipped between the gap in the blackwood double doors and entered the massive chamber her aides had chosen for the war council.

Rose-tinted sunlight fell in shafts through the stained-glass ceiling thirty feet above. A shudder passed along her spine as she took a moment to gaze up at the twelve lead-framed panels that converged in a central apex. No wonder everyone else in the chamber sat in hushed awe—she wanted to call it reverent. The panels depicted Niyandrian men and women, naked save for the skull masks that completely encompassed their heads. At some immemorial time, this had been a shrine to that most prehistoric of Niyandrian gods, Kaythe Nurglich, tenderly known to his bloodthirsty worshippers as the Corpse Maker. The skull-masked shamans in the panels cavorted around each other, many in evident states of arousal, the way the Corpse Maker allegedly liked them: enslaved by their own lusts and amenable to his own.

In conformity with the twelve ceiling panels and following the lines of their lead frames, the room was twelve-sided. Flush against each wall was a low dais, atop which sat a blackwood throne. These would have been the niches for the shamans of Kaythe Nurglich, from within which they would have intoned their barbarous cants while the most terrible sacrifices took place in the center of the chamber. She didn't allow herself to think beyond that; some images should never be allowed to enter the mind, lest they leave their indelible mark. Lest they corrupt. Niyas had a dark and stygian past, compared to which Queen Talia's reign had been a veritable golden age. Although she had to wonder... The things she had witnessed, the rituals Talia had performed, the ever-deepening chill that afflicted her flesh... According to those old enough to know—poor Eadgith, for one—Talia hadn't always been the Necromancer Queen the mainlanders described her as. Had she done something... compromised herself in some way? Made a pact?

Carred's two aides—she couldn't believe she had aides!—waited patiently either side of the entrance, a young man and a young woman Vilintia had picked sometime before dawn; they must have loved her for that. Why Carred needed aides was anyone's guess. Hers was because things were about to get serious, and she was the one best placed to deal with them. Maybe.

Over a breakfast of hot tea and gallons of water to flush out the effects of too much mistberry wine, she had asked Vilintia to invite nine of the most proven among the rebels: those who had led their own units over the past eighteen years, those who might yet still believe in Carred despite the change of direction. The rebellion had all been about resistance until such time as the Queen returned, but now, with Talia at least partially back—within Marith!—it was not quite so simple. Would these men and women be loyal to Carred or to Talia? Because there was no doubt that a rift had been introduced, one she suspected had been forming for quite some time. Marith had been the final straw, along with what Talia had made her do. Was Talia unbalanced from having been so long removed from the world? Was she so deluded that she actually believed the Niyandrians could win a war against the mainland allies?

Carred needed to find out where these rebel leaders stood because, speaking for herself, she was done with blind obedience to a queen she had started to believe, in all earnestness, was better off staying dead. Her loyalty was to Marith and to the abyss with taking back the isle from the mainlanders. Without Marith, what would be the point?

She looked around at the commanders seated on the blackwood thrones. Most she recognized. Some she knew fairly well. One or two even better. Vilintia looked worse than she had at breakfast: drawn and haggard, with dark rings around her eyes. She had told Carred she couldn't sleep and had been up all night planning and preparing—which didn't sound at all like the Vilintia of old, a capable enough warrior and a safe pair of hands, but an order taker not exactly known for her logistical skills or her strategy. She had dressed in armor, as if they were going to fight this day. Despite her evident fatigue, she cut an imposing figure, looking more of a leader than Carred, who had thrown on the same filthy clothes she had worn yesterday and run her fingers through her tousled hair to get out the worst of the knots.

Theltek's eyes, she was in a state. No wonder Anskar had rejected her. Not that it was any skin off her nose. She'd had an itch; how it got scratched didn't matter in the slightest. But just to be clear, last night was the only offer he'd be getting. Truth be told, she was embarrassed about the whole drunken business. She'd made a fool of herself, and probably should apologize. But at the same time, she couldn't stop herself from feeling angry towards him. She'd not been blind to the predatory way he used to look at her. She could read men—knew what most of them wanted. But when, with a little help from the wine, she'd practically begged him to take her, he had refused. If there was one thing she couldn't stand, it was game playing. She realized then she'd not yet clapped eyes on him this morning.

And then she saw the empty throne.

"Where's Ansk… the *Melesh-Eloni*?" she asked.

She had debated whether or not to invite him to the war council, or whatever it was Vilintia was calling it. Vilintia had advised against it, but Carred had overruled her. Without the *Melesh-Eloni*—without his devastating powers—the war against the mainlanders would be over before it started.

None of the others met her gaze, and when Vilintia did, it was with an insolent roll of her eyes, and a "How should I know?" shrug.

"Shall I fetch him?" the female aide asked—Carred really ought to ask her name, but with her mind so full of plans and fallback plans, not to mention the litany of her failures, she knew she would never remember it.

"I'd sooner you fetched me a glass of mistberry wine."

"At once…" The woman looked momentarily flummoxed.

"Uhm," the male aide said, "what is it we are to call you?"

"Carred? It is my name, and I believe that's the custom here in Niyas."

"They're right," Vilintia said. "This isn't the Last Cohort, and it's way beyond our ragtag band of rebels hiding out in Rynmuntithe."

"Your official title is the first thing we should decide," an older man said.

Because, of course, there were no more pressing matters.

"Name's Senvil," the older man said. He glanced either side, at the others seated on thrones. "Commander Senvil Dartoom."

They all nodded. Clearly, they were big on titles and had already decided upon their own. Wasn't she meant to have confirmed their positions? She glanced at Vilintia, then decided to let it go. She had already betrayed too much weakness, and out of all of them, the aides included, her appearance, after a night of drinking, was the least evocative of leadership.

"Anskar is supposed to be the focal point of our resistance," she said. "He is the rightful heir to Niyas. Compared with him, I am…" She was going to say *nobody*, but that would have been disingenuous. "Well, I used to be a captain, and I never had a problem with that."

She was met with stoic looks. She was winning no one over with her tongue-tangled rhetoric.

"We bent the knee to him, remember? After the battle in the streets?"

The way they said nothing, it made her wonder if she were going mad. But she knew she hadn't imagined it. She'd been the first to kneel to Anskar, and hundreds had followed her example.

"He's the *Melesh-Eloni*," she continued, undeterred.

"Whose role is to bring back the Necromancer Queen," a woman said. "Is that still what we are trying to do?" She cocked her head and arched an eyebrow.

"You tell me," Carred asked. Far better to get them to commit to answers than to give her hand away. Not that she had one, exactly. Or if she did, it was as lousy as the one that lost her the game of Five-Card Malice at Lowanin and landed her in bed with a porcupine demon thing named Count Vasseyli ap Murbian.

No one answered. They might as well all have been playing cards, and they were a darned sight better at it than she was. Why did things have to be so complicated? She guessed she had Marith to thank for that. Or, rather, Talia working through Marith.

"First," Vilintia said, "we establish chains of command."

"With me at the top?"

"Not necessarily," the same woman as before said.

"Sorry, do I know you?" Carred asked.

"Commander Hemlit Wuleta. I served under Fult Wreave."

Fult the Weasel. Carred had been wondering when his name would come up. An opportunity like this, with war brewing and the rebels dithering, where they weren't outright divided, seemed too good for the heir to the Ickthal Dynasty to pass up.

"Any idea why he didn't make it to Dorinah?" Carred asked. She had one or two of her own.

Wuleta shrugged, every bit as insolently as Vilintia.

"So," Carred said, moving on, "we establish the chain of command. What next, seeing as you've all made such good progress without me?"

"We defend the isle against a new mainland invasion," Vilintia said.

"And part of that," Dartoom said, "is that we go on our own offensive."

"Against the Order's strongholds on the isle?" Carred said. "I agree. It's something I've given a lot of thought to. But let's not forget, the mainlanders have ships patrolling the isle. Within days, they'll likely set up a blockade. What about us? How many ships do we have?" A rhetorical question. Everyone knew the answer. War-ships: none. Traders: a handful. Fishing vessels: quite a few, though considerably fewer since Monash and the refugees from Branil's Burg had used them for the voyage home across the Simorga Sea.

"And what about..." She almost couldn't say it. Her lips were suddenly dry. "That mistberry wine," she told her female aide. "I wasn't joking. On second thought, make it water. As to what you call me," she said, as the aide turned to leave, "can we all settle for now on General? Until I think of something better."

"Water coming right up, General," the aide said, then scurried from the room.

"You were saying?" Wuleta prompted.

"I was? Oh, yes... What about Marith?" She directed her question at Vilintia, who gave a sad shake of her head. "What about Queen Talia? Do we all at least agree that things have changed, given what happened here yesterday?"

"We do," Anskar said from behind her in the doorway. "At least, I do."

Carred almost couldn't look at him. His eyes—like glistening spheres of onyx—sat within dark cavities. Since she had seen him last night, his cheeks had grown sunken, his lips thin, and his skin, usually dusky with just a tinge of red, was now almost as crimson as her own. To her revitalized sorcerous senses, he bristled with power. A hazy aura surrounded him, and in his proximity, she felt a throbbing pressure in her head.

Over his clothes, which looked every bit as filthy as her own, he had thrown on a white Order cloak, which he pulled tight around him as if he were cold. That immediately had Carred on the alert. If anything, it was too warm in the hall. So, either he had picked up a chill, or it was a cold not of this world, just like his mother used to feel. First his eyes, and now this. She wanted to ask what he had been doing, but this was hardly the time or place.

She wasn't the only one to have noticed. Anskar had the attention of everyone in the hall. Fear would do that, and whatever else these commanders might have thought of Anskar, she could see from their faces that they feared him.

"So," Carred said warily, "what do we do now?"

"After what happened yesterday, does anyone here really want the Necromancer Queen back?" Anskar asked.

The commanders exchanged looks, but no one dared speak. What if he were testing them, was the sense Carred got from their expressions. Better to let someone else stick their neck out. Someone like her.

"I don't think this…" She couldn't bring herself to mention Marith. "I don't think this is how she meant to return. Not originally. Else why the need for a guardian? Why the need for…?" And again she hesitated.

"Why the need for me?" Anskar asked. "I'm sure she had a use in mind, but somehow I have—*we* have—scuppered her plans."

"Vulthanor?" Carred asked. She didn't want to say more in front of the others; it would take too long to explain.

Anskar seemed to sense her reticence and merely nodded. "She was forced to make a desperate move."

And now Carred breathed the name she had been avoiding: "Marith…"

"A temporary fix, I'm sure," Anskar said. He even looked as though he hoped it was, and that Marith's possession would soon be over. "I don't know how I know, but I don't think a sorcerer, even a necromancer as accomplished as my mother, can commandeer someone else's body for too long. Else why didn't she do so before? My theory is, she still needs the Armor of Divinity to make herself fully manifest. This is why she is going to Naphor."

"Naphor?" Vilintia asked. She had ridden with the Last Cohort under Carred's command when the city had fallen. "Does she mean to take on the garrison by herself? Is that her goal, to occupy the capital? That's suicide—even for Queen Talia."

"Maybe she has an army of her own waiting for her," Carred said. "What do you think?" she asked Dartoom.

Of course, the response she got was a shrug.

"I have a feeling," Anskar said, "that my mother's not quite ready for Naphor yet. She's after something else, and I need to stop her from getting it."

"A feeling?" Vilintia said. "That's the best you have to go on?"

Anskar ignored her. He seemed to be waiting for Carred to say something.

And then she worked out what it was. "There's a suit of Armor of Divinity nearby." She didn't add the precise location—a mansion that had once belonged to Domatai, the demon lord. Talia's father. Anskar's grandsire.

"Which is why I'm going after her," Anskar said. He let his cloak fall open to reveal the sword at his hip.

"You mean to kill her?" Suck the life out of her, more like.

"If I have to."

"But you can't. Not without killing Marith."

"Trust me, Carred, I will do all in my power to avoid that."

"You'll do more than that," she said, advancing on him. "You'll take me with you."

A frown furrowed his face. Mercifully, for a few seconds, he shut those empty black eyes. His nod, when it came, seemed to indicate agreement, but then he opened his eyes and turned them on the commanders. He had been thinking about something else entirely.

"What are these people doing on the thrones?" he asked in a soft voice—the voice of a boy, naive, innocent, as if he had not walked in the dark places. As if he'd changed personalities. "This is the Dodecagon, and those seats are reserved for the holiest knights." He grimaced and pinched the bridge of his nose.

"These are our new commanders," Carred said. "Vilintia hand-picked them."

That was when Carred noticed Vilintia glaring at Anskar with narrowed eyes. When she saw Carred looking, she dropped her gaze and affected a look of nonchalance. What was going on?

Anskar ran his eyes over each of the commanders in turn. They all sat rigid, trying to hold his gaze yet sagging with relief whenever he moved past them. He paused longer at Dartoom, looking her up and down. Carred felt an outpouring of… something, from somewhere within Anskar. Not a repository as such. It was more than that, as if his entire being were infused with sorcerous currents. And whatever she felt, it wasn't the dawn or the dusk.

"This one's a traitor," he said.

Dartoom's eyes widened, and she started to protest.

And suddenly, the innocent Anskar was gone. He might even have snarled as he made a rending motion with one hand. There was an accompanying sound: the rip of a sheet, the patter of rain, a skirl of wind. Dartoom screamed as she slumped forward and toppled out of her throne, a raw and bloody mess.

Her skin…

Theltek, her skin!

Carred covered her mouth to keep down her rising gorge. The commanders were frozen rigid on their thrones, scarce daring to blink.

Dartoom had been flayed alive, her skin ripped away in one go. No sign of it now. It had just been… taken away. Somewhere. Disappeared.

Blood oozed from all over the crimson corpse, pooling beneath it on the floor. Dartoom twitched once or twice, and then she was still.

"So," Carred said from behind her hand, "I guess that means Fult Wreave is plotting something."

But how had Anskar known? She immediately tried to bury her train of thought beneath a jumble of memories—most of them sexual. Not because she wanted to dwell on such things right now, but because they were the strongest, the easiest to develop into attention-grabbing scenes that might deflect an intruder from her real thoughts. Because what he had just done to Dartoom he could do to any one of those present. Was he even now trying to plumb the depths of Carred's mind? And if he was, if he got past her sordid defenses, what would he discover? Betrayal? She didn't think so. Theltek, she didn't even know where her allegiances lay now. The only thing she was sure of was Marith.

"It matters not what this Fult Wreave is plotting," Anskar said, "so long as we take down my mother. So long as I do."

He turned to leave—he'd not even stepped from the doorway into the hall, as if he'd never planned to stay even so long as he had. He'd come to announce his departure, nothing more. He cared even less about the war his mother had just started than Carred did. Yet he should care. They both should. They were supposed to be leaders.

She grabbed him by the arm—icy cold.

"I'm coming with you," she told him.

He yanked his arm away. "I don't think so. What can you do against the Necromancer Queen, you with your paltry excuse for a repository? Stay here. Make plans to retake Naphor before someone else does. But before that, march on Quolith. That way we cement our position here at Dorinah."

Carred looked at Vilintia, who nodded that she understood. Well, that was a start.

"You're in charge, General Yoenth," she said.

Vilintia bucked up at her promotion, but then she looked even more uncertain of herself. "And what exactly am I supposed to do?"

Carred had never seen her like this—unsure of herself, shrill, close to tears.

Anskar started to protest, but she talked right over him.

"Don't think you can stop me, even with your fancy sorcery. Marith's my responsibility, understood?"

For a moment, she thought he was going to do to her what he'd done Dartoom, but then he dipped his black eyes. When he raised his head and nodded, he was the young knight again, though the strain on his face showed the effort it took to control himself. Not from rage, for he had been cold in his condemnation and murder of Dartoom. It was as if he had to remind himself he wasn't some all-powerful tyrant, like Talia had been. That he was a living, breathing person, the same as the rest of them, and not some contemptuous god.

Internally, Carred breathed a sigh of relief, then turned away from Anskar before he could change again.

"Delegate," she told Vilintia. "You have all these commanders now. Form the rebels into divisions. Establish chains of command. You were in the Last Cohort. You know how it's done."

Vilintia clenched her jaw and nodded. Give her a task, and she'd do it. Leave her to come up with plans of her own, though…

Carred turned a slow circle as she addressed the hall. "I want to see a disciplined army when I get back. First priority: secure the Burg and the city, then make plans and gather supplies for an assault on Quolith. Once we're secure, we can turn our attention to Naphor. Anything else?" she asked Anskar.

"The citizens are to be treated with the utmost respect," he said. He might have been thinking about specific things he'd seen. "If anyone harms a Niyandrian citizen—any citizen—or enters their home, have them flogged. If they offend again, hang them."

Carred could almost hear the gasps that no one dared to utter.

"And," Anskar said, "have our people forage and hunt for their own supplies. I don't want them being a drain on the city."

"And recruit," Carred added. "See if any of the locals will join us."

"They will," Anskar said, "as soon as they know there's a war coming, whether they like it or not."

"Is that enough for you to get on with?" Carred asked Vilintia. She took the miserable nod as a yes. "There will be an inspection when I get back."

"I can't believe you're leaving her in charge," Anskar said, as they left the hall together.

"You have a problem with that?"

"No problem."

"Good. Then let's get a move on. I take it we're not walking."

He smiled then. If not for the eyes, she would have believed in his innocence.

"I used to work at the stables. We can grab ourselves a couple of horses there."

"Three," she said. "I'll take one for Marith."

Anskar hesitated, then gave a decisive nod. "Good idea."

FIFTEEN

HE AND CARRED HAD RIDDEN so long, Anskar felt as though his horse were part of him, that some unforeseen effect of the earth-tide had transformed him into a hybrid, part animal, part man. The stallion was no Fellswain, to be sure, but he had done well to carry him so far through Rynmuntithe Forest with only the occasional stop for water and rest. An older thoroughbred of fifteen hands, the black stallion he'd selected on account of the scars that riddled his face and flanks. The horse had seen his share of fighting, and was unlikely to balk at the first sign of danger. Rosie he hadn't been so sure about, though Larson always used to claim she was a great hunter and ferocious in fights with other dogs. To be on the safe side, he had left Rosie with Orix. If nothing else, she might give Orix something to think about, other than Noni—a situation Anskar felt he would be unable to fix, not without making concessions to the dark, to Kaythe Nurglich, he wasn't prepared to make.

Carred rode a little ahead of him on a sorrel horse with white spots that had a peculiar shuffling gait and inquisitive eyes of hazel. Hers was a lighter horse than Anskar's, selected for the trek through the wild woods that smothered central Niyas. Carred led a second steed on a long rein, a spritely bay palfrey. Marith's horse, if they found her. If there was anything left of Marith to bring back with them.

The sun had been ascending blue skies with only the wispiest strips of cottony cloud when they left Dorinah, but within a few miles, dark clouds had blown in from the Simorga Sea, and had pursued them ever since. The horses kept ahead of the gathering storm, but Anskar kept glancing back through the trees as the wind rose and thunder rumbled off in the east.

But the horses were slowing, the churlish clouds scudding overhead now, bringing the first few fat drops of rain. Another half mile, and the wind howled through the branches, the rain building to a driving downpour, icy and unnatural for the time of year. Lightning forked across the sky, the booming crash of thunder mere seconds behind. The forest acted as a wind barrier, but on the periphery of Anskar's vision, trunks swayed and branches thrashed in the gale. A too-close bolt of lightning blasted a trunk to his right, causing his stallion to whinny and rear. Anskar leaned over its great neck, patting the horse and speaking to calm it, even as the tree burst into flame, portions of its trunk already charcoal and giving off plumes of smoke.

Carred reined in beneath the branches of a colossal oak, looking back at him, her cat's eyes wide with worry. Anskar nodded. He could feel it too: a tickle at the nape of his neck, a tingling along his spine. Every sense, the mundane and the sorcerous, was pricked, fully alert. Something wasn't right. It felt as though the gods or some other supernatural force were working against them.

"Talia?" Carred asked, but he shook his head.

"I fought her at Branil's Burg, remember? She is powerful, maybe powerful enough to influence the weather, but I would know if it was her. I would sense her taint." And besides, she wouldn't dare. He had beaten her soundly. She had screamed under the assault of his sword.

So, who or what, then? Kaythe Nurglich, angry at his refusal? Anskar refused to think about that. Was it Menselas? What if the God of Five Aspects was real, after all, and Anskar had rejected him? Not only rejected: blasphemed against him and betrayed the Order he had consecrated. If Menselas was behind the storm, which seemed all too purposeful, too malignant, to be pure chance, then was this a chastisement, or was it a warning not to go to Naphor? If the latter, why would Menselas try to warn him? Did the god still care? Did he want to forgive Anskar his trespasses? He shook his head. It was too late for that. And in any case, he had come too far, grown too powerful. What need had he for gods and their mercy, when he was so close to… He severed the thought before he could complete it, before it became irrevocable. He was no god, nor did he aspire to be one. That was someone else's ambition, a temptation set before him. An entrapment. He recognized those words of warning as Brother Tion's, from back when Anskar had been a willful child, always convinced he was right, always believing others were given unfair advantages over him. "I am special!" he had once belligerently complained. "We are all of us special in the eyes of Menselas," Tion had replied, which was as good as saying no one was.

"We should find shelter," Carred said. "There's a steading not too far from here."

"We press on," Anskar said, undeterred by the battle raging in the heavens, by the sleet stinging his skin and drenching his cloak. Lightning fizzed behind the clouds, limning them with flickering fire. Thunder shook the forest and caused his horse to shy.

They rode on, drenched and shivering, the horses' hooves gouging the slick ground and leaving a muddy trail. Not that Anskar feared being followed. He'd not forgotten the taste of power that had fully bloomed within him back at Dorinah. Nothing on Wiraya could rival such sorcery. And yet… Marith-Talia had, until *Amalantril* turned the tide. And not just that, a niggling voice wormed its way into his consciousness: he had been unable to fully restore Noni. Which implied there was more power to come, or powers he possessed as yet untapped. Images like pesky flies flittered across his inner vision—of the wraithe who had accompanied him on his spirit journey to the core of the world, of the wolf-headed horror, the scaly monster that was Kaythe Nurglich, perhaps the oldest of the Niyandrian gods and maybe even the oldest of all the gods. Kaythe Nurglich, who had evoked terror so primal that Anskar couldn't bear to dwell on the memories, and prayed to Menselas—to Menselas!—to take them from him. The wind-rustled leaves above his head seemed to snigger at him, to whisper that he was snagged, that sooner or later he would return to the depths of the world and enter into a pact with the Corpse Maker.

"Never!" he uttered through chattering teeth, cursing the cold and the rain, but at the same time embracing them, as if their harshness could keep him grounded and safe.

Hour after hour they rode, the horses maintaining only a plodding pace, the unrelenting storm lashing the trees, tearing at his hair and clothing. But at last they came in sight of Hallow Hill, jutting up out of the woodland like a gigantic grass-tufted skull, the chalk of its bones showing through where the topsoil had eroded. Light, stark and gray, seeped through the gaps in the clouds, causing the sheeting rain to glisten.

Anskar dismounted and tethered his horse to a low-hanging branch. Shivers repeatedly sent his muscles into spasms, more so now he was deprived of the warmth of the beast beneath him. He waited for Carred to climb down from her roan horse and tether it, along with the spare palfrey, then he wove a dull and near-invisible ward sphere from strands of the dawn-, dusk-, and dark-tides around them both, shutting out the driving rain.

"That would have been nice before," Carred said.

"Maybe." But Anskar hadn't wanted it before. He had embraced the cold and the damp as a penance, as a refusal of the blasphemous thoughts that he couldn't quite put down. Gods, after all, did not suffer from chills and exposure to the elements.

He unleashed a steady flow of dusk-tide to warm the interior of the ward sphere and dry their hair and clothes. At first Carred frowned, then she sighed with relief.

"Why did you bring us here?" Anskar asked.

"Prudence," she said, indicating that they should walk to the foot of the hill. "You can see Naphor from the summit. If there are Order patrols…"

"And this house, this mansion, is near the city?"

"A little way farther through the forest. Hidden away. Secluded, which is apparently how Talia's father… Domatai, your grandfather… liked it."

"And my mother lived there?"

"You would think. But there's another reason. You said we were going to have to take back Naphor, and I don't disagree, not if war is coming. I tried once before, but even with the new citadel far from complete, we were out-thought and outmatched."

"You want another look at it before we attack?" Anskar asked.

"What if they've increased the garrison? The more intelligence we have, the better our chances."

"You ask me," Anskar said, "like I said back at the Burg, we take Quolith next, cement our position. A few more strategic victories, and we can isolate Naphor."

"Ordinarily, I'd agree," Carred said, "but will we have time for a siege?"

"I hope so. Things don't move quickly on the mainland. I saw as much from the Order's dealings with the Kingdom of the Thousand Lakes. The Grand Master took months to respond to King Aelfyr's request for aid, and when he finally sent a force, it was arguably too small. But we won, though at a cost."

Carred blew out air between pursed lips. "Isn't that always the case? Come on," she said, "last place I want to be after sundown is atop Hallow Hill."

They had gone no more than ten yards when dozens of figures slipped out of the trees, congregating at the foot of the hill. Spindly, pale figures, with eyes like boiled eggs protruding from their flat faces and mouths like black gashes rimmed with razor sharp teeth.

"Dead-eyes," he whispered, putting a hand on Carred's shoulder.

Still more of the creatures came from the shadows of the forest, forming up in ragged lines to block their way. The deads just stood there and watched with their macabre, lifeless eyes, a hundred at least, more hanging back within the trees. An entire tribe.

And suddenly Anskar's belief in his newfound powers was shaken. He had seen what such a vast pack of dead-eyes could do when he was a novice; when the only thing that had saved the Order knights he was with had been Sareya and her moontouched abilities. But even then, it had been a close thing.

He reached within himself, feeling out the disparate threads of tidal sorcery, picking some, discarding others, then weaving threads of the dusk and the dark together.

But now it was Carred touching *his* arm.

"They're not doing anything," she breathed. "It's as if they're waiting."

Anskar emerged from his inner world and let his eyes rove the massed creatures in front of them. Save for a slight swaying motion, unified, as if they were in some sort of communal trance, they simply watched.

"Whatever you do," Carred said, gripping his hand now, "just make sure you don't let your ward down. I've a nasty feeling they're here for you, and that, by myself, I would just be dinner."

"Oh, you would be far worse than just dinner," Anskar said. Dead-eyes were notorious for defiling their prey in the most hideous ways. To his mind, they weren't much different to the lowest orders of demons, save for their sickly pale appearance and their lack of spines and horns. There was something almost translucent about the flesh of dead-eyes, like a cross between fish and corpses.

Anskar drew *Amalantril* as he and Carred advanced, still within the protection of his hybrid ward sphere. The sword's blade grew lambent, a wavering moonbeam, and upon his wrist, the vambrace's glow was visible beneath his shirt sleeve.

As one, more than a hundred dead-eyes prostrated themselves, hissing and making clicking noises with their tongues. As Anskar and Carred threaded a course between them, not a single dead-eye looked up at them. Anskar glanced this way and that, not quite trusting his ward sphere, angling his sword so he could counter any sudden attack. But then they were through, and climbing the sheer bank of Hallow Hill.

As they made the ascent, Anskar kept looking back at the dead-eyes, unable to suppress the panicked feeling that this was a trap. What if there were more dead-eyes all around the base of the hill or on the summit, waiting for their prey? Did dead-eyes do that? Did they possess the cunning, and the restraint, to set traps? Before, at the farmhouse, the tribe had been utterly chaotic, uncoordinated, and ravenous.

Several times, his boots caught on protruding rocks of chalk, and he had to look twice to reassure himself they were not skulls. Almost the instant they crested the summit, the clouds choking the sky dispersed as if blown away by some unnatural wind—because there was no wind now, not even the slightest breeze. It had all gone still, as if he and Carred had crossed into some other place, some liminal space between this world and the next. The late afternoon sun appeared through a watery haze, patterning the sky with a full rainbow. Was that a sign? For good or ill? From Menselas? He gave up speculating. How could he tell?

In the clear air over the summit, the ruined temple or tomb or whatever it was at the top stood out in stark contrast, a squat, lifeless mass that made him think of a bloated tick sucking blood from a dog. He didn't want to look at that place; didn't want to remember the day he had found the vambrace, the day he had collapsed, only to be found by Rosie and the team Vihtor had led in search of him all the way from Branil's Burg. He strode for the far side of the summit, but Carred gripped his shoulder and forced him to turn.

There in a doorway that had not been there a moment ago, silhouetted by the crimson glow from within, stood three figures in cowled robes. At first, Anskar thought they were wraithes, but then one of the cowled figures emerged into the open air. The sky instantly darkened, the sun plunging toward the horizon like a scuttled ship, leaving trails of blood in the watery firmament.

It was a man who came towards him, not a wraithe. A man with pallid skin and sunken cheeks and dark eyes set in deep calderas. The other two remained in the doorway, fingers interlaced in an attitude of prayer. He thought they might both be women, though skeletally thin. Something about their crooked stances implied arthritic pain or unnatural contortions of the spine.

The robed man stopped five feet from Anskar and Carred, though even that was too close. He exuded the stench of rotten meat, of ulcers and pus. In the dwindling light, his lips appeared blue, curling back as he spoke to reveal yellow teeth filed to points.

"Ah, brother," he said with a rasping wheeze, "we were told you would pass this way."

"Told?" Carred said. "By whom? I didn't even think of coming to Hallow Hill till we were halfway to Naphor."

The man ignored her, black eyes fixed to Anskar's—eyes the same as his own.

Anskar glanced at Carred, willing her to say more, because he could find no words.

"You accepted the gift?" the man asked.

Anskar managed to shake his head.

"Not fully, then; but a little, I see. You carry the taint of the dead. What did you do, bring a hapless shade back from the realm of the dead?" When Anskar said nothing, he went on. "How did that work out for you? Let me guess: not altogether satisfactory?"

"Anskar," Carred said, tugging at his sleeve. "We don't need to stay and listen to this."

Her eyes were wide with supernatural dread. He felt it too, only there was more. He felt inquisitive; on the precipice of a compelling mystery.

The man gave a smile with bluish-purple lips beneath his cowl, and nodded as if he understood what Anskar was feeling; as if he were a fisherman who had snagged his first catch of the day.

The two women emerged from the entrance, one impossibly ancient, strands of lank gray hair visible beneath her cowl and teeth missing, save for two elongated fangs. The other was young, and would have been beautiful save for how emaciated she was, her skin parchment thin and scraped over the protruding angles and ridges of her skull. He couldn't tell if any of the three were Niyandrian. If they were, every last trace of red pigment had been diluted from their skin, leaving them almost translucent—not dissimilar, he thought, to the dead-eyes waiting at the foot of the hill.

"He has great potential," the old woman said, but all Anskar could think about as she approached and her rancid stench hit his nostrils was the Abbess and what she had done to him. Carred's hand gripping his sleeve was suddenly unbearable, and he pulled his arm away.

The young woman sneered. "But he lacks control. He needs tutoring." She reached out gnarled, bony fingers and lifted his chin, forcing him to look her in the eye—dark, soulless eyes, just like his own. Her sneer turned into a cackle. "Could you endure that, young man? Do you have the resilience to survive my training?"

"I thought we agreed," the man said. "This one is mine. The last was yours, and let us not forget the mess you made of him."

The young woman released Anskar's chin and flowed back toward the entrance—literally glided backwards across the grass-tufted summit an inch above the ground.

"You are correct," the ancient crone said. "The boy is yours to teach." She too drifted back to the entrance.

"I don't want to be taught," Anskar said.

The man turned up his palms, crimson motes swirling around the skin of both hands. "I will not force you," he said, then added, "even if I could."

"Good," Carred said, her voice tight with fear. "Then leave us be." Her fingers were curled in a sign of warding, and Anskar felt the play of essence within her dusk-tide repository—paltry, compared with his, but it had grown somewhat, and seemed to still be in the process of developing.

"Wait," Anskar said as the man turned away from them. "What is it you think I need to learn?"

Without looking back, the man said, "What is it you most desire? What do we all desire, ultimately?"

Anskar looked hopelessly at Carred. *I don't know,* he said with a shrug.

"As Niyandrians," Carred said, "we are told to hunger for immortality."

The man turned back, a half-smile on his pallid face. "Go on."

"But to live forever is not the path of every Niyandrian. It is the provenance of kings and queens and necromancers."

The man nodded. "And which of those three is first? Which is most favored by the old ones?"

"Old ones?" Anskar blurted, heart thudding in his ribcage. "You mean Kayth—"

"Do not utter that name here!" the man said, and suddenly the two women were beside him, eyes black and forbidding. "You have not earned the right to speak it."

"Gently," the old woman said. "Else you might frighten him away."

"I don't fear you," Anskar said. Power swelled within him, but the three robed figures didn't retreat as he had expected. The man raised an eyebrow, goading Anskar on.

"A suggestion," the young woman said. "Show him what we have prepared inside." In a voice insipid with fake innocence, she said, "What harm could it do?"

"Anskar…" Carred warned.

"It's all right," he said. "I'll be all right."

He walked toward them, and the three figures turned and drifted inside the tomb, where the crimson glow seemed to devour them.

"Anskar," Carred said, "we didn't come here for this! Marith, remember? The Armor of Divinity…"

"I won't be long," he replied over his shoulder.

And then he stepped inside.

SIXTEEN

TREES SPED PAST MARITH IN a blurry haze. Steadings and crop fields, rivers, lakes—nothing but passing glimmers. Landmarks shot by too fast for her to recognize. Without the compass of Queen Talia's spirit sense, she would have lost her way many times. Then again, without Talia's compulsion, she would never have made it this far. One bout of the haste sorcery was enough to drain her repositories and leave her in need of a week's recovery in bed; but one haste sorcery would only take her a mere few miles. After the third bout of unnatural speed came to an end and she stuttered to a standstill, she had collapsed to her hands and knees, palms abraded by the rocky ground she had come to a stop upon. Talia had screamed at her to get up, and she would have, if it had been a simple matter of choice. But it was her body that was failing, not her mind, which was no longer in control of her actions, dispersed as it was throughout her being. Her body was no more than a chariot like those once driven into war by the ancient kings and queens of Niyas, Talia's spirit the charioteer steering it, Marith's ebbing reserves of sorcery the horse pulling it under the constant bite of the whip. But the haste sorcery took so much tidal essence, and she hadn't fully recovered from the clash with Anskar at Branil's Burg.

When she fell a second time, Talia had lashed her consciousness with dark sorcery, flaying her nerves, beating her as if she were a truculent dog that refused to move. After, when Talia must have realized it was no good torturing her for the failures of her body, the queen had flooded her with cold energies that rose up through the ground. Involuntarily, Marith's possessed body had gagged, but when the nausea passed, she once more regained her feet.

She fell for a third time amid emerald pasture land and grazing sheep, flat on her face, tasting mud and grass and Theltek only knew what else. Her stomach clenched, and her heartbeat was a ragged pounding that seemed to come from far away, as if it belonged to someone else.

Talia cursed as bile rose in Marith's throat and she vomited. The Queen's spirit roiled about within her like a ship that had lost its mooring. Marith's awareness rushed up from her marrow and her veins, from its dispersal beneath her skin, coalescing within her skull, reasserting itself as Talia seemed to drift away from her. But then Marith felt a violent surge of essence as Talia dredged putrid forces from deep below ground and flung them far and wide, ripping the life force from several sheep and flooding Marith's body with new energy. At the same time, Talia shoved Marith's consciousness out of her skull, forcing her to seek refuge throughout her ailing body as the Queen once more resumed control.

"Up!" Talia commanded. "I command you to rise!"

Invisible strings tugged Marith to her knees, then yanked her to her feet. She swayed, arms outstretched for balance.

I don't think I can go on, no matter how hard you push me. My body is too weak. Another haste sorcery and it will fail. You must know this.

"Your body will not die," Talia snapped through Marith's lips. "I will not permit it."

Again a vile flow rose up through the ground, entering Marith's feet and filling her veins. She could no longer hear her heartbeat. Her arteries felt lifeless, clogged with icy sludge. The bleat of the sheep all around her grew more and more remote, reaching her through the walls of some invisible cave. She grew numb all over; couldn't even tell if she continued to breathe. She became aware of her boots, soles flapping free from the dozens of miles they had covered in the space of minutes, and she somehow knew that her feet within them were lacerated down to the bone, though she could feel nothing. If she could have made herself look behind, back the way she had come, she felt certain there would be a long trail of blood.

"Your sacrifices are duly noted," Talia said. "But they are not yet over."

And Marith knew then: she would never again feel the wind and the sun on her face, never again drink mistberry wine nor feel the warmth of Carred pressed against her.

"It won't last," Talia said. "This is nothing but a necessary phase. Once we have the Armor of Divinity, I will restore you."

Tainted essence moiled within her repositories, the earth's stagnant flow still flooding them, filling them to bursting; and then, with a death-rattle breath and sheep scattering before her, Marith was off again, tearing through the pasture faster than a bolt of lightning, through the trees beyond, through mile after mile of the great forest of Rynmuntithe. In the distance, she glimpsed the passing blur of a massive citadel and restored city walls, streets, roads, and houses under construction. Naphor. And then she was permitted to slow as she came to a path through the brambles, the briars and thorns, the ferns and the tall grasses of untamed wild growth. At first she didn't see it. The dilapidated mansion was so overgrown with creepers, it could have passed for a hillock. But then she saw the caved-in roof, the trunk of a huge oak tree growing up out of the house.

Under Talia's control, she approached the partially collapsed portico and pulled aside the vines that covered the doorway, the splintered door lying on its side against the jamb. A baby rabbit froze in the hallway beyond as she entered, watching her. She feared that Talia was going to drain it, but to her surprise, the Necromancer Queen forced her to look away—the rabbit's cue to flee outside.

"What?" Talia said. "I like rabbits. For Theltek's sake, Marith, I am not the monster you take me for."

The entrance hall had more the feel of a gigantic burrow, it was so riddled with tree roots. The wooden floorboards had been reduced to sawdust by termites through which soil showed, tufted with weeds and grass. The ground itself seemed alive, writhing as it was with earthworms and maggots. It was ornamented with the bones of small birds and rodents and a more recent carcass, a badger, still bubbling with decomposition. The place should have stunk like a slaughterhouse or a sewer, but Marith could smell nothing, only see and hear in a muted sort of way. Judging by the black mold that covered the crumbling ceiling and the mildew that speckled the wall coverings, she guessed her dead sense of smell was a good thing.

"It was once beautiful," Talia muttered, causing Marith to turn a slow circle, looking around. "If prisons can ever be said to be beautiful."

You were imprisoned here?

"It was my childhood home. What more is there to say?"

Your father…

"The demon lord Domatai," she said, as if she'd swilled vinegar, "has many vices and cruelties. Come, we waste time dwelling on what is past."

It was oddly disconcerting, walking through the unfamiliar mansion with supreme confidence, mind ignorant, body knowing exactly where everything was, where not to step, which doors to open. And a good job, too, as the hallway Talia took her down started out with intact flooring but then suddenly dropped away, the flooded basement ten feet below teeming with rats. Before reaching the collapsed section of floor, though, Talia stopped beside a discarded mop and bucket and made Marith open a closet door. It was dark within, but Talia did something to her eyes—again that sensation of effluent sludging through Marith's veins—and she could see shelves stacked with empty bottles and jars, a large fishing net on the floor, something bulky bundled up inside it. Whatever Talia had done to Marith's eyes— some quality of the earth-tide to alter matter, or augment it—caused a limning of everything inside the closet with emerald light. Within the net, plates of armor glinted green, and Marith's repositories gave off a little shiver in response.

You want me to put it on? she asked.

"All but the helm," Talia said. "Carred was supposed to bring me void-steel, but she left it somewhere in Dorinah, somewhere I have no access to, which must mean Sheelahn's place."

The Ethereal Sorceress? Carred knows her?

"She returned from the abyssal realms with Anskar. They must have traveled in the *izindel*—lore stolen by the Ethereal Sorceress from the most sacred, most ancient sanctuary of the Orgols, and I don't mean Lorestone Citadel. Somewhere hidden away from the world, yet at the hub of all that transpires in Wiraya."

Like the Ethereal Sorceress herself, then, Marith said.

"And for the same reason. The *izindel* permitted the expansion of Sheelahn's once fledgling business across the entire span of Wiraya. The Orgol shamans, however, use the lore for an entirely different purpose. Believe me, when I retake the throne of Niyas, my first act will be to wrest this power from them and stop the Orgols interfering in the affairs of our world."

And the Ethereal Sorceress?

"I once offered her an alliance."

And she refused you?

"A large part of why Niyas fell. Sheelahn hates demons. I told her I felt the same way, but my blood is tainted and she would brook no exceptions. Until now, when apparently my son's demon blood does not have the same effect on her. I wonder why."

It is said Sheelahn makes and breaks kingdoms, Marith said.

"She is not alone in that, and is sometimes at loggerheads with a consortium of the mainland elites, though not averse to working with them when it furthers her ends. I will not forgive her for the aid she rendered the mainland armies during their invasion of Niyas."

As if she feared dwelling on the matter, as if she were on the brink of losing control, Talia made Marith take hold of the net and drag it, the armor clattering and scraping within, to the front of the mansion, to the entrance hall with the mold and the vine-covered doorway. Marith's hands fumbled at the knot closing the net. Talia, it seemed, was not used to untying knots, and she was also too anxious, too much in a hurry. Frustrated, she ripped at the net, but only succeeded in slicing the skin of Marith's fingers, blood staining the netting. Marith didn't feel a thing, save for surprise that she still had blood, that it was still red and not the color and consistency of tar.

"I did not lie to you," Talia said through clenched teeth. "I have pushed you beyond mortal limits, but not so far that one versed in necromancy cannot restore you to life."

Or a semblance of it, Marith thought, no longer caring that Talia could hear her. What did she have to lose?

"Believe me, you do not want to know," Talia said.

The earth-tide once more sluiced through Marith's veins as Talia directed its filthy flow through her fingers, reshaping the substance of the net to create an opening. One piece at a time, she removed the armor. In the scattered sunlight coming through the vines covering the entrance, each piece glinted, pristine silver with no hint of rust or tarnish:

pauldrons for the shoulders, greaves, vambraces, sollerets to cover the feet, a gorget for the neck. Last of all, Talia removed an immaculate great helm with a hinged face plate and not even a slit for the eyes.

"Put everything on," Talia ordered, "but not the helm. The helm completes the armor and seals the wearer in. We—your body—would be transfigured, translated from this realm, incapable of returning."

Before she realized she was doing it—that her body was complying—Marith had strapped on both vambraces.

They're way too big, she thought, but then the metal surrounding her forearms grew liquid and molded itself to her form. Same with the greaves, the sollerets, with every piece she held against her body; no buckles, no need for a padded gambeson beneath. It was as if the plate armor formed a second skin.

Talia caused Marith to stretch, to move about—silently, the armor light, almost insubstantial, yet it looked as though it weighed more than she did. There were only hairline gaps between each piece, but as she flexed and extended her limbs, she felt the slurry of tainted power rising through her veins, and even those gaps closed up, until it seemed as though the armor were forged from one seamless piece of divine alloy. Talia had done something—some application of the earth-tide. Marith started to panic. What if she couldn't remove the armor? What if she needed to pee?

"You won't," Talia said with smug satisfaction. "Never again."

Because of what you did to me? Because you turned me into a corpse?

And not just a corpse: an animated carcass encased in a seamless suit of armor. Marith wanted to thrash, to scream. If her lungs had still been under her own control, she wouldn't have been able to breathe.

"A little while longer, Marith, and your body will live forever."

But I won't? My body will live, but my spirit will… Will what? What will you do with my spirit? Send me to the realm of the dead in your stead? Is that what you planned to do to Anskar? To your son?

"Perhaps," Talia said. "But circumstances have forced me to find another way. And no, I will not oust you entirely from your body. I cannot, in any case. Without the presence of your spirit, the body would be an empty shell, a husk. It would break down and decay, and, in time, my shade would be forced to flee."

Compelled, Marith stooped to pick up the great helm and tucked it under her arm.

So, we're stuck with each other? And I'm as good as a corpse, a prisoner in my own body and mind.

"It means you had better hope we fare better against my son next time. Together, we are too much for him."

How do you figure that, considering what happened before?

"Because the armor will thwart his sorcery."

It made sense. Divine alloy was said to negate the dusk- and the dawn-tides.

But what about the dark?

"Let me worry about that. Anskar has but recently come into his dark-tide powers. Mine reached their fruition long before he was even born. And the earth-tide…" She made a scoffing noise. "I showed him scraps, nothing more. To challenge me with the earth-tide, with power over matter and over the dead, he would have to make sacrifices that no one should."

But you did?

Talia didn't answer that.

What about his sword? Marith suddenly thought. *It nearly drank both our souls.*

"Then it is a good job that a key component of divine alloy is *astrumium*, star metal, which is anathema to demons."

The sword is a demon?

"Perhaps it is an outgrowth of Anskar's own demon nature?" Talia wondered aloud. She seemed distracted by something outside; a scent, perhaps, that Marith no longer had access to? A movement? A sound?

"I did not foresee this," Talia said as she pulled aside some of the vines covering the entrance and stepped outside. "But then again, I worked hard to suppress what I had inherited from the abyssal realms. Now, be silent, Marith, for it seems we are being spied upon."

Marith had only ever seen one dead-eye before, and it had been dead, appropriately enough, but not before it had killed one of her goats. Her husband had still been alive back then. He'd caught the creature in the act of defiling the goat, fetched his woodcutting axe, and cleft its skull in two. Upon hearing the creature's last shrieks, Marith had come outside, and wished ever after she hadn't. She could still see its pallid, near-translucent skin, its bulging, lifeless eyes, the rank ichor spilling from its ruined head.

And now here she was confronted with a dozen or more of the creatures, loosely arrayed in a half circle facing the mansion, watching, twitching each time their blunt faces turned to keep her body in sight as Talia strode towards them, exuding confidence. She stopped mere feet from them, fixing each with a stare until it averted its boiled egg eyes.

Tidal forces shifted within Marith's body. She felt Talia's revulsion, her reluctance to draw upon such power; glimpsed flashes of scaled skin, slavering jaws, a wolf's head. Her mind was filled with thrashing, gurgling, hissing sounds. It felt as though a veil shadowed her consciousness, plunging her into a state not dissimilar to the depression that had crippled her upon her husband's death—nothing so dramatic as dead-eyes; he'd died of the lung rot and taken a long time about it, Marith watching him waste away before her, scarce daring to leave their house in case he passed away while she was out. She'd had the odd feeling that, so long as she could see him, some hidden power of hers could keep him in life. The fact that he'd breathed his last while her eyes were wide open, her hands frantically warming his cyanosed fingers, showed how wrong she could be. All that sorcerous power, that moontouched ability, and still she could do nothing when it really counted. And she could do nothing now, with Talia in full control of her body.

Talia forged some kind of connection, an accord of shadows that the dead-eyes seemed to recognize. There was a brief struggle, as if some other force, some other person or entity, were trying to keep Talia out, but then Marith felt tendrils of awareness retreating from the dead-eyes, all of whom stood rigid before her, obedient as well-trained hounds.

"There are three necromancers nearby," Talia whispered to herself in a drawn-out monotone. "Slaves of Kaythe Nurglich. Old rivals of mine. Huh!" she gasped. "Anskar is with them. Not just him: Carred."

Carred? Where? How near?

"Hallow Hill," Talia said, snapping out of her reverie. "Too near."

She flung out an arm, taking in the dead-eyes. "Guard the way to the house. If anyone approaches, kill them. Defile them. Eat their flesh."

The creatures screeched shrilly and loped off into the undergrowth.

Can they can stop him, if he comes? Marith asked.

"*When* he comes. Of course they can't stop him. See, I told you he was after the Armor of Divinity."

Maybe he's just after you, Marith said. *After both of us, seeing as it was my soul he was drinking with his sword, not just yours.*

"You think we should flee?" Talia said. "Where would we go? Your body would likely disintegrate before we made it back to your farm using the haste sorcery. Naphor? Fult Wreave and his warriors won't be in position for days, and in this condition—in you—I may not have the strength to defeat an entire garrison of Order knights on my own. No, we stand our ground, Marith. We end this now."

You want to kill your son? Truly?

"There are hands other than mine pulling the strings, Marith."

Whose hands? Theltek of the Thousand Eyes? This bloody Consortium I keep hearing in my head? Your father, Domatai?

"You forget Menselas, the Five."

He's real? I mean, how can a god have five faces? I thought Menselas was just some kind of mainland joke, or a lie they fabricated to control people. Menselas is the one pulling the strings?

"Maybe he tugs on a few strings, but not all of them. There are older powers even than he, and powers you could not even dream of. Even I..." And now Talia seemed to waver, Marith's voice regressing to the one she had used as a child. "Always there are hidden hands. Things change. Circumstances change. I never planned for this, wished it even less, but it has become necessary."

She sounded scared, a little girl frightened of the dark—or more likely terrified of her own father.

"Anskar is not who I prepared him to be. Always there are other influences out there in the world, those which would thwart a mother's right to raise her child as she sees fit. So, in answer to your question: yes, I do want to kill my son. I have no choice."

SEVENTEEN

THE TOMB WAS NOT AS Anskar remembered it. That first time he had been drawn to Hallow Hill, there had been ancient corridors, miraculously free of dust, and there had been violet light exuding from the scaleskin fungi that coated the walls. He remembered an unnatural chill and stairs into the depths, chambers and sarcophagi, the statue of a queen—his mother.

But this time it was stifling inside, the light red not violet. This time there were no steps to descend; he had the sense he was already as deep down as it was possible to go. And yet how had he come to be here? There had been no sensation of dislocation when he passed through the entrance, no explosion of white light behind his eyes, as with the *izindel* that he had traveled through between the Ethereal Sorceress's depots.

A quick glance behind showed no sign of the entrance. There was just solid wall there, not even the outline of a door. He stiffened, fought down the urge to lash out with sorcery. Far better to keep calm and play along for now, until he knew what this was about.

He turned back, blinking till his eyes adjusted to the crimson glare, taking in the chamber he found himself in: three walls that formed a triangle, the ceiling some thirty feet above molded or carved to resemble a gigantic wolf's head with gleaming rubies for eyes—the source of the infernal glow. The walls themselves were ribbed with dark stone, the seamless floor a pool of shadow with the sheen of black ice.

A triangular altar sat at the center of the room, upon it a Niyandrian girl of perhaps five or six, her nightdress besmirched with mud and the detritus of the forest. It was ripped in several places, as if snagged by brambles, and scored with thin lines of blood. The child stared at him, her cat's eyes wide, lips cracked and quivering. Her wrists and ankles were chained to the black stone of the triangle she lay upon.

Around the altar, one at each of its three points, hooded and robed, stood the man and the two women who had been outside the tomb. They had entered the building mere moments ahead of him, yet he had the impression they had been waiting for him, standing in these exact positions, for quite some time. Had they been mere illusions before? Spirit projections, similar to how Anskar had traveled to the core of the world for his meeting with Kaythe Nurglich? Were they projections now, or solid to the touch? Even if he did touch them and they proved tangible, how could he be sure his perceptions were true? He felt disoriented, in the panicked grip of a nightmare. His head began to pound. Nausea rose to swamp him.

"It will pass," the man said—the man who had offered to teach him. Anskar's eyes kept being drawn back to the girl on the altar. But teach him what?

"Am I really here?" Anskar asked, half-expecting to see Carred, to feel her hand clutching his, pulling him back to reality. "Or am I traveling in the spirit once more?"

"You are here," the old crone said.

"We all are," the young woman said.

A curved blade appeared in the man's bloodless hand: a rust-scabbed sickle. Had he conjured it out of thin air? Plucked it from within one of the voluminous sleeves of his robe?

The girl on the altar screamed, a scream that bounced from wall to wall, resonating shrill and strident all the way up to the wolf's head on the ceiling, where it died, swallowed by those ravenous jaws.

Anskar clutched his ears against the din despite the fact that it had ended. That cry of terror, of despair, had been rendered unnaturally loud by the configuration of the chamber, amplified to an earsplitting shriek. The wolf head's ruby eyes flashed, then seemed to narrow in anticipation of more to come. Moisture dripped from its jaws to spatter the girl's face, causing her to whimper. A leaking ceiling, or something else?

Anskar's every muscle clenched against a reoccurrence of such a banshee wail. *Don't feed the wolf!* he wanted to cry, but would have felt foolish doing so. He racked his brains for something else to say, something that wouldn't give credence to his rising fear that the wolf's head on the ceiling was alive and salivating.

"What is this girl doing here?" he asked.

The old woman touched a finger to her lips. "Do not startle the prey. You are shouting."

"I am?" Anskar said with measured softness. His voice sounded muffled in his ears.

"It was a loud scream," the man said, hand clamped firmly over the little girl's mouth as she wriggled beneath him, chains rattling. "An effect of the chamber. But it is how the Ancient of Ancients likes it. He prefers our terror to be unmitigated, absolute. A scream that does not shred the throat is no true scream. It is why we take great pains to follow the master's desires in every exacting detail, to serve him without concession, to be willing to do all things solely because he wishes it."

Anskar stared up at the ceiling, at the unrelenting glare of the wolf's eyes. "You serve the Corpse Maker?"

"He desires you, Anskar DeVantte," the young woman said, in a voice that suggested she was the one who desired him. Her voice had grown thick and husky, suggestive of unnatural lusts, her eyes beneath the hood lambent and green. "That means we three are sworn to do everything possible to make sure he has you."

But I already told him no, Anskar thought. *Did the wraithe lie to me, by giving me the impression I had a say in the matter? That taste of the Corpse Maker's power over the dead, my ability to raise Noni but not in the manner I had intended, or Orix, for that matter: was it just a game, the wraithe and its master all too aware of where it would lead me, where I would end up, whatever I might decide?*

"Let me guess," he said, swallowing bile. The thought of the young woman's desire for him made him think of maggots and rot. Nevertheless, images of her lying with him forced their way into his mind. He refused to consent to them, and drove them out with a scourging blast of dusk-dawn tide before they could root themselves in his flesh, when there would be no turning back.

"Careful," the man said. "You could injure your mind with such a crude banishing, and then you would be incapable of serving the Corpse Maker in all but the basest of ways, and then only the once, before your putrefied flesh sloughed from your bones and your bones crumbled to ash."

"Embrace the images you are given," the crone said.

As an image of the Abbess of the Hooded One started to arise, Anskar wove a barrier of tidal forces around his mind, the dawn, the dusk, and the dark intertwined. He gagged at the impression of slimy tendrils squeezing through the gaps in his eldritch net, insinuating their way into his imagination, boring deep into his thoughts and memories. He flooded his mind with the vileness of the earth-tide, and the tendrils withered and died.

"Good," the man said, nodding in approval. "You are a quick learner."

"Yet still he resists," the crone said. "Our path, Anskar—yours—is not to go the way of all things that perish, that die and decay. Accept the Ancient of Ancients. Give him death that you may live forever. Is this not what all Niyandrians desire?"

"Why did you not accept the Corpse Maker's gift when you went before him?" the young woman said. "Why do you refuse it even now?" She might as well have asked why he had not accepted her gift either. Why he never would.

But there was the thing: Anskar couldn't place his finger on when the very idea of intimacy had started to repulse him. Back at Branil's Burg, Vilintia had aroused such a violent reaction in him; had that been the start of it? She'd had the opposite effect on him before, when they had made love in her tent in Rynmuntithe, so what had changed?

The girl on the altar craned her head to look at him, something like hope in her fear-wide eyes.

"Here," the man said, holding the sickle out to Anskar.

"Why?" Anskar asked.

"Do not play dumb," the crone said, as if she were growing bored. As if she had given up on him.

"Kaythe Nurglich," the man said in an awed whisper, eyes flicking toward the ceiling, fearful, so it seemed, of offending the wolf's head, not wanting to provoke it into falling on him and devouring him with those razored jaws, "is a patient god. He understands your earlier reticence."

"I haven't changed my mind," Anskar said.

"Oh, but you could," the young woman said. Her robe fell around her ankles, exposing her emaciated body, her alabaster skin. Her ribs protruded, as did the ridges of her pelvis. Her breasts were flat, her chest boyish. Her head was a skin-covered skull, utterly bald, her eyes like a witch's lanterns of searing emerald set within deep and shadowed cavities.

"I could persuade you," she said, touching herself between the legs.

"By making me sick?" Anskar said, his voice thick with urgent need despite himself, despite the revulsion that crawled like maggots through his veins.

She fondled her boyish breasts, some foul discharge seeping from her nipples where she squeezed them, as she edged round the altar toward him, stepping out of her crumpled robe.

Anskar's heart began to gallop. His mind screamed horror, but his body didn't agree. He closed his eyes. Saw the Corpse Maker, wolf-headed, scaly, the cloaca opening on his chest, the thrashing tendrils that emerged. With a gasp, he opened his eyes just as the young woman leaned in to kiss him, her tongue sinewy and black, flicking from her mouth.

And he punched her full in the face, his fist coming out the back of her head in a shower of soot and ashes.

Anskar stumbled away, mouth gaping with shock, the hand that had hit her shaking beyond control. The woman's body hit the ground with a sound like the rustle of falling leaves, then dispersed in a billow of black smoke.

Silence.

Even the girl upon the altar ceased to move, not even the hint of a whimper leaving her lips.

Anskar glanced at the crone, at the man, but could see nothing of their expressions beneath their cowls. But there was something about the man's bearing, some hidden aspect of his demeanor that suggested a smirk.

"Is she dead?" Anskar asked.

The crone let out a harsh, grating cackle.

"Aren't we all?" the man said. "Dead or dying, or forever undying, once an accord has been struck between life and death. But smoke and ash: it is not the mark of the living, so, yes, she is gone. For now.

Maybe for good. How much more necessary you have made yourself. How much more… vital." Once more, he offered Anskar the sickle. "Take it."

"No," Anskar said, backing away to the wall, willing it to dissolve and let him outside. "I won't do it. I won't kill the girl."

"Idiot," the crone said. "How can you raise her, if she is not first killed?"

The girl was back to watching Anskar, her eyes glistening with unshed tears, chin trembling.

"Raise her as what, exactly?" he asked. *As a prisoner inside her own decomposing body, like Noni?*

"There are many levels to the mysteries of the Corpse Maker," the man said in a kindly tone. He was starting to sound like Brother Tion, the man Anskar had trusted above all others, until he hadn't. "But we all must start somewhere. Let us see where you are at. Have faith in us, Anskar. What you are being offered is the prehistoric dream of our most primal ancestors, granted to but a few."

"To my mother?" Anskar asked. "Did Queen Talia of Niyas come here to you? Did she…" A lump clogged his throat. It felt like knotted eels, bundled together, wriggling and coated with slime.

"Did she accept the gift of the Corpse Maker?" the crone asked. "Only she can answer that question. For us to do so is forbidden."

"And we do not want to offend…" The man pointed a finger at the wolf's head on the ceiling.

"So you're saying she did, then?" Anskar challenged. "Did my mother kill an innocent child, like this one?" *Of course she did,* he told himself. *After all, she abandoned one. She abandoned me. She permitted hundreds to be taken by the Order of Eternal Vigilance as they sought the true heir of Niyas.*

Again there was silence, the man still holding the sickle out to him, the crone folding her arms across her chest, the child swallowing repeatedly, her body shuddering with suppressed sobs, as if she knew what Anskar would decide. As if she had despaired of any last lingering threads of hope.

Anskar smiled at the girl and tried to reassure her with the merest wink.

Opening his arms wide, he let power rise within him, the four tides moiling about each other, each seeking dominance until he forced them to compromise. There came the sensation of sparks scalding his innards, of acid clouds and fire. As his feet left the floor, the crone flinched and stepped back. The little girl's eyes grew bright with awe; she propped herself up on her elbows, as much as her chains allowed.

The man lowered the sickle. He radiated not so much fear as disappointment.

"You overestimate your powers," the crone said. "You cannot stand against us."

The man said nothing, merely watching Anskar like a predator not quite ready to strike.

"Release the child!" Anskar demanded, volcanic forces roiling within him. "I assume my mother was able to stand against you, which is why she is called the Necromancer Queen. What makes you so certain I cannot?"

The man and the crone exchanged a look.

And suddenly Anskar was outside the tomb, back in the fading light of day atop Hallow Hill, the little girl's despairing scream a skirling memory from a distant place. Claw marks of red scored the horizon as the sun sank below the height of the trees. There was only solid wall in front of Anskar, and he hammered at it with his fists, crying out for the little girl and knowing he had failed her. But what else he could have done?

"Let me in!" he raged. "Face me, you bloodless cowards!"

His voice died where it struck stone, unheard, unanswered. Power bloomed in his chest. A corona of emerald-veined shadows formed around each fist. Thunder boomed with each blow. Luminous green sparks showed upon impact. The earth beneath Anskar's feet grumbled and shook. And yet the wall of the tomb was completely unscathed. With a roar of defiance, he redoubled his efforts, drove all four tides at once down his arms, into his fists, but suddenly there was a hand on his shoulder, gripping him and pulling him back. Spittle flew from his mouth as he spun round.

Carred let go his shoulder. She recoiled at the expression on his face; would not meet his dark eyes. Power ebbed away inside him, and he took several deep and labored breaths to quiet his pounding heart.

"Forgive me," he said, scarce above a whisper. "In there… What I saw… The screaming… What they wanted me to—"

Carred silenced him by sweeping out an arm to indicate the dead-eyes fanned out around the hilltop the side she and Anskar had ascended. The creatures must have followed them up, but they just stood there, motionless and mutely watching.

"The screaming was our horses. The dead-eyes grew frenzied the minute you disappeared inside. Much longer and I imagine I would have been next. Whatever were we thinking, leaving horses unprotected amid a pack of deads?"

"I wasn't… Thinking, I mean," Anskar said.

"Neither was I. Well, we have only ourselves to blame. It's going to be a long walk back to Dorinah. Thank Theltek it's not far from here to the mansion."

"Are you sure it was just the horses screaming?" Anskar asked. "You heard nothing from inside the tomb? There was a little girl—"

"I don't need to know what happened in there," Carred said. "Unless you did something you ought not to have…?"

Anskar swallowed thickly and shook his head. Then he realized what Carred was implying—or at least what he thought she implied. "No!

How could you…? I was trying to save her."

"Those three… what were they, necromancers? They wanted you to harm this girl?" She started back toward the tomb.

"It's no good," Anskar told her, gripping her arm.

There were tears in her eyes as Carred turned around. "Was she alone? Had they snatched her away from her home? Was she lost and all alone?"

"There's nothing we can do," Anskar said, ashamed of his own failure, shocked he could be so powerful yet so impotent when it mattered. "I can't find a way to re-enter the tomb, and even if I could…"

"She's dead?"

That last wailing scream… Now he had calmed down, it seemed unmistakable. Undeniable. He nodded, and Carred stiffened then wiped the tears from her eyes. A new resolve came over her—that of a General used to defeat and knowing no good could come over bemoaning her losses. The only way she knew was onwards, deeper into futility.

"Come on, then," Carred said, heading towards the far side of the hilltop, opposite the dead-eyes. "We should go."

"But Naphor…" Anskar said, starting after her. "The sentries atop the walls will see us."

"Not if we don't get too close," Carred said. "And not if you use that dark-tide power of yours to hide us."

"Yes," Anskar said. "Yes, that will be easy."

Relieved there was something he could do, he wove a cloak of shadows around them both, and they began the descent of the hill, nascent moonlight outlining the rebuilt central tower of the ancient Niyandrian capital, defiled as it was by the occupation of the Order of Eternal Vigilance.

Suddenly he longed for the old days, when the Order had been everything to him; when he'd been tucked away inside the safety of the

Burg's walls, with Tion as his guide and mentor, and Vihtor the model of what every good servant of Menselas should be. So simple. So pure. So innocent.

So bloody naive! Anskar thought.

And still the little girl's cries echoed around his head.

EIGHTEEN

IN THE DAYS BEFORE THE fall of Naphor, the city's air was known for its intermittent smog, a pall of shadow-like mist that roiled in the atmosphere and drove the inhabitants indoors. At such times, the air smelled of tar and something Carred was inclined to think of as rotten mushrooms. People complained of difficulty breathing, of chills, and of bad dreams—for those who could sleep at night. And now here she was, within a sphere of the same fuliginous smog that encompassed her and Anskar as they walked. Her once dormant repositories shivered in protest at the murky tidal forces that powered Anskar's sorcery. When she tried to identify the source, the actual tides that he used, her dawn-tide repository convulsed so hard she almost retched. The dusk-tide repository grew hot within her mind, as if it sought to ward itself.

It seemed obvious now, why the strange pollution had visited Naphor at odd, apparently random times. The reason had everything to do with Queen Talia and the sorcerous experiments she used to conduct in the catacombs beneath the palace—all that remained of the foundations of the first, pre-historic city upon which Naphor had been founded. A city that, according to the myth, had been reduced to dust by the newly ascended gods—Theltek among them—who opposed the tyranny of Kaythe Nurglich. Nothing grew on the site of the original city for centuries, but always the catacombs remained, a locus of the ancient powers and the haunt of necromancers still loyal to the ways of the Corpse Maker. It made sense that the Necromancer Queen was behind the smog and that the same powers now issued from her son. Talia had been half-demon. But Carred felt certain there was more to the obscuring sphere than a manifestation of the dark-tide by the way the threads of shadow almost seemed to congeal, the way the sorcery stank. Whether Anskar was aware of it or not, there was something impure about his casting, as if the powers he wielded were in some way corrupted or had a mind of their own.

And it wasn't just the sphere, designed to keep them from sight as they passed within a quarter mile of the city walls, that felt wrong. It was Anskar, too. Whatever had afflicted his eyes and turned them into orbs of obsidian seemed to have spread like a contagion to the rest of him. He had started to lose weight, far too rapidly for it to be natural. His skin had grown pale, his cheeks sunken, and his black eyes were set in ever-deepening pits. Lank hair, like seaweed smothered in oil, plastered his scalp and half his face. His muscles, once so full and defined, were atrophied. When she had put a hand on his shoulder to pull him back from the tomb, he had been frigid to the touch, just like his mother. He had done something, she just knew it; made some sacrifice in return for his burgeoning powers. Talia had been the same, always making compromises, maybe even pacts, in order to strengthen herself against threats real and perceived. And the more powerful she had grown, the more frightened she had become, to the point that she couldn't sleep alone, and if she could, she would likely have frozen to death.

Carred threw repeated glances at Anskar, but visibility was poor within the sphere, a shade darker than the twilight without. Her skin tingled in his proximity, screamed at her to get away from him—far away; but when she started to lag behind, he turned to her and snapped at her to keep up.

"There are sentries," he said, with a sharp nod at the partially restored curtain walls, little more than a thickening of the darkness at the extent of her vision. The fact that she could see no one at this range only made her that much more uncomfortable. Anskar clearly could. "And besides," he said, "I need you to lead. I don't know the way to this mansion."

"Then it's a good job I came," she retorted. He had wanted to leave without her. Theltek help Marith if Carred had permitted that! But she suspected he could have found the way by himself, if he had needed to. Or he could have asked Noni, or whatever it was that now inhabited her corpse.

Carred led them in a wide loop, putting as much distance between them and the city as she could, despite adding more than a mile to their journey. They plunged deep into Rynmuntithe Forest. In the crepuscular light, overhanging branches became the gnarled arms of giants ending in savage claws. Every sound, every hoot and scamper and growl, became demonic, until it felt as though they were back in the abyssal realms. All in Carred's mind, she assumed. Anskar showed no sign of wariness, striding through the woodland as if he couldn't contain his need to pit himself against his mother. Carred had to half-run to keep up with his long, loping strides. Old childhood fears of abandonment, of floating helms, of lost ragdolls, lurked at the edges of her awareness.

They continued the way they had been going until the city was out of sight, then struck a new course through the trees. So long as she felt the city was off to her left, Carred was confident she was heading the right way. After another hour stumbling through the thickening dark, Carred spotted a flicker of light in the distance. They slowed down, proceeding cautiously, as more lights appeared through the trees to their right.

"What are they?" Anskar asked.

"Are your spooky eyes failing? I thought you could see the sentries atop the walls?"

"I didn't see them. I sensed."

"If you ask me," Carred said, "those are fire lights." And now she thought about it, she could smell the smoke and the scent of something roasting—it might have been deer.

He nodded. "I thought as much. I can sense people—upwards of two hundred. Niyandrians."

Now it was Carred's turn to nod. "I saw them from the top of Hallow Hill, coming in through the forest. They could be rebels, but not mine, if they are. And I told Vilintia to do nothing other than organize things back at Branil's Burg."

"Then whose?"

She ground her teeth together. "I don't know for sure," she answered, "but I can guess."

It had been an organized force she had seen weaving through the woods—or rather, several of them, coming from different directions. Forming an advance party, no doubt. Those in the local vicinity who had received the word to assemble. Talia's so-called sleepers? There was only one person she could think of who a sizable portion of disaffected Niyandrians might follow instead of her.

The only problem was, the only thing that didn't quite make sense, was that Fult Wreave hated Queen Talia and everything she stood for. She was a usurper queen to him, the one to end the Ickthal Dynasty and deprive him of his birthright. So, if it was Fult Wreave, what was Talia offering in return for his allegiance? Unless Wreave didn't know it was Talia. But why would he follow Marith? Because he was following one or the other of them, she was certain. There was no way on Wiraya

Fult Wreave had the guts or the resources to go up against the Order's garrison at Naphor on his own initiative. She should know. She had tried before, and it hadn't exactly turned out well.

"You think my mother is gathering an army?" Anskar asked.

Carred shrugged. "If Noni is right and she's returned to the mansion…"

"For the Armor of Divinity," Anskar said. "Noni said my mother came here looking for the armor, not to wage war against the Order of Eternal Vigilance."

"And what then? What will she do when she finds the armor? Disappear to some other realm, never to be seen again? That's not the Talia I know. It's this world she wants—this island. She wants to rule here and live here forever, not in some distant place. She must have plans to modify the armor. Theltek's multi-pronged…!" She realized what those plans involved; the sole purpose of her mission to the abyssal realms: "My void-steel! It's not as if Talia was hiding her intentions from me."

"The void-steel is still in the ethereal Sorceress's depot," Anskar said. "Along with the star-metal I brought back."

"But what if she's retrieved it?"

Anskar shook his head. "When would she have had the time? Noni would have said something, had Talia and Marith teleported to the depot before coming here. And in any case, Sheelahn hates demon bloods. Menselas alone knows why she tolerated me."

"Sheelahn is dead," Carred said. "She was stabbed in the back, remember?"

"By Blosius," Anskar said. "I trained with him. Fought him in the first trial. I thought we were friends."

"Presumably, so did the Ethereal Sorceress."

"But there was no body. Afterwards… just an empty robe."

"We'll deal with it later," Carred said. "First, we have to help Marith."

Anskar's expression was hard to read, given his black eyes, but it seemed to suggest a shrug, an "If we can."

They left the scatter of firelights behind them as they plunged into the deep thicket at the edge of the woods.

"There!" Carred said, pointing through the brambles, to where she could see the bulk of the mansion. There was a wavering emerald light coming from the doorway, a lone figure silhouetted within its ambit.

Marith.

Something pale and spindly emerged from the thicket off to Carred's right. Another appeared to the left, then another, until a cordon of dead-eyes surrounded Anskar's shadowy sphere.

"Can they see us?" Carred asked anxiously.

Anskar shook his head as he sighed. "I'm not sure they can see at all with those bulbous eyes. But they can sense us."

The creatures—there were upwards of a dozen of them, bow-legged, skeletal arms that terminated in filthy clawed fingers. No movement of their boiled egg eyes, which were somehow luminous in the dark, counterparts to the twin moons now showing through the clouds.

Anskar dispelled his sorcerous sphere. "What's the point?" he asked. "Might as well save energy."

He needed to? It was good to know he wasn't quite the god he had appeared back at Dorinah.

Carred realized her hand was tightly wrapped around the hilt of her sword. She had pulled the blade an inch out of the scabbard, when Marith called from the doorway of the mansion, a strangled cry that turned into a scream: "Carred!"

"Marith!" she called back, but then a pallid limb slashed at her face, and she only just jerked aside in time, air whipping past her cheek. She pivoted as she drew her sword, but the dead-eye was too close—so close she almost gagged on its fetid breath.

All around her pale forms blurred as the other dead-eyes swarmed to the attack. She heard the rasp of Anskar's sword leaving its scabbard, and immediately her skin crawled. Carred ducked beneath the swipe of a claw and rammed her sword through the dead-eye's belly, spilling guts. And not just guts, she saw as she stumbled back, ripping her blade free: half-digested carcasses of lizards, frogs, and insects slopped to the forest floor, and among them an ear and an eyeball—the slitted pupil giving it away as Niyandrian.

A dead-eye shrieked behind her. She turned to see Anskar's sword embedded in its chest, the dead-eye twitching as it shriveled before her eyes, its skin wrinkling, sagging, deflating. The creature's bulbous eyes sank within their sockets, and the head shrank till it was a desiccated husk. To Carred's nascent sorcerous senses, Anskar's sword seemed to throb. Dark essence gushed from the wound it had made in the dead-eye and coursed along its blade. She caught a glimpse of Anskar's eyes, black and gleaming, and his lips were curled in what she took for a smirk. All seen in one timeless instant, while she imagined the sound of the sword slurping, then singing out for more as Anskar ripped the blade free and the dead-eye's corpse flopped to the ground, flaccid and empty.

Pallid fingers grabbed her wrist. She spun, elbowing the dead-eye in the face, then chopped down with her sword. Black blood spurted from the artery in its neck. She kicked another in the chest as it surged toward her. Claws raked her thighs and grabbed at her boots. All around her was a chaos of snarling and panting, the sounds of lust as much as of savagery.

Anskar's sword pierced another chest, but before it could drink, two more dead-eyes dragged him to the ground, and he lost his grip on the hilt. Carred tried to reach him, but an arm wrapped around her throat from behind, pulling her back. She kicked and she cursed, spat in a fiendish face, hammered her sword pommel into a pallid head.

Black fire erupted around Anskar, sending the two dead-eyes pinning him shrieking into the air, only to smack down into the ground ablaze with dark flames that wouldn't go out no matter how the creatures thrashed and rolled. Like a puppet suspended from invisible strings, Anskar rose effortlessly to his feet. Shadows effused from his skin, molding themselves into plates and bands of dark, gaseous armor that engulfed him completely. He flung shards of shadow Carred's way, and the dead-eyes holding her slumped to the ground. Then he ripped his sword free from the dead-eye's chest and kicked the creature violently aside, sending it crashing into a tree with a pulpy splat. Almost disdainfully, he hurled shadows, and his blade rose and fell.

Carred turned at movement from behind her—a dead-eye fleeing into the thicket. With three quick steps she caught up to it and sliced it across the back of the legs. The creature squealed as it fell, and she shoved her blade through its neck, then bent double, panting, her heart thundering in her ears.

A shadow passed over her, and the hairs on the back of her neck stood on end. She glanced up to see Anskar, wreathed in his armor of shadow, striding towards Marith.

"Don't hurt her!" she pleaded, straightening up and running after him.

He held up a hand without even turning back to look at her. Her knees buckled and she pitched to the ground, her legs refusing to obey her.

"Leave this to me," Anskar said in a voice like distant thunder.

"Anskar!" she cried, crawling after him on her belly, dragging her sword with her.

Marith stepped from the mansion's doorway. Away from the emerald light, she ceased to be a silhouette, but even so, Carred almost didn't recognize her. Marith's hair hung lank, and it was encrusted with filth—dirt, dust, the detritus of the woods. The skin of her face had lost almost all trace of its natural red hue. It looked as though Marith wore a death mask carved from alabaster. Her cheeks were sunken, her blue-tinged lips stretched in a rictus grin. And her eyes… black like Anskar's, glistening orbs of obsidian set within the shadows of deep calderas.

Marith was sheathed in armor—full plate armor that left only her head exposed, somehow the separate pieces all seamlessly melded into one skin-hugging whole.

There was a slight discoloration above the heart, where the Necromancer Tain had mended the armor. When Carred had found it in the wreckage of a sunken ship, a sword had pierced the breastplate. But it had been a set of armor then, a suit comprised of many pieces. The metal—divine alloy or whatever it was—seemed to have molded itself to every contour of Marith's body, like a second skin, impassable.

Carred's heart lurched. Not only did Marith look like a dead woman walking, but there was so little of her visible. Marith held the armor's great helm under her arm, a piece with no hinged face plate and no eye-slit to see through. *Please no,* Carred thought, *don't put it on.* The head was all that remained of her beloved Marith. If the helm took even that from sight, there might be no coming back. Theltek, what would happen if every last part of Marith were encased? Translation to another realm, as the Necromancer Tain had claimed? Or had Talia done something to prevent that, worked some dark sorcery that would keep Marith's body here, enslaved, forever buried beneath a skin of metal?

Carred groaned, the sound coming from the pit of her stomach. If the armor could never be removed… All in the time it took to gasp one strangled breath, Carred grieved the death of sensations she would never feel again, not with Marith: the warmth of their bodies pressed together beneath the sheets, the soft caresses; those times Marith would brush the back of her hand as they sat together sipping mistberry wine; those tender goodnight kisses and those last tired words before sleep. And yet even without the helm, Carred knew her lover was gone. Whatever was left of Marith beneath the metal, if it was anything like her face, was no more than an animated corpse.

The groan grew in pitch and volume, till it opened her mouth in a wail of disbelief, of horror, of despair. Something in her cry caused Marith to flinch, to shiver and spasm. Her black eyes rolled up into her head and came down white as a dead-eyes'. Marith flung out her arms for balance. Like a woman who had fallen asleep standing, she stumbled, then lurched a step toward Carred.

Anskar moved to intercept her, a mournful drone coming from his sword. It caused Carred to shudder even as she struggled to her knees. The sword didn't sound as if it were mourning for what had happened to Marith; it was grieving for its own hunger, because it hadn't been given permission to feed. Not yet.

But Anskar showed no restraint as he strode purposefully toward Marith, accepting what Carred could not: that the body that confronted them might once have been Marith's but now belonged to another, and Carred could feel the hatred coming off Anskar in waves of shadow.

Carred reached her feet as Anskar drew back his sword. She stretched out an arm in a vain attempt to draw him back. There was no sign of alarm on Marith's death-mask face, no attempt to defend herself.

Carred, help!

A strangled cry within her mind caused Carred to stumble. She leaned her weight on her sword, both hands wrapped around the hilt.

"Marith?" she cried. "Marith, is that you?"

Anskar hesitated. He turned back toward her, his face hidden by the helm of shadows, conveying nothing.

Here… Marith's voice said in her mind. *Quickly. I can't do this for long. Drowning…*

"It's Marith," Carred said. "Really Marith, inside and out."

Anskar looked back at Marith. "You're sure?" The shadow helm encasing his head dissolved, leaving only his body protected—just like Marith's.

"That's right, isn't it, love?" Carred asked, a sliver of hope giving strength to her legs. "You're fighting back."

Using her sword as a walking stick, she advanced a couple of steps till she was at Anskar's side. Her heart screamed at her to get closer, to take Marith in her arms; but her head had yet to be convinced. "Keep talking to me, Marith. Tell me what you need me to do."

A sound like a wheeze inside her mind, then a series of jumbled thoughts, barely started sentences, throttled at birth.

"Help her!" Carred screamed.

She recoiled from the power streaming from within Anskar, an amalgam of tides that crashed into the armored body.

"Marith!" Carred screamed.

I'm sorry, love… I'm trapped… I'm…

"Gone, is what she is." It wasn't Marith's voice now; it was Talia's. "You made me do this, Carred. This is all your fault."

Carred wailed. Lost herself in a despair-driven rage. She charged at the armored figure and swung her sword in a murderous arc. There was an earsplitting boom, then the sensation of flying backwards through the air. She hit the ground hard. Air burst from her lungs. Stars exploded in her skull. She could smell blood. *That's funny,* she thought: she still had her grip on her sword.

She heard the crunch of boots, the hungry growl of Anskar's sword, the fizz and crack of wild sorcery.

And then she was falling through the soft and enveloping dark.

NINETEEN

AMALANTRIL YEARNED FOR BLOOD AND souls. The sword screamed for them as it squirmed in Anskar's grip. And he did nothing to hold it back as he flung volley after volley of shadow-shards at the armored thing that housed his mother. Because that's all he saw: a *thing* that had once been Niyandrian. Had once been Marith. All that remained was the ghoulish head, black eyes gleaming, blue lips drawn back a snarl that evoked a savage beast fighting for its life. Only it wasn't Queen Talia's life, was it? She had already died, and now here she was, having dispelled Marith's soul—for he had *seen* it the instant it happened, same as he could still hear Marith's terrible wailing as she spun away in a vortex not perceptible to normal eyes, to a place that was somewhere and nowhere. He had been there, albeit briefly: the realm of the dead.

Shadows bounced off Talia's armor, streaking skywards in long, inky ribbons; so many shadows they formed a pall across the sky, smothering the twin moons. *Amalantril* scraped along the breastplate with a high-pitched screech, sending up sparks but not even scratching the divine alloy. Talia staggered back under the ferocity of his attack, her blue lips moving with the words of a cant—of several cants—as she warded her unprotected face from shadows.

Before she could recover, Anskar cast again, masking his sorcery with a vicious chop of his sword that connected with a shoulder guard, sending a jolting pain up his wrist and arm from the impact.

This time Talia barely even flinched, the Armor of Divinity absorbing the brunt of the blow. As he had known it would. Lighting sparked from his free hand, striking the breastplate in a coruscating blast that briefly blinded him.

When the glare died down, Talia was still standing. Black fire erupted from his mother's eyes, and Anskar threw up his dark-tide ward sphere; but before the flames touched the ward, they retracted until they were just flickering eyelashes of flame.

"We don't need to do this, my son," Talia said. "It wasn't meant to happen this way."

"Too late," he snarled. "You should have thought of that before you provoked the attack at Branil's Burg. Before you ousted Marith's spirit. Before you started a war Niyas can't win!"

He swung for her unarmored head, but a sword of shadow parried his blade, springing up from Talia's fist faster than he could blink. *Amalantril* glimmered with silver radiance, emitting a wail of hunger and rage. Talia glided to one side and thrust for Anskar's heart. He barely blocked in time, then angled off, gasping for breath.

"You put all your effort into knock-out punches," his mother told him as she began a predatory circle, shadow sword extended, keeping him at range. "Sorcery is an art form, not brute force. You must learn to measure your attacks."

"And you must learn to keep your mouth shut!" Anskar cried as he darted in, feinting low with his sword, drawing her defenses downwards, and then lashing her unprotected head—her mind—with the Wracking Nerves.

His mother screamed. Her shadow blade dissipated as she threw up a frantic defense, a mesh of interwoven strands of the dark-tide designed to keep his attack out.

But Anskar was relentless, and the Abbess had taught him too well. He had flayed far worse than Queen Talia. He had wracked the nerves of full-fledged demons.

She wailed, froth spilling from her mouth, as he excoriated her thoughts, her memories, the very fabric of her mind, and every nerve of every part of her—Marith's—body.

See? he thought cruelly. *That'll teach you to take over someone else's flesh!* "You'd have been better off without a body!" he snarled. "You still might be! Go now! Go on, get out!"

Talia's face contorted with excruciating pain, oily tears bleeding from her black eyes and tracking down her hollow cheeks. Spasms made her limbs dance.

He intensified the attack, and her back arched. She gasped, spewed blood, and convulsed from head to toes. But still she was defiant. Still she refused to depart, clenching her teeth as blood drooled from cyanosed lips. Slowly, little by little, she raised the great helm above her head.

"You wouldn't dare," Anskar said, redoubling his attack and hoping to make her drop the helm as she shuddered and spasmed. "Without void-steel added, it's a one-way journey." Carred had told him what had happened to the necromancer Tain, whose body remained trapped in some other realm, head kept alive within his helm, until Carred had grabbed him by the nose and ripped him from it. "Is this what you want—to cease to exist? Go ahead, then. It's fine by me. I don't care, *mother!*"

Talia's entire body clenched as power surged within her. Phenomenal power that made Anskar step back—the unmistakable vileness of the earth-tide boiling within her, threatening to explode. And not just the earth-tide; there was a colossal outpouring of the dusk—enough to incinerate a small forest or destroy an entire town.

Frantically, he sought a defense. He plunged his senses through the ground and ripped what he thought of as tidal waste from the buried depths. Husks of insects, casts of worms, fragments of animal bone emerged from the topsoil and shot into the air, disintegrating, their combined dust adding itself to the dark-tide that surrounded him in a glistening sphere of shadow.

Talia literally throbbed with unbridled power. The air around her head shimmered, casting the helm she held aloft in a pulsating blur. Her face twisted under some unimaginable force, and the Armor of Divinity glowed red hot, as if heated from within, then white.

Anskar took another step back, then another. His mother was going to unleash an explosion, the same as she had done when she'd destroyed the old city of Naphor, taking herself with it. He braced himself, praying to Menselas that his sorcerous defenses would be enough.

But then he realized the earth-tide and the dusk- that threatened to burst Talia asunder weren't aimed at him. He didn't need his sorcerous senses to tell him that she had turned the power on herself. He could see it at work, rendering her armor incandescent, causing its metal plates to ripple then melt, one piece into another, the exposed flesh beneath bubbling and blistering. Talia's scream was part pain, part exultation, a scream of terror and triumph. Liquid metal combined with melting flesh, intermingling, becoming one. And within, at the core of this burning horror, Anskar could perceive the wavering dance of Talia's shade as it expanded to every inch of her molten form. There was no distinction now between armor and flesh, between flesh and spirit. The three had become one, Talia's body a white-hot statue of melded divine alloy, muscle, skin, and bone. Her form changed before his eyes: a little more height, the limbs longer and thinner, the waist so narrow he could have snapped it like a twig had it not been formed from a hideous composite of tissue, bone, and metal. Could it even be called a body now? Did it still have organs within—lungs, a beating heart, a brain inside the skull? She had made herself a statue. A living, moving sculpture, impossible to harm by normal means.

Too late, he realized what she had done; what desperate sacrifice he had driven her to make.

She lowered the helm over her head, and Anskar watched in awed fascination as it grew instantly fluid and conformed to the shape of— not Marith's face, but his mother's: the way Queen Talia had appeared when he'd glimpsed her shade in the realm of the dead.

An unnatural wind funneled down from the sky—he was too stunned to tell if it was the dawn or the dusk-tide. Lambent with unimaginable heat, Talia spread her arms wide and let the chill gusts cool her. She clenched and unclenched her fists, threw back her head, and opened her mouth in a cry of exultation.

And then she fixed Anskar with her eyes—not the twin black orbs they had been earlier: they were stars of burning argent within the iron gray of her flesh. He wanted to look away from her nakedness, but fear and awe compelled him. She was lithe and willowy, one step shy of skeletal. He looked with part unease, part resentment. Her narrow hips evoked scorn. Her arms, long and sinewy, resembled smooth-barked tree limbs. No hair—not on her head, nor anywhere else. Smooth all over, like a casting of steel. But she had a strange sort of beauty, a macabre attraction that made him hate her more than he already did. Brazenly, as if she knew she held him enthralled, as if she knew she could compel by the sheer fact of her appearance, she stalked toward him.

"You know, of course, what this means?" Talia said as she turned her palms upwards, seeming to enjoy his helplessness.

"That you no longer need me?" Anskar replied.

"Need is never a good thing," Talia said. "Isn't it better for both of us if I want you, rather than need you?"

"Want?" he asked, looking up, hoping she didn't mean what he thought she meant—remembering Uspeth and the unnatural attentions he received from his mother, the Abbess.

"Stupid boy," Talia said. "This body has risen beyond such animal lusts."

"Then why is it still here? I thought the gods ascended to a higher plane."

"It is here," Talia said, "because I so will it."

"Because you used the earth-tide to alter your Marith's flesh and the Armor of Divinity?" Anskar asked. "Because you somehow changed the nature and the purpose of the armor? How did you know what to do?"

Talia let out a tinkling laugh. "I didn't. I took a wild gamble." She ran her metallic hands over her gleaming body. "I never did enjoy Five-Card Malice—that was Carred's game. But this time, the gamble paid off."

Anskar glanced behind, to where Carred lay slumped on the ground, blood trickling from her nose and ears.

"Sad, isn't it?" Talia said. "I never envisaged things turning out this way. I thought Carred would be my ever-loyal servant, and you my heir apparent, my eternal champion. Of course, you still could be…"

Anskar ripped his gaze away from Carred and let his black eyes pour their ire on his mother.

Talia's shoulders drooped, but rather than express her disappointment in words, she continued to stare at Carred's prone form. "She told me about her childhood. About the day her mother left her in the woods to teach her a lesson. When the bitch finally revealed herself, she dragged poor Carred away, leaving her ragdoll lost amid the trees. Funny, I bet Carred never thought she'd end up looking just like that little ragdoll."

"You think this is amusing?" Anskar said. His veins pulsed with power. The tides—the dark, the dusk, the dawn and the earth—hissed and writhed and surged within him, demanding to be unleashed. *Amalantril* growled in his mind.

"Not in the slightest," Talia said, and she did a good job of sounding genuinely sad.

"Is she dead?" Anskar asked.

"Why don't you go and see?"

He almost did, but he didn't want to turn his back on his mother. His ward sphere hummed and throbbed around him—darkness reinforced with bones and rot. Was that why Talia hadn't attacked? Did she need him to lower his guard first?

"By the way," Talia said, hands on hips now, brazen in her steel-sculpted nudity, "what were you doing with those three necromancers?"

"You know about them?"

"Clearly. I do hope you paid them no heed. They are old rivals of mine. Bitter foes."

"Then perhaps I should have stayed longer and listened more."

Talia held a hand in front of him, fingers twitching. Her silver eyes flickered, metal brows furrowed in a frown, and Anskar felt the caress of feelers of awareness that slid with ease through his ward. He shut them out by weaving a net of intermixed tidal forces, but a little too late.

"You carry the taint of Kaythe Nurglich, the Corpse Maker. There was no need for you to tread that path, my child. How far..." She hesitated, as if speaking of such things were distasteful, abhorrent. "How far did you go?"

"Not as far as you, I'd wager."

A quiver passed through her flesh-metal chin as she studied him for a long, uncomfortable moment. Anskar couldn't look away from his own reflection in her mirror-bright eyes. His face looked gaunt, diseased, his eyes black and soulless. It was easy to deny what he was becoming, what he had become, when he wasn't confronted with his own appearance. But this... Marith had looked bad enough, a living body in a state of advanced decay, but he had done this to himself.

Talia's voice, when she next spoke, was tight with restraint. "We don't have to fight, you know."

Tension prickled between them. Motes of dark sorcery moiled within his mother's armor-infused body, black sparks to his sorcerous sight. The earth-tide's effluence boiled at her core, seeping from her metal flesh to form a bruise-colored aura.

Amalantril begged in Anskar's mind to be unleashed, to maim and to drink. The sword hilt bucked in his grip, each judder more violent than the last. He held on now with both hands. He could no longer distinguish between the four tidal powers that swirled within him; they had dissolved one into another until all he felt was sorcery, wild and threatening to utterly engulf him if he didn't give it its head.

"You think I wanted to do this to Marith?" Talia asked. "You think I wanted to hurt Carred?"

"Yes."

"This is your fault!" Talia stormed. "You summoned me while you were in the abyssal realms. You handed me over to that monster… my father."

"I'm sure he thinks of you in the same way," Anskar said. "As do I."

"Truly? Then why do you keep coming to me for help? Answer me that! Each time you get into trouble, you call me back and beg for more power. Admit it. You know it's the truth."

"Not any more," Anskar said. "I hoped… I believed… But not now. I've seen enough. I know exactly what you are."

But did he? Did he really? He had been so certain; but now, face to face with her, listening to what she said…

A glamor! he told himself. *Don't listen to a word she says. Lies. It's all lies.* The story of his life.

"What were you even doing in the abyssal realm?"

"I was sent," he said. A debt repaid.

"By the Ethereal Sorceress. I know. But why, Anskar? Why would you enslave yourself to her, a woman sworn to oppose me on every level?"

"Maybe that's why," Anskar said, readjusting his grip to stop the sword from shooting out of his hands and piercing Talia's heart—if *Amalantril* could penetrate her armor-flesh. If she still had a heart. "What other reason would I need?"

He could hold back no more. The four tides that were now one surged down both arms and along his extended sword, erupting from the tip in a blistering stream of fire so golden it could have come from the sun itself. The blast hit Talia square in the chest, her armored flesh incandescent with red then white so intense she should have melted. Only she didn't. The massive tidal charge from Anskar's sword kept pouring into her, making her so bright he had to shut his eyes against the glare, the raging heat causing him to back away. The powers surging within Anskar sputtered, fizzed, and spat, then died out. His sword let out an exhausted moan, the hilt in his grip suddenly cold as ice.

He opened his eyes onto Talia's smirk. She gave a condescending chuckle as she stepped towards him. Anskar swung with all his might, but she caught *Amalantril's* blade between her palms. He twisted the sword, trying to slice through her flesh, but she gripped the keen edges now in one fist and wrenched the sword from his hand.

Anskar stumbled back, panting for breath. Tried to rustle up tidal forces—anything—but his heart pounded so fiercely he feared it would rupture.

"Not as strong as you thought, are you?" Talia said as she took a two-handed grip on his sword and held it above her head.

Amalantril screamed with rage and frustration, and in response, Talia lashed it with the dark-tide.

Anskar felt the sheer virulence of her power pouring into his sword; felt *Amalantril's* excruciating pain as if it were his own. He pitched to one knee, hands clutching the earth as if he could wrest power from it with enough effort. He had to get up. He had to run. He knew he had lost; knew that he could never win. Talia had been powerful before, but now she wielded Marith's immense powers alongside her own. She reminded him of the demons he'd encountered with Blaice Rancey in the abyssal realms—demons who had slain other demons and absorbed their power, their memories, their very souls. He'd done it himself, without really knowing what he was doing. It was in his blood. And he could feel *Amalantril* still trying to do the same to his mother—turn the tide on her and suck out everything she was. But Talia was wise to the sword's attacks; she was clearly well schooled or experienced in countering them. She intensified her use of the Wracking Nerves till *Amalantril* ceased struggling and let out a last pathetic whimper.

Talia switched her attack, dredging up torrents of earth-tide through her feet and flooding the sword with vileness, molding and reshaping the matter that constituted the blade, undoing the painstaking work of Anskar's forging.

He stood, extending his hand; he cried out lamely, fearing she was unmaking his sword. But then the blade shivered and turned to a glistening black, coruscating runes of scarlet running along its length.

With a tilt of her head, Talia smiled. She made a few practice swings of the sword, then suddenly flowed toward him.

Too exhausted to run, Anskar plunged his senses deep within himself. His heart stuttered. Something pinched deep within his brain. A fist of ice clumped in his skull and then shattered, a dam broken, admitting a fresh rush of tidal force, a confused blending of the dawn and the dusk, the dark and the earth. Particles of dirt and fragments of decaying matter swirled around him, coalescing into a sphere of darkness and light, a chiaroscuro of brilliance and shadow.

Then Talia's black sword struck. Anskar stumbled under the impact, and his dazzling ward sphere buckled. Through its flickering barrier, he saw his mother, a whirling demon, the crimson runes on her blade weaving trails of red through the air as she pivoted and struck again, and this time his ward sphere dissolved in a puff of soot and sparkles.

Anskar tripped as he retreated from Talia's relentless attack, landing flat on his back as she stood over him. He rose to his elbows, his mouth open in a scream that would not come.

Then he gasped as the black sword's tip—*his* sword… *Amalantril!*—pierced his chest at the very point his catalyst had been removed. Shock numbed the impact, his eyes wide, staring at the blade embedded in his sternum, the crimson runes pulsing as *Amalantril* sucked.

Anskar wailed as everything he was, everything that defined him, recoiled from the sword's hunger. But already he was losing. Little by little, he felt himself being drawn into the blade.

TWENTY

CARRED…

It was a familiar voice from far away.

Mother?

No, the tone was all wrong, more plaintive than eviscerating.

From somewhere in the background, even more remote, came a man's terrible keening and a woman's gloating laugh.

Then that voice again, so familiar:

Carred!

And now it was urgent. Carred mistook it for passionate need, felt herself wriggle in anticipation, moan at the touches to come.

Oh, Marith. I've missed you.

It was odd the way her own voice sounded in her head, no sensation of moving her lips. Theltek, was she talking in her sleep, yet aware she was dreaming? Dreaming of Marith…

The voice sounded again, coming from everywhere and nowhere, the urgency turning into a desperate cry, like that of a mother for her child—a real mother, not the cow that had spawned Carred—pouring her whole being into a piercing shriek:

Carred, wake up!

She sat bolt upright, as if blasted by lightning. She had no idea where she was. All she could see was white brilliance slowly dissolving into black. But the voices were still there—outside her head: the man's anguished cries and the woman's laughter. Her hand was clasped tightly around something… the hilt of her sword.

A pressure started in her skull, forcing its way down her spine, then exploding within her.

Not a dream this time; this was real. She was convinced there had been an incursion into her mind, into her very being, triggering her dreams.

Just like with Noni, someone was trying to possess her.

Just like Talia had possessed Marith.

But who, or what, was the intruder?

She recalled Talia then, armored and carrying a great helm, waiting in the entrance to the mansion. And she remembered traveling there—here?—with Anskar… Where was he? Had he failed and left her prey to his mother?

She started to panic, her innards churning with revulsion. *Get out!* she wanted to scream. *Leave me alone!*

It's all right, love, said a voice from between her ears, a gentle breeze that blew right through her. *Calm yourself.*

She could feel another presence within her, quite distinct from her old familiar sensations of self, and there was a slight shifting in her sense of where her consciousness was centered in her skull, as if she had been nudged a little to one side or the other. This new presence had a definite *scent* to it, a *heat* and a *weight*…

"Marith?" she asked, blinking her eyes into focus, grimacing at the pounding in her head, the pain in her back and hips. It felt as though a mountain had fallen on her. She could smell the iron tang of blood, and wiped warm stickiness from her nose. She tasted its salt on her lips.

I'm here, love, came the reply in her head, beside the locus of her self-awareness, closer to her than anyone had ever been.

Carred could see now, eyes slitted against the pain in her head. Not Marith—she was nowhere to be seen. Theltek, Marith had been possessed by Talia, then driven out. Marith was—had to be—dead. But it was indeed a woman she saw looming over a fallen man, and she recognized those contours. She had been forced to feel them often enough. But Queen Talia looked different. She seemed molded from silver, shimmering with unnatural radiance under the moonlight. Talia held a black sword in one hand, its tip piercing the man's chest— Anskar! Crimson runes on the sword's blade pulsed as Anskar grimaced in pain, his wails now muted whimpers, his cheeks growing hollower by the second, his body convulsing as it slowly lost substance.

I am here, love, the inner voice repeated. *Carred, don't you recognize me? I'm right here.*

"Here where?" Carred whispered, afraid of being noticed. "Inside me?"

Relax, love, Marith said in her mind. *Permit me to enter fully. I will not possess you by force. Not you. Not ever.*

"How do I consent?" Carred asked.

You just did.

Warmth flooded Carred, old and familiar. Blissful warmth. A pleasant heat. She almost forgot then, where she was, that she was in danger. That Anskar was bleeding out on the ground; that the black sword buried in his chest was drinking, slurping, draining him dry. Tears blurred her vision and tickled their way down her cheeks. She didn't want to see clearly. All she wanted was to retreat inside the shell of her body, never again to emerge. She had felt the same with Marith after they made love, never wanting to climb out of the warm bed, fragrant with their scent.

There, Marith said, her voice closer to Carred than her own thoughts. *Isn't this snug? Two girls in one flesh. Just what we always dreamed of.*

Carred could feel the presence of her lover's shade within the very marrow of her bones, permeating every organ, churning about in her skull, wearing her like a suit of skin. But all she felt was bliss, without fear of being ousted. Instead, she grew aware—for the first time—of her own essence, whatever it was that really defined her and gave her life, intermingling with Marith's shade. She gasped as they wound around each other, not quite solid, giving, sharing, blending, caressing. And she wanted to keep things exactly as they were, just like this, forever. Theltek, was that too much to ask?

Love… Marith's voice said—it could just as easily have been Carred's, the two were so intertwined. Not an expression of affection this time. A warning.

Under the prompting of Marith's will, she turned her attention outward, onto Talia, who had noticed her at last, and now studied her with eyes of quicksilver as she stooped over Anskar, twisting her black sword in his chest.

The Necromancer Queen's pliant metal form screamed wrongness to Carred; didn't seem quite alive. All the curves, the features, even the facial expressions were the same, as if she had been perfectly molded by a master craftsman. Even the eyes were silver, differentiated from the face only by their shape and brightness. And yet, before Carred had been flung back and lost consciousness, it had been Marith's body the Necromancer Queen had been wearing, not her own.

My body! Marith said, hearing Carred's thoughts as if they were her own. *She still has my body, but she's molded it into the form of her spirit.*

"Oh, Theltek, no…" Carred could see it now—what had happened. The armor Marith had been wearing, the Armor of Divinity, was now one with Talia's—Marith's—skin. Talia hadn't just possessed her lover's body, she had assumed it as her own, and reshaped it till there was nothing of Marith left save the base matter that had once constituted her form in life.

Pleasant heat in her veins turned to scalding anger. Talia had taken what was not hers to take. But then, why wouldn't she? The Necromancer Queen had always been a taker. It hadn't been love between them when Carred had been commanded to share her bed. The Queen had merely used her. Not Marith, though. Marith had loved her. Really loved her.

And I still do! Marith said. *Whatever happens next, never forget that.*

"Hello, Carred." The Queen threw out her free arm. "I'm back, like I said I would be. You worked so hard, so long for this. I do hope you still desire my return."

Talia glanced down at Anskar, his struggles growing weaker as he visibly lost weight under the sword's hungry guzzling. She affected an expression of pity, though it was tinged with resentment and malice.

"Anskar, however, did not exactly receive me with open arms. He has proven a huge disappointment. How about you?" she asked, turning her silver eyes back on Carred. "A few transgressions I can overlook, but what about now? Are you still my loyal servant? Will you honor what we had together? Will you accept me once more as your queen?"

And pay homage to your bed? Carred thought acerbically. *Not bloody likely. You'd have to kill me first.*

Marith let out a wry chuckle inside Carred's skull. *Maybe she will. She is the Necromancer Queen, after all.*

Not funny, Marith, Carred replied. Though she would have laughed out loud, if fear hadn't throttled the breath in her throat.

Queen Talia's metallic brow knitted with consternation. She looked either jealous or suspicious. Had she overheard their thoughts? Carred felt the probe of feelers of awareness. Felt also Marith's forbidding sorcery, refusing them entry. Talia stared directly at her hand—still gripping the hilt of her sword.

On the ground, Anskar shuddered. His back arched, blood spraying around the blade embedded in his chest. The crimson runes on the sword blazed with a new intensity as the sword siphoned off the dregs of his life force.

Carred gasped at all these new perceptions; her senses were sharper than ever before, Marith's own moontouched powers mingled with them. She could see how hard Anskar fought against the sword's devouring lusts, how even now he frustrated it with obfuscating wards as he dredged up energy from the earth. But he was losing. Little by little he was being drawn into the blade.

We can stop this, Marith said. *I can, if you wish it.*

"Then stop it!" Carred cried. "Stop it now!"

Talia's silver eyes widened. "You care about my son?" she said with evident amusement, before twisting the sword again in Anskar's chest wound, her lips curling in a tight grin at the renewed sound of his screaming.

Keep her talking, Marith said. *Get her to stop, if you can. And whatever you feel inside, try not to react.*

Feel? Carred wanted to ask. *React?* But there was no time to ask. Anskar was dying. In that moment, he had ceased to be the *Melesh-Eloni*, the heir to Niyas, the key to Queen Talia's return. He was just a young man to her now, confused, misled, used, and discarded; and she of all people knew just what that was like.

"Stop!" Carred cried. Did she sound too theatrical, too over the top? "Talia, please…" Better. "He's your son. My friend." Stretching it, maybe, although she did feel something for Anskar. Empathy, maybe? Some misplaced sense of responsibility?

"Why, Carred, I'm touched. And not a little surprised."

There was an outpouring of sorcery from the Queen. The pulsing red runes along the black blade grew dull and inert, and a cocoon of shadow wove around Anskar, stilling his feeble motions and muffling the sound of his ragged breaths. "You want me to remove the sword from his chest?"

Carred shook her head. "He'll bleed to death."

"Not if I cauterize the wound." Black flames sprang up on Talia's open palm. "It won't be easy. This is a hungry sword, and quite temperamental. You know it's inhabited by a demon, don't you? And you know how much I abhor demons. I think the sword senses that. It might even turn on me."

Something pinched within Carred's mind. She started to lift her hand to her head and then remembered Marith's warning not to react.

"So, what do we do now?" Talia asked.

"I don't know." Carred thought frantically, but it didn't help when the pinching sensation in her mind turned to a rip, and she felt the slow ooze of tidal force coming from a repository—the dawn-tide.

"Are you still angry with me over Marith?" Talia asked. Her metallic eyes narrowed as she stared at Carred. Had she sensed whatever it was Marith was doing?

"Angry?" Carred said. "With you? You are my queen. I could never, never, never... Marith was nothing to me. Just another lover to pass the time with."

Thanks! came the voice inside her mind. *Almost there...*

"You always were a terrible liar, Carred," Talia said. "Nevertheless, I appreciate your attempt to save my son." She glanced down at Anskar's shadow-wrapped body, then with a wave of her hand, dissolved the inky cocoon that surrounded him. "Alas, it will be numbered among your many failures." The red runes ignited once more along the blade, and Anskar began to thrash like a fish on the line.

Got it! Marith cried, and a second rupture opened in Carred's mind, widening, deepening her dusk-tide repository.

Talia's eyes blazed with starfire. "Carred?" she asked, and sounded genuinely shocked. She ripped the sword from Anskar's chest in a spray of blood and surged toward Carred, the black blade singing its dire song of lust and hunger.

The tides of dawn and dusk collided within Carred's skull. Her teeth clamped down hard before her tongue could get out of the way. Needles of pain lanced through her nerves. She tasted blood—not for the first time today. And then her back arched as white light exploded in her head, a force so colossal, so volcanic, it could only have been Marith's moontouched abilities working through her. As if a puppeteer pulled her on strings, Carred flung out her arm, scintillate fire blasting from her hand, her lips moving with the words of cants she neither knew nor understood. There was a concussive boom and a blinding flash as the sorcery struck.

But it wasn't Queen Talia it hit—she had proven to be resistant to such things.

It blasted the ground beneath her feet.

Divots of earth, stones, and the bedrock beneath exploded into the air amid billowing black smoke and fiery motes. Talia shrieked as she plummeted down into the crater, lost within the pluming dust, and then the glittery conflagration retracted, drawing the displaced sod and stone and rock to it like a lodestone, and burying Talia beneath.

Her legs moving as if they belonged to someone else, Carred sheathed her sword as she ran to Anskar's side and dropped to her knees, her palm pressing of its own accord to his gushing chest wound. He was frail, ebbing away before her, but her senses showed that his essence, the undergirding of sparkling motes that gave form to his ailing body, were intact, and that he still had a soul.

The removal of the sword saved him, Marith explained, her inner voice frail and reedy. *A few more seconds, and there would have been no coming back.*

"Marith?" Carred asked. "Are you all right?"

One last thing, my love… One last…

Carred's hand on Anskar's chest grew lambent with white fire. Her mind rippled then turned inside out. Heat poured from her core, from her marrow. So much power. Too much to be her own. Beneath her palm, the rent skin of Anskar's chest melted together, the flesh sizzling and smoldering as it fused. Within herself, Carred felt a receding presence, like water seeping away between her fingers, no matter how hard she tried to keep hold of it. She started to shake all over with the need to scream.

But what came out was instead a whisper. "Marith?"

Bye, love, came the reply—a distant echo.

"No!" Carred cried, pulling her hand away from Anskar's chest. "I'll take no more of your power, Marith. You hear me? I refuse it! Stop this. Don't do this to yourself."

Too late. A sound like the tide going out.

"Oh, no, Marith! Please… Please, no! Please, please, please! I'll find you!" Carred wailed. "Even if I have to travel to the realm of the dead, I will find you!" Theltek, it was an echo of Queen Talia's last words to her when she had sacrificed herself at the fall of Naphor: *Please, Carred… don't leave me long in the realm of the dead.* Carred had not known what to do then; she was even less certain now.

Pressure built behind her eyes, but no tears would come. She gripped Anskar's elbow with almost savage intent, as if he were to blame for the loss of Marith, as if he were the cause of all her losses. He had been too weak to prevent this. Marith had been too weak. Both of them… they were supposed to be gifted sorcerers. They were supposed to do better.

The cascade of rubble caused her to turn. Rocks and stones slid into a depression where she had blasted the ground from beneath Talia's feet. The surface of the earth undulated. Talia was still alive down there. Big bloody surprise!

"No time," Carred muttered through gritted teeth, tasting the salt of her tears as they reached her lips. No time for weakness, for grief.

She tugged on Anskar's arm and he started awake, black eyes wide, the skin of his face parchment thin and etched with lines of pain. His brow knitted with confusion; then, as if his nerves had just come back alive, he screamed in excruciating torment. He touched his chest, where the skin still smoldered, embossed with the charred imprint of Carred's hand.

"Get up," Carred hissed, her words lost in his screaming. She yanked on his arm again, harder this time, leaning back and using her body weight to bring him to his knees, where he shook and shuddered, staring in shock at the mark on his chest.

"My sword…" he uttered with trembling lips. "My sword tried to…"

The ground erupted behind Carred, and she turned in time to see a slender hand burst up through the soil and stone, fingers twitching.

"Theltek's balls," she said. "Get up," she told Anskar, hoisting him to his feet, where he swayed, looking but not seeing, not even knowing where he was.

Another eruption of rubble and Talia's second hand appeared, tongues of dark flame dancing on her fingertips, black lightning arcing between her palms. A crushing weight pressed against the sides of Carred's skull, building in pressure, straining to explode.

"Move!" she said, starting towards the trees at the edge of the property, taking Anskar with her. His knees buckled and he pitched to the ground.

"Move, you useless idiot!" she cried, her skull rattling as the pressure approached its zenith. She could smell heated metal, hear the fizz and pop of lightning, arcing faster and faster. "It's your mother!" she yelled, hoping fear would instill strength into him. "We have to get out of here."

When he just lay there, supine and panting, she stooped and took hold of his collar with both hands, walking backwards, leaning into every step as she dragged him after her.

And she could see now, amid the arc of the lightning between Talia's hands, a burgeoning ball of black fire that throbbed as it grew.

"Move!" she yelled, switching her grip to beneath Anskar's arms. "Bloody move!" she roared.

The fiery black sphere ascended into the air, and as it did, a mound of earth and rubble rose up in its wake, falling away to each side in a fearsome crash and clatter. And there, caked in mud and covered with wriggling worms and maggots, stood the Necromancer Queen, the silver of her new flesh glinting from beneath the dirt of her brief interment.

"No…" Anskar groaned, kicking out with his legs, pushing himself backwards along the ground. But at least it was some help, as Carred heaved him into the thicket at the edge of the woods, cursing as brambles ripped into her skin and snagged her clothing. With a violent effort, she was through and into the trees, still pulling Anskar in her wake.

White light exploded around Talia, and when it died down, she was silver all over once more, no trace of mud and grime. The Queen turned her head, luminous eyes of argent staring straight through the trees at Carred, then dropping to Anskar, still on his back as Carred dragged him behind.

"For Theltek's sake, will you bloody stand up!" Carred yelled, and this time Anskar found the strength to help her as she drew him to his feet and looped his arm over her shoulders. "Run!"

It was more of a staggered walk than a run. She glanced behind as they lumbered in among the trees, expecting to see Talia pursuing them, but perhaps the Queen had learned her lesson. Talia just stood there, watching them from the edge of the forest as sorcerous cants spilled from her lips. Her hands, fingers splayed, made circular motions above the ground. There was a succession of cracks, and the forest floor juddered. Fissures opened in the earth, spreading out beneath the trees.

"Sweet Menselas," Anskar groaned. "She's raising the dead."

"Then it's a good thing we're leaving," Carred said, urging him to greater speed, taking half his weight.

"How?"

"You're about to find out," she said. Or, rather, she hoped he was.

She was relieved to be right when they came upon the moss-covered flagstone path that wended its way through the trees. Strange sounds followed them—rasping, groaning, clattering noises. The air amid the branches fizzed and popped with the aftereffects of sorcery, and once or twice, Carred glimpsed Queen Talia gliding in pursuit when she looked behind.

The path twisted eternally. It seemed far longer than she remembered. Anskar grew weaker by the minute, till Carred's shoulder burned from the effort of supporting his weight. His boots scuffed and scraped along the flags, more from her efforts than his own ability to walk. Their flight took on the quality of a nightmare—of *the* nightmare, when Carred had fled through the trees with a floating helm in pursuit, seeking safety in the thorny arms of her mother. Worse than that, it was the abyssal realms all over again, but that was a parallel to be expected, given this was the route she had taken when Talia had sent her to Vulthanor in search of void-steel.

At length they came to a clearing within a circle of yew trees. At the exact center of the clearing, as if the trees had been deliberately planted to protect it, stood the dark structure of the portal chamber that had sent Carred to the abyssal realms. It was taller than she was and twice as wide; not cylindrical, as it might have appeared from a distance, but eight-sided, each of its metallic panels green with patina. And, of course, they were all closed.

"Shit," she said, her free hand flying to her neck, where her void-steel ring used to be. Without the ring—the key—they would never be able to enter the chamber.

In the surrounding forest, in among the trees, the earth blistered all around them. Skulls burst up from the ground. Skeletal hands wriggled their way to the surface, some clutching rusty weapons that the dead had presumably been buried with. So many animated cadavers—hundreds, too many to count. Talia's old home—her father's mansion—must have been built over the site of an ancient cemetery, or some horrific battle lost to time.

Several of the skeletons that crawled up out of the earth had the remnants of wings protruding from their backs, some still with the tatters of scaly membranes between the bones. These winged skeletons had elongated skulls, horns, and ridges of bone plates running along their spines.

"Demons…" Anskar said. "This must be one of the battlegrounds of the demon wars."

Of course. It made sense, what with the portal chamber being a gateway between Niyas and the abyssal realms.

"Well," Carred said, unhooking Anskar's arm from her shoulder and making him stand by himself so that she could draw her sword, "I'm glad we've solved that particular archaeological mystery. Not that we'll get to tell anyone. You still got any sorcery in you?"

Anskar shut his black eyes tight. For a moment, an inky aura surrounded him, but then it dispersed. She felt the probe of his senses in her mind, and wished Marith's shade was still with her, able to shut them out. A gulf opened up inside her, almost swallowing her whole. *Marith…* All this power she had awakened within Carred, but no instructions on how to use it. It had been the same in life, with everything they did together: Marith, the provider, the voice of reason, the one who nurtured and guided; Carred still the little lost child clutching her ragdoll. By herself, she was useless. Worse than useless: she was nothing.

"You…" Anskar said. "You have power. Your repositories… I sensed them. They've grown. You have to do something."

"Such as? You think I wouldn't have already done something if I could?"

"But before," Anskar protested, "when I was… when you saved me… I felt the outpouring of tidal force from your repositories."

"That wasn't me," Carred said. And that was the only answer he was getting. It had been Marith controlling her lips, speaking the cants necessary to shape the tidal forces, working the mental calculations. Without such knowledge, all Carred had was a reservoir of power she couldn't use, save for a few minor tricks every Niyandrian was taught as a child.

Back to back, she and Anskar turned a slow circle as skeletons, both Niyandrian and demon, continued to rise from the earth.

And then Queen Talia came gliding through the trees, Anskar's black sword held in one silver hand, red throbbing like engorged veins along the blade, lusting for blood, hungry for souls. The sheer power radiating from the Necromancer Queen was staggering. It made Carred want to fling herself on her knees and plead for mercy, plead for forgiveness for ever daring to stand against her one-time lover, her queen, her… goddess?

"Sorry, Marith," Carred breathed. "I tried."

Anskar turned to look over his shoulder, as if warned by some undisclosed sense. An instant later, crimson light splashed the forest floor at Carred's feet. It was coming from behind.

Talia stopped in her tracks, silver eyes incandescent with rage. Carred risked a look behind, and terror struck her so hard, her resolve failed, and she pitched face first to the ground, trembling from head to foot. She dared not look again, but she had seen a massive figure silhouetted in the doorway of the portal chamber, backlit by the hellish glow of the octagonal interior. A second look, and she might not live. Not that it would have made any difference. She had already seen enough to know they were finished.

But Anskar showed no such fear. If anything, the arrival of this gigantic horror seemed to give him—if not a second wind, then a last gasp of effort, and now he was the one pulling Carred to her feet.

Panting, almost choking, with fright, racked with uncontrollable shivers, she looked up to see the giant step away from the portal chamber. At first she perceived only a monstrous skull atop a gargantuan man twice her height—closer to two-and-a-half times. The giant was wrapped in shadows and would have been spectral save for its mountainous density. Carred felt the giant's mass tugging at her, pulling her towards it—the same sensation she had whenever she stood to close to the edge of a cliff. The skull was the size of a horse's, with a blunt snout, jagged fangs, and crescent-shaped eyes. On either side of the ridged, bony jaw was a curved tusk as big as a scimitar.

Her initial reaction was to flee, but flee where? With Talia closing in from behind and the disinterred dead all around them. The sheer violence of her trembling was the only thing that kept her conscious, though she was pressed flat by a dread she had not experienced since a child, her teeth chattering so hard she feared they would shatter. As a little girl, she would have pissed herself—and then she would have felt the back of her mother's hand. If Father had been home from the tavern, it might have been worse. In spite of her fear, she felt certain she knew this gigantic being, that she had seen him before, only her terror wouldn't allow her to put a name to it, wouldn't let her string a single cogent thought together.

Not so Anskar.

Still he showed no such fear. Probably he was too weak from his injury, from the depletion of his tidal power. He did, however, manage a shallow bow.

The giant gestured behind at the portal chamber, at the infernal glow coming from its interior. "Flee!" he commanded in a voice like thunder.

Talia hissed—a serpent sound she sometimes made in bed, whenever her passion turned to fear and fear became rage. Carred glanced back at the queen, still frozen in her tracks, but defiant now, her ebon blade held aloft, its crimson runes blazing.

When neither Anskar nor Carred moved, the shadow-wreathed giant's voice boomed out again. "Flee to Vulthanor. You are expected."

Talia shrieked as she glided toward them, the black blade howling. Skeletons, both demon and Niyandrian, crashed and clattered through the trees on every side.

"Now!" the giant commanded. "I will hold your mother off."

"You can do that?" Anskar asked.

"That is not what matters," the giant said. "What matters is that you survive."

With a long arm, he shoved Anskar behind him, and Carred numbly followed. But not into the portal chamber. They stood with their backs to the entrance, Carred compelled by the terror the giant evoked, Anskar with his eyes on Queen Talia as she came to a stop. The black sword hummed in her grasp and the blade bucked, straining for sustenance.

"He cannot stop me," the Necromancer Queen said. "Not now I have absorbed the power of a moontouched. I am beyond even you, am I not?" She splayed her arms, rendering herself defenseless. "Scour me with your vile senses, like you did when I was a child. See for yourself how much I now surpass you. Tell me it isn't true. I no longer fear you, demon. It is you who should fear me!"

Carred's repositories shivered at a discharge of sorcery from the giant. The distraction was enough to weaken her new resolve, and she started to lower herself to her knees, only Anskar wouldn't permit it; he held her up with his arm looped under hers.

"You speak the truth, daughter," the giant said, and Carred's mind squealed that it knew who this was, but she was too numb with fear to name him. "I had hoped," the giant said, "that you would still be prone to the glamor of terror I project."

"You might have frightened me as a child," Talia said, "even as a young woman, but I am dead, Father, or at least I have been, and death rids us of most—if not all—of our fears."

"And this moontouched… a Niyandrian, I suppose. You absorbed the power of a sorcerer?"

Bitch, Carred mouthed, surprised she was able to find such venom within herself. She clung to the hatred. Sooner that than terror.

"I guess I got that from you, Father," Talia said. "It must be an innate ability of my demon blood—to steal the power of those I vanquish."

"And your sword is no better," the giant said as he reached up with shadow-gloved hands and removed—not his skull, as Carred had first thought, but a helm made from bone.

"*My* sword!" Anskar protested. "I forged that blade at Branil's Burg."

"Apparently, you were careless during your sojourn in the abyssal realms," the giant said, no thunder in his voice now; it was thin and rasping, the voice of a tired man resigned to meeting his end. The shadows that obscured him dissolved away until he no longer resembled a god of storms and thunder whose very presence could crush mere mortals; he was withered and gray, some kind of bony exoskeleton holding his flesh and his innards together. He still radiated a mass that belied his frailty, a gravity almost impossible to resist, yet he was gangly and thin to the point of emaciation. His head was elongated and wizened, etched with deep wrinkles and the scars of some virulent pox or the wounds of a thousand battles. His mouth drooped on one side, displaying a solitary snaggletooth that implied a past ferocity long-since worn out. The hands that clutched the bone helm were knotted and arthritic.

Fear's ice-cold shackles fell away from Carred then, and clarity penetrated the cloud of terror that had settled over her mind like a spear thrust. Domatai! Talia's demon lord father. Anskar's grandfather. His being here made no sense. In Vulthanor, she and Anskar had been Domatai's prisoners. They had barely escaped with their lives.

"The sword has become infected," the demon lord said, licking dry lips with a forked tongue, yellow and sinuous, veined with purple. "It is sentient, Anskar, inhabited by a particularly nasty mezzo-demon, one who lusts only for souls, to absorb the power and memories of its betters. A demon like this will stop at nothing to become a lord, and it won't rest until it is a god."

Carred started at Anskar's hand on her shoulder. He jerked his head to indicate the cordon of skeletons that surrounded them. Their eye sockets were far from dark and empty. Red-hot embers smoldered in place of pupils, leaving pinpoint reflections on Anskar's skin and Carred's. Those who in life had been demons rattled the bones of rotted-away wings—some stubborn instinct telling them to fly when hunting their prey. While Talia and Domatai had been speaking, the noose had tightened, and yet Carred hadn't seen the undead move. A glance behind reassured her there was still a clear path to the portal chamber.

Domatai noticed the encroaching horde and let out a weary sigh. "This could end here, daughter."

"Yes, it could," Queen Talia said. "And it will. With your death!"

She flowed toward him, her feet leaving the ground as her body corkscrewed through the air, the sword extended like a spear.

"Flee, Anskar!" Domatai cried, his old man's voice cracking. "Both of you, flee!"

Fuliginous waves rippled out from the demon lord, shunting Talia to one side, so that her sword thrust missed its mark. Instantly, Domatai pivoted to face her again, bringing the bone helm down to cover his head.

Fear slammed into Carred once more, even though it wasn't aimed at her. Anskar gripped her wrist, urging her toward the open portal chamber. As she stumbled in his wake, she craned her neck to see plates of shadow armor manifest all over Domatai's gangly, stooped frame. He seemed suddenly twice as wide, twice as dense. Shadow wings tipped with glistening spikes sprouted from his back and a wave-edged sword of darkness extended from his now gauntleted hand.

The forest undulated with movement as the skeletal horde surged forward, bone-demons flinging themselves at Domatai and incinerating on impact, crumbling into dust and ash. But there were so many— hundreds, if not thousands. Carred was overwhelmed with the sight of mottled bones and rust-scabbed blades, the collision of silver on black as Domatai and Talia hacked and parried, dancing around one another with bewildering speed.

And then Carred's vision was ablaze with red as they entered the portal. A droning hum filled her ears, punctuated by the boom and crash of sorcery from outside in the clearing. There was an overwhelming stench of sulfur.

"Domatai!" Anskar cried, his black eyes swallowing the crimson glare coming off the eight panels of the interior.

But the door panel was already closing—of its own accord, or under some sorcerous control of the demon lord's?

A thunderous scream rent the air, in its wake a triumphant roar— Talia's.

The Necromancer Queen's outstretched hand reached almost to the portal, and then the door panel clicked shut, and the low drone within the chamber escalated to a piercing shriek.

TWENTY-ONE

WITHIN THE EMBRACE OF THE algae-streaked walls of Sansor's principal harbor, the Simorga Sea grew placid, a welcome change from the buffeting waves and the gusting winds that had harassed the *Callixonis* for the best part of the day.

Sareya had remained on deck the whole time, trusting the brine in the air to settle her queasiness. That last voyage to Sansor, with then-General Varensi Monash, she had spent the entire trip shut up in Varensi's cabin, sharing her bed and Theltek alone knew how many bottles of blood-red Kailean Vancouro. Oddly, alcohol did wonders for her seasickness, and Monash's attentions even more so.

But now, this time around, Sareya didn't dare let her guard down in order to drink anything but the brackish water in the rainwater barrels. She might have been aboard an Order vessel with a contingent of fellow knights, but she'd never felt so alone. Well, she had, but that was in the days and weeks after she had been taken from her family, examined—a little too thoroughly, if you asked her—then forced to remain at Branil's Burg, where she was disabused of her Niyandrian heritage and trained to be a knight in the service of Menselas.

Well, she had made the sacrifice, albeit grudgingly. She had served the Order—even the previous Seneschal of the Burg, Vihtor Ulnar, had commended her. And she had risen somewhat on high, thanks to the favoritism Monash had bestowed upon her. But it all counted for nothing now. Monash had stayed behind to defend the Burg, ordering Sareya to flee to Sansor for help.

She had not wanted to go, not without settling her score with Anskar—not without proving to herself, and to the new Seneschal, that her sorcerous powers were still greater than his; that he had not surpassed her, a moontouched, the only accolade that she felt truly deserving of, one that anchored her to her Niyandrian roots.

And she had certainly not wanted to make the trip overseas by herself. Because she had known deep down that she was still a nobody in the eyes of her mainland comrades. The only reason they had respected her before was because she was with Monash, and she suspected they'd sneered at her behind her back even then. The only reason the knights aboard the *Callixonis* remained civil was on account of the fear she evoked in them. They had seen what she could do. The Captain had seen, and against his better judgment, he had agreed to abandon his role in the blockade of Niyas and set sail for the mainland a week before he was due to be relieved. He had not said another word to her since, but she felt certain Captain Ilaire Gulbert was plotting some kind of petty revenge against her for the loss of lucrative bribes and tariffs from the traders he was supposed to keep away from Dorinah's port.

Above the protection of the harbor walls, feathery clouds scudded under the lash of the wind, the strips of sky in between washed out and limpid, the sun, on the occasions she caught a glimpse of it, dull and radiating, so it seemed, cold rather than heat.

The score or so of long stone piers that jutted into the sea were crammed with fishing vessels, many covered with oilskin tarps against the expected rain. The wharves were largely empty, and besides the *Callixonis*, there was only one other galleon in dock, her sails furled and decks abandoned. To the north of the harbor—the exclusive end, Monash had told her when they had left Sansor together, bound for Niyas—the yachts of the wealthy were moored, at least a dozen, same as before. Maybe the rich merchants, the bankers, and the Kailean nobles never actually used their yachts and just kept them for show. More likely, they had forgotten they even owned them.

Sareya was surprised when the *Callixonis* didn't head for a vacant berth and instead stayed out in the harbor's deep waters, where the Captain ordered the anchor dropped. Soon after, a small row boat was lowered over the side, and Captain Gulbert waddled down from the poop deck, pipe in mouth and a slice of pie in hand, with a sullen looking, wide-shouldered sailor woman in a red bandana and hooped earrings trailing behind.

"Grelda will take you ashore," the Captain said around the stem of his pipe. "And then she'll row straight back, without stopping to browse for junk no one wants or needs, nor fancy food, nor a quick beer in one of the taverns. Ain't that right, Grel?"

"If you say so," the woman said.

"You're not staying in Sansor for a day or two?" Sareya asked. What she meant was: *No one is coming with me to the Mother House?* She had assumed she'd have an escort, though why she should have assumed that, given the way the crew and the knights aboard shunned her, made no sense now she came to think about it.

"And answer questions about why I abandoned the blockade of Niyas?" Gulbert said.

"You had no choice," Sareya said. "You were given a command."

"I was threatened, more like. And I don't deny you had your reasons. You were right: someone had to reach Sansor with a message about what's happened. Only…"

"You wish it hadn't been you?" Sareya could guess why. She wondered, not for the first time, how much this detour from his underhand practices was costing him.

Gulbert shrugged then turned away, waggling his pudgy fingers at her over his shoulder.

Perhaps the Captain was right to grumble about coming all the way to Sansor. To her mind, Sareya's mission was a waste of time. By the time she met with the Grand Master, Branil's Burg would have already fallen. Either the Seneschal and all the knights were dead, or they had escaped to the mainland, in which case they could make their own reports when they arrived. There was never any chance of help being sent in time to make a difference. So why had Monash sent her, particularly when Sareya was the only one whose sorcery even remotely rivaled Anskar's? She refused to believe it was out of concern for her life, as if she were more than a maritime distraction for the new Seneschal. Because she was an Order asset? Monash had hinted as much on the voyage to Niyas: "The Grand Master has his eye on you," she had said as they lay in bed. "And not the same way I do. Vihtor made a most interesting report about your battle with the dead-eyes and your use of your innate Niyandrian talents. He asked me to make sure you don't let such gifts go to waste."

Remembering the conversation now made her uneasy. Is that what she was in all this—an asset? A power to be preserved, even at the sacrifice of a major stronghold and hundreds of lives?

She shook her head and banished such thoughts. All nonsense. She was just tired, with a malingering seasickness. She was just resentful at having been sent, and worried about how she—a despised Niyandrian in a white cloak—would be received this time around.

"Right, then," Grelda said, striding towards the rope ladders hanging over the gunwale. "Best get a bloody move on."

Grelda didn't say another word to Sareya as she leaned into the oars then pulled them back with powerful strokes. She kept her eyes slitted, turned up to the churlish skies, or staring out over Sareya's shoulder at the *Callixonis*, as if she couldn't wait to get back on board and away from Sansor.

When Grelda brought the boat alongside one of the jetties, she didn't even bother to secure the craft to a mooring post, but merely cocked her thumb, telling Sareya to get out. The boat rocked and swayed as Sareya clambered onto the jetty, and then Grelda was pushing away from the side with an oar before turning the craft and rowing back out to the *Callixonis*.

Sareya watched her go, pointedly sniffing her armpit, then regretting doing so. She'd not had a chance to wash properly while at sea, not since the fight with Anskar in the streets of Dorinah. To say she stank was an understatement, but at least it allowed for the possibility that there might have been another reason—other than the fact she was Niyandrian—for Grelda's surliness.

She turned away from the water and headed toward the wharves, jangling the coin purse Monash had sent her away with. It felt like a payoff now; the salary of a whore. How quickly things had changed. One minute she had been on the up, the envy of the Niyandrian recruits at Branil's Burg; the next, she was a messenger, deprived of the honor of staying behind to fight. *Fight for what, though?* she thought as she untied the knotted cord that held the coin pouch to her belt. For the mainlanders who had won her over, just so they could trample all over her pride and dignity? For the invaders of her homeland? For the people who had stolen her from her parents?

She had to stop herself from casting the coin pouch into the sea. This was a foreign land to her. Despite her white cloak, she didn't belong—

certainly not without Monash's protection. The money might be all that stood between her and starvation, for it was well known there was no charity in Sansor. Even when she reached the Mother House, there was no guarantee they would put her up, let alone return her to Niyas. Monash might as well have thrown her to the dogs. Once her message was delivered, Sareya would be totally at the Grand Master's mercy, something that was in short supply, judging by the way he had punished the Niyandrian rebels at Branil's Burg who had converted the Chapel of the Hooded One into a vault for mainland wealth.

She refastened the coin pouch to her belt and hid it beneath her cloak. She glanced up at the waterfront restaurants on stilts or at the end of purpose-built piers. No one was seated outside due to the inclement weather, but within she could see smartly dressed waiters fawning over men and women of the highest rank, decked out in the latest fashions—many of which seemed to be derived from the traditional dress of Niyas. The scents of spiced fish, sautéed onions, garlic, and yeasty, fresh bread overcame the tang of the brine and set her stomach rumbling. Suddenly her coin pouch felt woefully inadequate. Probably all she could afford in such establishments was a glass of stagnant well water, and then only if she sat outdoors waiting for rain. Not that she would have long to wait, she thought, as a fat drop hit her in the face. Soon after that, it began to bucket down.

Sareya pulled up the hood of her cloak and hurried into an alley between eateries. The alley smelled of something astringent, and it was spotlessly clean, with not even a rat or a cockroach in sight. She wondered how they did it—or rather, who did it, who was employed to keep things so pristine. Perhaps that was why she had seen so many Niyandrians here on her last visit. Sansor had a reputation to keep, no doubt, and slaves would be the best way to get the work done while keeping the costs down.

As she passed in front of a ramshackle warehouse, she was startled by movement from within the open doorway. She glanced back to see a massive figure hunched beneath a threadbare burnoose that did nothing to hide his bulk. Feral eyes burned with an amber radiance, watching her as she passed, the rest of the face obscured by a deep hood. Something—some questing sense—brushed against her repositories then instantly withdrew as if it had touched fire. She caught a glimpse of a thick, muscular arm as the man gripped the doorjamb and lurched out onto the wharf. His skin resembled obsidian, glistening and dark.

An Orgol? Here in Sansor?

Sareya quickened her pace, her heart hammering in her ribcage.

She'd never seen an Orgol before; only heard of them. Beof, the priest of the Warrior at Branil's Burg, had spoken with awe about the giants of the Jargalan Desert, claiming he had seen a single Orgol crush the skull of a knight with its bare hands, then slaughter half a dozen of the man's companions as if they were defenseless children. What the Order had been doing so far south, in Jargalan lands, Beof had never said. How Beof himself had survived the encounter was a question no one had dared ask. Beof was not known for his gentleness. The man had been a terrifying bully—until Anskar stood up to him with dark sorcery.

She checked behind once more to see if the Orgol was following her, but he had come to a stop mere feet from the warehouse entrance, as if he feared being noticed by anyone else. Anyone other than her, for he was still watching her.

She turned into another rain-lashed alley, making for the paved street at the far end, which led up through sprawling tenements toward the business district of the city—or rather one of the many, for Sansor was the mainland's main hub of commerce, whether the rulers of the City States, the Pristart Combine, and the other major players wanted to admit it or not.

A ripple passed through her dusk-tide repository. Sareya sent her awareness inward, to make sure everything was as it should be, then winced at a popping sensation in her head. Suddenly, she had no access to the repository; all she felt was a knot of hardness somewhere within her mind. She *scraped* at its shell, then felt a fierce heat in her chest, just beneath the sternum. Instantly, the heat turned to icy cold, and then her dawn-tide repository was nothing but a disconnected bubble free-floating in her mind.

What in the name of Menselas?

"Madam, a word, if you please."

The voice, a woman's, clipped and officious, startled her, and she looked round at an alcove she had walked past without noticing. Within the alcove stood a wooden shed, painted midnight blue, a sodden flag hanging limply above, depicting the scales of justice beneath an all-seeing eye: the symbol of Zihanna, the so-called goddess of justice and mercy. The door of the shed was ajar, and a woman in a gray coat stepped out into the rain. Her mousy hair was cut severely short, forming a border around the white mask that covered her face, two glass spheres for eyes. In one black-gloved hand, the woman held a slender metal rod about the length of Sareya's forearm. In the other she clutched a cudgel.

Rumor had it the mask bestowed powers upon the wearer, but Sareya didn't believe it. Gods and goddesses made their own decisions about who they chose to wield their power.

As the woman stepped away from the kiosk toward Sareya, a white-masked man emerged behind her, the hilt of a sword visible beneath his open gray coat. Was there enough room for two people inside? Perhaps if they were intimate…

"Icon Jindaya Uthrall of the Watch," the woman said, her voice not at all muffled by her mask in spite of there being no mouth hole. It might have been enhanced by sorcery.

Not that Sareya could tell, now that her repositories were no longer functioning. She supposed that was on account of something the

Watch woman had done to her. A precaution?

"This is my colleague, Icon Halden Turv," the woman said, as the man took up a position at her side, one hand resting atop the hilt of his scabbarded sword. Stance was everything, given the lack of facial expression to go on, and this Halden Turv's posture warned of trouble to come if Sareya didn't cooperate.

"What's this about?" she asked, wanting nothing so much as to get out of the rain. The woman stiffened at her tone, and the man seemed to swell in size as he puffed out his chest. "Would it be too much to hope that you've been sent as an escort?" Sareya asked, turning on her charm with a smile and lightening her tone.

"Depends what you mean by escort," the woman said.

"Where are you heading?" the man asked.

"Order business."

"Hence the white cloak," the woman said.

"That's right. So, whatever you've done to my…" She was about to say "repositories," but the followers of Menselas were forbidden from using all but the dawn-tide. "Whatever you've done to nullify my catalyst, please undo it so I can be on my way."

Icon Uthrall and Icon Turv exchanged looks—no more than that: just a simple glance, as if they communicated by some other means that didn't require gestures and speech.

"We received no notification of an Order ship coming in," Icon Uthrall said. "Especially one that simply turned around and left again, with only you coming ashore."

"From Niyas, I assume?" Icon Turv said.

"How do you…? Oh," Sareya said, realizing he meant the color of her skin. "If you people were as all-seeing as you're said to be, you would know that I've been here before. Twice, actually. Last time, I left aboard ship with *General* Varensi Monash, who is now Seneschal of Branil's Burg and Governor of Niyas."

Again an exchanged look.

"So," Icon Uthrall said, "you were under the General's protection then. Why not now? Why have you returned to our country alone?"

"*Your* country?"

"A figure of speech," Icon Uthrall said. "You have papers, of course?"

"I have a letter from Seneschal Monash to Grand Master Hyle Pausus."

Icon Turv held out his gloved hand.

"Aren't you paying attention?" Sareya said. "I said I had a letter for the Grand Master. Or are you going to explain to him why you opened it?"

Icon Uthrall took a step toward Sareya. "We have the authority to intercept and question anyone we deem out of the ordinary. Please try to understand."

"By out of the ordinary, you mean red-skinned?" Sareya said.

"Or blue," Icon Turv said helpfully. "Or green, like the Ilapa. Anyone who stands out."

"Of course," Sareya said. "And would that include obsidian?"

She cocked her head to indicate where the Orgol had emerged at the mouth of the alley. Apparently he had been following her. The dark-skinned giant stood motionless, his amber eyes glinting in the light of the sinking sun—not watching Sareya, as she had first thought; they flicked between the two Icons of the Watch.

"You," Icon Turv said, sword rasping as he half drew the blade from its scabbard. "Stay where you are!"

The Orgol spun away, burnoose whirling around him like a cloak of shadow.

"Halt!" Turv cried, striding after it.

But the Orgol was already gone, seemingly vanishing into thin air.

"I guess that showed him," Icon Turv said as he slammed his blade back into the scabbard and sauntered back.

"You'll have to make a report," Icon Uthrall said.

"Me?"

"You're the one who got closest."

"You think there'll be a manhunt? You think I'll get to lead?"

"It was an Orgol, Turv, not a man. And good luck catching it. But yes, there will have to be a hunt. This is… most unusual."

"You think it's the start of something?"

Uthrall glanced at Sareya, then motioned for her colleague to say no more.

"What about this one?" Icon Turv asked.

"Most irregular," Uthrall said. "Coming in on an unscheduled Order ship, then disembarking alone. I don't mean to imply anything by it, but it's not often we see red-skins in white cloaks, not here in Sansor."

"Then get used to it," Sareya said. "Niyas is under mainland control. Or didn't they teach recent history at Watch school? There are dozens of us serving in the garrison at Branil's Burg, and dozens more still in training. Now, are you going to let me get on with my mission, or do I have to speak with your superior?"

The two masked Watchers exchanged looks.

"It would be better for you if you did not disturb our superior," Uthrall said.

"Oh? And why is that, then?"

No answer. Uthrall merely stared at her through the glassy eyes of her mask. Eventually, it was Icon Turv who broke the tension.

"This letter you say you have…"

"She does," Uthrall said. "That much was true."

"That much?" Sareya asked. "Everything I've told you is the truth." Monash had told her of the Watch's uncanny ability—some said it was a divine gift from Zihanna—to discern truth from falsehood.

"I agree," Uthrall said. "But what about the things you have not told us?"

"A lie of omission?" Sareya said. "Is there such a thing?"

"If it concerns the security of Sansor, perhaps," Uthrall said.

Icon Turv took a renewed grip on his sword hilt and stepped in a little too close for comfort.

"If you think I'm going to open up and tell all my dark secrets, you have another thing coming!" Sareya said, inching away from Turv, only to have Uthrall intercept her retreat. "Theltek's balls, I thought the priests of the Healer were bad enough, wanting to know every last sordid detail of—"

"Sordid, no," Icon Uthrall said, slapping the metal rod she held from one hand to the other. "Dark, yes. When were you going to tell us about the sorcerous power you possess?"

"I figured you already knew all about it," Sareya said, "considering you shut my repositories down. How did you do that, by the way?"

"There is something different about you," Icon Uthrall said. "Something… special?"

"I'm moontouched. So what?" Sareya said. "If you knew anything about Niyandrians, you would know it's… Well, it's not exactly common, but I'm far from the only one. You should also know I'm no threat to you or anyone else. Even with my repositories working, I'm consecrated to the service of Menselas. Or doesn't that mean anything to you? Please don't tell me Zihanna is at odds with the Five."

"She is not. We are not," Icon Turv said, rivulets of rain running off his mask.

"All right," Sareya said. "You've had your fun, but I don't have the time for this nonsense. I have a message to deliver. An urgent message. Or perhaps you two will want to explain to the Grand Master why you prevented me from alerting him to the plight of Branil's Burg? The citadel came under attack from Niyandrian rebels."

Again the masked Watchers exchanged looks.

"Not me, idiots. There's been an uprising, a rebellion, and the longer you delay me, the worse things will get."

"She speaks the truth," Icon Turv said.

"And yet she still does not disclose all," Uthrall replied. "We must be prudent and follow procedure, especially now there's an Orgol on the loose—an Orgol that, in my estimation, was following her. Put her in the holding cell?" he asked, nodding towards the midnight blue kiosk they had both come out of.

"Until we hear back from the Mother House," Uthrall explained to Sareya. "We will send word of your arrival and await the Grand Master's instructions."

"You want to lock me in there?" Sareya asked. "Are you insane? Haven't you heard a word of what I just told you? There isn't time!"

Icon Uthrall clamped a gloved hand on her shoulder.

Instinctively, Sareya reached for the dusk-tide, only to be rebuffed by whatever carapace now sealed her repository. She bounced over to the dawn, all the while knowing it was in vain. She clenched her fists and spun around to face Turv, slicing her elbow towards his chin, but he was quicker than he looked and blocked with an arm before grabbing her hood and snapping her head down toward the ground.

Something ruptured in Sareya's mind, radiating out through her head, streaming through her veins—an outpouring of... she could only describe it as soot, then tiny motes of darkness exploding into black flames. She swelled with power, and Turv cried out as tongues of umbral fire erupted all over Sareya's skin. He started to swing his sword then dropped the blade, screaming as it burst into shadowy flame, leaving his glove a smoldering ruin, melted into the flesh of his hand.

And still the dark-tide flooded her—for what else could it be? She had tasted it before; felt its nascent flow back at the Burg when she was still a novice; assumed it was a contagion she had picked up from Anskar after they lay together.

The scuff of a boot came from behind her. Something prodded her between the shoulder blades… something hard and icy cold.

"I knew there was something wrong about you," Icon Uthrall said as the fire inside Sareya died down and left her hunched over and panting for breath.

Icon Turv held his suppurating hand in front of his masked face. "What is she, a demon?"

"Maybe," Icon Uthrall said, coming to stand in front of Sareya, her metal rod firmly in hand. "Void-steel," she explained to Sareya's bemused expression. "Nullifies the dark tide. What I want to know is what a knight of the Order of Eternal Vigilance is doing with dark-tide ability. It's bad enough that you are in possession of the dusk. That I could understand. They say the Grand Master has use of such forbidden sorcery. But the dark-tide…" She turned her glassy eyes on Turv. "Shackle her."

"You shackle her," Turv said miserably. "I can't use my hand."

Uthrall sighed. Probably, beneath her mask, she rolled her eyes. "How ever will you get to sleep tonight? Here." She tossed him the void-steel rod, and he caught it with his good hand. "One hint of sorcery, use it again. Better still, crack her over the skull with it."

Sareya tried to straighten up, but her every muscle clenched, and her teeth ground together as she spoke. "I need to see the Grand Master."

"You will, in time," Icon Uthrall said. "If he agrees that you were indeed sent by Varensi Monash and are not here for some other, more nefarious, purpose."

Uthrall took hold of Sareya's wrist and yanked it behind her back, then unclipped a set of manacles from the belt she wore beneath her coat.

And at that instant, Sareya's clenched muscles went into a violent spasm and she screamed out in excruciating pain. But no sound came from her lips, merely a torrent of fire, golden and incandescent. Uthrall yelped and leaped out of the way as Sareya threw her head back and spewed flames high into the air, searing through the clouds and setting the sky ablaze. Heat raced through her bones. Her red skin was ablaze with aureate brilliance, sunlight expanding out from her, growing, growing—

Something slammed into the back of her head, and the fire went out.

Her face slamming into the ground briefly woke her, and she saw through bleary eyes the cloaked figure of the Orgol watching once more from the mouth of the alley, before he turned and slipped away.

After that, a blanket of darkness swooped down to cover her.

TWENTY-TWO

WHATEVER STRENGTH REMAINED TO ANSKAR leached from his limbs as a pounding thrum filled his skull. Crimson light strobed all around him, causing him to shut his eyes and forcing him inside his head. The last dregs of tidal essence trickled through his veins and seeped from his pores, leaving him utterly spent, turned inside out.

Without warning, the red light flickering behind his eyelids ceased, and when he opened his eyes, the interior of the chamber was now a dull gray, the only illumination coming through a door-sized panel that had opened in the wall. Whether it was the same panel they had entered by or a different one, he was too disoriented to tell.

He hadn't realized he had slumped to the floor of the strange chamber until Carred hefted him under the arms and dragged him outside.

Heat prickled his skin, as if he were too close to a fire. He gasped in dry, scalding air that burned his throat and lungs, leaving an acrid taste in his mouth and the stench of sulfur in his nostrils. There was another underlying smell… alcohol? Some strong spirit? Not coming from Carred, else he would have noticed it before. All she smelled of was stale sweat and blood. Probably he smelled just as bad, given the amount he had bled—so much blood, he was lucky to be alive. Or unlucky, depending on he looked at it. He had failed. He had deluded himself into thinking his powers were unmatched. And he had paid a severe price.

His hand instinctively went to his chest, and he snatched it away again with a whimper.

"Are you all right?" Carred asked. She sounded disinterested, her attention elsewhere.

No, he wanted to say. *Of course I'm not all right.*

He was floundering through a blurry haze, drifting in some liminal space between waking and sleeping, between death and life. Pain was his anchor, and he used it to orient himself. The flesh where Carred had cauterized his chest wound still smarted, and it was still hot to the touch. Carred had healed him? How? He had seen her shrunken repositories; even though they had grown, such a feat was beyond her.

Talia had stabbed him right through the bony protection of his sternum, in the exact spot his catalyst had once been, reopening the wound where the old Niyandrian sorcerer had removed the crystal embedded there. Stabbed him. His own mother. The recognition of that deed was all the confirmation he needed. Talia had never been anything more than the sow who had brought him into this gods-forsaken world. Forced him into it, more like. He was nothing to her save a tool to be used, the key to her triumphal return from the dead. But then she had found another way back that didn't involve him. Once he was of no further use to her, she didn't need to fake affection. Of the two faces she had always presented to him—vacillated between—she now had only the one: the face of the Necromancer Queen. The Order of Eternal Vigilance was right to demonize her. With that thought, he realized the next logical inference with a sickening clarity. He had made a terrible mistake betraying the Order.

Nausea filled him as he lost his mind in agony. He rushed upwards toward the surface of the emptiness that defined him, seeing nothing but oblivion above and beyond and extending into all eternity. His heart lurched. He snatched at breath as he caught hold of the burning pain in his chest once more and used it to reel himself back in. This time, images flooded him: flashes of memory, pangs of despair.

It was a wonder Queen Talia hadn't pierced his heart, but he suspected that was never her intention nor the sword's. The sword's! *Amalantril* had turned against him—by choice or compulsion? The sword he had labored so hard to forge during the trials had drunk of his essence, his very soul. It was infected by a demon, Domatai had said. The idea that such a thing was even possible had never occurred to him. A demon that could inhabit a blade and render it sentient, hungry? But then again, he had never imagined that he could imbibe the life force of a demon that he had vanquished, that he could absorb… what, exactly? A few scattered impressions of memory. Sorcerous power. But any other traits—strength, endurance, intellect, wisdom—he had seen no sign of any of those, not judging by his recent stupid acts. Going up against his mother, believing himself a god! He was a fool; an idiot. Worse, he was a blasphemer of the Five.

And with that last wispy thread of thought, he knew Menselas still had his hooks in him. For some reason that made him angry, and with a curse and a vow never to return to the ways of the Five, he shut out the voice of his conscience as if it were an evil spirit to be exorcized, the way the priests of the Healer had exorcized Queen Talia's shade when she had haunted him.

He heard Carred mutter something under her breath as she lowered him to the coarse, grainy ground and stepped away from him. The back of his head hit something giving that crunched and shifted beneath him. He jolted upright, eyes snapping open onto a sea of blood swirling overhead. He thought at once of Kaythe Nurglich as he craned his neck, expecting the Corpse Maker to slither out of the shadows. But there were no shadows, not beneath the glare of the sun, a ball of molten brass twice the size of the sun on Wiraya. Clouds the color of bruises scudded across the crimson sky, and he remembered the time he had come here before and the voice of Domatai telling them to flee to Vulthanor.

He was back in the abyssal realms.

He fell back to the ground, his fingers brushing through diamond-hard granules of… He looked and had to shield his eyes from the reflected sunlight, a prismatic radiance that made the ground seem to shiver. He clutched a handful of granules and let them fall through his fingers in sparkling cascades. Crystal.

He and Carred were within a circle of standing stones, the rock of which had the appearance of fossilized sponges. Through the spaces between dolmens he could see another circle, wider than the first, and another, wider yet, beyond that. The sight made him disoriented, giddy. Concentric rings of megaliths extended as far as he could see in every direction. He felt like a fly trapped at the center of a gigantic spider's web.

Carred was watching him, giving him time to find his bearings. She looked away when he met her gaze, as if she couldn't bear to see his black eyes.

"Recognize this dump?" she asked, kicking the crystal sand.

Anskar nodded. "I never thought we'd be back so soon." His voice came out little more than a rasp.

"This is where I started out in Vulthanor before," Carred said, "and it wasn't pleasant. Be on your guard."

She looked around warily, sword in hand.

Anskar managed to get to his knees, but when he tried to stand, a wave of dizziness overcame him, and he remained kneeling. "Domatai…" he said. "Domatai said someone would be here to meet us."

Carred shrugged as she squinted up at the blistering ball of brass in the sky. "So Domatai lied. Isn't that what demons are good at?"

"No!" Anskar wanted to protest. He was part demon—a quarter, at least. Demons weren't the malign beings the Church of Menselas made them out to be. Not all demons, unless he had been mistaken in that as well. He had started to believe there was more to demons than the horror stories he had heard from Brother Tion, but how could he be sure? According to Domatai, the higher demons ascended through their orders, the more cultivated they became, the more their intellect and wisdom increased. But not necessarily their morality. Domatai had said nothing about that. Maybe higher order demons didn't lie quite as crudely. Maybe their every word was designed to manipulate and trick. How could he know if he were being hoodwinked? And not just by Domatai. How could he know if anything were true: the things people said, the world around him, even his own thoughts and memories? Nothing was knowable. Nothing at all.

He refused to believe that. That path led only to despair. If he couldn't even trust his own mind to discern fact from fiction… No, he had to believe there was truth out there somewhere, a way things were in reality, a concreteness to existence that could be known. And he had to believe there was something that approximated to goodness in demons, no matter how paltry, else what did it say about him?

Domatai was his grandfather, and while their first meeting hadn't exactly gone well, the demon lord had come to his aid. Domatai's final screams still echoed through his head. He imagined his grandfather assailed by some excruciating agony, such as the Wracking Nerves. Although there was an alternative explanation for those terrible screams. He turned wide eyes on Carred.

"What?" she said. "You think just because Domatai showed up when he did that demons are creatures of honor? More than likely this is all just some ruse to get us out of the way, out of your mother's power. Although… why?"

"I think Domatai is dead," Anskar said.

Another shrug from Carred, but this time the gesture angered him, and Anskar made it all the way to his feet.

"My mother is half demon," he said, advancing towards her. "What if she has the ability to absorb vanquished demons? Even the lesser demons do that. How do you think they rise to one day become lords?"

He could see from her expression that her mind was playing catch up. "You think Talia has absorbed Domatai?"

Anskar stopped a pace from her, her eyes forbidding him to take another step. She was afraid of what he had helped her to realize, and she had every reason to be.

"The essence of a demon lord," Anskar said with a slight nod. "All his memories, his powers, locked away in a knot of protective sorcery within her, waiting to be released. But she'll have to fight him for it," he said, recalling the spirit battle he had fought against the demon Sicth Na'Jagalot in the presence of the Adjudicators.

"And she'll win," Carred said, as if it would be no contest. "She has Marith's powers, remember?"

"It won't be easy," Anskar said. His battle had been anything but. He had been lucky to survive. At the end, when he had triumphed, the Adjudicators had done something to him as he was flooded with Sicth Na'Jagalot's memories and powers, robbing him, at least in part, of the spoils of his victory.

But surely the powers were still within him—that would explain why he had grown so much in his dark-tide abilities, beyond anything his mother had intended. But he had no conscious access to Sicth Na'Jagalot's memories nor the abilities the demon had honed over the course of his long life in the abyssal realms. It was all there somewhere within Anskar, an untapped reservoir of dark-tide power and demon lore. And he wondered, then, if that was what had happened to *Amalantril*. Had some of Sicth Na'Jagalot's essence fled into his sword at that critical moment? Was that particularly unpleasant demon still somehow alive, still sentient within the blade, still seeking revenge?

Too late to worry about that now. The sword was his mother's. As was the essence of his grandfather. Of that he was growing more and more certain.

"So, Domatai might win?" Carred said.

"If he's not already lost," Anskar said. "Why has he not come back through the portal?"

"He never said he would," Carred reminded him. "He said someone would be waiting for us."

She rested the blade of her sword on her shoulder as she turned in a slow circle, visoring her eyes with her free hand. Abruptly she stopped and moved towards a dolmen, gesturing for Anskar to keep quiet and follow.

He swooned as he started after her, then steadied himself with a deep breath. The sun's heat was so intense it seemed to pound the top of his head, and already he was bathed in sweat.

It was an effort picking his feet up, and he left furrows through the crystalline desert from where he dragged them.

And then he saw what had alerted Carred: a pair of boots protruded from behind the standing stone, the toes turned upwards. And not just boots: they were attached to legs, and presumably there was a body behind the wide bulk of the dolmen.

Carred approached the booted feet at a tangent, beckoning for Anskar to take the other side. He wished he had a sword of his own—any sword other than *Amalantril*. Not that he would have had the strength to wield it. And as for sorcery… Just the thought of raising a ward sphere made his heart stutter in his chest. He stumbled and had to reach for the neighboring standing stone in order to stay on his feet.

But he had come close enough to see now the figure on the ground in the shadow of the dolmen: a man, lying supine, his massive chest rising and falling erratically as he snored. Anskar he could *smell* that it was a demon. Not with his nose but with some nascent sense he had not been aware of before, though he suspected it had been there all along, lying dormant with so much else that was awakening within him. It was a maddening scent he perceived, but not the scent of madness. Confusing, perhaps. Overwhelming. Competing signals that shouted different degrees of danger amid slivers of kinship.

The sleeping demon—or unconscious rather, judging by the empty liquor bottle clutched in one shovel-sized hand—was a giant of a man, at least a head and a half taller than Anskar. Huge slabs of muscle strained against the fabric of his rough-spun shirt and pants. The contours of his pectorals invoked the impression of armor. His thigh muscles spoke of immense power, and his arms were thickly knotted, the biceps swollen even at rest, the triceps shaped like horseshoes and probably just as iron-hard. The demon's skin was gray with a silvery sheen, his hair black and satiny, bound into intricate braids, some of which had come undone. Like his hair and his exposed flesh, his clothes were dusted with granulated crystal that he must have picked up from rolling about on the ground. It glittered a myriad different colors as the clouds shifted overhead. Where his shirt was open to the navel, the skin was crisscrossed with old scars—the slash of blades, the rake marks of claws, puckered puncture marks that had been badly sutured, leaving the imprint of stitches. It was a wonder the demon was still alive. Any one of those wounds might have killed a human. The realization only added to the prickles of warning in Anskar's veins.

Carred prodded the demon with her boot. No response.

"You think this is who was meant to meet us?" she asked.

Anskar shrugged, then looked around. "There's no one else here…"

"Huh," Carred said, crouching down beside the demon and sniffing his breath. She stood back, fanning her nose. "Whiskey. And a strong one at that. Did I tell you about the time I…? Forget it. This is hardly the time."

She pried the bottle from the demon's grasp, threw back her head, and emptied the last dregs down her throat. "Theltek's nipples!" she rasped as she grimaced. "That is no ordinary whiskey. It tastes like— and don't get the wrong impression here, because I've not tried them, but it tastes like I imagine goat's turds would taste."

"Maybe that's because I added them for a bit of extra punch," the demon said without opening his eyes, without moving in the slightest, save for his lips. His voice was a low rumble that reminded Anskar of Borik, the hero who had died when his legendary Sword of Supremacy had shattered in the Kingdom of the Thousand Lakes. The only difference was, Borik had spoken Nan-Rhouric.

"You speak Niyandrian?" Anskar said, keeping a wary five feet from the demon's unmoving body.

"You're a sharp one." The demon cracked open an eye then instantly closed it, as if the sunlight pained him. "I bet nothing gets past you. I also speak Nan-Rhouric," he said in that tongue. "And…" There followed garbled sounds, guttural noises, the clacking of teeth, the flicker of his sinuous, purplish tongue.

"What is that?" Anskar asked. "Nazgrese?"

"And Ilapa, Soreshi, slagwight, and a smattering of gryll-ensis. Do not ever let it be said that I am not studious… when given the right incentive."

"So," Carred said, "a scholar, a polyglot, *and* a drunkard. I'm impressed."

She dropped the whiskey bottle, and with startling speed, the demon's hand lashed out and caught it. Both the demon's eyes opened, jaundiced and bloodshot. He shook the bottle, upended it above his lips and waited for a drop to roll down the throat of the bottle and drip onto his tongue. When the drop merely clung there, too stubborn to fall, he flung the bottle away from him with a growl of disdain.

"I thought demons couldn't get drunk," Anskar said. He thought Brother Tion might have divulged that particular snippet of useless information during one of the tall stories he used to tell Anskar growing up.

"So did I," the demon said, pushing himself into a seated position and clutching his head in both hands. "Blood and fire!" He rubbed his head as he sat up. "Spirits don't normally have much of an effect me, other than to dull the feelings a little. Bloody blood and fire! Now, if only I could remember what I did differently this time… I distill my own whiskey, you know. Actually, I'm getting quite good at it. A little too good, perhaps," he said, pinching the bridge of his nose. "In any case, it's a demeaning habit, one I picked up on your sordid little world of Wiraya, where it pays to keep a demon's heightened emotions in check."

"Alcohol does that?" Carred said. "In my experience, it only makes feelings worse."

The demon squinted at her between his fingers, then dropped his hands and cocked his head to one side. Almost disinterestedly, he said, "Oh, it helps with the emotions, and by Shimrax, I needed it to back in the day. Have you ever been bound by a sorcerer? A slave forced to do unspeakable things?" He gave her a long, appraising look. "No, I suppose you haven't."

Anskar exchanged a glance with Carred and she turned away, staring out at the concentric circles of stones expanding like fossilized ripples from where they stood.

"Sore point?" the demon asked, looking at Anskar for confirmation. "Don't tell me you bound her? If you have, I may be forced to reassess my mission here."

"Me? Bound Carred? Of course not," Anskar said. "She's upset for other reasons. Carred's not the one who was… I don't even know if *bound* is the right word. Her… Her friend was possessed by—"

"My lover," Carred snapped without turning back. "Marith was my lover."

The demon beckoned Anskar closer with a wag of his finger. Anskar took a single step, and that was close enough for him. Within the inky vapors that underlay the demon's physical form—the dark-tide essence that defined all demons—something festered. Something scorching, some immense force with intimations of fire, compressed into a tiny kernel that rippled as it pulsed, straining to explode. Anskar's proximity to the hidden force sent vibrations through his skull, and his heart began to pound like a drum from some indefinable deep.

"She seems a little tense," the demon whispered.

"I'm not deaf," Carred said, turning at last. "But I am way beyond tense. So, answer me this, demon: are you the one Domatai sent to meet us?"

"Domatai? Ah," the demon said, "I assume that was the name His Grandiosity gave you. Did he ever tell you his real name? No, I don't suppose he did. He's not an idiot. Names have power."

"Well?" Anskar asked. The demon's presence felt scalding to his senses, as if he were standing too close to one of Hrothyr's unnaturally hot forges in Wintotashum.

"Well what?"

"Did Domatai send you?"

"He requested my presence here," the demon said. "Not me specifically, but he sent a plea for help, and his plea was answered. I just happened to be in the vicinity, in need of penance, and out of favor enough to make me disposable. I have no evidence for the latter, so please do call me paranoid, if you must." He made an effort to get to his feet then decided instead to scoot his back up against the dolmen he had been lying behind.

"No," Carred said, "don't touch—!"

"The stone?" the demon said, leaning back against it and once more closing his eyes. "The alarm only sounds for intruders. I have diplomatic immunity."

"Diplomatic?" Anskar asked. "You're not from here?"

"From Vulthanor? I wish. Shimrax is—was—my abode. Not a nice place. Unless you enjoy the sport of hunting, while playing the part of the prey. And of course, being a prisoner. I am here in Vulthanor merely as an ambassador, and now, it seems, as your chaperone."

"His?" Carred asked, nodding toward Anskar. "Not mine?"

"His Grandiosity only mentioned the lad: Antsy Demon, I think he said it was. Correct me if I'm wrong."

"Anskar DeVantte," Anskar said. "Domatai is my grandfather."

The demon studied him with bloodshot eyes. "You don't say. I must tell you, he was in quite a fluster before he left, a panic unseemly for a demon lord. I do not know what he would have done if I had not been sent to his tawdry brass citadel for a secret meeting…"

"A coincidence?" Carred asked.

The demon smiled. "Do not be so absurd. The long and the short of it is, His Grandiosity was extremely worried about young Antsy here, and asked me to wait here for him, then convey him to a place of safety."

"Why you?" Anskar asked. "Domatai is a demon lord. He controls Vulthanor. Why you, a stranger to his realm, and not someone else?"

"You will have to ask him that when next you meet," the demon said, "but if you ask me, it is a trust issue. I am a demon. I know about these matters. As should you, being—what is it? A half-blood demon? Less than that?"

"Quarter, I think," Anskar said.

"You think?"

"My mother is—"

"I know who your mother…" The demon's voice trailed off as the innermost circle of standing stones started to flash crimson. "That's not good," he said.

Already, the next circle out from the one in which they stood had started to flash. It was followed by the next, and the next, till the stone circles strobed with glaring red light all the way to the horizon.

"I tried telling you," Carred said.

"This is no mere alarm," the demon said. "It is a call to arms, to open warfare. It is the start of the selection process."

"Selection?" Anskar asked.

"For the next demon lord. It means…" The demon fixed Anskar with a hard glare. "It means that your grandfather is dead. And before you ask, it's not a hereditary monarchy. If you want it, you have to fight for it like everyone else. But what would be really worrying is if your mother, the Necromancer Queen Talia, were the one to kill him. As a half-demon herself, she would have the ability to—"

"Absorb him," Carred said. "Tell us something we don't already know."

"Of course," the demon said, "it is no easy matter to absorb the essence of a demon lord, then break open the shell protecting it, and assimilate without drowning your own consciousness. For a half-blood demon, impossible, I would have to say, without the power of—"

"A moontouched?" Anskar said. "She has that."

"Oh," the demon said. "Well, that changes things. My… My colleagues? Confreres? The way they outnumber me, I want to call them my sorority. They probably didn't see this coming. They knew the Necromancer Queen was powerful, well on the way to becoming a minor goddess; but now, with the added power, the memories, the intellect of a demon lord… Even if the entire might of the mainland came against her, there may be no stopping her. You think I am overreacting? I suppose it could be the whiskey. Now, do please make yourself useful and help me to stand."

Anskar merely stared back blankly, eyes refusing to focus. He blinked back spots of white light, wishing he could attribute them to the oversized sun; but he knew he wasn't right, that he had one foot in the realm of the dead. *Amalantril*—or rather the demon that inhabited the blade—might have been prevented from completely drinking his soul, but it had harmed him right down to the core. He felt dizzy, and not at all himself. As if even now he were dissolving away into some light-starved void.

It was Carred who leant the demon a hand and helped him to his feet.

"I was speaking to the man here," the demon said, yanking his arm out of her grasp. "And I was not being entirely serious. As if I would require the help of an inferior."

He arched an eyebrow, watching for Carred's response. When she gave him none, save to turn her back on him, he shrugged at Anskar. "Do not take me at my word, quarter-demon. I find prodding my new acquaintances—verbally, I hope you understand—to elicit a response most enlightening."

"Do you now?" Carred said, without turning back to face him. "And what have you learned?"

"Only that you remind me of another non-demon I once…"

Even through his blurred vision, Anskar could see the change that came over the demon: he dipped his head, his jaw working as if he were chewing gristle.

"My…" the demon started, and then seemed to change his mind. Carred faced him now as he addressed her. "You remind me—just a little—of… someone."

"Someone?" Carred asked.

"It matters not. And someone else. There are two people you remind me of, both of them women, and neither of them demons."

"And that's a good thing?"

"You would have to ask them. Only you can't. The first is long dead.

The second… Well, maybe you will ask her, and maybe she will recite fond memories, or maybe she won't." He looked utterly forlorn for a moment, dragged down by an ancient wave of melancholy. "Let me ask," the demon said, "before the savagery begins: I don't suppose you happened to bring any whiskey with you? I am rather partial to Widow's Malt. It doesn't just dull the emotions and blunt the memories. These days, I need it for… other reasons."

"What other—?" Anskar started, but the demon cut him off.

"No, of course you don't have any strong spirits on you. You're barely a man. Do you even shave yet?" He peered at Anskar's chin then tsked. "You missed a bit. Come on now. Then sooner we get a move on, the better. Coming?"

"Where?"

"Away from here," the demon said, making an elaborate gesture that took in the circles of standing stones flashing with red light.

In the far distance, Anskar could make out hundreds, if not thousands, of dark specks on the horizon. He blinked in case it was a matter of the white sparks turning black, but when he looked again, the specks were still there. They billowed through the blood-hued skies, amid the contusions of clouds. Insects, or swallows? Or something larger, still too far off to see clearly, but he thought they were coming nearer.

"Of course," the demon said, visoring his eyes so he could gaze off at the gathering specks, "we may be cutting it a bit fine. Can either of you run? Foolish question," he said, moving towards Anskar, who could barely stand, let alone run. "I will carry you."

"Why?" Carred asked.

"Because he will not make it otherwise." The demon rolled his eyes. "I'm starting to think your resemblance to my former lady friends is merely physical, and then only if you discount the color of your skin."

"Why should we trust you?" Carred asked.

"Fine, then don't," the demon said, sauntering away toward a gap between standing stones and waving over his shoulder.

"At least give us your name," Anskar called after him. "A token of trust…"

"Trust?" the demon said, spinning round to face him. And now there was tightness in his bearing, in the smolder of his eyes. When he advanced a step, there was something coiled about his muscles, a balance to his movements that betokened danger. "You would speak to me of trust? You want to be able to trust me? Well, don't, and see if I care. Trust is for fools—I should know. Come with me, or stay here and die. My instructions were to meet you, which I have done. I will not force you to accept salvation at my hands."

"You don't need to force us," Anskar said, as his knees gave way and pitched him to the ground. "But what… what do we call you?"

"Other than demon," Carred said, coming to Anskar's side and trying in vain to pull him to his feet.

"They're getting closer," the demon said.

And he was right. Anskar raised his head to see winged shapes like large birds racing against the wind. But he knew these were no birds. "Demons?"

"The stones have read your blood," the demon said. "You were spawned from Domatai's seed, and so they have marked you out as a likely contestant for the realm. Hence this place is to be the battleground of succession. Usually, when these wars of succession occur, there is great devastation. Some realms have perished entirely. The cataclysms of your own Wiraya are nothing in comparison."

"You still haven't given us a reason to trust you," Carred said.

The demon sighed. "Names are fraught with peril, and should never be dispensed without compulsion. But seeing your predicament, and in honor of my mission, you may call me Yahsh."

"Yahsh?" Carred said. "That'll do. After all, it rhymes with—"

"It is short for Tarrik," the demon said, then grimaced as if he had made a fatal mistake. "All right, you can call me Tarrik. Satisfied? But that is all you are getting. Just Tarrik of Shimrax, formerly of the Thirty-Ninth Order—very briefly Fortieth. Is that enough for you? Though you probably don't understand. It is not enough to bind me, and in any case, I would gut you if you tried."

"Tarrik," Anskar muttered, half-expecting to feel the tingle of power on his lips, some measure of the ability to bind; but there was nothing, save some inner conviction that, while not the whole truth, the name the demon had given was certainly not a lie.

"Tarrik it is, then," Carred said. "And you can get us away from here?"

"What do you think I've been trying to—?"

The ground bucked and trembled, then pitched like the deck of a ship, rolling Anskar onto his side. Low, rumbling tremors sifted through the crystal sand, causing it to leap into the air. He glanced sideways to see Carred in a wide stance, hands thrashing about for balance. Tarrik swayed as if he were drunk—the fact that he was probably didn't help matters. The entire surface of the land as far as Anskar could see was rocking, sending great sheets of crystal dust sliding this way and that, then cascading into depressions that had not been there moments before.

"Blood and fire!" Tarrik said. "This is going to be a problem."

"What's happening?" Anskar asked, trying and failing to roll to his knees.

"Vulthanor is home to more than the ubiquitous winged demons you see closing in from the west."

Fifty yards from where Anskar lay, the ground ruptured in a shower of crystal, and a monstrous three-clawed hand reached above the fissure that had opened. It was followed by a second hand, hard and glistening, colored a livid red with purplish mottling. The head emerged next, wedge-shaped and broad, tusked and horned, its mouth a jagged gash of razor-sharp teeth, above which a row of emerald eyes—ten at the very least—blazed.

"A bloody grahveed," Tarrik moaned. "Even on a good day, without all the alcohol, I would sooner stick my head in a vat of boiling oil than face once of these execrable behemoths. I had quite forgotten about the bottom dwellers, primitive demons who live in the bowels of the abyssal realms and surface only to slaughter and feed. It seems as if everyone and his dog—to coin a phrase I picked up during my first enslavement on Wiraya—wants to be king now that the throne is growing cold."

The grahveed's muscular shoulders emerged above the top of the fissure, then it levered its gigantic, squat body over the lip and came to stand in a deep crouch, coiled with immense power, long arms dangling in front of it, claws raking the crystal ground. Even stooped as it was, it must have been over fifteen feet tall. The entire demon shimmered red, its torso, shoulders and thighs armored with some kind of natural carapace, with chitinous plates with spikes at the knees, elbows, and shoulders. It turned its broad head, exhaling noxious plumes of brownish smoke as it oriented itself.

"Blood and f..." Tarrik started. "Did I say that already? It's going to—"

The grahveed ducked its wedge-shaped head and charged, scattering crystal dust in showers of prismatic glitter. The monster's jagged maw opened in a fierce, ululating shriek that sent Anskar's hands flying to cover his ears. Weak and helpless, he just lay there and watched in horror as the grahveed pounded across the intervening space—not towards Carred and Tarrik, both of whom were standing, but towards him.

Carred stepped in front of Anskar, sword clutched in a trembling hand. Her protectiveness—her loyalty?—stunned him. The futility of her defense only added to his despair. She was a reed in the path of a hurricane. Each lumbering stride of the grahveed sent up columns of crystal dust, as its massive feet pounded the ground. The weight of the thing… To send such shock waves through the desert, it must have been impossibly heavy, unbelievably dense. And it bore down upon Anskar, single-minded and unstoppable. Twenty yards distant. Fifteen. Ten.

Carred cried out as Tarrik shoved her aside, sending her sprawling to the crystal-strewn ground. The grahveed's shriek turned into a thunderous, booming roar as it raised its taloned arms above its head, arching its entire body for a blow of awesome power that would pulverize Anskar.

But at the very last instant, Tarrik uttered a guttural curse and burst into flame. Heat scorched the skin of Anskar's face as the demon streaked forward like a blazing comet and smashed into the charging grahveed. There was a colossal impact, and Anskar was born skyward on the crest of a wave of crystal. When the wave receded, it dumped him on the ground, and Carred fell beside him.

"Get up!" she gasped, grabbing his arm and trying to heave him upright. "Come on, run!"

But there was no need. Anskar could see that from where he lay slumped in the sparkling sand. Where the grahveed had been standing, there was now only a smoking crater, crystal scree sliding down its sides, slowly filling it up. On the other side, through a haze of heat, he could see Tarrik, wreathed in flame, his entire frame burning but not consumed, his skin, his hair, his clothes visible through the conflagration that licked and crackled around him. Even from some fifteen yards distant, Anskar's eyes watered and his skin prickled from the intense heat.

Carred gave up trying to move him and relaxed her grip as she stared in awe and horror at the burning demon. A corona of golden brilliance expanded outwards from the flames that wreathed Tarrik's flesh. Each rise and fall of the demon's barrel chest seemed like the action of a bellows on a forge fire. Higher and higher the flames around Tarrik reached, the aura of golden light stretching, expanding. A few more seconds and it would encompass Anskar and Carred. She must have realized the same thing, and renewed her efforts to haul him back. But then, like a man straining against chains that bound him head to foot, Tarrik arched his back and threw out his arms as he roared. The flames engulfing him guttered and went out. Tarrik slumped to his knees, smoldering yet unharmed—no marks of charring, no blisters, nothing. For a few seconds, his skin remained lambent with gold, the veins iridescent streams of pulsing sunlight, and then even that died down.

"Whiskey…" Tarrik said from a parched throat. "Blood and fire, give me a drink."

Anskar crawled toward him, fingers abraded by the coarse ground. "We don't have any," he said. "But I have to know: What just happened?"

Tarrik turned to face him, his eyes like silver stars blazing from their sockets. He grunted as he stood, throwing his arms out for balance, and the silver glow receded from his eyes until they were once more dull and bloodshot.

"What in Theltek's name did you just do?" Carred demanded.

To Tarrik's bemused look, Anskar said, "That power…?" Like nothing he had ever experienced. A power so intense, so puissant, he felt it could have incinerated the world—all the worlds—if Tarrik had not kept it in check.

"Just remember this," Tarrik said, "before I take you where we are going: Everything we are taught incurs a debt of servitude to someone or other. No exceptions. Do not forget this, and make no pacts lightly—if at all."

Shadows dappled the ground, as if from clouds scudding overhead. But these were no clouds. Anskar looked up to see hundreds— thousands—of winged demons circling them high above.

"We really should get going," Tarrik said, sucking in air through gritted teeth, and with it seeming to inhale new resolve. He stumbled toward Anskar, then stooped and scooped him into his arms as if he weighed nothing. "There's a canal not far from here. It will take us directly to the citadel of brass. Keep up, Red," he told Carred, then ran with great loping strides across the crystal desert, between the flashing dolmens of the stone circles.

And in the umbral skies, a storm of beating wings blotted out the sunlight as myriad ravenous demons circled above their prey, gyring ever faster, spinning down towards the ground like the funnel of a tornado.

TWENTY-THREE

SAREYA SMELLED OF VARNISH AND fresh paint when she came to. She was slumped on the floor of a cramped room, its wooden walls whitewashed, the door unpainted but with a glossy new coat. Her hands were above her head and her wrists shackled to the wall by a short chain. There was a low bench on the adjacent wall, upon which was a half-eaten sandwich next to a pair of mud-caked boots. The new coat of paint on the wall here failed to disguise the dark spatter marks beneath—possibly blood. Above the bench hung several sets of manacles, keys on chains dangling from them. A sliver of dirty light came through the transom window above the door.

The blue box or cubicle or whatever it was she had seen in the street—the holding cell the Icons of the Watch had wanted to put her in. Well, they had gotten their way, and they were going to regret it. She delved into her dusk-tide repository, aiming to dredge up enough tidal power to burn through her shackles, but all she got for her efforts was a pinching pain at the back of her head. She glanced around. Was there something in the holding cell that was nullifying her powers? Or maybe she was just out of tidal essence. How long had she been here? Surely not long enough to run dry. The light through the window might have been dirty, but it was still evidence of daytime outside.

She rattled her chains in frustration. She didn't have time for this. When she got out of here, she was going to… Going to what? Fight the Watch? With what? Her sword, or the nascent power they had detected within her. Was that why they had locked her up? Because of the threat they thought she posed, because she had manifested this… infection? Because she had to think of it that way. Niyandrians didn't possess the fiery power that had all but consumed her. Nor was the dark-tide one of their innate abilities. She refused to believe she was part demon. Both her parents were Niyandrian. She'd grown up among Niyandrians. For a sickening moment, she wondered if that had been a lie, if she had been duped about her origins every bit as much as Anskar had been. Sweet Menselas, she wasn't… couldn't be… his sister, his twin? She had slept with him, for Theltek's sake! But no, she couldn't have been. If Queen Talia had birthed twins, how could she be ignorant of the fact? The Necromancer Queen would have contacted Sareya, wouldn't she, the way she had contacted Anskar? Unless the Queen were playing an even more elaborate game than they had all credited her with. But Anskar her brother? And then she realized how ridiculous the idea was, how her ability to reason had been truncated by her mounting fear. Anskar was half mainlander. Sareya was a full-blooded Niyandrian. So, unless Talia had given birth on two separate occasions, to the children of different fathers… No, it made no sense. Didn't add up. This dark-tide manifestation, whatever it was, had started after she and Anskar had first made love. Somehow, she had contracted it from him, or their intimacy had awoken a latency within her. But was it really the dark-tide? Was there any such thing as the dark and the dusk and the dawn? When she had erupted with golden fire, the disparate tides had felt like no more than fragments of this wild and pure power. She feared another such eruption; feared spontaneously combusting and losing control until everything around her was reduced to ashes.

Her stomach rumbled. She'd not eaten aboard ship. If she had, her meals would have ended up over the side. She became aware of the pressure in her bladder. She badly needed to pee.

Footsteps approached from outside. She yanked on her chains and readied a particularly vile Niyandrian curse for her captors, but when a key turned in the lock and the door opened, admitting a waft of warm air, it wasn't either of the icons who stepped inside. It was an old man in a threadbare and much-patched robe—a priest of the Elder. The man's long white beard had a dusting of breadcrumbs and was stained yellow in patches, no doubt from tobacco smoke.

He squinted at her with rheumy eyes. "The apostle with a missive from the periphery? By which I mean to say, the outpost of Niyas?" he asked, then looked left and right as if to reassure himself there was no one else there. Beyond his stooped shoulders, Sareya caught sight of the two Icons who had imprisoned her. Again she reached for her repositories, and again she found nothing, not the slightest dreg of power.

"In terms of personal nomenclature," the priest of the Elder said, "I am Brother Gordiz, personal tutor to Grand Master Hyle Pausus, of elevated esteem atop the hierarchy of the Order of Eternal Vigilance. And if your white cloak is to be believed, your *boss*." He raised his eyebrows, either in appreciation or surprise. "Good solid word, 'boss.' Hefty, one might say, as is the preponderance of the vocabulary that has infiltrated Nan-Rhouric by way of the Jargalan Desert. Or do you prefer 'superior'? Please tell me that you don't."

"The Grand Master knows I'm here?" Sareya asked. "He sent you?"

Brother Gordiz looked crestfallen she had not answered his question, but there were more pressing matters on Sareya's mind than the finer points of language. Menselas, she hated priests of the Elder—nothing but senile old idiots with drool in their beards and the practical sense of an artichoke.

"Indeed he did send me," Brother Gordiz said, glancing behind and nodding. Icon Uthrall entered and set about releasing her manacles with a key.

"Indeed I was sent, but not wearing my personal tutor hat, you must appreciate. After the passing of my esteemed confrere Brother Bonavir of some repute—not all of it ill—I have risen, as the soldiery would no doubt say, through the ranks and must add to my accolades Chief Advisor to the Grand Master. On behalf of Hyle Pausus, I beseech you, young woman, to accept my lacrimonious contrition for this little misunderstanding."

Icon Uthrall snorted as she released Sareya's wrists and stepped back outside.

"Come along now," Brother Gordiz said. "The Grand Master does not suffer procrastinators lightly. We must make haste."

The old man looped his arm in hers as they left the shed-like holding cell, more for his own support, Sareya felt, than for hers. As they headed away down the street, her brain seemed to fizz and pop. Something fluttered within her mind, causing her to stop and wince.

"My repositories are back," she said in response to Brother Gordiz's raised eyebrow. "You're not afraid I might do something?"

"At my age," the old man said, "there is a little left to fear. Though I must confess," he said with a worried frown, "your assets—sorcerously speaking—are quite sizable." He looked as though he wanted to ask something then wagged a finger, chastising himself. "Know your place, Gordiz, you old fool," he muttered as they resumed their walk through Wintotashum's streets.

When they reached the Order's compound, Brother Gordiz was drenched in sweat and leaning most of his negligible weight on Sareya.

"Why did the Grand Master send you and not someone else?"

Sareya asked.

"Someone younger and without a palsy of the lungs?" Brother Gordiz said. "Because the Icons were quite agitated about the powers you tried to unleash on them."

"And, as a priest of the Elder, you could counter any offensive sorcery I might attempt to use?"

"Oh, I sincerely doubt that," Gordiz said, then paused to cough into his fist. "I imagine it is simply a matter of extreme age rendering me somewhat expendable."

There was more activity than Sareya had seen last time she was in Sansor, with long lines of Order knights drilling maneuvers and practicing activating their ward spheres in a unified fashion, causing them to overlap and reinforce the barrier each offered. If she didn't know better, she'd have said the compound was on high alert. Either that or news had already reached Sansor about what had happened on Niyas. That didn't seem likely. She had come as fast as she could, and there had been no other ships anywhere near Dorinah when she had left.

She walked with Brother Gordiz past the cluster of brick priests' houses, past the cloister, outside of which robed men and women in broad-brimmed hats scuttled about the allotments with baskets and trugs as they harvested vegetables and mushrooms for the evening meal. One thing she had liked about her brief stay at the compound before: the freshness of the food and the excellence of the cooks. The Grand Master was an exacting man, so Monash had told her. He knew what he liked and how to get it. Sareya had spoken only briefly with Hyle Pausus, and he had seemed distracted throughout, as if he struggled to take a young woman, and a Niyandrian at that, the least bit seriously. Of course, her first impression of the man had been even worse, when he had visited Branil's Burg. She still recalled his air of righteous indignation as the Niyandrian workers who had converted the Hooded One's chapel into a banker's vault were executed for spying. And maybe they had been. Maybe they deserved what happened to them.

A man in the black robe of a priest of the Hooded One sat on a bench outside the cloister, watching the gardeners. It was a rare sight these days. The Hooded One's devotees had distanced themselves from the Order since the desecration of the Branil's Burg chapel. More so since the incident at their Abbey outside Sansor, where two hundred of their priests had been found dead and the Abbess gone.

Even with his face shadowed by his hood, there was something familiar about the man, and Sareya became aware that he had switched his attention to her.

"I've seen him before," she muttered.

Brother Gordiz stopped to take a look, then tsked to himself as he shook his head. "Lanuc of Gessa, poor fellow. A penitent now, but once a good knight, and highly favored by the Grand Master."

"Penitent?" Sareya asked.

"A novice of the devotees of the Hooded One—who used to be known as Death, by the way."

"I heard," Sareya said. "I thought the Hooded One was out of fashion."

"The aspects of Menselas wax and wane," Brother Gordiz said. "The Hooded One's devotion might be on the decline, but it will return, doubtless after some disaster or other—a lost battle, an outbreak of plague, a sorcerous cataclysm. Did you know, we haven't had a world-shattering cataclysm for more than…"

But Sareya was no longer listening. The robed man, Lanuc, had stood and wandered inside the cloister's open door.

"It makes no sense," she said. "Why would such a knight dedicate himself to the dark aspect of Menselas?"

"Because," Brother Gordiz said, not sounding the least bit put out that she had cut him off mid-sentence, "Lanuc holds himself accountable for the misfortunes that overtook his daughter, Gisela."

"She is dead?"

"In spirit, perhaps, but alas, she still partakes of the gratuities of Wiraya."

"What happened to her?"

"The Tainted Cabal happened, when Gisela accompanied her father and a small army to aid the king of the Thousand Lakes. What occurred was... most lamentable. Horrible, actually. Lanuc blames himself, though how he could be held accountable beggars belief! It is a foolish kind of pride that convicts oneself of events beyond one's sphere of control. Men!"

"You're a man," Sareya observed.

"Am not," Gordiz said with venom—the first hint that he could be anything other than affable. He stuck his nose in the air and released her arm so he could scurry along ahead. "Come on, the Grand Master is waiting."

When Sareya and Brother Gordiz arrived at the Mother House, they were ushered in by a knight with mutton chop whiskers who walked with a pronounced limp. The man gave Gordiz a deferential nod. Sareya he practically ignored. He led them not to the wood-paneled room in which she had briefly met with the Grand Master on her last visit but to a large and much more formal hall with a high, vaulted ceiling.

The atmosphere was heavy with the smoke of oil lamps set all around the walls. Three lifeless alchemical globes were suspended on silver chains from the ceiling, all cracked and cloudy and smothered in cobwebs. Not for the first time, she wondered why the Order let such precious lore go to wrack and ruin. It wasn't as if they didn't have the wealth to maintain the alchemical globes—unless the impression of riches within the Order was as illusory as the impression of morals. She shut the lid on that particular train of thought. Monash had several times chastised her for her cynicism—not a commendable trait for those who wanted to rise through the ranks. Well, if she ever did rise, if she should one day become Grand Master, she'd see to it that lights were serviceable and morals were clean. If she was going to give a hundred percent to the service of Menselas through the Order of Eternal Vigilance, she expected the Order to live up to the ideals it liked others to believe. Not that the Order would ever accept a Niyandrian as its supreme head. It smarted, that she had only achieved status because she was favored by the Burg's new Seneschal. Smarted more that her favor seemed to be on the decline, given how readily Monash had sent her away.

The Grand Master didn't deign to notice her as she entered. He was seated at the head of a long table so glossy with varnish, so polished, that it reflected the faces of all the men seated along its length. No women, and certainly no Niyandrians. They were all dusky-skinned Kailean inbreds, judging by their turned up noses and the looks of disdain they flicked her way when they could be bothered to raise their eyes from the papers in front of them on the table. Some of them murmured; might even have shaken their heads. One of them, a ruddy-faced fat man with a thick mustache, smiled kindly at her and winked. The gray-haired knight next to him elbowed him in the ribs.

Hyle Pausus was eating from a plate laden with cheeses, sweetmeats, olives, and dates, a half-filled carafe of red wine beside it. He took a sip from his glass then popped an olive in his mouth, chewed noisily, then turned his head aside to spit the pip on the floor. A server promptly picked it up and added it to the basket he was carrying.

Brother Gordiz made his way around the table to stand beside the Grand Master's chair. Hyle Pausus ate a piece of cheese and took another sip of wine.

"It has been quite the wait, Brother Gordiz. Quite the wait. We are, all of us, busy men."

"Forgive my tardiness, Grand Master," Gordiz said with an

obsequious bow. "The rheumatism that afflicts my joints impedes locomotive efficiency."

The Grand Master chuckled as he drained his glass. "You think I should have sent a boy as a runner, eh? Perhaps I would, if I could find a fresh one. The buggers are quite worn out."

One of the knights at table looked up at that. "We are too soft on them, Grand Master. Hard work and discipline is what the young ones need."

"Quite," Hyle Pausus said, switching his gaze to Sareya. His cheek twitched. "Perhaps we could send the young postulants to Branil's Burg. I am sure Seneschal Monash would love that. And lo and behold, here is the Seneschal's new favorite. Forgive me, my dear, but I am abysmal with names…"

Sareya started to introduce herself, but the Grand Master spoke right over her.

"Oh, please don't trouble yourself. In one ear, out the other. Come closer, where I can see you properly." He patted the chair adjacent to his own.

With a glance at Brother Gordiz, Sareya crossed the hall and seated herself. Immediately her eyes started to itch and she felt the urge to sneeze. There was a strong scent coming from the Grand Master—something at the same time musky and floral that made her head swim.

"Now," the Grand Master said, "the Icons of the Watch sent word that you brought urgent news from overseas."

"Niyandrian rebels have—"

"Seized Branil's Burg. Yes, I know. Old news, my girl, old news. You might have noticed the young men limbering up and preparing for war, vying for who will be picked to go. All that sweat and muscle. There is nothing like a whiff of pending war to bring out the nobility of men, don't you think?"

It wasn't just men Sareya had seen training in the compound. "And women," she said.

"Yes, them too."

"But, Grand Master, how did you know?"

"Monash and others came ashore in the Pristart Combine some few hours ago, according to the Patriarch. Menselas knows how he gets news so quickly!"

"I would have been here before then," Sareya said, "had I not been waylaid."

"By the Watch, yes. All resolved now, I trust. No harm done? Good."

"The Watch can't be blamed," one of the knights said. "It's not every day they see Niyandrians dressed like one of us."

"Now, now, General Klimpth," Hyle Pausus said. "The dear girl is not dressed like one of us; she *is* one of us. I really must have words with the master of the Watch. One really should not discriminate on the basis of skin color. I thought Kaile had progressed beyond such things. My dear," he said to Sareya, "please accept my apologies."

"It wasn't your doing, Grand Master," Sareya said.

"Indeed, but can't I feel the teensiest bit bad about it? Personally, I find crimson skin if not delectable then exotic and rather charming. Do you consider delectable a good word, Brother Gordiz?"

"Oh, more than good, Grand Master. Splendiferous."

"Splendiferous, eh?"

"Etymologically speaking, it is derived from the Skanuric splen—"

"Blah, blah. You must forgive Brother Gordiz, my dear. He has been my tutor for longer than I care to remember, and tends to be over-zealous, full of aplomb, and somewhat loquacious—all terms that I am indebted to his tutelage for. Oh, don't look so crestfallen, Brother. Splendiferous is the best word you've come up with in ages. You must remind me to use it sometime. But if we may return to your treatment, my dear girl, you should not be too harsh with the Icons of the Watch. I'm sure you can appreciate that white-cloaked Niyandrians are not something you see every day in Sansor."

"Neither are Orgols," Sareya countered.

"Yes, the Icons said something about that. They wondered if there was a connection. All nonsense, of course. A mere coincidence. The Watch can be so paranoid, spurious in their theories of conspiracy. Don't concern yourself with this Orgol. My people are already looking into it."

Sareya glanced around the table, but no one seemed particularly interested—in the Orgol or in her. She had the impression they were waiting for her to leave, so they could get back to whatever they had been talking about before. She felt a fraud, a child, a fool for ever thinking she could be accepted by the likes of these Kailean aristocrats.

"Will Seneschal Monash be coming here?" she asked.

One of the knights made an odd mewing noise, as if he were trying not to laugh out loud.

The Grand Master's eyes were bright with amusement, but he was all seriousness when he spoke. "I would have arranged for Seneschal Monash and the other refugees to come here via the Ethereal Sorceress, but… Well, things are not as they once were."

"The Sorceress is dead." Sareya had seen her killed. "Stabbed in the back by her own functionary."

The Grand Master's jaw dropped. "I am… I am… Help me out, Brother Gordiz. What am I?"

"Flabbergasted, Grand Master?"

"Quite." He turned back to Sareya. "And you saw this happen? Then it will be an age before Monash arrives to explain her failures. We will have to act without her. The world is changing, my dear. It is in a state of flux, and it is up to us to decide what its new shape should be."

There were nods of approval from around the table, though from the frowns no one seemed to have fully recovered from the news of the Ethereal Sorceress's death.

"There are more disturbing reports coming in from your homeland,"

The Grand Master said. "My contacts tell me the Necromancer Queen has returned. Tell me, Sareya, how do you feel about that?"

"Queen Talia, back from the dead?" Once, Sareya would have been elated by the news, but now, she didn't know how she felt. She was acutely aware that the Grand Master was reading her expression for a reaction. Queen Talia alive? How? Lamely, she asked, "When?"

"Right after your Seneschal went and lost Branil's Burg."

"But how could you know this?" Sareya asked. "Even I didn't know, and I left Dorinah as soon as it was no longer defensible."

"As I said before, contacts. *A* contact, who has subsequently disappeared. I fear he may have been killed or worse. Still, life goes on."

"What…" Sareya said. "I don't understand. What does this mean?"

"It means you must return to Niyas, my dear. I can think of no one better for the job. Can you, gentlemen?"

There were murmurs of assent.

"As a daughter of Niyas, you will be our expert on the ground. I wish you to lead a team of experienced operatives, a sort of clandestine—you approve, Brother Gordiz?—a clandestine vanguard while we iron out old alliances and assemble a fleet."

"You—we—plan to invade Niyas?" Sareya asked.

"And do a darned sight better job of it this time. As for your little mission…"

"You want me to go after Queen Talia?"

"If you have the opportunity. If you are up to it."

Was she? She knew she was powerful, and growing stronger, but though it burned to admit it, Anskar had gotten the better of her. Surely Queen Talia was a level above even her son.

"But for the most part, I need you to take out the rebel leaders at Dorinah. Put them into disarray. If it's possible—and I know this is a big ask—I want the port of Dorinah back in our hands before the fleet arrives."

"You want me to conquer a stronghold by myself?"

"You will not be alone. You will be with an elite group, all of them experts of one thing or another. You have heard, of course, the legends of the three heroes?" He gestured to the fat man and the gray-haired knight next to him. "Two of them are here with us now. Alas, Borik has gone on to brighter and better things in the bosom of Menselas."

"Nul," the gray-haired knight said as he stood.

"Rindon," the fat man said, also standing, and adding an elaborate bow with a flourish of his arm. "Charmed to make your acquaintance."

As Sareya left the Mother House with Rindon and Nul to meet the rest of the team, a woman in a filthy black robe scurried towards her, wailing and shrieking. Sareya's hand went to her sword, but Nul steadied her with a hand on the shoulder.

"Be at peace," he said. "She will not harm you."

"Gisela," Rindon said, standing between the woman in the black robe and Sareya, "where is your father?"

She stopped screeching and hung her head, then turned as Lanuc of Gessa, also robed in black, came running in from behind, like a man whose dog had slipped its leash.

"Let me speak, Father," Gisela said, her voice tight, on the verge of screeching. "I have to speak to her."

Lanuc looked distressed as he met Rindon's eyes, then Nul's, before settling on Sareya. "She has… She has started to have visions," he said, his tone suggesting a shrug his shoulders did not give. Perhaps they were tired of the gesture. "Come, daughter, we should return to the cloister."

Gisela held her head in her hands and began to sway. A low murmur escaped her chapped lips, rising to a moan.

"It's all right," Sareya said. "Say whatever it is you wish to say to me,

Gisela."

Rindon stepped aside, and Gisela lowered her hands as she smiled—a mad smile of twisted lips and fever-bright eyes. She hitched her robe up above her knees as she came towards Sareya, like a child wading in the sea. She had broomstick legs, purple with bruises and scored red with hair-thin cuts. Her throat, too, had been nicked by a knife or a razor, and when she spoke, her breath was sour. Sareya had to will herself not to turn her face aside.

"Anskar loved you. Made love to you. I see you glistening with sweat, hear your lustful breaths, see what you do to each other with hands and mouths, behaving like husband and wife."

Sareya retreated a step, tried to say something, glanced at Nul for what to do. Rindon, she noted, raised an eyebrow at her, as if he approved.

"He came to me," Gisela said. "Made his confession."

"Confession?" Sareya said.

"Gisela was once a priest of the Healer," Lanuc explained.

"I can't tell," Gisela said, pressing a finger to her lips. "Shush. Shan't tell a word of what he said to me. But I want you to know this: Menselas was not angry, as Anskar feared. The Five smiled, and he cried. Wept and laughed. Laughed and wept."

"How do you know this?" Sareya asked.

"Because that's all he ever does—to me. Laughs, weeps, mocks, and chides, all of him, save one. Save one!" she repeated, tugging at the front of her robe to make her point clear.

"The Hooded One?" Sareya said.

"She finds solace in—" Lanuc started.

"In Death?" For that was what they used to call the Hooded One, before the Church tried to soften the image of that particular aspect.

Gisela sank to her knees, eyes wide and staring. She held out trembling hands, gnarly like an old woman's, though she couldn't have been much older than Sareya.

Something about this madwoman fascinated Sareya; drew her like the edge of a cliff. Was it horror, disgust, pity? Fear, she realized. Some pending doom or dread that prompted her to ask, "What do you want from me?"

"You are afflicted," Gisela said in a little girl voice. "As afflicted as Anskar." Gisela bobbed her head like a demented woodpecker.

"I am nothing like Anskar," Sareya said through gritted teeth.

"But you are," Gisela said happily. "You are. That is why Menselas laughs and cries. He mocks you as he mocks me. But he is a merciful god." She showed Sareya the crisscrossed scars on her forearms. "He taught me to cut away my pain. The Hooded One slays sin—that is the greatest function of death."

"What do you want, Gisela?" Sareya asked again.

"To heal you."

"I don't need healing."

"You won't know that till you are healed." And now Gisela sounded perfectly sober, a woman of great wisdom who had not lost her mind.

Sareya looked for the glint of a knife among the folds of the black robe. As if to reassure her, Gisela stood and pulled her robe over her head, revealing nothing underneath, only the scars on her belly and breasts, and the ribs pressing up against her paper-thin skin.

Lanuc turned away, ashamed. Nul went to his side and put an arm around his shoulders.

"I only need to touch your face," Gisela said, extending spindly fingers towards her.

Sareya stiffened, her mouth suddenly dry. She tried to swallow but couldn't make enough spit. Her cheek twitched as Gisela's fingernails neared, blurring in her vision. Their touch sent shivers of lightning up and down her spine, and then suddenly she was sucking in great gasps of cool Wintotashum air that seemed to scour her inside and out. And she was weeping, sobbing and laughing all at the same time, and wondering if this was as close as she had ever been to Menselas.

An image of Anskar ghosted behind her eyes—not the shadow-armored god who had flung sorcery at her and bested her, but the naive boy she had mocked growing up, the young man whose innocence she had ruined. But she remembered things differently now; saw them more as they had been, not as they had been reconstructed by bitterness, by life. There had been days of joy, of peace in each other's arms. Of love.

What trickery was this? She grabbed Gisela's wrist and forced her fingers away from her face. She glared defiance at the lunatic: *It wasn't like that!* she shouted with her eyes, all the while knowing that it had been, and that Gisela knew as much as she did, that it was the truth she now saw, the truth reclaimed. She turned her head aside as a pang of longing ripped through her stomach.

"Come on, daughter," Lanuc said as he picked up Gisela's robe and handed it to her. "It's time for your meal."

Gisela seemed reluctant to leave Sareya like this, and just stood there naked and unabashed. "I'm not hungry…"

"Then it's time for prayer."

That seemed to satisfy her. She pulled on her robe, and without a word of goodbye, took her father's hand and walked with him toward the cloister.

"What are you two looking at?" Sareya said, pulling her cloak around her body, not against the cold but against her own feelings of nakedness.

"Nothing," Nul said.

Rindon clamped a pudgy hand on Sareya's shoulder. She flinched, then saw only amiability in his ruddy face, and for the first time since arriving in Sansor, she felt like she belonged—if not in the Order's compound, then with these two men, these heroes she barely even knew.

"Nothing that can't be fixed by a quick drink, eh, lassie?" Rindon said.

TWENTY-FOUR

CARRED'S LEGS REFUSED TO RUN, as insubordinate as any number of her bloody rebels. Her feet were numb, her thighs hollowed out, the blood in their veins the consistency of molasses. Was it an effect of the transport from Wiraya? A niggling thought told her it was the loss of Marith and that she was dissolving away, following her to oblivion. She beat it back with a barrage of curses. It didn't matter the reason. All that mattered was that her legs obey. Run, and run fast, or it was all for nothing.

Darkness thrashed and flapped and circled above her, a vortex of shadow-black wings. Demons filled the sky, shading her from the merciless heat of the sun, which she supposed was one good thing. Tarrik ran ahead of her with easy, long strides, despite carrying Anskar in his arms.

From time to time a demon would flutter down and reach for her hair with clawed fingers. Always it was the smaller ones, no doubt urged to take all the risks by those higher up in the pecking order of the abyssal realms. A quick thrust overhead with her sword and the demons would ascend with the fierce flap of shadowy wings—near insubstantial, smoky in consistency, and no doubt the result of their innate ability with the dark-tide. But the longer this went on, the farther she lagged behind Tarrik and Anskar, the more emboldened the little demons became. And she started to notice larger demons with amber eyes and spiny carapaces dropping down nearer to the ground, biding their time, judging when best to attack.

The demons seemed more wary of Tarrik, despite the fact he was carrying Anskar and couldn't use his arms to defend himself. As with her, it was the smaller demons that drew close to Tarrik, harassing him but not fully committing to an attack. Even so, their proximity drove Tarrik on to greater efforts, his strides lengthening, his lead on Carred growing ever longer.

"Bastard," she muttered. He was leaving her behind. But why wouldn't he? He had been sent for Anskar. Her part in all this was over. She was nothing.

She started to jog in order to catch up, but several small demons took that as a sign of weakness and swooped down at her. The first she gutted with an upthrust of her sword, and purplish ichor splashed down around her, sizzling where it hit the crystal sand. A second demon slashed at her face. She got her arm in the way at the last instant, then grunted as curved talons raked the skin of her forearm. She thrashed about wildly with her sword, driving the demons back—there were five of them buzzing her—only to have them wheel around and come straight back at her. They had the scent of her blood now, and more descended from the vortex overhead. She batted one away with the flat and thrust for another, but missed when it swerved aside. Talons grabbed her hair. A demon drove its teeth into her thigh. She shrieked and slammed the pommel of her sword into its head, but already more demons were swarming her, and not all of them small. She turned this way and that, hacking about blindly, her blade sometimes biting into flesh. And then an obscuring column of flapping wings surrounded her, blotting out the last chinks of sunlight. Claws grazed her back, teeth nipped at her arms, her legs. She felt fetid breath on her neck.

Blackness pressed in around her. Howls and screeches and the flutter of wings filled her skull. Still she swung her sword, still she thrust, but her strikes were getting slower. She found she no longer cared whether she lived or died. She was ready. *Marith,* she thought as a demon latched onto her breast and she ripped it away, casting it to the ground and stamping on its head. *Marith, I'm coming.*

Spears of sunlight burst through the surrounding gloom, dazzling her eyes and blinding her for an instant. Demons fell smoldering to the ground all around her. Others soared for the heights, one or two of them trailing smoke, their wings alive with tongues of flame.

Through the clearing column of darkness, she saw Tarrik striding towards her, Anskar over his shoulder, unmoving. The demon's eyes were radiant with silver, his free hand outstretched, the fingertips lucent with golden brilliance.

In the skies above, demons swarmed their own injured who had fled upwards, ripping into them with teeth and claws. Blood and gore rained down amid the chaos in the air, but out of the confusion a massive demon soared straight at Tarrik, sensing the opportunity. It was wreathed head to toe in armor of shadow, and as it streaked into range, a shadow axe materialized in its hand, the inky blade arcing towards its prey. At the last moment, Tarrik swayed aside. The axe grazed his shoulder and sent up a spray of dark blood. But Tarrik lashed out with his hand, caught the arm that held the axe, and yanked the big demon out of the air into a vicious headbutt. The demon roared as it slammed into the ground amid showers of crystal, then surged to its feet, launching itself back to the attack. Tarrik kicked it in the chest, and the demon flew back, righting itself by extending its shadow wings, then using them to propel itself forward again.

Only this time, Carred was right behind it, and she thrust her sword with all her strength into its back. The demon screamed, and its wings vanished, its shadow armor dissolving into the air. The demon thrashed and shrieked, then tried to turn and face Carred. When that failed, it wrenched itself sideways, blood spraying from its chest, where the tip of her sword protruded. Driven by rage, the demon jerked left and right and managed to yank the sword from Carred's grip. With a triumphant roar, it staggered around to face her, a jagged grin splitting its scaly face.

But then Tarrik was between them, Anskar still over one shoulder. Tarrik's hand lashed out, and he grabbed the demon by the throat. It was far larger than he, and stronger. Tarrik's muscles knotted with the effort of throttling it, but the demon merely bared its teeth and laughed. Until Tarrik's fingers erupted with golden fire and the demon burst into flames, its scaly hide sloughing away till only its char-blackened skeleton remained in Tarrik's grasp. He let go, and the bones turned to ash when they hit the ground.

Tarrik shook with power, silver eyes ablaze, veins golden and smoldering.

"Anskar!" Carred cried. "You're going to kill him!" He already looked dead, he was so still, slumped over Tarrik's shoulder. But he hadn't burned the way the demon had. He was completely unscathed.

With a violent shudder, Tarrik closed his eyes. When he opened them again, the power had left him, but the strain was written all over his face.

"I can contain it," he said in a tightly controlled voice. "But not for much longer." He glanced skyward, where more and more large demons were emerging from the ranks of the fodder and building the courage to attack. "We need to keep moving."

"Is he…?"

"Still breathing," Tarrik said, patting Anskar on the rump. "But only just."

Carred retrieved her sword, hurled a curse up at the circling demons, and then followed as Tarrik resumed his course between the standing stones.

They quickly came to the brink of a ridge at the edge of the concentric circles. Tarrik disappeared over the edge, and Carred followed him down a steep bank of crystal shale toward the valley at the bottom and the glimmering ribbon of silver that ran along its length—the canal.

The spinning funnel of demons rose high above them, then wafted out over the valley. Carred could feel hundreds of eyes boring into her, appraising the three of them, gauging their remaining strength. Some of the demons high up in the funnel started down, plummeting the last few feet as their wings of shadow dissolved. Did that mean they had run out of dark-tide power? Had they delayed too long in their attack? Whatever the case, these grounded demons began to follow on foot, still keeping their distance.

Ahead of her, Tarrik slid and surfed down the bank of crystal scree till he reached the bottom of the valley. Carred sheathed her sword as she followed. Last thing she needed was to stumble and stab herself. When she reached the flat ground at the bottom and trailed Tarrik along the banks of the canal, she could see a barge moored some way down stream, with a child, or a very small demon, on board, hopping from foot to foot and waving to make sure Tarrik had seen him. She glanced behind to see dozens of demons gliding down the scree bank, while in the sky, the bulk of the dark funnel flowed above the valley, plunging it into shade.

Fear lending her strength, Carred ran to keep up with Tarrik. He gave her a narrow-eyed look, as if he were surprised she was still with him, surprised she hadn't fallen behind and been picked off.

The barge, she saw as she drew near, was deep-bellied and long, and it seemed molded from some kind of dull gray metal, with no sign of rivets or joins. The bulk of the keel was below water, the deck and a foot or so of gunwale above.

The little demon at the stern, waving them on and still hopping in an agitated fashion, was dressed in striped pantaloons of red and yellow and brocaded doublet of black velvet. He wore a ruff of fine lace around his too-long neck. His skin was turquoise and mottled with darker shades of green and blue, and his head dome-shaped, the jaw long and jutting, gave the impression of a bird. His deep-set eyes were aflame, miniature suns with pinprick pupils at their center. Perhaps she had been wrong. Maybe he wasn't a demon after all. But what, then? Some kind of hobgoblin from myth?

The turquoise man was livid with barely suppressed rage, pressing his fists into his hips and pointedly stomping his feet as Tarrik climbed aboard and lay Anskar down on a bench that ran along the length of the gunwale.

"Well, you certainly took your time! When we saw the wingers coming in, we almost left without you."

We? Carred scanned the barge for someone else, but there was only this one little fellow.

"I am surprised you didn't," Tarrik replied, then patted the turquoise man on the head—an action that only served to inflame his anger.

"You realize what this means, of course?" the little man said, cocking his thumb at the sky, where the demon swarm circled overhead, not coming any closer. Perhaps they saw the barge and its tiny occupant as a new threat to be assessed. The demons following on foot stayed back fifty or so yards from the canal bank.

"I think it is fairly obvious," Tarrik replied.

"What are they afraid of?" Carred asked as she climbed aboard.

The little man wrinkled his bulbous nose at her, then averted his eyes, as if he couldn't bear to look at her. As if her appearance offended him in some way.

"They," Tarrik said, "are afraid of smelling their own feces, in case the stench should kill them. But give them long enough to grow some testicles and they will have a go at us."

"They already attacked us," Carred pointed out.

"The foolish ones did," Tarrik said, "and now they are dead."

"Pah," the little man said, arms folded across his chest as he looked down into the water, watching the reflections of the demons circling overhead. "These are no more than harbingers, a foreshadowing of worse to come. You didn't answer our question, Yahsh," the little man said.

"It's all right, Oddy," Tarrik said. "They know my name."

"All of it?"

"You think me an idiot? No, do not answer that. They know enough to address me, no more than that."

"Ah, Goat-Breath, then. Of all your multifarious titles, that is the one we find most apposite."

"Tarrik, you odious little turd. They know to call me Tarrik."

"And we will too, so long as you refrain from calling us Oddy. Unless your aim is to make us sound peculiar?"

"Forgive me, my friend," Tarrik said. Then to Carred: "This is Odopek Gethern dan Semong—a descriptive name in his own language, one he adopted since his… accident. And before you ask, he is no demon, so don't even try to bind him. As to what he is…"

"They!" Odopek objected. "Do please use the correct pronoun. It's plural, not singular. Goodness, I can't remember when it was last singular. Or rather, singulars, as in two and not one."

"As to what *they* are," Tarrik said, "Well, you will have to ask them, and you will no doubt get the same answer as everyone else."

"Mind your own business," Odopek said.

"Whatever," Carred said tiredly.

The little man peered at her as if he expected more curiosity from her. Well, she had better things to do. Like check on Anskar, for one thing.

His skin was the color of ash, and she only knew he was still breathing when she pressed her ear to his lips and felt the tiniest tickle of breath.

"*They* are going to love this!" Odopek said with another stomp of his foot.

"They?" Carred asked. "Not you… plural you?"

"Oh, the ignorance!" Odopek said. "When speaking of others, is it not the custom where you come from to use the third person?"

"It is a complicated matter," Tarrik explained, "but Odopek is two in one."

"In the same way Menselas is five in one?" Carred asked.

"Oh, the very idea!" Odopek said. "We are offended you would suggest such a thing."

"Really?" Tarrik asked. "Even if *they* are right about who Menselas really is."

"*If* being the operative word," Odopek said. "As to Menselas's connection—nay, identity—with *the* power, that remains to be seen. I am not given to theological speculation, only to tangible things… like tea. And biscuits. And those yummy little cakes made with molasses and seeds and big chunks of chocolate."

He shook his head mournfully then directed his sunlit eyes at Tarrik. "Now, perhaps you will not mind telling us why you had to take so long."

"I didn't," Tarrik said. "I couldn't very well bring them here until they had arrived in Vulthanor."

"You've been waiting for them all this time? Have you been drinking?"

"You would sooner I didn't?" Tarrik said, as he raised one end of a deck panel and pulled out a bottle from beneath, where Carred glimpsed dozens of bottles packed in straw.

The little man shuddered. "We would sooner you took instruction, rather than placing everyone else at risk. But what do we know? We are just the bloody barge crew."

"Then shouldn't you have us underway?" Carred said. "Before Anskar slips completely into the realm of the dead."

"And then who do you think *they* would blame?" Odopek said. "Us, of course. It is always our fault!"

The little man harrumphed as he stomped his foot, rocking the barge as if he weighed ten times more than he appeared to.

"I didn't mean to—" Carred started to apologize, but Odopek turned his back on her and shuffled to the prow. He raised one finger overhead, waggled it in a good impression of an earthworm peeking above ground, and in response the barge juddered as it began to move out into the canal.

"I think I might have upset him," Carred said. "It wasn't my intention."

"Do not worry about my little friend," Tarrik said, pulling the cork from his bottle with his teeth and spitting it over the side. He proffered the bottle to Carred but didn't wait for her to accept or decline, instead upending it and taking a long, glugging pull. He came up for air when the bottle was two thirds empty, wiping his lips with the back of his hand then continuing what he had been saying. "Ever since his—their—accident, he has been—"

"*We* do have excellent hearing, you know," Odopek called from the prow. "And you might at least be consistent with the pronouns. 'He' we are prepared to tolerate, so long as it is used in conjunction with 'his' and 'him.' As to which 'him' the singular pronoun refers to, leave that to us to decide."

"He it is, then," Tarrik said. He opened his mouth to go on, but Odopek interrupted him for the second time.

"Oh, and we are not paranoid. That is what you were going to say, isn't it?"

"Not exactly," Tarrik said. "Beset with persecutory ideas, perhaps."

"Wouldn't you be, in our situation?" the little man asked.

"Depends who I had to share a body with," Tarrik said. "Either of you two, and I would seek out a sturdy tree limb from which to hang my noose."

"Charming," Odopek said. "Clearly you are more of a coffee drinker than tea."

"Actually, I prefer strong spirits," Tarrik said, finishing off the bottle.

Odopek shook his head and tsked, then looked up, startled, as a huge winged demon swooped down out of the gyring funnel.

Tarrik hadn't noticed. He was still licking out the neck of his bottle. Odopek seemed in two minds about what to do—which he probably was.

But Carred was already running for the front of the ship, pulling her sword from its scabbard. She screamed a curse as she lunged with the blade, and the demon veered aside before climbing high in the sky with lazy strokes of its shadow wings. As it reached the whirling black vortex, other large demons began to separate out from the funnel, berating their companion and mocking him with laughter.

"I think I preferred the little ones," Carred said as she watched five of the big demons start a spiraling descent toward the barge.

"They have the measure of us now," Tarrik said, tossing his empty bottle overboard and forming a two-handed sword out of shadow. "They must have worked out you are just a comedy midget, Odopek, and nothing to be afraid of. So, humans and other, either we fight or we die."

The dark funnel dispersed with the roar of a hurricane, shadow-winged demons separating out from it and soaring on their own trajectories above, around, or straight toward the barge—hundreds of demons, filling the sky like a murder of crows.

"Can you not make this infernal craft go any faster?" Tarrik asked as he took a two-handed grip on his shadow blade and stepped to the stern.

"We are doing our utmost," Odopek said, "but that is no regular sun overhead, and there is no moon to reflect it. We are relying solely on the power that lingers in our blood."

"You are moontouched?" Carred asked as she took up a defensive position at the gunwale, her sword a ponderous weight in her hand. She was too exhausted to put up much of a fight, but it wasn't as if she had a choice.

Wings the consistency of smoke propelled the demons closer with long, languorous strokes, but only so close before they veered away, circling the barge, looking for an angle of attack. But no sooner had one broken off its approach than another took its place.

Carred moved to the prow, keeping the tip of her blade aimed toward incoming demons. She glanced behind to see Tarrik doing the same thing. As a spiny, livid-skinned demon flew to the edge of his range, Tarrik's shadow blade suddenly extended another foot and pierced the demon's guts. Purplish ichor spilled to the canal, the demon's wings exploded in a puff of soot, and it plunged into the water in a seething mass of bubbles.

"That showed them," Tarrik said.

But it hadn't cowed them. This new death only seemed to enrage the horde, and with uncanny coordination, the demons dive-bombed the barge.

Carred ducked beneath a claw and smacked her sword upwards into a demon's face. Already she was turning, ramming the blade deep into another demon's chest. She felt the claws of sorcerous senses in her mind, gauging her abilities, and then shards of shadow shot toward her, a volley of midnight arrows.

Before she could even gasp, the barge shot forward at an impossible speed, pitching her backwards, where she smacked into the deck and hit the back of her head, shadow shards skimming over her. Demons thrashed all around her, beating their insubstantial wings, jostling for position, trying to react. And then the barge was beyond them, shooting along the course of the canal, leaving the swarm in its wake.

Tarrik's shadow blade dissolved into the air as he held onto the gunwale with both hands, his braided hair streaming behind him. The bodies of three demons lay at his feet, deep gouges in their flesh.

Carred pushed herself into a sitting position, shaking her hair out of her face. Wind whipped past her, roaring in her ears as the canal banks whizzed by on either side, the shimmering crystal desert a glinting blur.

Almost as soon as it started, the barge's impossible speed began to slow, but already Carred could see the brass citadel up ahead, growing faster at an alarming rate.

But then the speed dropped again, and the barge began to coast under the momentum it had garnered, and Odopek slumped down to a bench at the gunwale, panting hard, his turquoise and green-spotted skin sheened with sweat.

"Good job," Tarrik said, relaxing his grip on the gunwale. "Are you all right, old friend?"

Odopek held up a hand while he sucked in big gulps of air. At last he said, "Friends. The word you are looking for is friends. And yes, we are perfectly all right. Nothing a nice cup of tea won't fix."

In the receding distance, the sky was alive with demons, swirling around each other, clashing with blades of shadow, with teeth and claws. Sorcery roiled round them—noxious clouds, sprays of black darts, shadow flames. Dark blood rained down. Gore and entrails slopped to the waters of the canal. Bodies pitched from the sky, impacting the crystal desert in sprays of shimmering granules.

"They're fighting each other now?" Carred said, sheathing her sword.

"Of course," Tarrik said. "They're demons. The common target has eluded them, and they were already wary of us—well, me, if we are to be brutally honest. I am an ex-resident of Shimrax, but my exploits are not entirely unknown in the other abyssal realms. So now it is a war amongst themselves, the victors supping on the essence of the vanquished in the hopes that they will grow strong enough to challenge ever higher demons and arrive at the ultimate goal."

"To become lord of this realm?" Carred asked. "It's a free-for-all?"

"They think it is," Tarrik said. "But there are far more advanced demons at large in the citadel, and they are the real challengers for Domatai's throne. These minor demons will effectively cull themselves, with only the strong remaining, perhaps to challenge another day in a hundred years, a thousand, maybe even longer."

"But the real threat lies ahead?" Carred said, glancing at the looming citadel as the barge moved towards the circular harbor beneath the main body of the tower. "Where we just happen to be heading."

"I never expected Domatai to perish," Tarrik said. "Indeed, the possibility was never discussed."

"That's demons for you," Odopek said.

"Our assignment here was to open talks with Domatai," Tarrik said, "to posit the idea of an alliance. I am starting to think we were sent on a false pretext."

"Do you think Domatai knew what was going to happen?" Odopek asked.

"Of course he knew," Tarrik said. "The only question is, why did he go so willingly to his death?"

"For Anskar," Carred said.

"The boy must be important indeed," Tarrik said, "if a demon lord is prepared to lay down his life for him."

"He is Domatai's grandson…"

"Even so. Demons routinely slay and absorb their own kin. But it is starting to make sense to me now…"

"Isn't it just!" Odopek said. "*They* did send us here, after all. To parley with Domatai, our feet!"

"As if we two—or is that three?— had anything to offer a demon lord," Tarrik said. "All this booze *they* insist I drink, to dampen down the power, perhaps it has eroded my ability to reason."

"They make you drink?" Carred said. "Personally, I never need much persuasion."

Tarrik stared at her as if he were appraising an interesting insect.

Odopek made peculiar clucking noises with his tongue. "*They* set us up. *They* must have known this was going to happen, and they wanted you here to protect the boy."

"Against a bunch of ambitious higher demons?" Tarrik said. "*They* may have overestimated my abilities."

"Of course," the little man said. "But *they* also knew that we would be with you."

The barge continued to cruise down the center of the canal, and Carred felt a tickling sensation at the edge of her mind, brushing against the boundaries of her repositories. She glanced at Odopek, who stood at the prow, a hand shading his eyes as he peered ahead. The power came from him, she was sure of it, but what power, and how it propelled the barge, she had no idea.

"Well, it's still standing," Odopek said as the barge drifted toward the mountainous tower of brass that stood upon huge pylons that emerged from a vast circular lake. The impression at first was of a floating citadel, but as they drew nearer, Carred could see that the pylons rose a good fifty or more feet above the surface of the lake, and the base of the citadel rested upon them. It was a feat of engineering she had not seen before; on her previous visit, she had been captured and taken inside the citadel while insensible, but here, now, approaching from the canal, she could see what people meant when they said that demons were not just brute creatures driven by lust and hunger. The light of the bronze sun, no longer obscured by the spread of a thousand shadow wings, reflected from the brass citadel, giving it a sorcerous radiance. She almost wanted to call it sacred.

"Of course it's still standing," Tarrik said. "The new incumbent, when the war of succession is over, will hardly want to build a new one. If I know demon lords, and those who aspire to be lords, they will proceed with great care once they come to terms with what has happened. No doubt they will pick battlegrounds that have no value, then unleash the maximum of destruction on their rivals."

"It would be so much easier if they all just got together and had a chat over a good cup of tea," Odopek said. "Then, once they got to know one another, they could take a vote on who is most suited to rule over them."

"That is not demon nature," Tarrik said.

"Nor is it in the nature of the peoples of Wiraya," Carred said. "People are drawn to war like flies to sugar."

"Demons are the same," Tarrik said. "Another point of convergence between our races."

"There are far more differences," Carred said, and Odopek was watching her, his head cocked to one side.

"Agreed," Tarrik said. "Demons start life much lower than humans are even capable of going… well, most humans. Lesser demons are aptly named: less than the beasts, driven by unnatural lusts."

"Unnatural?" Carred asked. "Then where do they come from?"

Tarrik narrowed his eyes, and Carred felt it as a chastisement. She had strayed, apparently, where she should not.

"But," Tarrik said pointedly, as if he did not appreciate being interrupted, "we also rise much higher than humans can ever rise. Save, again, in some very rare cases."

"He is referring to *them*," Odopek said.

Them again. Why the need for secrecy? "I assume by *them* you mean gods?" Carred asked. Ascended humans; those who had succeeded in the crafting and use of Armor of Divinity.

Apparently not, judging by Odopek's wince and Tarrik's world-weary sigh.

"*They* would like you to think that," Odopek said, folding his arms over his chest.

"Not all of them," Tarrik said. "And if I ever... Not that that will ever happen."

"It might if you were not so guarded," Odopek said. "It is now we who are paranoid!"

"You would be too, if you had endured all the things I have. Far better that things stay as they are."

"Until the whiskey runs out..." Odopek said.

They coasted into the circular lake and the blessed relief from the sun's glare beneath the base of the city. The lake was virtually an inland sea, though perfectly circular, with eight evenly spaced canals leading to and from. Hundreds of jetties extended from the lake's retaining walls like the spokes of a wheel, and there were innumerable barges moored at them, some covered with tarps, cargo bulging beneath, others uncovered and half-filled, as if loading or unloading had been abruptly abandoned. Above, Carred saw dozens of trapdoors in the underside of the citadel, some trailing ropes with pulleys, hooks and nets dangling from their ends. A vast crate hung suspended from one such hook, mere yards from the open trapdoor above.

"Welcome to Artuum-Nak'Urdim," Tarrik said, ending by spitting a wad of phlegm into the glimmering waters. "The hub of Vulthanor. There's something similar in each of the realms, save for Shimrax, of course. The hub of that place is a gigantic cesspit."

"Hence Tarrik's charming smell," Odopek said.

"So," Carred said, "you're not tempted to vie for control of Vulthanor?"

"Pah!" Tarrik said. "Why would I want such a thing?"

Odopek raised an eyebrow. "Not tempted in the slightest?"

"You think I could prevail against demons of the forty-fifth order and upwards?" Tarrik asked.

"We think you know the answer to that, old friend. What intrigues us, what we most love about you, is that you do not think it is your place to rule."

"Huh," Tarrik grunted. "Well, maybe I'll change my mind."

"You won't."

Odopek weaved his hands through the air above the prow, and the barge steered a course for the base of a jetty close to one of the massive pilings that held up the citadel. The piling was constructed from girders of black metal. It might have been void-steel.

As the barge came to rest, Odopek uncoiled a length of rope he took from beneath a bench, clambered over the gunwale to the jetty, and secured the rope to a cleat on a mooring post. Tarrik leapt to the jetty and then, to her surprise, offered Carred his hand. His was coarse in her grasp, the palms callused.

No sooner had her feet touched the jetty than a robed demon emerged from the far side of the piling. He was a head and a half taller than Tarrik, willowy where Tarrik was heavily muscled. He wore a long stately robe of some kind of shimmering cloth bedizened with metallic scales of silver and gold. The skin of his face was leathery, crisscrossed with scars and pitted with the tiny craters of some affliction. He only had one eye; where the other had been was a jagged scar across the socket. In one gnarly hand he gripped a rod topped with a heavy iron ball, covered with wicked looking spikes, some with strips of flesh and tufts of hair clinging to them. The ball itself was spattered with dark blood.

TWENTY-FIVE

A QUICK BEER TURNED INTO a night of drinking, and when Sareya awakened in a room above the tavern—a room she didn't remember paying for—she looked around for whoever had taken advantage of her in her drunken state. Only she was alone, with no signs that anyone had done anything other than fold her cloak on a chair, place her boots beneath it, and tuck her into bed.

After she had splashed her face with water and run her fingers through her tangled hair, she fastened her cloak, tugged on her boots, and went downstairs. She found Rindon and Nul still drinking at the same table by the fire they had occupied all night.

"Don't you two ever sleep?" she asked blearily.

Nul poured her a beer from the pitcher on the table.

She waved it away. "Tea," she croaked at the woman behind the bar. "And something to eat—dry toast, if you have it."

She suddenly needed the latrine and hurried away out back. When she returned, a steaming mug of tea awaited her on the table, beside it a rack of toasted bread with flecks of oat and seeds baked into it.

Rindon and Nul had cleared away their beers and both now nursed their own mugs of tea. They looked up from their discussion of the papers before in front of them—scrawled notes, from what she could see, with the names of people she didn't know and lists of what looked like supplies.

Nul glanced up as he noticed her reading over his shoulder. "I hope you are not too shocked to realize it is late afternoon. Rindon and I took the rooms next to yours. Contrary to popular opinion, even heroes need to sleep."

"Though I got little enough of it last night," Rindon said, waggling his fingers at the woman behind the bar. He frowned and then reached under the table to scratch his crotch. The bar woman saw and flung a sodden dishcloth at him.

As Sareya sat down and took her first appreciative sip of tea, the server arrived with plates of sizzling bacon and scrambled eggs for the two heroes.

Nul waved one of the papers he was reading at Sareya. "The thing I hate most about going on missions of this ilk," he said. "Logistics."

"Ah, but where logistics are concerned," Rindon said, "Nul's your man—or rather, the Grand Master's."

Nul gave him a sour look, and Rindon chuckled before stuffing his face with eggs and toast.

Sareya took up a well-thumbed piece of parchment and scanned the cursive text. "Skanuric?" she said.

"Aye," Rindon answered as he brushed crumbs from his mustache. "Nul's always been the brains of our trio..." He closed his eyes and pinched the bridge of his nose. "Duo, nowadays."

Without looking up from his papers, Nul reached over and squeezed Rindon's forearm. "My father wanted me to be a priest of the Elder," he explained.

"What happened?"

"He met me, is what happened," Rindon said. "In the Black Swan tavern in the western suburbs of Sansor."

"My fresher year at the Academy," Nul said, still reading. "This reprobate was singing to the accompaniment of a hand drum and a piper, and, foolish youth that I was, I thought he had a passable voice, so I stopped to watch the entire performance and drank too much in the process. I inadvertently insulted a giant of a man, who divested me of a couple of teeth." He grinned to show Sareya the gap. "Rindon here came to my rescue."

"And fought the giant on your behalf?"

"Good grief, no," Rindon said. "I introduced the fellow to a strumpet I knew rather well, and she popped his anger like a Mingolian balloon. Do you remember how much he itched and scratched for a year after?"

"I remember," Nul said, finally looking up, smiling fondly.

"You're talking about Borik," Sareya said. "I heard what happened in the Thousand Lakes. I'm sorry for your loss."

"Our loss is Menselas's gain," Rindon said, clashing his tea mug with Nul's as if they were beer mugs.

Sareya set her paper down. She couldn't read a word of Skanuric, only recognize the shape of the letters.

"Do you have any idea," Nul said, "how much jerked meat, oats, double-baked bread, and salted herring it takes to supply a team of thirty for a three-day sea crossing followed by a week on land?"

"Say you do," Rindon said, "else you'll be here for the rest of the day, bored out of your pretty mind while he runs through every last calculation, then goes through his list of favorite suppliers, the cost of whetstones, how to keep tinder dry, the prediction of weather patterns, the ebb and flow of the tides... every last tedious, insignificant detail you could imagine, and many you couldn't."

"If Rindon were organizing our mission, we'd likely miss Niyas altogether and end up on the isle of Ak-Settur with nothing to drink save beer, nothing to eat, and the other twenty-seven members of our company painted whores."

"Aye, but it'd be a good trip, eh?" Rindon said, grinning at Sareya as if they were old friends.

She couldn't keep herself from smiling back. One day, she hoped, they really would be friends; but that only brought back memories of the friends she had lost—colleagues at the Burg who had resented her rise through the ranks as Monash's favorite, and poor Naul who had been murdered when the kidnappers had come for her. And Anskar, she thought, wishing Gisela of Gessa had never revealed to her the truth of how she felt.

It was a far easier thing to hate.

The moonlit docks were serene, the water lapping against the pilings of the jetty Sareya walked along with Nul soothing, almost musical. With an hour to kill before they met Rindon and the rest of the newly assembled team for drinks in the quayside tavern they had taken over for the night, Nul had offered to show her the carrack they were to board for Niyas at first light. Its three masts were stripped bare like trees in winter, the sails heaped on deck as sailors inspected and repaired them by the light of oil lamps and a single alchemical globe.

"Taken unawares," Nul explained as he waved to a crewman. "The *Pulchritudinous Princess* wasn't expected to sail again for weeks. Normally, there's ample time for repairs. The Order is paying the captain and crew thrice the normal rates to have us underway by morning."

"Pulchritudinous?"

"It's ancient Skanuric for beautiful. Captain Donalsiom's pretentious like that, but good company for a voyage by sea. Plays the fiddle, has a fine baritone voice, and a personal library that would be the envy of the Elder's priests. He's also a friend of Rindon's."

"So, he likes to drink, then?"

"He has been known to."

Sareya stood at the water's edge, breathing in the cool night breeze, watching the sway of yards and the bob of keels. Every berth seemed full: caravels, yachts, several massive galleons, and hundreds of fishing vessels, all shadows on the star-spangled black water. Out past the calm of the harbor, moonlight fell on another ship: a carrack, she thought, its sails furled, dragging anchor amid the choppy seas. Waiting for room to berth, she had to assume. Waiting for something.

She turned at the clatter of a cart pulling up at the edge of the docks, then watched with Nul as crewmen came down the gangplank of the *Pulchritudinous Princess* and ambled over to unload it.

"The provisions you ordered?"

Nul was hardly listening as he counted with a pointed finger each crate and barrel that came off the back of the cart. "We may have been short-changed. Too late to do anything about it now, but when we return from Niyas—*if* we return—a certain merchant will be getting an unpleasant visit from two irate heroes. Come on," he said, already setting off for the tavern. "An hour must have passed by now. I don't want Rindon insinuating there's anything going on between us. If that man has one fault, it's jealousy. And flapping lips. And a penchant for mockery."

"That's three faults…" Sareya pointed out as she followed him off the boardwalk and into a cobbled alley.

"Don't get me started on the fourth."

The moonlight failed to reach the alley, but the tavern lights at the far end shed an artery of homey light through the center of the gloom. The muffled sounds of music—drums, a guitar, and some kind of skirling pipe—drifted on the air towards them. A man's voice began to sing, a rich tenor, the words distorted by the distance.

"Rindon always likes to perform before we set off on a mission," Nul said. "We should hurry before there's no more beer left in the tavern for us. The others should have arrived by now. They're an interesting team. You should like them. I know they'll like you."

Sareya started at the pad of tiny feet then saw a rat scamper away from the trade door of a store to her right. She started again as she walked into Nul, who had stopped, and now held her back with one hand as he drew his sword with the other.

Three men stood in the alley ahead of him, blocking the way to the tavern. Sailors, Sareya deduced, from their billowing shirts and headscarves, and the cutlasses that glinted in the overspill of light from the far end of the alley.

"Where are the Watch when you need them?" Sareya asked. She reached into her dusk-tide repository.

"Don't waste your energy on riffraff like this," Nul said.

The three men backed away as he stepped toward them. One of them wore a smug grin, and with a "Come on, then" gesture of his hand, goaded Nul on.

"Fine," Nul said, not stupid enough to take the bait. "Use your sorcery."

Flames ignited around Sareya's clenched fist, and the men scattered before she could unleash them, disappearing down intersecting alleys.

But then she felt a weight behind her, a presence so heavy it seemed to drag her towards it. She turned and froze. Twin eyes of amber glared at her out of the gloom. At first she could see nothing else, but then her eyes adjusted, and she could pick out an immense shape, as if the shadows had coalesced into the form of a large and powerful man. The great bulk stepped toward her, and there, a mere ten feet from her, stood the Orgol she had seen upon her arrival in Sansor, its coal-black skin hungry for the scant light. Maybe it was the effect of shock or fear, or some kind of sorcerous glamor, but the Orgol seemed bigger than before, a giant who filled the alleyway, a being so dense it felt as though a mountain had been compressed into his seven or eight-foot frame.

Nul pulled her back and stepped in front, his sword arm trembling. So he felt it too: the elemental dread this creature of the Jargalan Desert radiated.

"Go to the tavern," Nul hissed through gritted teeth. "Get Rindon and the others."

"I'm not leaving you," Sareya said, again reaching for her dusk-tide repository, and this time not holding back. Power swelled within her, the kind with which she had once incinerated half a tribe of dead-eyes. She threw out her arms, and a wall of violet flame sprang up between them and the Orgol.

"Back up," she told Nul, and slowly, one step at a time, they retreated down the alley.

A vast silhouette appeared within the wall of flame, then the Orgol stepped right through it, unharmed.

"Run?" Nul suggested.

"Run," Sareya agreed.

But before either of them could turn, the Orgol surged toward them so fast there was no time to react. A massive fist came at Nul's chest, and he collapsed before it even struck him, his sword clattering to the cobbles.

Sareya lifted herself into the air on a crest of tidal power, but the Orgol made a clutching gesture and she pitched to the ground, her teeth jolting at the impact. She tried to push herself upright, but a shadow fell over her.

Through blurred vision, she saw the Orgol's shovel-sized hand above her face, fingers splayed, ripples of dark energy dancing between them. An impossible weight drove her back down, pressed her head into the cobbles. She couldn't scream, couldn't breathe. She thrashed with her arms, but it was as though she were trapped beneath a fallen tree. A fierce ringing started in her ears, a pressure in her head. Fissures seemed to rip through her skull. She smelled blood in her nostrils, then felt it trickle from her lips. And then she sagged beneath the relentless pressure and the crushing dark.

TWENTY-SIX

CARRED DREW HER SWORD AS the robed demon confronted them. She couldn't take her eyes from the gore-spattered spikes of his mace. The little man, Odopek, hid behind her, while Tarrik confronted the demon with an air of supreme confidence.

"Tarrik Nal—" the demon started, before Tarrik cut him off with a raised fist, shadows already dancing across the knuckles.

"The fool demon was about to divulge Tarrik's actual name," Odopek hissed.

As the little man spoke, Tarrik stooped down and placed the unconscious Anskar on the ground. Anskar twitched, but was otherwise deathly still. His cheeks appeared sunken, the skin covering them thin and taut.

"Revelation of a demon's full name," Odopek continued in a whisper, "is the supreme discourtesy in the culture of the abyssal realms—a remarkably high culture, if you ask me, and I must confess to having considerable experience of such things. Actually, to reveal another's name is tantamount to a declaration of war."

"Then how does this demon know Tarrik's name?" Carred asked.

"Shush now," Odopek said. "And listen carefully to all that transpires. Every word might decide whether we live or we die. I will translate for you."

"I urge you to be discreet, Warder," Tarrik said in Nazgrese, Odopek translating into Niyandrian almost before Tarrik's words left his mouth. "Unless you would like me to divulge your full name and rank in the demonic orders? Do not think I will not. I sacrificed a good deal to gain such valuable information while I was under your loving care in Shimrax."

"Warder?" Carred whispered.

"Tarrik was an exile," Odopek explained, "confined to Shimrax under the Warder's charge."

Which would no doubt explain how the Warder had come to know Tarrik's full name.

The Warder let his spiked mace hang limply at his side, then decided to hide it behind his back and pretend no one had seen it. He grew suddenly officious, tilting his pointed chin and somehow managing to convey disdain with his one eye. "It is surprising to see you here, Tarrik, and at such a critical time. How did you escape your exile?"

"Who said I escaped?" Tarrik said, as Odopek rapidly finished translating the Warder and rushed to keep up. "Maybe I earned my freedom."

"A likely story!"

"The funny thing, Warder," Tarrik said, "is that you should know how and why I came to leave Shimrax, given your famed *omniscience*."

Carred could hear the sneer in that last word, even without the aid of Odopek's translation.

"Yes, well, I left my duties in Shimrax quite some time ago. I thought you might have noticed. Tell me, did the place grow lax in my absence?

I bet there is unbridled violence and lust now, the inmates predating upon one another."

"That is about the measure of it," Tarrik said. "And so, Warder, you have gone up in the realms. I suppose you have a nice abode here in Vulthanor? How many higher demons did you have slaughtered just so you could absorb them and gain their privileges? Because I refuse to believe you killed them yourself."

The spiked mace chose that moment to reappear from behind the Warder's back.

"I have killed, Tarrik. And I will kill again, if I must. Anything in order to get ahead of the others, and survive."

"If you did not know me better, Warden," Tarrik said, "I might take that as a threat."

The Warder's demeanor shifted. His eye widened, but it was hard for Carred to know whether it was from fear or surprise.

"A threat? You jest with me, Tarrik! There are no threats between us. Oh, we might not have always gotten along, but I had a job to do, and you… well, I am sure you worked out your penance admirably. I pride myself on how well I treated my charges. You were lucky to be under my care. I did right by you, did I not?"

Tarrik's only answer was a low chuckle.

The Warder switched his attention first to Carred, then to Odopek, who was still translating the last exchange in Carred's ear; and finally to Anskar lying prone on the ground beneath the piling.

"Might I ask, Tarrik," the Warder said in a deferential tone, "what you are doing with this filth? They are from one of the slaver realms, are they not?"

"That," Tarrik said, "is between me and the Lord Domatai. Or was. You do realize he is dead?"

The Warder gave a grim nod, then leaned in conspiratorially to Tarrik. Odopek held a hand to his ear, the better to hear. "I would advise against entering the citadel. It is turmoil inside, everybody vying for position, forging alliances that we all know will sooner or later be broken."

"You know how it is," Tarrik said. "An old demon like you, you must have been through many successions."

"Actually, I have not," the Warder said. "Hence my lowly position as an overseer in Shimrax. You really think I would have gone to that cesspool by choice?"

"So, what you are saying is that you prefer to run away whenever the chaos of a war of succession ensues," Tarrik said. "Just think—if you had a spine, you could have been a demon lord by now."

"Or dead," the Warder said. "Absorbed by some brute bloody gurnap or other. I tell you, those monsters seem to breed just for such occasions. No, thank you! And besides," he said slyly, "there are other ways to ascend than by engaging in bestial combat." He tapped the side of his flat, broad nose. "I have, shall we say, contacts. Perhaps, Tarrik, old friend, my contacts could be of value to you…"

"In return for what?" Tarrik asked, seemingly growing bored with the conversation and beginning an inspection of the outer casing of the piling, where Carred now noticed the outline of a closed circular hatch.

The Warder grew agitated. "What are you doing? You can't go down there!"

"Because this is your escape route? I have known you a long time, Warder," Tarrik said, "and it does not surprise me that you are once more running away."

"Running? Running away! All the way down there, so far beneath the citadel? Wherever would I go?"

"I think we both know the answer to that," Tarrik said. "I assume you heard the rumors, but have not yet established for yourself whether or not they are true."

"Rumors? What rumors?"

Tarrik stepped back from the pylon as the hatch popped open onto a gloomy shaft with dark metal rungs set into the wall.

"Rumors of a recent addition to the citadel's trade routes: a portal with near infinite possibilities of travel between worlds."

"You know of it?" the Warder said.

"The Ethereal Sorceress's depot," Carred whispered to Odopek. "Anskar brought it here in his pocket, a model that grew once he—well, it was me, actually—triggered it. It's how we escaped Vulthanor that first time."

"Yes, yes, yes," Odopek said. "This we already know."

"How?" Carred asked, aware that both Tarrik and the Warder were watching her.

"The Ethereal Sorceress told us."

"Told you when? She's dead."

"Nevertheless…" Odopek said.

"Well," Tarrik said in Nazgrese, Odopek resuming his translation, "if you are heading the same way as us, Warder, make yourself useful and carry the boy."

"Carry?" the Warder said, frowning down at Anskar.

"Or do not," Tarrik said. "But that is the only way you are getting to the depot."

The Warder's eyes flicked left and right as if he were considering every possible avenue. His shoulders sagged as resignation set in. "Very well, if you insist," he said, leaning his mace against the piling and stooping down to pick up Anskar. The instant his fingers connected with Anskar's shirt, the Warder recoiled.

"What is this… this power?"

Odopek glanced at Carred, and she mouthed, "The earth-tide?"

The little man shook his head, as if she were an idiot, then raised a hand to prevent her from saying anything further as he resumed his translation.

The Warder's shock turned to indignation. "I cannot—will not—participate in this… in whatever it is you're up to, Tarrik. This… human… Power such as resides within him does not belong here in the abyssal realms. It is an offense. It should not exist!"

An inscrutable look crossed Tarrik's face as he stood in front of the open hatch, appraising the Warder. "Power such as what?"

The Warder edged to his right, and Tarrik mirrored his movements, circling away from the doorway. "I want no trouble, Tarrik, and nothing to do with this… abomination." He cocked his thumb at Anskar. "Go, all of you. I will not hinder you. Nor will I accompany you. I will remain here, and for once I will fight."

Tarrik frowned, then gave a curt nod. "I wish you the best of all luck, Warder."

"And I you."

Tarrik crouched down so that he could lift Anskar into his arms, then gave a curious look to Odopek. He might even have winked.

As Tarrik turned his back and walked with Anskar toward the open hatch in the pylon, the Warder's hand slipped inside the folds of his robe and reemerged clutching a curved silver dagger. With speed he had not shown until now, the Warder surged after Tarrik, slashing with the blade at the back of Tarrik's neck.

At the same instant, Odopek made a sweeping gesture with his arm and uttered a cant in a language Carred didn't recognize. Tarrik shunted to one side as if blown by a sudden gale, and the Warder's blade struck only air. Off-balance, he stumbled toward the opening in the pylon. A second gesture from Odopek—a shove this time—and the Warder screamed as he shot through the opening and plummeted from sight.

Tarrik turned a wry grin on Odopek, who thrust his fists into his hips and looked far from amused.

"You do realize that was a star metal blade he was going to cut you with?" the little man said.

"It was?" Tarrik glanced over his shoulder, then shrugged, shifting Anskar's unconscious body in his arms. "Then I am doubly grateful for your intervention, old friend. Forgive me: old friends."

Carred remembered Queen Talia telling her that star metal was inimical to demons. It was star metal she had brought—a pouch of powdered *astrumium*—to trade for void-steel during her first visit to Vulthanor. The Lord Domatai had apparently been stockpiling weapons of star metal. Anything to gain an advantage, it seemed.

The Warder drifted up inside the pylon atop an inky cloud of blackness, his eyes ablaze with violet light.

Tarrik spun on his heel, but his arms were full, and the Warder's dagger came straight at his face. Odopek was too slow to react, and Carred was out of range. But then a shadow blade shot from Tarrik's hand, knocking the Warder's dagger from his hand and punching through his skull. The star metal blade went spinning back through the opening, and the Warder convulsed for a second before pitching backwards into the void as Tarrik's shadow sword retracted into his hand.

By the time Carred reached the opening and peered down, there was no sign of the Warder or his blade. Then she heard the muffled thud of his body hitting the bottom.

"See you down there," Tarrik said as he stepped into the opening, a disk of shadow appearing beneath his feet as he began a slow and measured descent into the darkness.

"Just make sure you don't touch the void-steel rungs, if you must show off and use dark-tide sorcery!" Odopek said. He gestured for Carred to go ahead of him, indicating the rungs set into the wall inside the pylon. She sheathed her sword and gritted her teeth.

It was like climbing down into a vat of oil, the darkness beneath Carred's feet was so thick. Her wrists ached from where she gripped the rungs too tightly, fear of falling making her tense every muscle in her body. The darkness above her softened, and she glanced up to see

Odopek limned with silver light as he climbed down after her.

"What have you stopped for?" the little man asked, craning his neck so he could frown at her. His face was lambent, the silver glow emanating from his beady eyes.

"I was…" Carred bit her lip to stop from confessing that she was afraid. "I was just waiting for you to catch up."

"Really?" Odopek said. She couldn't read his expression in the burgeoning glare, but he sounded genuinely surprised. "That is most considerate of you, Miss Carred. We are grateful."

The light from Odopek's eyes brightened until it illuminated the inside of the piling, a shaft of dark metal that dropped beneath the ambit of the silver glow.

"The void-steel in the ladder," Odopek said cheerily as they resumed their descent, "fortunately has no effect on my moonshine." He chuckled, as if at a private joke.

They climbed down for what seemed an age, until they reached a solid metal floor at the bottom. There they found Tarrik standing at a crossroads of four intersecting tunnels, all of the same dark metal as the shaft they had come down and each wide enough for three people to stand abreast.

Anskar sat slumped against the tunnel wall, chin on chest, barely breathing. Odopek's radiance only extended about thirty feet in every direction. Beyond that, Carred could see nothing. It was a wonder the little man could see at all with such a conflagration blazing from his eyes, but he saw enough to muster a frown, which was directed at the body lying at Tarrik's feet, beside the star metal dagger.

It was the Warder; or rather, what was left of him. His corpse was desiccated almost to the bone, shriveled up and emaciated, little more than a mummified husk.

"I thought you weren't going to do this demon stuff anymore," Odopek said. "*They* will not be pleased to hear about this."

"Then do not tell them," Tarrik said. His voice grated, as if he had drunk nothing for days, and his body was knotted with tension. His eyes were tightly shut, his breathing labored.

"As always, we will be discreet," Odopek said, "though our discretion is never without a cost."

"I will fix your blasted teapot."

"You said that years ago."

"And I have been too busy," Tarrik said. "Gone through too many changes. But this time it will be different. I just need one more component to get the job done."

"And it will work?" the little man said, the silver glare from his eyes wavering as his voice rose in pitch. "All will be restored? One will become two again?"

"The Ethereal Sorceress thinks it will work," Tarrik said, "and she should know."

Odopek danced an excited jig.

"Teapot?" Carred asked.

"And what," the little man said, indignant now, folding his arms across his chest, "is wrong with teapots?"

"Nothing," Carred said, glancing at Tarrik for help.

The demon's eyes remained shut, his chest rising and falling as if he had just been for a sprint. "Always so paranoid, little friend. She meant no disrespect." Then to Carred, "The teapot is his…" He grimaced as if in great pain. "It is his pride and joy."

"To put it mildly," Odopek said.

Tarrik began to pant, faster and faster, until he threw his head back and let out an exultant roar. His eyes snapped open, blazing violet for one blistering second before dimming to their usual gray. Shudders ripped through his massive frame, and then slowly faded away until he stood perfectly still.

Odopek sighed, while Tarrik shook himself then let out a theatrical belch.

"I will digest the Warder's essence when there is more time."

"If he permits it," Odopek said.

"Oh, I do not expect him to put up much of a fight." Tarrik rapped the side of his head with his knuckles. "Be a good boy in there, Warder, and I will absorb what remains of you as swiftly and painlessly as I can. Though, really, I do not know why I bother. I cannot imagine he has much in the way of knowledge I do not already possess."

"Then why do it?" Carred asked. It wasn't hard to understand what he had just done. She had learned from Malady the dwarf demon that absorption of one's vanquished foes was the means of ascent in the abyssal realms. She could feel her ire rising. It was all a bit too close to what Talia had done to Marith.

"You sound angry," Tarrik said. "Bitter."

Carred made no attempt to disguise the fact, and Tarrik raised an eyebrow at her tone of voice—surprise, or a warning not to push him too far? "The higher you demons rise through the orders, the more cultivated you become, you say?" she said. "I'm not convinced."

"Nor need you be," Tarrik said. "I am rarely inclined to seek the opinions of humans. My mission here does not even concern you." As if to illustrate his point, he scooped up Anskar and settled him once more over his shoulder.

Tarrik led the way along the right-hand tunnel, always at the very edge of Odopek's radiance. The clangor of their boots on the metal floor was deafening, no matter how softly Carred tried to step. She expected at any moment every demon in the citadel to come running, but when none showed, she guessed they had more pressing matters to attend to, such as ripping each other to shreds in the war of succession.

They came to a ramp that led down at a steep gradient. At the bottom, the corridor turned back on itself, and then they were following a succession of switchback ramps deeper and deeper underground.

Tarrik never slowed, never tired, despite the weight of Anskar slung over his shoulder. If anything, the demon's energy seemed to have increased since absorbing the Warder.

When the switchback descent stopped at a corridor leading off into the gloom, Carred felt an overwhelming urge to run. Odopek placed a reassuring hand around her wrist, and she drew in a deep and calming breath. Without the illumination the little man provided, she would be blind in the dark.

"Do not be affrighted," Odopek said. "You are sensing the residue of feeble sorcery, nothing more. The sorcery of the enslaved."

He was right. Now she thought about it, she could feel a prickling sensation beneath her scalp, and her reawakened repositories seemed to bubble and boil in anticipation.

Tarrik strode ahead, as if Anskar weighed no more than a baby, until he came to a door at the far end, where he turned back to wait for Carred and Odopek to catch up.

As she drew nearer, Carred became aware of a voice, high-pitched and tinkling. It was answered by a second voice, this one bestial. Both were speaking guttural words, but nothing that she could understand. Presumably it was Nazgrese.

The door Tarrik had turned his back to was of the same dark metal as the corridor. Set into the center of the door were two gemstones, one amethyst, the other clear quartz. Phosphorescence glowed green either side of the door, drawing her eyes. There, formed from emerald light, were two mouths, one to the left, the other to the right of the door. Both had thin lips and razor-sharp fangs. There were letters in curlicued script beneath each mouth—also Nazgrese.

The tinkling voice spoke again, the lips of the left-hand mouth rippling as they shaped the words. Though Carred couldn't understand what the mouth said, she could hear the urgency in its utterances, the demand.

The right-hand mouth growled in response, a hungry growl with intimations of blood.

Tarrik swung round to face the door, at the same time barking guttural words in Nazgrese. Instantly, the green light that defined the sorcerous mouths faded away to nothing, and the door slid to one side. Hot air rushed out of the entrance, hitting Carred in the face.

"Subtle as ever," Odopek said.

"What did he say to them?" Carred asked.

Tarrik replied without looking back, as he strode ahead through the doorway, carrying Anskar. "I merely told them to be silent and to open the door."

"And they obeyed, just like that?"

Odopek was chuckling to himself.

"I might have mentioned," Tarrik said, "something about flaying the spirit nerves of their pathetic shades before I absorbed the last dregs of their essence. Blood and fire, I loathe the unbodied."

Odopek released Carred's wrist and gestured for her to go next.

The corridor beyond lacked the dark metal paneling of the passageways they had thus far followed. The walls, ceiling, and floor were of some porous rock, glistening with dew and thick with black mold. A peppery stench irritated Carred's nostrils and made her want to sneeze. Her eyes started to water, and when she breathed, very little air seemed to reach her lungs.

"What does he mean, 'unbodied'?" she asked Odopek.

"The sorcerous mouths by the door we entered by," Odopek said, "were formed from the lingering essence of lower order demons whose bodies had been destroyed."

"Demons live beyond physical death?" Carred said. "They have shades like we do?"

"Similar, but not quite the same," Odopek said. "For one thing, pureblood demons never go to the realm of the dead. Usually, their essence—their intellect, memory, the sorcerous abilities they have accrued—is absorbed by the one to vanquish them. But sometimes…"

"Sometimes," Tarrik cast back over his shoulder, "their putrid essence isn't worth the effort of absorbing, and so they are permitted to linger, albeit in service to the one who slew them."

"Which is to say," Odopek explained, "they become the components *and* the energy source of certain fixed sorceries, like the speaking mouths you just witnessed."

"Sounds horrible," Carred said.

"That is because it is," Tarrik replied.

Carred's heart thumped at an explosion from somewhere high above. It was followed by a succession of thunderclaps and muffled screams.

"It sounds like the war of succession has commenced in earnest," Tarrik said. "Which means we should not linger. Every inch of Artuum-Nak'Urdim will be scoured for resistance and for possible contenders."

"Him," Odopek said, cocking a thumb at Tarrik. "They will scent his mightiness and assume he is in the running."

"I doubt they will scent anything much over the odor of your flatulence," Tarrik said.

A second explosion came from above, this one not quite so muted.

Odopek waved his hands in denial. "That was not us!"

A sound like the crash of waves followed, the cascade of rubble and water.

Carred turned a wide-eyed look on Tarrik, but the demon was already running, Anskar's head bobbing over his shoulder.

"Do not tarry," Odopek said as he scampered past her.

Fear got Carred's blood flowing once more, and she followed at an easy jog, fingers wrapped around the hilt of her scabbarded sword. She kept glancing behind but saw no sign of pursuit; yet the roar of a waterfall went on increasing, and screeches echoed along the corridors behind her.

Tarrik brought them to an intersection where the walls were no longer ragged and rough; they were coated in a smooth substance that might have been a kind of plaster. He took the right-hand path, Carred and Odopek following, past dozens of circular doors formed from some sort of frosted crystal that studded both walls of every corridor they went down.

After the fourth or fifth turn, Carred was utterly lost, each passage the same as the last, the only difference being that some of the crystal round-doors were open onto storerooms crammed with barrels and crates, one or two with the carcasses of giant lizards hanging from meat hooks set into the ceiling. One opened onto a cell, where a yellow-skinned lesser demon with a spine-covered head and burning orange eyes was nailed to the opposite wall. It looked up forlornly as they passed, then let out a plaintive cry, devoid of all hope.

"Do you know where you're going?" Carred called to Tarrik. She was convinced she had fled along these very corridors with Anskar when they had escaped the abyssal realms, but that didn't make her any less lost.

"This is the way we came when we were sent as ambassadors to the Lord Domatai," Odopek explained.

"We had an escort when we arrived," Tarrik called back over his shoulder, "but one of the benefits of absorbing so many superior intellects is that I have a near-perfect memory and have no trouble following a route once traveled."

"When he's not drinking," Odopek said.

They rounded yet another corner and came to a dead end, where the corridor terminated at one of the ubiquitous crystal doors.

Tarrik raised his palm toward the frosted surface, then pulled it back when Odopek tapped him on the back.

"Do you think the depot is still guarded?" the little man asked.

"Blood and fire!" Tarrik swore. "I had quite forgotten."

"Must have been the whiskey you were downing while you waited for me and Anskar," Carred said. "So, we're reliant upon your less-than-perfect memory for our survival now. That's reassuring."

Tarrik scowled at her.

"Last time, we were on official business," Odopek said. "We may not be afforded the same courtesies now that the Lord Domatai is dead."

"It is a bit late to worry about that," Tarrik said, pausing to listen as a roar went up from somewhere behind. It sounded like the battle cry of an army.

Tarrik pressed his palm to the crystal surface and the round door slid open, disappearing within a groove cut into the plastered wall. He stepped through the doorway, and Odopek gestured, with a little flourish, for Carred to go next.

As she crossed the threshold, her every sense was pulled towards the monstrous demon looming on the far side of the chamber, standing in front of what looked like an enormous buttress, a growth of un-mortared wall, almost as if it had grown like a tumor of granite to take over much of the room.

Steam plumed from the demon's flared nostrils as it took a lumbering step toward the intruders. It was as wide as it was tall—and it was a head and a half taller even than Tarrik. Thick cords of sinew stood out on its bullish neck, and its ape-like face was slate-gray, with a single amber eye set in the center of its forehead. The demon was naked save for a thick leather gauntlet that covered one hand, the other with only three fingers and a thumb. The gauntleted hand was clutching what looked like a short sword, given the immense size of the demon, but to Carred it would have been a long sword. The demon's torso was riddled with fist-sized warty growths that had the consistency of rock. Its muscular legs bent backwards at the knees and terminated in bird-like talons. No phallus, though, Carred couldn't help but notice; just a jagged scar surrounded by an unruly growth of spiny black hair.

"Leave this to us," Odopek said. "The demon must remember us from our arrival."

"With a brain the size of a pea?" Tarrik said. "I sincerely doubt it."

"Then we are sure it will respond to our charm," Odopek said. "It did before, and was quite professional in its conduct."

"Odopek…" Tarrik cautioned. "It's a gurnap, barely even worthy of the name demon, a beast from the slag pits of Shimrax. You would have more luck using your famed charms on a raging bull."

"Have you so little faith in our abilities, even after all this time?" Odopek said. The little man took a step toward the demon, stopping when its massive head swiveled in his direction.

"Would it be all right if we just take our leave from Vulthanor and head back the way we came?" Odopek asked, still speaking Niyandrian.

The little man edged toward the granite buttress of the depot, where there was a rectangular outline partially submerged beneath the floor—double doors of stone. Carred had seen them only from the inside, when the depot had grown up around her and Anskar.

"Speak in Nazgrese!" Tarrik said, then backed away in a half-circle to his left as the demon turned toward him. "Actually, do not bother. Gurnaps rarely possess the ability to speak. You could try grunting, I suppose."

The demon growled then lurched toward Tarrik, and Tarrik barked something back in Nazgrese as he set Anskar down on the floor.

"What did he say?" Carred asked.

"You do not want to be fighting me, lesser demon, spawn of goats!" Odopek translated for her. "Tarrik is not renowned for his diplomacy. He does, however, have an indecent amount of experience with goats—do not ask!"

A shadow blade extended from Tarrik's hand, growing to a length of at least five feet. He reinforced his grip by curling the fingers of his other hand around the misty hilt.

The gurnap let out a rumbling laugh that caused the chamber to rock. It raised its gauntleted hand, brandishing its silver sword.

Tarrik started to say something in Nazgrese, then stopped, his eyes narrowing as he glanced at Odopek and said in Niyandrian, "Is that star metal?"

Carred glanced at the depot. There was more star metal inside—she had seen it last time she was here—an entire stash. But then she remembered the servants of the Ethereal Sorceress carting it away. Probably it had already been sold.

Despite its ponderous bulk, the gurnap glided like a dancer as it sped straight at Tarrik, taloned feet clattering over the floor. Silver arced through the air, the sword on a trajectory to slice through Tarrik's neck. Tarrik blocked it with his shadow blade, at the same time pivoting to lessen the brunt of the impact. But he was so intent on avoiding the star metal that he didn't see the gurnap's free fist coming at him from the other side, a ferocious left hook that slammed Tarrik into the wall. Tarrik's shadow blade dissolved into thin air as he slumped to the floor, and the gurnap rushed in to finish him off. But it stopped in its tracks when Tarrik burst into flame, at the same time lifting into the air, back arched, arms splayed wide.

"No!" Odopek yelled. "Tarrik, you must not!"

The gurnap turned at the sound of the little man's voice. It hesitated, glancing between the conflagration that was Tarrik and Odopek, who saw the danger he was in and backed away behind Carred.

The flames engulfing Tarrik died down then immediately flared up again, and the gurnap turned back to him, as if it had sensed a weakness.

"Tarrik is fighting the power," Odopek said.

"And that's a good thing? Now might be a good time to use it," Carred said as she drew her sword and started after the gurnap.

Black smoke effused from Tarrik's skin, and his eyes smoldered. His face was contorted in a grimace as he struggled to contain the fire burning within him, but the gurnap had already launched into its gliding attack.

Carred pounced then, slamming her sword into its back. Steel struck the rock-like carapace of its warty hide, and the blade bounced off, and sending shooting pains up Carred's arm. The gurnap's free hand lashed out, grabbing her sword by the blade. With a grunt, the gurnap squeezed, and the blade shattered. Carred glanced at the hilt in her hand and the jagged piece of blade protruding from it, then flung it in the gurnap's face. The demon swayed out of the way effortlessly, and the hilt clattered away across the floor.

The gurnap showed its palm to her: not a cut, not a scratch. There was nothing she could do to harm it, and it remained fixated on her as she backed away, following as if it had all the time in the world and nothing to worry about from any of the three that faced it.

The gurnap lunged for Carred, then drew up sharp when the floor of the chamber bounced under the impact of a concussive boom from above. There followed a succession of blasts and a sound like an earthquake that went on and on. Through it all, pressure continued to build in Carred's skull, and she felt the quiver and tug of her repositories responding to the sheer magnitude of sorcery being unleashed above ground.

The instant the rumbles died away, the gurnap swung its star metal sword at her with such ferocity, she didn't even have time to scream. Before the blade met her neck, something popped within her mind. Lightning streaked from her eyes, and the gurnap wheeled away with a shriek, shielding its face with an arm.

A shadow shifted behind the wailing gurnap—a solid shadow with something dense moving within: Tarrik, wreathed in a second skin of black mist, armor woven from dark-tide sorcery. A new shadow sword extended from his hand, arcing toward the gurnap's head. Warned by some instinct, the gurnap spun round and brought up its star metal blade to block. Where shadow met *astrumium*, shadow lost, and Tarrik's sorcerous blade dissipated into the air. But the gurnap's sword was still moving, grazing the edge of Tarrik's shadow armor as he swayed out of the way. Immediately the second skin of inky vapors that shrouded Tarrik disappeared, leaving him stunned and utterly open. But only for a moment. As the gurnap stepped in to finish him off, Tarrik ducked beneath its swing and pivoted off to one side. The gurnap turned, and Tarrik delivered a crushing roundhouse kick to the side of its knee, causing it to stumble.

"Keep out of range!" Odopek yelled. "One touch of star metal and you are finished."

"Then get the depot open!" Tarrik cried back. "Blood and fire, must I do everything myself?"

Odopek produced a silver bell from his pocket and rang it three times.

The gurnap roared and spun towards the little man even as the double doors to the depot started to grind open. Tarrik whistled, and the gurnap turned back, straight into a right hook.

"Blood and—" Tarrik swore as he shook out his fist and nursed his wrist, but the gurnap's sword was already flashing toward his face. He ducked and shoved the gurnap in the chest, but the creature just stood there, immovable as a mountain.

"Come on!" Odopek shouted from the doorway. "Oh, shit. We quite forgot the boy!"

"Go on ahead, I'll get him," Tarrik said, backing away to where Anskar lay.

Odopek grabbed Carred's arm, pulling her toward the entrance, but she broke free, shadowing the gurnap as it made a beeline for Tarrik.

Again the gurnap began its gliding offense, swinging for Tarrik as it came into range. Tarrik ducked again, but this time the gurnap's attack had been a feint, and it caught him by the throat with its free hand and hoisted him kicking and spluttering into the air.

Carred ran at the gurnap, grabbing its sword wrist with both hands. Tarrik slammed his palms against the creature's ears—little more than holes in the sides of its massive head. It roared and flung him into the wall with a sickening thud. Tarrik slumped to the floor.

The gurnap tried to shake Carred off, but she clung to its wrist with tenacity, determined to make it drop the sword. When the gurnap reached for her with its other hand, she kicked out hard, striking it in the mutilated groin—a direct hit on the scar. The gurnap squealed, so she kicked it again, harder. The gurnap thrashed about in a fury, dropping its sword as it strove to protect itself.

The instant the sword clattered to the floor, Carred let go of the gurnap's wrist, jarring her knee as she landed awkwardly. The gurnap lunged for her, but she rolled beneath its grasping hands and came up holding the star metal sword. The creature saw the danger and hesitated, its tiny brain trying to work out the best course of action. And in that moment, Carred thrust the blade with all her strength into the only place the gurnap seemed to be vulnerable: its groin.

The gurnap's single eye widened, then rolled up inside its head as it let out a piercing, ululating shriek. Carred expected the creature to pull away from the sword embedded to the hilt in its groin, but it seemed frozen in place, unable to do anything but scream. And then its massive frame began to convulse, warty flesh sloughing from the bone to spatter the floor in steaming puddles. For a moment, the gurnap stood there, a glistening, dripping skeleton, shuddering around the blade that impaled it, and then it disintegrated, showering the floor with dust and ash.

"Theltek's nostrils, that stinks," Carred said, covering her mouth and nose with her free hand as she stepped away from the sludge—all that remained of the gurnap.

She turned at a scuff from behind to find Tarrik cricking his neck and popping his back. He didn't exactly look impressed with her handiwork. If anything, he looked concerned.

"You can put the sword down now," he said, eyeing the star metal blade warily.

"Bastard gurnap broke mine," Carred said, "so I'm taking his in reparation. But I can see now why you demon types are so afraid of star metal."

"If I had my way, it would be banned," Tarrik said. "Otherwordly space junk. Keep it if you must, but do not think to draw the blade in my presence."

Or what? Carred thought, but she didn't dare voice the words. Something had changed in Tarrik's demeanor. He seemed edgier, dangerous.

And then she realized what it was. Not the star metal blade, although he was undeniably worried about that. "You think you should have done better against the gurnap."

"Do not think that I am being boastful," Tarrik said. Odopek was watching from the doorway to the depot, an odd expression on his face, something between sadness and pride, the sort a parent— a real parent, not Carred's—might have for a child who had learned a valuable but painful lesson. "I have more power than you, and yet I was impotent against the gurnap."

"Because you elected to be," Odopek said. "You could have incinerated it with your... other power, but you did not."

"Then perhaps I am a fool," Tarrik said.

"On the contrary, old friend," Odopek said, "you may have just saved all our lives, and you may have taken a vital step on the journey you have undertaken."

"Not entirely voluntarily," Tarrik said.

"When is it ever?" the little man replied.

Carred tried the star metal sword in her scabbard. The blade was slightly narrower than her old sword, so it wasn't exactly a snug fit, but at least she would have no trouble drawing it in a hurry.

Then the thought occurred to her as Tarrik stooped to pick up Anskar and drape him over his shoulder again: a star metal blade might be a good equalizer, and not just against demons. Talia was a half-blood demon. Carred did nothing to combat the vengeful images conspiring in her mind, the burn of acid in her veins, but then doubt poured the cooling water of a slack tub on them. What if star metal only worked on full-blood demons? After all, hadn't Anskar once blended *astrumium* with his sword? More than that, wasn't star metal one of the ingredients for the Armor of Divinity that was now melded with Talia's—Marith's!—flesh?

"Do not tarry," Odopek said, disappearing inside the depot.

Tarrik shot Carred a glare then followed the little man.

"Don't mention it," Carred muttered.

Her arm shook from where she gripped the hilt of the scabbarded star metal sword too tightly.

Marith, she thought as hot tears squeezed from her eyes. This wasn't about Tarrik. It was about Marith. It was about Queen Talia, and how the bitch was going to pay.

One finger at a time, Carred released her grip on the sword hilt, then with a deep breath, she entered the depot.

Inside, the stash of star metal weapons might have been cleared away by servants, but, oddly, the Ethereal Sorceress's orichalcum mask and her blood-drenched robe—the blood was golden—still lay on the checkerboard floor, even though she had been killed in Dorinah. Beside the robe lay the masked functionary who had slain the Sorceress. Blosius—Anskar had known him. He still held the murder weapon in his hand, a dagger with which had had then killed himself.

And there, right where she had left them when she and Anskar had been accosted by Sareya and the knights sent by Archduke Peleus to arrest Anskar for some crime he had apparently committed against the

Archduke's son, were Carred's two caskets of void-steel.

Her head swam with the implications. She had brought the caskets back through the *izindel* from Vulthanor to the depot in Dorinah, and yet here they were in the Vulthanor depot. She knew these were the same caskets: one of them was still open from where she had dropped it, ingots of void still scattered before it on the checkerboard floor. And the Ethereal Sorceress's robe, her mask... Blosius. How could they be both here and there?

A quick glance back through the depot's double doors showed her they were still in the chamber where she had slain the gurnap. She covered her mouth to contain her rising bile.

"Do you think Sheelahn will notice if I take one?" Tarrik said, striding for the caskets and picking up an ingot of void-steel.

"Hey!" Carred said. "That's mine!"

"You can spare a single ingot, surely," Tarrik said. "I shall consider it payment for services rendered."

"So much for your touted demon honor," Odopek said. "Return the ingot to the poor lady, else we shall be ashamed to call you our friend."

"Void-steel is the missing component... for your teapot."

"Oh, well in that case, a single ingot is but a drop in the ocean of void-steel." Odopek gave Carred a toothy smile. "No harm done?"

"Fine," she said. "Just the one, mind. But that's it. Consider yourselves paid in full."

Odopek crouched down and lifted the Ethereal Sorceress's mask, peering into its empty eye holes. "We still think we should take it to her."

"Whatever," Tarrik said, pocketing the ingot and striding for the far side of the chamber.

Carred and Odopek shared a look, then Carred crossed to the twin caskets and began returning the spilled void-steel to the one that was open. She stacked one casket atop the other and hefted both to her chest.

Tarrik and Odopek awaited her in the cage that traveled between levels. As she entered and Odopek shut the cage door, she caught sight of Anskar's face hanging over Tarrik's back. She lifted one of his eyelids with her thumb. No reaction. Nothing there save the black pebble of an eye that had appeared lifeless before, but now really was.

"He's dead," she said in a tremulous voice. All these years looking for the heir to Niyas, a lifetime of fighting and failing, and now, at the last, she had failed again.

"Continue on?" the demon asked, as if it didn't matter to him either way.

"The power still resides within him," Odopek said, "even if the outer shell no longer lives. We say, go on. *They* will know what to do."

Carred withdrew into herself, startled back into the world outside her head only when the cage juddered and began to descend.

She vaguely registered exiting the cage and shambling along behind Odopek and Tarrik, down the same green-carpeted corridor as before until they reached the room with the polished granite floor, a circle of orichalcum at its center, inscribed with Skanuric runes.

Odopek and Tarrik awaited her in the middle of the circle. Tarrik could not meet her eyes as she joined them.

"How are we going to operate it?" Carred asked. Last time, Anskar had mouthed words of sorcery in a strange, mellifluous voice.

"You forget," Odopek said, shoving the Ethereal Sorceress's mask under his arm, "that Tarrik and I came to Vulthanor via the *izindel*, and that the Ethereal Sorceress is an associate of ours."

The little man shuffled from foot to foot, keeping time with the tinkling song that spilled from his lips.

A storm of gold and silver motes swirled around the circle, and then Carred was falling through the void.

TWENTY-SEVEN

THE PITCH AND ROCK OF a ship brought bile to Sareya's throat when she awoke in the gloom below deck. From somewhere above—it sounded miles away—yards creaked and men laughed as they cried out to one another in an unfamiliar language. She was seated with her back to a beam, arms above her head. Chains rattled as she shifted position, manacles pinching her wrists. The air in the was stultifying, made worse by the stench of spilled wine turned sour, of vinegar, and bad meat, rat dung, and human. Not a cabin, then. The ship's hold? She was beyond caring that hers was among the smells. Embarrassment was a privilege she no longer enjoyed. Of course, it could have been coming from Nul, chained to the post opposite her, unmoving.

"Nul," she whispered.

No response.

"Nul," she said again, louder this time.

He grunted something, but before he could speak, the trap door above opened, spilling unnatural light into the hold.

A man backed down the steps and cast his eyes over them. The billowing pants he wore had a fine coating of salt, and his turned-down boots were dark with damp. Strips of black cloth were wound about his head and face, save for the almond-shaped eyes. His bare arms were crisscrossed with scars; nothing accidental about them, either. They formed white ladders that covered virtually every exposed inch of skin.

"Jargalan," Nul said in a thready voice. "Pirate…"

"Silence!" the man said in Nan-Rhouric, his accent thick. He stooped so he could glare into Sareya's eyes. His sclerae were a sickly yellow, the blue irises almost luminous, the pupils pinpricks, despite the gloom.

Sareya's heart began to pound in her ears. Some force she couldn't see, couldn't perceive with her sorcerous senses, prickled between them.

"Touch me and I'll bite your face off," she said.

The man let out a throaty chuckle.

"If what I hear about Jargalans is true," Nul said, pausing to cough, "it's me you want to worry about. Although I'm probably a bit too long in the tooth for his likes."

The Jargalan spat in his face. He raised his fist, let it linger for a long moment, then turned and headed back up the ladder.

The trapdoor slammed shut, plunging them back into darkness, the only sounds the scratch and pad of the rats among the cargo and the creak of timbers.

Nul let out a rasping sigh, and after that he said no more. Probably the few words he had spoken had exhausted him, and sure enough, now Sareya could hear his fitful snores.

She breathed deeply to calm herself. She'd felt certain the pirate was going to defile her, and bound like this, her repositories insulated from the replenishing tidal winds, there would have been nothing she could have done.

But once they reached land, if they ever did, she'd imbibe all she could of the tides, and then she would send the bastards kicking and screaming to the Corpse Maker.

The next time the trapdoor opened, two Jargalans descended into the hold. She couldn't tell if either was the man from before: their faces were bound as his had been, and they wore virtually identical clothing—a uniform of sorts.

"It is time, worthless ones," the first down the steps said. The other stood by with cutlass in hand. "To cleanse the filth from you."

The man leaned over Sareya to release her manacles. He smelled of sandalwood and sweat, brine and sour wine.

"If I am contaminated by my proximity to you, I will be most displeased."

Finally, the manacle snapped open, and the Jargalan went to work on Nul.

"This one is not long for this life. Perhaps we should feed him to the sharp-tooths."

"I'm better now," Nul said with a forced smile.

The Jargalan backhanded him round the face.

"I bet that's how you treat your wife," Sareya said. "Or maybe she does that to you—slaps you around like a little bitch."

"Be silent!" The Jargalan drew his short sword and held the tip in front of Sareya's eye. "Unless you would like me to slit you open, you speak only when I say, yes? Now rise. You are going up top, yes you are."

He grabbed a fistful of Sareya's hair and dragged her to her feet, then turned her around and shoved her toward the steps. He followed close behind, poking her in the back with the tip of his sword.

The second Jargalan brought Nul, hitting him each time he stumbled.

Up three decks they went, never stopping long enough to see more than a glimpse of cabins, a mess area, and a room stacked with wooden crates.

They emerged from a trapdoor into a gale. Freezing spray hit Sareya in the face, and her feet slipped on the rain-slick deck. The ship heaved and pitched and bobbed. Sailors yelled to one another from the ratlines. The sky was shrouded with black clouds. Sails bellied in the wind, mid, aft, and fore, straining on their yards.

A sailor cried out, pointing at the main mast.

Blue sparks ghosted around its heights, causing the hairs on the nape of Sareya's neck to stand on end.

"Curse the Orgol god," a woman cried in Nan-Rhouric, snapping Sareya's focus back to the deck. "Get down from the rigging!"

"Indeed, Captain!" came the reply from up in the heights.

The ship's captain was a dusky-skinned woman in a tricorn hat and a brocaded jacket. It might have been a disguise, because it didn't suit her in the slightest. "Out of the crow's nest. There's more lightning on the way."

A distant rumble lent emphasis to her words, and men scurried down the ratlines toward the deck.

Sareya glanced nervously at the churning skies. She had always hated lightning; feared the randomness of its strikes. It was a foe she had no defense against, not even sorcery—although she might have done, if she'd not been taken by the Order as a child; if she'd had the time and the training for her moontouched abilities to fully develop. If the choice had been hers, she would have headed back below, where even now Jargalan pirates were scurrying.

Nul flung his arms wide and raised his face to the pelting rain. His hair and clothes were sodden. "Menselas is angry!" he hollered. "We're all going to die!" He proceeded to sing a song that seemed to need a mug of beer and the accompaniment of Rindon.

"Someone shut him up," the Captain said.

The Jargalan with him slashed Nul's forearm with his cutlass, drawing blood. Hero that he was, Nul didn't even flinch.

"Cheers," he said.

"I will cut your face next time if you do not keep your mouth shut."

"I'd like that," Nul said. "But not as much as I'd like watching you die after."

"Insolent dog! You think to threaten your betters?"

Nul said nothing further, just stared at him with mad eyes until the man swallowed and looked away.

Nul winked at Sareya, and she dared to hope. Heroes always had a plan, didn't they?

The storm gave the impression of an angry god. More than angry, it felt capricious, granting them long respites, only to circle back round and come at them twice as hard.

Sareya stumbled at a shove from behind.

"Move along, worthless one."

With the point of the Jargalan's cutlass needling her back, Sareya approached the gunwale, where two men stood waiting.

One was a pig of a man, rolls of fat visible beneath his sweat-stained robe, sickly eyes glinting from the narrow slit in his head bindings.

The other was a tall man, made taller by his conical helm with only crescents for the eyes. A black cloak shrouded his shoulders and fell to his iron-booted feet. A breastplate of burnished bronze glistened in the rain, then flashed in reflection of the lightning that forked overhead.

There were two coiled ropes behind them at the gunwale, the ends tied to cleats.

"Ah, so the merchandise lives," the fat man said. "But that stink! Worse than a week-old corpse, no? Do not tell me that does not excite you, Malugin. Everybody knows the preferences of you magi."

So, the man in the conical helm was a sorcerer—a Jargalan magus. She knew of them, but not what they could do. Jargalan sorcery was as steeped in mystery as their sword smithing techniques.

"Where is the Orgol?" Sareya asked.

"He does not transport the merchandise, only hunts it," the fat man said.

"He's still in Sansor?" Nul asked.

"What is it to you? You will not be returning to the mainland. Not now. Not ever."

"How long have we been aboard?" Sareya asked. How long had she been unconscious? Quite some time, judging by the state of her soiled clothes."

"If not for this storm," the fat man said, "we would be able to see the Jargalan Coast. But before we dock, you will be clean, yes? And you will cease to smell. After we disembark, we will have an overland march of several days, during which we will be entering towns. With you two unworthies looking and smelling the way you do, they would indubitably not let us in, out of fear of the pestilence. So, it is my humble opinion that we should give you both a good bath before we reach land."

"You have a tub on board?" Sareya asked.

"Captain, do we have a bath tub on board?"

"This is a ship, Galban, not your mother's brothel."

"It would seem not," the fat man—Galban—said. "Humbly, I beg your forgiveness. I am so terribly sorry for the inconvenience. We will just have to go with what the gods provide. Truss them."

The Jargalans who had brought Sareya and Nul on deck grabbed the loose ends of the coiled rope at the gunwale. Sareya backed away.

White light blazed through the eye-slits of the sorcerer's conical helm, and ice froze in Sareya's veins. She couldn't move as one of the Jargalans tied rope around her ankles, and the other did the same to Nul. No sooner were they bound, feet together, than the light went out of the magus's eyes and Sareya could move again.

"I must warn you, Galban," the Captain called down from the helm. "The sea here is rife with sharp-tooths. And even if your precious merchandise is not eaten, they may get struck by lightning, if that is the will of the gods."

"But at least they will not stink of feculence," Galban said. "Over the side, I say!"

The two Jargalans grabbed Sareya's arms and dragged her to the gunwale. Then, lifting her, they tossed her overboard.

She gasped when she hit the water. Salt stung her eyes. She thrashed about in panic, unable to kick with her legs bound.

There was another splash and a chaos of bubbles. Lightning lit the water, revealing Nul, limp as he drifted at the end of his rope, mouth open, taking in water.

Sareya tried to reach him with frantic strokes of her arms, but the churning sea pulled them farther apart. She struck for the surface, her lungs screaming for air.

But she could no longer tell which way was up.

Something thumped Sareya in the back. She gasped, and water spewed from her mouth. She tasted salt, smelled the brine. Yards creaked above her. Thunder rumbled.

She was lying face down on the deck, her shirt and trousers clinging to her, sodden and freezing.

Two Jargalans threw Nul down beside her, shivering and blue, eyes wide with shock as he spewed seawater. Sareya couldn't feel her fingers—as blue as Nul's lips. But her dusk-tide repository… It wasn't as empty as she'd believed…

"Better," a Jargalan said—she was sure it was the man who had roused her in the hold. "The worthless one doesn't stink so bad now." He ran his fingers through her sodden hair, then screamed as he flew back through the air and slammed into the gunwale. The man slumped to the deck, hair stood on end, smoke spilling from his smoldering eyes.

All around Sareya, sailors pulled back, muttering and touching their foreheads.

"Dead," someone cried. "He's dead!"

Sareya chuckled into the waterlogged deck. Someone rolled her over and stood astride her.

"What happened?" Galban demanded, dagger in hand. "Tell me, or by my ancestors, I'll—"

"The Five happened," Sareya said, not meeting Galban's eyes and instead gazing up at the cloud-choked sky. "The Five loves me. It did not love him."

"The Five!" Galban said. He grabbed a fistful of Sareya's hair and hauled her to her feet. "Menselas is an impotent god. An imposter. In my country, you would be boiled in oil for uttering the blasphemy of his name."

Sareya ignored the pain and let her body go lip, her head off to one side, like a corpse hanging from a gibbet.

Nul pushed himself up on an elbow. "Leave her alone!" he yelled.

A sailor kicked him in the face, and Nul's head smacked into the deck.

With Galban still holding her up by the hair, the magus in the conical helm touched his fingertips to Sareya's forehead. She could feel him probing her repositories.

"Where did you learn this power?" he asked. "It is my understanding your Order does not permit the use of the dusk-tide."

"I was born with it," she said.

His fingers grew hot, and pain ripped through every nerve in her body. She gritted her teeth as she shook, refusing to scream. When the pain stopped, she tasted blood in her mouth from where she had bitten her tongue.

"Where?" he asked again.

"I wasn't lying," she said. "I was born with the power. My people call me moontouched."

"Demonic," the magus said to Galban, who wore a concerned frown.

"I can draw off her power for now, but we will have to watch her closely."

"Do it," Galban said. "A lot hinges on this delivery."

The magus withdrew his fingers from her head. Filaments of lightning danced between his splayed fingers. Sareya smelled burned metal. Silver fire burst from the magus's hands. Sareya screamed as it engulfed her, but the fire didn't burn. For a moment she thought she'd been let off with a warning, but then every muscle in her body clenched. Her teeth ground, and her scalp pulled taut. She started to buck and writhe. Then came the pain: every organ, every bone, every nerve, shredded, pulped and mangled as she thrashed upon the deck. When it was over, drool trickled from her mouth, and her repositories were empty.

"Well?" Galban said.

"It is done."

"Excellent. A little longer, and we will be rich men."

"I still do not know about this," the magus said. "Why does *he* even want her? Sell them both in the markets. We'll still come out of this richer than we went in."

"The man, yes," Galban said. "But the girl is spoken for. Have faith, my friend. Trust me. All will be well, you'll see."

"You don't know that."

Galban threw an arm around the magus's shoulders. "You are too cautious. Too frightened of myths and shadows. I say again, all will be well."

TWENTY-EIGHT

SKITTERING. SLITHERING. THE CHITTER OF insects. The clack of tiny mandibles. It felt as though maggots were gnawing on Anskar's flesh; but the pain was remote, almost someone else's, a distant resonance of stings and bites coming slowly into focus. There was so little feeling left in his body—an impression of coldness, limpid and liquefying skin. And that smell! The odor of putrescence. His every sensation coalesced into a pinprick of blackness that tugged at him with an inexorable hunger. He shrieked, a scream as soundless as it was eternal, hearing nothing, seeing nothing, feeling only the relentless, crushing unrelenting pressure as an infinitesimal speck of void stuff sucked him in, reducing him to nothing.

And then, with a plop, he was *something* again, though something quite different, something he didn't recognize as himself. His hands, when he raised them to his eyes, were comprised of black mist. Same with his arms, his torso, his legs, his feet. He touched his face but felt nothing, save a tingling vibration and an icy chill. But he could see now; not that there was much to look at, only a circular space of woven shadows that contained him like an air bubble in the vast emptiness of eternity. The prick of a pin, and his bubble would burst, and what then? Would even his consciousness cease to exist?

Dead, then.

That much was obvious.

Amalantril's wound, the sword's voracious feeding on the essence that defined him, had been worse than anyone had thought. Flesh could heal, but his soul, not so much. He had exhausted himself in his battle with his mother, dredged up every last dreg of sorcery from his blood. He had pushed himself to his limits, and beyond.

And still it hadn't been enough.

Queen Talia was more powerful than he could ever have imagined—especially now that she had absorbed a Niyandrian moontouched.

Marith.

Poor Carred. He had barely given a thought to her loss; merely expected her to carry on as if she were every bit as much his tool as she had been his mother's. Or if not a tool, a sidekick, expendable, scarce worthy of his consideration. Sweet Menselas, when had he grown so self-absorbed? When had he grown so callous?

A shiver passed through the shadows that contained him, and then a rent split the blackness, and a translucent tendril slid through the parting, white and glistening, thrashing through the shadow-space in search of sustenance. A second tendril followed, then a third, a fourth, until dozens of slimy feelers writhed in the darkness, forcing the rent wider, creating an opening through which a massive figure passed. The tendrils had their points of origin in a scaly chest. Eyes of puce lit up the penumbral dark like evil crescent moons, illuminating the wolf's head they sat within.

Anskar felt a renewed panic as his vaporous form start to break up and waft apart. All his hopes and fears condensed into a knot of dread, and his self-perception abruptly altered. Now he was no more than a delicate sphere of glass no larger than a pea, and he was clutched between the thumb and index finger of this most ancient, most vile, must demanding of all gods.

Kaythe Nurglich smiled down at the little glass sphere that was Anskar. Razor fangs protruded from the god's black lips, wet and glistening. The smile was a poor attempt to appear reassuring; probably it was no attempt at all, merely some capricious game.

"Your existence is such a brittle thing," Kaythe Nurglich said.

"Yes," Anskar said. "It is. Please, can you help me?" His voice was the wind whistling through the mountain tops. It was a testimony to his lack of substance, his reduction to the state of no-thing.

"*Will* I help you, you mean?" the god said. "I offered to help you before, and you refused my aid."

"I was afraid," Anskar said. "I feared making a pact."

"Fear," Kaythe Nurglich said. "Always it is fear that stands in the way of greatness, of true and unbridled service. Your mother feared me, Anskar, enough to make her vows to me. But"—and now a hard edge crept into the wolf-head's voice—"not enough to remain faithful."

"She betrayed you?" Anskar asked.

"She reneged on a promise, and so she suffered the consequences. Is not this the way of justice? Does not your beloved Menselas teach as much?"

"What happened?" Anskar asked, acutely aware of the pressure of the thumb and finger pressing against his little sphere of fragility. "What did you do to her?"

"Naphor happened," Kaythe Nurglich said. "The mainland invasion happened. The Consortium, ever loyal, did as I bade."

"The Consortium serve you?"

"Not all of them, but some. A sizable and influential minority. But what of you, Anskar? Are you ready to serve me now?"

Every instinct screamed at him to say yes, to take the one slender chance he had of clinging to life. Every instinct but one, and he couldn't say what it was, where it came from, only that it seemed like a guttering candle in the night. His voice was now no more than a whispering breeze. "I would sooner die."

"Would you now?" Saliva dripped from the wolf-head's jaws. "And despite your flirtations with necromancy, you really believe death would be the end?"

Suddenly Anskar was enfleshed again, pale and naked, kneeling before Kaythe Nurglich, who now stood impossibly tall, a colossal presence, his wolf's head as far above Anskar as a mountain peak.

"You think the mark of Menselas will spare you?" Kaythe Nurglich said.

Anskar's bones rattled within his flesh, pounded by the voice of the god. Light blazed on his abdomen, and he looked down to see a five-pointed star emblazoned on his skin in iridescent gold. His eyes burned as he stared at it, and he had the sense that Kaythe Nurglich expected him to look away, to reject all that the five-pointed star had come to represent: the Order of Eternal Vigilance, the Church, Niyandrian slaves and subjugation, priests of the Elder and their lust for knowledge at all costs. The violence of the Warrior's priests—two had tried to kill him. The judgments of the Healers, who loved to hear confessions but seldom owned up to their own faults. The impotence of the Mother's priests to do anything more than utter useless platitudes. The morbidity of the Hooded One—and how could he forget the evils he had witnessed at the Abbey?

But no, he thought, that was unfair. He had so little experience of the Hooded One, especially after the Grand Master had ordered the chapel at Branil's Burg converted into a banker's vault. And the Abbess had been an agent of the Tainted Cabal, not a true representative of the Hooded One.

Warm wetness oozed from his eyeballs—were they still black? He could see only crimson, as if he were looking through a haze of blood.

"Avert your gaze from the enemy's mark," Kaythe Nurglich said, an insistent rumble. "The longer you look, the worse it will—"

"I can't!" The pressure in Anskar's eyes increased till they started to bulge from their sockets. Excruciating pain ripped through his head. Acid tears spilled from his eyes, melting his flesh, eating through bone. Skin sloughed away from him, everywhere but his belly, where the five-pointed star pulsed faster and faster, burning, scalding, threatening to explode.

"Look away!" Kaythe Nurglich said. "I demand it! Look away or perish, and by perishing know this: you will not cease to exist. You will be mine. Mine! I am the source of the earth-tide, Anskar. All those who use the earth-tide are mine. Necromancy is mine. I am the god of the dead and the undying."

"No!" Anskar cried, as his newfound body dissolved, leaving only the blazing star of Menselas. "I want to live."

"One word!" Kaythe Nurglich said. "One word, and I can save you. Without your consent I can do nothing. Will you serve me, Anskar? Yes or no?"

"I said—"

"Yes or no? I need your answer. Yes or no, Anskar, yes or..."

The five-pointed star etched in light into the very fabric of the shadow-space flashed erratically.

"Look away!" Kaythe Nurglich roared. "And give me your answer. Yes... Yes... Yes!"

Anskar was nothing again, just a tiny point of awareness. Yet he still saw the blazing star, strobing ever faster. Still he felt the fragility of his existence, as if it really were clasped between the god's thumb and forefinger. An ascending whine filled his... did he still have ears? Then where... How...? What...?

With a world-shattering boom, the star of golden light exploded.

TWENTY-NINE

A THOUSAND SPECKS OF DUST, scattered throughout the heavens. Ten thousand. A million. A hundred million. And Carred was every last one of them, each individual mote; and she was all of them at the same time. She felt stretched in all directions, ripped apart fiber by fiber, then drawn back together, like iron filings attracted to a magnet, bees returning to the hive, a trillion grains of sand taking on the identity of a beach. Or a desert.

Her eyes snapped open, and now the motes were white and burning, swarming around her head and giving the impression of a starry crown. She blinked several times, and the motes dissolved into the air.

With a jolt of disorientation, she realized she was standing, just as she had been when she had entered the *izindel*. She swayed for balance, then adjusted her hands on the topmost casket she was holding before it tumbled to the floor. Void-steel. A fortune's worth. Enough to buy Niyas, if it were for sale. It was a hefty load she carried, but necessity— and the need for vengeance— made it lighter.

She had her bearings now, and looked around without the barest hint of surprise. As she'd known she would be, she was still in the granite-floored chamber, within the orichalcum circle of the *izindel*. The atmosphere was thick with the stench of burned metal, but there was something subtly different about it, about the quality of the air she breathed. The depot might have looked the same—might even have been the same—but she was someplace else, no longer in the abyssal realms.

She glanced about for Tarrik, Anskar, and Odopek, but they were nowhere to be seen. That made her frantic, and she turned this way and that, seeing nothing but the walls of the chamber, the open door leading to the corridor beyond. She was alone.

Her guts clenched, like they had that day when her mother abandoned her in the woods. Suddenly, the caskets of void-steel felt heavy as boulders, her need for revenge retreating before a child's primal terror of abandonment.

Where were the others?

Tarrik and Odopek said they had traveled to Vulthanor via the *izindel*, and Odopek had given the impression that he knew how to get them back. But back where? And why just her? Had they gone somewhere else without her? Why? Because she was too challenging? More likely, she thought, because she was of no use to them. No use to anyone, now that Talia had returned from the realm of the dead without her help, and Anskar no longer needed a guardian.

But you're still a leader, she told herself as she tried to fight the tremors ripping through her arms and legs. *Oh, really? Leader of what, exactly? Talia's rebellion?* Because it had never been about ordinary Niyandrians. What sorcery had the Necromancer Queen put her under to make her believe otherwise? *No sorcery at all,* she thought bitterly. *Why waste sorcery when my gullibility will do the trick free of charge? And let's not forget my pathetic need to belong. Theltek, I can be such an ass. Nobody wants you, Carred. Nobody needs you. Not even Marith.*

Oh gods, Marith was gone.

It felt as though a serrated blade had sliced her in two, from head to toe. Inside she was hollow, nothing but darkness and void. And yet she was still there to observe the dark, to fill the emptiness with her pain, her grief, her steadily mounting rage.

Falter now, she told herself, and there would be no one to avenge Marith. No one to administer justice… to Talia.

As if she, of all people, could do anything against the Necromancer Queen!

But she had a star metal sword, and she had void-steel ingots, a metal that nullified the dark-tide. Surely that counted for something.

She winced at a stab of pain in her head. It came from her repositories.

And she had her burgeoning sorcery, too. Nothing special, like Marith's moontouched abilities. Nothing out of the ordinary for any Niyandrian. Or maybe it was. How could she know until she had pushed herself to her limits and found out what she was capable of?

Steeled by resentment and anger, and the hope—illusory, for all she knew—that she was equipped to do something, to make some tiny difference, she marched from the chamber, each step faster than the first, till she was jogging, running, sprinting along corridors, the void-steel ingots clacking together in their caskets, till she reached the cage and went up.

When she came to the entrance hall with the checkerboard floor, the Ethereal Sorceress's robe still lay there beside the corpse of her functionary, Blosius. But the Sorceress's mask had gone, thanks to Odopek.

The air that blew through the open double doors was familiar, carrying with it the odors of refuse and hop beer, pungent smoke, and horse dung. And she knew where she was, even before she stepped out into the street and gazed up at the imposing walls of Branil's Burg in the near distance.

Clouds hung heavy and dark over Dorinah as Carred made her way through abandoned streets. Shattered glass crunched underfoot, from the broken windows that seemed the latest fashion. Rain-drenched clothing—the items discarded by the looters—lay strewn across the road. Rats gamboled in the gutters amid scraps of food that had been drunkenly thrown away. So much for a free Niyas for Niyandrians. This was the result of her people, her rebels, sating their needs after the fight for the city. She could have counted on the fingers of one hand the number of battles they had won, so she didn't blame them for wanting to celebrate. But like this? Looting from the people they were meant to liberate?

And looting wasn't the half of it. As she turned down an alley to bring her within spitting distance of the bailey walls of Branil's Burg, she came across the body of a Niyandrian woman, her dress ripped down the front, breasts covered with angry welts and legs splayed. She averted her eyes in disgust at the blood and other fluids, and her simmering rage started to boil over.

This had to stop.

Theltek's eyes, what in all the hells was Vilintia doing? She was supposed to be in charge.

"What you got there?" a man said, coming up behind her in the alley. He spoke Niyandrian.

Carred turned. One of her rebels—she vaguely recognized him, probably because he had such an unforgettable face: livid with some cantankerous rash and scarred with the craters of a previous pox. His nose had been broken at least once, and his lips were twisted from being split open so often. She caught him half-leering, half-eyeing the caskets she held against her chest. The idiot must have thought she was a looter making off with something valuable. She stiffened when she caught sight of the dagger in his hand. By the looks of it, it had already been used.

"You don't know who I am, do you?" she asked, stooping to set down the caskets on the road.

"Darling, I don't need to know your name. Come here, give us some of that," he said, waving his dagger to indicate her breasts.

Carred raised her fist above her head, drawing his attention. Slowly, one at a time, she opened her fingers, revealing the two that were mere stubs.

"Carred Selenas?" He hid the dagger behind his back. "I didn't mean nothing by it. How was I supposed to know it was you?"

"And if it wasn't me?" Carred drew her sword as she stalked toward him. "If I was some defenseless town-girl on her way home—what would you have done then? The same as you did to her?" She jerked her head toward the dead woman's corpse.

"That weren't me!" the man protested. "You gotta believe me!"

Carred winced at a sharp pain in her temples. Within her mind, her repositories seemed to blister. The dusk-tide one burst, and she felt something almost tangible, like a hot seepage in her brain. A tremor passed through her body. Her sword arm stiffened. White-hot needles lanced through her fingers, and then filaments of lightning danced along the keen edges of her star metal blade.

The man took a stumbling step back, almost tripped on the dead woman's body, and then turned and ran away back down the alley.

The skin of Carred's face was taut as she watched him flee. She became aware that her teeth were bared. She turned her head and spat, and there was a metallic aftertaste in her mouth. Not blood; something else. Some residue of the dusk-tide that had surged through her.

She turned to retrieve her caskets but then stopped herself, instead crossing to where the dead woman lay. Carred drew together the woman's torn dress to cover her exposed flesh. She looked less vulnerable that way, less a victim. She knelt and closed the woman's eyes with her fingers; then, fighting down her gorge, leaned in to kiss her on the forehead.

"I will make this right," she swore under her breath. "I will make Niyas right."

And with that, she stood, collected her caskets, and strode for the side gate that led into Branil's Burg.

The Dodecagon was packed when Carred barged through the double doors, still clutching her twin caskets of void-steel to her chest. She ignored the shocked looks of the slovenly guards outside, a couple of rebels from one of the fringe groups she'd not seen before—or if she had, they hadn't left much of an impression. Neither guard made a move to stop her. They knew who she was.

It was gloomy inside, no light coming through the rose-tinted glass ceiling. Outside, it had started to rain. There were upwards of fifty rebels seated on the floor, some of them decked out in shiny armor, no doubt stolen from the Burg. Many had plates of food—hunks of beef, turkey drumsticks, corn on the cob—and they ate as the twelve commanders seated on the blackwood thrones around the room talked among themselves.

Vilintia paused mid-sentence, a frothing mug of beer halfway to her lips, as Carred stormed into the chamber.

"Don't you people have anything better to do than sit here stuffing your faces?" she asked. "I do hope this isn't the same meeting you were engaged in when I left."

"So what if it is?" Vilintia said. Carred bridled at the insolence in her tone. "Where's Anskar?" Vilintia asked, peering past Carred's shoulder as if she expected him to come through the doors.

"The *Melesh-Eloni*," Carred said, "is…" She thought about telling them how he had failed, how his own mother had almost killed him. Thought about telling them where she and Anskar had been and how they had been separated by the *izindel*; but she was too angry for explanations. "The *Melesh-Eloni* ordered that the local Niyandrians were to be treated with respect. You do know the meaning of the word, I assume?" She swept her arm out to indicate Dorinah beyond the walls of Branil's Burg. "This is not who we are! Out there, the looting, the fighting, the raping… that is not what we do!"

Vilintia rolled her eyes. "Perhaps you should have thought of that before you left us, yet again."

Carred dropped her caskets, spilling ingots of void-steel onto the floor. She strode across the room and grabbed Vilintia by the throat, drenching her with beer as she knocked the mug from her hand. The other commanders gasped. One or two stood, declaring their outrage. The rebels seated on the floor exchanged wide-eyed looks and muttered words. She expected the same level of shock from Vilintia. She expected submission. But Vilintia had always been a strong woman; physically, at least. Much stronger than Carred. She grabbed Carred's wrist and squeezed, causing the fingers to open, then forcing the hand away from her throat.

But Carred's other hand wasn't idle. Her fingers—even the stubs, so far as they could—curled around the hilt of her sword. The blade rasped as it came clear of the scabbard, and Vilintia froze at the touch of cold steel against her throat, where moments ago it had only been fingers.

"You wouldn't dare," Vilintia breathed, eyes flicking left and right to gauge her support.

No one came to her defense. Anger radiated from Carred like a knight's ward sphere, and they seemed afraid of what might happen if they collided with it.

She withdrew the edge of her sword from Vilintia's throat, never once relinquishing her glare. Her dusk-tide repository fizzed in her mind, and once more filaments of lightning ran up and down her blade, arcing and flashing.

Vilintia dropped back down in her chair, shielding her eyes from the sword's glare. No one else in the Dodecagon seemed capable of looking away. They were shocked, dumbfounded, enraptured. Carred held the sword aloft until she was sure she had full command of the hall, then slammed it back in its scabbard.

"You, you, and you," she said, jabbing a finger at three of the commanders. "You command divisions, don't you? Then you are accountable for what's happening in the streets." Before anyone could protest, she went on. "Get out there and round your… *people* up. I was going to say 'dogs.' From this moment on, if anyone is guilty of looting, flog them. If they harm a local, flog them harder. If they kill or rape, string them up. And if you don't mete out my justice, understand this: the sentence falls on you. Now go!"

The three exchanged looks, and then scurried away.

The fifty or so rebels seated on the floor watched like a hushed congregation at one of the ancient rites of Theltek, where to speak was an offense against the god's thousand mouths and could cost you your tongue. Many had unchewed food in their mouths and proceeded to remove it as discreetly as they could.

"That's better," Carred said, her new tone of calmness sounding fake even to her. She let out an exaggerated sigh as she slumped into one of the blackwood thrones vacated by the three chastised commanders. It just happened to be adjacent to Vilintia's.

Carred crossed her feet one way then the other, but her attempts to appear relaxed were inept, and frankly, embarrassing. She elected instead for poise, and sat upright in the throne, arms on the rests, not caring in the slightest if there was an imperious tilt to her chin. Her failing in the past, she realized, was her reluctance to fully embrace her role as leader. How quickly she had relinquished command after the capture of Dorinah, so she could rush off with Anskar, leaving Vilintia at the helm. Marith was dead, she reminded herself. No one left to mother her, no one left to lean on. It was time, at long last, that she grew up. And if that put people's noses out of joint, then so be it. But there was no need to be a cow about it.

"Sorry," she said, with a sideways glance at Vilintia. "I shouldn't have left you with all this responsibility."

Vilintia's eyes widened. "No," she said. "You should not. I never wanted to lead, Carred. I might be older than you, but I was cut out for following orders, not giving them."

"I'm sorry," Carred said, louder this time, making sure everyone could hear. "I went running off after the rabbit and left the herd unattended. Not that I consider you a herd. I don't mean to imply Queen Talia is a rabbit. She's far more dangerous than that."

That drew a reaction—mutterings that seemed to infer she was being disloyal.

"I didn't order the attack on Dorinah," Carred said. "I don't think it was what any of us wanted, was it?"

Silence. Most seemed to agree with her. A few—the younger men, notably—apparently did not.

"Marith… My Marith was possessed by the Queen Talia's shade. She gave the order, and now she is…"

She shut her eyes as Vilintia squeezed her hand. She kept her tears at bay, but there was nothing she could do about her trembling chin.

"We were duped," Carred said. "Used in a scheme from beyond the grave. Talia doesn't give a damn about Niyas. She doesn't care about you or me. All she wants is life and power. I see that now."

The hall grew appreciably colder. The rebels seated on the floor looked lost, uncertain. But without exception, they were looking straight at her, imploring her to go on. Expecting her to lead.

"What does this mean for us?" Vilintia said. "For the rebellion? For Niyas?"

Carred extricated her hand and stood.

"We have to decide who is the greater foe," she said. "The Order of Eternal Vigilance, or a queen who refuses to stay dead."

"But what if Queen Talia can take back the isle?" a middle-aged woman said. Carred thought her name might be Parva. "She promised to bring us to eternal life."

"You're free to go to her and see that she keeps her word," Carred said. "But the things I've seen lately make me question terms such as 'eternal life.'" The only life beyond death she had witnessed from Talia's hands had been animated corpses. "Believe what you like, all of you. I can only speak for myself: I can't go on believing."

"Then what will you do?" Vilintia asked, standing beside Carred, as if the purpose of her whole life depended on the answer.

"Nothing noble," Carred said. "One way or another, I will avenge Marith."

"She's dead?" Vilintia said. "What happened?"

"Please don't ask me that," Carred said, and now the tears were streaming from her eyes.

Vilintia drew her into a hug, stroking her hair as she addressed the room.

"You know me," she said. "I am Last Cohort—one of the last of the Last Cohort." Several people laughed halfheartedly. Vilintia wasn't exactly known for her humor. "I stand with my captain," she said, holding Carred out at arm's length. "And I too am sorry."

Carred wiped tears from her eyes. "Sorry for what?"

"Blaming you for Taloc. He was a grown man. He went with you by choice."

"If I could have—" Carred started, but Vilintia cut her off.

"I know."

An awkward silence ensued, the commanders on the thrones exchanging looks, the rebels on the floor shifting uncomfortably. Vilintia motioned for Carred to return to her blackwood throne, and they both sat down.

"Before I ask my own," Carred said, "does anyone have any questions?"

A young woman seated on the floor raised her hand, causing Carred to smile, though it wasn't exactly a happy smile. She had last raised her hand for permission to speak back home with her parents. Failure to do so had always resulted in a slap or a thump.

When Carred nodded for her to go on, the woman asked, "So, Queen Talia ordered the attack on Dorinah? Through the moontouched woman?"

"Marith," Carred said. "Her name was Marith."

"And we all just went along with it?" the woman asked, running her eyes over the commanders, as if it were all their fault.

"Queen Talia influenced all of..." Carred was about to say "you," yet had to accept that they had all been swayed by the queen's powers one way or another, even she. "Queen Talia influenced all of us. She wielded a sorcerous glamor. Many of our people were possessed. Do any of you remember feeling strange, out of control?"

More looks were exchanged—worried, befuddled, crestfallen.

"What can we do," the young woman asked, "to make sure it doesn't happen again? How do we protect ourselves?"

"That is my job," Carred said. "From this moment on, I will not be leaving you—any of you—to fend for yourselves. I served Queen Talia all these long, dark years, but instead I should have been serving you, the people of Niyas."

"The Queen promised to return," an older man said. "Promised us immortality."

"Of course she did," Carred said. "It's what every Niyandrian wants and expects. It's written into our culture."

"She used us," Vilintia said, and Carred nodded, relieved to have an ally.

"Talia has no interest in you," Carred said. "In any of us. Not even in her own son."

"Where is the *Melesh-Eloni*?" the young woman asked.

"I don't know," Carred said, "and right now, I don't care. Any more questions? No? Then perhaps someone can bring me up to date. Did you decide anything during this meeting, before you stopped for food?"

Vilintia rolled her eyes, but this time she at least mitigated it with a smile. Then her face grew hard, and her lips pressed together in a tight line. "We agreed to march on Quolith."

One of the commanders, a gray-haired man, puffed out his pigeon chest. "That way, we control the port here at Dorinah and the nearest stronghold. With enough time, we can turn Niyas into an island fortress. But first we have to defeat the enemy closest to hand."

Carred nodded slowly to show she was following. Defeat the Order of Eternal Vigilance one stronghold at a time, and as quickly as possible, before help from the mainland could be organized. She might have followed a similar strategy herself, had things been different. Had she not seen Fult Wreave's warriors outside of Naphor. Had she not seen what Queen Talia had done to Marith. To Anskar.

"So, occupy Quolith," she said. "That's your plan? I can think of a better one."

THIRTY

THE SCENT OF HONEYSUCKLE CLUNG to Anskar's nostrils, coaxing him awake, though he was too exhausted to open his eyes. He was bathed in a cold sweat, but his blood felt on fire. Something was irritating his throat, causing him to cough. Incense? Like the kind they burned in the chapel of the Healer back at Branil's Burg?

He let out an involuntary groan as he rolled his head from side to side, picking up a new scent. This time it was grass, fresh and sweet. His fingers brushed through blades of lushness, scrabbled about in soft loam.

He became aware of the crash of surf upon a shore, a rhythmic rush and retreat that echoed the beat of his heart. There were voices too, a little way distant: a woman's. A man's. Another woman.

"Carred?" he uttered through dry lips. His throat felt as though it were full of sand. Perhaps it was granules of crystal.

That thought, that memory of the abyssal realms, finally made his eyes snap open.

Everything was a blur, and there were bright spots dancing across his vision, sparkling motes of golden light. He saw patches of green and blue, glimmers of silver and white, like oil on water. But he could tell at once this wasn't Vulthanor. The light held a different quality, for one thing; not a relentless glare from a stationary sun, it was wavering and less harsh. The air was pleasantly warm, a far cry from the scalding heat of Domatai's realm.

He blinked his eyes into focus on limpid skies of washed-out blue, the haze of water vapor lingering in the air. Through wisps of cottony cloud, he could see the faded arch of a rainbow.

He was lying in verdant meadow, surrounded by cat's ears and buttercups, splashes of yellow that struck him as the spoor print of the sun—the old familiar golden sphere of Wiraya, not the bronze fireball of Vulthanor.

So, he was back. But back where, exactly?

He sat up, and the skin of his chest pulled taut, causing him to wince. With tentative dabs of his fingertips, he examined his wound: gone. Not even the scar where his catalyst had been removed, just a shiny patch of new skin where he had been stabbed.

He was naked from the waist up, but the trousers he wore—had been dressed in—were not his own; they were smooth and black, some kind of soft leather, and they smelled of must and mildew. Beside him, folded neatly on the ground, were a shirt to match and a pair of knee-length boots with turndowns. All the clothes seemed ancient, as if they belonged to a different era.

His veins prickled with sorcerous essence, but when he sought out his repositories with his inner senses, he found no loci of tidal power, no differentiation between dusk and dawn, nor even dark. Like the blurry colors he had perceived upon waking, the three tides had intermingled within him and were dispersed throughout his body. A sea of power resided within his every fiber, and when he plumbed its depths, he grew giddy and had to withdraw his senses. Not new. None of this was entirely new. It just felt different. *He* felt different: healed, harmonized in a way he had not believed possible. Zek had hinted at such a possibility; had even inferred that it was natural.

And yet, beneath it all, or rather, surrounding it, he became aware of the penumbra of the earth-tide's reach and its claims on him, its opposition to all that felt good and vital and filled with light.

What did this mean? What had happened since he had passed from consciousness in Vulthanor? Who had done this to him—separated light from dark and left him with a critical choice? Because the tides were not passive within him: they were vying for his attention. They had taken sides. And it was a surprise how they had been aligned—or aligned themselves: three against one, as if even the dark-tide had no accord with the earth.

His head swam with the magnitude of the changes that had taken place inside him, with the implications, with the pressure to choose.

Because he was certain that was what he had to do: decide between the triad of dawn, dusk, and dark and the bubbling filth of the earth-tide, the provenance of Kaythe Nurglich.

The sky lurched, and Anskar fell back against the soft grass. Nausea swamped him, and he felt himself sinking through the loam towards the core of Wiraya. He fought against it tooth and nail. He didn't want to go there. Didn't want to return to the horror that awaited him below.

"Carred!" he cried out, flailing around blindly.

A hand caught hold of his and gave it a reassuring squeeze.

"I have you, Anskar," a woman said in a voice that both chimed and crackled, a voice of mellifluous fire. It wasn't Carred. An unfamiliar face filled his vision as he came back to his senses. "Anchor yourself in my touch."

She was… a goddess? An angel? Eyes like twin suns gazed down at him, not with searing heat but with warm compassion. Her face was lambent with golden light that effused from her skin. Her hair shimmered with the same aureate brilliance. Her whole being glowed, and he had the impression that, if she had wanted to, she would have burned.

"I…" he began, then turned his head to one side so that he wouldn't be drawn into those smoldering eyes.

"I?" she prompted

"I thought I was dead."

"So you were," she said. "And now you are not."

She released his hand and he groaned internally, fighting back the urge to plead with her to touch him once more. The blood in his veins surged in anticipation of a renewed contact. When he looked at her again, he caught the tail end of her smile, luminous as the stars.

"What happened?" Anskar asked. "Where am I?"

"The nascent power within you—I imagine you have already felt the first pangs of its gestation—went into bloom. Not full bloom. Untrained as you are, that would have spelled disaster, and not just for you."

"Like with Tarrik?"

The woman shifted her position, and Anskar could dimly see other figures beyond her, sitting, moving, but her visage was too bright for him to make out any details. He could hear voices too, the sound of men and women speaking to one another, all muffled and far away. His every sense was attuned to the woman sitting on the grass beside him, as if she were the only thing that mattered in all the worlds. As if the two of them were the only things that really existed.

"I died?" Anskar said, images of the Corpse Maker shooting though his mind and making him shudder.

"The power preserved you. But only just, I think. Tell me, what did you see?"

He told her about Kaythe Nurglich, and how close he had come to accepting the pact.

She sucked in a sharp breath, the only indication that she might once have been—might even still be, in some sense—human, that there was more to her than radiance and suppressed flame.

"And then the golden star exploded?" she said, as if needing to confirm what he had just described to her.

"It was a five-pointed star," Anskar said, and she smiled once more as if she had known that all along. "Like the star of Menselas."

"Yes?" she prompted, her golden eyes shimmering with amusement.

Anskar felt awkward then, the butt of some joke. Not a malicious joke, he concluded. He could never imagine this woman being malicious in the slightest.

"Are you a goddess?" he asked, feeling heat rush to his cheeks.

She chuckled. "Tell me, Anskar, what do you believe this power to be that kept you alive?"

"I thought maybe… necromancy," Anskar said.

She narrowed her eyes, till they were slits that bled gold. "What happened to you," she said, "*happened.* It was pure gratuity, nothing you did of and by yourself. It was no self-worked necromancy that you used in refusal of death. And no, it was not the power of the Corpse Maker, either. You did not make that pact."

"I almost did," Anskar protested. "I wanted to. I was scared, and he gave me no time."

"Because Kaythe Nurglich is a liar. He offers ultimatums that do not exist. Believe me, you did not accept his pact. Had you done so, you would still exist, but I would not call that existence life. You would have been lost, Anskar. Far better to be trapped in the realm of the dead forever. Far better to be dissolved into the void."

"Then help me to understand," he said. Heat suffused his palms, and when he raised them to his eyes, they glowed golden for the merest instant, then returned to their usual red-hued duskiness.

"The seed of the god's mark—you perceived it as a five-pointed star of light etched into your belly—died and brought forth new fruit, nascent life, still gestating."

"Pure gift, you say?"

"This only happens once, Anskar. Do not forget that. There are no more new starts."

He nodded, but he was still thinking of something else. He met her eyes—wide again, shining, welcoming. "A gift from whom?"

"Oh, Anskar, is it not obvious?"

Her eyes alighted on his chest, on the fresh new skin that had grown over the gushing wound where his own sword had pierced him and drunk his essence.

"My wound?" he said. "You are a priestess of the Healer?"

Almost disinterestedly, she shook her head. "There are no priests here."

"I was taught growing up," Anskar said, "that only Menselas can heal."

"And maybe that is true. It depends on what you mean by Menselas."

He couldn't help it; everything he said made him feel more foolish, out of his depth, but he still had to ask. "Are you… Are you Menselas?"

"Do I look like I have five faces?"

"One of his aspects, then. The Healer? The Mother?"

"Would you like me to be? Are you in need of a mother?"

Pain stabbed through Anskar's chest, and he checked with his hand in case the healing sorcery had failed and his wound had re-opened. But this was no physical pain, he realized. It was the barb attached to the word "mother."

The woman was watching him intently, as if her words had been carefully chosen and she wanted to see how he reacted. He bit back his anger and looked around, still seeing everything else as a hazy blur.

"Where is Carred?"

The woman raised an eyebrow, but at least this time she had the decency not to smile. "Only a select few can ever come here," she said.

"She's not good enough for you, you mean?" Anskar instantly regretted his tone. "Carred was—is—my guardian."

"Assigned by your mother," the woman pointed out.

"So, she means nothing to you?"

"Everybody means something," the woman said. She glanced up at the skies. "The sun shines on all Wiraya's creatures."

"Now you sound like my old mentor, Brother Tion," Anskar said. "Always going on about how Menselas bestows his blessings on the wicked as well as the good."

"You think he does not?"

"Tion explained that what is important is how we respond to his blessings."

"The god makes the first move?"

"As I understand it." But this theological conversation was making him edgy, and it was taking him farther from the things he wanted to ask.

Again his hand strayed to his chest wound, fingertips brushing against the new growth of skin, tracing its smooth contours. It seemed odd, having no ridge of scar from where his catalyst had been removed.

"Yours was a complex wound," the woman said, wisps of golden mist coiling away from her lucent skin.

"The sword," Anskar said, pausing to make spit and swallow. "My sword tried to drain me. It drank my soul. The sword was infected by a demon, and my mother did something to it—turned the metal dark."

"A working of the earth-tide, perhaps," the woman said with a shrug. "Possibly blended with the dark-tide."

"What I don't understand," Anskar said, "is how a blade that contained astrumium could fall prey to a demon. Surely the star metal would repel any attempt to possess the sword."

"You would think," the woman said. "Unless it is the flesh of demons that star metal affects, and not their disembodied essence."

Anskar nodded slowly to himself as it all started to make sense. There had been something awry with the sword from very early on, some inkling that it was growing sentient. That, he'd attributed to an overspill of his own developing dark-tide abilities. But after his trip to Vulthanor that first time, it had been different. The sword had grown stronger, more willful. It had adopted a personality far from his own.

"I think it was a demon called Sicth Na'Jagalot."

The woman frowned. "Why do you think this?"

"Because…" And now he hung his head. What he had done to Sicth Na'Jagalot—what he had been forced to do, he reminded himself—felt sordid in front of this golden woman. Depraved.

"Because you absorbed him," a deep voice said.

The woman shifted to one side, making way for a tall, muscular man with gray skin. Anskar recognized the roiling dark-tide flow within the demon's veins, and something brighter, something explosive at his core.

"You know the name, Tarrik?" the woman asked.

He eyed her curiously, then swallowed and crouched down next to Anskar. "Sicth Na'Jagalot is—was—a festering piece of shit, a particularly violent and ambitious demon approaching the highest of our orders. If you vanquished and absorbed him, I am duly impressed."

"I don't know if I did," Anskar said. "Fully absorb him, that is. I know I was on the cusp of it, but then something happened. I was interrupted."

"You did not feel the exultant rush?"

"I don't think so."

"Believe me," Tarrik said, "you would know it if you felt it. Tell me, do you have access to his memories? Are there images of blood, of rending and ripping and pain?"

Anskar closed his eyes in order to concentrate. "Nothing."

"Anskar thinks the demon may have fled into his sword," the woman said.

"That is possible." Tarrik reached out with both hands for Anskar's face. "May I?" he asked.

"Go ahead."

Tarrik's fingertips were coarse and hard, and they somehow managed to convey the demon's great strength. If he had wanted, he could have crushed Anskar's skull. But instead, the demon's touch, his hands splayed either side of Anskar's face, was light. There was an exchange of dark-tide essence as Tarrik pressed his forehead to Anskar's. After a few seconds, he pulled back and let go.

"Nothing," Tarrik said. "No residue of Sicth Na'Jagalot within you. You are lucky, Anskar. An interrupted absorption often leads to the strengthening of the vanquished foe and gives him access to the byways of your mind. A demon with the guile of Sicth Na'Jagalot could have worked an ungodly amount of mischief under such conditions. He might have even wrested control of your body and mind from you."

"Then it's a good thing he was such a coward," Anskar said, though he was unsettled by the thought. "And that he fled into my sword."

"And this *Amalantril* is now in the possession of your mother?" the woman said.

It pained Anskar to admit it. He had slaved over a hot forge to create that blade. He had studied the writings of Jargalan swordmasters for weeks on end so that he could make a superior weapon. Gone now. All that effort wasted. Something else, in addition to his childhood, his mother had taken from him.

"So, Sicth Na'Jagalot now serves the Necromancer Queen," Tarrik said.

"You sound sympathetic," the woman said.

"You know me, Ren, always harping on about the injustice of demons being summoned and enslaved by humans."

"As if it never happens the other way around!" the woman—Ren— said.

"Not to you it didn't. But it happened to me, and not just the once."

She reached out a golden hand and rested it on his forearm. He snatched his arm away as if burned, then winced and smiled an apology.

This time when she reached for him, it was to run her fingers through his braided hair. He closed his eyes and sighed.

Ren craned her neck to look behind, and Anskar could see clearly now, as if a veil had been lifted.

"Odopek is pouring tea," she told Tarrik. "You know how he hates it if we don't drink with him." For Anskar's benefit, she explained: "Tea is for communal consumption where he comes from."

"Which is?" Anskar said.

"Come on," Tarrik said, standing and then hauling Anskar to his feet. "Put on the shirt and boots. You like the clothes?"

"Where are my own?"

"We thought about washing them, but they were too frayed and bloodied. And by all the cesspits of Shimrax, they stank. Ren incinerated them."

"Where did these come from?" Anskar asked as he shrugged into the shirt, trying not to think about the smell.

"Me," Tarrik said. "I wore them an age ago, when I was first enslaved by a human. Ren thinks it will do me good to let them go."

"You were summoned and bound?" Anskar asked. "What was that like?"

"Pray you never find out."

"Who did that to you?"

Tarrik's mouth twisted into the semblance of a smile. "Ren's father."

Ren was already gliding away across the beach toward where the little man sat filling a teacup from a steaming pot. There was a kettle before him atop a heap of smoldering coals—violet coals, no flames and no smoke.

The beach…

The grass they stood upon was a circle of green between the arms of a forest on the one side and giving way to a sandy shoreline the other, where rills of golden sunlight danced across the gently lapping waves.

The waters were azure, almost crystalline in their clarity, save for the froth of white horses around submerged reefs and the spray and splash of silver fish that leapt from the water. Overhead, gulls circled, pristine and white, their cries nothing like the grating screech of the seabirds at Dorinah; they were soothing and musical. Almost, he could have believed, they were crooning to him.

"This place…" Anskar said, leaving his jaw hanging open as he turned around in wonder, taking it all in. The forest that encompassed them on three sides was treed with gray elm and ash, their branches sparsely leaved, admitting beams and splashes of sunlight. Golden figures, misty and incorporeal as wraithes, flitted between the trees, sometimes pausing to stare out with eyes like suns before gliding back to whatever tasks consumed them. It felt like an island of gods. Or angels. Squirrels scurried from limb to limb, and there were large insects hovering nearby, as if supervising or simply observing. Not insects, he realized as he squinted. They were tiny birds that seemed to just hang in midair, their wings a blur of movement, almost too fast to see.

The act of squinting caused Anskar's hands to fly to his eyes. "Are they still…?" he asked.

"Black," Tarrik said. "Which never bodes well. Boots…" he prompted, and Anskar stooped to pull them on.

Steadying him by the arm, the demon led him off the grass and over the sand to where Ren stood waiting. Odopek was seated on a rock, sipping tea. There were four empty teacups beside the teapot on the sand, but of the kettle and the fire there was no sign. It was as if they had simply vanished into thin air. In their place there was a circle of brass embedded in the beach, partially covered with sand. There were markings around the perimeter, inscriptions in what might have been an early form of Skanuric. Possibly they were numerals. A triangular gnomon, like a sail made of brass, stood up from the center, and where the sunlight struck, it cast a shadow on the circle.

Anskar felt the stab of recognition when the woman who had been lying by the fire sat up, sand clinging to her dark, starched-stiff robe. Her back was to him as she shook out her shimmering silver hair. Her robe had been stitched with golden thread, presumably where Blosius's blade had penetrated. She half turned, then seemed to remember to reach for the orichalcum mask that sat beside her on the sand. As she lifted the mask and settled it over her head, Anskar glimpsed the side of her face—or rather, where the side of her face should have been. Through the strands of silver hair, there was nothing, only an indefinable absence that made his guts clench with the wrongness of it all.

"Sheelahn?" he said, immediately wondering if he had gotten the name right. "Or is it Haeth Ho'Akopeth?" He didn't think so—Haeth Ho'Akopeth had a face like a faceted black diamond, not no face at all.

The empty eyes of the orichalcum mask turned to take him in. "I am both and neither," the Ethereal Sorceress said in her mellifluous voice. "But you have been accorded permission, and so you may call me by the name you were given."

"Sheelahn, then," Anskar said. "I thought you were... I mean, Blosius stabbed you."

"You thought I was dead?" Sheelahn said. "Whereas you really were."

"Only for a short time," Ren said.

"Indeed," Sheelahn said. "I am still not convinced by this course of action."

"Nor need you be," Tarrik said.

"This is our island, after all," Odopek said above the rim of his teacup as he took a noisy slurp.

"And thus I cede to your authority in this matter," the Ethereal Sorceress said, inclining her mask toward the little man, who beamed affably back at her. "But do not say I did not warn you."

"With guidance," Ren said, then peered into Anskar's eyes, as if her luminous ones could turn his black orbs another shade. "With guidance, Anskar, the power could come into full bloom within you."

"And I would be like you?" he asked, then jerked his head toward the forest, where dozens of golden figures watched from the tree line. "Like them?"

"It is our hope."

Anskar shook his head, biting down on his confusion, his frustration. "Then you're going to have to explain…"

"What would you like to know?"

"For one thing, where I am." He glanced out across the sparkling waters. They struck him as too perfect to be real. "What is this place?"

"That," Odopek said, gesturing with his cup and spilling tea, "is the Trackless Ocean. Our isle is surrounded by thousands of miles of sea, about as far from so-called civilization as it is possible to get on Wiraya."

The realization made Anskar giddy.

"Then how did we get here?"

Sheelahn spread her gloved hands, then used one of them to buff a section of the brass circle embedded in the sand.

"Is that an *izindel?*" Anskar asked.

"The original."

"Stolen from the Orgol god," Tarrik muttered, then desisted at a sharp look from Ren.

Odopek gave a polite cough and nodded towards his teapot.

Tarrik rolled his eyes. "Did I not say I would fix it? Patience, old friend."

"We have been! It has been many years, Tarrik. The absence of freedom stifles us, and we are tired of being one."

"What's wrong with it?" Anskar asked. "It seems fine to me." He took a step toward the teapot, then stopped when Odopek snatched it from the sand and held it protectively in his lap.

"Steeping tea is but one of its functions," Tarrik explained. "But do not worry, Odopek, it will be fixed. I am a demon of my word."

The little man let out a sigh. "I know you are, friend. Forgive my impatience. Now, drink your tea. It will help your contusions to heal."

One of the teacups rose into the air and floated over to Tarrik, who grimaced before he took hold of the cup and sipped the contents.

Anskar felt something akin to a cold breeze ruffling the hairs on his forearms and brushing the back of his neck. He glanced at Ren for an explanation.

"Odopek calls it his moonshine," Sheelahn said with an amused shake of her masked head.

"And so it is," the little man said. "So what if we wish to go on bathing in its reflected radiance? Not everyone aspires to such lofty goals as you. Each to their own, we say. The moon's power is perfectly to our liking, and there is no concomitant danger of our head growing so big to the point that it explodes and takes the whole world with it."

"I am beginning to think Odopek has a point," Tarrik said.

"We have spoken of this," Ren said, even as a teacup drifted toward her and she reluctantly accepted it. "The power does not manifest in individuals just for us to ignore it, or to accept a dim reflection of its true puissance and rest on one's laurels. Your growing power, Anskar, is the same as Odopek possesses, only in its pure, unmitigated form."

"And Sheelahn?" Anskar asked.

The Ethereal Sorceress glared at him with her empty eyes. "I do not walk this way. Neither, I think, should you, Anskar."

"Get too close to the light," Odopek sniffed, "and you will be rendered blind… to your own hubris, if nothing else. And we, for two, do not wish to be held accountable for the death of nations; nay, even the ending of the world."

"Which is why those who are coming into their power," Ren said, her golden eyes on Anskar, "are in need of guidance."

"Our method is safer," Odopek said.

"Yet it stops before the journey is complete," Ren said with measured patience.

"You assume it is a journey worth taking," Sheelahn said.

"I do not see how it can be," Tarrik concurred.

"For me it was." Ren's tone softened as she touched his cheek. "For you it will be."

"Maybe." Tarrik passed his half-empty teacup to Odopek. "Does anybody have strong spirits? The Widow's Malt kind, not the metaphysical."

"Your stash is where you left it," Ren said, and it was hard to miss the note of amusement in her voice.

Tarrik grunted something and trudged away up the beach, crossing the green sward and entering in among the trees.

"So," Anskar said in an effort to break the awkward silence that followed Tarrik's departure, "this moonshine power of yours, Odopek, is it the same as what Niyandrians call being moontouched?"

The Ethereal Sorceress let out a tinkling laugh.

"Hardly," the little man said.

"The moontouched have the potential to experience what Odopek calls the moonshine," Sheelahn explained. "It depends upon the degree to which they are able to reunify the tides."

"Reunify?" Zek had theorized that the differentiated tides came from the same source; that it was unnatural for them to be compartmentalized.

"The tides were not always separated," Ren said. "They are now, for our own good—save for those who are chosen, and those who have been burned by sufficient trials."

"Huh," Odopek said. "More likely, so that those who have ascended can continue to lord it over the rest of us."

"Then why do you not strive to ascend, if you believe that?" Ren asked in a voice like a whiplash.

"Because…"

"Because what?" Anskar prompted when the little man seemed too lost in his thoughts to go on.

"Because we are not altogether sold on the idea that this world is fallen to a lower, denser state from its original inception. Because we do not wish to return to some mythical realm of the gods."

"Ah, the wisdom of the little one," Sheelahn said.

"Two!" Odopek said indignantly. "We are two. And no, Sorceress, you and we do not agree. On anything."

"Certainly not on tea," Sheelahn retorted.

"The ascended are not gods," Ren said.

"But you act like it," Odopek said, "hiding away out of view, influencing, drawing people along the paths of your designs, but never getting your golden hands dirty."

"You know why that is," Ren chided.

"Yes, yes, yes. Because a direct war of the ascended against the descended would tear apart the very fabric of Wiraya. Who says? To our mind, it is mere speculation, scaremongering, and an excuse to sit on the sidelines and do nothing."

"We are doing something now." Ren said. "You and Tarrik did a great deal by going into the abyssal realm to bring Anskar to us."

"Only because we are not ascended."

"Not yet…"

"Nevertheless, not. We sometimes wonder if that is why you keep us around, one foot in the heights, the other firmly on solid ground. You need intermediaries to do your heavy lifting."

"And the descended," Anskar said. "Who or what are they?"

"You have seen," Sheelahn said from within her mask. "I feel the taint of them on your spirit. You came close, did you not? Nearly acquiesced?"

"Kaythe Nurglich?" Anskar asked.

"We have already discussed this," Ren said. "He did not acquiesce.

The power erupted within him. Saved him."

"So much for free will," Odopek said.

"I knew there was a reason I favored you," Sheelahn said. "Your mother's blood must have been diluted by your father's, for she did acquiesce, before she sought to back out of her contract with the Corpse Maker, thus setting into motion the events that led to her downfall."

"Which was by no means decisive," Anskar said. "My mother is far from finished."

"This does not surprise me."

Ren gave Anskar a reassuring touch on the arm. "Your mother made choices she ought not to have," she said. "She chose the descending path. But in your case… The fact that the power manifested when it did is a sign that you belong with us."

Anskar glanced at Sheelahn, but she sat motionless, looking the other way.

"Oh, how remiss of us!" Odopek said. "We quite forgot to pass you a tea."

The cup didn't float toward Anskar. This time, the little man got up from the sand and handed it to him. "Drink," Odopek said. "Let it bring you calm and clarity."

Anskar was acutely aware of everyone watching him as he prepared to sip. He hesitated, suspecting this was some kind of joke at his expense, but when he frowned at Odopek, the little man merely nodded and smiled his encouragement.

"Careful, it's hot," Odopek warned as Anskar raised the cup to his lips.

Just that one sip brought a rush of flavors to his palate—a pleasant sweetness, a woody note that reminded him of cinnamon. It was mildly bitter as well, with a hint of salt. Anskar took another sip, then drank a little more deeply. His airways seemed to open up, and an invigorating lightness filled his head.

"Good?" Odopek enquired.

"Better than good," Anskar said, finishing off the cup and holding it out for a refill. "It's exquisite."

"Excellent," Odopek said, snatching back the cup. "But that is all you are getting. Tea of such quality is not easy to procure."

"Not to mention," Ren said, "a second cup will leave you with a bad case of the jitters, and a third… You will have to ask Tarrik about that when he returns. The one time he drank three cups, he was insensible for hours."

Odopek lifted the hinged lid of his teapot and peered inside. Apparently satisfied, he collected all the used cups and stacked them atop the pot, as if he intended to fit them inside, which was absurd. They were far too large. Odopek's lips moved in a silent cant, and the stacked cups grew blurry and indistinct. Anskar blinked to adjust his focus, but when he could see clearly again, the cups had disappeared.

"I trust you are refreshed?" Ren asked, as she seated herself on the sand at the edge of the brass circle.

"Thank you, I am," Anskar said as he joined her.

Sheelahn stood stiffly, brushing sand from her robe, and then moved to sit across the *izindel* from Anskar. Odopek reached inside his teapot and withdrew something before closing the lid.

"Impossible…" Anskar breathed, as a folding chair grew in the little man's hand, a wooden frame with striped blue and white canvas.

With an arch of his eyebrows that seemed to ask, "What?" Odopek opened up the chair and slumped into it with a satisfied sigh.

"You must have many questions, Anskar," Ren said.

Anskar glanced at the Ethereal Sorceress, seated cross-legged, totally serene, no reaction from her empty eyes of void space. He switched his gaze to Odopek, who was in the process of popping something bright into his mouth—something orange, or rather, salmon-pink.

"Candy-cap mushroom?" Odopek said, offering Anskar a white paper bag.

"Thank you, I won't," Anskar said.

"Tastes like maple syrup," Odopek said. "No? Suit yourself." He returned the bag to his pocket.

"You've already told me where we are—roughly," Anskar said.

"There are no charts that show the island's location," the Ethereal Sorceress said in her musical voice. "As far as the rest of Wiraya is concerned, this place does not exist."

"And a good thing, too," Ren said, "if we are to remain aloof from the world, untainted by its corruption."

A guttural sound came from within Sheelahn's mask. It may have been a scoff.

"You have also indicated how I came to be here," Anskar said. "But you won't tell me how my chest wound was healed?"

"Does it matter?" Ren countered.

"But it was you?"

Silence.

"Menselas? The awakening power within me? Why won't you tell me?"

"All in good time," Ren said.

"What she means," Odopek put in between chews of his candied mushroom, "is that she is not quite one hundred percent sure of you yet. Our Ren is paranoid like that. She has never been the most trusting of people."

Ren smiled. "I thought I had improved."

"You have," Odopek said. "Immeasurably. But, Anskar, you must understand this. We took a great risk bringing you here. Call it an act of faith, if you like. Your nascent power caused a… resonance here on the isle. The avatars…" He dried up when Ren shot him a warning glare.

"The golden folk of the forest," Ren said, "grew excited and then scared. There was much debate as to how involved we of the isle should become in your fate."

Sheelahn peeled off a long, black glove. The hand beneath was shiny and white, as if made from alabaster. The nails were immaculate and silver, curled like claws. She clicked them together, a sound that seemed to unsettle Ren. Odopek merely rolled his eyes.

"And are you one and the same with them?" Anskar asked Ren.

"On account of my golden glow?" She smiled almost bashfully. "You…" She grimaced, as if uncertain how much she should say. "Some things cannot be explained, Anskar, at least, not with words."

"They have to be experienced?"

Ren nodded, at the same time closing her eyes and swallowing. Remembered pain?

"What must I experience?" Anskar asked, not sure he wanted to hear the answer.

"She will not tell you," Odopek said. "Believe me, we have tried to probe, and always the answer is the same."

"The power, fully manifested," Ren said, "is not really power at all—for those who are chosen. It is not an ability earned through merit. It is pure gratuity."

"A gift again," Anskar said. "Like the god's mark?"

"You are wasting your breath," Odopek said. "Perhaps I should make more tea?"

"No," Anskar said, rising. "I've had enough of mysteries and obfuscation—a lifetime. I'm ready to leave now."

Sheelahn turned her masked face toward Ren, as if she wanted to see how she would react. The Ethereal Sorceress might even have been amused.

"You must be patient with us, Anskar," Ren said. "Trust us."

"Trust! I didn't agree to come here. What if I don't want to join your little cabal?"

"Calm," Ren said, though there was a hint of menace in her tone. "All will be revealed, if that is your lot."

"If that is my lot!" Heat flooded Anskar's veins—a different heat, new and virulent. He could no longer feel the dark-tide within him, nor the dawn or the dusk. It was as if they had been subsumed.

Ren raised her hands in a placating gesture. Odopek swallowed. Sheelahn's posture grew as stiff as her robes. Anskar felt the bristle of strange sorceries within her.

Magma bubbled and surged within him. Golden light, like a second heart, pulsed beneath his borrowed shirt.

"Anskar," Ren said, her voice close to a whisper. "Breathe deeply. You are in no danger here. We are all friends."

"Of course we are," he said. "But would we be if I did not possess this power? Now answer me: Where does the power come from? What am I supposed to do with it?"

"I'm sorry," Ren said. "That is for you to discover. We can merely monitor and guide you through the…" Again, she stopped short of a complete explanation.

"Guide me through what?" he demanded. Heat scorched his cheeks. His hands, when he raised them to his face, gave off little whorls of steam, and the veins were golden and throbbing.

"Please," Ren said, "be seated. Calm yourself. Let us help you."

"You can help me, all right," he snarled, then jabbed a finger at Sheelahn. Flame flickered on the tip. "Activate the *izindel*. Send me back."

"Back where?" the Ethereal Sorceress asked, her voice still lyrical, but it had risen a notch.

"I'm sure Vulthanor wouldn't mind having him back," a deep voice said from behind Anskar. "He'd be a nice addition to their war of succession, being the grandson of the previous lord."

He turned to find Tarrik looming over him, a spear of dark metal clutched in one hand, a bottle of spirits in the other.

"No shadow blade this time?" Anskar asked, clenching his fist, swelling with confidence as fire wreathed both hands.

"It is my hard-won experience," Tarrik said, raising the bottle and finishing off the contents before casting it aside, "that steel is far more reliable against sorcerers than anything the tidal powers can manifest."

Anskar's confidence started to gush away from him. He knew he could take Tarrik; knew he could devastate all of them—the entire isle—and yet something about the demon's surety unnerved him. What if he were wrong? Not just about the extent of his power or the extent of theirs; but what if he were wrong in his suspicions? Yes, he had been duped all through his short life, one way or another, fed lies atop lies; but what if Ren were being truthful with him, and he was just too damaged to see it?

He pulled himself together. It didn't matter either way. He wasn't staying here. He had matters to attend to. A matter.

"I need to return to Wiraya."

He could no longer face Tarrik's looming presence, and so he turned imploring eyes on Sheelahn, the fire within him starting to abate.

Ren breathed a sigh of relief. "Good," she said. "You show remarkable control, Anskar."

"I am not an animal to be trained!" he snapped.

"Where would you like me to send you?" Sheelahn asked.

Odopek and Ren shared a look. Tarrik took a step closer.

"Wait," Anskar said. Suddenly, his head was pounding as memories, images, questions flooded his mind. He turned back to Tarrik, who held his spear two-handed now, the tip aimed at Anskar's chest. "Why did you come to Vulthanor?"

"Because Domatai asked," the Ren said. "And in times of peril, we must all make alliances of one sort or another."

"Basic business sense," Sheelahn said.

"Peril?" Anskar said. "My mother?"

"You," Odopek said quietly. "The peril we foresaw was you."

"I suspected when first we met," Sheelahn said, "though your dark-tide ability was then coming into the ascendance, and so I could not be sure. The power you possess is the only reason I tolerated your presence."

"Because you hate demons? So why do you mix with Tarrik?" Anskar almost slapped himself for his stupidity. "Because he has this power too. But I still don't understand. If you're opposed to demons, why would you work with Domatai?"

"In business," Sheelahn said, "it is not unusual to trade with one's ideological opponents. The Lord Domatai and I had many dealings throughout the decades. It was never more necessary than during the war with your mother. In Domatai's case, I would describe him as the lesser of two evils."

"So he was evil, then?" Anskar said. He had long since given up hoping his mother was anything but. "Am I evil, too? Is that why Domatai came through the portal to save me? My grandfather gave his life so that Carred and I could escape." Actually, he doubted Carred had had anything to do with it. Domatai couldn't have cared less about her. This was all about him.

"If Domatai did indeed sacrifice himself," the Ethereal Sorceress said, "it must have been on account of his fully evolved demon intellect. Always, the Lord Domatai showed an ability to see far in advance of the rest of us, a bigger picture that most can scarcely imagine."

"But you can, I suppose?" Anskar said.

"What I think," Ren said, "is that Domatai saw what was coming if the Necromancer Queen, his daughter, went unchecked. The powers she wields are no secret. Old enemies united once before in order to stop her bringing about a new Niyandrian Empire, one that would have ushered in the next great cataclysm."

"Well, if she was capable of that in the past," Anskar said, re-living the feeling of futility he had experienced when facing her onslaught, "it's going to take more than an alliance of mainland nobles and the Church to stop her this time. She possessed—assimilated—another moontouched. She may even have absorbed Domatai himself."

"So much for his famed omniscience," Tarrik said. "Why would Domatai oppose the Necromancer Queen if he knew she would beat him and take his power?"

"To keep Anskar from her, of course," the Ethereal Sorceress said. "He would have perceived the power burgeoning within his grandson. We all know the hatred Talia had for her father, and where it would have led. Domatai could not prevent her return to life, but perhaps he saw a way of ultimately defeating her."

Ren shook her head. Some of her radiance seemed to have departed her, leaving her still golden but less luminous. It made her appear more solid, a creature of flesh and blood. "I find it hard to believe," she said. "A self-sacrificing demon…" She trailed off when Tarrik dipped his head. Something like regret crossed her face, and she stood and went to him and brushed his hand with her fingertips.

"So, you all think I'm just a weapon to be used against my mother?" Anskar said.

"No," Odopek said. "Absolutely not! How could you think such a thing?"

"It certainly sounds that way."

"And perhaps it has played out that way," the Ethereal Sorceress said. "But you were originally Queen Talia's plan, the means of her return. None of us—not even she—expected things to turn out the way they have."

"That is because our fate is in other hands," Ren said.

"On this, we disagree," Sheelahn replied tersely.

"And what if Domatai merely acted out of protectiveness for one of his own flesh and blood?" Anskar said. "Maybe he just wanted to keep me safe."

Sheelahn laughed melodically. "The Lord Domatai's vast intellect did not make him more compassionate. If he cared about you—"

Ren cut her off. "Domatai was a demon lord, advanced in the ways of culture, of reason, and, yes, compassion."

"Thank you," Tarrik said. "You, at least, get it."

"You have taught me all this," Ren said.

"So, my grandfather cared?" Anskar said.

"I, too," Ren said, glancing at Sheelahn, "used to revile demons. Observing Tarrik has taught me how wrong I was. In some cases. We do not know the real motives for Domatai's self-sacrifice, but we should at least be grateful for it, and to him."

"Because I'm useful?" Anskar said.

Ren looked deflated by his question. "This is not about utility," she said.

"Maybe not for you," Tarrik said. "Me, I am not so sure."

"Which is why you continue to resist your ascension, no doubt," Sheelahn said. "Perfectly understandable."

"You don't have to remain here," Ren said.

"And I will not stay any longer than I need to in order to recover," Sheelahn said. "I am grateful for your aid with my convalescence, but I do not ever let a favor grow into a debt. I will grant you one service. Whatever you desire."

Ren met Anskar's eyes. Somehow, even through the brightness of her golden orbs, she managed to convey pity. "There is still darkness within you," she said.

When his fingers went to his eyes, she nodded.

"The choices you have to make," Ren said, "are yours alone. We cannot—nor would we, if we could—compel you to stay here with us. But know this: you are wanted here. We"—and now she turned to take in the golden figures who stood at the edge of the forest—"would all like to see you ascend, and we fear for what might happen should you go about your new birth in your own way."

"The people of this isle are not the only ones who will be concerned,"

Sheelahn said. "Some will not want to take the risk of permitting Anskar to go his own way."

"Hush," Ren said, waving the Ethereal Sorceress to silence. "We must—difficult as it is—relinquish control. We must have faith."

"In what?" Anskar asked."

"In you, of course. Now, what is it you most want?" Ren asked.

He saw visions of Kaythe Nurglich, tendrils wriggling in the dark. Heard again promises of power. He saw the golden-eyed crow at his bedroom window, then drinking his blood. He saw Hallow Hill, the wraithe, the necromancers inside the tomb, the little girl on the altar. He heard again the offer of power, enough to avenge himself on Queen Talia. And he started to grow angry once more. Angry at all the duplicity, the lies, the betrayals. Angry for Marith, for Carred. Angry with himself—for not knowing right from wrong. Angry at Tion for being such a poor example. At Vihtor for dying.

Sareya.

Why Sareya? Her image flared behind his eyes, luminous like Ren for a moment, then faded to red and then to nothing. But he was left with the unnerving conviction that she was going to kill him.

She had tried before, at Dorinah.

And then he saw Queen Talia laughing in his face, mocking him for his impotence, telling him he was nothing, just a thing of blood and bone. He had failed her, she seemed to say, but she had found another way. He was useless. Worse than useless. She had no need for him, so why not just stay here on the isle? Why not ascend—whatever that meant—and vanish from the affairs of the world? He might as well. Surely that was better than seeing the world turn to rot under the Necromancer Queen's rule. Because, she intimated in his mind, that was what was coming. No compromises this time. No attempt to share the world's stage with the mainland. Death and devastation were coming. A new goddess had arisen, and even Kaythe Nurglich was quaking in terror.

And then he was—in his memories—back in the chapel of the Hooded One at Branil's Burg, amid the coffers and the Sandoval safes, and he was face to face with the ruby skull, all that remained of the original chapel, an icon of the aspect of Menselas that had once been called Death.

And he knew then what he had to do.

What he was *called* to do.

"You asked what is it I want," Anskar said.

Ren nodded warily.

"I want free access to the *izindel*, at least for a time."

"Never," Sheelahn said.

"You offered me a service," Ren said to her. "A payment now rather than a debt incurred. This is what I ask, and thereby any debt you may owe us is redeemed."

Sheelahn looked away, thinking it over. Finally she turned back. "We have a contract," she said. "Your terms are agreeable."

"Good," Ren said. She drew in a deep breath, then squeezed Tarrik's hand, as if she needed his strength. "I have prayed that my faith in you be increased, Anskar, but I will tell you that I am still weak, more human than I would wish. Tell me, please, what is it you intend to do?"

"Ultimately," he said, noting the anxiety on Odopek's face, Tarrik's stoicism, Ren's abject fear; even Sheelahn seemed on tenterhooks. "I intend to kill my mother."

THIRTY-ONE

HANDS MANACLED BEHIND HER BACK, Sareya stood at the gunwale. Her clothes were scratchy and stiff from where the sun had dried them. A Jargalan stood beside her, one hand on the hilt of the cutlass hanging from his belt. The man's ability to withstand the new and sudden heat would have seemed inhuman but for the occasional pant that came from beneath his face coverings.

Yards creaked overhead. Canvas flapped with each gust of wind. Waves sloshed around the keel. The decks were alive with sailors tying off stays, hazarding the rigging, scrubbing, lifting, carrying loads.

Nul sat slumped on a bench, head cocked to one side, eyes unfocused.

The fat pig, Galban, was leaning out over the prow with the magus, gazing at the dark smudge of approaching land. All Sareya could see was a shimmering heat haze, the sea of the bay they were coming into bedizened with rills of reflected sunlight. Little by little, she started to make out the masts of ships moored in a vast harbor with gargantuan walls that looked as though they had risen from the deep, grown rather than built.

The stench of roasting meat wafted over the becalmed harbor waters to greet them, heavy with fat and oil. A handful of flat-roofed buildings hemmed the wharves. A cliff loomed above them, and there were more buildings above. To either side of the harbor, there was nothing but rolling desert, and to the west, a single sand-dusted road wending away between the dunes.

Mooring posts as tall as trees ran from the harbor walls into the sea, with boarded walkways between them. The helmswoman brought them in slowly, then sailors leapt from the gunwale to the jetties and secured the mooring lines to cleats.

Upwards of fifty Jargalans, wrapped head to toe in black bindings and carrying tall wicker shields, marched down the gangplank two abreast, Sareya beside Nul at the center of the column. In the lead, Galban was deep in conversation with the magus. Sareya glanced back to see the ship's captain leaning over the gunwale, watching them depart. She spat a dark wad into the gently lapping water then shook her head.

Nul stumbled and dropped to one knee. His breaths were ragged, his face drawn and haggard in the unforgiving glare of the sun. Sareya wanted to help him up, to support him as they walked, but with her hands as bound as his, there was nothing she could do. The Jargalan behind kicked Nul in the back, pitching him to his face.

"Leave him be," Sareya snapped, instantly regretting it as they man raised his hand to her. *Do it!* she said with her eyes. *Go on, hit me, and see what happens when I greet the dusk-tide. If,* she corrected herself. If she were permitted to see the sun go down.

The pirate wavered, hand trembling as he decided whether or not to strike. The man next to him muttered something in their own language, and the pirate lowered his hand. "Speak again, red bitch, and you will suffer."

The column passed along the wharves and began the ascent of the sheer stone steps cut into the cliff face. Nul tripped repeatedly, and several times he fell.

Galban and the vanguard were there waiting at the top, where a well-worn trail led to the outskirts of a clifftop town.

As she caught her breath and waited for the rearguard to come off the steps, Sareya took in the view of wave-like sand dunes on the horizon, a scatter of palm trees, and a range of jagged mountains in the hazy distance. Beyond the close-packed buildings of the town, dust plumed in the wake of a departing camel train.

Once the column had reformed atop the cliff, Galban led the way across fields of giant cacti planted in rows upon the sand. Women in flowing burnooses and straw hats with gauze veils worked amid the cacti, cutting into them with augers and inserting tubes of stitched-together animal gut, through which the cacti's milky fluids flowed into wooden pails. Boys in baggy trousers and silk vests stood atop rickety ladders as they cut off the uppermost spines and brilliant yellow flowers, stowing them in bags that hung at their hips. The boys' heads were uncovered, and they were completely bald, their scalps adorned with intricate ocher tattoos.

Beyond the cacti fields, the column meandered past a cluster of homesteads on the edge of town, then picked up a paved road that brought them in amongst dilapidated cottages of baked clay, where old women in drab colored smocks mended fishing nets, watching with dour faces as the column went by.

Farther in, the houses were of painted brick—yellow, pink, violet, and blue—packed together in long and winding terraces two, even three, stories high. Two old men on a balcony smoked long-stemmed pipes as they played a game with carved wooden pieces on a checkerboard. They paused to watch the column pass by below. One of them made a gesture with his finger; it had more the feel of a curse than a blessing.

As they entered in among narrow lanes, the column moved to

single file, so they could weave in and out of the crowds entering and leaving the stores either side or perusing the market stalls that ran down the center of the road. About half the men and women wore head coverings. Those who did not were more often than not attired in shabby, much-patched clothing. Many of them walked barefoot, despite the occasional scorpion that scuttled by.

Above the hubbub, Sareya became aware of the grating drone of some kind of music coming from the open door of a restaurant. Menselas alone knew what kind of instrument it was that made such a dreadful noise, but none of the locals seemed to notice, as if it had become a background to their daily lives.

The air was redolent with spices and the succulent aromas of fish and meat. Sareya looked longingly at vendors cooking over hot coals; at the carts laden with olives, dates, and figs, all dusted with sand. Her stomach growled, but there was no sign of her captors stopping. Not one of them even looked at the fare on display.

Hawkers held up trinkets of crystal and wood, leather and bone—all ignored. A silk-clad prostitute glided in and out of the column, glittery tassels hanging from her full breasts, a scarlet cloth bound about her face, leaving only her sultry eyes visible. She too was ignored by all the pirates. That struck Sareya as strange. At sea, she could have sworn she smelled their arousal, felt their lusts; but here, on dry land, they seemed as dispassionate as priests of the Healer. Then again, appearances could be deceptive. She'd learned that lesson at Branil's Burg.

"Remind me to come back this way," Nul rasped. The effort of speaking sent him into a coughing fit. "Don't suppose you have any beer?" he asked the nearest pirate. No response. "Water, then?" Still nothing.

At length they came to a barracks ground on the far side of town, where Jargalan warriors manned the fighting platforms of a weather-beaten palisade formed from scaly palm trunks, their tops whittled to spikes. An officer wearing a red sash over his black burnoose met

Galban at the palisade's crude wooden gate and somewhat sullenly
ushered the troop inside.

The Jargalan pirates lined up for bowls of gruel and mugs of watered
wine, served outside in the dry midday heat. Beneath their head
wraps, they were all bald. Like the boys in the cactus field, they had
scalp tattoos—some kind of cursive script in ocher ink. Their wicker
shields were stowed against the palisade. How effective such flimsy-
looking shields would be against the Order's lances or their astrumium-
enhanced swords, Sareya would like to see. Not much, she thought.

Sareya and Nul sat together, backs to a stone well, so close yet so far
from the water. Her mouth was so dry, she couldn't make spit, and her lips
were cracked and sore. From time to time a burnoose-clad warrior would
descend the ladder from the fighting platform, draw up the bucket, and
ladle cool water into his mouth. The Jargalans seemed a sullen race, never
joking, barely even speaking, and when they did the conversation was
terse, as if they resented every word. Of course, it might have been down
to discipline. Off-duty, they might have been different.

Sareya dozed off in the unforgiving heat, but was sharply awakened
by water splashing her face.

"Galban says drink," a scrawny pirate said.

"Beer?" Nul asked with feigned jollity. But he was fooling no one.
His face was badly burned from the sun, dried out and riddled with
new creases.

He took the proffered ladle and swilled the water around his mouth
before swallowing.

"More," he said, but the man dipped the ladle into the well bucket and
offered it to Sareya this time. It was lukewarm and tasted of grit, but she
swallowed it as if it were the finest mistberry wine. Of course, that had

been Monash's favorite drink. Menselas, she must have spent a fortune, the amount she had plied Sareya with on the voyage to Dorinah.

"What about food?" Sareya asked.

"What about it?" The Jargalan moved away and took his place at one of the tables.

Galban made an announcement to his men when he came out of the hut he had entered, the officer with the red sash behind him, but he was speaking in a language Sareya didn't know. The pirates seemed to relax at whatever he said, but then the commander beckoned for two of his warriors and pointed at Sareya and Nul as he gave instructions.

Grabbing Sareya and Nul by the arms, the warriors roughly manhandled them into one of the buildings and down a flight of stairs to where the air was blessedly cool, yet tainted with the iron tang of blood and the stench of ordure. One of the warriors unlocked a heavy wooden door and pushed Nul into the moldering darkness beyond. The second warrior shoved Sareya in the back, and she landed with a jaw-crunching thud face-first on a pile of stinking straw.

She groaned and rolled onto her side as the door slammed behind them and a key turned in the lock. She managed to get to her knees, then stood, head touching the low ceiling. A chink of dirty light bled through a crack high up on one wall, dust motes dancing in its narrow beam.

But it was enough light to see that the cell they had been thrown into had another occupant, emaciated almost beyond recognition, his hair and beard long and bedraggled. It took Sareya a moment to recognize him—he had acted as Seneschal at Branil's Burg following Vihtor's death, until Monash had arrived with Sareya and relieved him.

Nul bucked up immediately, as if he'd been reunited with a long-lost friend. And perhaps he had.

"Eldrid DeVantte!" he said. "I would shake your hand, only..." He turned to show Eldrid his shackles.

"Nul?" Eldrid said. "I assume you're not here to pay my ransom, then?"

THIRTY-TWO

THE CLASH AND CLANG OF blades was deafening as Carred left the cool interior of the citadel and stepped out into the stifling heat of the bailey. A light mist rose from the waterlogged grounds, where the grass seemed to have grown several inches overnight. The air was thick with gnats, and she didn't envy the training rebels, who repeatedly cursed as they swatted away the horseflies that always seemed to proliferate at this time of year.

It was a brief interlude between storms, and she was pleased to see her commanders making the most of it, seizing the opportunity to run drills and to continue beating the ever-growing rebel force into a half-decent army. The problem was, so few of the commanders had seen war—Carred herself, Vilintia, and a handful of others had served at Naphor, and though there were a good few veterans among the soldiers, most were not leadership material.

She stood in the shade of the portico, not so much inspecting the training as observing the glistening red flesh on display. Several hundred

Niyandrians were engaged in the drills, stripped to the waist—both the men and the women. Not because they had returned to the ancient tradition of fighting naked, which had earned Niyandrians the name of demons among their more civilized enemies, but because it was so punishingly hot. She almost couldn't wait for the break in the clouds to close over and for the next bout of rain.

For a blissful moment, Carred grew lost in the distraction of muscles and sweat, until she realized she had allowed old habits to draw her away from her purpose. Without her need for vengeance, without her anger, she was brittle as dry kindling, and could just as easily be consumed. She focused instead on the scrape and clash of blades, the barked commands of the drill instructors—she wanted to call them sergeants, and maybe she would, when this became a real army.

And then she recognized one of the instructors, after he acknowledged her with a perfunctory nod. Sef Ap'Lian, she thought his name was. She thought she might have slept with him once, a long time ago. If she had, it wasn't exactly memorable.

"General Selenas," Sef said, thumping his hairy chest in salute and sending up a spray of sweat.

If she had slept with him, she must have been extremely drunk.

She returned Sef's salute and stepped away from the sheltered portico. "Good work, Sergeant," she said, almost wincing at her use of the rank. Sef arched an eyebrow, but at the same time his chest puffed up with pride. The trainees under Sef were quick to take advantage of the distraction, and put down their weapons so they could drink water from the pitchers set on trestle tables around the bailey.

Carred pulled her shoulders back as she approached Sef and clasped his hand, wrist to wrist in the warrior's way—something she hadn't done since her Last Cohort days.

"Forgive me for being a little vague," she said, "but weren't you with the Queen's Royal Guard?" She would have remembered if he'd been with the Cohort.

"I wish," Sef said. "Spearman in the Second Battalion, General. Just a bloody grunt." He grinned, and she wondered if there was more to it than self-effacement, some little joke, some innuendo she was supposed to pick up on.

"Well, your military experience has reaped dividends, Sergeant," she said, releasing his wrist. "These warriors"—she spoke loud enough for everyone to hear—"are clearly benefiting from your instruction. Uhm, carry on."

She began a circuit of the citadel, moving from section to section of the bailey, stopping briefly to watch the other drills underway: archery, the arrow-heads enhanced by dusk-tide sorcery that sent plumes of smoke curling away from the straw-stuffed mannequins being used as targets; unarmed combat, during which the grapplers were entirely naked, presumably to avoid fraying or ripping their clothing. She didn't linger long there but passed on to a broad swathe of grassland south of the Burg's herb and flower gardens, where several of the commanders were teaching their wards the basics of maneuvering in phalanx formation, armed with long spears and tall, curved shields they must have found in the Order's storerooms. If they had, that might be a good thing, if the shields were made to the Order's usual high standards and enhanced with astrumium. As to the phalanx work, shield walls were a throwback to a bygone age, and yet she had employed them herself back in the day. With the right support on their flanks, phalanxes with spears could be a formidable defense against cavalry charges. Someone had been doing her thinking for her, it seemed.

She moved on to the horse yard, which, according to Vilintia, the Niyandrians had commandeered while she was away with Anskar. Another good idea, and upon learning of it, Carred had immediately ordered mounted messengers sent to Quolith. Without giving too much away, she let it be known that this was part of her "better plan."

The corralled exercise yard was pitted with craters from the heavy rains, but still an old Niyandrian woman was engaged in ground work with a big chestnut stallion, lunging it around the enclosure by standing in the center and cueing it with movements of her body, sweeps of her arms, and the odd whispered command carried by dawn-tide sorcery.

Others were practicing their riding skills around the stable yard, though not with the heavy destriers, for what would be the point? There was no way unseasoned riders could rival the Order's knights, even if they had years to train, let alone the days and weeks they actually had. What she needed were scouts to scour the way ahead and report on Order activity all over Niyas. And not just the Order; she needed to know what Talia was up to, how quickly her forces were moving, what their objectives were. For she knew Talia. The Necromancer Queen hadn't returned from the realm of the dead just to breathe the fresh air of Wiraya and find herself a quiet spot to live out her second life. And it was too much of a coincidence for Talia to be within spitting distance of Naphor while Fult Wreave and his allies assembled in the woods outside the city walls.

The smell of damp grass and manure conspired to trick Carred into relaxing, into forgetting that she was not all right. She ambled over to the corral and leaned on a fence post, watching the old woman lunge her horse, feeling the reciprocal resonance in her own repositories as the woman whispered commands and the horse seamlessly obeyed.

"One of the veterans recommended her to me," Vilintia said, startling Carred, and spoiling the moment.

"Are you following me?" Carred's eyes returned to the paddock.

"A little, perhaps." Vilintia leaned on the crossbeam next to her, nodding behind to where several armed warriors were fanned out around the stable yard, keeping a close eye.

"Protection?" Carred asked.

"A precaution. If we're to be an army, and if you are to lead us…"

Carred took in a deep breath and then nodded as she let it out. "Thank you. I'll get better at this. More focused."

"You've been through a lot," Vilintia said.

"No excuse. You have too, and you're doing all right. Better than me. So, any word from Quolith?"

"Nothing yet."

"Maybe the Order's captured them."

Vilintia shrugged. "They bloody well shouldn't have. It's against the rules of war."

"Depends on whose rules," Carred said. "And who's winning. You should have learned that from the last war."

Vilintia shook her head. "I thought the Order knights prided themselves on their honor."

"As I pride myself on my celibacy," Carred said, and Vilintia slapped her on the arm. "A lot of things are said that aren't necessarily true."

"You should hear what they're saying about you," Vilintia said.

"Do I want to?"

"I think they were afraid before," Vilintia said. "Afraid of Talia's return and what that might mean for them, for all us ordinary Niyandrians."

"I can understand why."

"But when you came back, when you spoke about what Talia had done to Marith…"

Vilintia hesitated when Carred turned a glare on her, which she instantly softened with an apologetic smile and a nod for her to go on.

"When you announced your intention to stand against the Necromancer Queen, a change came over them. It's as if they had wanted this all along, a chance to live their own lives without submitting to unnatural sorcery—depraved, some of them are now openly saying."

"Are they?"

"Niyas isn't an island of necromancers, Carred. It never has been. Sorcerers, yes, with a natural affinity for the tides, but necromancy…

I was always told horror stories about that when I was a little girl. All the children were warned against dabbling with the affairs of Kaythe Nurglich. What are you laughing at?"

"I'm sorry," Carred said, "but I can't think of you as a little girl. I always just sort of assumed you came into the world fully grown."

"I'm serious," Vilintia said. "The earth-tide isn't natural to us. It's a perversion of the true tides, a step in the direction of the beasts—or rather, the demons."

"But not the demons, eh?" Carred said. "They're all about the dark-tide. And of course, Talia's no stranger to that, either. So, what you're saying is, the people see me as a leader, even after all the failures?"

"A leader for them, not for Queen Talia," Vilintia said. "And that brings them hope." She rested her hand on Carred's shoulder as they watched the old woman feed an apple to her horse. "It gives me hope."

Carred rose just before dawn and went to greet the tide—something she had not done since a child.

A filament of crimson outlined the horizon as she found herself a stone bench beside one of the Order's herb gardens. She settled herself down as the red bar in the sky widened and breathed deeply of the scent of lavender and sage, rosemary and basil.

At first she felt nothing, and when she turned her senses inwards, her dawn-tide repository felt clenched, as if it were holding its breath. But then a slight resonance passed through her dusk-tide repository, passing swiftly to the dawn.

Carred's breath caught in her throat, then she threw her head back and shuddered as she sighed. A cool breeze blew through her, easing every ache and filling her lungs, flooding her veins and coalescing within her dawn-tide repository. The repository swelled till it threatened to split her skull, and just when Carred thought it was over, the tidal wind gusted, then wailed, then screeched. Her hair blew out behind her, and her shirt whipped and snapped. She gripped the bench with white-knuckled hands, resisting the invisible forces that buffeted her, driving her backwards as if they sought to slam her into the wall of the citadel.

In her mind's eye, a vivid memory of Nally took form. She could almost feel the ragdoll lying in her lap as the ethereal winds blew through her hair, her body, her soul. And it was the same wind now that she had experienced as a child, though it felt stronger, buffeting her core, pummeling her like fists. Maybe that was on account of the growth in her repositories, her increased capacity to harness the tides. It could have been a trick of her memory, but the tide had felt cooler back then, cleaner. By comparison, the tide blowing through her now, though blissfully invigorating, seemed a little less pure.

Without warning, the gale died away, skirling off into the west, and Carred slumped forward, head in her hands, gasping for breath. She half-expected to be resting her elbows atop Nally, but the ragdoll wasn't there; she remained in the woods where Carred had lost her all those years ago, no doubt frayed, sodden, ripped apart by wild animals. If there was anything at all of the ragdoll left.

She started to weep with the shock of it all, then her tears turned to laughter as a never-before feeling of euphoria flooded her veins. For the briefest moment, she felt cleansed inside and out; scoured free of her doubts, her regrets, a lifetime of failures. She felt forgiven—though for what, she couldn't say. She felt redeemed, unified with all that was, that had been, that ever could be.

But already the feeling was starting to fade. And so she let it go, suddenly wanting it to leave her as quickly as it had come. She needed her failures, needed her grief. But most of all, she needed her anger.

She stiffened.

Was that horses she could hear?

Yes, the clop of hooves. Lots of them. There was a flurry of activity in the bailey—armored Niyandrians rushing toward the barbican. And then, out of sight, Vilintia was calling her name.

Carred stood from the bench. When she reached the barbican, she could see Vilintia, flanked by a dozen Niyandrians, facing off against a group of white-cloaked riders wearing armor that seemed too bright to be natural. Not just a small group, either. As she made her way to the front of the barbican, and Vilintia acknowledged her with a nod, she estimated upwards of two hundred riders, her own Niyandrian messengers in the front ranks. So they had returned, and they both looked unharmed. The knight at the head of the force raised a gauntleted hand then dismounted.

Carred fought hard to keep the sneer off her face. He was young enough to be her child—well, almost. Probably in his mid-twenties, dusky skinned, save for the raw patches on his chin that could have passed for Niyandrian—evidence of a recent shave, and an inept one at that. He was willowy, swamped by his white cloak and dazzling breastplate. He removed his open-faced helm and tucked it under his arm as he approached.

"Aren't you hot in all that armor?" Carred asked in Nan-Rhouric.

He replied in perfect Niyandrian. "A prudent sacrifice. The Order of Eternal Vigilance has very precise rules for engagements such as this. Think of the armor as, if not purely ceremonial, a precaution."

"Makes sense."

"I could not help noticing your maimed hand," he said discreetly, between the two of them, as if he feared offending her. "So I trust I am speaking with the infamous Carred Selenas?"

"I prefer notorious," she said, and he smiled—a warm smile without any guile. Of course, that might just mean he was good at disguising it.

"I am Antarry Bennetavian, Seneschal of Quolith." He dipped his head in a perfunctory bow.

"Aren't you a bit young to be a seneschal?"

"I was chosen by Vihtor Ulnar, the Five rest his spirit, neither for my age nor my good looks."

"Merit, then," Carred surmised. "Now, that's a rarity."

"I am a stickler for organizing things," Bennetavian said. "People, supplies, money. My mother said it was an affliction, but it has proven its worth over and over. And so here I am."

"Yet you left your stronghold unattended…" Carred said.

"Not so. A skeleton garrison remains at Quolith, under the charge of one of our most experienced commanders. You will be pleased to hear she is of advanced age."

It was hard not to like this man. "Antarry…" Carred started, but he held up a finger, glancing behind at the mounted force who had followed him to Branil's Burg. "Forgive me, but I must insist on my formal title in front of the troops. Please call me Seneschal Bennetavian."

Already Carred's opinion of him was starting to change. She bit her tongue to avoid telling him she could think of something better to call him, and instead offered her hand. "General Selenas."

He almost smiled, then squeezed his lips into a tight line. He clicked his heels when he shook her hand.

Carred indicated the riders she had sent to Quolith with a jerk of her head. "I see you received my message."

"We did," Bennetavian confirmed. "It was not an easy one to believe, until…"

He turned toward the riders. At a gesture from Bennetavian, the ranks parted, their horses skipping to either side, and a man in a blood-drenched white cloak kicked his mount to the head of the group.

It was hard to decide who looked worse, rider or horse. Both were caked in dried blood, and the man's tattered cloak was more red than white. Half the horse's face was a melted ruin, and the man hadn't fared much better. There was an angry burn mark on one cheek and a blistered patch of livid skin on his temple, where his hair had been burned away. He raised a hand to Carred, not in greeting, but to show the purple mottling of the fingers and the black veins that crawled from his wrist up his arm.

"I take it that's not frostbite," Carred said.

"In this heat?" the blood-caked man muttered. "Sorcery. Spread from man to man like a contagion. Must have run out of steam when it reached me." He hawked up phlegm and spat from the saddle.

"Are you…" Carred started as it dawned on her. "Are you from Naphor?"

The man's lips moved, but he seemed too angry, too bitter to answer. The glittery hardness in his eyes put Carred on her guard.

"Corporal Starn is a survivor from Naphor," Bennetavian confirmed. "Scarce a dozen reached Quolith. Only Starn is able to speak about what happened. The others managed to ride out of danger, but since their arrival, they just lie there in their beds, not talking, not eating or drinking, barely even breathing."

"Because they were unprepared," Starn said, eyes locked to Carred's, as if his every word were a curse on her—on every last living Niyandrian. "I seen horror afore, growing up like I did in Nagorn City. But the others who survived, they were too well brought up, too privileged, too bloody weak. I tell you, Seneschal," he told Bennetavian, "your knights better harden up, and harden up fast, because the same thing's coming to Quolith—to all this gods-forsaken isle. If it was up to me, we'd set sail for the mainland this very day."

"If we could find a ship," Bennetavian said. "General Selenas here now controls the port of Dorinah."

Carred was barely listening, still trying to piece things together.

"And the rest of the Naphor garrison?" she asked.

"Dead," the blood-drenched knight said. "Or worse."

A familiar feeling crawled over her flesh—and it wasn't nostalgia. She knew what Talia was capable of. During the early days of the war with the mainland, she had seen the dead walk and the living decompose before her very eyes. So much horror she had seen without *seeing*, believing it was all for the greater good of Niyas, that it was in defense of the Niyandrian way of life against mainland oppression. And maybe it had been, but now she wasn't quite so sure.

Shame washed over her, and she had to look away from the survivor's eyes, back to the spattered ruin of his cloak.

"You might at least have patched him up, helped him wash, change his clothes," she said to Bennetavian. She knew it was an unjust accusation, a deflection from the way Starn seemed to blame her.

"I refused their help!" Starn said. "I'll not change my cloak till my colleagues are recovered, and if they don't recover, I'll keep wearing it till every last one of them Niyandrian bastards lies choking on their own blood."

Angry murmurs sounded from behind Carred, where Vilintia stood with an ever-growing group of Niyandrians.

Bennetavian frowned as he noticed the gathering threat. He waved Starn to silence. "Please, General, forgive Corporal Starn's tone. He is still suffering from shock."

"I can understand that," Carred said.

Bennetavian met her eyes. She found him hard to read: calculating, yes, but of ill-intent? She didn't think so.

"You are not unfamiliar with horror and loss, I think, General," he said. "I will pray for you."

"You pray to Theltek?"

His eyes widened, and he spluttered, "No!"

"Then thanks," Carred said, "but no thanks."

Vilintia was a bristling presence at Carred's shoulder. As if she were the mouthpiece of all the other Niyandrians presents, she asked, "Why did you come here with such a large force? Were you thinking you could take back the Burg?"

"Oh hush," Carred snapped. "If you think two hundred riders is a large force…"

"Two-hundred knights of the Order of Eternal Vigilance," Vilintia said. "Or have you forgotten how well we fared last time, when you tried to take back Naphor?"

"Point taken. Seneschal?" Carred asked with a raised eyebrow.

"I will admit," Bennetavian said, "that we are ready for war against you, should it prove unavoidable, but that is not our wish."

"One of them, are you?" Carred said.

"I beg your pardon?"

"Plan for the worst, hope for the best."

"Oh, I see. Yes, that is about… What is the Niyandrian idiom? The long and the short of it?"

Carred turned to face Vilintia and the other Niyandrians. "So, as I suspected, Queen Talia has taken back Naphor. Does anyone here think that's a good thing?"

"Well…yes…" a woman said uncertainly.

"You would have thought so yourself not that long ago," Sergeant Ap'Lian said. She hadn't seen him arrive, nor the three dozen spear fighters he stood at the head of.

Carred's eyes flicked to Vilintia. Was this a challenge to her authority?

Sef Ap'Lian grinned, his chipped yellow teeth somehow homey and reassuring. "But then you woke up to reality," he said, "and the rest of us woke up soon after. Well, most of us did," he said to the dissenting woman, and she shot him a withering glare.

"What do you want to do?" Vilintia asked.

"That all depends," Carred said, "on Seneschal Bennetavian here."

Bennetavian glanced behind at his mounted force, as if he too needed reassurance they were still under his command. "There is an old saying in the Pristart Combine, where I grew up: The enemy of my enemy is—"

"A useful idiot," Carred interrupted. "Yes, we have the same saying in Niyas."

"I was going to say 'my friend,'" Bennetavian said.

"But that's so seldom true," Vilintia said.

"Even so," Carred said, "am I to understand you are proposing an alliance with us mere savages?"

"Savages?" Bennetavian said. "I never… never… How can you think such a thing? I have spent half my life studying Niyandrian culture, learning your language. I… I…"

"It's all right, Seneschal," Carred said. "I was joking. I know what kind of man you are."

"You do?"

"Which is why I would like to invite you into Branil's Burg. We're still in a state of disarray, but there are food stores and half-decent livestock. If you're not in a particular hurry, I think we could rustle up a meal in the knights' refectory."

"For all of us?" Bennetavian said incredulously.

"Unless you think I'm being imprudent."

"What about their weapons?" Vilintia asked.

"What about them? Trust has to start somewhere. Might as well be with us. Sergeant Ap'Lian and his warriors will show you to the stable yard, Seneschal, where you can rest and feed your horses. After that," she told Sef, "bring them to the refectory. Vilintia…"

"Food? I'll handle it. Before you arrived, I employed a bunch of locals to slaughter livestock and to cook for us. I'm sure they won't mind a bit of extra work for a bonus."

"Excellent," Carred said, then sought out the dissenting woman with her eyes. "You, locate the wine cellar. We can all get acquainted over a glass or two while we wait for dinner."

The knights' refectory was truly a vast hall, and as she grew numb on wine, Carred found herself dropping out of the conversation at her table and staring about at the Niyandrian stonework, as if it were a portal onto the past.

Theltek alone knew what the refectory's original function had been, back in the days when Branil's Burg had been a Niyandrian stronghold. In Carred's imagination, the hall could once have been a gymnasium or an indoor training ground for warriors. Equally, it could have been a shrine devoted to any one of Niyas's ancient gods. She wondered what those gods would think now, about the rows upon rows of trestle tables that filled the floor space, making it seem like some barbarian jarl's feasting hall.

And the smells—spiced meats, grease and fat, the bitter aroma of the hop beer brewed and cellared by the Order's priests of the Elder, the sweet scent of the strawberry wine, and the more robust reds that had been disinterred from their dust-covered racks in the bowels of the Burg: how would the gods react to such smells? Did they prefer them to incense and the coppery smell of freshly spilled blood?

In place of the sonorous chanting Carred imagined, and the screams of sacrificial victims—all too commonplace in the times of the Ickthal Dynasty who had ruled before Queen Talia—the refectory was filled with the clink and clatter of armor, the clash of scabbarded swords against chairs, the scuff of the servers' feet as they brought plates of steaming meat and vegetables to the tables, and the hubbub of voices, half the room speaking Nan-Rhouric, the other half Niyandrian.

Carred hadn't thought to arrange the seating, and so the visitors from Quolith had all clumped together, two hundred enemy knights and the handful of priests they had brought with them on one side of the refectory, and an equal number of Niyandrians the other. And neither side seemed to want to communicate. Save for the leaders; they had no choice.

Carred found herself seated beside Vilintia along one side of a trestle table, with Seneschal Bennetavian and his senior officers on the other. A wizened priest of the Elder stood leaning on his staff behind Bennetavian's chair, a surly looking priest of the Warrior looking on from where he perched atop a stool in the corner. The rest of the priests were healers, who insinuated themselves among the white-cloaked knights as if to ensure no one got out of hand.

She could infer from the way several of the Order knights gazed around and gesticulated at the refectory's grand features—the ornamental corbels, the beams of the vaulted ceiling that resembled the underside of a ribcage, the elaborate double doors carved with death's heads and demons—that they were familiar with the place. Presumably they had trained at Branil's Burg and had eaten in the hall many times over the years.

While everyone around her tucked into the surprisingly lavish feast with gusto, Carred touched nothing but the mistberry wine she'd brought from her chamber. She wasn't in the least bit hungry, though she knew she should have been famished. Her anger might have cooled from a violent boil to a simmer, but it filled her to the brim, leaving no room for food.

"General…"

Bennetavian pulled Carred back into the conversation and out of her head. His confreres—all but the priest of the Elder—exchanged annoyed looks because he had again spoken in Niyandrian.

"General, I would like to share some intelligence with you: disturbing reports from our scouts returning from Naphor."

As the Seneschal spoke, the others clearly had no idea what he was saying, and they looked decidedly uncomfortable. Not the priest of the Elder, though, whose keen eyes flitted from Bennetavian to Carred as he monitored every word. If Carred didn't know better, she would have thought the old man had some sorcerous means of burning every last word into his memory so that it could be retrieved at a later date as circumstances demanded.

Bennetavian paused in his speech momentarily as he saw Carred observing the priest of the Elder, then smiled at the old man. It occurred to Carred that the priest might once have been the Seneschal's tutor.

Vilintia looked as though she were about to grab Carred's arm but then thought better of it.

"Let me guess," Carred said. "An armed group of Niyandrians who had been hiding in Rynmuntithe Forest made a surprise attack on the citadel?"

Bennetavian grimaced. "Naphor was still under construction, its garrison insufficient."

"I know," Carred said. "Yet I still failed to take back the capital when I tried."

"Eldrid DeVantte is a remarkable knight," Bennetavian said. "Always one step ahead of the enemy. But alas, Eldrid was not at Naphor this time."

"Oh?" Carred said.

"Overseas. Order business from on high."

"Even so," Carred said, "I refuse to believe the citadel fell to a ragtag bunch of deserters. I would have thought twice about going up against Naphor even with the force we have here. Order knights are no pushovers, not the way they coordinate their ward spheres, and don't get me started on the superior weapons and armor." She realized then she was tapping the pommel of the star metal sword at her hip, to reassure herself it was still there.

"The Niyandrians had help," Bennetavian said, and now there was silence as everyone waited for him to explain what help. Judging by the sober looks on the faces of the knights on Bennetavian's side of the table, they didn't need to understand Niyandrian to know what he was talking about. "Dead-eyes," the Seneschal said. "An entire tribe of them that came down from Hallow Hill."

"I saw…" Carred started, but Bennetavian hadn't finished.

"And the dead walking. Risen corpses. By all accounts, thousands of them. I have since received reports of the earth rupturing for miles around Naphor, the mass graves from ancient battles spilling forth their dead—skeletons whose ligaments had long since rotted, somehow held together, somehow able to walk, to fight, to kill. And fresher corpses, too: the recently buried. Even knights of the Order who had been buried on consecrated ground."

"Talia," Carred whispered. The Necromancer Queen had done such things before, but dead-eyes… This was something new. The creatures had been more or less docile when she and Anskar had gone to Hallow Hill. She'd had the sense they were under the control of the three necromancers Anskar had seen within the old tomb. Had Talia formed an alliance with those throwbacks to the time of Kaythe Nurglich? It didn't seem likely. The Talia Carred knew had despised that vile god and all his servants. Though not at first. Talia had revealed making a pact with the Corpse Maker, something she had ever since regretted and rebelled against. So, what, then? Had Talia wrested control of the dead-eyes from the necromancers?

"These Niyandrians who had encamped outside Naphor," the priest of the Elder said. He looked in Carred's direction, but she had the impression he couldn't see her; that he was blind. "Our scouts reported that they were rabid, men possessed, berserk. I have… consulted. They are under a glamor, one deeper than the norm. An application of the earth-tide that has… reshaped their brains. Myths of ancient Niyas— all that my brethren have been able to find out about the prehistory of the isle—allude to something similar: the creation of what the legends refer to as 'ragers,' more beast than man, savage killers with unbridled aggression. Very difficult to stop."

Bennetavian sighed and pinched the bridge of his nose. "Whatever was done to them," he explained, "is apparently contagious."

"We don't know that for sure," the old man said, "but if the myths are anything to go by, we must assume the worst."

"How does it spread?" Vilintia asked. She seemed to be taking it all rather well, and Carred nodded her approval. Perhaps being in charge had been Vilintia's problem, and now she was doing what she did best: being a soldier. Being the strong right hand Carred needed.

"Bite, according to the legends," the priest of the Elder said.

"Then we knock their teeth out," Vilintia snarled. "Cut off their heads."

"Or we stay out of range," Carred said. "Fight them with arrows and sorcery."

"Our ward spheres…" Bennetavian said.

"Yes," Carred said. "If we work together, strategize together."

"I was hoping you would say that," Bennetavian said. "As I am also hoping you will agree with my next suggestion."

"And that is?" Carred asked.

"That we send word to the mainland, and ask for help."

Vilintia turned a glare on Carred.

"I assumed you would have already done that," Carred said.

"Oh, we did, after news reached Quolith about your attack on Dorinah. But we have yet to receive a reply. And, as you can appreciate, matters have gotten decidedly worse."

"So, you want to wait for a mainland fleet to arrive before you attack Naphor? How will that work out for us?" Vilintia asked. "You think the mainland rulers will just want to shake hands and forget about Branil's Burg?"

"That I cannot say," Bennetavian said. "All I can do is give you my word that I will speak on your behalf. And surely you must realize, a mainland force is coming, sooner or later. There were survivors from your attack, weren't there? Refugees?"

"Unfortunately," Vilintia said.

"I knew I was going to regret letting them go," Carred said. "Actually, that was Anskar's decision."

"And where is Anskar DeVantte?" Bennetavian said.

"Theltek knows!" Carred said. "But last I saw, he was in no position to help us. What concerns me is how much larger Talia's army will grow if we sit on our asses and do nothing. Ordinarily, I'd be all in favor of a defensive war behind the walls of Branil's Burg, but what about the people of the isle—the villagers, the farmers, even the other Order strongholds? The longer we do nothing, the more dead Talia can raise."

"Don't forget the dead-eyes," Vilintia said. "An entire tribe! And what if she summons more?"

"To my mind," Carred said—and already she was starting to mistrust herself; her judgment hadn't exactly been sound in the past when it came to military matters—"we need to go on the offensive, before Talia gets too strong."

But what if she were already too strong? And the Queen's sorcery… Even Anskar hadn't prevailed before.

"I fear Quolith may be next," Bennetavian said. "And then, if it were me, Dorinah."

"You want us to reinforce your stronghold?" Vilintia said, and there were angry murmurs from the Niyandrian commanders.

"On the contrary," Bennetavian said. "I plan to leave Quolith virtually defenseless, with a minimal garrison who have been instructed to use… chicanery to make their numbers look greater than they actually are."

"Chicanery?" Vilintia said.

"Spears lined up along the battlements, helms on poles, mannequins stuffed with straw, the local farmers and market gardeners dressed in white cloaks."

"You want Talia to take Quolith?" Carred said.

"I want her to take the bait."

As the Seneschal unfolded his plans, beer and wine flowed, Dorinah locals waiting on the Order knights and Niyandrian warriors with great attentiveness. It made Carred wonder how much Vilintia was paying them, and from what funds. Her own mistberry wine didn't last too long, but somehow, rather than making her drunk, it helped her to focus on the deliberations for war.

The priest of the Elder joined them at table, translating key points for Bennetavian's commanding officers and then translating their responses. Once the chief details were settled, the commanders grew deeper in their cups. Niyandrians began to try out their scant Nan-Rhouric, a gesture that was much appreciated, and the knights showed a willingness to learn the odd word of Niyandrian. Mispronounced words were a cause for laughter on both sides, and soon enough, no one was speaking clearly even in their own language. Beer mugs were clashed, wine glasses clinked together, and the bonhomie spread out from the commanders' table to the rest of the refectory.

The evening culminated in good-natured wrestling bouts, in which the Niyandrians got to show off their traditional unarmed combat skills—isolating an opponent's limbs and locking the joints till they elicited a tap of submission. Carred declined to join in. She'd finished the mistberry wine and started on a bottle of Kailean red that had been brought up from the cellars. Now that the serious business of war planning was over, her head began to throb, and she grew woozy.

Bennetavian rose and proposed a toast, speaking each line first in Niyandrian and then in Nan-Rhouric. A hush descended over the hall as he spoke of this new alliance, of the challenges they all faced, the evils, and of his assurances that he would do all he could to ensure that this peaceful coexistence between the knights of Quolith and Carred's rebels would extend to the mainland armies when they arrived—not if.

Everyone knew it was only a matter of time.

Then, to Carred's amusement, which quickly turned to surprise and then admiration, Bennetavian started to sing in a perfectly tuneful yet rasping voice that somehow managed to project around the refectory. The Seneschal's men and women watched with evident pride as Bennetavian sang frivolous lyrics about love and romance, about birds and flowers and butterflies. It was hardly the usual sort of pre-war ballad, wherein bards would sing of battles past and glory yet to come. Yet Carred liked that it wasn't. Bennetavian's song felt more wholesome, more real; and to be honest, she was sick to death of the lies propagated by the bards. Bennetavian's was a song for the ordinary people, who could recognize themselves in the things he sang about. The bards sang only for the aggrandizement of the elite, be they lords, kings, queens, or the shady members of some bloody mainland consortium.

After the song, Carred made her excuses. Wine had numbed her capacity for thought or speech, and she just needed to get to bed. Bennetavian stood to bid her good night, and the entire refectory stood with him. Carred did her best to fix her posture, to acknowledge the respect she was being shown in a manner befitting a General, and then she marched from the refectory, only stumbling once, leaving the sounds of raucous laughter and Bennetavian's next bout of singing behind her.

Long shadows flowed across the floors of the corridors as she made her way to her chambers. Moonlight flooded through the clerestory windows, bathing every surface in an otherwordly sheen. By some miracle of Theltek, she found her door without falling and breaking her neck. It was mercifully unlocked—had she left it that way?—and so she pushed her way inside, leaning against the door as she closed it beside her.

A dark figure rose from the couch, and she fumbled for the hilt of her sword.

THIRTY-THREE

THE RED LIGHT OF THE lowering sun glinted from the myriad granules of the crystal plain, surrounding Anskar with a prismatic brilliance. For an instant he was a being of motes and sunlight, a spirit as ethereal as a wraithe. But then the sun dipped behind a cloud and the crystal desert was solid once more, hard and abrasive, scarred by the tracks of the sled that had brought him here from the Ethereal Sorceress's depot.

He glanced at Uraxa of the Agalot, seeking reassurance in her doleful eyes. It would soon be twilight. They were running out of time. Once the sun set, the crystal plain would turn to liquid, Uraxa had told him on his last visit, a sea alive with predators.

Uraxa's russet skin was sheened with sweat. There was a time Anskar would have followed the trail of rivulets glistening on her lean chest, but that time was not now. Now he was consumed with a new passion: to end everything that had been set into motion the day the golden-eyed crow had visited his room at Branil's Burg. Uraxa adjusted one of the black braids of her hair and then held up a finger for silence. Anskar dropped his gaze to the crystal ground, noting the bloodstains where Uraxa had cut her bare feet and not once mentioned it.

The granulated crystal rippled in several places, then started to bounce as tremors ran beneath the surface. Anskar moved his feet to avoid the sifting of the crystals, the little depressions that formed, as if the surface of the desert were being sucked downwards. He stumbled backwards as the ground erupted and millions of crystals blasted into the air, raining down in a glittery shower, sparkling with reflected sunlight. He shielded his eyes with his arm, only removing it once the hail ceased.

Surrounding him, there now stood five shimmering *nietan*, like children formed from crystal, each with a single crystalline horn protruding from its forehead. Two resembled boys, the other three girls.

Anskar glanced at Uraxa, who stood outside the circle of *nietan*. Her eyes were wide with awe as she dropped to one knee and dipped her head.

A chiming, chittering sound came from one of the *nietan*—a girl.

"They know why you have come," Uraxa said, still averting her eyes.

"Will they help me?"

One of the male *nietan* responded with an airy sound, like a flute.

"This one aided you before," Uraxa said. "Now it discerns your purpose is greater, yet tainted with strong passion. It fears for you."

Anskar too feared for himself. He knew he was on the edge, that the slightest teeter could send him plummeting toward disaster. He could feel the brush of the shadows, the insistent pull of dark tendrils. But he could see no other way. Either he was an utter failure, an heir who had missed the point of his creation, his formation since the day he was spawned; or he had a different fate, one his mother could never have guessed at when she had foreseen a use for a child begotten with guile and dark sorcery.

"But will they help me?" Anskar said. "I need what only they can offer. But I need more than I took before."

All five *nietan* began to chime and whistle at the same time, their musical voices blending in shifting harmonies before stabilizing in a single, sustained chord that resonated within Anskar's skull. And now he heard their voices for himself—or rather, the single voice of all five.

"Be faithful. Be prudent in your choices. Do not succumb to temptation."

One of the males reached up with crystalline fingers and snapped the horn from its head. One by one, the others followed suit.

"For the glory of the one who is five," their conjoined voices said in his mind as each in turn lay its horn at Anskar's feet.

Anskar sought out Uraxa's eyes as she stood and leaned on her spear. She looked totally exhausted. "The one who is five?" he said. "Do they mean themselves?"

Uraxa shook her head, one side of her mouth curling in an enigmatic smile.

"Menselas?" Anskar asked.

Light bloomed within the crystalline chests of each *nietan*, an effulgence that hurt Anskar's eyes. He buried his face in his hands. It was like staring into the sun.

When he felt Uraxa's hand on his shoulder, he looked again.

The *nietan* were gone, the crystal sand still settling back into place from where they had presumably sunk back beneath the surface.

"They must have great faith in whatever it is you plan to do," Uraxa said. "I am not sure that I could give so much of myself and remain uncertain of the outcome."

Anskar drew in a deep breath then let it out in a sigh. "Me neither," he said as he stooped to pick up the horns and stow them in the large satchel he had brought for the purpose.

On the sled ride back to the depot, the sun sank toward the horizon and the dusk-tide blew through Anskar, though not violently as previously; it filled him like a breath of cool mountain air, and when it passed, it left him the gift of a fire smoldering in his belly.

The Ethereal Sorceress was waiting inside the entrance hall of the depot when Anskar arrived, the satchel of *nietan* horns slung over his shoulder. She wore her orichalcum mask, the eyes dark and empty. There was a stoop to her shoulders, and she was leaning on a polished staff of ivory or bone. It seemed strange seeing her here like this. In the past, she had always met him in the levels below. Always there had been a masked functionary to greet him at the door.

She acknowledged Anskar with a nod of her masked head and then turned to look over her shoulder as dozens of green-skinned men and women streamed into the hall through roundalls that opened up in the walls. They were naked save for scanty clothes woven from vines and leaves and the tattoos in a darker shade of green that adorned their exposed flesh. One glanced at Anskar, amber eyes glinting, then crossed the checkerboard floor and exited through a portal on the opposite side.

"Ilapa?" Anskar asked.

The Ethereal Sorceress switched her attention back to him. "It is easier to trust one's own people after a betrayal such as I have suffered."

"You are Ilapa?"

"Once, perhaps. The Ilapa are a diminishing part of me."

Anskar tried not to think about what that might mean. What was the point? He would be answered only with riddles, and there were more important things to attend to. But one question still bothered him.

"Why did Blosius betray you? I mean, how? I was under the impression you controlled the minds of your functionaries." If not also their bodies and souls.

"I did for the longest time," the Ethereal Sorceress said, "but I no longer employ such practices. Ren and I spoke on this subject. She believed it immoral, and that it might jeopardize our future business arrangements. In Blosius's case, I did not use it. But as to why Blosius betrayed me: money. It is always about money."

"Archduke Peleus…"

"Is an old associate of Blosius's father."

"Will you replace him?"

"In time, if I can find someone to trust. For now, you will have to do all the work yourself. There will be no further debt incurred. I see you were successful. The *nietan* are a good judge of character. As I used to consider myself, though I no longer enjoy that certainty."

"You no longer trust me?"

"No longer? Anskar, I did not trust you before."

"On account of my demon blood, I suppose."

Sheelahn let out a sigh that was more like a musical chime. "I made an exception in your case. You did not know your heritage at first. But I will reveal this to you: the demons of the abyssal realms were not kind to the Ilapa in the days before the demon wars. They kidnapped my people from their forests and removed them to Shimrax. For what, I cannot say. Perhaps as prey, or fodder for their games? No one ever returned to tell us. Do not look so concerned. The kidnapping ceased."

"What happened?" Anskar asked.

She spread her arms. "I happened."

She brought the tip of her staff to bear on Anskar, glanced at him as if for permission, then touched it to his belly. Instantly she withdrew the staff, as if she had plunged her hand into flames.

"Ren was right. Seldom have I seen such rapid growth. You are at a junction, Anskar DeVantte. Much depends on the next choices you make. *The* choice. Expect danger. Expect threats. Others will not stand idly by and risk you heaping destruction on Wiraya."

"Others? What others?"

"To speak his name would open a connection I do not wish to open. Our actions are monitored, Anskar. Yours far more than mine. Those who watch prefer the shadows; prefer to be left alone. But power such as gestates in your belly cannot go unnoticed, and in some people's minds, unchecked."

"What if I don't want this power?" Anskar asked.

"That is not the choice you face."

"Then what is?"

The Ethereal Sorceress studied him with her empty eyes as she leaned on her staff. "How will you defeat your mother, Anskar? Ask yourself—how? That you must is unquestionable, but the path to victory—should victory even be possible—is of the utmost importance… to some, at least."

"But not to you?"

"Huh," she said, an uncharacteristic glimmer of humor in her mellifluous voice. "Unsavory alliances must sometimes be forged. Pacts made. That is the way of business. Why would it be any different in the affairs of the wider world? Come now, you tarry when haste is of the essence. My Ilapa will bring all the other things you need to Wintotashum."

"Even void-steel?"

"You require void-steel? That was not part of our agreement."

"But you can get me some, yes?"

"No, Anskar, I cannot. Will not. As with the *nietan* horn, you must procure void-steel for yourself. You will have to return to the abyssal realms."

"No," Anskar said. "I don't think I will."

THIRTY-FOUR

WATERY MOONLIGHT BLED THROUGH THE latticed windows of Carred's rooms, rendering the intruder's skin lucent and not quite solid. The rest of him was shrouded in a hooded robe so dark it could have been an extension of the shadows that pooled in the corners. Within the pallid face, pinpricks of black stared at Carred, eyes the same as Anskar's. The man's cheeks were hollow, his lips cyanosed, the exposed teeth yellow and filed to sharp points.

"You," Carred said, suddenly sober as she looked about for the other two necromancers she had seen outside the tomb on Hallow Hill. A shudder ran the length of her spine as she remembered the muffled screams that came from within—a little girl's. Anger that had been quenched by wine and cooled by fatigue returned to the boil.

"I came alone," the man said in a rasping voice. He opened his palms to her. "It was not my intention to startle you."

"With a face like yours," Carred said, "I doubt you can help it."

He didn't laugh; didn't even smile. She had expected neither. She was just buying time till she could figure out the threat he posed and the best way of thwarting it. She started to back away to toward the door, but her legs wouldn't move. They had grown unnaturally cold, frozen in ice.

"I just want to talk."

"Of course you do," Carred said. "An old friend of mine said that the first time we met, and we did everything but."

The necromancer's brow knitted in a frown, and then his eyes grew even darker, as if he were irritated by her flippancy. Good. Let him be.

"Kovin," she muttered as she discreetly tried to draw her sword. Her fingers were numb, as cold as her legs. "My friend's name was Kovin. He's dead now. Perhaps you know him?"

And now he did smile, though it was a cruel smile, all razor-sharp teeth. "Perhaps. Though the name is unfamiliar."

He glanced about the room, as if seeing it for the first time. Carred followed his gaze and lingered on the wine rack she had been slowly emptying.

"You'd better not have broken in to steal my mistberry wine," she said.

"I am very selective about what I drink," the necromancer said. "Not water, never wine. Only life."

"By which you mean blood." All the ancient Niyandrian sagas referred to blood as "the life," presumably because they had been written during the dark times, when the isle was governed—terrorized might have been a better word—by people such as this.

He didn't deny it, but instead continued to appraise the room. "My colleagues and I came here during the war, to these very rooms, when they were occupied by Seneschal Vihtor Ulnar. He declined our offer of an alliance, though we held a foe in common."

"Talia?"

"About whom you know a great deal," the necromancer said. He might even have leered. "I am here to make you that very same offer."

"An alliance with you? I don't think so. I don't slaughter little girls."

"A transfer of life, nothing more, nothing less," the man said with a shrug. "A simple transaction of essence."

"Define it however you wish," Carred said, "but I still say you're a rancid turd clinging to the ass of a maggot-ridden goat." She'd never been good with insults, but she was getting better. Jada would have been proud of her.

Kovin first, and now Jada: two dead lovers to add fuel to the blaze that had started with Marith's death.

"Be careful, General Selenas," the necromancer said. "By insulting me, you also profane the name of the one who sent me."

Carred's heart clenched. When it released, it began a fierce pounding in her chest. "Kay—" she breathed, but the necromancer forbade her with a raised finger.

"Do not utter his name, unless you are willing to serve him."

"The Corpse Maker," she said, trying and failing to hawk up enough phlegm to spit. "He sent you? I'd have thought he would have approached Talia first, being that she's the Necromancer Queen."

"Approach her he did, a very long time ago. Even before she was a queen. She entered into a pact with him, and he gave her the power to achieve her ends. Afterwards, she refused to repay the debt. She reneged upon the agreement."

"So, this is about debt collection? Or should we call it revenge? A subject close to my heart right now. I don't suppose you have any advice?"

"This is about judgment."

"Is it now?" Carred said. "Then why doesn't your all-powerful god exact his judgment? Why does he need my help?"

"No god is all-powerful," the necromancer said. "Save..." He clamped his blue lips shut, as if he had said too much.

"Go on..." Carred prompted.

"Your Queen Talia," he said, "did not pay her debt to my master in life, nor did she pay it in the realm of the dead."

"So now that she's back, you thought you would collect?"

"Her powers have increased," the necromancer said. "Inordinately."

"I noticed." And so had Anskar. It was a miracle he was still alive—if he were still alive, wherever Tarrik and Odopek had taken him.

"The dead-eyes you saw during your visit to Hallow Hill," the necromancer began.

"They were yours? Then you owe me a horse. Three, to be exact."

"The dead-eyes are no longer under our control," the necromancer said. "Like Queen Talia, they have become adulterers to their lord and master."

"Adulterers? Kaythe…" Carred stopped herself as the man appeared right in front of her, so close she could smell the mildew on his robe and the coppery tang of his breath. "The Corpse Maker marries dead-eyes? Each to their own, I suppose."

"The Necromancer Queen drew them away from our influence," the necromancer said. "They are now hers to command."

"And I bet your master just loves that."

"She must not resume control of Niyas," the man said. "You know this, I think."

Carred nodded. "There, at least, we agree. So, what else do you know? I heard she has an army, that she has retaken Naphor."

"Without the dead-eyes, we are blind to the Necromancer Queen's activities. Her wards thwart our attempts at scrying. The master has conveyed to us what he perceives, but even he is locked out by her sorcery."

Had Talia really grown so strong? Powerful enough to challenge Kaythe Nurglich, a god?

"There are ragers with her," the necromancer went on. "Men and women whose minds have been warped by the earth-tide. Ordinarily, these would belong to my master, but Talia has arrogated the power to herself. And for miles around Naphor, the dead rise and march to her side."

"I know all this," Carred said.

"Usually…" the man started.

"You would be able to control the dead, same as you normally control the dead-eyes? You're not making a very strong case for an alliance. What's in it for us?"

"We are not entirely powerless," the necromancer said. "I will let you in on a secret that not many share. There is, among the wealthy and powerful of Wiraya, a network, if you like, a—"

"The Consortium?" Carred said. "I know. I've met some of them. They're nothing but plunderers, ravagers of other people's lands. Sorry, not interested."

"Hear me out," the necromancer said. "You are right, in part. The Consortium is all these things, and more. But just think: we will use them, use the influence our master has over some of its members. With their say-so, a mainland invasion force is already in preparation. It will be a long war and hard, but in the end, we will prevail."

"And the Consortium will just hand over Niyas to the likes of you?" Carred said.

"To you, if you like. We will make persuasive arguments to that effect. The Consortium will require reassurances, a pledge of allegiance, but—"

Carred was shaking her head, and in response, the necromancer grew more urgent.

"They had an accord with the master's servants before…"

"Before Talia usurped the throne from the Ickthals, you mean?" Carred said. "And you would have us go back to that? To be honest, I think I'd prefer Talia. What I would like most of all is Niyas governed by ordinary Niyandrians, not mainland oligarchs or the necromancer slaves of a vile god, and certainly not a queen come back from the dead."

"Listen to reason, General. Await the mainland fleet, which my contacts tell me will be underway within two weeks. You must hole up here at Dorinah while we work to undermine Talia's influence over the dead. The master willing, we will wrest control of one or two cadavers from her. Perhaps when she sleeps… a knife in the dark…"

"Talia won't sleep," Carred said. *Not without me.* "And the Talia I encountered outside Naphor is made from divine alloy. You really think a knife is going to stop her?"

"You will join us!" the necromancer growled, reaching for her throat with pallid fingers. "You will serve the Corpse Maker. As a Niyandrian, it is your duty."

Carred couldn't move. Every muscle was frozen stiff, crystals of ice metastasizing throughout her body and mind. She hurled her anger at the enclosing cold, and her dusk-tide repository responded with fire that melted away the frost within her skull. She managed at last to hawk up her rage and spat it in the necromancer's face.

He didn't so much as react; simply curled bloodless fingers around her throat and started to squeeze. Carred grabbed his wrist, at the same time unleashing the full force of her dusk-tide repository.

The necromancer cried out, releasing her throat and holding his arm up to his face. The white flesh dripped like hot wax, the impressions of her fingers deep within the muscle and sinew, in places exposing the bone. The livid skin on the edges of the burn started to crawl, dark maggots wriggling to the surface and forming bridges with their loathsome bodies, packing the wound then dissolving into it. Within moments, the flesh of the necromancer's wrist was fully restored. A corona of crimson flared around the black sclerae of his eyes. Dark pustules erupted on his fingertips, and still Carred could not move as he guided the diseased flesh toward her face.

In her peripheral vision, Carred saw the shadows behind the

necromancer shiver. At first she thought it was something he was doing, some use of sorcery designed to cow or punish her, but then a figure emerged, details lost in the penumbra.

"Leave her alone," Anskar said. "It is me you want, not her."

The pustules faded from the necromancer's fingertips as he turned away from Carred. Immediately the cold left her, and she ripped her sword from its scabbard. She swung for his back, but the sword bucked in her grip and flew across the room, clanging and clattering as it hit the floor.

The necromancer ignored her and spoke only to Anskar. "You have come to your senses? You will serve?"

"Not you," Anskar said as he emerged from the edge of the shadows. He looked dour, serious, dressed in a black leather shirt and trousers and knee-length boots. The clothes were a bit on the large side, though not unbecoming. A bulging satchel hung at his hip from a strap across his chest. "Heed my advice: Do not approach me ever again. If I have anything to say to Kaythe Nurglich, it will be between me and him. I do not speak with underlings."

"Then you are an insolent—"

Anskar's eyes—balls of obsidian—rolled up into his head and came down golden and excoriating. Light exploded with such force it slammed Carred into the wall, and she slumped to the floor, covering her face with her hands. Heat rushed toward her, then recoiled before it burned her skin.

She peered through the gaps between her fingers, seeing wavering patterns and blurry shapes through a film of red. It felt as though she were on the edge of a furnace, with only the thinnest barrier of cold air between her and a painful death by melting. Then, with a sound like a gusting wind, the red haze withdrew and coalesced around Anskar, a silhouette at its center. With a rush and a snap, the light and the heat were gone, and Carred removed her hands from her face.

She expected to see devastation, smoldering furnishings, piles of ash; but miraculously the room was unscathed. There wasn't even a trace of acrid smoke—in fact no indication that anything had been burned at all.

Save for the charred bones that lay on the carpet. Odd, she thought, as she rose in a daze and reached out to touch them. No plumes of smoke. They were cold to the touch.

She glanced up at Anskar. His eyes were once again black, his face contorted into a look of bemusement or shock. His hands began to tremble. "I didn't mean to… Menselas, what have I done?"

His face grew lambent with gold, and a fiery corona surrounded the dark pits of his eyes. He clamped his jaw shut, shoulders rising towards his ears as he clenched every muscle in his body.

And once more, the light died, and the fire surrounding his eyes went out.

"Pity you didn't do that to Talia," Carred said. When he didn't respond, but just stood there trembling, she said, "Anskar, what just happened?"

"Control…" he uttered. "I lost control."

"Of what?"

"I'm not sure. Something tidal, but as if they were all one. It doesn't make sense."

She extended her hand to him and lightly brushed his face. Cool, just like the necromancer's bones. She let out a sigh of relief.

"I didn't mean to kill him," Anskar said. "Just to warn him."

"Oh, I wouldn't worry," Carred said. "I imagine he was already dead, for the most part. Service to Kaythe Nurglich has a reputation for leeching the life from you."

"I know," Anskar said, his hands going to his black eyes. "The Corpse Maker wants me, Carred."

"But you refused him, yes?"

"I thought I did, but the wraithe—I thought it was a servant of Kaythe Nurglich's, but now I'm not even sure about that—it granted me a taste of the power I could expect from the Corpse Maker. I used it to reinstall Noni's spirit in her body—for Orix."

"And it was a lie," Carred said. "Or, at best, a half-truth."

"It was designed to make me go back for more."

"But you won't, right?" Carred said. When he just stood there, dumb, she led him to the sofa and encouraged him to sit.

"Why are you here?" Carred asked, as she seated herself beside him. "Did you know that necromancer was…?"

"The void-steel you took from Vulthanor," Anskar said. "I need it."

So he hadn't come to save her, then. Not that she needed his help, her returning anger told her. She'd have found a way to kill the bastard herself, given enough time. *Of course you would,* an errant thought told her. *Then how come your sword's lying on the other side of the room? You couldn't even stab him in the back.*

"Oh, fuck off," she said.

Anskar looked up.

"Not you. Me. My sarcastic bloody inner voices. I don't have time for doubts and self-effacement. Someone has to stop your mother. Stop her from taking over Niyas and enslaving us all. Raising the dead."

"All my life, I was told that was what *you* wanted," Anskar said.

"And it was, till whatever glamor Talia had over me snapped and I started thinking for myself."

"You're sure it was a glamor?"

"What else could it have been? Other than a young woman's infatuation with royalty, of being honored to share the queen's bed. Of being played for the idiot she was, and then spending years trying to convince herself she wasn't a complete and utter fool and a failure."

"You want revenge, don't you?" Anskar said.

Carred nodded.

"For Marith," he said. "For the life you've lived."

She swallowed. Tears stung her eyes.

"Give me the void-steel," Anskar said, "and you will have your revenge. It's the missing ingredient from the armor I must make if I'm to face her again."

"Because it nullifies the dark-tide?" Carred said. "That means yours as well as hers."

He shrugged, as if that were of no matter, as if he no longer needed the dark-tide. "I think void-steel has properties other than nullification of the dark-tide."

"Tain thought as much," Carred said. "And your mother apparently agreed, which is why she sent me to Vulthanor in the first place. How much do you need?"

"Maybe half of what you brought back from Vulthanor."

"I'll do you a deal," Carred said. "You can have the void-steel… if you do something for me."

"I don't… I can't…" he said, standing from the couch and backing away from her. "I'm changing, Carred. I'm not like that anymore."

"What?" she said. "Not that, you silly fool." It was at that moment she realized he wasn't the only one to have changed. She had changed too. Since Marith's death, she couldn't imagine lying with another person. While Marith still lived, it had felt all right, sleeping with whomever she chose—though she was starting to suspect Marith hadn't really been all right with that. *And neither was I,* Carred realized. *I just thought…* She had always assumed no one, not even Marith, could possibly want more from her than sex and a drinking partner.

Teetering from her revelation, Carred stood and crossed to her sword. She picked it up and held it up for Anskar to see.

"You want me to take your star metal sword," Anskar said, "to use against my mother?" He shook his head. "I think it will take more than that. She has *Amalantril,* also forged using star metal, but sentient now.

Powerful beyond any sword I've ever heard of."

"You're not getting me at all, are you?" Carred said. "I don't want you to take this blade. Same as I don't want you exacting vengeance for me. You have a rival, Anskar. There are two of us hunting the same prey. What I want is for you to add void-steel to this blade. Do you think you can do that?"

He frowned, thinking. "To work with divine alloy, a far hotter forge than those we have here at the smithing hall would be needed. But void-steel? I have no idea of the temperatures needed for that. You have the void-steel here?"

She nodded.

"Then let's go find out."

Carred followed Anskar to the smithing hall. She could barely find her own rooms in the Burg, but he'd been brought up here. He carried one her chests of void-steel ingots. The other they left in her rooms, for him to take with him when he left.

"I used to spend most of my time here," Anskar said as they entered. A lone Niyandrian guard stood from the bench he had been sitting on and tried to pretend he hadn't been dozing.

"Then it's a wonder you can still hear," Carred said, "what with all that hammering on an anvil."

Anskar shrugged as if it were nothing, then moved over to one of the forges.

The Niyandrian—she thought his name was Malric—looked at her for some indication of what he should do.

"Dismissed," Carred told him. "I'll take over here."

"But…"

"Anyone says anything to you, refer them to me. Now go get some well-earned sleep."

"General," he said, as he gathered his things and left.

As she watched Anskar lay fresh coals and kindle them, a thought occurred to Carred, spawned by the memory of what the necromancer Tain had done with Orix's sword.

"Why don't you just use the earth-tide to meld void-steel to my sword? You could even use it to make the Armor of Divinity. All you would need are the components."

Anskar paused, clutching a hand bellows to his chest. "I considered that, but each time I even think about using the earth-tide now, I see…"

"Kaythe Nurglich?"

Anskar nodded. "I can almost feel him salivating. The earth-tide is his domain. Every use brings me one step closer to his clutches."

"It must have been the same for Tain," Carred said. "And your mother. Then you're better off sticking to the conventional way."

"If there is a conventional way," Anskar said. "I've no experience of working with void-steel."

Carred wandered the smithing hall as Anskar set the forge aglow. While he waited for the coals to heat, he topped up the water in the slack tub with a bucket. He then dug around for a large ceramic crucible and some tongs with which to hold it in place over the coals.

"This will take some time," he told her, "so if you have anything else to do…"

"I'll stay," she said. "I want to see how it's done." The truth of the matter was that she didn't want to let her new sword out of her sight. It was an irrational thought, she knew, but she couldn't quite suppress the suspicion that he might run off with it, a replacement for the sword Queen Talia had taken from him.

"Is that for the void-steel?" she asked, indicating the crucible.

"Menselas alone knows how much heat it will take to melt it," Anskar said. "Might as well get started."

He selected an ingot from the chest and used a second pair of tongs to lower it into the crucible. After that, he disappeared into a storeroom off to one side of the smithing hall. Carred heard him clattering around inside.

She approached the forge, holding her hands out to the heat. Flames still licked over the coals, and it was barely hot enough to roast a sausage. Maybe Anskar was right: maybe she should find something else to do. But then she peered into the crucible and recoiled. The ingot was still solid, but it writhed like a living thing. As she watched, it grew glutinous, malleable, sinking down in the crucible and conforming itself to the shape of the base of the vessel.

"Anskar," she called. No answer, so she called again, louder: "Anskar!"

He reappeared in the doorway to the storeroom, carrying a steel breastplate and an entire arm-segment of armor.

"What is it?"

He wandered over to her, depositing the armor on a workbench. Glancing into the crucible, he frowned. He took up a quartz stirring rod and used it to poke the semi-liquefied void-steel. The magma-like sludge clung to the rod, slurping and sucking, then began to crawl up its length. Anskar withdrew the rod and stepped back. A residue of void-steel still clung to the rod, moving around it as if seeking purchase. He shook it off over the crucible, and it clumped back together with the central mass.

"Metal," Anskar said, snapping his fingers. "Something metal."

"My sword?" Carred asked, drawing it and handing it to him.

This time, Anskar dipped the sword's tip into the crucible. The liquid void-steel sprang at the blade, oozing along its length until the entire surface was coated with a bubbling, blistering layer of dark-gray. Tendrils of void-steel began to climb onto the hilt, and so Anskar set the sword down on the coals and stood back to watch. Carred expected the void-steel to drain away onto the coals, but if anything it clung more stubbornly to the sword, smothering the hilt now, as well as the blade.

"Look," Anskar said, pointing. "The void-steel is melting into the sword. That shouldn't be possible."

Carred couldn't believe it either. As she watched, the thick, gloopy coating began to thin and dissolve—but not into the air. It seemed to drain away into the very metal of the sword itself.

"The forge isn't anywhere near hot enough to melt iron," Anskar said. "It's as though the void-steel were ice or butter."

They waited a few more minutes, until all the void-steel had disappeared, leaving the sword somewhat darker than it had been before, and starting to glow orange from the heat of the forge.

Anskar selected two pairs of sturdy tongs and used them to remove the sword from the heat. "I was planning on finding a mold and melting the blade down, then combining it with the contents of the crucible," he said as he plunged the sword in the slack tub amid the hiss and rush of steam. "But I don't think that's going to be necessary. There's something almost living about the void-steel. I wonder if that's why my vambrace…" He stopped mid-thought and withdrew the sword from the water. Gingerly, he touched the blade with a finger. "It's already cold."

Carred ran a finger along the flat of the blade. Icy.

"Did it work?" she asked. She had started to wonder if the star metal would prove as inimical to void-steel as it was to demons.

Anskar handed her the sword. He uttered a cant, and wings of shadow extended from his back.

"Anskar?" Carred asked, stepping away from him. "What are you—?"

"Touch me with the blade," he said.

Carefully, she extended the blade and touched the flat to his shoulder. Immediately, the shadow wings vanished.

Anskar nodded decisively. "I'd say it worked. Now, if only divine metal would prove as easy to work with."

He returned to the storeroom and came out with more pieces of armor, enough for an entire suit, including a full-faced great helm. "I thought it might come in handy to have a template," he said. He sounded weary, as if the task ahead of him were starting to seem too much.

Anskar went back to the storeroom and brought out two large canvas bags fitted with leather handles and set them on the bench. He collected the chest of void-steel ingots and proceeded to pack the individual ingots into one of the bags. "I'll take these, and you can keep the ones we left in your room."

It seemed a good deal to Carred, and so she simply shrugged.

Once Anskar had packed the ingots, he started to stow pieces of armor in the same bag.

"Promise me you'll have nothing further to do with Kaythe Nurglich," Carred said. "If we are to reclaim Niyas for the people, it must be a different Niyas, a better one."

"I agree," Anskar said, buckling shut the first bag then starting to fill the second with the remaining pieces of armor, the chest plate, and the helm.

"But?"

"One thing I have started to learn: in this world, compromises sometimes have to be made. Even the Order…"

"Promise me!" Carred insisted. "The last thing Niyas needs is the rule of any more necromancers. Theltek, I'd sooner be oppressed by the mainlanders."

"Just trust me," Anskar said. "I know what I'm doing."

He held her gaze with his black eyes. The tiniest corona of gold that surrounded the void-stuff of the sclerae hinted that all was not lost.

"I'll do what I can," Carred said. "But trust? I've been played for so long. Duped. Used."

Anskar closed up the second bag and then lifted the two of them off the bench. "Just worry about the tasks before you, not the bigger picture."

"Your mother's the task before me, Anskar. I'd say she's a pretty big picture."

"Leave her to me."

"I did last time, and look what happened."

"Do all you can to impede her progress," Anskar said. "Stop her cementing her position on Niyas. Do not let Dorinah fall."

"We already have plans," she said. "And an alliance with Quolith."

"Quolith? With the Order? But that's…"

"I thought you'd be pleased."

His face became a battlefield of emotions. Finally, he said, "I am. I think. Good. All the help we can get. I'll be as quick as I can. There are things I need to prepare. And there's someone I need to see before I leave Dorinah."

Carred glanced at the sword in her hand, and imagined plunging it into Talia's throat and watching the queen bleed out before her. With a shudder, she rammed the blade back in its scabbard. "Who do you need to see?"

"Someone who can tell me exactly what my mother's up to. I need to stay one step ahead of her, Carred, if I am to have any chance at all."

"Well, you sound confident."

He stood before her, a laden bag in either hand, and stared into her eyes. "Realistic is what I am. But if it's down to effort on my part, we will succeed, mark my words. I'll not fail again. And," he said, as he turned to leave, "neither will you."

"*Melesh-Eloni,*" she muttered. It sounded hollow coming from her lips. A bad joke. She hadn't intended him to hear, but he did.

"Guardian," he replied, as he headed out of the smithing hall. "Not of me: of all Niyas."

Carred closed her eyes and pinched the bridge of her nose against the pounding in her head. He just had to go and say that, didn't he?

Guardian of all Niyas!

THIRTY-FIVE

THE STENCH WAS OVERPOWERING AS Anskar stood in the doorway of the room Orix shared with Noni. Rot and decay. Putrefaction. The stink of bodily waste. He turned his head aside to snatch a last gasp of air from the corridor outside then stepped across the threshold. Flies buzzed all around him as he dumped his twin bags of armor and ingots on the floor.

Noni had the bed all to herself. Not that she needed a bed. She lay there, blue and rigid, more of a waxwork effigy than a woman. Nothing about her indicated life: no rise and fall of her chest, no movement of her eyes, empty and white. Nothing but her mouth, agape in a perpetual scream, her tongue thrashing, her lips curling in torment. No sound came out. Her larynx was beyond making noise. She had screamed herself hoarse, and then she had screamed herself silent. She was as mute as she was dead, and yet she still went on howling against her condition. And he had done this to her.

Orix sat in a corner, slouched on the floor. His face might have resumed its original form, but it was etched with worry lines, and dark circles surrounded his eyes. He was gaunt, his cheeks pinched and thin. It looked as though he hadn't eaten in weeks. Probably he hadn't been able to eat much when his mouth had been on his forehead, and it didn't look as though he gave food much thought right now. He was too bleak, too full of despair.

"She never stops," Orix said, barely glancing at Anskar. "All she does is scream, though thank Menselas her throat's given out at last. The noise was…" He grimaced, and his hands covered his ears as he remembered.

"What do you want me to do?" Anskar asked.

"Heal her. Bring her back fully."

"I tried, Orix. I can't." With the aid of Kaythe Nurglich, maybe he could, but at what cost? Not just to himself, but to Noni. That monster had caused this. He'd used the wraithe to entice Anskar with the merest taste of necromantic power, knowing all along that Anskar would have to return for more—if not by choice, but because Orix, or Noni, would compel him. He knew that now. But he couldn't do it. If he ever returned to Kaythe Nurglich for help, it would be for a far bigger cause, and even then, he hoped it never came to that. Noni was already dead—something she'd brought upon herself.

"Surely you can stop this," Orix said. He lifted his head to display the redness of his eyes, the tracks of tears that cut through the dirt on his cheeks.

Anskar nodded grimly. The best he could do for Noni was release her from her suffering. He felt certain he had enough ability with the earth-tide to do that. But before he could do that, there was the matter of the real reason he had come here.

"Noni," he said, kneeling beside the bed.

Her mouth remained agape, lips and tongue moving, but nothing coming out, not even drool.

"She can't hear you," Orix said. "Or if she can, she can't show it. She can't answer."

"Noni!" Anskar snapped. Same result. He touched her shoulder, meaning to shake her, but it was like touching bad meat. Her skin had lost integrity, and he feared it sloughing away if he pressed too hard.

"It's no good, I tell you," Orix said. "She heard me at first, but it's like she screamed herself deaf. She might as well be dead and fully gone. This is worse than death."

"I'm sorry," Anskar said. "This is my fault."

"Not yours," Orix said. "Mine. I pressured you into doing it."

"And I should have been stronger, had more knowledge, had more power."

Orix pushed himself to his feet. He moved like an old man, he was so exhausted and weak.

"When did you last eat?" Anskar asked.

"Don't worry about me, worry about her." Orix placed a hand on Anskar's shoulder. "Just help her."

"I will, but first let me try something."

Anskar had been able to hear the dead speak since his catalyst had awakened latencies within him. Perhaps if he concentrated, he could speak to Noni—not with his lips, but to whatever lingered of her spirit.

He closed his eyes, then steeled himself to rest his hand on her forehead. He didn't know whether he needed physical contact to make the connection, but it felt the right thing to do. All he could feel, other than her coldness, were little tremors, slight vibrations from where her lips still moved in an eternal wail.

Noni, he spoke with his mind. At first there was nothing, but then he heard the distant howl of wind, so muffled, so muted, it seemed to come from a cavern deep in the bowels of Wiraya. Or a grave.

He tried again: *Noni.* This time, the howling wind seemed to veer towards him, as if he had attracted its attention. And he knew then:

this was no unearthly gale, it was what Noni heard within her head—the sound of her own screaming.

Encouraged, Anskar redoubled his efforts. It was a matter of focus, of reattuning his senses. Noni had died, but she wasn't quite dead. She occupied some liminal space between Wiraya and the realm of the dead. All he had to do was find her, even if it meant following the sound of her screaming all the way to its source.

He plunged his senses deep within her skull, and immediately a violent gust slammed into him, like the full force of the dawn and the dusk combined. Noni's screaming took on the cadence of thunder that pounded Anskar's senses and threatened to blast him into a million fragments. He opened himself to the tortured wind, allowing it to buffet his spirit, to sling him this way and that, to catch him in its current and drag him into the vortex raging at the core of Noni's being.

And there he found her, a wavering gray flame, guttering yet bound to life by the dark motes that swarmed around her like flies—the sorcery he had used to pull her back from the realm of the dead.

Noni, he said again, only then realizing that he too was screaming.

The gray flame flickered then expanded in his *vision*, and the wall of noise that had threatened to blow him apart ceased.

"I want to go back," Noni said, her voice the same as it had been in life. "You lack the power to restore me to Orix." There was a hint of spite in her voice, as if she had somehow bested him. But then her tone changed, and she sounded conciliatory. "You did fix Orix's face. I tried, but it was beyond me."

"As it's beyond me to help you, Noni. If I can, I'll dispel the sorcery that keeps you bound to your body. Perhaps then you will find peace."

"In the realm of the dead? The brief time I was there, it did not seem a peaceful place."

"Perhaps, given time…"

"Maybe. Time is something I will possess in abundance in death. I imagine the realm of the dead will be a relief after what you have done to me. I know this is what Orix wanted you to do, but Orix is a child in his desires. A lovable child, but a child all the same."

"Believe me," Anskar said, "I know. Before I release you, Noni, there's something I would like you to do for me—for us. For the sake of Niyas."

"You want me to commune with your mother one last time?"

"I thought you might still have a connection with her. I need to know what she is up to, what she has in mind. Carred and I went up against her. We—I—lost. She was more powerful than I could have believed. And Carred now realizes she was wrong to serve my mother."

"Carred was infatuated at first, then the victim of her own desire to be wanted," Noni said. "A desire that was stronger than any sorcerous glamor. This I know from my possession by Queen Talia. Your mother, Anskar, is callous. She used Carred for warmth, and then as a diversion while her true plan came to fruition. You. But you did not turn out as she expected. She had not figured in the external factors—the people who raised you, the effects of your training, your devotion to Menselas. She assumed you would be just like her."

"And so, I disappointed her." Anskar didn't understand why it hurt so much. He barely knew her, and what he did know, he wished he didn't. She was nothing to him. Even Vihtor, while hiding his paternity, had been more of a parent than the Necromancer Queen.

"In her mind," Noni said, "she has already discarded you. If she could go back in time, she would rip you from her womb."

The gray flame that was Noni grew again in size and enveloped Anskar's spirit, seeking to succor him. Suddenly Anskar was aware of his physical body, boiling with emotion—rejection, grief, and spite. The urge to find Talia, to challenge her again and this time send her screaming into oblivion was so strong, it threatened to pull him back into his body. With a desperate reassertion of his will, he clung to the gray flame, but even now he was slipping back.

"Please, Noni, I need to know what she is doing; what she has planned next."

The gray flame shuddered as it released Anskar's spirit and started to diminish. Its wavering became erratic.

"I am…" Noni said. "I am with her."

The flame grew still, then condensed into a ring of dark fire.

"She is at Naphor," Noni whispered, as if she feared being overheard. "There are men and women—Niyandrians. I see Fult Wreave. They are wild, frenzied, like rabid beasts."

"I know all this," Anskar said. "What are her goals? What is her next objective?"

"The dead march, and the dead-eyes follow them," Noni said.

"Already?"

"There are so many, Anskar. The dead of all the ages rise and come to her side. Naphor will soon be a necropolis."

"And those that march?" Anskar asked. "Where are they going?"

Noni's spirit voice seemed to choke. "Quo…" she said. "Quo… Quolith."

That last word ended in a shriek, and then Noni was screaming once more. Ripples passed across Anskar's *sight*. There was a resounding pop, then a slitted eye appeared within the ring of black fire. It stared straight at him.

"Still alive, boy?" Queen Talia said. "Well, I'll just have to change that."

With the concussive force of a punch to the head, Anskar slammed back inside his body. His eyes snapped open as intense pressure constricted his forearm. His vambrace shivered as it tightened, clamping down so hard it cut deep grooves in the surrounding skin. Anskar cried out, his fingers trying to find purchase beneath the metal of the vambrace in a vain attempt to rip it off.

"What is it?" Orix said, crowding Anskar, flapping his hands because he had no idea what to do.

"Get back!"

The vambrace contracted again, and Anskar gasped. Blood seeped from beneath the metal edges. Skin, muscle, sinew squelched. Something burst, and he screamed. He could feel the vambrace grinding against bone, then tightening still more, crushing.

"Tell me what to do!" Orix demanded.

Ignoring him, Anskar plunged his senses through the floor, gagging as the earth-tide's effluence rose in response. Cold sludge sluiced through his guts and entered his veins. He had nothing but instinct to guide him, and the vague recollection of how the tide had reshaped Orix's face. He ground his teeth in an effort to suppress the screaming, focused on the intense pain and the slow fracturing of bone, and harnessed it to his will.

With a defiant roar and an eruption of earth-tide force, he ordered the vambrace to expand. Instantly the pressure was relieved, but that only seemed to intensify the pain as constricted nerves could once more convey their distress. Rank essence flooded his body and swilled through his brain. He doubled over and vomited a steaming, foul-smelling discharge, but even that didn't deter him from his aim.

Another release of earth-tide essence, his will implacable, and the vambrace opened, releasing his forearm. He ripped it away from his skin and threw it down on the floor. Already it was rattling, bouncing, coming back toward him. He retreated a step, then hit it again with the full brunt of the earth-tide he held within him. Divine metal warped, and dark veins of void-steel were now visible, pulsing within—and that must have been what gave the vambrace the semblance of life, its malleability. It must also have been the void-steel's compatibility with her demon blood that gave Talia such control over it, even from such a distance. Thoughts of his mother, what she had tried to do to him, how quickly she had turned on him, how she saw him as nothing but an ill-thought-out plan, kindled his ailing powers. Again he lashed the vambrace with the earth-tide, catching it in midair as it leapt at him. He clenched his fist, and the vambrace hit the floor, dented all around its center. With both hands, he made a twisting motion, and the vambrace contorted. Another twist, and the metal became a mangled mess. He clamped his hands together, compressing the vambrace into a lumpy ball. One last squeeze, and it grew still.

Panting for breath, Anskar stumbled closer, watching for any sign of movement. There! Just a brief twitch, but it was all he needed to know. Reeling on his feet, tired beyond exhaustion, he dredged up more earth-tide through his feet and unleashed it in a long, steady stream, until the vambrace was a bubbling, liquefied mess that slowly dissolved away before his eyes.

"By the Five," Orix whispered.

"The Five had very little to…"

Before he hit the floor, Orix caught him and helped him sit on the edge of the bed, where Noni still lay silently screaming. "The Five…" Anskar started to say again, but he was suddenly falling in the spirit. It felt as though chains were wrapped around the essence that defined him, attached to an anchor that plummeted to the depths. He could see nothing, feel nothing, and through the emptiness and the dark, a voice like the rustle of leaves in the wind said, "Good. Your power is growing. But it is not enough to defeat your mother."

And now his spirit took bodily form, though it was airy and mist-like, the body of a ghost. He was drifting now, not plummeting, always down, down, down. In vain he flapped insubstantial arms, trying to gain height, but still he continued his wafting descent. Beneath him when he looked down, it was not an anchor he saw. It was the wide-open maw of a gigantic wolf, its body covered with scales, thrashing tendrils emerging from the center of its chest.

"Come to me," Kaythe Nurglich growled. "Let us try again. I wish only to talk with you."

"No!" Anskar cried. "Release me! I do not come willingly."

"Anskar, Anskar," the wolf's head said.

He was so close now he could feel the chill of Kaythe Nurglich's breath, see the glistening saliva on his curled black lips.

"At least hear this," the Corpse Maker said. "Your mother once came to me, as all who discover the earth-tide must eventually do. She asked me for the power to mold matter with the earth-tide, and she used this power to embed the sentience of a dead necromancer in the vambrace you have just so masterfully destroyed. The vambrace recognized only her power. If you had done her will and completed the Armor of Divinity, you would have been encased in an armor that was under her sole control. She planned for you to translate to the realm of the dead, where the armor would have absorbed your life force and granted it to her. You were the Necromancer Queen's key, Anskar, the material means of her return."

"Why are you telling me this?" Anskar asked. The news didn't shock him in the slightest. He had started to suspect something similar, and there was nothing he would put past his mother.

"Talia reneged on her agreement with me," Kaythe Nurglich said, and now Anskar's spirit-body stood on the very tips of the Corpse Maker's fangs. "She took the power but refused to serve."

"Then do something about it," Anskar said.

"Oh, I did. From the moment of her refusal, her fortunes changed, as did the fortunes of Niyas. But I am not the only one with influence. Always there is a war of power, Anskar. It has ever been that way."

Anskar started to drift slowly upwards, away from the Kaythe Nurglich's slavering jaws.

"You're letting me go?"

"I am a reasonable god. I merely propose, never coerce. Think about what I have said. You cannot defeat your mother without my help. All I ask in return is your service. You would give your allegiance to Menselas; how is it any different to turn to me? This power that grows inside you, Anskar, should not be the provenance of one god. Power must be evenly distributed in order to maintain balance. You, as a devotee of Menselas, know this. Yet I say Menselas is a god of balance only insofar as it pertains to his own splintered nature. Like all gods, he seeks supremacy. Do not let him become a tyrant. Bring your burgeoning power to me."

Lies, Anskar thought as he felt once more the weight of his body and became aware of Orix lightly slapping him round the face. But was it a lie? Yes, he had a plan, but would his modified Armor of Divinity be enough against his mother? It was a huge gamble, going up against her again. If he lost a second time, he'd not get a third chance.

"I can't," he said. "Everything you are is evil."

"Who told you that?" Kaythe Nurglich said. "Priests of Menselas? Yet I do not sell the people of Niyas into slavery; only Menselas's Order of Eternal Vigilance does that."

"You call for the murder of little girls!" Anskar said.

"Do not be a fool, Anskar. The world is built upon transactions and compromises. The girl's essence was merely shuttled from one form to another."

"What form?" Anskar demanded. "What did those bastards use her for?"

"Do not be naive. She was nothing. You are all nothing. You only exist because we gods will it. And yet you could be something. You could ascend…"

"If I served you?" Anskar said. "Didn't my mother promise the same thing?" Didn't the people of the isle—Ren and the others? Isn't that what the theologians of the Five—the priests of the Elder—said lay in store for the most devoted? Ascension. Even Niklaus du Plessis, consumed with desire for the goddess Sylva Kalisia, was spurred on by the prospect of sharing her godhood. Always it was about ascension.

Why couldn't the gods just leave everybody alone?

He expected Kaythe Nurglich to reply, but instead he felt a sharp slap to the face and opened his eyes to see Orix looming over him, a hand raised to strike again.

"I thought I'd lost you," Orix said, as Anskar pushed himself up on his elbows.

The stench of rot made Anskar gag. He feared he had gone too far, re-immersing himself in the earth-tide for the purpose of speaking with Noni. But then he realized the smell wasn't coming from him, only from Noni. Still she howled in silent torment, the remnants of her soul imprisoned within the tomb of her decomposing corpse.

"Anskar, what is happening?" Orix asked. "Was it your mother?"

"And other things," Anskar said, but he was still looking at Noni, remembering what she had said about the torments of the realm of the dead being better than what he had done to her.

"Did you get through to her?" Orix asked. There was no hope in his voice. He knew what had to happen next.

"I got through. Orix, she can't remain like this. It's cruel to keep her in this condition."

Orix dipped his eyes. "I know." He took hold of Noni's lifeless hand.

"She begged me to release her," Anskar said, and now Orix was nodding as tears tracked down his cheeks.

"Do it."

If I can. Though what would the price be for another use of the earth-tide? It didn't matter, he thought, gritting his teeth. It still had to be done.

Go on, Kaythe Nurglich's voice said in his head. *Consider it a gift. The power the wraithe awakened within you will be sufficient. I will not require payment. Just come to me when you require your full strength. I will be waiting.*

As Anskar once again plunged his senses into the bowels of Wiraya and felt the earth-tide rise within him, he was aware of tendrils not-quite-solid weaving around him, and the icy breath of the Corpse Maker blowing over his skin. He directed the earth's current at the body on the bed and used it to unfasten the chains that locked her soul in place. He felt her sigh as she floated free. And then Noni was gone, nothing but a corpse now, an empty husk.

"Will we…" Orix said as he sniffed back tears. "Will we bury her?"

"Wrap her in the bed linen," Anskar said. "Carry her outside. "

He could feel anticipatory heat growing in his belly, the prompting of his nascent power, enticing him to use it just as Kaythe Nurglich encouraged him to use the earth-tide. Tarrik had spoken of the risks of giving into the power. Odopek had hinted that it might lead to devastation, a new cataclysm if the wielder lost control. But Anskar was no Tarrik, he told himself. He had a lifetime of discipline in the Order, and he had grown swiftly into an accomplished sorcerer. He wouldn't lose control.

While Orix wrapped Noni in a sheet and scooped her into his arms, Anskar collected his bags, the armor and ingots clattering as he followed his friend outside to the bailey. They made their way to the knights' graveyard, flames already encompassing his fists.

Once there, Orix set Noni down on the ground, and Anskar provided everything they needed to send her off.

And he had been right. Ren and the others might have urged caution, but only because they wanted to control his new power. Like everyone else—Vihtor, his mother, even Carred and her cause—they wanted to control him. Well, he was done with being controlled. It had led him nowhere, save disappointment and defeat.

So he did what had to be done, and comforted Orix as smoke plumed into the sky above Branil's Burg.

And the world did not burn.

Only Noni.

THIRTY-SIX

ODDLY, THERE WAS NO SMELL of smoke and burned flesh on Anskar's clothing as he re-entered the Burg. Fire had consumed Noni's remains, but it was no natural fire, and it had burned with abnormal heat.

Orix lagged behind, toting Anskar's two bags—not because he had been asked to but because he didn't seem to know what else to do. He'd said nothing at Noni's pyre, merely stood watching the flames that burned without need for wood or any other fuel. And when it was over, when nothing remained of the woman he loved, not even ash, he had simply muttered, "The flames were pure," before nodding his thanks to Anskar.

Orix was right: the fire had been pure. It had come not so much from his belly, which was where he had previously felt the heat rise, but from his sternum, in the same spot his catalyst had been fitted, and subsequently ripped from him. Since Ren had healed the site, it had become the locus of his new power.

The corridors of the citadel were teeming with Niyandrians as he made his way to Vihtor's old rooms—he still couldn't think of them as Monash's, and even less, Carred's. And yet, of the three, Carred was the one who had lied to him the least, if at all. As he paused outside her door, waiting for Orix to catch up, he felt ashamed at the lust for Carred the Abbess had aroused in him. But when he tried to think of that foul hag and the things she had done to him, his stomach no longer clenched. He saw the situation from outside now, or above, as if it had happened to someone else. Or if it had indeed happened to him, it no longer possessed him, as if the images of that night had been burned away along with Noni's corpse.

"You don't need to carry my bags," he said, as Orix joined him in front of the door.

The Traguh-raj lad's eyes were red-rimmed and vacant, focused on some other place.

Anskar knocked and let himself in, Orix shuffling behind.

To his surprise, Vilintia was seated on the couch, a steaming mug of tea in hand. Her face was impassive, her eyes cold as she acknowledged him.

Carred emerged from the bedroom, toweling her wet hair. She had changed into a white tunic and black trousers—Order issue. Anskar raised an eyebrow.

"I stank," she said, "so I decided to change. Can't say I care much for Monash's taste in clothes, but at least they weren't Vihtor's. So, how did it…?" She hesitated as she saw Orix standing there, still holding Anskar's bags. "Not good, then."

"I had to set Noni free," Anskar said.

"Oh, Orix," Carred said, approaching him and brushing his face with her palm. "I'm so sorry."

Vilintia frowned and drank deeply of her tea.

"What will you do now?" Carred asked, and Orix shrugged, the armor in the bags clattering. "We could use a decent fighter like you."

No response.

"He's coming with me," Anskar said.

That drew a glance form Orix.

"I need your help," Anskar explained.

"Can't you carry your own bags?" Carred said.

"Not with that. Something else. I'll make sure he's all right, trust me."

"I suppose I'll have to." Carred seated herself beside Vilintia on the couch and continued to rub her hair with the towel.

Anskar couldn't help wondering what was going on here and began to feel awkward, the butt of some joke.

"Oh, don't worry, Anskar," Vilintia said with the slightest of sneers, "my presence here is purely professional."

"Military," Carred said. "We have been strategizing in advance of the full war council in the Dodecagon. Have to keep one step ahead of that Bennetavian. He's quite the know-it-all."

"Sounds as though he impresses you," Anskar said.

"Oh, he's not so bad. So, did you achieve what you set out to achieve? Did you learn anything new?"

Anskar nodded, at the same time rubbing his forearm where the vambrace had been. "My mother is raising a massive army of the dead."

"Well, that was predictable," Vilintia said.

Carred shushed her with a hard look. "How many?"

"Noni didn't say. A lot. She has already sent a force against Quolith."

"As Bennetavian's scouts reported," Carred said. "How quickly can the dead march?"

"Assuming it is just the dead," Vilintia said. "There's still the matter of the weasel, remember?"

"Fult Wreave," Carred said. "Did Noni say anything about him?"

"She didn't have the chance to. She was cut off."

Carred nodded as she considered what she was hearing. "Talia. And you still have things to prepare?"

Anskar indicated Orix and the two bags he was holding. "I'm going to need a few days to get ready. I can't risk going up against my mother until I've made some adjustments."

"No," Carred said, standing and meeting his eyes, as if they weren't black and inscrutable. "Well, just don't be too long. Theltek knows how this is going to end. In the meantime, I'll do my part."

"I know you will," Anskar said.

"You'll meet us at Quolith?" Vilintia asked.

"I thought you were staying here at Dorinah," Carred said.

"We both know I'm no commander, and certainly no seneschal," Vilintia said. "I was going to raise it in the war council, but you might as well hear it now. I'm coming with you."

"I take it you have a replacement in mind?"

"Several, actually," Vilintia said. "I thought we might interview them together."

"Did you now?" Carred said. "Another bloody job. See what I have to put up with?" she asked Anskar.

"I don't think there's time for me to join you at Quolith," Anskar said. "I've never made plate armor before, and even with experience, from the little I gathered in the smithing halls when I was a novice, it usually takes weeks, not days. Something tells me Queen Talia herself won't leave Naphor anytime soon. She's up to something. I can feel it."

"So," Vilintia said, "no need to fear her sorcery, is that what you're saying?"

"Not directly, but be careful. I don't know what she's capable of."

"It's almost as though she read Bennetavian's script," Carred said, and now she looked concerned. "He hoped to draw Talia into an attack on Quolith, where we would counter and take her by surprise."

"And it's a good plan," Anskar said, "so long as you remember that Talia is not likely to be there. The important thing is that you don't let her take Quolith and strengthen her position. If Dorinah should fall next…"

"It won't," Carred said.

"Will you be joining us for the war council?" Vilintia asked.

"I can't," Anskar said. "There isn't the time."

"Any suggestions you would like us to make?" Carred asked.

"Just make sure you hold Quolith. Defeat whatever force Talia sends. Make sure Dorinah has enough warriors to defend the walls, in case we missed something. Do the same at Quolith. Then bring everyone you can muster and march on Naphor."

"Attack Talia?" Carred said. "Without you?"

"I'll be there. I promise." *For what it's worth,* an errant thought said. And it was right: he hadn't exactly been a man of his word in the past.

"Good luck, Carred," Orix said, startling everyone.

She stiffened, then seemed to wilt. She leaned in and kissed him on the forehead. "Thank you. I'm going to need it."

Sheelahn was waiting in the open doorway when Anskar arrived at her Dorinah depot. It had stopped raining, but there was a watery quality to the sunlight shafting between the clouds, a wavering, limpid glow that made the Ethereal Sorceress hazy to his sight, a being who did not quite belong in the outside air.

Orix dragged his feet as he came up the steps, lugging Anskar's two bags. When he reached the top and saw the Sorceress, he glanced at Anskar with wide and fearful eyes. Good. Fear was better than grief; a sign that he still had something left to lose. Anskar had grown increasingly concerned about his friend as they passed through the streets in silence on the way here. Orix resembled a dead man walking, and images rose unbidden in Anskar's mind of the lad hanging from a tree or lying in a bathtub filled with pinkish water, blood swilling into it from his lacerated wrists. Orix's seemed an excessive grief to Anskar's way of thinking. Ridiculous, even. He had only known Noni for a short time.

But maybe that wasn't the point. It felt as though some kind of clay cast that had been constricting Anskar's mind and heart had crumbled away, releasing not so much the heat that had burned Noni into oblivion as a warmth of understanding. Compassion, Tion would have called it. Noni hadn't been Orix's only loss. Orix had been friends with Naul, who had been murdered outside his rooms at the Burg. Then Carred had lured him away from the Order that had raised him. It wasn't just the disciplines of knighthood that Orix had been bereft of but the sense of belonging to something bigger than himself, not to mention the colleagues he had left behind. Anskar felt the same. And Orix had been there when Taloc had died. He had suffered horrendous disfigurement from the sorcery of the necromancer Tain, and Noni had been the only one to bring him any degree of comfort. Of course he was devastated by her passing.

And, of course, they had both lost Sareya.

Odd how she, a pureblood Niyandrian, had been faithful to her vows, whereas they had not. He would have followed that particular chain of regrets down into the pit of despair that had always sat at his very core if Sheelahn hadn't slipped back inside the depot. She expected him to follow.

By the Five… Sareya. It caused near-physical pain just thinking about that first time they had made love in the smithing hall, about the countless times after. It hadn't just been lust, he was convinced of that. He had… He shook his head as if he were an idiot. He'd not loved her. Or, even if he had, she hadn't loved him. How could she, when she had come to capture him on behalf of Archduke Peleus? How much money had it taken for her to betray him? And when she had fought against him in the streets of Dorinah, she had done everything in her power to kill him. He'd seen the hatred in her eyes. And the feeling had been mutual. A funny kind of love that was.

"Come on," he muttered to Orix as he stepped through the doorway into the hall with the checkerboard floor.

Orix lingered on the threshold. "Take these," he said, offering Anskar the bags. "I don't belong here." He set the bags down, eyes on the robed and masked figure of the Ethereal Sorceress.

"You do not," Sheelahn said. "Why have you brought him here, Anskar? Merely as your baggage carrier, or is he to be another Blosius?"

"Another Blosius? You can't blame me for that. How was I to know that Blosius was a traitor?"

"I do not blame you. I have, however, grown wary of uninvited guests."

Orix was still staring at the Sorceress, not with fear now, but with something more akin to awe. "Blosius served you?"

"I thought I told you about—" Anskar started, but Orix cut him off.

"How? What did he do here?"

"Orix…" Anskar warned.

The Ethereal Sorceress said nothing; merely studied Orix with her empty eyes.

"Oh, no," Anskar said. "I didn't bring Orix here for you. I need his help."

"You do?" Orix said.

"At Wintotashum. You can help me with the armor."

"Anskar," Orix said, "I'm the most useless smith who ever lived. You know that. I'd not have passed the trials without your help."

"Then I need you to watch my back."

Orix shook his head. "I've seen what you can do. I've felt your power. You need nothing from me. I'm a mouse compared to you, an insect. You are… Hells, Anskar, I don't know what you are. Too powerful for the likes of me. I'm nothing. Worthless."

"Not to me you aren't," Anskar said, his heart pounding as Sheelahn glided across the checkerboard floor to stand right in front of him.

"Your eyes remain black," she said.

"As do yours."

"Empty is not the same thing as black. I—we—had hoped the power growing within you would have purified you by now."

By "we" he had to assume she meant Ren and the others. "Maybe it will, when I'm done with my mother."

"Did you find what you were seeking in Branil's Burg?" Sheelahn asked.

"I have the void-steel, and I brought a suit of plate armor as a template. Did your people procure the rest of the ingredients?"

"They have left them for you in Wintotashum, as our contract stipulated."

Anskar tried not to think about the cost that would incur. If he survived the coming conflict, he'd need a lifetime to repay his debts to Sheelahn.

The Ethereal Sorceress moved gracefully, weightlessly to Orix, appraising him like a piece of merchandise. "I thank you for bringing your friend, Anskar. I accept. Consider your remaining debts to me repaid."

Anskar started to object, but Orix's face was bright with excitement. It was as though a lightning strike had shocked him back to life.

"And I'll get paid?" Orix asked.

"You like money?" Sheelahn put her arm around his shoulder. "Not as much as your predecessor, I hope."

"Orix will never betray you," Anskar said.

"You accept, then?"

It was tempting. All his debts wiped out… But… "Orix is not mine to give," he said. "He's his own person."

"And I choose to do this," Orix said, face radiant with new purpose, new meaning.

"But there must be no curtailment of his freedom," Anskar stipulated. "No blackwood mask, no mind control, and Orix must be allowed to leave whenever he wishes."

"That is unsatisfactory," Sheelahn said.

"I mean it," Anskar said. "You have to learn to trust him as I do. If Orix says he'll work for you, he'll do that to the best of his ability. Try it, Sheelahn: employ him without coercion. I know Orix. You're getting a bargain."

"You trust him, you say?"

Anskar's eyes met Orix's. "With my life."

"Very well," Sheelahn said. "No mask, no coercion, no glamor upon his mind."

"And my debts are still repaid in full?"

"A trial period. If Orix performs his duties with aplomb for the period of one year, then your debts are forgiven."

"Forgiven?" Anskar said. "You make them sound like sin."

She pressed her hands together in an attitude of prayer. Was she mocking him?

"Orix?" Anskar said.

"A year," Orix said. "I can do that. At least this way, I'd feel I'm doing something to help. And these depots, you say, are all over the place? I've always wanted to see the world."

"Then we have an agreement," Anskar said, offering Sheelahn his hand.

She declined to take it. "No need to shake," she said. "My new functionary has borne witness. I wish you luck with all that you must do, Anskar. Be wary of temptation, and nurture the power growing within you. It is not yet stable. Do not use it indiscriminately, because others are watching, measuring the risk you pose to Wiraya."

"I'll be careful," Anskar said. He nodded at Orix. "Take care of him."

"I would not dare do anything less," Sheelahn said, and her voice chimed with what sounded like laughter.

THIRTY-SEVEN

THE NIGHT-BLACKENED STREETS OF WINTOTASHUM were empty, save for the one warrior on patrol Anskar spotted, looking miserable beneath the hood of his sodden fur cloak. Rain pelted down from an unbroken canopy of clouds that smothered the moons and stars. Anskar hurried, keeping to the shelter of buildings whenever he could, his arms aching from carrying the two bags filled with armor and void-steel ingots. The satchel containing the *nietan* horns was slung over his shoulder.

When he reached Hrothyr's forge—technically, King Aelfyr's—he didn't even think about how he was going to break in, he just did it. The sorcery that erupted from his fingertips came as easily as breathing. It sparked, flared, and melted straight through the heavy lock that had been fitted to the door in his absence. He assumed it was the dusk-tide. Even though he could no longer feel individual repositories, there was a flavor to each of the tidal powers. Or at least there had been. He hesitated before opening the door, mind awash with possibilities.

Traditionally, the dusk-tide was associated with destruction, so it made sense that it was the dusk he had just used. And yet…

Heat bloomed in the area of his heart—again, where his catalyst used to be. There was an answering burn in his stomach that radiated down his legs to his toes. He stepped back from the door, stumbling over one of the bags he had left on the ground. As he flung his arms wide for balance, he saw his hands wreathed in golden flame. Heat surged up his spine, and he spun round in panic. Flames burst to life all over him, dancing across his clothes but not consuming, not even sizzling in the rain. He flung himself to the ground, intending to roll, but the fire suddenly died down—no smoke, no char marks, not even any residual heat.

He lay there panting, expecting at any moment to burst into flames and this time to be incinerated. When a minute passed and nothing happened, he rose shakily to his feet and collected his bags.

He turned at the sound of footfalls moving away. No one there, but he was sure he'd been seen. *Too late to worry about that now*, he thought, as he entered the forge and set his bags down on a workbench before returning the door and shutting it. He was about to fuse the lock shut with another burst of sorcery but held back. What if the flames had been a warning last time?

He plunged his senses within and could find no trace of the dawn or the dusk, just an overwhelming sense of fire when he tried to focus on the tides. But the dark was still there, flowing through his veins, and when he directed his senses beneath the ground, the earth-tide began to bubble and stink. But there was a different quality to both, a sense that they were no longer fully themselves, that they had started to dilute.

He considered using the earth-tide to warp the lock, to cause it to expand and jam the door shut, but he rejected the idea. He wasn't ready for Kaythe Nurglich, and use of the earth-tide seemed the surest way of attracting the Corpse Maker's attention.

He looked around the forge for something he could use to barricade the door for now. Beside the original cartload of components Sheelahn had sent to Hrothyr, there was now a second cart, laden with sacks, crates, and barrels. How had her people gotten in? Did they have a key? Probably not. Quickly, he unloaded the contents onto the workbenches and then dragged and pushed the cart into position in front of the doors. It wouldn't stop anyone entering, but it might buy him some time.

His stomach sank at the sight of all the bags, sacks, crates, and urns of components he was going to have to combine to produce divine alloy. Even if he could find the copy of the Necromancer Tain's notes Brother Bonavir had made for Hrothyr, so that he could add the correct ratios, he still needed to make an entire suit of plate armor with the alloy. How did he even start?

"Somewhere," he muttered with grim determination. He had to start somewhere.

First prepare the alloy, then worry about shaping it. But it had to be done, either way. Only a fool would go up against the Necromancer Queen a second time without coming up with some way to nullify her sorcerous advantage. His new ability might still be growing, but Queen Talia had taken decades to perfect her craft, and unless Kaythe Nurglich were lying, she had made sacrifices and entered into pacts. Maybe he should have done the same. Maybe he still could.

Anskar left the components in their various containers and set about firing the main forge. It was hotter than all the other forges throughout Wiraya, so they said, so Hrothyr used to claim. Well, now it was time to test that claim.

First thing he needed was fuel. There were no coals, only a thick layer of ash coating the bed of the forge. He found a pan and a brush and started to clear the ash away, then stopped as he caught sight of something glinting beneath. Carefully now, he brushed more ash aside to reveal coarse granules of some kind of reddish crystal that covered the hardened ceramic base. Quickly, he cleared the rest of the ash and set the brush and pan aside so he could inspect the forge.

It was like no other forge he had seen. The red crystals were arranged in geometric patterns, each no large than the span of his hand: circles, triangles, squares, rectangles. At the center of each shape, some kind of nozzle stuck up from below. He crouched down to peer beneath the forge, where thick brass pipes ran down through the ground, their ends terminating at the nozzles in the forge bed. Toward the underside of the forge, on both sides, there were metal valves painted red. Curious, he gave one a turn, and immediately there came a hiss and the stench of something rotten.

Anskar turned the valve off and stood, pondering. There had been nothing like this at Branil's Burg, and he had noticed nothing unusual when he'd spent time at Hrothyr's forge during his first stay in Wintotashum. But then, why would he have? Hrothyr had been the only one doing any smithing, and the forge bed had been heaped with coals, obscuring the crystals and nozzles beneath.

It made him feel uncomfortable, these innovations to a standard forge. He wasn't keen on using something he didn't understand— although hadn't he done just that with the dark-tide and later the earth? Even so, there was no sense in taking unnecessary risks, and so he wheeled over the large coal scuttle and heaped lump charcoal onto the forge bed. It took forever to find something to get the blaze going, but at last he found a rusty lamp and drained what was left of its oil over the coals. He got the fire started with Hrothyr's tinder box and then located the copy of Tain's notes, stuffed between two metal boxes on a workbench.

He proceeded to unpack the components for divine alloy one at a time. First a consignment of blackwood from the forests of Sevalio beyond the Trackless Ocean. According to Tain's notes, when heated, the wood would produce no smoke and would not reduce to ash, only to an ocher resin that would meld with the metals. Tain had said nothing about the resin's function, only that it was necessary. The next package contained thee Khorun pearls, each the size of his fist. Already he was wondering about the size of the crucible he was going to need, then assumed he would have to measure out ratios of each ingredient and melt them down in small quantities, producing each plate of armor one at a time. Surely there had to be another way, else this could take weeks. If he were to keep his word to Carred, he had mere days.

He felt dumb as the last dregs of confidence ebbed away from him. He'd considered himself a master blacksmith on account of having made a single sword and a coat of chain! If only Sned were still alive, he'd pop back to Branil's Burg for a consultation. Better still, if only Hrothyr hadn't been killed by the vambrace, then hacked to pieces by the priests of the Warrior in some bizarre funerary ritual. Even Braga, Hrothyr's wife… but she'd been scattered to oblivion when a demon had pulled her from Anskar's shadow step.

He pried open the lid of a wooden crate next, shielding his eyes form the glare inside. A single sunstone sat within, the size and shape of an eagle's egg. It appeared formed from golden light, but it was solid when he removed it from the crate.

Next he opened a sack of astrumium—star metal combined with orichalcum, the former some kind of ore contained in rocks that fell from the sky.

The final thing to be unpacked was a small casket that contained ingots of red gold from Ruruc in the Wastes. He arranged all the components on the workbench, studying Tain's notes to see the quantities he would need of each. Sheelahn had been generous. He had more than enough for his purposes.

He took his void-steel ingots from his tote and the *nietan* horns from his satchel. Everything he needed—save for the knowledge of how to assemble a full suit of plate armor, and the skill.

With a sigh, he began to remove the plates of armor he'd brought from Branil's Burg, laying them out on the floor in the form of a man and scanning the forge for the tools he would need to hammer out similar pieces.

He turned at the sound of a rasping chuckle, but there was no one there. The sound had come from within his head. With an effort of will, he shut out the clamor of his doubts and decided to deal with each task as it presented itself, starting with the matter of combining the ingredients into divine alloy.

He selected a good-sized crucible and set it atop the white-hot coals, then with a selection of hammers, tools, and scrapers, chipped and shaved away fragments of each ingredient. The little sunstone he collected was a fine crystalline powder that continued to radiate golden light. He combined the approximate ratios of each in the crucible, save for the void-steel, which he would add last.

The blackwood was the first to change, shriveling, condensing, melting into an amber sludge, within which the other ingredients settled. The red gold turned to liquid next. The astrumium was stubborn, but at length began to turn molten. Not the dust of Khorun pearl, though, nor the shavings of *nietan* horn. They just sat on the surface of the liquid alloy as if the heat didn't affect them. Or as if the forge simply wasn't hot enough.

The valves… He crouched down so that he could reach them, then jumped at a fierce hammering on the doors, banging his head on the underside of the forge. One of the doors started to open inwards, but it stopped when it struck the wagon.

"Open up in there!" a man's gruff voice called. "By order of the King."

Anskar stood, rubbing his head, all manner of lies running through his mind. He rejected them at once. He didn't do that anymore. He considered hiding, or slipping out into the alley that ran alongside the forge—though they probably knew about that and had it covered.

More voices from outside, consulting with the first man. The door that had hit the wagon started to move outwards. They had realized the doors were hinged both ways. *Idiot,* Anskar chastised himself. He should have realized as much.

Figures appeared within the widening gap, half a dozen men rendered bulky by the fur coats they wore against the cold and the rain. Mail glinted with reflected forge light. All carried round wooden shields. Three had swords drawn, two held spears, one a long-hafted axe.

"Stop whatever you're doing," a bearded giant said—the man who had first spoken—"and step away from the forge."

Anskar hesitated a split second. King Aelfyr could be a harsh ruler when it came to transgression of his laws. He had warned Anskar about breaking into the Scriptorium, and given him a second chance. But this—returning to Wintotashum without announcing himself, then breaking into the royal forge… He didn't need to follow that thought any further to know the consequences would be severe.

The six men of the watch entered the forge and made their way around the wagon-barricade. Anskar lashed out instinctively, the dark-tide shifting within his veins as he flung shadows at the watchmen. Three went down; not dead, merely stunned—he had made sure of that. The others backed away outside, muttering and cursing.

"Get out!" Anskar told the three downed men, then advanced, inky tendrils of blackness thrashing about him.

The downed men didn't need telling twice. They stood and scrambled back behind the cover of the doors.

Anskar ignored the rising heat in his chest, the flames of gold that licked across his skin. He focused instead on the dark-tide, willing it to flow, wresting it from the flames burgeoning within him, and forming it into a ward sphere of glistening blackness. He strode to the entrance, unperturbed as an axe crashed against his ward sphere, its head shattering on impact. All six men retreated after that, then turned and ran.

But they would be back, and next time there would be more of them. Likely they would bring the priest of the Warrior who acted as the king's chief councilor of war. Brother Kennaith, he thought the man's name was.

Well, let them come, Anskar thought. But no one was going to stop him from what he had to do.

You should speak with them, a niggling voice said. *Speak with the King. Once he knows why you are here, who you are up against…*

"There isn't time," Anskar muttered to himself. He couldn't just walk into the King's hall and expect to be heard. He would be arrested, and probably thrown in the dungeons for a day or two. There might even be a trial. He couldn't risk it. He'd given his word to Carred.

He found himself considering the sphere of darkness that surrounded him, then recalled what he'd been taught to do with his dawn-tide ward sphere, how he could expand it to encompass others, or refashion it as a weapon.

It was hard to concentrate with the heat rising within him, threatening to explode. Once more, his hands were lambent with gold, and it felt as though his brain were floating in lava. Gritting his teeth, he willed his ward sphere to lose density, till it was light and gaseous. He caused it to expand, out through the walls and the ceiling of the forge, till it encompassed the entire building, and then he willed it to resume its solidity. He discovered that he could keep the barrier in place with a barely expressed intention that required little to no effort. As an afterthought, he directed the dusk-tide's virulence into the barrier, instilling it with lightning—a nasty shock for anyone who came too near.

And again, he wondered at the vagueness of all that had previously distinguished the tides, the ease of blending them together—beyond even the melded repositories Zek had taught him.

He staggered as flames erupted from his skin, sheathing him in a flickering corona. It felt as though forge coals burned in his belly and magma oozed through his veins. He tried calming himself with slow breaths, but it was like using a bellows to put out a blaze.

He looked frantically around the forge, remembering how Tarrik had contained his own power. There, beneath a workbench, was a half-empty crate of bottles. He stumbled to the crate, snatched a bottle, and removed the cork with his teeth. The beer within was warm and had the tang of hops. Hrothyr had never strayed far from alcohol. Anskar downed the entire bottle as quickly as he could, and when it had no effect, he drank another. By the third bottle, the flames receded.

As he lined up the empties on the workbench, he felt a little woozy, and when he turned back to the forge, he stumbled. He almost burst out laughing. Almost gave up on his ridiculous plans and went back to finish off the crate. Menselas, he was drunk; but it had done the trick.

So, what now? he thought as he surveyed the sludge in the crucible. The flecks of *nietan* horn and Khorun pearl still floated on the surface, stubbornly holding onto their solid form.

Emboldened by the drink, Anskar reached beneath the forge and turned a valve. There was a sharp hiss, a rush of air, and a huge explosion of flame. He ducked down as fire surged toward the ceiling. Frantically, he screwed the valve back the other way, and the flames died down.

The shock sobered him in an instant, and he cursed himself for an idiot. It was no good: he didn't know what he was doing, and he didn't have the time to experiment, to find out how to bring the forge to its fullest heat without burning the whole place down.

He stood and moved to the pieces of plate armor he had laid out on the floor. Was there some way he could reuse this suit of armor, some method of adding the ingredients of divine alloy without having to melt them down over hot coals? It would certainly save him time if he didn't have to hammer out new plates or construct molds for the more complicated pieces. He knew he could add the void-steel without any problem, but the other components... Perhaps heat wasn't the only way to reshape them.

He grabbed another beer and sipped on it—not to cool off his inner fire this time, but to grant him courage, the audacity to use power and not think about the cost.

Setting down the bottle, he retrieved a portion of each of the components—more than he had estimated he should need—and set them in amongst the pieces of plate armor on the floor: five entire *nietan* horns, the Khorun pearl, chips of sunstone, staves of blackwood, ingots of red gold, shavings of astrumium. As before, he left out only the void-steel: he would add that last.

Once he was ready, he stood amid the armor and the ingredients and plunged his senses down through the floor.

He expected trouble—a rush of tendrils to impede his spirit-journey to the world's core; the whispered growl of Kaythe Nurglich, goading, cajoling, promising much; the ghost-image of a wolf's head atop a body covered with scales. But there was nothing, not even the sense that his access to the tide had diminished, as had been the case with the dark. If anything, the earth-tide's effluence came too easily, rising up through his feet and flooding his body as if it were as natural to him as blood. It felt like an invitation.

Staving off his mounting concerns, Anskar directed the earth's flow into the assembled ingredients and pieces of armor. He held nothing back. If this was going to work, he needed to do it in one fell swoop, warping, buckling, reducing each component part to a liquid state, mixing them all together, then recombining the new alloy into the form of a suit of armor. It didn't even have to resemble the original suit: anything that covered him head to toe would be fine.

In response, the metal plates rocked on the floor, creating a clattering din. A vambrace twisted, the breastplate contracted then expanded, as if it drew breath. The helm collapsed in on itself. The gauntlets twitched like the hands of a man dying in agony. Some of the ingredients began to alter, too. The blackwood repeatedly liquefied then congealed. The *nietan* horns spun around on the floor then started to corkscrew. The Khorun pearl vibrated so much it began to bounce.

All the while, pressure built behind Anskar's eyes, but there was no gathering heat within his chest and belly this time. Instead, cold rot sluiced through his guts and entered his throat. He dropped to his knees and turned aside to vomit—an unbroken stream of foulness that he thought would never end. And when it did, he lacked the strength even to wipe the filth from his lips.

He dropped to his side and curled up, praying his efforts had achieved… something. But when he brought bleary eyes into focus on the armor and ingredients, nothing had combined. Each piece, each component, lay where he had placed it, back in its original shape, all evidence of earth-tide warping now gone. So much energy expended, and all for nothing.

The voice that had been hiding from him chose that moment to speak within his head. *You over-estimate your powers, Anskar,* Kaythe Nurglich whispered. *You cannot do this alone.*

He didn't want to believe that, but the evidence was against him. Only a few short days ago, he had been a virtual god during the fight in the streets of Dorinah. The rebel army had bent the knee to him in the face of his power. But now… He was a child once more, where sorcery was concerned. Everything had changed since his mother had defeated him. Was it a matter of confidence alone, or had there been other, more tangible changes since his escape to the abyssal realms, since his "healing" on the isle of the avatars?

He clenched his fist as he struggled back to his knees. After few deep breaths, he reached up for a benchtop and climbed to his feet.

Wiping foulness from his mouth with his shirtsleeve, he decided he'd had enough. He needed a change of course.

"I lack sufficient power?" he asked the voice in his head. "Then help me."

Instantly, he found himself deep below ground in a cavern that resembled the inside of a skull. There, on a throne of bones, sat the reptile-wolf-thing that was Kaythe Nurglich, smaller than before, no more than Anskar's height, yet utterly solid even here in the spirit, so dense the god formed the heavy center of the cavern. Anskar felt himself pulled toward the throne, and he fought against the compulsion to drop to his knees. He wasn't ready for that. But a compromise, he could handle.

"You wish to defeat your mother so much?" Kaythe Nurglich asked.

"I do."

The god studied him with feral eyes, stroking his slavering jaws with taloned fingers. As regular as breathing, tendrils of fuligin sprouted from the god's chest, thrashing before retracting within the scaly carapace once more.

"You are but a vessel for the earth-tide, Anskar, a frail and limited one. To do what you desire requires more tidal force than you can weather. You must opt for more orthodox means—a worker of metals with skills and experience in advance of your own."

"A blacksmith?"

"Who knows how to generate sufficient heat to combine the components you have gathered," Kaythe Nurglich said, "and then to mold them into the requisite shape."

"Hrothyr?" Anskar said. "But he died…"

Even as he said it, he knew that meant nothing to a god with power over the dead. Yet… "I was at Hrothyr's funeral. They diced him into pieces."

"Have trust, Anskar," Kaythe Nurglich said, standing from his throne. "Accept my aid. In return, all I ask is your service."

He had no choice, or if he did, he felt no desire for one. His mother was going to pay for the things she had done—to him, to Marith, to Menselas knows how many others—and it didn't matter what he had to sacrifice to make that happen.

Anskar nodded. "Fine. I'm ready."

The eyes of his physical body snapped open upon the forge, and he staggered. It was like waking from a bad dream, yet he still carried the strong resolve of what he had to do.

He stepped over the puddle of black vomit he had left on the floor and strode for the open double doors, passing through the bubble of darkness that encompassed the forge and leaving it intact against intruders.

THIRTY-EIGHT

SAREYA SLEPT ONLY FITFULLY ON the straw bedding. The stench was something she just couldn't get used to. Eldrid had been a prisoner for several weeks, and he'd not once left the cell. It was doubtful, he'd said in his defense, that anyone had scrubbed the place out before he took up residence.

She dreamed of being aboard ship with Monash, of making better decisions this time. But all the while in her dream, she knew what she had done couldn't be undone, that she had sacrificed her dignity as a Niyandrian for preferential treatment from a superior. She knew in her heart Monash was to blame, but still, she could have said no.

She also dreamed of Anskar. Or rather, she had nightmares. He was a horned demon, bigger than Branil's Burg, looming over her with malice and lightning in his eyes. She tried to fight him with sorcery, but he laughed at her attempts, and then he opened his fanged mouth and incinerated her with a blast of abyssal fire.

She awoke screaming.

A hand was on her shoulder, shaking her.

"Time to go," Galban said. He was silhouetted in the gray light coming through the open door.

"Good," Nul said. "I can hardly wait to get out there in all that heat and sand."

"Not you," Galban said. "You two are staying here, till the next caravan leaves."

"Leaves for where?" Eldrid said.

"All these weeks and no response to our legitimate request for a ransom," Galban said with a sad shake of his head. "This Order of Eternal Vigilance does not put much stock on the lives of its people, no?"

"We don't treat with pirates," Eldrid said. "But you already know this: I told you upon my capture, and I am not given to lying."

"No," Galban said. "And I respect you for that. A pity. If I had only listened to you back then, I could have sold you at the salve pits for a goodly sum. But now, wasted away as you are, you would fetch only a pittance."

"Might as well let me go, then," Eldrid said. "And Nul here. I doubt he'd have fetched much even before you beat and starved him."

As Galban stood from his crouch, he pulled Sareya to her feet.

"Sadly, I must decline. A pittance is still money, and money feeds mouths. I have a family, you know—six boys and three girls, with another baby on the way. Every little bit helps."

"Glad to be of service," Nul said. He sounded cheerful, as did Eldrid, but they both looked—and smelled—like death.

Galban dragged Sareya out of the cell. Just before the door closed, she looked back over her shoulder, and Nul winked.

When Galban finished locking the cell, Sareya said, "You should feed them both. That way you'll make more money when they're sold."

Galban inclined his head, as if he were giving her suggestion serious consideration. "They might grow strong again, and attempt to escape.

Eldrid DeVantte was not an easy man to capture, and this other, this Nul: I have heard of his fame. There were three of them, no? Three heroes? I do not, as a rule, like heroes. They tend to cause a good deal of trouble. No, to the slave pits with both of them. It is of no matter that they will not fetch their full worth, not now that I have you to make me rich beyond my wildest dreams."

"Rich how?"

"The Orgol that caught you paid me good money to cross the sea with you, and he promised me much more upon delivery. I'm inclined to believe him, though my crew are not altogether convinced. They think we're being used, that your would-be purchaser will simply kill us when you're within his reach. He has the power, or so they believe. Me, I think it is all superstition."

"Why me?" Sareya asked. "And who is it that wants me?" It made no sense. She'd never before been to the southern lands, and knew of no one who lived there.

"A myth?" Galban said with a shrug. "A demon? A prophet? A god? All I have are instructions on where to take you and what to ask in return."

"And you trust the word of an Orgol?"

"Like I said, he paid well. I trust solid coin."

"Not if you end up dead at the other end, and he gets his money back."

"Do not worry yourself on my account, girl," Galban said. "Risk is our way of life, and we Jargalans are not easy to overcome. You, I think, know this."

"In a fair fight—" Sareya started.

"Goodness gracious, girl, there is nothing fair about fighting. At least, there shouldn't be."

Sareya dragged her blistered, sand-caked feet along the winding road that led into the mountains; not fast enough, apparently, because a Jargalan pirate shoved her in the back. At the center of the marching column, she was flotsam buffeted by the waves. She walked at another's pace, went where they wanted her to go. It had been the same with her novitiate, after the knights had abducted her from home.

Again the warrior behind shoved her in the back, and she pitched to her knees. Rough hands grabbed her under the arms, raised her to her feet, and pushed her on.

Little by little, the bloated, blistering sun listed toward the horizon in thickening bands of red and gold that leached away to a crepuscular gray and then dark. It was a supreme effort, disguising her imbibing of the dusk-tide. It scoured her inside and out, despite no one else—not even the magus, as far as she could tell—aware of the eldritch wind. When it had passed, her dusk-tide repository was filled to the brim, and she was itching to use it. But not now. At some more opportune time.

And still they didn't stop.

The magus cast an orb of fire into the sky, and it kept pace, hovering above the column, engulfing them in the ambit of its light. Sareya kept a close eye on the magus after that, intent on any sign of how he did it. There had been a faint odor of burnt metal, but other than that, nothing she could discern with her senses. Again, she thought, it had to be the conical helm hiding his repositories.

Sareya's walk became more of a shuffle and a drag as her blisters burst and the soles of her feet grew sticky from their seepage. Mile after miserable mile, she grew delirious. She began to look at the warriors differently; no longer oppressors, now they were cattle to be slaughtered with devastating sorcery whenever she chose. She would have to take out the magus first, else he would drain her repositories, as he'd done before. But could she really do it? What if she were too weak from all the walking, the lack of food and water? Perhaps that was why they neglected her welfare.

She ripped her gaze from the man in front of her. The need to lash out with power and hurt someone was too strong. It possessed her, though not with enough to force her to act. If at once she gave in, she'd be dead in an instant, a Jargalan sword in her back. That was her realistic assessment. And she realized then she was in the unrelenting grip of despair.

Her eyes were drawn to the fiery sphere above. In her delirium, she craved it, wanted to feel it embrace her like a loving mother. Not that she could remember what that was like anymore. If only it had been a real fire, one that expanded till it filled the sky and burned her to a cinder.

But it wasn't, and it didn't. The sphere merely winked out.

Sareya turned to see the magus conclude dispelling his light source with a flourish of his hand. One of the rings he wore over his glove sparkled for a second or two. Again, the smell of heated metal.

No more need for the sorcerous sphere, she assumed.

The moons, gibbous and close to full, had come out from behind a veil of clouds.

Did that mean his power was finite, too precious to waste?

The moons' wavering glow turned the paved road they now followed into a silver ribbon that wound its way through a long and winding pass between mountains. Miles they trudged beneath saw-toothed peaks, where shadows untouched by moonlight flowed down the mountainsides, concealing Menselas-knew-what. Animal cries came from ledges high above: cackles and gibbers, hoots and caws. From time to time, stones clattered down, as if something had deliberately dislodged them. Jargalans cast nervous glances into the pressing dark, suddenly human, despite their hidden faces, suddenly vulnerable;

things that bled and breathed.

Progress was faster once the road leveled out, but that only meant more stumbling, more scuffing and scraping for Sareya. She no longer felt the sting of burst blisters; the nerves of her feet were as dead as she was inside.

The column slowed and then came to a halt. Ahead, the moonlight reflecting from the walls of the pass was joined by flickers of orange and gold. A ghostly mist plumed skywards, a veil not to be crossed. Sareya could smell woodsmoke and roasted flesh. On either side, the outlines of spindly tree trunks, stripped of their branches, flanked the road, quivering in the maddening chiaroscuro of silver and shadow.

The magus raised his palm and sent his sphere blazing ahead. As it passed between the trunks, it flared, and a collective gasp went up. The stripped trees had sharpened tips that protruded from the mouths of warped horrors—huge human-like creatures with horned heads, their naked bodies smeared with black blood, at least two dozen that Sareya could see, impaled on spikes.

Warily, conferring in hushed voices, the Jargalans passed between the spikes. Sareya cocked her head to take in the grisly scene, the contorted faces, the buzzard-pecked eyes.

It was a warning, but who was doing the warning? At the head of the column, Galban seemed, if anything, more at ease, exchanging soft-spoken words with the magus. He might even have laughed.

Farther along, the impaled bodies gave way to heaps of rocks and hills of piled sand. Then came single-wheeled barrows packed high with stone slabs, stacks of picks and shovels, barrels of tar. Shapes moved against the dark skirt of the mountains, and there was a musky animal stench. Camels, at least a dozen. Beasts of burden, standing from rest as the column went by.

Last, there were tents, simple canvas structures pegged out beside the road where hardy weeds had cracked the stony ground. Men poked their heads out of the openings, exchanging hushed words. One man emerged onto the road, tucking his shirt into patched trousers. He was clean-shaven like the Jargalan pirates, his scalp a script of tattoos.

"The impaled bodies along the road…" Galban said. "They are sand wights, yes?"

The man stepped into scuffed sandals outside his tent's entrance and laced them up his shins. "It wasn't my idea."

A robed Jargalan in a turban stepped out of the shadows behind the tents. A scimitar hung from his belt. Not quite separated from the dark, more warriors advanced on either side of him—a dozen or so, certainly not upwards of twenty.

"I figured it might deter the sand wights," the armored warrior said. "I know you: the esteemed Galban, procurer of slaves." He dipped his head as if that were a noble profession. "We are indebted to your service, Galban. Your trade is the lifeblood of the desert. I am, humbly, Corporal Vamulgar of the Scorpions."

"This is ill news for our journey," Galban said. "I thought our people rid these coastal regions of sand wights."

Corporal Vamulgar clasped Galban's wrist and gave the most cursory bow. "The great salamanders have started their once-in-a-century swarming in the central desert. A shaman predicted it, but such a thing was hard to believe."

"And the salamanders have driven the sand wights east?" Galban said. "Ah, Providence, why do you defecate in my general direction? It is the curse of the Orgol god, I tell you. They should never have killed him."

The Corporal released Galban's wrist and tucked his thumbs into his belt. "It is an unsavory situation, to be sure. The road repairs still have some way to go. It could be many months before we're done here, but at least the sand wights keep mostly to the mountains."

"Why did I know you were going to say that?" Galban said.

Nervous mutterings passed among the Jargalans waiting in column.

"You need refreshments for your men?" Corporal Vamulgar asked.

"I would not deprive you. We will survive. We are Jargalans, born in fire."

Corporal Vamulgar grinned. "As are we all. Then you will not stay to rest awhile?"

"We will march through the night."

Deeper into the frigid pass they moved, hour by hour, the night's dark made blacker by the shadows that flowed down from the peaks. The Jargalans behind gave up pushing Sareya. She'd become so slow, they took hold of her under the arms and dragged her along. She almost thanked them, she was so numb with exhaustion and frozen to the core.

She started to reassess whether the Jargalans really were mortal. Save for two short breaks to relieve themselves and drink water from canteens, they pressed on through the night. Nothing but the odd mouthful of water for her, though. That told her they weren't just cruel; they knew with great exactitude the bounds of endurance, and wanted to push her to the absolute limits. Would the experience make her more valuable to whomever Galban wanted to sell her to? She didn't see how, unless they not only wanted sorcerers, but also wanted them especially strong and durable. Or maybe delirium was making her over-think things. More likely, Galban was just a bastard. A charming one, and polite, but a bastard all the same.

Imperceptibly, the sky lightened to gray, and a blood mist shrouded the heights. Sareya winced as the dawn-tide scoured her skin and blasted through her, then tried her best not to show it, same as she'd done with the dusk. She wanted to cry out in exultation; wanted to revel in the tidal force flooding her repository.

The grips on her arms grew tighter, till they hurt. Not intentional, she realized. They hadn't realized she had imbibed the tide. The men holding her were gazing up at the heights. In front and behind, the Jargalans began to whisper. Fingers pointed above, where atop a rugged plateau a silhouetted building stood, a crude, blockish fortress with domed towers. She couldn't hear what the Jargalans were saying, but she could feel their growing fear as if it were a solid thing.

The mountaintop fortress was lost from sight as they passed around a bend and entered the winding ascent of a gully with sheer walls on either side, here and there overhung with outcroppings of rock and protruding ledges.

A savage, ululating cry went up, echoing along the gully. Steel glinted in the burgeoning sunlight ahead of the column, and above, the ledges swarmed with fur-clad giants, horns rising from their shaggy heads, axes and spears in hand. Sareya caught glimpses of blue-streaked faces, lips curled back and showing crooked yellow teeth.

The clash of weapons came from up front now. All around Sareya, Jargalans drew cutlasses and knives and raised their wicker shields. The hands gripping her let go. Someone cried out, and heads lifted.

With cries of rage, the horned beasts surged forward and flung themselves from the ledges, arms outstretched, as if they thought they could fly.

"Sand wights!" someone cried above the din.

Hatchets glinted in the reddening dawn light. Scree scrunched underfoot as the Jargalan slavers scrambled to protect themselves.

The skin of Sareya's wrists chafed as she struggled against the manacles that held her hands behind her back. Panicked Jargalans bumped into her as they turned this way and that, trying to defend against an enemy that seemed to be everywhere. Thuds and cries. Sparks flew from the clash of steel.

An explosion shook the mountains, echoing through the pass. Sand wights shot into the sky, trailing plumes of smoke, then slammed into the rock walls. Sareya caught sight of the conical helm of the magus arcing with lightning.

An axe head came down, glancing from the head of the Jargalan in front of Sareya. The man stumbled back. A second strike—this from a hatchet—and his skull caved as he spun away into her.

Sareya slipped on blood and slush and hit the back of her head as she fell, the Jargalan landing on top of her. Boots stomped around her head, and cutlasses clattered to the blood-spattered ground.

Sareya uttered a cant and her ward sphere flickered on, surrounding her, and then died out before it fully formed. Her head was pounding from where she had struck it, and she couldn't focus her mind.

A sand wight fell to the ground beside her, eyes frenzied, the pupils massive. Gurgling, spitting hate, the wight snapped his jaws in Sareya's face. Unable to do anything else, she crashed her forehead into the savage's face, shattering his nose. The sand wight shrieked then bit Sareya's ear with needle-sharp teeth.

With a fierce thrust of her hips, Sareya turned beneath the weight of the Jargalan who pinned her, ignoring the pain as the savage ripped her earlobe away and spat it out. The sand wight suddenly arched his back, blood gushing from his mouth—too much blood to have come from Sareya's ear. The savage writhed like a dying serpent, thrashing his arms and legs. His face contorted with madness, he snapped once more at Sareya, and then he stiffened and stilled.

A Jargalan woman ripped her knife from the savage's back and pulled her fallen comrade off Sareya.

"You say you are a knight," the newcomer said—she sounded young beneath her helm, her words stammered between rapid breaths. With trembling hands she produced a key and inserted it into one of Sareya's shackles, turning it repeatedly. With a second key, she did the same to the other manacle, then popped them both open and let them fall to the ground. "Then you are trained to fight. Do so now, or you die. We all—"

A spear tip ripped through the woman's chest, spattering Sareya with gore. Shock cleared her head, and she leapt at the sand wight who had killed the woman, who was struggling to free his spear. She hit him hard on the jaw, and then threw a kick at the liver. For a second, the savage froze, and then he collapsed, clutching his belly in agony. Sareya ripped the spear out of the fallen Jargalan and ran the savage through.

Already more were coming, and she saw her doom. The Jargalans had formed a defensive square, wicker shields on every side, with those in the center holding shields overhead. Sand wights crashed against the shield square like an angry tide, but Sareya was isolated on the outside.

Eyes blazing beneath the wolf heads that encompassed their faces, three sand wights pounced at her before she could throw up her ward sphere. She caught one coming in, impaling it on her spear. The savage dropped her hatchet and clutched the haft with both hands, pulling herself along its length, spitting blood and cursing. Sareya let go the spear so she could catch the wrist of a sand wight swinging a cleaver for her head. She smashed a knee into the man's ribs then swung him into the path of the third attacker, knocking him from his feet.

Snatching up the woman's hatchet, Sareya delivered quick, fierce blows that left two men twitching in the snow. She hurled the hatchet at a fourth savage she hadn't seen at first, shrieking as he tore toward her, screaming as the hatchet smashed through his teeth.

The sand wight impaled on the spear frothed at the mouth as she struggled to stand. Sareya took hold of the haft and rammed the tip deep into the ground, then pulled it free with a sucking, slurping sound as the sand wight quivered and stilled.

Sareya dropped to her belly, hiding behind the bodies of the dead. Her heart beat a thunderous tattoo in her ears. Blood was thick in her nostrils, some of it her own. Her ravaged ear stung now she had a moment to think about it. Hot blood gushed down the side of her neck. With scarce a thought, she covered her ear with a hand and discharged a measured burst of dusk-tide fire, cauterizing the wound. The searing pain made her cry out, but her scream was lost amid the howls of the sand wights. Not knowing what else to do, she pushed her ear into the snow and moaned with relief at the numbing cold.

More and more skin-clad wights streamed down from the heights, an avalanche of fur hides and frenzied eyes, hatchets, spears, and cleavers. Dozens threw themselves from low ledges to crash against Jargalan shields and buckle the defensive square. From within the shield square, Galban's voice cracked orders, muffled by the shields overhead. In response, daggers ripped into the savages, spilling blood to the trampled slush the snow had become and turning it pink.

Another command, and this time the ceiling of shields parted around the magus's conical helm. Lightning forked from his raised hand, striking a sand wight in a bearskin cloak as he leapt from the rock face, then arcing from savage to savage, setting their animal hides ablaze. The magus seemed to swoon, and Galban held him upright until they were taken from sight by the shield ceiling closing up once more.

That was it? That was all the magus had? Not so tough as Sareya had been led to believe.

She crawled like a lizard toward the backs of the massed sand wights attacking the Jargalans' defensive square. Screaming to startle them, she charged, hurling her spear with such force it ripped through a wight's back and exited her chest. Stunned, the woman teetered round to see what had hit her then crashed face-first to the ground.

Leaving her spear jutting from the savage woman's back, she reached into her repository and unleashed a storm of lightning from her fingertips. Fur went up in flames and smoke, sand wights screamed, and then they turned and ran for the rock face.

Galban yelled commands. The shield wall opened. Jargalans advanced with sweeping strokes of their cutlasses, daggers in their off-hands, as they tore into the fleeing savages. Bodies heaped on the ground before the Jargalan advance.

Sareya weaved between the sand wights as they ran, slashing about her with a cleaver she scooped up from the ground, thrilling each time it bit. And still the Jargalans came on, driving the savages before them, turning certain defeat into a rout.

Galban barked a command, and the Jargalans ceased their pursuit.

Not what Sareya would have done. With a unit of knights at her command, she'd have given chase and cut every last sand wight down. Never leave an enemy standing was what the priests of the Warrior taught, lest they return when you're not looking and stab you in the back.

Hands grabbed Sareya's arms and pulled them behind her back, snatching the cutlass from her. She started a cant, but stopped when she felt the cold edge of a blade at her throat. Shackles snapped shut about her wrists.

"I fought for you!" she raged. "I saved you!"

Galban emerged from the remnants of the shield square. "You did, but let us be honest: only to keep yourself alive. And now that our mutual foes have fled, we do not need to pretend to be friends anymore."

The magus loomed over her, and she felt the probe of his senses. He said something in the Jargalan tongue to Galban, who nodded and spoke with the man holding Sareya.

"One hint of sorcery, and he will slit your pretty throat," Galban said. "Sometimes it is more prudent to cut one's losses, no?"

The sand wights had regrouped on the ledges, howling and cursing as they pelted the Jargalans below. Stones bounced from shields to clatter away.

Galban growled something at a group of Jargalans ransacking the bodies of their own dead. They desisted at once and skulked away beneath the shelter of an overhang.

Sareya counted a dozen Jargalan fallen, but there could have been more buried beneath the corpses of sand wights piled up along the pass.

Stones continued to rain down as the Jargalans began to move out, sprinting between patches of shelter. Sareya ran with her hands shackled behind her back, then stopped at a sudden break in the bombardment.

And she saw then: the sand wights hadn't run out of rocks to throw; they were standing on their ledges, watching her, as if they feared what might happen if they targeted her. They had seen what she could do, how she had blasted them with lightning. She would have blasted them with something far worse, if she hadn't been saving her dusk-tide essence for the right opportunity.

Galban ordered a halt while they waited for Sareya to catch up, which she did at her own unhurried pace.

"What are they doing?" he asked, once she was in among the warriors.

"They're conserving their rocks," Sareya said. "And they're taking a parallel course along the heights."

"Herding us into an ambush, you think?" Galban said.

She shrugged.

Galban bristled with tension and rammed his fist into his palm. "I thought after we bloodied their noses…"

"They were just testing us," the magus said, joining in the Nan-Rhouric exchange. "Forcing us to expend energy."

"And you fell for it," Galban observed.

"Rest will restore my power."

So he did indeed have limitations, and from what Sareya had seen, far more than she did. It was tempting to make a break for it now, but a glance at the Jargalan guarding her showed just how attentive he was, how close his dagger was to her throat. She forced herself to relax, hoping it would rub off on him.

Renewed cries echoed down from the heights.

"By the rotting flesh of the Orgol god, how many are there?" Galban said.

"Our greatest chance is to run," the magus said.

"Fine." Galban started back the way they had come. "Follow me."

No more protests, no hesitancy; the Jargalans did as he commanded, and Sareya was bundled along with them, as they rounded another bend and began the ascent of a winding path of scree that led to the heights.

THIRTY-NINE

THE WARRIOR'S CHURCH EMERGED LIKE a stone giant's fist out of the pitch night, its contours defined by the sleet spattering its sagging roof. When Anskar had come here before, for Hrothyr's funeral, it had been daytime, and the church had appeared quaint, even homey, with its flintstone walls and lead-framed embrasures—for they were hardly wide enough to be considered windows. But here, in the dark and the storm, the basilica seemed to squat like some malevolent beast, waiting for him, daring him to enter.

He shrugged off the feeling, all too aware it was an effect of guilt for what he was about to do. He knew it was wrong. Menselas, he knew! But evil like his mother couldn't be vanquished by sticking to the rules. The Warrior aspect of Menselas knew that better than most. That was why his priests were encouraged to seek every advantage, no matter the cost. Hrothyr would understand. He might not have made it as a priest, but he'd commenced the training and imbibed the culture, and for the remainder of his life had attended services at this very church.

Anskar took shelter from the icy torrents beneath the modest portico and glanced back at the empty streets he had come down. No lights on anywhere, save high up on Wintotashum's walls, where the sentries must have been grateful for their roofed watchtowers and the braziers that stood between them and the frigid night. Even the King's hall was in darkness. Wintotashum felt like a city of the dead, but he knew he didn't have long till it would resurrect with the coming of dawn.

He was surprised not to hear the sounds of gathering warriors, coming in response to his break-in at the forge. Surely word had reached the King's advisors by now. But then again, Aelfyr was a prudent king, not just a capable one. Warriors would come, but only when the king was ready, and likely only when they had been equipped with some means of defense against Anskar's sorcery. The Scriptorium was filled with such things—books, scrolls, and artifacts that only saw the light of day when the king decreed they were needed.

Anskar turned back to the church's bowed wooden door, lifted the latch, and let himself in.

It smelled of incense inside. It smelled of blood.

At first he could see very little, it was so dark, and the narrow windows conveyed only the blackness outside. But swiftly Anskar's black eyes adjusted, and he began to pick out shapes in shades of gray: the rows of pews, the anvil-like altar, the blood-drenched axe suspended above it, dripping into an iron bowl. It was the same ceremonial axe they had hacked Hrothyr's corpse apart with. Perhaps there had been another funeral recently, or maybe it was the blood of some animal or other. Back at Branil's Burg, the priests of the Warrior were rumored to keep their religious relics wet with the blood of oxen or sheep.

He remembered Hrothyr's remains being slopped into a lead-lined sarcophagus and slid down a ramp behind the altar, into the crypt beneath the church. He located the entrance, which was covered with a stone slab, an iron pull-ring set at one side. When he took hold of the ring and heaved, it wouldn't budge. For his efforts, Anskar grew dizzy and his head started to pound. He looked up in case there was some kind of pulley system to open the crypt, but there was nothing save rotting rafters and dust-filled cobwebs. For a moment, he considered blasting his way through the stone slab with lightning or flame, but he knew it was foolish to risk the use of such sorcery. He'd already come close to losing control of the new power that had awakened within him. Next time, he might not be so lucky.

That left only the earth-tide, the only sorcery he possessed that seemed independent of the new power. It hardly surprised him that the provenance of Kaythe Nurglich had no accord with the other tides. All the theories he'd heard implied that the earth-tide was the tainted residue of the other three tides that had seeped below ground, through layer upon layer of corruption. If those tides were analogous to winds and the position of the sun in the sky, the earth-tide was more akin to a cesspit's effluence. And yet, as he had learned, it had the power to warp and shape matter. Back at the forge, he'd only had limited success with the armor; the tide had failed to do anything other than slightly warp the plates. Maybe it would be easier with stone…

He knelt beside the slab and placed one hand on it, then plunged his senses down through the earth.

The foul currents came much more easily than before, and the nausea he usually experienced gave way to little shivers of exultation. The slab beneath his palm started to shake and groan. It wasn't a new shape he sought to give it, but rather a new weight. Little by little, as he grew cold with the sludge coursing through his veins, he drove the tidal waste into the slab and, with his will directed by his imagination, made the slab less dense, lighter, as if it were made of wood and not stone. Something like a click and a pop inside his skull told him he was done.

He stood, expecting to feel drained, but if anything he was more energized. The slab still resembled stone, but when he gripped the iron ring and pulled, this time it opened with ease to reveal a steel ramp with well-oiled runners on either side, leading down into the gloom.

Almost at once he could hear the dead whispering—not the words they spoke as such, just a rising susurrus that sounded like a warning, an imprecation to leave this place.

As he descended the ramp, one sibilant voice rose above the rest, and now he could discern the words it spoke. Two words, uttered through some unimaginable agony, or dread:

"Anskar, no!"

"Hrothyr?" he answered, the name echoing away through the crypt as he reached the floor. No reply. This time, he dredged up more of the earth's flow and sent his voice skirling into the realm of the dead. "Hrothyr?"

Silence—not just from Hrothyr; the whisper of voices had ceased. But he was sure the blacksmith's shade had heard him. Heard him and hidden. Playing dead, he thought with wry amusement. Hrothyr knew what Anskar was going to ask of him—was going to make him do—and he was afraid. Demons were the same, Anskar had learned back at the Abbey of the Hooded One: petrified of being summoned against their will and bound to a human. Get the summoning and binding wrong, and the demon would punish you for it; more likely, it would devour you body and soul. That put him on edge. Did the recalcitrant dead present a similar danger?

In his grayscale vision, he could see niches cut into the walls of the crypt from ceiling to floor, dozens of them holding stone sarcophagi. The crypt extended away into the deeper dark, the niches farthest from the entrance empty, awaiting those still living—probably for generations to come, given the sheer size of the chamber. The crypt was much larger than the little church above it, and gave the impression of a vast necropolis beneath the city of Wintotashum. Cobwebs hung from the ceiling. At the center of one he saw a fist-sized spider and couldn't shake the feeling it was watching him.

Rendered jumpy by the silence, he made a quick preliminary search of the occupied niches, but it was impossible to distinguish one from another. There were no plaques to indicate whose remains lay within. He reasoned that the most recent dead would have been interred farthest form the entrance, and turned his attention to the sarcophagi at the extremity of the filled area.

He needed to hurry. For all he knew, the King's warriors were on their way to the forge at this very moment; and while he doubted they would be able to pass the barrier he had erected, the priests of the Elder would work out a way sooner or later, even if they had to scour the Scriptorium for the requisite lore.

Have trust, Anskar, Kaythe Nurglich had said. *Accept my aid. In return, all I ask is your service.*

Well, he had already agreed to that pact, and it was too late to back out now. *Fine,* he thought. *I trust you. And I have pledged my service in return for your help. So, help me.*

No response. No presence. Nothing.

"Kaythe Nurglich," he whispered. "Corpse Maker."

His words echoed back at him, hollow and weak. They seemed to mock him.

He sighed and clenched his fists. Closing his eyes, he diverted his senses to the realm of the dead, and far quicker than at any time before, he felt them punch through the veil between worlds.

His body grew cold, as if plunged into icy water, and he opened eyes of the spirit onto the swirling gray limbo he had visited before. Still his senses went ahead of him, snaking through the crepuscular gloaming, ignoring the shapeless shades that were tugged this way and that by invisible winds. And then he felt his feelers thrash with excitement. He tried to follow them, but clouds of formless spirits coalesced in front of him, blocking his path. When he tried to force a passage, they surged toward him, driving him back.

He retreated, drifting, as ethereal as the shades of the dead, and focused on what his senses had perceived. He could see nothing, as if the eyes of his spirit senses had no permission to be here. Yet he could hear: voices, boisterous and drunk. There were roars of laughter, snatches of song, the clank and clash of metal mugs. Amongst the revelry, he recognized Hrothyr's deep baritone. Anskar called to him—a soundless summons, and he heard Hrothyr growl in return, not in the realm of the dead but here, in the crypt. He called again, this time with his eyes open, his worldly senses alert, and Hrothyr responded with cuss words and threats, warnings to leave him alone. The sound of his voice was unnatural—haunting, a howl of unearthly wind. And it was coming from one of the sarcophagi high up on the right-hand wall.

Anskar went over to it, reached up, and touched the end of the sarcophagus with his fingertips. His senses plunged inside, to where he could see the tail-end of a spirit, all that had come through from the realm of the dead. He snagged it with his senses and tugged. Hrothyr screamed. There was a moment's resistance, and then the entire spirit popped into existence within the sarcophagus. Drawing upon the knowledge of demons he had learned at the Abbey, Anskar uttered words of binding, but a voice intruded upon his mind to correct him.

Not like that, Kaythe Nurglich growled. *Like this.*

It felt as though a part of his mind dissolved, releasing knowledge that had been there all along, yet hidden away or calcified from lack of use. Not for the first time, he felt his mother had deliberately kept things from him, limited his powers till they could be of use to her, till she was sure he would pose no threat.

The words he now spoke were Niyandrian, not Skanuric, forbidding Hrothyr from straying from his physical remains. As he spoke the commands, Anskar could feel the spirit's horror, its revulsion at the dismembered corpse within the sarcophagus. Hacked into pieces it had been, and now Hrothyr screamed again, his scream splitting into a hundred voices as his spirit split apart to vivify each and every chunk of flesh and bone. In response to Hrothyr's fragmented cries, the other sarcophagi in their nooks began to rattle and shake. Dust cascaded down from the ceiling, and the voices of the dead screeched at Anskar to relent and leave them in peace.

He clutched his ears, trying in vain to screen them out as he focused all his awareness on Hrothyr's shattered spirit, on the chunks of desiccated flesh it now animated. With the unimpeded power of the earth-tide gushing up through the floor of the crypt and sluicing through his veins, he coerced Hrothyr's remains back together, slapping them in place like slabs of clay, fusing sinews, cartilage, muscle, skin and bone. Hrothyr's screams rose in pitch till Anskar reeled away in agony, warm blood seeping from his nose and ears. But then the disparate shrieks drew together in one long and torturous cry.

"Enough!" Anskar shouted. "Be silent."

Hrothyr ceased his wailing and instead whimpered and moaned.

"I said, be silent."

No sound now, save the ragged panting of his own breath. Even the other sarcophagi had stilled.

"Come!"

A fierce pounding started within Hrothyr's sarcophagus. A crack appeared in the base, a widening fissure, and then with a decisive crack, the end of the sarcophagus split open, chunks of stone falling away to crash on the floor. The soles of two lumpy feet were visible within, angry red ridges crisscrossing them from where the flesh had been crudely fused together.

Suppressing his revulsion, Anskar reached up and grabbed clammy ankles, then tugged with all his might. Hrothyr slid free of his tomb and slammed into the floor with a gurgling thud. Bent limbs twitched. Broken bones grated as they snapped back into place. Hrothyr's face was a mass of slapped-together chunks of meat, his eyes white and starting to rot. His body was a mess of lumps, a sculptor's abandoned first attempt, badly in need of smoothing out and forming into a truly human shape. But Anskar had neither the time nor the patience for that. He had seen for himself that Hrothyr's hands were intact, his fingers and thumbs in place. That was all he needed from the blacksmith. That, and the experience he had acquired in life working with divine alloy. Hrothyr had forged the vambrace as the first part of Talia's Armor of Divinity. Well, now he could finish the job for the Necromancer Queen's son. And if he worked well, if he proved successful, he would be permitted to return to his well-earned rest.

But not until.

"Follow me," Anskar said as he turned and headed for the ramp up. He stumbled. His legs felt hollowed out and weak. He raised his hands to his eyes. In the dark, he saw them as gray and lifeless; and worse, they were skeletally thin.

FORTY

A FOUL BREEZE BLEW ACROSS the top the cliffs that overlooked the Order stronghold of Quolith, swaying the tall grasses and carrying the stink of rot.

Carred lay on her belly at the cliff's edge, hair whipping about her as she peered through Bennetavian's spyglass. The Seneschal had already seen for himself the desperate plight of the tiny garrison he had left behind, and Carred could hear him cursing under his breath, then berating himself for cursing. Worshipers of Menselas! She would never understand why people devoted themselves to such weak gods, especially a god who didn't seem to know his own mind and had divided himself into five warring aspects. About the only aspect that would be of any use right now was that of the warrior, and she doubted even the pious Bennetavian could refute that.

Queen Talia had been busy.

A sea of shambling corpses surrounded the stronghold—Theltek alone could count them… ten, fifteen thousand? More were snaking in from the north, east, and west, columns of the marching dead, disinterred from all the tombs, graves, and burial grounds for miles around. Some were fresher than others, still decked out in their funerary robes, though with gray and blue skin. Most were skeletal, bones connected by fraying ligaments, the merest scraps of desiccated skin clinging to ancient frames. Hundreds wore age-rusted armor and carried chipped and pitted blades too dull to reflect the sunlight.

The twin settlements that had been there before the Order commandeered them and turned them into Quolith had grown together into one, connected by the massive tower under construction at their center. All around the conjoined settlement, trees had been stripped of their branches, their tops whittled to spikes, and they had been driven into the ground, their bases packed with soil and rocks. The trees were set closely together in a sturdy palisade, the only thing keeping the undead at bay.

"That your work?" Carred asked.

"Standard Order practice. We are taught to build a temporary fortification before commencing work on something more permanent. My predecessor at Quolith was, shall we say, remiss in her duties, and thought the felling of trees for a palisade a waste of time and resources. After your people attacked a group of trainees led by Vihtor Ulnar on their way to inspect the progress at Quolith, she was assigned other duties overseas."

"Looks like you got it built just in time."

The footings of a more permanent fortification were visible inside the defensive wall of trees. A rough parapet had been assembled all the way around the palisade, and sunlight glinted from the helms and spear tips of the knights. Most of them weren't knights at all; they were stuffed effigies clothed in spare parts of armor and white cloaks—to give the impression of a far larger garrison. Perhaps twenty real knights moved about among them, most carrying heavy crossbows.

The tower itself, the centerpiece of the stronghold, was close to being finished, though still surrounded by wooden scaffolding. The community's livestock had all been brought inside the palisade, where cows and goats grazing, oblivious to the threat from outside. Knights on horseback rode the perimeter, while the ordinary folk, the farmers and herders, the builders, merchants, cooks—everyone who kept Quolith going—congregated in nervous gaggles or went about their duties as if the palisade were not the only thing standing between them and their doom. But they must have known it was coming. Even here, atop the cliffs, the stench of decay and disease was overpowering.

"How are they going to breach the walls?" she asked, passing Bennetavian the spyglass back then scooting backwards away from the edge.

The walking corpses pushed and shoved, as if they sought to topple the palisade by sheer weight of numbers. They hacked at the stripped trees with rusty blades, but there was no other purpose to their movements, no indication of a plan. They seemed utterly mindless, not even focusing their assault on the palisade's massive wooden gate. If it had been she leading the attack, there would have been fire, arrows, a battering ram. There would have been dusk-tide sorcery.

"Maybe they don't need to breach the walls," Bennetavian said. "Maybe the Necromancer Queen is content to starve the garrison."

"And then what?" Carred asked. "March on to Dorinah and do the same there? Makes no sense. It will take weeks, if not months, to starve Dorinah, if it's even possible. They would have to block supplies coming in from the sea. No, there's something else going on here. I know Talia. She's no fool."

"Then what do you suggest?" Bennetavian said.

She thought about that as they both stood and together tramped back down the grassy slope to where their army was waiting, two hundred mounted knights of the Order of Eternal Vigilance and three thousand Niyandrians on foot, perhaps a fifth of them well-trained veterans, and the others… Well, she had done the best she could, given the lack of time, but they were mostly fisherfolk and farmers, or herders of sheep and goats. But all were in the prime of life, and all had at least some sorcerous ability, honed to military use by Vilintia and the commanders during long hours of practice in Branil's Burg's bailey.

Besides her elite force of veterans, Carred had given the Order knights authority over the inexperienced Niyandrian units. Drills had repeatedly shown that three knights with overlapping ward spheres could shield a closely packed unit of up to thirty Niyandrians. It would have to be enough.

One thing was still unclear to Carred: Why had Talia not come herself? And why had she sent no one else—someone with brains, rather than these mindless corpses? Had other necromancers flocked to her side? Doubtful, considering the creep who had visited her rooms in Quolith. He had shown no love for Talia. Quite the opposite. So, if Talia had concentrated so many undead here at Quolith, what was her game? Had she held back enough undead to defend Naphor? Maybe that was a job for Fult Wreave and his traitors—but would they prove enough?

"You want to leave Quolith under siege and move on to Naphor?" Carred asked. Strike now, cut off the serpent's head, and this could all be over before Talia was fully prepared.

Bennetavian swallowed. "I don't think I could live with myself if I abandoned the garrison. But," he quickly added, "I have pledged myself to your command."

She eyed him coolly for a long moment, then clapped him on the shoulder. To be honest, she was relieved. She'd seen Talia's sorcery firsthand. Married with Marith's moontouched abilities, and worse, if Talia had indeed slain and absorbed her demon lord father, she doubted even a force ten times the one she had assembled could prevail. Not without Anskar. She needed to give him more time.

"Tell your commanders and I'll tell mine," she said over her shoulder as she made her way to where Vilintia stood waiting with several of the Niyandrian leaders. "We attack within the hour."

Flies swarmed around Carred in a suffocating cloud. Some of them were big, with painful bites. She swatted and cursed, always thrusting with her sword at the endless bodies of the undead, hacking, slicing, blocking a clumsy blow from a rusty blade. Her star metal sword was lighter than any she had ever wielded, but her sword arm had grown heavy, and her sweaty palm was blistered from gripping the hilt too long. The blade had darkened since Anskar had added void-steel to it, and it glistened, perfectly clean, as if it had nothing but disdain for the gore of battle.

But that was just her sword. Diseased blood, slops, and viscera covered her clothes and skin, and she repeatedly wiped it from her eyes. But she was too deep within the horde, one instant her blade grating against bone, the next splatting through pulpy flesh and showering her with putrescence. Theltek, she'd put down dozens, and she wasn't alone. All around her, Niyandrians scythed about with swords and axes, evading the lumbering dead with ease. Knights advanced with discipline and precision strikes. Ward spheres flared on and off as they conserved energy, only using what they had to. Horses baulked at the stench and the horror before them, and then charged, trampling ancient bones to dust beneath their hooves.

Carred slipped on some blood straight into the arms of a cadaver. She tried to reverse her sword, but the corpse had a tight grip on her arm, cold and inhumanly strong. She stomped on its foot and heard it squelch; elbowed it in the ribs and met with a satisfying snap. But she couldn't break free. She butted her head back into its face, but the thing just wrapped an arm around her neck and started to squeeze. All around her, corpses pressed in. She saw the flare of Niyandrian swords ablaze with dusk-tide lightning. To her right, three Order ward spheres blazed into life, repelling the undead that surrounded the knights. Immediately, flies swarmed to the light, smothering the wards, then fizzing and popping and dropping to the ground like black rain.

Carred couldn't breathe now; the corpse had its other arm over her mouth and nose, squeezing so tight her jaw started to creak. She reached into her repository, not sure what she was looking for. Dusk-tide sorcery ignited in her veins, but before she could direct it, the pressure on her face fell away and the corpse slumped to its knees, a sword skewering it from ear to ear and spilling brains.

"Surest way to kill them," Vilintia said as she yanked her blade free, immediately turning to counter a rusty sword blow that came at her almost comically slow.

"Thanks for the advice," Carred said, thrusting her star metal blade through an empty eye-socket. The thing she had struck was virtually a skeleton, but still it convulsed before clattering to the ground.

One after another, ward spheres blazed on in quick succession, the knights within moving with drill ground discipline into a wedge formation, wards overlapping and growing denser where they met. With a yelled command from the commander—actually, it was Bennetavian, she saw—the wedge powered through rank after rank of undead, burning them up where the sorcerous barriers touched, swords snaking out where they did not. Dozens of undead fell.

Niyandrian archers moved into the cleared space, unleashing volleys of arrows enhanced with dusk-tide flames. Bodies pitched over, rank and smoldering, then ignited. The unnatural fire spread, leaping from walking corpse to walking corpse. Theltek, they should have thought of this earlier, Carred thought as she found a pocket of calm within the battle and stood watching, catching her breath.

All across the fields in front of the palisade, Niyandrians fought with steel and sorcery. Nothing grand, nothing devastating, such as Anskar might have used, or Marith, or Talia. But it was enough to turn the tide. The white cloaks moving among them were drenched with red. Corpses—nearly all of them dead for the second time—were heaped up all over the battlefield, piled high up the side of the palisade, some spitted by spears thrown from the fighting platform above. Severed limbs twitched and grasped. A skeletal hand scuttled across the grass looking for its arm. Here and there, she saw dead Niyandrians, fallen to the sheer weight of numbers, nothing else. Talia's army was big, but it was inefficient and lacking in speed and intelligence.

A change in the wind brought acrid smoke into her eyes and made them water. Plumes of black spiraled skywards, and the air was heavy with the stench of roasting flesh. Adding to the pall were the ever-present swarms of flies, harrowing the troops, biting exposed flesh.

"This is too easy," Vilintia said, coming to stand beside her. There was no more either of them needed to do. With more and more knights adopting the wedge formation with their ward spheres, and Niyandrians shooting volley after volley of flaming arrows, it was just a matter of time.

"That's what worries me," Carred said.

She wondered if she had made the wrong decision. Perhaps she should have gone straight to Naphor and trusted that Anskar would be there on time. Or maybe she could have taken on Talia alone.

No…

No mortal army would stand a chance against the Necromancer Queen, not now Talia had Marith's powers as well as her own. Carred's repositories might have started to develop, but it was too little, and she lacked sorcerous experience. *So, stop being an ass,* she told herself, *and think.*

But she couldn't think. All she could do is stand with Vilintia and watch the massacre of the already dead. The work before her Niyandrians and Bennetavian's knights was more akin to reaping wheat than fighting, there was so little effective resistance. But there was a limit to how many times a soldier could kill before he dropped from exhaustion; a limit to how much foulness and horror a person could endure. She could see from the resolve of her Niyandrians that no one was going to stop till this was over, and the knights were too disciplined to know when to quit. That realization guilted her into setting off once more into the fray, Vilintia groaning as the tagged along behind.

"All this is going to take is time," Carred said, as if that made it any easier.

But what if that had been the point all along?

Flies and bodies were everywhere she looked. Carred was used to the stink of a battlefield, the sickly tang of blood, the stench of open bowels, but this was worse. When the last of Talia's undead fell, the entire vicinity of Quolith was heaped with corpses, most of them rotten or pared to the bone. Vilintia directed Niyandrians to search through the piles of the dead for Niyandrian casualties, but there were comparatively few. Of the three thousand warriors who had left Dorinah, perhaps a hundred were gone. Of the knights, even fewer had fallen, no more than a handful. They had been protected by their ward spheres, not to mention the sluggish movements and the brittle blades of the enemy.

Carred was exhausted from her efforts and spattered with rank blood. Flies flitted all around her, landed in the drying blood that caked her skin and clothes and seemed to stick there. Some of the palisade timbers were smoldering, struck by stray arrows. Knights on the improvised parapet poured buckets of water down to stifle the flames, sending up plumes of steam.

A knight ahead of Carred, his white cloak drenched with crimson gore, bent double, clutching his guts and coughing. When he stumbled, Carred rushed forward and lent the support of her arm. The man teetered round to thank her then vomited a stream of black gunk over her mail hauberk, barely missing her face. He pushed her away and stumbled back, still vomiting. Foulness drenched his pants and slopped to the ground around him. He sank to his knees, trembling and groaning, then flopped onto his side, whimpering like a sick child.

And he wasn't the only one. Outside the palisade, men coughed and retched. A man came towards her, arms outstretched and face green with sickness. "Help me…" he rasped, then spewed blood and vileness.

Niyandrians began to separate themselves out from the knights, gathering in small groups away from the palisade. They all looked bone weary, and all were covered in filth, but not one of them appeared sick. That was just the knights.

She found Bennetavian by the palisade gate, which was open a crack, the man on the other side none too keen to bring the sick and wounded inside.

"Seneschal…" Carred said as she drew near.

To her relief, Bennetavian seemed merely tired, black rings around his eyes, a smattering of gore on his face.

"Some kind of blood contagion," the Seneschal said, indicating his sick knights with a sweep of his arm. He raised his voice for the benefit of the man on the other side of the gate. "These people need water and somewhere to rest."

"I'm sorry, Seneschal," the man within said, starting to close the gate.

"That's an order!" Bennetavian stormed. "So open the blasted gate, unless you are a mutineer?"

A moment's hesitation, and the gate creaked open.

"Forgive me, Seneschal," the knight said as he stepped warily outside.

"Orders from Colonel Wagstave."

"Whom I left in charge *until* my return!" Bennetavian said. "Now, where the in all the bloody abyssal realms is she?"

"I'll fetch—"

"Do not. I'll find her myself once the sick are taken care of. But if you see her, tell her I am displeased, soldier. Very displeased."

The knight looked fearfully at the sick, coughing and gushing fluids from both ends. Not all the knights: barely even half of them, though it seemed clear the sickness was spreading like wildfire.

"It's only affecting your people," Carred observed.

Bennetavian stared at her as if he had no idea what she was talking about, then let his eyes rove the carnage outside the palisade. "I wonder why."

"Talia," Carred said. "She's targeting mainlanders? I don't know. But this fight, here at Quolith, it doesn't feel right."

"I'll second that," Bennetavian said, wincing at some undisclosed pain.

"You all right?"

"A little queasy. Look, General Selenas, I'm sorry for my cursing just now."

"Perfectly fucking understandable," Carred said.

Bennetavian winced again, and then chuckled. "Looks like we'll be waiting for the mainland fleet after all." He stood aside as knights from the garrison came out of the gates and started to help the sick inside.

"I don't know that's a good idea," Carred said. "It feels as though Talia wanted to draw us here, to delay us."

"What choice do we have?" Bennetavian snapped, then proceeded to cough into his fist. He held up a hand in apology.

Murmurs sounded from the Niyandrians standing a good way from the palisade. Bennetavian's eyes followed where they were pointing, and Carred looked too.

Something like a black sun had appeared in the sky some miles distant—it had to be above Naphor. The glistening dark orb pulsed and rippled, and black filaments radiated outwards from it like some hellish corona.

"What in the name of Menselas…?" Bennetavian said.

"Sorcery," Carred said. She knew the kind. She'd seen Talia use it often enough back when she was alive. But never anything on this scale. "The dark-tide."

But for something on this scale… What in all of Wiraya was powering it?

"You should withdraw to Dorinah," Bennetavian told her. "Await the mainland army. The Order will send specialists—priests of the Elder; and the Grand Master has his elite units who will know what to do."

"No time," Carred said, already striding toward her waiting Niyandrians, signaling to Vilintia that they should move out. "Whatever Talia's up to, we have to stop it before it's too late. Theltek's balls, we were fools to take the bait and come here."

"I accept the blame for that," Bennetavian said.

"And I refuse to let you. Remain here, Seneschal. Be well."

"Wait!" he called after her, then issued commands to one of the knights who as yet showed no sign of sickness. "Take all the knights with you who can still fight. Please. Honor demands it."

Carred nodded then turned away.

She found herself a horse and rode to the fore of a swiftly forming column of Niyandrians on foot, the clop of hooves behind her as the remnants of the knights hurried after her. Vilintia, also mounted on an Order steed, joined her at the front.

"You have a plan, right?" Vilintia asked, low enough that no one else would hear.

Carred sighed, then kicked her horse ahead. "I'll think of something on the way."

But what could she do? Except pray to Theltek and hope that one of his thousand ears heard her. Pray that Anskar would show up on time, and that he had learned from his defeat at Talia's hands.

She tried to sit tall in the saddle. Tried to convey confidence to those marching and riding behind. But her hands on the reins trembled, and her nostrils were still clogged with the stink of rot and disease. Scabbarded at her hip, her star metal and void-steel sword seemed the only thing of permanence left in her world, something more enduring than flesh and bone, something that might be found in centuries to come when the rest of them had returned to dust. If they were lucky.

A thought wormed its way into her head as she rode: What would she do if Talia offered her terms, wanted her back, if not in her bed, then returned to her side?

She considered the scenario for a while as the trees of Rynmuntithe passed by the trail on either side and she waited for the column of Niyandrians to catch up. Behind them, she could see the spattered white cloaks of the mounted knights following, and the few who broke off and rode back toward Quolith, presumably starting to feel sick.

For a moment she felt a pang of longing for how things used to be, for the illusions she had lived under as a young captain in the Last Cohort. And though she knew it had been a lie, yes, she would have accepted Talia's invitation. She would have gone back.

If Talia hadn't done what she had to Marith.

FORTY-ONE

SAREYA COULDN'T SEE PAST THE Jargalan pirates in front as they reached the top of the winding path up the side of the gorge, but she felt their panic as they backed into one another, trying to get back down the slope. The problem was, those below were shoving from behind, as the wild hoots and shrieks of sand wights once more rent the air, and Sareya was caught in the middle. With her hands shackled behind her back, there was little she could do as the Jargalans on either side threatened to crush her. The pressure in front suddenly released as the man immediately ahead of her pitched to his knees in the snow, blood pumping from his half-severed neck.

A tall, slender woman loomed over the dying pirate, a long-hafted weapon that resembled a scythe held at the end of her follow-through, the curved blade dripping gore. At least Sareya thought it was a woman, judging by the desiccated flaps of skin that might once have been breasts. She—it?—was naked, mottled skin of yellow and pink smooth and polished, as if it had been scoured clean by a sand storm. Her wildly billowing hair was the same bruised and diseased color. Amber eyes glared dispassionately at the Jargalan, then switched to Sareya as the man keeled over onto his side and gasped his last.

The rest of the pirates who had reached the plateau lay in pools of blood, one or two of them twitching, but most of them already dead. She glimpsed Galban face down in the snow, a gushing hole ripped through his back. The warlock lay beside him, his conical helm dented by what must have been a crushing blow.

More slender beings—some that might have once been men—glided among the bodies of the dead, inexorably making their way toward her, their yellow-pink skin glistening, hair the only adornment, other than the weapons they carried—glaives, halberds, and billhooks.

The woman with the scythe stepped over the dead Jargalan and reached out with a jaundiced hand. Blood coagulated in Sareya's veins. Her heart seemed to spit and stutter. At a wail of absolute terror, she glanced behind to see hundreds of sand wights fleeing back down the gorge and along the main artery of the pass. They had seen what awaited them above.

The surviving Jargalans behind her peered above their wicker shields, nervously eyeing her as if, being at the front, she now led them.

She started as yellow fingers gripped her shirtsleeve, scorching her through the fabric. Sareya started to reach for her dusk-tide repository, but the scythe blade swept down before her eyes—a warning. She grimaced against the searing pain in her arm as the yellow woman drew her away from the Jargalans, into the mist that wafted above the bodies of the fallen and toward the squatting bulk of the building she had seen from below.

She craned her neck to look behind as the rest of the yellow-skinned beings glided down the gorge toward the surviving Jargalans, moving as though they skated on ice. With murderous precision, their blades flashed in the stark sunlight reflecting off the snow. The Jargalans, by way of contrast, seemed to move through molasses, their blocks tardy, their shields not quite protecting them where they were most needed. One Jargalan struck home with his cutlass, a massive blow fueled by terror. It should have cut the yellow-man's head from his shoulders, but instead the blade glanced off, and the yellow skin remained unscathed. After that, blood misted the air as the yellow beings advanced and the Jargalans fell so quickly, there was no time for anyone to scream.

The yellow woman's insistent grip tugged Sareya away from the grisly scene. As they approached the arched opening at the front of the building, all she could think of was that Galban should have heeded the advice of his crew and never come here.

Sareya shuddered as she passed beneath the arch. She wanted to turn about and flee, or fling herself to the floor and gibber insanely, but the yellow woman seemed to forbid any action save the act of following her.

It was a vast space Sareya found herself within, with massive archways open to the air on each of its six sides. The high domed ceiling was ribbed with glistening black stone, the faded azure plaster in between cracked and flaking. Fluted pillars of the same dark stone flanked each of the arches. One was crooked from where it had been split through about halfway up its height, the section of roof it supported sagging and crumbling. An enormous spiderweb comprised of rope-like strands filled the space inside the arch opposite the one Sareya had entered by. Skeletal remains stuck to its threads—large lizards, birds, something that might have been human.

Despite the light admitted by the six arches, a dingy pall hung over the chamber, and unnatural shadows accumulated on the floor. Something hissed, and Sareya lifted her foot as a wedge-headed snake slithered by. The yellow woman's scythe swept down, clearing a pathway through the undulating carpet that smothered the floor. A scorpion as big as a mule clacked its pincers as it scuttled to one side then watched Sareya from the gloom with silver eyes.

"What is this about?" Sareya asked, despising the tremor in her voice. "The people you just slaughtered—no friends of mine—were bringing me here of their own free will. You didn't have to kill them. Pay them, yes, but not kill them."

The woman's amber eyes studied her for a long moment, then glanced over Sareya's shoulder, where the other yellow beings were returning from their slaughter, no sign of their bloody work left on the blades of their polearms. With the grace of choreographed dancers, they each moved to take up positions beside the six arches. Even if Sareya's legs would permit her to run, there was no way out now.

"What are you?" she asked as the yellow woman drove snakes away from the center of the floor space to reveal the pattern of a seven-pointed star set within a broad-banded circle of stone. The design had been carved into the surface of the flagstones; or perhaps, Sareya thought as she peered closer, it was formed from intricate joins of the cut flags within the circle.

The woman cocked her head in response to Sareya's question. Something like a frown crossed her polished brow, and her amber eyes blinked in apparent confusion. She looked as if she wanted to say something, but then she dragged Sareya toward her, spinning away from her as if they were dancing, then releasing her arm as she propelled Sareya into the circle.

All at once, the sections of the star design fell inwards, and Sareya screamed as she plummeted into the dark. She flung out her arms, but there was nothing to grab hold of, nothing to arrest her fall. If there were walls lining the shaft of the tunnel down which she plunged, they were invisible within the absolute blackness. In terror, she called upon her repositories—for light, for destruction, something that might slow her descent—but all she got for her efforts was the sensation of burning coals in her stomach and a golden radiance that effused from her skin. Stunned, she could do nothing but gaze at her steadily glowing hands as she kept falling and falling—not tumbling, not plummeting now, but drifting slowly down. Seconds passed… minutes. At some point, the golden glow of her skin faded away, the heat left her belly, and the darkness closed in to reclaim her.

But the dark did not remain long. Light rose to meet her, pinkish and effulgent, and then she dropped the rest of the way, landing with bone-juddering force in a crouch, one fist hitting the ground in front of her, rock dust and sparkling motes pluming into the lambent air.

She should have been dead, crushed by her fall, but as she straightened up, she was bristling with energy and warmth.

Reflected light danced in patterns over her clothes and skin, and she looked about her to see that it came from the vast circle of crystal standing stones she stood at the center of. The dolmens were each the height of a tall man, and as broad. They were faceted like cut diamonds, yet they seemed to be rose quartz, each lit from within by a pulsing glow.

"Peace," a deep and resonant voice said from somewhere beyond the crystal circle. "You stand within the first *izindel*—the original, you might say. This is why you live after such a fall. The *izindel* dismantled your entire being, mote by mote, then reconstructed it, unharmed. It is a remarkable gift of our god, yes?"

A well-spoken voice, utterly at home with Nan-Rhouric, though there were some malformed vowels, as if the speaker's tongue were unsuited to such foreign utterances.

"*Izindel?*" Sareya asked, focusing her eyes on the movement of shadows beyond the circle as they coalesced into one, half again as tall as she was, and while it was not especially broad, she could feel the weight of its presence, a weight that seemed to press down on her skull. She smelled blood in her nostrils, and her hands began to tremble. It was an effort controlling her lips enough to go on speaking. "*Izindel* is a word connected in some way with the Ethereal Sorceress."

"Stolen lore," the shadow said. "Dangerous, forbidden knowledge.

But that was a battle lost an aeon ago and beyond remedy now. There are far more pressing dangers that demand our attention."

Shadow gave way to light as Sareya's interlocutor stepped between two crystal dolmens into the circle of the *izindel*. She couldn't work out at first if it was an Orgol. It had the height and the gravity of presence, the atmosphere of a storm about to break; but the Orgol that had attacked her at Sansor had been the color of coal, and every tale she had heard of the creatures concurred. The giant figure confronting her had skin the color of ash, like coal after it had been burned and consumed. Ridges of white scars covered every inch of its naked flesh, many joined together to perform patterns that might have been letters or might have been sigils and wards. Here and there, purplish welts and fist-sized swellings stood out on its belly, arms, and legs, and Sareya instinctively recoiled form the stench of weeping boils and disease. It had a blockish head like a lump of rough-hewn granite, and its deep-set eyes were sparkling and pink, the same color as the dolmens.

"I disgust you," the creature said.

Sareya shook her head in denial.

"I disgust my own race, so there is no reason why you should feel differently. It matters not to me. I was not placed here by the Orgol god to please others with my appearance. And for the work I have been entrusted with, I am better off out of sight, deep below the scorching sands, undisturbed."

"Until now," Sareya mustered.

"Until now."

"You arranged for me to be kidnapped and brought here?"

"It was necessary."

"Why?"

The gray Orgol studied her with his pink eyes. Sareya's skin prickled, and something popped within her head. She swooned, throwing her arms out for balance, then she dropped to her knees.

"Your so-called repositories," the Orgol said. "I merely quickened the process of their degradation and dissolved them."

Sareya clutched her head, staring up at the Orgol with wide eyes.

"You were born with exceptional sorcerous gifts, correct?"

She swallowed. She found it hard to focus with whatever was happening inside her skull. It felt as though sand were sifting from side to side, then began to cascade into a bottomless hole. "I'm moontouched."

"Yes, the Niyandrian term. Moontouched, moonshine, it is all one and the same: reflected light. Reflected power. Or nascent power not yet full grown."

The inner light that lit the dolmens pink flared, and Sareya cried out, covering her face.

And now she was watching herself from the outside, her skin afire with golden flame, her eyes burning orbs of magma. She rose into the sky, trailing fire, the ground where she had stood a melted devastation. She seemed a giant, a fiery spirit. A goddess. Flames blasted from her hands, incinerating the top of a mountain. She soared across the sky, burning farmland and forest, drying up lakes. She flew out to sea, where she reduced ships to ash. Then a city—consumed by a golden conflagration. Black smoke plumed into the sky. Everything she saw burst into flames, until the lands below her were reduced to lakes of lava and the sun was hidden behind a pall of acrid smoke. She screamed—even the goddess that she was in the vision started to scream in despair. But it was no good. She kept on blazing brighter, lambent with heat. And then she was far above the molten world, and the world bubbled and spat, then collapsed in on itself, and she wailed and knew she would never stop wailing.

Abruptly, she was back on the floor of the *izindel*, shuddering as she sobbed.

"Do you want this power?" the Orgol asked, his voice softer now.

"No," Sareya whimpered. "No, no, please, no."

"Good," he said. "That is good. Then we have a place to start from. Not everyone chooses as wisely as you have done. I will have your word, your oath that you will never again use sorcery."

"I can't," Sareya said. "I can't feel my repositories."

"Because they are gone," the Orgol said. "But the power they forced asunder and released only in trickles still remains latent within you. You must swear to me that you will not seek it out."

The Orgol loomed over her. When she didn't answer, he unclenched a gnarled hand to reveal an octagonal box of green stone that might have been jade. His other hand hovered over the box—a threat to open it. Warnings trilled throughout Sareya's mind, intimations of doom and oblivion.

"I promise!" she cried, pushing herself to her feet and stumbling back a step. "I swear never to use sorcery."

The Orgol relaxed and closed his fist around the jade box.

"Then we can proceed. Know this, though: Just because you do not seek out the power does not mean it is not there with a mind of its own. Should it unbind itself... Well, we must hope it does not."

"And this is why you had me brought here? To warn me off using some power I never knew I had?"

"It is not. You were chosen because, even passive, the power within you will protect you enough to do what must be done."

"Done?"

"To one who quickened your dormant power."

"Quickened? What do you mean?"

The Orgol's pink eyes flashed, and Sareya couldn't look away from them. Out of the corners of her eyes, she saw the crystal dolmens pulsing with the same pink light as the Orgol's eyes, and then she was once more watching herself from the outside, and this time she felt embarrassment and shame. She was on her knees in the smithing hall at Branil's Burg… in front of Anskar, trousers round his ankles.

Then she was in his bed, both of them naked and sweating. Scene after scene of the things they had done together played out before her, and she was powerless to turn away. But then, as the scenes repeated she began to see with a different kind of *sight*, and it showed her the bloom of golden light in Anskar's belly as they made love, then a reciprocal blossoming of light in her own, fainter, still nascent. She saw the agitation within each of Anskar's repositories, and within the dark-tide that sluiced through his veins. And again it was the same with her. Not the dark-tide so much—that was negligible, a recently awakened repository that felt as though it were an anomaly, or another contagion picked up from Anskar. But her dusk- and dawn-tide repositories moiled with bubbling fury as if they sought to break their bounds, as if they desperately wanted to come into contact, to touch one another as she and Anskar did; to meld together.

The vision faded as the pink light died back down to a gentle pulse.

"Anskar…" she murmured. "I didn't know. Does he know? That he quickened this… this power within me?"

"The son of the Necromancer Queen is an aberration. The sun-power that burgeons within him is not pure like yours."

"Sun-power?"

Golden fire blazed upon the Orgol's palm, and he turned and hurled it at one of the dolmens. The fire struck the crystal surface then emerged the far side, not a single golden stream but a scatter of rays of light—red, silver, and a purple so dark it almost looked black.

"The colored beams are the tides of sorcery," the Orgol explained. "The dawn, dusk, and the dark."

Sareya felt her jaw drop open. "They come from the same source…"

"They are the same power ripped asunder."

"But why? How?"

The Orgol dipped his blockish head, breathing deeply. "To prevent things like this."

The circle of the *izindel* once more filled with pinkish light, and then Sareya was looking upon more scenes of fire and devastation: mountains melting back into the earth, rivers scorched dry, entire cities turned to ash. And there, in the sky, arms outstretched, was a being of pure flame, and she knew at once this was Anskar. Sunfire burst from his skin, and the world turned molten. His eyes blazed like incandescent coals. Wiraya bubbled and steamed, then she saw the whole globe of the world collapse. Stars fell through the blackness of the heavens, until Anskar alone remained, a conflagration amid the void.

Sareya gasped as the vision faded, then she turned aside, bile rising to her throat.

"The power was divided for all our sakes," the Orgol said, "by a being far older than I, a creature of sublime puissance who ascended too high and paid the price of a self forever divided." He looked at Sareya as if he expected her to know what he was talking about.

Suddenly she understood. "Menselas?"

"That is what he is nowadays called."

"Menselas split the tides? And now they have come together again in Anskar?"

"Not just in him. Others have transgressed. Maybe their intentions are good, but the risk is too great. Far better that they are slain and any threat to Wiraya removed. But these others have been taken from my sight. I know not where to find them. And in coming here, tainted by your contact with Anskar, the tides have also come together in you. You are but an oath-break away from being removed as another risk to the world. But this Anskar, this child of the necromancer… he carries too many taints, too many other sorcerous influences. The sun-power fights back against them like the body fights infection. It strives to burn them up, to immolate them, whether or not he wills it. And yet, I fear from what I have observed that he does indeed will the power to manifest. He needs it; he fuels it with desires for vengeance."

"Then bring him here. Make him swear the oath."

"It is too late for that. He is too far gone."

"If this is going where I think it's going," Sareya said, "you should know that you're not the first person to ask me to kill Anskar."

"I do not ask this of you." The Orgol held out the jade box to her. "I merely want you to save the world."

"But he'll die in the process, won't he?"

"Open the box when you are this close to him." The Orgol's diseased skin pressed up against her as it took hold of her hand and pressed the jade box into it. "Wiraya will thank you."

"And what happens to me? Will I die too?"

"Must I seek another for this task?" the Orgol said, reaching for the box.

"No." Sareya hid the box behind her back. Refuse the task and she'd never leave this place alive. She didn't need to be a prophet to know that.

"Then do what must be done. Get close to Anskar—your own burgeoning sun-power will protect you, unless you leave it too late and he loses all control."

"So, Niyas it is, then. I would have been there already if you hadn't had me kidnapped."

"Without the box, without knowledge of the things I have shown you, your presence on Niyas would have made no difference. You would have died. Your companions would have died. And then the world would go up in flames. But yes, to Niyas you must now return. Certain things I have foreseen. The cataclysm, when it comes, will be centered upon Naphor. Anskar will be forced to fight his mother. That is when the world will end."

"Unless I prevent it," Sareya muttered. "Fine, so how do I get back to Niyas?"

The Orgol cocked his head as if listening. A crooked smile crossed his face, revealing the jagged stubs of black teeth.

"It would appear you have mighty friends. Friends with enchanted weapons."

"I do?"

"Friends with the ability to slay the undying." The Orgol sounded more intrigued than angry. His eyes flashed, and the crystal dolmens that surrounded the *izindel* flared.

Three figures materialized above her head, and Sareya stepped aside as they fell in a heap on the floor, a pair of swords and two hatchets clattering away across the circle.

"Rindon?" Sareya said, as the fat man who had landed on top of the others rolled to his feet with the agility of a cat, then rolled again, head over heels, to snatch up his hatchets.

"Nul?" She was too shocked to do anything other than stare as the second hero acknowledged her with a flash of white teeth and then held out a hand to help the third man up.

It was Eldrid DeVantte, whom she had last seen with Nul in a cell on the Jargalan coast.

Eldrid and Nul wasted no time retrieving their swords.

"We'll soon have you out of here," Nul said.

Eldrid weaved his sword through the air as he advanced on the Orgol.

"You'll have to think of a way to repay me," Rindon said with a wink, spinning his axes as he moved to flank the Orgol as Nul took the other side.

The Orgol merely bowed his head and interlaced his fingers over its belly.

"I don't think we need to fight," Sareya said.

"Shame no one mentioned that up top," Eldrid said. "It was all I could do to stay alive, facing those undying ones."

"You too shall have opportunity to repay me, though in your case beer will suffice," Rindon said. "The advantage of being a hero is that one procures weapons of exceptional quality."

"You killed them all by yourself?" Sareya asked.

"Alas, no. Age has diminished my powers somewhat. Nul accounted for two of them, although he too has a debt to pay, considering I brought his spare sword all the way from Sansor."

Sareya eyed the Orgol, waiting for it to speak. Its head remained bowed, but it gave the impression it was still smiling.

"You followed me here by sea?" Sareya asked Rindon.

"Commandeered the ship that was meant to take us to Niyas. The Captain's seething. Says the Grand Master will punish me. But I wouldn't worry about that. I know more about the Grand Master and his peccadilloes than he would like for others to know. I'm sure I'm quite safe. As for the Captain, he set sail for home before my feet had left the gangplank."

"Then how are you planning to reach Niyas?" Sareya asked. "We still have a mission to fulfill, don't we?"

And now she thought the Orgol was chuckling.

"Eldrid?" Rindon asked.

"Nul's the planner," Eldrid said. "Ask him."

The Orgol laughed out loud, and the three men backed away a step.

"You have nothing to fear from me," the Orgol said. "He who sees all is pleased with you. Three good men in an Order grown wicked; this is a rare thing."

"He who sees all?" Nul asks. "Menselas?"

"The Five who is one, not the one who is Five," the Orgol said. "You see the god through a prism that divides his light. Such is the blindness of men. My people are no better. Once we had a god all our own."

"Then you murdered him," Sareya said. "Not much of a god, if you ask me."

The Orgol stepped back behind the dolmens as they started to pulse with blinding light.

"Sareya?" Nul said. "What's happening? Do we fight?"

"With these three at your side," the Orgol said, no longer visible from outside the glare of the *izindel*, "my confidence in your success has increased."

"Success in what?" Rindon asked.

"Same thing we signed up for," Sareya said.

"Anskar?" Eldrid asked, and she nodded, just as the pink light began to strobe, and a whining drone filled the air.

And then the world about them exploded in a storm of burning motes.

Sareya came to herself—literally came back together—absorbed by a sweet fragrance and a frenetic humming noise. Cool air soothed her skin, so blissful after she had been scorched and blasted apart by the *izindel*.

She opened her eyes upon the source of the humming: a tiny bird with violet plumage, little larger than an insect, hovering mere inches from her face, its proboscis-like beak darting in and out of a tubular gold and silver flower.

Sareya was kneeling within a thicket of honeysuckle. Twenty yards from her, a doe and her fawn looked up from munching on the sweet flowers. They studied her momentarily, then went back to their feast. Above, the sky was the perfect azure of childhood memories— childhood before the Order knights had come for her. She was shocked at how cleansed she felt, renewed, and in some way forgiven.

She returned her focus to the little bird, marveling at the blurry speed of its wings as it hovered. Something changed in the atmosphere, an intimation of shadows, and with a succession of chirps, whistles and buzzes, the bird flew off. When she looked round, the deer had also fled.

Only then did she become aware of the three men standing around her.

"No need to kneel on my account, lass," Rindon said. "Unless, of course…"

Nul elbowed him in the ribs.

Eldrid shook his head, not in the least amused.

"I think she's found religion," Rindon said. "Real religion, the kind the mystics among the priests of the Elder are always going on about, which always eludes me."

"Because it's not to be found at the bottom of a mug of beer, old friend," Nul said.

Sareya was barely listening, her senses rapt by the sudden change in the air.

The clear sky was now but a narrowing circle within a ring of dark clouds that scudded in from every side. Was that even possible?

"You know this place?" Nul asked, dropping to one knee beside her.

Sareya nodded vaguely, but it was Eldred who answered.

"Rynmuntithe forest. Now, if I could just get my bearings and point us in the direction of Naphor…"

"There," Sareya said, standing. She pointed to where she had just seen a rippling of the clouds, and where now dark fractures radiated outwards from a central point.

"That doesn't look good," Rindon said.

Sareya palmed the jade box in her pocket but found no reassurance there. Whatever it was happening in the sky above Naphor felt wrong beyond anything she had felt before. She only hoped it was Queen Talia. She had set off from Sansor with the intention of killing Anskar, and the Orgol had provided her with the means; but now… Now she whispered prayers to Menselas that there might be another way.

When the Five didn't reply, she gritted her teeth with resolve. Shaking with the effort to hold back tears, she set off through the honeysuckle thicket toward the north, aware of the footfalls of her companions behind.

"So, let me get this straight," Eldrid said. "The Grand Master has ordered us to kill Anskar?"

"Us, not you, if we're going to be precise about it," Rindon said.

"And how do you feel about that?"

Like Menselas, neither Nul nor Rindon answered.

"Sareya?" Eldrid asked.

Tears broke free of her restraint, but she didn't turn back; didn't want the others to see. Her voice stiff with suppressed emotion, she said, "We let him kill his mother."

"And if he doesn't succeed?" Nul asked.

Sareya stopped. "Then we're in a lot of trouble, all of us. Even the mainland."

"And if he does?" Rindon asked. He appeared at her side and dabbed away a tear from her eye with his thumb.

She resumed walking, striding ahead of the group, no longer serene and expunged of all sin. How could she be, when she was destined to commit one more? She had grown up fueled by resentment, her homeland in the grip of invaders from overseas. But the passage of years had made her comfortable with mainland rule. She recalled how she had stood against her own people at the battle for Dorinah, and how righteous she had felt, how enraged by their uprising. The years hadn't just made her comfortable, they had made her complicit. And though she wavered every now and again, she realized that people fought for the things they were used to, not some bygone age they had never known— *she* had never known. The return of the Necromancer Queen had been a childish fantasy growing up, but the reality scared her. And not just Queen Talia, either: the thought of any degree of return to the old ways of blood and bone. The days of the necromancers were long gone.

"I ask again," Rindon said. She had never heard him so earnest, so sober. "What if Anskar succeeds in defeating his mother?"

Sareya shrugged. The Grand Master was right, and though she was loath to admit it, so was the pale-skinned Orgol.

"We do the job we were sent to do. Niyas needs no heir. Wiraya has had enough of necromancers and the undead."

FORTY-TWO

THE STREETS WERE STILL EMPTY when Anskar returned to the forge, the sullen, misshapen bulk of Hrothyr following behind, as if he had a choice. The blacksmith remained naked, but he was probably beyond caring about modesty, and the freezing sleet was no match for the cold of his flesh and bones. Once or twice, Anskar felt eyes on him, but when he turned to look there was nothing. He strode through the dark fog of his sorcerous barrier, skin tingling at its touch. Hrothyr passed through as if the barrier were not there. It was designed to keep out the living, not the dead.

It was warm inside, on account of the coals Anskar had left smoldering in the forge. Hrothyr's corpse looked in that direction, as if he too could feel the heat, or as if he were remembering his life as the King's smith.

The pieces of armor were laid out on the floor, as Anskar had left them, the additional components for making divine alloy among them. Hrothyr took it all in with eyes so white they shouldn't have been able to see.

"Still at it, then," the blacksmith said, his baritone voice an echo in Anskar's head. Though Hrothyr's desiccated lips moved, the only sound that came out was a gurgling rasp. "You'll not make divine alloy with just the heat of coals."

"I realize that," Anskar said. "Which is why you're here."

"Glad to be of some use."

"You don't mean that."

"No," the blacksmith said, "I don't. And I'll be waiting for you when this is over. Waiting in the realm of the dead. Forgiveness is not one of my strong points. If she were here, Braga would testify to that."

"Well, she's not here," Anskar said. "She's nowhere, and I suppose I'm to blame for that."

"I'm saying nothing," the corpse's voice said in his head. "So, you still want me to make Armor of Divinity for you, and won't even let death get me out of the task. Not what I would have expected of you."

"I promise," Anskar said, "that I'll release you as soon as it's done."

"Hmm," Hrothyr said, stooping to pick up an ingot of void-steel. "This wasn't in Tain's notes."

"No, it wasn't," Anskar said. "But it may give me the advantage I need."

"Because it cancels out dark-tide sorcery? Even your own?"

"I don't use the dark-tide anymore."

"Really?" Hrothyr said. "So what was that black shit you just had me walk through?"

"An exception. The last one."

"Of course it was."

"I've disavowed sorcery," Anskar said. "All but one kind."

"Found a new toy to play with, have you? You know what King Aelfyr does to necromancers, if they're stupid enough to step foot in his realm?"

"I'm no necromancer!"

"And I'm no corpse walking. By the way, you don't look much better yourself. You had more flesh on your bones last I saw you. And your eyes…"

He didn't need to say it. Anskar knew that he was, in some way, dead already, or dying. Changing into something, more likely, that had no right to walk in the world. Despair tugged him downwards, but he fought it back with a silent prayer to Kaythe Nurglich, to grant him the time to see through what he had to do. The fact that he'd appealed to the Corpse Maker made him feel damned. He followed it up with a muttered prayer to Menselas—that he would have his revenge on Queen Talia. That he would free Niyas from the menace of the Necromancer Queen, maybe even help it to shake of the yoke of mainland rule. After that, he would accept any punishment that was his due. Last of all, he prayed for forgiveness, for all he had done, for what he still had to do.

Hrothyr's malformed head was cocked to one side, as if he were listening, though scarce a whisper had left Anskar's lips.

The dead smith laid a lumpy hand on his shoulder. "The Five is merciful, Anskar, but you're pushing your luck. Come on. The sooner we get this over and done with, the sooner I can get back to the realm of the dead."

"It sounded…" Anskar started.

"As if I was having fun there? I was. There's a special place for the Warrior's devotees. Real or not, I don't care. If it was just a lingering dream, at least it was a dream full of beer and laughter and well-endowed women."

"I'm sorry…" Anskar said.

"I expect you are," the dead man replied. "But not enough to leave me alone. Is your need for this armor so great? Before, when I was alive, you seemed reluctant to pursue this course. You were dragged along by the whims of a foolish man."

Brother Bonavir. The priest of the Elder had become obsessed by the idea of creating a suit of divine armor, and he had been quite insistent about Anskar's participation. Not only him: Hrothyr's ex-wife, Braga, although she claimed she was influenced by visitations from the Necromancer Queen.

"Things have changed," Anskar said. This was no longer about the curiosity of an old man driven to possess every last scrap of knowledge and get one up on his confreres. It was about revenge, pure and simple. "And we don't have time for this. Everything you're going to need is here, laid out on the floor. Now, get on with the task you've been given."

Hrothyr started to protest, but Anskar choked off the blacksmith's voice in his head with a simple act of will. Little more than a petulant puppet, Hrothyr's clumpy form moved over to the forge and crouched on creaking knees to turn the valves beneath. With deft twists of the valve, Hrothyr controlled the gouts of flame, letting them initially kiss the ceiling, then turning them down till they rested mere inches above the forge. Within a few short minutes, filaments of red sprouted from the crystals on the forge tray, forming scintillant frills around the coals. Anskar had to shield his eyes as crimson flared and then went through successive changes of color till it settled into the iridescent silver of lightning.

"Are you ready to start?" Anskar said, anxiously eyeing the pieces of armor on the floor.

"Almost," Hrothyr said. "And I've a good idea what to do. Menselas alone knows how many years of my life I spent thinking about such things, dreaming of the greatest feats of smithing."

The dead man turned away from the forge, his white eyes narrowing at Anskar's belt. "Where is your sword? I thought we might modify it; add some of these divine ingredients. You'll not get far with just a suit of armor, no matter how well crafted and how divine. And if you're not going to use sorcery against the Necromancer Queen, I'd say the odds are stacked in her favor."

"*Amalantril*, my sword, is gone," Anskar said. He explained how Talia had taken it. Explained how the sword seemed possessed; how it had tried to drain his soul.

"Then you're going to need a new one, equally as good if not better, if you're to face her. Even if you do use sorcery, what happens if your sorcery and hers are evenly matched? It may come down to steel on steel."

"Why do you care?"

Hrothyr came face to face with him, so close that Anskar started to gag on the stench of rot. "I care because you weren't always like this, Anskar. I care because my Braga liked you, and that's saying something. And I care because Menselas cares."

"How do you know this?"

"Being dead, I hear things, see things, just sort of know things. No matter how far you fall, Anskar, it is never too far for the mercy of Menselas to reach you."

Anskar turned his back on the dead blacksmith.

"If you never believe another word I say," Hrothyr said, still speaking in his mind, "believe this. Menselas loves you. Loves all who have sworn to serve him."

"Even if they've betrayed him?" Anskar asked. "Even if they've sworn themselves to other gods?"

"Even if."

"No," Anskar said, facing Hrothyr once more. "I don't believe that."

"Do not despair…"

"I said no."

The blacksmith stood in somber silence for a long while, before turning back to the forge. "It's ready," he said. "I should start."

"How long will it take?"

Hrothyr threw him a sour look. "I don't require rest. If you will it, I'll have no choice but to work through the night, the next day, and the following night too."

"Good," Anskar said, realizing how cold he sounded, and choosing not to care. "Then that's what you'll do."

"You want me to make you a new sword while I'm at it?"

Anskar was about to say yes, then an idea flashed into his head. He wondered if it were an inspiration, a prompting form on high. And for a moment, though it was a brief one, he really did entertain the thought that there was some hope, that Menselas really did cling to what was left of his soul.

"If I'm to even the odds, you're right: I'm going to need a sword that can stand against *Amalantril*, and that blade I crafted as near to perfection as it's possible to get."

Hrothyr snorted in his mind.

"Something happened to *Amalantril* under my mother's influence. The sword was already corrupted. I think that happened during my time in the Abyssal Realms." Though he also feared the corruption may have initially come from him, another of the latencies that had been locked away inside him since birth. "The blade turned black when my mother wielded it."

"Void-steel?"

"I don't think so. My point is, I'm going to need something exceptional to compete with that sword." And not just in terms of the materials used. He needed something that would safeguard the remnants of his spirit—for that was what he thought the inspiration from on high meant. He needed a blade that was not only superior but one that *meant* something, a sword he could believe in.

"Wait here for me."

Hrothyr shrugged, as if to say, *It's not like I have a choice*, then went to examine the armor and the ingredients laid out on the floor.

Grabbing one of the empty sacks that had contained ingredients for the divine alloy, Anskar slipped out of the forge, just as the purple wings of night were starting to lift. Dawn was on its way, but he wondered if there was anything left of him that would feel the tide.

At first he considered shadow-stepping, or flying, as he'd done at Dorinah, but the thought that either might trigger an eruption of the fire within him made him baulk. Instead, he hurried through lightening streets that were slowly coming to life as Wintotashum's citizens rose from their beds. The few who saw him paid little heed; they were still bleary-eyed and had chores to perform. Only a street urchin reacted to his passing, when she looked out from the mouth of a rubbish-strewn alley and saw his eyes. With a yelp of fright, she was gone like a rat, back into the refuse.

As he passed along streets of brick houses toward the immensity of the city walls, he began to panic. Without sorcery, how would he ever get outside without being seen? The trade gates weren't open yet, and even if they were, people were routinely questioned going in and out, and by now the guards would have instructions to look out for him.

Before he could worry about that, he needed a horse, and so he made his way to the stables set within the surrounds of the Great Hall. As he suspected, there were patrols, and he couldn't risk being seen.

He continued on into the western quarter, where there was more land around the dwellings, and there were several smallholdings. Surely the peasants here made use of horses for tilling or deliveries of goods. All he found though were untethered oxen and a donkey.

The sun crested the walls behind him, which was when he realized he hadn't felt the dawn tide. That made him feel chastened, abandoned by the Five, despite what Hrothyr had said. But he had made a decision, he reminded himself. A sacrifice in the name of the greater good.

He was about to give up and return to the forge and make do with whatever Hrothyr could come up with by way of a sword when an old woman stepped from her cottage and crossed her arms over her chest.

"What do you want at this bloody time of day?" she said, noticing his eyes and merely grunting, as if black eyes were nothing unusual in this part of town.

"I'm looking for a horse," Anskar said.

"Lost it, did you?"

"To buy." He emptied his pockets, then realized he had no money.

The old woman raised an eyebrow.

"Borrow, then?" Anskar suggested.

"You was with them knights what came a while back," she said. "Saw you ride out onto the Iron Road. Saw you ride back in again."

"You recognize me?"

"Recognize the lot of you, I reckon. Never forget a face. That was a good thing you done. All of you. Them Tainted Cabal was a blight on the kingdom. Menselas did right by us in sending you."

"Praise be to…" Anskar started, but it sounded blasphemous coming from his lips.

The old woman smiled a crooked-toothed smile. "I got a horse you can borrow. Might need to feed him, should you find pasture on the way. Might need to water him, too."

She ushered him round the back of her property, where a single ribby horse was chained to a post, the ground around him a barren circle, lush grass just outside his reach.

"Why don't you move the post, or untether the horse?" Anskar asked, stroking the emaciated flanks, then rubbing his nose against the horse's muzzle.

"Thought about it," the old woman said with a shrug. "Would have gotten round to it one day."

Anskar stifled his rising anger.

"His hooves are still good," the old woman observed.

No thanks to you!

"Tell you what," the old woman said. "You can take him off my hands. Consider him a gift form Menselas, for what you and your lot did. Well, if you come by a little coin, or some bread, or beer—I do like my beer…"

"I'll find a way to repay you," Anskar said, as the woman unchained the horse, knowing he never would.

"His saddle and tack's in the shed," she said. "You'll have to get them and fit them yourself. Arthritis, see. Menselas has cursed me."

Anskar could imagine why.

"Thank you," he said as he headed for the ramshackle shed.

He led the horse away from the old woman's hovel and along cobbled streets, weaving his way north through the city, always in the shadow of the massive outer walls. He had all but made up his mind to risk a single shadow-step, taking the horse through with him, when he came in sight of the north gate that led on to the Iron Road. Oddly, for so early in the morning, the gate stood wide open, and the lone guard atop the parapet waved down at him. Nascent sunlight glinted from the man's helm, giving him a corona of gold.

"Can I go through?" Anskar called up, and the warrior gestured toward the open gate.

Anskar waved his thanks and led the horse out of the city. When he looked back to thank the man, the gate was starting to close, the lone warrior watching him, fully bathed now in sunlight. Anskar blinked against the glare, but then the sun passed behind a cloud, and the warrior was no longer there.

FORTY-THREE

PROGRESS WAS SLOW ALONG THE Iron Road at first. Anskar dared not ride the poor horse until it had eaten and drunk. He led it by the reins till they came to one of the kingdom's thousand lakes, this one merely a large pond a little off the road. He let the horse drink as long as it liked, then gave it free rein to chomp the long grasses, while he cupped water in his hands and refreshed himself.

After that, the horse nuzzled his face in gratitude and made no complaint when he mounted.

The sun shifted higher in the sky, taking the bite off the wintry air. Anskar began to feel relaxed and free, away from the curses that afflicted him and the battles that lay ahead. It was tempting to ride on forever and never look back; equally tempting to find some way to return to the isle of the avatars and to tell Ren and the others he was ready now, that he would embrace their otherworldly life of observation and guidance. But he knew he wasn't ready. He would never be ready, not now that he had pledged himself to another for the sake of revenge.

He reached Veranoth a little before dusk. The place was deserted, a ghost town. Presumably the survivors had moved away after the defeat of the Tainted Cabal. Too much devastation had been wrought here—at Anskar's hands, when he had incinerated the Soreshi enemy, cremating the fallen hero Borik in the process.

He tethered his horse to a rail outside a shuttered tavern and made his way to the ash-strewn ground that marked the site of his fatal eruption of sorcery.

The heat and the light had been intense. His sorcerous eruption had burned away flesh and reduced bone to dust, but it had not been the kind of heat Hrothyr was even now using to reshape metal and combine the ingredients for divine alloy. Nor, he suspected, could it rival the burgeoning power he now carried within him.

He sifted through the ash until he found a few shattered shards of the Sword of Supremacy, the blade that was above all blades, until it had broken deflecting a Soreshi sword.

Anskar wept at the thought of Borik's sacrifice, so pure compared with his own. So selfless.

Oh, Menselas, I'm sorry.

Borik had died that day, one of the three legendary heroes who had ridden to the Kingdom of the Thousand Lakes with the Order knights under Lanuc's command. And while Rindon and Nul had never blamed him for it, Anskar's hellfire sorcery had deprived the big man of a proper burial. There had been nothing left of him to take back home to Sansor.

The fragments of blade Anskar retrieved were tiny jagged pieces, nowhere near enough for what he had in mind. He ran his eyes over the ash-covered ground, knowing it would take days, if not weeks, to recover all the pieces. He shook his head. The old woman's gift of a horse, and the shining warrior who had permitted him to leave the city, had aroused a thready sort of hope within him, but already he felt an implacable weight dragging him back down.

Clutching the fragments in his hand, he drove his senses through the ground, down to the core of the world. When the earth-tide gushed up through his veins, he drove it through the fragments. The ash that coated the ground rippled, flecks of rust intermingled with it as glints of metal appeared on the surface and began to converge at Anskar's feet, leaving snake-trails in their wake.

As he stooped to collect the fragments of the broken sword into the sack he had brought from the forge, the sun finally set. He could hear the skirl of the dusk-tide wind, but it weaved around him as if he were too unclean to touch. He clenched his jaw and fought back a new wave of tears. How he felt was unimportant. He no longer mattered. Only Niyas. Only the promise he had made to Carred: to be there before the end.

He returned to his horse clutching his sack of jangling shards, then set off on the long ride back to Wintotashum.

The horse stumbled, righted himself, and continued on for a while, then stumbled again. His flanks were bathed in sweat despite the frigid night air. Anskar stopped for the umpteenth time, patting the horse's neck and allowing it time to chomp on the frost-covered grass beside the Iron Road. The horse needed to rest, but he suspected even a week-long sleep wouldn't change the outcome. The poor thing was dying from neglect and overwork. It was odd to Anskar how much he cared. He tried to get the horse to lie down, but it was either too proud or too concerned about the icy ground. Or maybe it lacked the strength to lower itself without simply collapsing in a heap.

Something howled off in the distance, and the horse whinnied in fear. Anskar turned a slow circle. He could see well enough in the dark:

the grayscale forms of trees and hills, the surface of a remote lake. But whatever had made that sound remained invisible to him. It conjured memories of the mulag who had stalked Lanuc's small force of knights on their way to Wintotashum only to attack out of the mist that followed them like a cloak. And he thought of dead-eyes and ghouls and the other horrors that prowled the wilds in search of flesh to eat. Tion had scared him half to death as a child, with stories designed to keep him within the safety of Branil's Burg's walls. If experience had taught Anskar one thing, it was that his old tutor was right.

He didn't remember sitting. Didn't remember lying down curled up like a baby, cloak wrapped around him for warmth. A hot breeze awakened him, only its feathery touch brushing his hair and skin, testing him out and finding him unworthy. As the dawn-tide passed him by, he blinked blearily at the pinkish sunlight cresting the horizon, then came fully awake with a start.

Now that the wind had passed, he was aware of how frozen his limbs were. His cloak was crusted with frost, and his teeth started to chatter. He stood, stamping pins and needles from his legs, cursing himself for being so weak, so careless, so late in returning to the forge.

And then he saw the horse.

It lay still beneath a blanket of frost.

Raise it, an insistent voice said in his head. *You have the power now. My gift to you. It will never tire again. Go on, welcome the earth-tide, and raise the beast.*

The putrid flow was already at his feet, though he had not yet summoned it. He wanted so much to open himself to the earth-tide, to bring back his horse the same way he had brought Hrothyr back, but when he looked down on the beast, he was overcome with sorrow. He couldn't understand why, but he again started to weep, and soon he was shuddering as he sobbed. Not for the horse, he told himself. *This is not about the horse!*

He crouched down, brushed frost from the horse's head, and looked it in its glassy, empty eye.

"Rest, my friend," he said, stroking its muzzle. "You've earned it."

The sack of blade fragments clinked as he slung it over his shoulder, and then Anskar set one foot in front of the other, determined to walk the rest of the way back to Wintotashum. In some indiscernible way, he felt he had earned a small, if ultimately futile, victory.

When he entered through Wintotashum's open trade gate late that afternoon, warriors stepped out from behind the walls and roughly grabbed him. There were six of them, and already more were coming from the buildings nearest the walls. One of the warriors snatched the sack of blade fragments from him. Anskar protested and tried to pull his arm free, but the warrior holding it twisted it painfully behind his back.

Sorcerous instincts thrashed wildly within him, but he quelled them with a thought. Again, the urge to use the earth-tide insinuated its way into his mind, and again he refused it. He could rot the flesh from their bones or turn the warriors into shambling dead, but they didn't deserve that. They were only doing their duty. He was the one in the wrong.

He took comfort from that thought. It was as close to confession as he had come since that last time with Gisela, when he had bared his soul and disgusted her, though she had disguised it well. He sighed with resignation. Perhaps it was better this way. Better to languish in the King's dungeons than to have to face his mother again. At least if he were locked up, he couldn't be accused of breaking his promise to Carred. Even if he got to Naphor in time, he was starting to doubt he'd be of any use. Talia was too powerful. He'd felt that firsthand. And all these wild hopes he had clutched at—better armor, a better sword— they amounted to nothing in the face of her sorcerous power, especially now he couldn't risk using his own.

He tried consoling himself that at last he was learning from his mistakes, coming to terms with the demands Menselas had made on him all his short life. But this was no valiant refusal of evil, no rejection of power in the name of the greater good. It was cowardice, he told himself. An excuse not to fight a battle he knew he could never win.

All tension drained away from him as the warriors marched him along the main street. A Warrior's priest came from an alley to join them, and he spotted several old men peering from the windows of houses—priests of the Elder.

So, the King's men were taking no chances. Probably the Elder's priests had some trick up their sleeve, some knowledge or artifact that could take him down if he used sorcery against them. Well, he would never know. They had him now, and they looked relieved at not having to fight.

He glanced at the warrior beside him when they passed the King's Hall without stopping. "You're not taking me to the dungeons?"

No answer. Not even a scowl.

The clang of a hammer on an anvil grew louder as they made their way through street after street, people lining the sides of the roads to watch the warriors and their captive pass. He should have felt shame, but all he felt was gratitude that, at last, it was over.

When they arrived at the forge, something was different. Not just the cordon of housecarls on guard outside. Anskar's sorcerous barrier was down. Odd. He had constructed it to last for days.

The warriors brought him through the open double doors and into the sweltering heat of the forge. A priest of the Elder clutching a black rod raised an eyebrow as the warriors forced Anskar to his knees. The Elder's priest gave Anskar a smug grin. Presumably he had been the one to dispel the dark-tide barrier around the forge. But then the old man stepped aside, and King Aelfyr himself loomed over Anskar. He was draped in an ermine trimmed cloak and had a woolen hat, not a crown, on his head. Aelfyr's cheeks were pinched, his pallor bloodless—but not in the manner of the dead. He had not been a well man during Anskar's previous stay in Wintotashum, and he looked less so now.

More royal housecarls were dotted about the interior, but no one detained Hrothyr from continuing his work as he hammered out a plate of armor on his anvil, then returned it to the forge with a pair of tongs. Hrothyr showed no sign of discomfort from being so near the forge's extreme heat. The dead, apparently, did not sweat. Nor did they ever tire or need sleep. Hrothyr had worked through the night, and there was no sign of him slowing down now.

And he had been busy, Anskar could see from the breastplate and helm, the gauntlets and greaves laid out on a worktop. They no longer resembled the pieces of armor he had brought from Branil's Burg: they were plainly formed, with no fluting or frills, merely sturdy and functional. And the metal they were forged from had changed color, from silver to a glossy black that seemed to ripple in the low light. If Anskar hadn't known better, he would have thought they had been lacquered, but they reminded him of his old vambrace under moonlight, though darker and much more menacing.

No piece was more disturbing than the great helm; it seemed to have been molded out of one piece of divine alloy blended with void-steel. It had no face plate or breathing holes, just the narrowest of eye slits to see out of. Hrothyr had read the Necromancer Tain's notes. He knew that not one inch of flesh could be exposed if the wearer were truly to ascend, but he also should have known that Anskar had no intention of ascending among the gods, if such a thing were really possible. He needed the armor for protection, and he needed to be able to see in order to fight. The helm was useless to him. Or was it? The glimmer of an idea began to form in his mind.

"Brother Jandros here has spoken with Hrothyr," King Aelfyr said, indicating the smug priest of the Elder with the black rod. "He has knowledge, shall we say, of the dead; knowledge we had hoped never to need. But one must always keep abreast of the lore of the enemy, don't you agree?"

"He's a necromancer?" Anskar asked.

Brother Jandros guffawed. "As if! A necromancer, my liege! Really!"

Aelfyr winced and put a hand to his stomach, momentarily closing his eyes in apparent pain. "Brother Jandros has studied keenly the ways of the necromancers of Niyas. Indeed, he has made it his life's work since the first break in at the Scriptorium, when your mother's minion stole the Necromancer Tain's notebook. I don't need to remind you about the second break in."

Anskar felt an overwhelming need to apologize—again, for he had done so when he had first been confronted by the King—but Aelfyr stopped him with an amused smile, a smile that said he was firmly in control and enjoying every moment of it.

"I have exchanged messages, also by sorcerous means"—several of the other Elder's priests present dipped their heads—"with the powers that truly rule in Sansor and throughout the mainland, the powers that even kings have no control over. It has been agreed to let you proceed. My housecarls will remain on duty outside the forge, as will Brother Jandros, whose rod, by the way, dispelled your unctuous barrier, so be warned. Make this armor you require, then leave my kingdom and never come back."

The King nodded at the warrior holding the sack of blade fragments, and the man handed it back to Anskar.

As Anskar stood on shaky legs, the King strode outside, followed by his warriors and priests.

Hrothyr turned away from the forge and spoke inside Anskar's head. "Did you find what you were looking for?"

Anskar carried the sack to a clear workbench and emptied the contents. The King's words discomfited him, but at the same time they had driven away his uncertainty, his fear. The powers behind the mainland? Did Aelfyr mean the Consortium? Or maybe they weren't the only powers working behind the scenes.

"Rusty shards," Hrothyr said.

"All that's left of the Sword of Supremacy. Reforge it, Hrothyr. Better than before. Stronger. Make it unbreakable. I assume there are enough components left?"

"A sword of divine alloy?" Hrothyr asked.

"All of them, even the void-steel. Put all your life's experience into it, Hrothyr, and the tirelessness of your death. Make this a sword you will be remembered by."

Anskar still didn't know why he felt compelled to include the rusty shards of Borik's sword. A blade with just the alloy and the steel was superior to any weapon he could imagine, and he had seen the original Sword of Supremacy shatter into a thousand pieces—clearly not indestructible, as Borik had claimed. And yet, he knew he wanted those shards as the basis for his new sword, as if they contained a power greater than void-steel, greater even than divine alloy.

"You don't exactly look filled with confidence," the dead smith said.

Anskar looked at him for a long while then dipped his eyes. "Because I'm not. Even with all this, Hrothyr... I don't know if I can beat her."

"Because your mother defeated you before?"

"Power like that... And how do you kill a being made from living metal? Even with this sword, how can I kill her?"

"You do the best you can. The void-steel in your armor will protect you from her dark-tide."

"And the dusk? The earth? If I use my own sorcery, Hrothyr, I might lose control. The world could burn."

"And you don't have any other options?"

Anskar grimaced then turned away.

"Even a bad option…" Hrothyr prompted.

"Once," Anskar said, "Brother Tion—my mentor at Branil's Burg—told me the tale of Menselas when he was a man."

"*If*," Hrothyr corrected. "Some say the idea that the Five began existence as a mere mortal is heretical."

"And maybe it is," Anskar said. Coming from Tion, that didn't seem at all unlikely. "But hear me out. I forget all the details, only that the world was in peril and the only way to save it was for Menselas to lose his life."

"The cost of sorcery, eh?" Hrothyr said. "Such things are not uncommon in the myths. It's a warning against growing too powerful."

"Maybe. But in dying, Menselas saved all things. Even himself, ultimately. He ascended. Became a god."

"And that's what you want, is it? To become a god?"

Anskar shook his head. "That's the last thing I want. My point is, we can try with the armor and the sword, and pray that they are enough. But just in case… I need a contingency. Remain here, and keep working. If I am permitted, I'll be back as soon as I can."

"Permitted by whom?"

"Just work, Hrothyr. Create for me armor that will transport me to the realm of the dead when I am fully enclosed in it. And be prepared to make adjustments when I return."

"What kind of adjustments?"

"That depends on the nature of the pact, and whether I still have anything left to bargain with."

"Be wary, Anskar," the smith said. "I still need you to return me to the glory of true death."

"I will," Anskar said. "Whatever it takes. And Hrothyr… Forgive me for bringing you back."

"We'll see about that," the smith said. "Once this is over."

If it's ever over, Anskar thought as he seated himself cross-legged on the floor. The clangor and bustle of Hrothyr working in the forge receded into the background as Anskar sent his senses inwards, then descended in the spirit into the bowels of Wiraya, where a dark and hungry god awaited.

FORTY-FOUR

ALMOST TWO DECADES SINCE THE fall of Naphor, and still the once massive curtain walls hadn't been fully rebuilt. Work had been started—several times, according to Carred's spies—but each time either lack of funds or complacency had brought the repairs to a halt. Now, as she surveyed the ancient capital from the top of Hallow Hill through the lens of a spyglass, she saw evidence of a recent return to the business of restoration. Scaffolding poked up above a section of wall that was still no more than half its previous height. Nothing but rubble had survived Queen Talia's devastating use of sorcery, and that same rubble, scorched black by unnatural flames of emerald, had been salvaged for the work of restoration.

She handed the spyglass back to Captain Ulvaes of Nagorn, whom Bennetavian had placed in charge of the remaining knights, those few dozen who had shown no signs of sickness as of yet. Ulvaes stank of sweat and rot—the latter coming from the diseased blood that speckled his cloak and armor. He was a brutish man, with a bull neck and barrel chest and legs too short for his torso. Probably he was immune to disease—it wouldn't dare to touch him. Not at all Carred's type, but now… He could have been Kovin reincarnated and she'd not have been interested. She doubted she would ever be interested again.

"No activity atop the walls," Ulvaes said.

"I know. Odd, don't you think?" She'd expected the makeshift wooden parapets to be packed with undead, but maybe there was a limit to what Talia could do, to the number of graves she could empty. Was it possible she had sent all her corpses against Quolith? Why? A gamble that she could end the war then and there? With such useless automatons? Unlikely. And besides, Talia must have known the mainlanders would send a fleet to retake Niyas. Then why send all her forces and leave Naphor undefended? The attack on Quolith might have bought Talia time, but time for what?

She glanced behind at the old tomb, half-expecting the necromancers to emerge. With any luck, she'd seen the last of them, thanks to Anskar's intervention back at her rooms. Even so, she kept thinking the dead-eyes would come back, that there would be shouts of alarm from her waiting army below, before the dead-eyes came racing up the hill. But there was nothing. Maybe because it was still day, though it seemed like dusk, given the choking smog that hung above Naphor and the throbbing black sphere that hovered a hundred feet or more above the city's central tower, its corona of dark filaments hissing and crackling as they flickered through the sky.

She put her eye back to the spyglass and focused once more on the city below. Beyond the lowest portion of wall, she could see partly built dwellings, corrals of horses, and fenced pasture with roaming livestock. The open ground between the scant new dwellings was pocked with dozens of craters, as if the knights had been digging for something. She offered Ulvaes the spyglass and bade him look.

"That's new," he said.

"Not your people, then?"

"Why would we dig holes in our own land? They look more like...
I don't know..."

"Disinterred graves?"

"My family were trappers back in Nagorn. I was going to say
burrows."

Carred shared a frown with him as she accepted the spyglass back
and took another look for herself. Burrows for what? Or did this have
something to do with sorcery? Perhaps Talia sought more direct access
to the earth-tide? Maybe. Carred didn't have a clue. All she knew was,
the holes made her uncomfortable.

But not as uncomfortable as what she picked out next.

Hundreds of people, dusky-skinned mainland settlers, Niyandrian
villagers, cloaked and armored knights who must have failed to get
away, were standing in a circle around the base of the tower. There
was something wrong about them. They remained rooted to the spot,
twitching and shivering in some grotesque parody of ecstasy. Her
vision through the lens grew blurry, then it gave way to a different kind
of *sight*, one she had buried since childhood, but which had started to
remerge, along with her repositories.

She could perceive dark tendrils now, connecting the people in
the circle, and others—filaments of black—that passed from their
foreheads into the base of the tower, pulsing with a rhythmic cadence.
High above the tower, the dark sun throbbed in time, its crown of
filaments flickering.

"I don't like this," Carred said, looking away and rubbing her eyes.

"Do you think it's a trap?" Vilintia asked.

"Of course it's a bloody trap," Ulvaes said, as he stood and collapsed
the spyglass.

"What worries me is *that*," Carred said, pointing at the sphere of
dark light that hovered above the central tower like a malignant sun.

"It looks bigger. Do you think it's bigger?"

Vilintia and Ulvaes shared looks that were difficult to read.

"Oh, for Theltek's sake, do stop competing, the pair of you," Carred said. "We're all in this together, and like it or not, we're allies now." At least for the time being. The gods alone knew what would happen when this was all over. Assuming any of them survived. It wasn't as if the mainlanders were going to turn up in their ships and simply hand Niyas back to Niyandrian rule. She almost didn't care. Anything was better than ceding control of the isle to Queen Talia. How had she not seen that before?

She began to head back down the hill to the waiting troops.

"So, what are we going to do?" Vilintia asked.

"Wait for the fleet, is my advice," Ulvaes said.

Carred shook her head. "My guts tell me if we don't put a stop to whatever Talia is doing with that black sphere in the sky, the arrival of the mainland fleet won't make a jot of difference."

"We attack, then?" Vilintia asked.

"We attack."

Carred had seen Griga do it when she previously mounted an attack on Naphor. The old sorceress had conjured a bank of fog that had obscured the advance of the fifty rebels and their cart of explosive black powder. But Griga had been moontouched, and an obsessive sorceress with it, dedicating her entire life to the secrets of the tides. Carred felt a fool for even trying such a feat. With her army of more than three thousand watching from the trees at the base of Hallow Hill, she grew self-conscious as she accessed her dusk-tide repository and uttered the cants she'd heard Griga use. She fumbled through the calculations she thought most appropriate, then shut her eyes and pictured what it was she wanted to manifest.

There was no bank of fog when she opened her eyes, just sparks dancing between her fingertips and the stink of acrid smoke. *No subtlety,* she thought to herself. She had none of the easy aptitude for sorcery Griga had shown, or Marith for that matter. Or Anskar. Yes, her wells had bloomed within her mind—she wanted to say they had been resurrected from the dead—but that didn't mean she had the knowledge and experience to use them effectively. All she could muster was lightning in her veins. She could hurl explosions. Nothing creative, nothing really useful except in a fight, and even then, would she have any control?

"What is it you're trying to do?" an old Niyandrian man asked as he stepped away from the trees, no trace of condescension in his tone. He watched her with moist eyes, as if he could see inside her. As if he understood.

Carred glanced at Vilintia, who nodded that it was all right. Maybe she knew the man. Vilintia had served in the Niyandrian army long before the battle of Naphor. Perhaps he had, too.

Carred could feel the strength of the old man's repositories, and not for the first time cursed herself for a fool. All Niyandrians were sorcerers to some extent, and until recently, she was the least among them in that respect. Why had she not thought to ask among her people? Pride? She didn't think so. Pride had never been her thing. Maybe, she conceded, it was because in the past she'd had Griga and Maggow, and now they were both dead. Or maybe she just wanted to be like Marith.

She noticed several of the Order knights murmuring to one another as she took the old man aside and told him what Griga had done, and how she wanted to take every precaution when they advanced on the city. He frowned as he nodded, then returned to the trees to consult with two young women, who might have been his daughters.

The three approached Carred.

"Join hands with us," the old man said. "That way they'll assume you're the one directing the sorcery."

"That's not what I want," Carred objected.

"But perhaps it is what the army needs."

Carred sighed. "You're a veteran, aren't you?"

The man gave her a gap-toothed grin. "Name's Hinrod, and yes, I'm a veteran, but not of Naphor. I was already too old to fight then."

"But not now?"

"Sometimes we don't have the luxury of hiding behind our infirmities," he said, and both young women smiled at him. "You've fought for our freedoms since the last war with the mainlanders. When the people at last rallied to your side, I couldn't stay behind and do nothing. I want my girls to live in a Niyas ruled by Niyandrians."

"But not by Queen Talia?"

Hinrod turned his head aside and spat out a wad of phlegm. "That woman ceased to be Niyandrian a very long time ago."

The old man waggled his fingers, and so Carred took his hand. One of the daughters took her other hand, and the four formed a circle.

"Let me guide you in the cants and calculations," Hinrod whispered in her ear. "Just shut your eyes and open your *sight* so you can follow what I do."

The hands clutching hers grew warm and started to tingle. Hinrod began to chant, and his daughters added their own harmonies, while Carred merely moved her lips as if she knew the words. Heat fizzed through her veins then burned within her dusk-tide repository. A stream of symbols flashed across her inner vision—letters, numbers, arcane runes; the same seven symbols permutating every which way until they became a jumbled blur that dissolved into a gray and heavy mist.

And the mist wasn't just within her mind; when she opened her eyes, it hung like a thick and obscuring blanket between her army and the city walls.

Oddly, she could still make them out in glittery lines of silver.

"So we can see where we're going," one of the daughters said, in a nasally voice that made it sound as though she had a cold.

"You're not coming with us," Carred said.

The girl released her hand and drew a curved blade from her belt, which was when Carred saw she was wearing mail beneath her dress.

"We're all coming," Hinrod said.

"For Niyas," the second daughter said, and she now held aloft a short sword.

Carred shrugged.

Several of the Order knights touched four fingers and a thumb to their chests in disapproval of the sorcery that now contained them.

"Pass the word," she said to Vilintia. "Advance."

Carred's heart thundered in her ears as they crossed the open space between Hallow Hill and the city walls. At any moment she expected figures to appear on the parapet, limned in the same sorcerous glow that outlined the walls. But there was nothing, only the dark forms of the army all around her, the only sound the tread of their booted feet, the clink of armor, and the creak of leather. Above, an oppressive weight pressed down on them; it had to be the black sun. The closer they came to the walls, the more the atmosphere grew pregnant, as if at any moment the sky might fall.

"Halt," she passed through the ranks as she came within yards of the main gates. They were bound to be guarded, if not warded with sorcery. She glanced at Hinrod.

"Think you can open a breach in the walls?" she asked, and the old man consulted with his daughters.

"If we drop the fog, maybe," he said.

"Drop it."

The sorcery had gotten them close enough, and in doing so had served its purpose.

Hinrod began a cant, while his daughters fumbled with the cords that hung from their belts, strung with beads and dangling bird feathers—fetishes to aid their sorcerous calculations. Most Niyandrians never used such charms; but then again, most Niyandrians barely scraped the surface of their innate abilities.

Hinrod extended a hand toward the city, and though she saw nothing, Carred felt the impact of compressed dark-tide essence as it impacted a section of the wall. Dust flew, and a few chips of rock dropped away, but the damage was negligible.

The old man shot an apologetic look at Carred and tried again. This time there was even less of an effect. There were tears in the eyes of both daughters, and Hinrod hung his head in shame.

"I'm sorry," he said. "I thought together we might effect a breach, but I'm no moontouched, and the girls are still learning."

Vilintia gave Carred a pained look.

"I'll try," Carred said. "What I lack in subtlety and knowledge, I suspect I make up for in anger." Then, affording Hinrod and his daughters the same consideration they had shown her, she said, "Try again, and I'll lend a hand."

Hinrod was about to protest, then saw what she was doing and smiled his thanks. This time, when he extended his hand, Carred reached into her dusk-tide repository and unleashed its vitriolic flow. Hinrod stiffened as the tide rushed into him, then a bolt of lightning slammed into the wall, throwing up rocks and plumes of dust.

"So we're abandoning stealth, then?" Vilintia said.

"Fine by me," Ulvaes said. The knight was standing right behind Carred, breathing down her neck, as if he couldn't wait to get started with the cut and thrust of battle.

Problem was, when the dust settled, Carred had only made the narrowest of gaps in the wall, a fissure no more than six inches across and a couple of feet high.

"Bugger," she said. She doubted she had enough dusk-tide essence to try again.

"Not a problem," Ulvaes said. "You've done the brunt of the work. Just need to widen the breach. Cortur, think you can do it?"

A lanky knight who had somehow managed to keep his cloak pristine slunk forward, stroking his wisp of a beard. He was young but had the bearing of an eighty-year-old. He seemed more suited to life as a librarian, or a priest of the Elder, than a knight.

"Ward fist, sir?"

"You read my mind, Cortur."

The young knight's ward sphere winked on around him, a silver island in the gloom. It flowed in front of him, compacting into a solid orb of force that streaked forward and smashed into the wall. This time, huge chunks of masonry burst apart, and when the debris stopped falling, there was a breach wide enough for a person to slip through.

Cortur slumped to his knees, gasping for breath.

"Good lad," Ulvaes said, laying a hand on the young man's shoulder. "Wait back here till you recover. Knights, with me."

"And take all the glory?" Vilintia asked.

Ulvaes grinned. "It's what we do."

"Idiot," Vilintia said in Niyandrian. The way Ulvaes raised his eyebrows, he must have picked up the local language during his time on Niyas.

"It's not just about glory," Ulvaes said. "Not at all about it, in fact. It's just… we were garrisoned here. We know the layout inside."

"Be my guest," Carred said, holding up a hand to tell Vilintia to let it go.

Motioning for his knights to follow him, Ulvaes went first into the gap. His front leg had barely crossed the threshold when he cried out and tried to back up. Emerald motes erupted all around him, steam pluming from his garments and skin wherever they touched. Ulvaes craned his neck to look back at Carred, his eyes wide with terror. He convulsed, reached a hand toward her, and then his entire body blazed with emerald light and collapsed in on itself. When the glare died down, there was nothing left of Ulvaes, not even his sword, his armor… nothing.

Overhead, the black sun throbbed and expanded. Murmurs passed among the Niyandrians and knights behind her as a deep shadow settled across the sky, and the air grew drastically colder.

And still there was no movement through the gap; nothing atop the walls. All eerily quiet. It would have been less stressful if Talia actually did something. All this anticipation was almost worse than a sorcerous attack or the advance of an army of corpses.

As Carred approached the breach in the wall, Hinrod laid a restraining hand on her arm.

"It's all right, I'm not completely stupid," Carred said. "I just want another look."

She made sure to keep a few feet from the opening, and let her eyes roam across the pitted ground the other side. Ulvaes had been right: the holes really did look like burrows. But burrows for what? Not large rabbits, that was certain.

She turned her attention to the base of the tower, where the circle of Niyandrians and knights twitched and shivered, flickering black filaments connecting them one to another and passing from the forehead of each into the tower itself.

She was about to turn away, not knowing in the slightest what she should do next, when she thought she recognized one of the convulsing knights standing around the base of the tower.

"Is that…?" she said, stepping back so that Vilintia could see.

"Ulvaes," Vilintia breathed.

Carred was startled by shouts that went up from the back ranks of the warriors. She met Vilintia's eyes. "Here we go," she mouthed.

Vilintia mouthed back, "Ambush?"

As Carred move in the direction of the commotion, the ranks of warriors and knights opened up before her, until she could see four figures approaching through the gloom.

"With me," she told Vilintia. "And you," she said to Hinrod. Because she feared it could be the necromancers. But four of them?

Under the dark glare of the sphere above the tower, the daylight had turned crepuscular, making it hard to see the approaching figures clearly at first. She could make out cloaks, but not much else. If they had weapons, they were not drawn.

"One of them is a sorcerer of some power," Hinrod whispered. "A moontouched, I think. Maybe more than that…"

"More than moontouched?" Carred asked.

"I can't explain. I've never felt anything like this."

"Be wary," Vilintia said, then gave an apologetic grimace. "I didn't really need to say that, did I?"

Warriors drew weapons as Carred stood among the front rank and waited.

It was a woman in the lead, she could see now, and as the four grew closer, she could make out the red skin and dark hair of a Niyandrian. But that did nothing to relax her. The woman, like the others, was dressed in a tattered once-white cloak, the rest of their Order clothing frayed and besmirched with grime.

"You!" Carred said, recognizing the woman who had caused so much trouble in the battle at Dorinah.

"Murderous cow," Vilintia said, drawing her sword.

One of the three men with the woman—they were all dusky-skinned mainlanders—stepped forward, hands held up placatingly. He was fat for a knight, with mutton chop whiskers flanking his jowls and a big bushy mustache covering his mouth.

"Ladies, ladies," he said, "this pulchritudinous scion of Niyas is

Sareya of Branil's Burg. These other scallywags are Nul, of some repute, and the illustrious Eldrid DeVantte, formerly stationed here at Naphor. For my sins, I am somewhat notorious, nay, even famous, as—"

"Rindon!" several of the knights among Carred's troops said at the same time. Awestruck looks passed among them, and even some of the Niyandrians seemed familiar with the name.

"Lads! Lassies!" Rindon declaimed, acknowledging them with the most ostentatious bow Carred had ever seen.

Of course, she recognized Eldrid, her bloody… she thought the word was "nemesis." He acknowledged her with a salute, the smug bastard.

"Knights of the Order of Eternal Vigilance alongside Niyandrian rebels?" Nul said. "Times must be tough."

"Tougher than you'd believe," Carred said. "You've not heard the news?"

"Alas, we've been out of town," Rindon said.

A few of the knights with Carred's force broke ranks and went to greet Eldrid. They were more deferential around Rindon and Nul, admiring them as if they were heroes of legend.

Sareya left the group and approached Carred. At first, the young woman couldn't meet Carred's eyes, as if she were ashamed. When she finally did, it was only fleetingly, and then her gaze flicked over the massed ranks behind.

"Is Anskar with you?"

Rindon and Nul waved off their admirers. They wanted to hear this. Eldrid, though, continued to talk with a handful of knights, who gestured towards the black sphere hanging above the city.

"Why are you here?" Vilintia countered, ever bellicose.

Rindon disarmed her with a toothy grin, and she did nothing when he laid a hand on her shoulder and spoke as though they were old friends. "We were…" He paused to cough into his fist. "We happened to be in the vicinity, when we saw whatever that is up in the sky."

Carred glanced at the pulsating black sphere above the tower then looked immediately away. It made her head throb and caused her innards to squirm. "You know what it is?"

"Well, it's sorcery," Nul said.

"You don't say. But what's it for?"

The two knights looked to Sareya. By way of response, she shuddered then shrugged. "All I can say for sure is that it's woven from the dark-tide, but that's not a tide I have much experience with. And there's something else… a taint."

"Earth-tide, no doubt," Carred said. She described the circle of corpse-like people arrayed around the base of the tower, each connected by filaments of black.

"Can we see?" Sareya asked.

"Not until you explain exactly how you come to be here," Carred said, "and why. I thought you would have fled with the others to the mainland."

"I did go to the mainland," Sareya said. "To Sansor."

"And she was sent back," Nul explained. "With us."

"Actually, it was more than us," Rindon said. "But before we could set sail…"

Sareya silenced him with a sharp look.

"You came by ship from Sansor?" Vilintia asked.

Rindon grimaced. "In a roundabout sort of way."

"And there are more than the four of you?"

"There might have been," Rindon said, "if we'd not mislaid our ship and its crew."

"Mislaid?" Carred said.

Again, Sareya flashed him a warning look.

"Did you sail with a mainland fleet?" Vilintia asked. "How many ships? How many knights?"

"Oh, they've not arrived yet," Rindon said. "Do you think they'll be underway by now?"

"How should I know?" Eldrid said. "Until you arrived, I'd sat in a prison cell for weeks on end."

"The Order imprisoned you?" Carred said.

"You'd like that, wouldn't you?" Eldrid said. "But no, not the Order." When Sareya tried to stop him from saying more, Eldrid held up a hand. "I refuse to continue with this charade. I'm told Queen Talia has returned, though Menselas alone knows how."

"You're well informed," Carred said.

"Where is Anskar?" Eldrid asked.

"Please tell me he hasn't joined forces with his mother," Sareya said.

"Are you really so stupid?" Carred said. "She tried to kill him, and Theltek alone knows how many of her own people she's turned into walking corpses. We faced an army of the dead at Quolith, and then this… this thing appeared in the sky. This is why there are knights among us. We have a common foe, and my suspicion is, if we wait for your fleet to arrive, it'll be too late. Whatever that aberration is in the sky, I just know it's not going to end well."

"You still haven't told us where Anskar is," Sareya said.

Eldrid rolled his eyes and looked about to say something, but Rindon waved him to silence.

"Not here," Carred said. "Which is all I'm prepared to say."

"Who among the knights commands?" Eldrid asked.

"Originally, Seneschal Bennetavian," Carred said, "but he fell ill at Quolith and has remained behind with the rest of the sick—some kind of contagion they picked up from the undead. And before you ask: no, none of my people caught it. The illness seems to target mainlanders. Those still with us show no symptoms… yet."

"And now?" Eldrid pressed. "If Bennetavian stayed behind, who leads?"

"Briefly, it was Captain Ulvaes…"

Eldrid barely suppressed a scowl, as if he were none too impressed.

Then he raised an eyebrow. "Briefly?"

She told him what had happened.

"A dusk-tide ward?" Sareya said. "If only I'd been here, I could have warned him… If I'd thought to detect it."

"You could have disarmed it?" Carred asked.

"I…"

Before Sareya could answer, Eldrid said, "So, who is next in command?" His eyes roved the knights who remained in Carred's army. At length, one of the men he had earlier been speaking with stepped forward. "You are the senior ranking officer, sir. You should take command."

Eldrid nodded. "So, General Selenas," he said, "what is your plan?"

"Well, it's a bit vague, after what happened to Ulvaes. But essentially, get inside the walls, storm the tower, and take out Queen Talia, hopefully before that dark ball in the sky does whatever it's supposed to do."

"And you can do that?" Eldrid said. "You can kill the Necromancer Queen?"

"Probably not… without Anskar. And even then it might not be enough. I was hoping he'd be here by now."

"And we can't wait for him?" Rindon said, eyeing the black sun nervously.

"Change of plan," Eldrid said.

"Oh?" Nul and Rindon said at the same time.

"We go in," Eldrid said. "All of us, together."

"What about Anskar?" Sareya asked.

"If he turns up… We'll deal with that situation when it arises."

"Deal with what situation?" Carred said.

"Can you get us inside?" Eldrid asked Sareya.

She hesitated before replying, emotions warring across her face. "Depends on exactly what's keeping us out."

Carred turned her palm up and gestured to the gap in the wall. "See for yourself."

Sareya approached the wall, Rindon, Nul, and Eldrid following so that they could see. A couple of feet from the gap, she stopped and raised her hand. "You'd have thought one of my fellow Niyandrians would have sensed this," she said, glancing at Hinrod and his daughters, then letting her eyes rove over the massed warriors and finally settling on Carred. "There's a dusk-tide ward around the entire city, following the contours of the walls."

"We're not all moontouched," Vilintia said with some bitterness.

"No," Sareya said. "I don't suppose you are. But the power required for a ward on such a scale… it's staggering. I doubt even a moontouched could do this. I know I couldn't."

"You looked accomplished enough at Dorinah," Carred said. "Seeing as Anskar's not arrived, maybe you should go up against Talia."

"I…" Sareya stumbled over her words. "I can't."

"Don't be so defeatist, lassie," Rindon said. "You will not face the Necromancer Queen alone."

"And you've defeated many necromancer queens, have you?" Vilintia said.

"Several," Rindon said with a wink. "And bedded a fair few, too."

"You're not the only one," Vilintia muttered to Carred, earning herself a dark look.

Sareya was back to peering through the gap. "There are dark filaments passing between those people around the base of the tower," she said.

"I know," Carred said.

"They're powering whatever that dark sphere is above the tower, and causing it to grow."

"Not by choice, either," Carred said, pointing out Ulvaes, twitching and shivering along with the rest of the cadavers. "That one died when he entered the breach in the wall. He reappeared there."

Sareya grimaced. She looked younger, somehow—her actual

age, rather than the image of maturity and authority she had been projecting. But there was a weight upon her, etched into her brow and reflected in her eyes. Again, Carred wanted to know the real reason for her coming here. Why had she and the others come ahead of the mainland fleet? To help, or something else?

"Can you dispel the ward?" Carred asked.

"Maybe. Perhaps. I don't know. The ward has the characteristics of dusk-tide sorcery, but it is no mere dusk-tide repository that powers it. It's fueled by another source. But even if I could dispel the ward, I can't. I mustn't."

"Do please translate," Vilintia said.

"I can't use my sorcery."

"Because of your vows to Menselas?" Carred asked. "That didn't stop you before."

"If I may," one of Hindon's daughters said, "while you have been talking, my sister and I have been scrying. This Sareya is right: the ward is dusk-tide, but it is powered by the dark. And we think we know how."

"The people at the base of the tower?" Carred said.

"All we would need is a piece of void-steel…" Hindon said, putting his arms around his daughters and kissing each on the forehead.

"I have void-steel," Carred said, and shrugged at the frowns she received.

"Not much good if you can't get to the tower," Sareya said. "If what you say is correct," she said to Hindon's daughters, "then the void-steel would have to come into contact with those people around the base."

"Not the people," Hindon said. "They are aberrations of the earth-tide. The filaments that connect them. Sever them—I do not know how many—and…"

"And the ward around the city would lose its power," Carred finished for him.

"And maybe even the dark sphere in the sky," Sareya said.

Carred's heart was thumping against her ribcage. So near, but still so far. "Back to square one, then. How in Theltek's name do we get inside?"

"I have an idea," Nul said.

Rindon covered his face with his hands. "Here we go…"

"Seriously," Nul said, "I think it might work."

He explained to Carred what he had in mind, and she looked to Hindon for an opinion. The old Niyandrian merely shrugged.

"You've had worse plans," Rindon said. "Shame Borik isn't still with us. Three ward spheres are better than two."

"I'll not ask anyone else to risk it," Nul said. "Not even you, Eldrid. Should anything go wrong, the knights here need you. You are necessary, whereas Rindon and I…" He gave a self-effacing smile. "We're heroes." He held out his hand to Carred.

"What's that for?" she asked.

"The void-steel."

"Oh, no," Carred said. The thought of loaning her sword to anyone sent waves of panic through her. It was *her* power, her only power, her only chance of avenging Marith's death. But she didn't need them to know that. "No one else gets to take risks unless I share them." It was the best she could come up with.

"As I said to Eldrid," Nul started, "I'll not risk anyone else."

"I wasn't asking permission," Carred said. "I may not be a bloody hero, but it's about time I started acting like one."

Rindon grinned. "Always room for another hero. Nul, you go first. Young lady, place your hands on his shoulders and keep as close as you can—skin to skin, unless of course you're prudish about such proximity?"

"As if!" Carred said as she rested her hands on Nul's shoulders. "Young lady?"

"I, of course," Rindon said, pressing up behind her, "will provide the second slice of bread for the sandwich."

"Ready?" Nul asked.

"Ready," Rindon replied.

In perfect synchrony, silver ward spheres sprang up around each knight, then expanded till they overlapped, forming a single, denser sphere, with Carred, Rindon, and Nul within.

"Close your eyes and wish for luck," Nul said as the trio started into the breach, pressed so tightly together Carred could smell stale sweat, not to mention Rindon's beer breath on the back of her neck.

Almost at once, emerald light flared behind Carred's eyelids. She opened her eyes to see green iridescence surrounding the silver ward sphere, flashing and sparking where it touched. It seemed an angry conflagration, raging and crashing against the ward sphere, trying to break in. Nul's progress into the gap slowed to a torpid crawl, and Carred felt a crushing weight pressing in all around her. She could hardly breathe. Invisible forces pounded at her flesh and bones; made her want to sink to her knees. Teeth grinding with the effort, she remained standing, but perhaps only because Rindon now held her around the waist, refusing to let her fall. Around them, the ward sphere started to buckle.

"Hurry!" Rindon growled.

"Can't..." Nul shot back. "Can't move. The pressure..."

The ward sagged, till it barely covered the three of them. The emerald blaze was mere inches from their skin.

Suddenly, Carred was inside herself, swimming within a sea of golden light. Then, before she knew what she was doing, she burst a dam she had not known was there, and the full force of her dawn-tide repository flooded into the ailing ward sphere, forcing it outwards, expanding it and driving the emerald glare back.

With a desperate roar, Nul lunged forward, and as he reached the threshold, he yelled, "Dive!"

All three dived at once, hitting the grassy ground inside the walls just as the ward sphere collapsed and emerald light rushed in to fill the breach in the wall they had just passed through. It wavered there for a moment, and then was gone.

The grass beneath Carred's back felt as hard and sharp as shards of glass, its scent strong and heady and threatening to drive her delirious. Not just the grass, either: she was aware of the weight of her body as if it were a new thing. Her breaths came deep, swelling her belly then her chest. With each inhalation, she seemed to grow. But it was a readjustment, nothing more; a reset to normal after transitioning through the ward around the city. Theltek, what sorceries had Talia learned in death? The only wonder was that the three of them had survived, and were not now standing in the ring of shivering corpses around the foot of the tower.

Nul stood over her and helped her to her feet, and she nodded her thanks.

Rindon still lay flat on his back, his big belly rising and falling as he sucked in air and found his bearings. Carred lent him a hand and hauled him up.

"Thank you, my dear," he said. "That little experience has left me quite discombobulated."

"If you hadn't reinforced our ward sphere…" Nul said.

He didn't need to complete the sentence. They all knew how close it had been.

Carred sent her senses inward and did a quick check. Her dawn tide repository was drained dry. Not the dusk, though. The dusk-tide repository was like a vat of acid waiting to be unleashed.

When she looked back through the gap in the wall, she could see Hindon peering through from the other side, Vilintia and Eldrid DeVantte behind him. The old man stepped back and threw a divot of earth into the breach. Emerald flared. There was a shower of sparks, and the divot vanished. So, the ward around Naphor was still intact.

She turned towards the great tower at the center of the enclave, not really expecting to be able to see whether or not the divot of earth reappeared—not from this distance.

Still the circle of people—dozens of them—encircled the tower's base, connected by black threads of sorcery as they convulsed.

Carred glanced at her companions and then drew her sword, advancing warily along the scorched remnants of the once-mighty central concourse toward the tower. It was odd: being here in Naphor didn't feel in the least like a homecoming. It had been eighteen years, but even so, she should have felt something. But then, the city she knew had been devastated. Save for the blackened stones of the road and the foundations of a few ancient buildings, and despite the reclaimed materials, everything within the reconstructed walls was new, even the tower. And it showed. Save for the tower, which had been built by enslaved Niyandrians, the rest of the buildings had a very temporary feel. Mainlander immigrants had probably done the best they could, felling trees and constructing dwellings, stables, and barracks that would have struck the local Niyandrians as primitive in the extreme. Not that the mainland didn't have its share of stonemasons and architects; it was just that they hadn't enticed any to come to Niyas. That was a good thing, she thought. Maybe they weren't planning on staying for good. She wished! With Talia's coming, Niyas was even more divided, and that much easier to subjugate. She knew that, just as she knew she was now treating with the enemy. But what choice did she have? It was either work with the mainlanders and hope for the best, or submit to Talia. Since the Queen's return from death, there were few indications that she would be a benevolent ruler.

Carred kept checking over her shoulder to make sure Rindon and Nul were still with her. The knights were uncharacteristically quiet, as if the atmosphere of this place affected them as much as it did her. The log cabins, the ramshackle stores, even the barracks ground seemed deserted. There were a few sorry-looking horses watching them as they passed the stable yard, but nothing else. The white cloaks among the dead surrounding the tower told her they were knights of the Order garrison at Naphor, but there were only a few dozen of them. Where were the rest? Dead? But then where were the bodies? Some had escaped to Quolith, but there must have been a hundred or more missing.

She glanced nervously at the holes that dotted the ground in between the buildings. She half-expected to see the corpses of knights lying in them, waiting to be covered with soil, but there was nothing. Each crater was a deep depression, with fresh soil heaped around the edges.

As they came within twenty yards of the tower, the stench from the spasming corpses was overpowering, and Carred had to cover her mouth and nose with a hand. Rindon produced a metal flask, unscrewed the lid, and took a swig. Nul declined when Rindon offered it to him, and Carred waved the flask away. She needed to do what she had to do before her nerve failed, and no amount of alcohol was going to strengthen her resolve.

"On second thought," she said from behind her hand. She grabbed the flask and took a long pull. "Pearlescent brandy? Who've you been hobnobbing with?"

"Friends in high places, my dear," Rindon said, accepting the flask back. "As well as friends in low."

"Stay here," she said as she started toward the base of the tower.

"A hero does not—" Rindon started.

"Please. I don't know what's about to happen, and there's no point risking all of us."

Nul put a hand on Rindon's shoulder. "We'll watch your back."

Still covering her nose and mouth against the stench—for all the good it did—Carred edged toward the circle of corpses. Their backs were to her as they faced the tower, swaying and twitching.

Now that she was closer, Carred could see that the inky threads of sorcery that connected the corpses and ran from them to the tower like the spokes of a wheel pulsed with dark light, and that each time they pulsed, the corpses jerked.

Her scalp started to prickle as she came beneath the corona of the black sun high above, and a deep drone thrummed though her skull.

As she drew within arm's length of the corpses, they paid her no heed. She looked away as maggots flopped from the ear of a convulsing Niyandrian woman. And then she saw that all the corpses had wounds infested with maggots, their wriggling adding to the grisly animation. Bodily fluids stained legs and pants, the hem of cloaks, and pooled on the ground. Carred's guts hit her throat and she grimaced as she swallowed bile.

Through the twitching bodies, she could see the tower's door: thick planks of oak reinforced with iron. Like the stonework, it was of Niyandrian build. It would not be easy to break down or force open.

She raised her sword, bringing its void-steel enhanced blade within a hair's breadth of one of the flickering black filaments that connected the corpses.

And hesitated.

What if her action alerted Talia—presumably within the tower? What if it triggered some catastrophic response?

She glanced back at the breach in the city walls. Anskar hadn't come. They had agreed on no set time, but he had given the impression—the reassurance—that he would be here. Had he been delayed? Changed his mind? What if something had happened to him? Theltek, what if Talia had somehow gotten to him, persuaded him his best hope was to join her? Given the defeat he had suffered at her hands, the humiliation, he might agree.

She met Rindon's eyes, then Nul's, not as reassured by the presence of these two heroes of the Order of Eternal Vigilance as she would have liked. It only made matters worse that her army remained outside the walls, kept from entering by whatever unholy ward Talia had put in place.

Even more reason to get a move on! Wars weren't won by second guessing yourself, by being afraid of taking the right action—the only action available to her, for she could think of no other.

She touched her sword to the black filament, and the filament dissolved in a shower of dark motes. The two shuddering corpses it had connected collapsed to the ground, desiccated and unmoving. The shadow thrown by the black orb above wavered, and when she looked up, the dark sphere itself juddered.

Rindon was beside her now. He raised an eyebrow, then nodded for her to continue.

Carred severed another filament , then another. Four more corpses fell, and in the sky, the black sun gyred chaotically, its fuliginous corona starting to retract.

"Keep going," Nul said. "A few more filaments, and—"

He was cut off by yells and cries, hoots and jeers.

Carred turned, a knight on either side of her.

"We should have checked the buildings," Rindon grumbled.

All across the enclave, doors crashed open, and dozens of red-skinned men and women charged, froth spilling from screaming mouths, eyes feral and bright with madness. And still more came, shrieking as they emerged from the barracks, the barns, the warehouses, until there were hundreds, a sea of raving Niyandrians.

FORTY-FIVE

IT WAS ALL MOVING SO fast, and events were getting away from her. Sareya no longer knew what she was doing, why she was here, whose side she was on. Was Anskar really a risk to Wiraya, and she the person best placed to stop him? Hopefully, he wouldn't show, and she wouldn't have to decide.

The black sun wobbled above the tower, casting long, wavering shadows.

"It's working," the old Niyandrian sorcerer said, peering through the breach in the wall. He thrust his arm into the gap. Nothing happened. He glanced back at Eldrid and grinned a gap-toothed grin. "The ward is down."

Sareya looked back towards Hallow Hill, as if she expected to see Anskar atop the summit. And there *was* something there—the dark forms of two watchers on the brow of the hill. She sensed an outflow of putrid essence, as if they felt her eyes on them. Feelers of awareness probed her mind, but before she could shut them out, before she could use powers that had been forbidden her, the feelers recoiled as if they had touched fire. Upon the hill, the dark forms dissolved into the darkling sky. But they had left a taint. Necromancers. They had been merely curious, waiting to see what happened below. She had the sense they would not soon be back, that they were diminished somehow, but that they were patient, and planned and schemed in terms of centuries, not months and years.

Even amid the massed ranks of Carred Selenas's army, Sareya felt suddenly alone and insignificant, her life as ephemeral as that of a mayfly compared with the things that haunted the ancient ruins, creatures who, she suspected, steered the course of history every bit as much as the gods.

She came crashing back to her senses when a thunderous roar went up all around her, and she was jostled by the press of bodies. Then she was stumbling, trying to keep on her feet, as a sea of Niyandrians flowed around her, interspersed here and there with the white cloak of an Order knight. The army surged toward the breach in the wall. She saw Eldrid shove the old sorcerer aside and duck into the gap. The lean, gray-haired Niyandrian commander went next, a woman whose hard body and grim visage belied her years—not unlike Monash.

And then the front ranks were funneling through the opening two at a time, and she was swept along with them. She felt vulnerable without her sorcery as she passed through the breach, but there was no chance of backing up, not with the weight of thousands behind.

On the other side, there was fierce fighting up ahead. Hundreds of wild Niyandrians converged on the base of the tower. She couldn't see Carred through the horde, only twin ward spheres—presumably Rindon and Nul. The sight of them fired her courage. She hadn't known the two men long, but she had seen enough, owed them enough, to know she could never stand idly by and watch them die.

Drawing her sword, she joined her voice to the Niyandrian battle cry that ripped through the air, and charged.

As Eldrid and the vanguard slammed into the enemy, berserk Niyandrians turned away from Rindon and Nul—not to defend themselves, for they showed no defense, but to roar and spit and curse at this new foe. Swords clashed in a fearsome din. Sparks flew. Niyandrian dusk-tide sorcery fizzed and scorched, sending up plumes of smoke and the stench of roasting flesh—all from Carred's force. The raging Niyandrians they faced seemed incapable of sorcery. They were little more than beasts.

Sareya darted into a gap, catching an enemy blade on her sword before it could eviscerate a Niyandrian. She side-stepped and thrust, taking the aggressor in the chest. But still the man raged on, foaming at the mouth. She ripped her blade free just in time to parry his overhead hack, then reversed her blade, slicing it across his throat. The man's eyes were bright with fury as he tried to lunge for her, blood spurting from his opened jugular. And then he fell.

It was chaos all around her. Swords, axes, fists, and clubs came at her, glanced from her blade, slit her cloak, thumped into her arms. Behind, she could hear the pound of boots as more of Carred's warriors rushed into the fray. They massively outnumbered the enemy, but the ravers just didn't know when to die.

She glimpsed Eldrid thrashing about with his sword, warded by a silver sphere. The gray-haired woman had carved her way to the front, visible for a moment between the ward spheres of Rindon and Nul. And then she saw Carred Selenas, battling furiously to stay alive, on the inside of the circle of shivering dead. Three ravers slashed and hacked at her, and Carred showed deft defense, moving laterally, blocking with her dark metal sword, flinging scorching sparks from her free hand— not enough to kill, but enough to distract. Why was she holding back?

Sareya redoubled her own efforts, powering forward, skewering a raging woman then whipping her blade free and hacking into the woman's neck. Suddenly she was in the thick of it, bodies pressing on every side, the clangor of blades deafening. She blocked a thrust, swayed aside from a club, but her arm was numb and she could hardly breathe. A berserker leapt for her, swinging an axe, and even as she brought her sword up, she knew it was too little too late. But suddenly a ward sphere extended to encompass her, flinging the enraged man back, and she looked round with gratitude to see Eldrid wink at her.

"Stay close," he growled, even as he swung through his ward sphere and sliced deep into a rager's shoulder. "We're winning."

And he was right. Though the battle was fiercest here, they were pressing forward, toward the base of the tower and the macabre twitchers who surrounded it. Behind, more and more of Carred's people were advancing.

And then she looked back at the tower, as she realized there were more ghastly bodies held up by invisible strings, connected one to another by thready black filaments. She gazed about the battlefield in horror. Save for the severed limbs and heads that dotted the ground, there were no bodies of the ragers. They were now among the circle of the dead, twitching as their essence was sucked through those evil black threads. And above the tower, the dark sphere throbbed and expanded, till it seemed it must fill the entire sky.

A vast shadow fell over the combatants, and the air grew frigid. The dark sun pulsed and gyred, spinning faster and faster. And still the battle raged. Still blades struck blade amid showers of sparks. Screams. Blood. The stench of open bowels.

"Eldrid, look!" she yelled.

He threw a glance at the ever-growing circle around the tower and cursed. Each berserker they killed only added to the power source and sent the expanding sun above their heads racing toward its dread purpose.

Shrieks went up from the rear—not just the odd cry of the mortally wounded, but an entire chorus of panic. She turned back to see blood misting the air as Niyandrians fell screaming. Ward spheres converged on the chaos—knights trying to stem this new assault. A ward sphere's glare was suddenly blotted out by the sheer number of bodies hitting it. Not human; these were no possessed Niyandrians. Dead-eyes streamed out of the holes that pocked the ground, flowing amid the ranks of Carred's army, ripping and biting with such ferocity that warriors began to panic.

And then their lines were sundered.

FORTY-SIX

SCREAMS ROLLED OUT ACROSS THE battlefield, distracting Carred from her task of cutting through the black filaments that connected the circle of corpses. At first she saw Rindon and Nul surrounded by their ward spheres, fighting with measured blows, holding back the rabid onslaught of wild Niyandrians intent on stopping what Carred was doing.

Beyond the two heroes, where the battle was thickest, dead-eyes swarmed the combatants, ripping into them, no matter which side they were on. There were hundreds of the stick-limbed horrors crawling up out of the ground. The burrows! They had been holed up beneath ground and now emerged in waves like the opportunist killers they were. Not for the first time, Carred had walked into a trap. Theltek's hairy assholes, Talia knew her too well!

Blood mist filled the air. Crimson spattered the ground. Pockets of silver light formed islands amid the slaughter—the ward spheres of the few dozen surviving knights, expanding to protect as many of their allies as they could.

A snarl startled Carred as a berserk Niyandrian slipped past Rindon and Nul to launch himself at her. She barely got her sword up in time. Blades collided, and a jolt of pain shot up her arm. She staggered back under the impact, falling against one of the juddering corpses. Tingles of wrongness pricked her veins, pulses of vileness; and there was something else: a taint that she recognized from her time in the abyssal realms. Whatever sorcery coursed through the quivering bodies that ringed the tower, it wasn't just the earth-tide; they were, in some way, conduits for the dark.

She recoiled from the contact with the corpse, and the sensation passed at once. Not the oppressive weight from the dark sphere above, though; that only increased as the black sun gyred and grew.

The raver came at her again, slavering, his feral eyes bright. Before she could react, she was forced to shield her eyes against the scintillant glare of two ward spheres that came to overlap between her and the madman. Rindon smashed a hatchet into the raver's head, and at the same time, Nul skewered the man's guts, spilling entrails to the ground. Still the raver spat and cursed, but each time he touched the ward spheres, he rebounded, skin blistering. Rindon's second hatchet swung in a glittering arc, cleaving almost clean through the raver's neck. A second swing and the head rolled away across the ground. The body, though, remained on its feet, and a thread of dark sorcery arced from the circle of the dead and set it twitching.

Carred sliced her void-steel enhanced sword through the filament, and the headless corpse flopped to the ground. Before she could reach the next spasming body, two more dead Niyandrians materialized in the circle, black filaments leaping from the circle to connect them.

"It's no good," she cried. "For every thread I sever, two more new corpses appear."

And she had the dread feeling she was running out of time.

Above, the black sun swelled. It spun so fast that an icy wind blew across the battlefield. White cloaks flapped and snapped as fighters leaned into the wind, struggling for every step. Carred swept hair out of her face as she glanced up at the pregnant sphere of darkness. Pressure built in her head, and a droning thrum pounded through the air, escalating in pitch.

There was no time. Anskar hadn't come. She had to get inside the tower.

Before she could turn toward the door, dozens of ravers burst clear of the battlefield, their numbers swollen by dead-eyes. Like the incoming tide, they surged toward her. Talia must have realized what she'd been trying to do with the filaments.

Rindon and Nul met the onslaught by once more merging their ward spheres and then expanding them into a wall of force between Carred and the enemy. But already, while the enraged Niyandrians crashed into the silver barrier, screeching where it burned them, dead-eyes began flowing to the sides. As a couple made it past the left flank and came at Carred, the knights altered the configuration of their ward, curving it into a horseshoe. The two deads recoiled, hissing and growling.

"Keep close!" Nul yelled as the ward contracted into a large sphere that surrounded the three of them.

"I need to get inside," Carred said. She was unsure if the knights heard her. Ravers and dead-eyes threw themselves against the ward, and the sphere of light started to buckle. Rindon's hatchets were a blur, splitting flesh, cracking bone, and sending up sprays of gore. Nul was more measured in his attacks, each thrust of his sword ripping through a chest, a throat, an eye.

Ten feet from the tower door, Carred left the ward sphere, ignoring Rindon's cries for her to come back. She reached into her dusk-tide repository, shocked at the rampant force within, just waiting to be unleashed. The dead-eyes and ravers hurling themselves against at Nul and Rindon in an effort to get to her suddenly relented. Silver wards spheres flared into life among them as knights cleaved into their ranks, Niyandrians among them, the flames of the dusk upon their fists and blades. Theltek, they had rallied, and now advanced with devastating force. Already her people were coming in from the sides, cutting down the flanking dead-eyes and ravers.

Out of nowhere, a raging Niyandrian came through the gap between the knights' ward and the tower, screaming her name, sword flashing toward her head. Carred's scream caught in her throat. Her own blade seemed to lag through the air, too late to save her. She blinked as the sword came crashing down, then opened her eyes to sparks and the clang of steel on steel.

And suddenly Vilintia was there, sword held in both hands as she turned the attacker's blade. Carred recognized him then, despite the feral eyes and the foaming mouth.

Fult Wreave!

Vilintia recovered with a quick pivot and a hack, but this time it was Wreave that parried her attack. And not just parried; he followed up with blistering strikes, all rage and no finesse. Vilintia was as good as anyone with a blade, but even when she side-stepped and thrust her sword deep into Wreave's guts, he kept on coming, driving her back against the wall.

Carred shook herself free of her stupor, trying to forget how close she had just come to being killed. She darted in and sliced her blade across Wreave's hamstring. He snarled and back-fisted her with such force that she fell toward the circle of silver light surrounding the knights, stumbling to a stop a hair's breadth from its thrumming power. Her hair stood on end and her skin tingled. Seeing her plight, Rindon and Nul separated their wards, drawing the light tight around themselves until they were wreathed in second skins of argent.

"Go!" Nul cried, too busy defending himself to help her or Vilintia.

Blood gushing from his mouth, Wreave continued to hack with wild abandon, Vilintia slowing each time she blocked, the force of the blows making her wince. Carred ran back in, swinging for the back of his neck… But not fast enough. Wreave's blade clove through Vilintia's wrist, and as her sword clattered into the tower wall, Wreave reversed the arc of his swing and ripped his blade up Vilintia's chest, her neck, her face, in a spray of blood.

Carred's sword crunched through flesh and bone. She barely registered Wreave topple over to one side, his head hanging by a sliver of flesh. She dropped her sword and caught Vilintia beneath both arms and lowered her to the ground.

Vilintia mouthed something through blood-smeared lips. It might have been an apology. And then she was gone, and Carred was screaming as she snatched up her sword and stood facing the doors. Dusk-tide power exploded from her, smashing through wood and iron. Flames and splinters roared into the interior. Black smoke plumed. Acrid fumes scoured her nose and throat.

Carred rode the wake of her sorcerous blast, racing into the tower, heedless that she could see nothing in the smoke and the wafting cloud of dust and debris.

But she heard something—heavy footsteps clanking on stone steps, and she ran in pursuit. Visibility was better as she reached the bottom of a spiral staircase that wound up to the levels above. A trail of thready filaments preceded her, trailing the footsteps. She could see now that the filaments came through the walls of the tower. She slashed at them with her void-steel sword as she hurried up the stairs. In response, a curse came echoing down at her. Talia! But sever one thread, and another took its place, just as had happened outside.

She ran with her sword before her, cutting through the filaments in a futile effort to dispel them all. One level, two. Her knees started to burn, and her breaths grew ragged. But she had to keep going. Outside, she could still hear the clangor of battle, the roars and the screams.

She reached the top and exited an open trapdoor onto the parapet. It was like stepping into a wintry midnight. The black sun above was so vast, its corona covered everything in a thick blanket of gloaming. Ice prickled her skin and sluiced through her veins. Pulses of wrongness throbbed beneath her scalp, all along her spine, causing her guts to clench and her teeth to grind.

Through the obscuring twilight, she could make out the dark filaments of sorcery that rose up through the parapet to converge on the lone figure standing beneath the gyring orb, arms extended toward it.

Even in the unnatural dark, Talia's new-formed body of divine alloy melded with Marith's flesh glinted and shimmered—silver, violet, moonlit blue. Her metallic flesh gave off an almost mystic radiance, not dissimilar to the phosphorescent glow of scaleskin fungus. There was no trace of the armor that had once encased Marith's possessed body. No trace of Marith at all. Even the great helm Talia had settled over her head had conformed to the contours of her head and face, a perfect sculpture, or rather a molding.

The Necromancer Queen turned toward Carred, her arms still aloft, still working whatever sorcery was fueled by the circle of corpses below. Besides the sword belt around her waist and the scabbard that sheathed Anskar's sword, Talia was naked, her every curve redefined in divine alloy, every birthmark, every blemish, every frown-line, even the contours of her apple breasts, her nipples, and the thatch of hair between her legs—all graven with the perfection of a master sculptor. Her metal face showed the same subtle expressiveness, the fleshy malleability it had possessed in life. The divine alloy that constituted her skin, and perhaps even her muscles and bones and the organs within, had a sort of viscous fluidity, like the torpid ooze of magma, only in this case, it exuded no heat. All Carred felt coming off that statue of living metal was coldness, frigid and leeching. With just a simple bemused gaze, the quizzical raise of a molded eyebrow, Talia cooled Carred's rage and then froze it altogether.

Carred's sword in her hand—the slender hope she retained— felt suddenly cumbrous, ridiculous, even, as if it were a child's plaything. The metal orbs of Talia's eyes conveyed emotion with a soft inner glow, one that suggested surprise, hurt, desire, and even a hint of amusement. How, Carred couldn't tell, but she felt… felt…

For an instant, she was a young recruit once more, bedazzled by the Queen's grace and unquestionable beauty. She recalled how she had gone meekly to Talia's bed, how easily she had been aroused—when till that moment she had never given such love between women a thought, nor even known it existed.

And now, as Talia stood atop the tower, beneath the sphere of gyring void stuff, her shimmering body fully exposed, arms weaving through the air, she looked… she looked utterly desirable. She also seemed vulnerable now, a little child left alone in the woods, in desperate need of protection. Carred felt an overwhelming need to go to her, to cuddle her, to melt away the frigidity of that metal body. It was a glamor, she knew, and yet…

With an almost audible groan of grief and longing, she willed her eyes shut, doing her best to ignore the blooming heat in her belly. She savagely cut down every thought, every image of what she wanted to do to Talia—with Talia. The pain of resistance was excruciating.

"Good girl," Talia said. "Lay down your sword and come to me."

And Carred almost did. She wanted to obey, as she had long ago obeyed. Wanted to provide her service of warmth. But there was a second intrusion in her mind: the image, then the touch, the sounds, the taste of her and Marith drinking mistberry wine in bed together. Their conjoined laughter wrenched at her awareness, arousing in her a different kind of longing, a need to be held and comforted, not to assuage unnatural lusts. She saw Talia's metal form in a different light now. The matter that formed it was Marith's, not hers. First Talia had violated Marith's mind, then she had stolen her body and reshaped it into her own.

Carred's anger reignited, incinerating whatever glamor the Queen had placed upon her. She tightened her grip on her sword hilt and took a step toward Talia, then stopped as a circle of purplish dusk-tide flames sprang up around the Queen.

"You can't harm me, Carred," Talia said, her arms still weaving beneath the pregnant sphere. "Why do you even want to? You were always my favorite—and Marith's. You could be again."

Talia broke off as the black orb above her head shuddered and expanded till its underside covered her metal hands to the wrists. She gasped with exaltation.

"What are you doing?" Carred demanded as she backed away. "What is that thing?"

"Oh, this?" Talia said, withdrawing her hands from the dark sphere to the accompaniment of a faint plopping slurp. "Dark-tide sorcery, of course, though of a superior kind. The one thing my father gave me— and even then not by choice: the essence, the knowledge, the *power* of a demon lord."

"So you killed him, then. I suspected as much."

"Killed and absorbed. But even his essence has a gristly quality. He does not easily divulge all his secrets. But I have time. I am used to playing the long game. Oh, don't look so disapproving, dear Carred. You'd have done the same to your mother. See, I *was* listening when you told me about her. I was not untouched by your tears."

"You could have fooled me," Carred said. In a moment's weakness, she had broken down and wept after their lovemaking yet again failed to restore warmth to Talia's frigid body. Carred had read the disappointment in the Queen's face; knew she had failed in her duty. And she had heard the lash of her mother's chastising voice in her head:

Useless, good-for-nothing. Is there anything you can do right?

"Let's not make this about you," Talia said. "This is about Niyas, and it is about my triumph over death and the even greater triumph to come."

"What triumph?"

The Queen thrust her hands overhead once more, into the pulsating dark of the black sun. "All those years fighting your little rebellion, Carred… Don't tell me you didn't dream of revenge."

"Against the mainlanders?" Again the black sun shuddered, and Talia threw her head back as she cried out in ecstasy.

Carred squeezed her sword hilt, steeling herself for a desperate charge across the flaming circle between her and the Queen. Because whatever was happening with the black sun, whatever Talia meant by revenge, she had the conviction she needed to act now or never have another chance. And maybe Talia sensed that, for she resumed their conversation as if they were out for a gentle stroll together. As if they were old friends.

"Remember how I was always afraid in life? I expect you of all people can understand how crippling, how crushing, how devastating it is to have a parent try to define you, all the while letting you know you are not good enough. Well, with my father, it was worse. He had always wanted to shape me into his instrument, and when he could not, he strove to kill me."

"And yet you would do the same to Anskar," Carred pointed out.

"No…" Talia said, though there was uncertainty in her voice for a second. "Anskar was my… my…"

"He was a tool you created to bring you back from the realm of the dead," Carred said, and now she did advance on the circle of flames, stopping only when the heat grew too intense. "And when you no longer needed him—when you stole new life from my Marith!—you tried to kill him."

"That is a lie!" Talia said. "And from you, Carred! You of all people. How could you think so little of me? You used to love me. You used to be loyal."

"All those years fighting the mainland occupiers… I'd say I was loyal to a fault. But then I started to see things differently. Observing Anskar and what you did to him was a big part of that. Marith was the final straw."

"She's still here…" Talia started, removing her hand from the underside of the dark sphere and touching it to her chest.

"No," Carred said, "she's not."

Her dusk-tide repository surged as she stepped into the ring of flames. Essence flowed from her, not directed by any conscious purpose, only by her grief and anger. An unnatural wind skirled across the parapet, snuffing out Talia's circle of fire.

"Where did you learn…?" Talia said, then she seemed to notice the dark-metal blade in Carred's hand.

Talia thrust both hands hard against the underside of the black sun, sending the pulsating sphere high above the tower, trailing the black filaments from the corpses below. A churning tide of emerald sorcery formed beneath her feet and carried her after it. The sight brought back memories of the fall of Naphor, when Talia had released the cataclysmic burst of power that had destroyed the city and then herself.

Carred turned back to the open trapdoor that had brought her onto the parapet. There was no more to be done here; she had delayed too long. Missed her chance. But maybe she could still do something. Maybe she could stop another slaughter. She started toward the trap, the sound of fighting still fierce below. Her people needed to break off. They needed to flee.

Movement out of the corner of her eye froze her. Something pale rose into the air above the parapet, and she stared in shock. It was a human skull, its empty eye-sockets ablaze with emerald light. Its jaws clacked at her, but then it rose high above and began to orbit Talia beneath the black sun.

And then she saw the others: skulls that had lain unnoticed all around the tower top began to rock and clatter. One after another, their eye-sockets lit up with emerald radiance, and they launched themselves skywards. There must have been twenty… closer to thirty of the macabre, clacking skulls revolving around Talia as she once more thrust her hands into the black sun, too far above now for Carred to do anything but watch.

Filaments of emerald arced between the skulls then shot from the mouths of each to strike Talia: thirty streaks of iridescence like the spokes of a sorcerous wheel, with Talia its hub. Theltek alone knew what kind of sorcery this was: the earth-tide of the Necromancer Queen, the moontouched abilities of Marith, and the dark-tide abilities of a demon lord? The tower shook as Talia's metal body grew lambent with emerald light, and in response the black sun gyred with renewed ferocity, so fast it became a dizzying blur, casting crazy shadows below.

Cries went up from the battlefield. A raging thrum rattled Carred's skull as she tried to reach the trapdoor. Her sword fell from her trembling hands to clatter to the parapet. She bent to retrieve it, but her knees turned to water and she slumped down, covering her ears against the pounding in her head. Blood trickled from her nose. All resolve left her, and she could do nothing but curl up on the parapet and watch enraptured as in swift succession the orbiting skulls exploded with emerald brilliance then rained down in showers of bone dust.

With each eruption, Talia grew iridescent, till she was a blazing column of emerald fire. And then the Queen discharged all that lucent force into the dark sphere above her, where it crackled and bloomed into a conflagration.

Carred lost sight of the Queen as the sphere grew brighter than the sun. It undulated and then collapsed briefly in on itself, only to reform as a vast opening in the skies, a gigantic maw surrounded by a corona of flame—no longer emerald but bronze.

Carred rose to her knees, gaping in horror. The corona was the same color as the sun above Vulthanor. A gateway? A portal between Wiraya and the abyssal realms? The last time something like this had happened had been the start of the demon wars.

She could see Talia again now, hovering to one side of this vast hole in the sky, held aloft by strange and sorcerous currents. The Necromancer Queen was radiant with reflected light from the corona of bronze fire that surrounded the portal. No mere being cast from divine alloy, now she actually did look divine, though not in a good way. To Carred's mounting horror, she realized that Talia's appearance recalled the horrific tales from Niyandrian pre-history, of ancient gods who could just as easily have been described as demons.

The thought had barely taken shape in her mind when the eclipse at the center of the portal began to sparkle with ripples of violet, and like sharp-tooths breaching the surface of a midnight sea, figures started to come through from the other side.

Not sharp-tooths. It might have been better if they were. Demons. Half a dozen; a score. Fifty, seventy, a hundred… And still they kept emerging from the portal one after another, the bestial lesser kinds first, though these were winged like butterflies woven from shadow. They spiraled down past the tower, then swooped toward the combatants below.

In their wake came greater demons, almost human in appearance, though with gray skin and vaporous wings of black. Behind them loomed something massive, some shadowed behemoth with horns and scales and a flaming sword.

By every one of Theltek's assholes… Talia commanded a demon lord? A lesser lord, presumably; one who would have served the lord Domatai.

For too long, she looked up, spellbound by the horror unfolding in the skies; but then she was jolted to her senses as a demon broke off from the pack descending to the battlefield and came straight at her.

She leapt to her feet, bringing up her void-steel blade two-handed to block the demon's shadow spear. It was a sinewy giant, a gray-scaled man of eight or nine feet tall. Eyes of maroon bored into her as the demon's spear vanished on contact with her void-steel. The creature touched down on the parapet, its shadow wings retracting. Dark vapors roiled from its open mouth then snaked toward Carred. The instant she swiped her sword through them, they dissolved into the air.

The demon let out a hawkish cry, and three more winged warriors changed course to come to its aid, each no larger than a regular human, and their weapons were steel not shadow. The giant demon darted in at her and tried to grab her sword wrist, but Carred snatched her blade back and sliced it across a gray-scaled forearm. The flesh smoldered, then bubbled and blistered. The demon shook as it staggered back, shrieking, then it slopped to the parapet in a pool of slime. She had almost forgotten the astrumium her blade was initially forged from.

Instantly, the three smaller demons were on her, slashing and thrusting with blades of steel. She parried and twisted, ducked beneath a sword, and rammed her own through the demon's throat, reducing the creature to steaming liquid. The remaining two grew wary then and began to circle her just out of range, every now and again glancing up at the portal and barking words she assumed were in Nazgrese.

Shrieks and roars reached her from below. Cracks and fizzes of dusk-tide sorcery. The tumultuous clash of steel. And was that… a snatch of song? She wanted so badly to glance over the wall of the parapet but didn't dare take her eyes off her assailants—nor the gigantic horned demon lord slowly wafting down towards her, as if it had all the time in the world. Perhaps it had seen what her sword could do and was hoping these lower demons could get the job done. Or it was simply having too much fun watching her hopes crumble into ruin.

The pair of demons pounced, too quick for her to defend herself properly. It was all she could do to stumble back against the wall of the parapet, narrowly avoiding an eviscerating slash. She bounced off the wall and countered with a thrust. Her blade barely scratched the demon's skin, but it was enough, and the creature slopped all over the parapet.

The other demon turned, extending its shadow wings as it tried to flee, but Carred was faster and ran it through the back. As it puddled at her feet, the singing from the battlefield reached a crescendo, briefly drowning out the roars and the screams, and she just had to see.

Below, there were demons everywhere. Amid the carnage, knights formed protective circles with overlapping wards of silver. Among them, shielded by them, her Niyandrians were growing bolder with sorcery. Not folding, as she had expected. It was a miracle. And then saw Rindon fighting alongside Nul, and he was leading the singing of some bawdy shanty. All around him knights and Niyandrians joined in, lifting their voices against the horror.

But it was no more than a valiant last stand, Carred realized. There were too many dead-eyes, and there were still ravers fighting with savage fury. More and more demons continued to pour through the portal. Glancing up, she glimpsed Talia, an almost disinterested observer by the portal's side, waiting for the battle to be over so she could descend in victory.

The demon lord no longer wafted lazily down like a leaf in the breeze. He suddenly plummeted toward her, sword ablaze in his massive fist.

Carred ran for the trapdoor, but with a sweep of shadow wings, the demon lord was there before her, landing with a thunderous impact that shook the tower.

Carred came to a trembling halt, her eyes locked to the towering demon lord. It—or rather, she—stood twice Carred's height, her body, which had seemed so dense and so massive, lean and muscular beneath its roiling cloak of shadows. The demon was armored in the scales of some large reptilian beast. Her hair was intricately braided with silken ribbons, and bull's horns of brass jutted from her temples—Carred couldn't decide if they were natural or adornments. Waves of madness rolled off the demon, causing Carred to swoon and making her want to pull her hair out and claw her own skin. She did neither, fighting back against the glamor by clenching her teeth and reaching into her dusk-tide repository. She came up with fire that wreathed her in argent, purging the demon's corrosive presence from her mind.

The demon woman arched an eyebrow, surprised but not exactly impressed. Her eyes smoldered as she made a fist of her free hand, and black lightning shot from it. Carred's sword drew the attack, and where the lightning struck void-steel, it fizzled away to nothing.

Carred charged. Just one touch of her sword was all it would take, but before she could close even half the distance, noxious fumes rolled from the demon woman's gaping mouth, and Carred ran headlong into their suffocating pall. She coughed until she couldn't, until she was too weak to do anything other than pitch to her knees, shuddering, gasping, her body racked with shivers. Her sword was suddenly too heavy to raise, and she almost didn't care as the demon lord's fiery blade came swinging down at her.

Marith! she cried soundlessly, in her mind. But before she could finish her final prayer, gold streaked across her vision, and blistering heat prickled her face.

With an explosion of light and a concussive impact, something like a flaming comet slammed into the demon lord, blasting her from her feet and through the wall of the parapet. Masonry flew into the air and cascaded below in a rain of rubble. And the demon lord fell with it, wailing and smoldering. A few seconds later, the demon rose above the parapet on wings of shadow that burned as if they were paper. The demon's progress through the air was erratic, agonizing, her face half-melted, the scales that she wore like armor ablaze with golden fire too bright, too brilliant to be natural. And then, with a last, keening wail, she erupted in a swarm of sparkling motes that drifted down over the battlefield.

With the demon's demise, the sickness left Carred. But not the shock.

For the thing that had slammed into the demon and saved Carred's life was no comet. Nor was it a directed blast of sorcery. It was a man, incandescent with golden fire, a being too luminous for the world of mortals. She started to look away, blinking against the glare, but then the flames around the man died down so swiftly that it seemed a new darkness had fallen.

And there, glaring down at her with the thinnest corona of gold surrounding those terrible black eyes was Anskar, sheathed head to toe in the most intricate plate armor Carred had ever seen. The entire armor was fluted with broad ridges that ran vertically down the breastplate, the pauldrons, and the cuisses. Gauntlets with gracefully scalloped edges and long, pointed cuffs covered his hands and forearms. A bevor made from a single piece of shimmering metal protected his chin and throat. It was a miracle of forging, not a single inch of skin exposed save for his face above the bevor—and even that could be covered in an instant by the visor that was currently raised atop the crown. A visor, oddly, without sight holes or slits, nor any means of ventilation. There were symbols radiant with sorcery etched into the visor, crudely formed, as if scored there by claws. Over one shoulder poked the massive hilt of a sword scabbarded on his back that would almost certainly required two hands to swing.

"Anskar?" Carred breathed, her eyes tracking movement high above.

She groaned. Queen Talia glided across the face of the portal, scattering the demons still pouring through, then as she dropped beneath the gyring maw, she drew her dark blade, descending toward the parapet like an angel of death.

"I…" he muttered from behind the metal of the bevor. A frown knit his brows. It sounded a struggle even to speak. Sparks re-erupted all over the armor, limning it with golden flame. Anskar squeezed his eyes shut and closed his gauntlets into fists. He let out a low moan, and the flames once more died down.

"Don't suppress the flames," Carred said, drawing his eyes to Talia's descent. "Do to her what you did to the demon lord!"

"I can't…" Anskar growled—his teeth might have been clenched behind the bevor. "Can't risk it. I barely put the flames out just now. Another use and it won't matter if we win here. We'll all lose. Menselas, Carred, the power… too much. I think I could destroy everything if I unleash it again."

"I'm willing to risk that!"

"But I'm not," Anskar said.

Queen Talia—living armor, molded perfectly to her once comely form—touched down on the far side of the parapet, then with terrifying speed glided straight at them, no more words, no more games, her dark blade howling for souls.

Anskar shoved Carred toward the open trapdoor. "Get out of here!" he commanded, as he reached over his shoulder for the hilt of his giant sword.

FORTY-SEVEN

EVEN THROUGH THE GAUNTLETS, ANSKAR'S grasp of the new Sword of Supremacy's hilt anchored him, freeing him from the fear that threatened to unleash his power, and by so doing, usher in an unimaginable cataclysm, one every bit as devastating as those that had shaped and reshaped Wiraya over the aeons. He knew that now with dread certainty. Tarrik had been right to shun his own power. Ren and the others had been right to warn him. And yet… They had let him leave their isle, despite carrying within him the potential to ravage the world.

Queen Talia came at him like a whirlwind, and even as he widened his stance to receive her onslaught, he wavered. She had beaten him before, and now, with *Amalantril* extended before her, screaming for his soul, he feared he hadn't done enough.

And then there was no more space for thought. *Amalantril* bucked in her hand as the blade lanced at his chest. Anskar deflected the attack with the greatsword Hrothyr had slaved to forge from divine alloy, void-steel, and the shards of Borik's legendary blade.

Amalantril twisted in Talia's metal hand like a cat caught by the tail. Its shrieks turned to hisses. It wouldn't have surprised him if the dark blade sprouted teeth. Even Talia seemed shocked by the violence of her sword's attack, its independence.

Again Anskar blocked, moving nimbly to one side. Talia possessed no footwork. It would have been easy, save for the thrashing, snarling blade that led the dance for her. He swung for her neck, but *Amalantril* was there in a blur of movement, countering before Anskar could react. He grunted as the keen edge of Talia's sword slid along his chest plate, as if searching for the minutest gap. Not finding any, the dark blade reversed course, slicing upward, grating along the bevor that protected his throat and chin. At the last instant, he turned his face aside, and the sword merely nicked the skin of his cheek. Ice burned where he bled, and he heard *Amalantril* roar with frustration.

Bolts of pure darkness shot from Talia's eyes, only to fizzle out where they touched Anskar's armor. She shrugged as if she had expected as much. She tried creating space as the dusk-tide swelled within her, but *Amalantril* squirmed in her grasp, tugging her closer to Anskar—close enough to drink.

Before Talia could unleash her sorcery, Anskar made full use of his superior reach, thrusting the Sword of Supremacy two-handed as if it were a spear. She grunted as he struck her metal shoulder and spun her round. To his shock, the sword left a hole, a wound, molten and oozing, but already starting to close up.

Amalantril slashed towards his exposed face, but Anskar swayed back and countered with a sweeping chop that was meant to cleave through Talia's waist. *Amalantril* blocked and started into a hack of its own, but Anskar had anticipated that, and dipped beneath the arc of the swing, bringing up his great blade with such ferocity, the two swords moving towards each other doubled the force of the impact.

And he saw in his mind's eye Borik's shock as the original Sword of

Supremacy shattered.

But not this time. Hrothyr had made the new sword too well.

Better even than Anskar had forged his first blade.

It was *Amalantril* that shattered, screaming as its dark blade fractured. Jagged shards flew across the parapet and clattered down. And he saw it then: the demon that had possessed the sword, a roiling brume of shadows and soot that erupted from the broken blade and flowed straight into Talia's chest.

The Necromancer Queen staggered back, momentarily stunned. To Anskar's sight, the demon's essence thrashed about inside his mother with the fury of a rabid beast, but she was too powerful, too accomplished, and she had already absorbed her own father, a demon lord. Nevertheless, the struggle gave him precious seconds, and Anskar pressed his advantage, powering his blade toward her neck.

But she was no longer there.

Talia reappeared from the shadows on the far side of the parapet. He ran toward her, then stopped as she yelled something in Nazgrese— her father's tongue—and the hundreds of demons streaming from the mouth of the portal veered away from the battlefield below and swarmed straight at him, their wings of shadow obscuring his vision.

All he could do was thrash about blindly, the void-steel in his blade turning every demon it touched into liquid. It was quick work, a slaughter born of seconds, and already Anskar could see the Necromancer Queen as he forced a breach in the vortex of demons that swarmed around him like bats. And he realized too late that it had been but another distraction.

He gagged at the stench of rot that rose up through the tower. For a brief instant he saw the noxious essence of the earth-tide coalesce around Queen Talia, and then the vile brume was suddenly shivering with shards of bone.

Talia brought her metal hands together in a thunderous clap, and a storm of bone shards ripped into Anskar, clattering from his armor. He turned his back, protecting his face. He could hardly breathe under the relentless pounding, the stink, the suffocating pall. As the attack dwindled, he swung back round, already charging, but Talia was there waiting, hand extended, palm up, as she blew choking vapors in his face. His throat burned, all the way down to his lungs. He began to shiver violently. Ice sluiced through his veins.

And then he was spinning through a twilit void, wailing a long drawn-out cry that echoed away interminably.

He was smoke now, coalescing into a form recognizably his own, though immaterial, and if not quite naked, then veiled in wisps of something like light. No sign of his divine armor, and perhaps that was a good thing. The design had been altered from the Necromancer Tain's original. Three runes on the raised visor of the helm, inscribed by the clawed finger of Kaythe Nurglich. An agreement had been reached, a plan made, and that plan had not included the shifting limbo that was the realm of the dead.

Because Anskar had no doubt that was where he was. No doubt at all that Talia had hit him with a force his armor was not intended to withstand: the earth-tide—enough to dislocate him from his physical form. All she had to do now was destroy his body or sever the link between it and his spirit, and that would be the end. And he found he didn't care. Better this than the fate he had agreed to for himself. Carred and the others would survive without him. Or they wouldn't. But he was too tired to go on. He hadn't asked for this—for any of it. Sweet Menselas, when had he become so vital, so important? So tired…

His surroundings wavered into dim focus—some kind of caldera as misty as he was. The walls of the crater within which he stood extended upwards forever, the sky an infinitesimal speck of darkness high above. There were vague intimations of gigantic forms within the rockface, morphing one into another, never settling, never fully revealing themselves. He saw hints of a man's visage, a woman's; suggestions of age and youth, of wisdom, compassion; something stern, something fierce, something skull-like locked in the rigor of death.

"You mustn't stay here," a man's voice said, and his focus instantly sharpened.

"Vihtor?"

The Seneschal stood before him, solid as stone, armored in silver, his white cloak draped around his shoulders. No sign of the arrow wound that had killed him. And he looked younger; a man in his prime, no older than thirty.

"Father?"

Vihtor smiled, though his eyes were troubled. "You have only seconds remaining to you. You must go back."

"I don't want to," Anskar said.

"You must!" a woman said, so fiercely that Anskar spun round, the wisps of his immaterial arms raised to protect himself.

She was but a shade, only vaguely modeling the contours of a woman. There was so little left of her, barely enough essence for her to continue in existence, and yet still she compelled him as if he owed her.

"Marith?"

"Go back!"

She flung out shapeless arms, and a spark of silver grew out of thin air before Anskar's eyes. It started to expand but then faltered, as if she lacked the strength or the power to do what she planned. But then a silver ward sphere sprang to life around Vihtor. He drew its energy into a fist of force and punched it through Marith's spark; the two merged and expanded, and then slammed into Anskar like the end of all things.

With a gasp, his eyes opened just as Talia's metal foot kicked the Sword of Supremacy away from him.

He was lying on his back atop the parapet, sheathed head to toe in his armor, only his face exposed. And then Talia was standing over him, her open palm above his face.

"Void-steel in your armor?" she said. "A clever idea. But you really should have covered your face."

A spike of glistening blackness sprouted from her palm, lancing toward him. He jerked his head aside, and the dark spear drove into the parapet, sending up plumes of dust.

"Keep still!" Talia snarled. Dusk-tide swelled within her, and knotted balls of lightning manifested on either side of his head, too blindingly bright to look at, forcing him to keep his head in one place. Anskar started to dispel the lightning, then hesitated, afraid of losing control. He'd risked his powers to save Carred—there had been no other way of reaching her in time—but now… to save himself at the expense of the world?

Too late.

Talia's hand hovered above his face once more. The black spike came down.

And vanished.

Talia screamed as a dark blade punched through her metal chest. No blood, No molten gore. Just a sword blade impaling her as she thrashed about with her arms.

Behind the Queen, holding onto her sword with both hands, was Carred.

Talia juddered and arched her back, as she flailed around behind with her hands. Carred twisted aside to avoid them, only just maintaining her grip on the sword as Talia wrenched the blade this way and that in her effort to free herself. The Queen's screaming grew ever more shrill as her frustration rose, a deafening banshee's wail that caused Carred's face to contort in pain.

Anskar frowned against the pounding in his head. His gauntlets scraped the stone of the parapet as he sought to ground himself. He opened his mouth to cry a warning as he sensed the rapid build up of dusk-tide within the Queen. Lightning arced along Carred's blade, and she let go of the hilt as it grew incandescent. Talia spun toward her, the blade still protruding from her chest. Sorcerous fire streamed from her metal eyes, and Anskar cried out, "No!" But a scintillant ward of dawn-tide sprang up to encompass Carred, her eyes wide with shock as Talia's fire wrapped harmlessly around her.

Talia scoffed scornfully. "About time you learned to use your innate powers, lover," she said, "but it won't help against this."

A massive surge of earth-tide bubbled up through the tower as Talia took aim with her hands.

Anskar rolled to his knees and swept up the Sword of Supremacy, but before he could stand, a blast of battle song erupted behind him, and then Rindon was there, twin hatchets hacking into Talia. Chips of alloy flew sparking from the Queen's unnatural body as Rindon pressed his attack. Talia spun toward him, and Carred immediately grabbed the sword hilt sticking from her back once more, holding her in place.

Anskar stumbled as he stood, then almost fell as Nul tore past him to deliver a huge swing of his sword at Talia's neck. The blade bounced off amid a shower of sparks.

A hand on Anskar's arm steadied him enough to orient himself.

Sareya.

At first he couldn't understand what she was doing here; then he prepared himself for her attack, because last time he had seen her, they had fought.

"Too many demons diving below," she explained. "The battle is lost if we can't close that portal!"

"Lost?"

"It will be in a minute. Eldrid's gathered our people into a defensive square, protecting our backs. But there's not much time."

Eldrid De Vantte?

There was no time to ask. Ward spheres blazed around Rindon and

Nul as Talia countered with dusk-tide fire that drove them both back. Anskar could feel the dark-tide within his mother trying to lash out, but it died just as quickly as it formed—the void-steel he had melded into Carred's sword. Again sparks shivered along the blade that impaled the Queen, and again Carred was forced to let go.

Immediately, Talia tried reaching behind for the hilt jutting from her back; she found it, and shrieked as she began to draw the blade out an inch at a time.

"My idea," Rindon said as he met Anskar's eye. "One last desperate gambit. Better to go down trying." With a bellowed battle cry, he ran at Talia, only to be thrown back by a wave of dusk-tide force.

"Use your sorcery!" Anskar demanded of Sareya, even as he hefted his sword and stepped in to deliver a massive blow to Talia's exposed midriff. The blade bit deep, gouging a huge gash in his mother's belly. Yet no sooner had he pulled back his sword for another strike than the wound bubbled and oozed like magma and started to seal.

"I can't!"

Anskar glanced at her, but Sareya's focus was all on her target as she slammed her sword into Talia's face. The blade clanged and the sword flew out of her grasp. Dusk-tide exploded from every inch of Talia's frame, and Anskar shielded his exposed face with a metal-clad arm. Heat washed over him. His divine armor grew scalding. When it passed, he expected to see nothing but the charred husks of the others, but instead was met by the guttering radiance of the ward sphere that contained him. Not his own—for that would have led to disaster. There were silver spheres of wavering light around Rindon, Nul, Sareya, and… The realization stunned him. The dawn-tide essence powering the respective spheres all came from the same source. It came from Carred.

"Everyone, back!" Anskar cried as he leaned into the storm of sorcery that burst from his mother, enough to smash through any amount of warding.

Rindon grabbed Carred, shielding her with his body and the remnants of his guttering ward. Anskar swung the Sword of Supremacy, shearing through Talia's outstretched arm. Metal clanged to the parapet, then grew molten as the severed limb oozed over Talia's foot, where it was reabsorbed by the body. It only took an instant for the arm to regrow, sprouting from the shoulder and writhing like a serpent, till once more metal fingers made clutching motions as Talia prepared to incinerate Carred and Rindon.

And there was only one thing Anskar could think of doing. Reaching within, he clutched at the essence not of his disparate repositories, for he could no longer locate them. He pulled on the essence of his blood, his organs, his bones. A scintillant ward of blazing gold sprang up—not around Carred or any of the others; not even around himself. It manifested around Talia, at the very moment her destructive blast of dusk-tide spewed forth from her fingers. The flaming virulence crashed against the inside of the ward sphere and went out, and the golden sphere itself died.

Talia turned in shock as Anskar's innards ignited. His skin grew lambent with ineffable power. His teeth ground together as he fought against the swelling tides, all melded into one pure and terrible force that he knew he could never contain.

Talia stumbled away from him, her hands raised in a vain attempt to ward her face.

Rindon pulled Carred back toward the trapdoor. Nul was already there, beckoning them below. This was beyond them now. Beyond all of them.

Dimly, Anskar was aware that only Sareya hadn't moved. She stood, watching him, her crimson skin reflecting the rising conflagration that threatened to consume him. She held something—a box?—in her hand.

But then Sareya seemed to drift to the edges of his awareness as the sound of his mother's voice filled his skull. Talia was trembling with emotion, and tears of liquid metal seeped from her eyes. When she spoke through her sniffles, her voice was at once on her lips and embedded within Anskar's mind.

"Oh, Anskar," she sobbed. "What are we doing? What have I done? Please stop. Don't hurt me. Please—I'm your mother."

He continued to advance on her, his core ablaze with the heat of a forge.

"Anskar!" she wailed, pitching to her knees. "How did it come to this? You're my child, my heir. I… love you. You must believe me. Everything I've done has been for you. Anskar? My darling…"

He stopped to lay down his sword on the parapet. "Mother?"

Talia smiled through her molten tears. "My son."

"Why?" he asked, and his awareness closed in even more. It was just the two of them now; there was nothing else he could see, nothing else he could hear, not even the raging battle below.

"I love you," Talia said, rising unsteadily to her feet. "Truly, I love you. I always have."

Anskar received her words like a spear thrust through the heart. He faltered, the flames wreathing his skin guttering then going out. Heat left his core, replaced by a yearning need.

And now Talia's lips barely moved as she continued to speak in his mind, her tone soft and nurturing, the mother's voice he had never experienced growing up.

"All I want, Anskar," she said, "all I've ever wanted, was to be your mother. To hold you, to care for you."

He knew she was lying, using a glamor, and yet his need was greater than his reason. He wanted to believe her. In some way, he had to.

As the last of his power ebbed away, Talia came toward him, tears like quicksilver tracking down her metal cheeks. Her smile was full of warmth, and totally, utterly, disarming. Without warning, tendrils of glistening blackness edged with lightning shot forth from her chest, whiplashing toward Anskar's unprotected face. Dimly, he heard Sareya cry a warning. He turned aside, the necrotic tendrils sizzling where they brushed against his armor. They slapped in place on the divine alloy, squelching as they slid over the plates of armor, questing towards his face. In response, heat once more flared in his guts, but he stifled it with the full force of his will. With gauntleted hands, he ripped the thrashing tendrils from him, even as more burst forth from Talia's chest to engulf him. With a grunt of effort, he pushed forward into the chaos of tendrils, at the same time reaching up to the crown of his helm. Talia roared with triumph as a tendril slipped past his defenses and crept over the lip of his bevor, straining for his exposed flesh.

Anskar hurled himself at his mother as he slammed his visor down. Utterly blind now, for there were no eye-holes, he bore her to the parapet with the weight of his body.

But neither of them struck the solid ground.

Talia's screams wailed away beneath them as the two, entwined, rose giddily like smoke through a flue.

And then they were no longer atop the tower. No longer anywhere on Wiraya. Within her son's armored embrace, Talia's metal flesh lost substance. She grew wispy and indistinct, as insubstantial as mist. They both did. And when they arrived where they were going, they were but two inky shadows wrapped about each other, she twisting, screaming, and doing everything she could to extricate herself and go back.

"Release me!" she shrieked in his head. "Where have you taken me?"

"You don't know?" he asked calmly, as his weight returned and his mother grew once more solid, still restrained in his arms. Two metal forms—one encased in armor and the other made from it.

Anskar's visor popped up of its own accord. Its god-carved runes had served their purpose— brought them where no one would want to go, a place from whence there was no going back.

Their surroundings shifted and shimmered into focus. Not the gray void stuff of the realm of the dead—the place Anskar was supposed to have retrieved his mother's shade from in her original plan for him to craft the armor of divinity. This was worse. Much worse. The very atmosphere of the place seemed to wriggle like maggots. The pervasive stench of rot and disease filled the air. The colors of sickness and bruises abounded, every surface, every shadow, every glimmer of dirty light that entered this cavern seething with effluent and decomposing corpses.

And there, emerging from a pit like a sphincter in the ground, was the scaly, wolf-headed horror that was Kaythe Nurglich, the Corpse Maker.

"No!" Talia screamed as she saw the aberration rise from his pit and shuffle towards them. She struggled to free herself from Anskar's grip, and he released her, for there was nowhere she could run.

At the last instant, as the gigantic horror leaned down with slavering jaws, Anskar panicked, overcome by the sheer, loathsome horror of the god-thing that came to consume them. He turned to run, though there was nowhere to flee; the entire cavern wriggled and undulated with the presence of Kaythe Nurglich. The god's taloned hand grabbed his armored waist, partially crushing the metal as it held him in place.

"Fool!" Kaythe Nurglich said. "Did I not say my aid would come at a cost you would not be willing to pay?"

Anskar had known he could never defeat Talia, not without imperiling the entire world. And so he had returned one last time to the Corpse Maker, and offered to avenge the god for Talia reneging on the pact she had long ago made. Kaythe had inscribed Anskar's helm with runes that were old even before the invention of Skanuric.

Talia wailed in despair as the wolf's jaws clamped down over her. Metal screeched as gigantic fangs ripped into it. There was no crunch of bones, no spurt of blood, just the twisting and rending of metal, and Talia's terrible screaming, which only came to an end when the wolf's head chomped down on the last of her and she was no more than the lump sliding down the beast's throat. Totally gone, Anskar realized. Not even a wisp of her spirit remained. There was nothing left of his mother the god had not consumed.

But the Corpse Maker wasn't done yet. There was still the matter of their pact.

As the god lifted him into the air, towards those slavering jaws, Anskar's nerve abandoned him and he screamed too. Like a child crying for its mother, he shrieked the name embedded in his being since he had been an infant.

"Menselas!"

The name had scarce left his lips when sunfire erupted within him, and the world exploded.

FORTY-EIGHT

ANSKAR STRUCK THE GROUND WITH a skull-juddering impact. Air burst from his lungs, stale and stagnant and full of rot. He gasped and sucked in the fresher air atop the tower, then realized it was little better: heavy with the sweet tang of blood wafting up from the battlefield below and ripe with the stench of demons still pouring through the portal. Something felt different. A cold breeze licked over his skin, sending up plumes of steam. He was naked. His armor had gone, and his body smoldered like the dying embers of a forge.

"Anskar!" Sareya cried, leaning over him. "You vanished. What happened? Where did you go?"

"Talia?" he asked, rolling his head to the side.

A second body hit the parapet—a woman with crimson skin.

His heart lurched, and he reached for the hilt of his sword then rolled to his knees.

Red skin… Not metal.

He squinted his eyes into focus. The naked woman convulsing on the parapet was…

"Marith!" Carred gasped, dropping her void-steel sword and kneeling beside her lover, cradling her head.

"Carred?" Marith murmured, as if she'd just awoken from a deep sleep.

Anskar looked away as the two women sobbed.

"This isn't over," Nul said, as the sky blackened.

The gaping mouth of the portal stretched wider, disgorging hundreds of shadow-winged demons, who swirled around the tower top before diving below.

"They're still coming!" Sareya said, her cat's eyes fixed on Anskar. "And it's getting worse."

The portal shuddered, then expanded again, the blackness at its center giving way to vistas of shimmering desert and pinnacles of glinting rock. It was no longer a mere gateway between worlds, it was a tear, a rent in the veil between Wiraya and Vulthanor. With horror, Anskar realized he was looking directly onto the abyssal realms. And there were demons, so many demons, a gathering army forming up in ranks across the shimmering desert above them, blotting out the throbbing bronze sun, and thousands more massed in the sky like a churning storm head.

"Talia was holding them back," Marith said as she clung to Carred. "She summoned enough to gain control of Niyas, but not to challenge her. Now she's gone…"

"We have to help Eldrid!" Rindon said, as he and Nul disappeared through the trapdoor, heading below.

"It's too late!" Carred called after them. "There are too many!"

"I know what you can do," Sareya told Anskar. "I've seen your power… felt it. You can stop this."

When he frowned, she flashed her eyes at the portal, but already he was shaking his head.

"If you really knew the power within me, you'd never ask me to use it." It would take more than he had ever used to do what Sareya asked of him, and there would be no way back.

"I do know!" Sareya said. "And yes, it scares me. Anskar, the same power grows inside me. I dare not use my own, but you…"

"I'll not be responsible for the end of the world!"

"You won't need to." Sareya opened her hand to reveal an ornately carved jade box. "Trust me. I can help you."

Again the portal shuddered, and the breach filled the sky. Demons lined its maw from horizon to horizon. Hundreds soared through on smoky wings, circling then swooping below. Wild sorcery flashed. Swords clashed. Men and women screamed. And still the rift widened.

When Anskar looked at Carred for what he should do, she nodded. "I command now," she said. "Not you, *Melesh-Eloni*. The blame will be mine."

Anskar nodded, not believing her. Death had once again come for him, and he would embrace his end.

He turned up his palms and drew in a long breath. Heat bloomed in his belly, coursing through his veins. Tongues of flame licked all over his naked flesh, and then, lambent with golden fire, he soared into the air, straight toward the breach.

A monstrous demon broke off from its pack and streaked toward Anskar. It erupted into flames as it came within the corona of his fire, falling like ashen rain.

The army of demons on the far side of the portal's mouth scattered as Anskar drew near, growing ever more lucent, golden sunlight flaring from every inch of his skin. Arms outstretched, he came to a hover at the center of the breach, then opened himself to the full virulence of the power that burned within him.

He screamed, and for the second time, his world exploded. Blinding light blasted from him, incinerating everything it touched, even the sound of his own voice, the thoughts in his head, his vision, his every perception. The portal shuddered, then started to shrink as the sky around it closed back in, knitting together beneath the blinding conflagration.

Demons, afraid of being stranded, winged their way up from the battlefield, hundreds upon hundreds of shadow-winged monsters, slick with the gore of combat. As one mighty wave, they rushed toward the closing portal. Heat and fire exploded from Anskar of its own accord. Screams. The flash of a sunburst. And then there was nothing left of the myriad demons save a sky full of burning motes that drifted on the breeze.

Cheers came from the battlefield. Through the fire in his eyes, he looked down to see the remnants of Carred's army, a mere few hundred Niyandrians and a scatter of Order knights. Ward spheres winked out now the battle was done. Atop the tower, Carred held Marith on her feet. Sareya craned her neck to look up at him, imploring him, praying that he would stop now.

And he would, if he could.

With a remote awareness that seemed to belong to someone else, he heard the sound of his own roaring—bestial, insane, and despairing. He burned with such incandescence the very air hazed around him.

He couldn't stop himself as scorching flames shot from his hands, his feet, torching the ground. People ran for cover as flames leapt high from the surrounding trees. The tower top a hundred feet below grew molten, and the only thing keeping those who still stood there alive was the scintillant ward sphere that covered the parapet like a lucent dome—a ward that sprang from Marith.

And then Anskar was streaking across the sky, leaving a trail of fiery destruction. Beneath him, the ground trembled. Fissures split the earth. Steam plumed from the rents he caused, then flames sheeted into the air atop streams of bubbling lava. Clouds of black and acrid smoke billowed into the sky, and it was all Anskar could do in his madness to veer out towards the sea, away from the lands, the animals, the people he threatened to raze from the face of Wiraya.

As he soared away from the coast, the waters of the Simorga Sea bubbled and steamed, and all he could think to do was fly faster, hoping against hope that the speed and the wind would snuff out his flames. Fishing boats caught fire as he passed overhead. Desperate, he turned east, a churning missile of sunfire. He began to gain altitude, thinking perhaps of rising high above Wiraya, taking his flaming destruction out into the black reaches of space, where he was convinced the flames would die, and him with them.

Then he saw the white sails below, the wave-cutting prows of dozens of ships crossing the sea between the mainland and Niyas, and a new madness rose within him. The mainland fleet was coming, and though he tried his utmost to pull away, to continue with his plan to rise above the world and lose himself in the vastness of space, the fire within seemed to have a desire of its own, a need to burn and destroy. As if his will were consumed by his own blaze, Anskar sped through the sky on a direct course to intercept the fleet.

The mast of the lead galleon burst into flames as he neared. Crew members dived from the gunwale, then screamed as they hit the boiling water, where fish sizzled and sharp-tooths bobbed to the surface, their gray skin blackening from his heat.

Deep within himself, Anskar wept; he cried out like a forlorn child to Menselas, begging the flames to stop. Yet still they roared. Still they flared out from his burning body with the intensity of a small sun.

The fleet began to break formation, cumbrous galleons banking into the steaming waves as they tacked away from the devastation. The flagship, and by far the largest, sat within a vast golden ward sphere that emanated from the cloaked and armored woman on the poop deck: Seneschal Monash. It was a futile effort at self-preservation, but still an impressive one.

As Anskar shot past the flagship, flames licked across the surface of the golden sphere, which began to flicker erratically. But it was the galleon behind it that caught fire. Black smoke billowed from its mainsail, above which a banner depicting twin clenched fists started to smolder. Sailors balked before throwing themselves into the boiling water, and then with a rush of heat and flame, the ship was gone.

"Revenge, Anskar?" a sorcerous voice said in his head. "That was Archduke Peleus's ship, the man who hired me to capture you."

The man whose son Anskar had killed aboard the Grand Master's ship that first time he traveled to Sansor. He started to think it was no loss then stopped himself. There had been several hundred people on board. Menselas, he had killed them all.

He turned in midair, looking behind for the source of the voice. And then he saw her, streaking toward him, wreathed in flame the same as he was, burning a fiery trail behind her.

"Sareya?" he asked, knowing she was still too far off to hear him. But she had spoken in his mind… How did she do that?

"It's easy when you know how," she said. "Comes with being moontouched."

"Your flames…" Anskar said, trusting his voice would carry to her mind. "Just like mine."

"Too alike," she said, and there was no humor in her voice now as she approached within fifty feet of him and started to rise, high above the boiling sea, above the burning ships and those seeking to escape. Without his volition, Anskar followed her up through the clouds, flame drawn to flame, as if they recognized each other, burned for each other.

Clouds grew incandescent as he followed Sareya through them. Lightning forked across the heavens as if it too fled the danger. Thunder boomed, pounding Anskar's ears.

And still his flames flared about him, and it seemed the whole world was hazed with heat, trembling, on the verge of blistering and melting away to nothing.

Sareya hung in the air a mile or so above the sea, waiting.

"I can't stop!" he cried as he came level with her.

"I know," she replied sadly.

Her own flames grew more agitated in proximity to his. And he saw then, through the fire that consumed her face, she was grimacing as she tried to control the conflagration raging within.

"I don't want this," Anskar said, indicating the smoke rising from the ships below. "You said you would help me."

"And so I will," Sareya said, speaking with her true voice now, the words barely discernible through the roar of flame and the escalating crashes of thunder. "I only wish I could have stopped you sooner."

Flames uncoiled from her body and embraced him. His own fire surged in response, sending out flares of golden brilliance that wrapped around Sareya, drawing them both together.

Sareya's eyes blazed red, and he realized his own eyes must have looked the same.

"I saw this in a vision," she said. "Not so much me. I saw your eyes burning. The one who showed me… an Orgol… said I had to prevent this."

"An Orgol?"

Anskar's back arched and his radiance expanded, merging with Sareya's, till together they blazed and churned, a single sun set to explode and envelop the world in flame.

"I think he'll kill me for using my power," Sareya said. "And maybe he should. But what else could I do? How else could I have caught up with you?"

"It may be a moot point," Anskar said, his heart a pulsing fist of fire that seemed to grow denser with each thunderous beat. "If the world burns, we won't survive. And even if we do, would we want to?"

"You didn't choose this," Sareya said. "I told you to use your power. Carred commanded you."

"It was the only way to close the portal, to prevent another demon war."

"But still… you are not responsible."

She produced the jade box from within their conjoined blaze. Within the heart of the churning fireball, Anskar reached out, covering the box with his hand.

"Open it," Sareya said. She trembled as they locked eyes.

"And we both die?"

She nodded.

He opened the box.

Briefly, he glimpsed a five-pointed star within, inverted, formed from overlapping strips of black iron. Then suddenly the fireball that engulfed them shuddered before it imploded, its flaming residue sucked within the box. The fire that wreathed Anskar and Sareya went out, and he felt unseen forces pulling at his body. He started to lose cohesion as the box hungered for him, seeking to draw him after his flames. Then quickly, like a woman who had changed her mind, Sareya snapped the lid shut.

Anskar felt as though he had been frozen in ice. His skin prickled with cold and his teeth chattered. For an instant, he hung there in midair, the jade box in Sareya's hand charred black like coal, her other hand clasped in his.

And then they plummeted toward the sea.

FORTY-NINE

SAREYA OPENED HER EYES ONTO a dim and smoky cabin. She rolled her head on the pillow till she tracked the source of the dirty light: a rust-scabbed oil lantern hanging from the ceiling, black drip marks staining its corroded orange casing.

She was lying on a narrow bed, blankly watching the wisps of brown smoke seeping through the lantern's buckled door. From somewhere above, yards creaked, and she could hear the persistent squawk of seabirds amid the muffled hubbub of voices and the swell of waves. The smell of brine clung to her nostrils, and when she ran her fingers through her hair, it was crusted with salt.

She lingered in that liminal space between waking and sleeping, convinced she had come out of a nightmare in which the world had been about to end, till she and Anskar had sacrificed themselves and plummeted into the boiling sea.

And, as in every death dream she had ever experienced, she had awoken before the bitter end. With a groan she realized what that meant. She must still be a captive of the Jargalans.

Although… a cabin? Previously, she had been chained up in the hold among the rats.

"Sareya?"

A voice she had not expected to hear again, perhaps ever. She should have felt relieved—happy, even—but all she felt was the coldness that sometimes followed spent passion.

"Varensi?"

Seneschal Monash was perched on the end of the bed, watching her like a worried mother. Monash's eyes were rimmed with black, her face drawn and haggard. And Sareya remembered then. Remembered seeing the golden sorcery that protected the Order's flagship from Anskar's raging fire.

"I wasn't dreaming? I really did plunge into the sea?"

"And I fished you out," Monash said. "Well, not me personally, but I did give the command."

Sareya turned her head away, thinking, reliving her fiery flight towards the burning fleet. Reflexively, she made a clutching motion of her hand, remembering the feel of the jade box she had held. Dimly, she recollected dropping it as she fell. Whatever sorcerous artifact it had contained—a power that nullified and consumed—was now lost at the bottom of the sea, and perhaps just as well. And her own power… She had not felt her repositories since the Orgol had done something to her, and they were still absent. In their place, she had felt a nascent power at once pure and utterly terrifying, which the Orgol had warned her never to use. Well, she had disobeyed him, and likely she would be punished. Perhaps she had already been punished, for whatever it was, that power of flaming destruction, there was no trace of it now. All she felt was cold—in her heart, her body, and her mind, and a dreadful sense of loss.

But shouldn't she be dead?

She checked her skin. Not in the least scalded by the superheated waters. Her sun-power, the source of all tides, nullified when Anskar had opened the jade box, must have still been alive somewhere within her.

The mattress bounced as Monash plonked herself down beside Sareya's head and stroked her hair. Sareya winced but felt compelled to endure the touch. To her surprise, though, it didn't progress to anything more.

"You look…" Sareya said, resting her hand atop the Seneschal's on the bed.

"A bloody mess?"

"I was going to say exhausted."

"And you'd be right."

"From the sorcery? The way you warded your ship was…"

"Beyond the ordinary dusk-tide abilities permitted a knight of the Order of Eternal Vigilance. I know. Let's just say, the Grand Master has long selected those with exceptional abilities for special roles within the Order. But my sorcerous power, such as it is, pales in comparison with yours. And as for Anskar… It's a miracle you were able to stop him."

"You know what I did?"

Monash smiled as she indicated the neighboring bed in the cabin. "He told me."

Anskar lay beneath a single sheet. His face was ashen, no trace of the crimson tinge that marked him out as a half-blood Niyandrian. His chest didn't rise and fall beneath the sheet.

"Is he…?" Sareya asked.

"I fear he soon will be," Monash said. "He started to fade even as I spoke with him. I suppose he must have used too much power. Burned himself up from the inside. Either that, or the thing in the box—he said you had a jade box; that he opened it and that's what saved us all. Don't worry, you'll have plenty of time to tell me all about it before I return to Sansor."

"You're not going back to Branil's Burg?"

"After losing it so soon following my appointment? No, the Grand Master wants me back on special duties after that debacle. It's a wonder he entrusted me with charge of the fleet."

"He'll use you for your sorcery."

"In the service of the greater good," Monash said cynically. "But first I need to finish up here. We should be entering the bay shortly. The fleet will need time for repairs, and I plan to take a contingent to Naphor."

"The battle's over," Sareya said.

"There's the matter of the Niyandrian army…"

"I'd hardly call it that anymore. There are so few left. Without them… the sacrifices they made…"

"I am aware of that. Anskar said that was largely down to Carred Selenas. Who would have thought, the notorious rebel leader fighting side by side with the likes of Rindon and Nul and Eldrid DeVantte, her arch-nemesis?"

"So, what will you do with her?"

"With Carred Selenas? I imagine she'll be long gone by the time we reach Naphor. Whatever would she hang around for?"

"She'll assume you'll arrest her, to put an end to her rebellion once and for all."

"Of course she will. But nothing could be farther from the truth. Even before we set sail, I was informed that changes would be coming to Niyas, so long as the Necromancer Queen was out of the picture."

"Oh, she's gone," Sareya said.

"So Anskar told me. For good this time."

Sareya fixed her eyes on the Seneschal's, holding her gaze for the longest time.

"What about us?"

Monash smiled. "I am not completely insensitive. I am grateful for what we had, but… there is someone else. I didn't think you would be disappointed."

"Someone else?"

"I have a man now. Barely a man. He's rather young. I had to do something to pass the time on the journey back to Sansor after the loss of Dorinah. Tell me you don't mind?"

All Sareya could think of to say was, "Thank you."

"I'm sorry, Sareya," Monash said. "Not for my new love, but for you, for Anskar. He still has feelings for you." Monash raised an eyebrow. "And I suspect you do for him. Such a pity. The ship's doctor doubts he's going to make it."

Sareya swallowed, then nodded.

"I'll leave you alone," Monash said. "Rest more, if you can. Really, Sareya, I am sorry."

Sareya didn't see her leave, merely heard the click of the cabin door as it closed.

She rolled her feet out of bed and padded across the cabin to sit on the edge of Anskar's bed. She gazed down at him, her eyes moist as she thought back to the way she used to taunt him, then that first time they had made love in the smithing hall. Did she still have feelings for him? Did she still love him, after everything?

She began to shudder before she even realized she was sobbing. Something had happened when they burned together in the sky above the fleet. A reconnection. Powerful emotions—buried ones—had flooded back to the surface. Not for the first time. Something similar had happened when she was with the Orgol shaman. He had shown her the connection that existed between her and Anskar. Youthful passion, yes, but that had passed. This was something more, something deeper: a kinship of fire.

She hugged Anskar's neck as she cried into his hair. He was icy as a corpse. She pushed herself up from him to check he was still alive, and pressed her ear to his blue-tinged lips.

"Oh, Menselas, no," she cried as she cradled his head to her breast.

Her tears felt suddenly molten, scorching her skin as they tracked down her cheeks. A fist of coal burned in her belly, its heat radiating out to the rest of her. Flames danced on her fingertips, then flared where they contacted Anskar's skin.

He bucked beneath her, gasping as his back arched. And in that moment she felt the seethe of the Orgol's anger, reaching her across hundreds of miles. She had failed in her task, he seemed to say in her mind. She was supposed to have kept the box open till Anskar was consumed along with his flames. And he had forbidden her from using her own power. Her mind was almost overwhelmed by the Orgol's ill-intent towards her. He would send minions—there was no limit to his reach. He would snuff her from existence before she could grow too strong, too uncontrollable, too dangerous for the world to contain.

"Sareya?" Anskar whispered.

"It's all right," she said as she held him close, more for her own benefit than his. "It's going to be all right. We're going to be all right."

Some days later, Anskar stepped from the depot in Wintotashum, hand in hand with Sareya. Her cat's eyes shone golden. She shouldn't have used her power to revive him, but thus far she was doing a better job than he of controlling the power. But for how long?

Monash had let them go—even lent them a couple of horses for the long ride to Dorinah. Ultimately, it hadn't been the old Seneschal's choice, though. She had informed Eldrid that he was to replace her as governor of Niyas. Word had apparently reached the Grand Master of Eldrid's liberation from his Jargalan cell. The Consortium were no doubt already determining the fate of Niyas in the post-rebellion, post-Talia era.

Both were dressed in the standard uniform of the Order of Eternal Vigilance and wrapped in white cloaks with hoods against the sleet-spraying wind.

"I'll wait for you inside," Orix said from behind them, where he stood on the checkerboard floor of the vestibule. "No point getting wet if I don't have to."

He was wearing the gray jacket and trousers of one of the Ethereal Sorceress's functionaries. The only thing missing was the blackwood mask.

Sareya turned and planted a kiss on Orix's cheek, which immediately flushed. "It's so good to see you again, lummox," she told him.

"I would say it's just like old times," Orix said. "Only it ain't."

"This may take a while," Anskar explained, as he led Sareya down the steps and away from the depot.

"I'm sure I can find things to do," Orix said. "Say one thing for Sheelahn, she don't tolerate slackers, and there's always something coming in or going out."

Despite the pelting sleet and the blustery wind, Anskar felt better than he had in ages, energized and full of purpose. He knew what he wanted to do now; a decision had been made. And he couldn't wait to share it with Sareya. For once in his life, the future was a welcome friend beckoning him to better things. But first there was something he had to do. He had given his word. Not so long ago, he would have scoffed at the idea. His word! It had always been such a meaningless term. Until his mother had perished once and for all, engulfed by the jaws of the Corpse Maker. He knew who he was now—who he really was. And he knew just where he wanted to be.

Hrothyr shambled into the little church of the Warrior, escorted by twelve housecarls, a single priest, and King Aelfyr himself. Anskar followed behind with Sareya, palms sweaty as he thought about what he must do, what had led to this most unnatural of all events: Hrothyr's second funeral.

Inside, the church was empty, save for the forge-heated axe suspended above the iron altar, shedding a murky orange glow that somehow managed to feel homey.

"Courage," Sareya whispered to Anskar as she released his hand. "Menselas is with you."

Maybe, Anskar thought. Probably, the Five approved of what he was about to do, if not what he had previously done to Hrothyr. No matter how he tried to justify it to himself, he couldn't forgive himself for bringing Hrothyr back from the dead and using him as a slave.

The smith had worked without a break, forging the Armor of Divinity and the Sword of Supremacy, and now Anskar had neither. The armor must have remained behind in the Corpse Maker's domain, he figured, after his power had carried him free. The sword he had dropped atop the tower at Naphor. Eldrid DeVantte had found it and offered it back, but Anskar had no further use for it, and he could think of no better recipient for such a blade—especially now Eldrid seemed to have taken Borik's place as the third of three heroes.

Under the stern gaze of the officiating priest of the Warrior, and with the King, his housecarls, and Sareya as witnesses, Anskar reached into the bowels of the earth and made contact with the earth-tide for the very last time—another promise he intended to keep.

He kept his eyes open so that he could anchor himself on Sareya, just in case. They had spoken about this—about the possibility of drawing the attention of Kaythe Nurglich once more. Anskar hoped not. He wanted to believe that dark influence in his life was over, every bit as much as his mother's.

Sareya gave an encouraging smile when Anskar shrugged that he felt no presence of evil. There was nothing but the sluice of vile currents through his veins. It didn't seem likely that his eruption of golden sunfire had slain the Corpse Maker, but perhaps it had harmed him enough to make him think twice before accosting Anskar again.

He stepped up to the altar of iron, where Hrothyr was waiting, clumped together chunks of dead flesh that had no business walking abroad in the land of the living. Fighting back his revulsion, Anskar laid his hands on the blacksmith's misshapen head, siphoning off the earth-tide that animated the corpse and channeling it back beneath the ground.

"Thank you," Hrothyr mumbled as he swayed on his feet, the life literally leaching out of him. "For not forgetting. For coming back for me."

How could he not have come back? How could he have lived with himself knowing that he had condemned another to eternal torment? No, he was done with the earth-tide, done with Kaythe Nurglich, and he was done being the son of the Necromancer Queen.

With a smile of gratitude, Hrothyr slumped to the floor.

"He's free now," Anskar told the congregation.

The Warrior's priest nodded grimly, as if he might forgive but would never forget. The grizzled old man reached above the altar for the red-hot axe. The flesh of his palms sizzled as he gripped the iron haft. The priest barely even grimaced, as if he had trained long and hard for the endurance of such pain. Anskar had queried the need for the forge-heated axe, but the priest told him that the abomination he had committed on Hrothyr, the desecration, required extreme measures if the Warrior aspect of Menselas were to be appeased.

"You can all leave now," the priest said, as he raised the axe above Hrothyr's corpse, ready to chop it into pieces once more in preparation for the afterlife that lay in store for the Warrior's devotees: an eternity of beer and camaraderie. Anskar could think of worse things.

"Never again," Anskar whispered to Hrothyr's lifeless body. "Rest well, my friend."

Sareya's hand fell on his shoulder, and as he turned, she embraced him.

"Now, where else did you want to take me?" she asked, as they followed the King and his housecarls from the church. "And why the big secret?"

Anskar winced at the pulpy thud of the axe cleaving dead flesh.

"You said you were afraid to use your sorcery…"

She had told him as much, and yet her power had manifested aboard ship—just enough to rouse him.

"I can't. If I continue… Well, I've been warned. Probably, I'm already being hunted… and no, there's nothing you can do to stop this Orgol shaman or whatever he is, not without using your own power, and we all know where that would lead. I doubt he has forgotten about you, either. First, Archduke Peleus, and now an albino Orgol mystic! I never thought you would end up so… notorious."

Anskar smiled. "Fortunately, I may have the very remedy. Come."

As one, they bowed to King Aelfyr, then walked away through the sleet toward the Ethereal Sorceress's depot. Anskar didn't think he would miss the Kingdom of Thousand Lakes one little bit. He had experienced enough of the cold, both literally and figuratively. All he could think about was sunshine and sea. And Sareya. Menselas, how had things worked out for the good like this?

And perhaps that was his answer, he realized, with an amused look up to the blustery heavens.

Menselas hadn't been deaf to his prayers. A little tardy in replying, perhaps, but, as Tion never used to tire of saying, good things come to those who wait.

"I still maintain, Niyas is better as a trade partner and an ally than an occupied nation," a man's voice said.

Carred couldn't tell from where. Vaguely, she registered the crumpled sheets beneath her as she buried her face in the pillow.

"You would say that," a woman replied, "considering your company has a track record of turning old enemies into customers."

"Because it works," the man said.

"Not always the way we would like it to," a different woman said.

Then there were too many voices, pecking away at the inside of her skull like birds hunting for grubs:

"Niyas has a good deal to offer—minerals, timber…"

"And craftsmanship. Their stonemasons are second to none."

"And the sorcery?"

"Incentives must be given not to use it."

"Never? What if we allow select usage… for business purposes?"

"For defense."

"You really think that will be necessary? Who is there left to fight?"

"Let's not rest on our laurels. There are the Jargalan pirates, for one thing. The Orgols of the desert. And the Five alone knows what threats we face from across the Trackless Ocean. No, it's time for change, I say. Bring Niyas to our side. I propose a vote."

Someone was knocking. At first she thought it was a gavel on a block, or a fist pounding a debating table. A dog started to bark.

She cracked open a bleary eye, and saw Marith was already out of bed and wrapping a robe around her shoulders. Rosie growled in between barks as she stood at the front door. They had collected the dog from Dorinah before returning to Marith's farm. Someone had to look after Rosie, and she couldn't see Anskar doing it, not where he had decided to go.

"Someone's outside," Marith said, concern in her eyes, in the tightness of her voice. She didn't need to explain. Last time they'd had visitors at Marith's home, they had been assassins. Of course, Marith had dealt with them, much as she'd finished off the last of the ravers and dead-eyes back at Naphor. It was handy being the lover of a moontouched.

Carred rolled out of bed and threw on her shirt. As she stepped into her trousers, she glanced up at Marith.

"I still can't believe I've got you back."

Marith was distracted by the persistent knocking, only half giving Carred her attention. Rosie's bark had turned into a whine.

"Yes, well, I didn't have a pact with the Corpse Maker. That was Talia. Bitch might have stolen my essence, the stuff that made up my body, but without her soul infesting it, that all returned to me when she passed into the intestines of that vile god."

"I still say it's a miracle," Carred said as she finished buttoning her shirt and grabbed her sword, pulling the blade from its scabbard.

Marith stepped into the living room and peered through the slats on the shutters. She turned a wide-eyed look on Carred.

"There's Order knights all over the place." And still someone was knocking on the door—not pounding, though, just lightly rapping.

Carred felt the swell of her lover's repositories as she prepared to fight. Carred's own repositories thrummed in response.

"How many?" She peered over Marith's shoulder.

There couldn't have been more than a dozen. She shook her head. Marith was always exaggerating. But then whoever had been knocking stopped and glanced toward the window. They must have seen her and Marith looking out.

"Hello in there?"

It was a man's voice, and one she recognized. Rosie too, judging by the way her tailed wagged as she yipped excitedly.

Marith trailed Carred like an overprotective shadow as she went to the door, drew back the new bolt that had been installed after the assassins came, and pulled it open.

"Eldrid?" she said. Then she saw the two men with the knight. "Rindon? Nul?"

"At your service," Rindon said, with an ostentatious bow.

Nul rolled his eyes. Eldrid, though, looked utterly serious and more than a little awkward. The hilt of an enormous sword poked up over his shoulder, from where the blade was scabbarded on his back.

"Is that Anskar's?" she asked.

"He said he had no further need of it," Eldrid said. "Wanted me to have it."

"An appropriate gift," Nul said. "For you could never replace dear Borik without a sword as mighty as his."

"Minus the rust," Rindon said.

"Why are you here?" Marith said, coming to stand in the doorway beside Carred.

Rosie slipped past her and offered her tummy to Eldrid, who bent down to tickle her.

"Eldrid has been appointed Seneschal of Branil's Burg," Rindon said. "At least, until they can find someone from the mainland who will accept the commission. Ultimately, his seat of power will be Naphor, once the rebuilding has been finished."

"Work is proceeding apace," Nul explained. "Huge investments are coming in from the mainland, and they're paying only the best Niyandrian masons and carpenters to expedite the rebuilding."

"Mainland money?" Carred said, remembering the voice in her dream—if that's what it was. "Niyandrian workers?"

"Think of it as a new beginning," Eldrid said as he stood. Rosie continued to lie there, crestfallen. "I am to be installed as Governor of Niyas. My instructions are to usher in a new era of cooperation, and ultimately to hand control of the isle back to Niyandrians."

"You're joking," Carred said, sharing a look with Marith.

"It won't be an easy transition."

"I'll bet," Marith said. "No doubt a lot of tangled strings attached."

"A few," Eldrid admitted. "But together"—and now he was speaking directly to Carred—"we will do the best we can."

"Together?" Carred said.

Rindon was beaming at her, Nul gently smiling as he took over petting the dog.

"Niyas for Niyandrians," Eldrid said. "Isn't that what you fought for all these years?"

"You know it is," Carred said, "but I never expected you mainlanders to hand over the isle on a platter."

"I wouldn't exactly describe it like that," Eldrid said. "As I said, it will take a while to transition power to the locals. Probably years."

"And the terms?"

"Stacked in the mainland's favor, of course," Eldrid said.

"The Consortium?"

He shrugged, as if he didn't know about that—or didn't want to know.

"Over time, you'll be able to negotiate for more. I'll lend you my full support. Believe me, a working partnership with Niyas is more beneficial to the mainland than perpetual occupation. Now that the specter of the Necromancer Queen has been banished, now your rebellion is deprived of its primary hope, the future looks bright for the isle."

"Home rule?" Carred said, still not quite believing it.

"Partnership," Eldrid said. "Mutual trade."

"Why are you telling me this?"

"I came here to ask something of you," Eldrid said.

"Here we go." Marith folded her arms across her chest.

"When I'm installed as Governor, I would like you to be my deputy. In time, when the Order withdraws entirely from the isle, the governorship will be determined by a vote of the people of Niyas."

"With mainland money influencing the outcome!" Marith said.

"Nothing we can do about that," Eldrid said. "But with the experience you will glean from deputizing, not to mention your legendary status…"

"Infamous is what I'd call it," Carred said.

"Niyas still needs you," Eldrid said. "I need you too, if this is to work."

"I thought you two were enemies," Marith said.

"Nothing like old rivalries to keep new partners honest," Rindon said. "Or so a wise old woman once told me."

The tumult of a cosmic thunderstorm subsided from Anskar's skull amid the reintegration of the essence that defined him. No matter how often he traveled through the *izindel*, he would never get used to it. Each time was like being ripped into a hundred million pieces then slapped back together again. Reborn.

Solid ground formed beneath his feet, and his fingers were once more interlaced with Sareya's. They stood upon the brass circle of what Sheelahn had called the original *izindel*, its edges brushed over with sand. The symbols around the rim glowed faintly for an instant, shimmering gold and silver and a luminescent cobalt blue, then slowly they faded. The brass gnomon at the center seemed nothing so much as a triangle of pure sunfire, so bright Anskar had to look away, until it too faded, glinting now only with reflected sunlight and casting a thin line of shadow on the *izindel's* surface.

It took a moment to acclimate to the gentle breeze, the swell of the surf hitting the shore, and the susurrus of its receding. Lyrical birdsong sounded from gulls of pristine white, who skimmed the wavetops in pursuit of the silver minnows leaping from the water. Beyond the narrow strip of beach, verdant grassland replete with wildflowers stood in the embrace of the forest of gray ash and elm. But there were no golden people flitting between the trees this time; they were all on the beach, waiting, a circle of men and women lambent with gold, seeming only partially solid.

"This place…" Sareya said, her voice hoarse with awe and wonder. "Are we dead? Is this the paradise of Menselas? Are these angels?"

One of the ethereal beings stepped forward. It was Ren, her skin wreathed in flames that glowed but did not burn nor give off any heat. "Not angels," she said. "We are the ascended. Though not all of us. Not quite yet."

The glowing beings parted to reveal Tarrik.

The demon's gray skin had a sheen of gold, and his eyes were rimmed with sunfire. He carried a large teapot, and now that he could see it, Anskar became aware of a low, droning thrum coming from the spout and the merest rattling of the lid.

As he approached, Tarrik trod warily, on account of the two tiny men who walked a little in front of him, each no larger than a mouse. Anskar crouched down and squinted, the better to see them. They were both dressed in identical coats that sparkled with a myriad colors, curly toed silk slippers on their feet and pointed hats on their heads. One of them had skin of turquoise, the other a darker shade of green. There was something familiar about each of the little men—the shape of their noses, the gait, the glittery eyes that seemed to open onto dark and wide vistas filled with stars.

"Odopek?" he said.

"No longer," they replied at the same time, then each gave an irritable frown at the other. "We are no longer conjoined. The teapot has been repaired, thanks to the void-steel your friend Carred allowed us to take. The aberration that was Odopek is undone."

"Sareya," Anskar said as he stood up straight, "this is—"

"A demon," she said.

"This is Tarrik. A friend."

"You're sure about that, are you?" Tarrik let out a deep belly laugh, and for an instant, golden flames licked over his skin.

"You look different," Anskar said. "Have you accepted your power?"

"Tarrik has at last agreed to commence his training," Ren explained.

"Her constant nagging won out in the end," Tarrik said. "It was only a matter of time."

"And what of you two?" Anskar asked the tiny men. "Will you be training too?"

"No," one of them said.

"No, no, no," the other said, hiding behind his comrade. "Absolutely not. I'll stick with my moonshine, thank you very much."

Tarrik set the teapot on the sand, and the two little men quickly climbed up the side like spiders, then sat on the lid with their legs dangling over the edge.

"What's it for?" Anskar asked. "Besides tea, that is."

"Transport," one of the little men said with a harrumph. "Why, whatever else?"

"Now that it's fixed," the other said. "Thank you, Tarrik, for keeping your word. My colleague here might be a terrible ingrate, but I can't tell you how relieved I am to have a fully functioning teapot once more. All those places to go, things to see!"

Anskar glanced at Sareya, but she was as bemused as he was. The circle of luminous beings that surrounded them seemed to ripple with amusement.

"And what of you, Anskar?" Ren asked. "Why have you returned?"

"I think you know why."

"Then we will learn together," Tarrik said. "Brothers."

"I would like that," Anskar said.

Ren stepped up close and peered into his eyes. "Golden. Not a blemish. That is good. The shadow has left you."

"Melted away," Anskar said. "Incinerated."

"I assume Sheelahn sent you from one of her depots? She is recovered?"

"Not fully, but my friend Orix is fussing over her. She'll be fine."

Ren switched her attention to Sareya and began to circle her, nodding with approval. Sareya's eyes were golden orbs like Ren's. Presumably like Anskar's own were now.

"Sareya," Ren said.

"You know me?"

"I know of you. It is good, Anskar, that you brought her here. Her power has been prematurely awakened."

"By a pale-skinned Orgol," Sareya said.

"And now he seeks to prevent you from using the power? That is a familiar story. He is not evil, merely concerned, afraid of that which he does not possess for himself. There are far greater threats than he."

"But I used the power," Sareya said. "I think he'll come for me now."

"Undoubtedly. But not while you're here. Train with us, Sareya. Among your own people, you would have remained nothing but a wild moontouched—powerful, yes, but good for what? Grow into your power here. Understand what it is, where it comes from, and you will no longer present a danger to Wiraya. On the contrary, you'll become like us: guardians of this world, a balance to the dark. This is the way it has always been; the way it has been decreed."

"By Menselas?" Anskar asked.

Ren smiled. "If it helps, you may think of us as avatars of the Five—for now. You are right at the very beginning of your ascension, Anskar. You both are. And you both have much to learn."

"As do I," Tarrik said.

"Oh," one of the little men said, "I'm sure you have much more to learn than they do. Probably you need to be in a remedial class by yourself."

Anskar turned to Sareya and took her hands in his. "This is the reason I asked you to come here. Will you stay and learn with us?"

Sareya closed her eyes and gently nodded her head. Anskar started to release her hands, but she tightened her grip on his. When she opened her eyes to meet his gaze, they shone like miniature suns. "The Orgol shaman will not be happy."

"That," Ren said, "is a problem for another day."

THE END

TO MY READERS

As always, if you enjoyed the read, leaving a review supports the books and helps keep me writing! You can return to where you purchased the novel to review it or simply visit my website and follow the links: WWW.MITCHELLHOGAN.COM

There are also websites such as Goodreads where members discuss the books they've read or want to read or suggest books others might read: WWW.GOODREADS.COM/AUTHOR/SHOW/7189594.MITCHELL_HOGAN

If you never want to miss the latest book sign up here for my newsletter. I send one every few months, so I won't clutter your inbox. MITCHELLHOGAN.COM/NEW-RELEASE-ALERTS/

Having readers eager for the next installment of a series, or anticipating a new series, is the best motivation for a writer to create new stories. Thank you for your support and be sure to check out my other novels!

ABOUT THE AUTHOR

Photo copyright © 2018

When he was eleven, Mitchell Hogan received *The Hobbit* and the Lord of the Rings trilogy, and a love of fantasy novels was born. He spent the next ten years reading, rolling dice, and playing computer games, with some school and university thrown in. Along the way, he accumulated numerous bookcases' worth of fantasy and sci-fi novels and doesn't look to stop any time soon. For ten years he put off his dream of writing; then he quit his job and wrote *A Crucible of Souls*. He now writes full-time and is eternally grateful to the readers who took a chance on an unknown self-published author. He lives in Sydney, Australia, with his wife, Angela, and his daughters, Isabelle and Charlotte.